IN HO

Passi

Meet Nat, Mark and Michael—three sexy men who've been brought to their knees by passion! They're each in hot pursuit of the woman they want…but will they catch her?

Spice up your summer with these three exciting full-length stories in one brand-new collection!

ABOUT THE AUTHORS

Vicki Lewis Thompson was a journalist before she became a Mills & Boon® author, and believes she's probably a writer because her parents couldn't afford music and dance lessons, and pencils were cheap. She sold her first romance in 1983 and now, nearly forty books later and with a few awards thrown in, she can't imagine anything else making her happier.

Sherry Lewis can't remember when she *didn't* want to be a novelist, but she only began her writing career a few years ago. Sherry writes mysteries as well as romances, and says she draws her inspiration from the places she visits when she travels, and when she's behind the wheel on long drives. She makes her home in Utah, USA and is the mother of two daughters, Valerie and Vanessa.

Roz Denny Fox began writing in the mid-1980s. After freelancing a series of self-help and other articles, she began to try her hand at contemporary romantic women's fiction. When Roz's husband retired, she decided to write full time and, to date, she has had nearly twenty books published. Currently, she and her husband reside in Tucson, USA. They have two married children and five grandchildren.

IN HOT PURSUIT

Vicki Lewis Thompson
Sherry Lewis
Roz Denny Fox

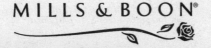

MILLS & BOON®

*First published in Great Britain 2001 by
Harlequin Mills & Boon Limited,
Eton House, 18-24 Paradise Road, Richmond, Surrey, TW9 1SR*

IN HOT PURSUIT
© by Harlequin Enterprises II B.V., 2001

The publisher acknowledges the copyright holders of the
individual work as follows:

THAT'S MY BABY! © Vicki Lewis Thompson 2000
FOR THE BABY'S SAKE © Sherry Lewis 2000
BABY, BABY © Rosaline Fox 2000

ISBN 0 263 82841 7

49-0601

*Printed and bound in Spain
by Litografia Rosés S.A., Barcelona*

CONTENTS

That's My Baby!
by
Vicki Lewis Thompson

With love to my husband Larry,
whose faith in me has never dimmed.

CHAPTER ONE

JESSICA FRANKLIN'S STOMACH gurgled with anxiety as she waited at JFK for the 5:45 flight from London. After seventeen months apart, she had to meet Nat Grady, the man she'd loved—still loved, damn it—disguised as a bag lady. Then she had to tell him about Elizabeth, the baby he had no idea they'd conceived, the baby she'd left in Colorado to keep her safe.

The embarrassing truth was, Jessica had picked up a stalker. She thought of it like that, as if she'd contracted a deadly disease and was no longer fit to be a mother. Growing up, she'd felt stifled by her wealthy father's attempts to protect her from kidnappers. She'd left home, spurning a life of bulletproof cars and bodyguards, insisting she could live quietly and anonymously without all that. It infuriated her to be wrong.

About ten feet away, a woman clucked and cooed at the baby in her arms. Jessica ached every time she saw a mother and child. For her own good she shouldn't watch them, but she couldn't seem to stop torturing herself. Babies drew her like magnets. When she spotted one, she'd stare shamelessly as she tried to guess the child's age and wondered whether Elizabeth would look anything like that, act anything like that.

This one looked to be around eight months old, Elizabeth's age, and he was a boy, judging from the outfit. Jessica couldn't imagine her baby this size. When she'd left her at the Rocking D Ranch, Elizabeth had been so tiny, just barely two months old. Jessica had never imagined that their separation would be this long. But now that Nat was home, she would see her baby again. Soon.

The little boy laughed and Jessica counted four teeth. Elizabeth would have teeth by now. She would be crawling, getting into everything, learning to make noises that were the beginnings of speech.

Like ma-ma.

Jessica endured the pain. At least Elizabeth was safe. She'd known she could count on her friends Sebastian, Travis and Boone to keep her baby that way until Nat came home and they could all decide what to do.

Weary passengers trudged into the gate area from customs and Jessica's pulse raced as she anticipated the meeting to come. She still hadn't decided on her approach. The thought of Nat Grady brought up so many emotions she had to ask them to stand in line and take turns being heard.

Usually the first feeling to shoulder its way to the front was anger. She'd fallen head over heels in love with the guy, but for the year they'd been involved, he'd insisted they keep their relationship secret from everyone but his secretary, Bonnie, a woman who had invented the word *discreet*. Even his best friends, the three men she'd left in charge of Elizabeth, didn't know she and Nat had been seeing each other.

She should have recognized the secrecy thing as a warning signal, but love was blind, and she'd accepted Nat's explanation that his friends were a nosy bunch and he didn't want outside interference in their relationship until he and Jessica knew where it was going. All the while he had jolly well known where it was going, she thought bitterly. On a train bound for nowhere.

If only she could hate him for that. God, how she'd tried. Instead, she kept thinking of what he'd said the night they'd broken up. *I shouldn't have let you waste your time on me. I'm not worth it.*

Then he'd left her, his real estate business and his friends to head for a tiny, war-torn country where he'd worked as a volunteer in the refugee camps. Along with her other emotions connected to Nat, Jessica battled guilt. If she hadn't pushed him to end the secrecy and marry her, he wouldn't have left the country. She was sure of it. He'd have stayed in Colorado, making love to her, the sweetest love she'd ever known.

Instead, to get away from her and the demons she'd demanded that he face, he'd plunged into a violent place where the lines of battle blurred and changed every day. As a civilian he had no weapons and no military training to protect him. He'd spent seventeen months in danger on account of her, and if he'd been killed or hurt, she would have blamed herself.

She was also to blame for the baby, after he'd told her flat out he never wanted kids. A woman her age should have known antibiotics canceled the effect of birth control pills. But she had some gaps in her sexual education, thanks to growing up shadowed by her own personal bodyguard. She hadn't known.

She needed to tell him it was her responsibility. Still, she thought he should know about the baby, in case the stalker got lucky. But before she told him anything, she'd have to convince him who she was. The dark wig, the baggy clothes and the thick glasses wouldn't look familiar to him. But once he'd figured out it was her, what would she say first?

Nat, we have a baby girl named Elizabeth. Too abrupt. A man who'd said he never wanted children might need to be eased into that kind of discussion. *Nat, I'm disguised like this because I have a stalker on my trail.* Too much, too soon. He'd just returned from dodging bullets. He deserved a little peace and quiet before she gave him that bad news, coupled with the information that if anything happened to her he'd need to watch out for Elizabeth, whether he cared to or not.

Her stomach felt as if she'd swallowed a bagful of hot marbles.

A man in a business suit came toward the woman with the baby, and the baby bounced happily, reaching out for the man. When the father lifted the baby into his arms and showered him with kisses, Jessica had to look away.

She took off the glasses she was wearing as part of her disguise and brushed the tears from her eyes. She had to pay attention. Nat could be coming along any minute, and she didn't want to miss him.

A tall man with a full beard and hair past his collar appeared in the stream of passengers. He wore a battered-looking leather jacket, jeans and boots. A scuffed backpack hung from one broad shoulder, a backpack not too different from the one she carried. Her gaze swept past him, then returned. He moved through the crowd with a familiar, fluid walk, as if he were striding along to a country tune. Nat walked that way.

She looked closer, past the rich brown of his beard, and her heart hammered. The mouth. She'd spent hours gazing at that chiseled mouth, classic as the mouth on one of her father's prized Rodin sculptures. She'd spent even more hours kissing and being kissed by that mouth, and her tongue slid over her lips in remembrance. Nat. In spite of the anger and guilt, pure joy bloomed within her at the sight of him. Nat. He was here. He was okay.

Suddenly whatever she decided to say seemed unimportant. She just had to get to him, wrap her arms around him and give thanks that he'd returned in one piece. Her nightmares had begun the day she'd learned where he was, and CNN had been her lifeline ever since.

No matter how furiously she'd counseled herself to remain calm when she saw him, she was miles beyond calm. She was weepy with gratitude for his safe return. He was an oasis in the desert her life had become without him.

Drinking in the sight of him moving through the crowd, she sighed with happiness. Thank God he looked healthy, his skin tanned and his hair still lustrous, reflecting the terminal's overhead lights. But she'd give him the herbal supplements she'd brought, anyway, and insist that he take them. He didn't eat right under the best of circumstances, and no telling what he'd existed on over there.

He was so appealing that she couldn't help wondering if he'd become involved with anyone while he was gone. A beautiful waif of a woman, perhaps, who spoke little English, but who had awakened his protective instincts. A woman who'd fallen deeply in love with the big, handsome American cowboy who'd come to help. Jessica knew how easily such a thing could happen, and her heart hurt.

But if he had found another to love, that wasn't her business. He was free to do as he chose.

Seventeen months. That was a long time for a single man of thirty-three to go without sex. He might not have fallen in love, but he might have taken a woman to bed....

She wouldn't ask. No, she definitely wouldn't ask. But the thought made her want to cry.

Moving closer, she focused on his face, trying to meet his gaze. They'd had a magic connection between them, and maybe if she caught his eye, he'd see beyond her disguise and recognize her, heart to heart. He'd be startled, of course, and might wonder if she'd gone crazy while he was out of the country.

In a way she had. Crazy with worry...and love. Still love. But she wouldn't let him know that she still loved him. She would be very careful about that, unless...unless he had gone a little crazy, too. Although she'd lectured herself to squash that hope like a bug, she'd let it live.

At last Nat glanced her way, and she opened her mouth to call to him. But instead of saying his name, she drew back in uncertainty. His gaze was so hard and uncompromising that it intimidated her. He'd changed.

For a minute she wondered if she'd been wrong in thinking this bearded man was Nat. No, she hadn't been wrong. It was him. But his blue eyes, once so full of good humor, looked like chipped ice. She wondered what he'd seen in those camps that had put that grim look on his face.

He gave no sign of recognizing her as he turned and headed down the terminal. Her courage failed and she closed her mouth. But she had to catch him, had to let him know about the baby before he called anyone at the Rocking D in Colorado. Sure as the world someone at the ranch would tell him immediately that she'd left Elizabeth there, although she hadn't named the father. But Nat would know, once he was told the baby's age. She couldn't let him find out that way.

She had to hurry to keep up with him. Dodging luggage, people and motorized carts, she kept him in sight as he followed the signs directing him toward ground transportation. She knew he planned to stay in the city for a few nights and take care of some business before flying back to Colorado. His secretary, the only person Nat had contacted before coming home, had said so.

Bonnie didn't know about the baby or the stalker. She just thought she was helping Jessica create a romantic homecoming surprise for Nat. During the year Nat and Jessica had been secretly involved, Bonnie had set up many of their rendezvous locations, and she'd seemed to relish the role of matchmaker.

When Nat and Jessica had separated, Bonnie had called Jessica, urging her to try to patch things up. Jessica had refused, convinced that Nat had meant for the affair to end from the beginning, which was why he'd kept it such a secret. But when her pregnancy was confirmed, she'd called Bonnie and learned that Nat was out of the country and unreachable. Since then, Jessica had made use of her friendship with the secretary to find out exactly when Nat was due back.

The escalator foiled Jessica's plans to catch up with him. People and wheeled carry-ons bunched onto the grooved metal steps between them and made it impossible for her to get close. But she didn't really want to confront him here, anyway, she finally realized. Her news was upsetting enough without being delivered under harsh overhead lights with the din of people and the clatter of baggage to interfere with an emotional conversation.

He'd undoubtedly take a taxi from the airport to his hotel. She'd follow in another taxi and catch him in the lobby. Much better. Maybe they could go for a drink to discuss their options.

The chill of an October night cooled her overheated system as she bustled outside and followed him toward the taxi stand. She gained some valuable time as he convinced the cabdriver to let him ride in front. How like Nat to hate the idea of being chauffeured. She'd been drawn to his democratic instincts from the beginning.

She hated being chauffeured, too, but she didn't have time to discuss that with the driver of the next taxi in line. With a quick no thanks, she brushed aside his offer to help with her backpack. "I'm in a big hurry," she said as she hopped in the back seat.

"Right." The driver hustled himself behind the wheel. "Where to?"

"Follow that cab," she said, pointing to the one Nat had entered.

He swiveled in the seat to stare at her. "You're kidding, right?"

"No, I am not kidding!" She panicked as the other cab pulled away from the curb. "That one! And don't lose it!"

"You better have money," the cabbie muttered as he started after Nat's cab. "You better not be some nutcase who's watched one too many James Bond movies, or I'll drive you straight to the nearest precinct station and turn you over to the cops."

"I have money." Jessica watched Nat's cab gain a little distance and clenched her jaw. "Just keep up with them. That cab has a vee-shaped scratch on the trunk. Did you notice that? That's how you'll know which one to follow."

"I see the cab. I just wanna know what's with the cops-and-robbers routine. I don't wanna be a whatchamacallit—accomplice."

"I'm not breaking the law." Jessica was losing patience with the cabbie. She was pretty much out of patience, anyway, and being back in New York put her even more on edge. The closer they came to the jeweled city on the horizon, the more she felt the tug of her father's influence.

"I don't wanna get mixed up in anything," the driver said. "I just wanna do my job, y'know?"

"In the movies, the cabdriver never complains about having to follow another taxi," Jessica pointed out. "He just does it."

"See? What did I tell you? You think you're in a damn movie or somethin'! I'll bet they just let you out of the nuthouse. Gave you a pack of meds and told you to have a nice life. And it's my bad luck that you picked my cab to act out your delusions."

"I'm perfectly sane." Jessica might not like being chauffeured, but she was used to it, and she'd never had a driver question her the way this one was doing. Of course, she was used to limos. And this guy didn't know who she was.

He didn't know the paper beside him on the front seat was the product of her father's news empire. "Quick, he just changed lanes!"

The driver sounded highly insulted. "I can see that he changed lanes, lady. I didn't start driving yesterday. Do you even know who's in that cab?"

"Yes."

"Yeah, right. You probably think it's Elvis."

"I know who's in the cab. I need to talk to him."

"Why? Who is it?"

Many times as a child Jessica had watched her mother deal with questions she didn't want to answer. Her mother would stiffen her spine and speak in what Jessica thought of as her to-the-manner-born voice. Jessica had never tried the technique, but she decided to give it a whirl.

Straightening in her seat, she lifted her chin and said, "I don't believe that's any of your business."

Her effort seemed lost on the cabbie. "It sure as hell is my business! I'm transportin' you in my cab! And I'd appreciate it if you'd lay off the high-and-mighty tone, unless you're about to tell me you're kissing cousins to the Rockefellers, which I sincerely doubt."

Close, Jessica thought. But apparently she didn't have the presence to carry it off. Then again, she did look like a bag lady. Maybe her mother's success in turning aside impertinent questions had as much to do with her elegant clothes and her position in society as her tone of voice. Yet in her heart of hearts, Jessica believed that even dressed in rags with no fortune to command, her mother would make people do her bidding. She'd certainly kept her husband and daughter in line for years.

Jessica sighed. Barring a personality transplant, she'd need to give the cabbie some explanation for why they were tailing another cab into the city, or she was liable to be dumped by the side of the road. "The man in the other cab is an old boyfriend," she said. "I've changed since we last met, and he didn't recognize me, but I really need to talk to him."

"Maybe he doesn't want to talk to you."

"Maybe not," she acknowledged, "but I have some information he needs to hear."

"Aw, jeez, I know where this is goin'. We're talkin' about the patter of little feet, right?"

Jessica couldn't think of anything but the truth. "You might say that."

"Poor bastard. But them that plays, pays. I learned that one the hard way. Do you have any idea where he's goin'?"

"To a hotel in the city, I imagine."

The cabbie heaved a sigh. "All right, then. I'll catch him for ya."

"Thank you." Jessica settled back against the seat as the sparkling skyscrapers of Manhattan hovered ever nearer. Habit caused her to pick out the Franklin Publishing Tower dangling between sky and earth like one of her mother's diamond chokers.

She spoke only briefly with her parents these days, stopping long enough in her flight to put in a quick call every couple of weeks. They thought she was "seeing the country." None of her conversations with them in the past few years had been significant, anyway, and she hadn't seen them since she'd left home.

They didn't approve of her decision to abandon their world and try to create her own life, and their attitude toward her had been curt ever since she'd moved to Colorado. Her current predicament, having a child out of wedlock and a stalker on her trail, would only confirm what they'd always assumed—that on her own she'd make a mess of things. She didn't want to give them a chance to say we told you so.

"How far along are you?" the cabbie asked.

Jessica blinked and tried to figure out what he meant.

"When's the baby due?" he asked, clarifying his question.

"I, um, already had her," she said. "I left her with friends."

"Wait a doggone minute! You already had the kid, and you're just now nailing the father? Are you sure he's the father and this isn't some kind of shakedown?"

"I'm sure. He's been out of the country. I couldn't contact him before."

The cabbie's gaze flicked into the rearview mirror. "Okay, I'm gonna believe you. The reason is that your voice sounded strong when you said that. After all these years of drivin' cab, I can tell when a passenger's blowin' smoke. You can hear it in their voice. So what did you name her?"

"Elizabeth." Speaking the name brought a lump to Jessica's throat and she wondered if she'd cry when she talked to Nat about the baby. She hoped she wouldn't cry. She didn't want his pity, only his support.

"Pretty name. I got two kids. Both boys. Rory and Jonathan. I had to marry my wife on account of Rory, but it's worked out okay."

Worked out okay. The lukewarm comment made Jessica shiver. She'd never in a million years want a marriage that *worked out okay.* Even if Nat had a burst of responsibility and proposed marriage to give Elizabeth two parents, Jessica wouldn't agree. But Nat wouldn't propose. Marriage scared him to death. The only thing that scared him worse was fatherhood.

"Your guy doesn't seem to be goin' into Midtown, like you thought," the cabbie said. "Looks like we're headed for the Hudson Parkway. Still want me to follow him?"

"Absolutely." The route made her nervous, though. She

knew it only too well. But it was only a coincidence that the first time she set foot back in New York since leaving her parents' estate, Nat would lead her back in the direction of the Hudson Valley, straight toward Franklin Hall.

"Like I said, I hope you got money," the driver said. "For all we know, the guy's headed for Vermont to see the leaves."

"I doubt it."

"You ever seen the leaves?"

"Yes." She'd taken a trip through Vermont in the limo with her parents the October she turned nine. The long black car had seemed to take up far too much space on the narrow back roads, and it had looked ridiculous sitting parked on the village square in one of the hamlets where'd they'd stopped for hot cider.

She'd been aware of people staring, but she'd grown used to that. She'd ignored them and gazed longingly at three children playing in a yard full of red, yellow and orange leaves. They'd rake them into piles and then dive into them, scattering the leaves in an explosion of color before raking them up and starting all over. Their laughter had made her feel so completely alone.

Her memory clicked over to a crisp fall day in Aspen. Nat hadn't really understood why she'd begged him to help her gather leaves into piles and jump with her right into the middle of them. But he'd helped her do it, anyway. The lonely child within her had loved every minute, and she'd loved Nat for being such a good sport about it.

"My wife's after me to take her and the kids up there next weekend," the cabdriver said, breaking into her reverie, "but I told her I do enough driving during the week. Besides that, it's bumper to bumper on those little back roads. The word's out about those leaves."

"You should take her, anyway," Jessica said, suddenly feeling sorry for the woman who had no passion in her life.

"Get a sitter for the boys. There are some nice bed-and-breakfast places up there. It's a good spot for couples."

"You mean couples with bucks. Those cozy little inns aren't cheap. My wife would probably rather have a new couch."

"Ask her. I'll bet she'd rather have the weekend."

"I'll bet she'd rather have the couch. You're gonna have that for a good ten years or more. The weekend's over and done, and you've got nothin'."

"You have memories!" Jessica protested, battling now for this unknown woman's right to be romanced, at least once in her life. "They're worth more than anything."

"I don't know. You can't sit on memories. Listen, we're headed out of the city entirely. You sure you want to keep going? This is turning into an expensive ride."

"That's okay. Keep going." As they left Manhattan behind, she could hardly believe the direction they were taking. They'd left the Hudson Parkway to follow the familiar route that wound along beside the river. If they kept going like this, they'd drive right past her parents' estate.

"High-priced real estate up here," the driver said. "But what I always think about, especially this time of year, is that story about the Headless Horseman. Sleepy Hollow, and all that. That story scared the daylights out of me when I was a kid."

"Me, too." She hadn't thought about it before, but now she realized that when she allowed herself to think about the person stalking her, she felt sort of like Ichabod Crane trying to escape the Headless Horseman.

"My boys love that story, but kids today don't scare so easy, I guess."

"I guess." Jessica wondered if Elizabeth would grow up braver than she was. Her self-image of strong independence grew shakier the closer they came to Franklin Hall.

Less than a mile from her parents' gate she told the

driver to slow down. At last she'd allowed her instincts to take over, and they had told her exactly where Nat was going. By the time the left-turn signal on the cab ahead of them flashed in the darkness, she was prepared for it. For reasons she couldn't begin to imagine, Nat was going to Franklin Hall.

"Pull over under that tree," she told the cabbie. "I'll get out here."

"What are you gonna do?" He pulled off the road as she'd asked, but gone was the camaraderie they'd established. He sounded nervous and suspicious again. "I can't let you get out here, in the dark. And you sure as hell can't follow him into that place. They got one of those automatic gates, and there are probably Dobermans running around or something. I should never have agreed to this. You're some psycho or something, aren't you?"

Jessica's teeth chattered from the adrenaline rush of being so close to Franklin Hall again, but she tried to stay calm. "I *can* follow him into that place," she said. "I used to live there. I know the gate code."

"No way!"

"Look, I'll prove it to you. First let me pay you what I owe." She glanced at the meter and handed him some bills, along with a generous tip.

He looked a little happier upon seeing the money. "Just let me take you back to Manhattan, okay? I won't even charge you. But I can't leave a woman on a lonely country road like this. If I was to read about you in the papers, I'd never forgive myself."

Jessica watched the taillights of the other cab disappear down the winding lane leading to the main house, which was obscured by trees. "Okay, you can pull over to the gate now. I'll show you I can open it."

"I'll pull over there." He guided the car across the road and stopped, his headlights shining on the ten-foot-tall gates

with the scrolled letters *FH* worked into the intricate design. "But you're not opening that gate. I know the kind
of people who would live here, and you're not that kind."

"Appearances can be deceiving." She opened the car
door. "You can stay here until I open the gate, and then
go on back. That way you'll know I'm inside the protection
of the fence."

"What if you're attacked by dogs?"

"There aren't any dogs. At least not the last I heard."
She opened the door and got out, hefting her backpack onto
her shoulder. "Thanks for bringing me out here," she said.
"And do ask your wife about taking that weekend trip to
a bed-and-breakfast." She closed the door.

He rolled down the window and stuck his head out.
"You just show me you can open that gate. When you
can't, I'll take you back to town, no questions asked. You
can stay at the Y."

She turned to smile at him. "Thanks. You're a nice man.
But I won't need to do that." She still wasn't sure what
she would do once she was inside the gate, but that was
her first step. The code came back to her the minute she
stepped up to the keypad, and she punched it in without
hesitation. The gates swung slowly open.

"I'll be damned," the cabbie said. "Who are you, anyway?"

"Doesn't matter." She gave him another smile. "Goodbye."

"This'll be one to tell the guys."

A chill passed over her. "Please don't. Don't tell anybody about this." She had no idea how close her stalker
might be.

"Look, if the police question me, because somethin' bad
happens, then—"

"They won't. I'm just asking you not to gossip to the
other cabdrivers. Can you promise that?"

"Yeah, I can promise that. Better get in there. The gates are closing again."

"Right. Bye."

"Take care of yourself."

She turned and ran through the gates before they clanked together with a sound that brought back that familiar feeling of claustrophobia. Once again she was a prisoner of Franklin Hall.

CHAPTER TWO

NAT HAD PREPARED himself for wealth, yet he was still blown away as the cab pulled up in front of the floodlit colonial mansion. In bandbox condition, the exterior was the color of ripe wheat, and the ivory trim looked as if it had been freshly painted that morning.

Jess had once lived here. The knowledge sent adrenaline rushing through his system, sweeping aside the fatigue of a transatlantic flight. Surely her parents would be able to tell him where he could find her.

The circular driveway had taken them up to an elegant entry, but the big draw of the house was obviously the view from the back, which sloped steeply down to the Hudson. On the way in, he'd caught glimpses of the majestic river through the trees, and the driver pointed with excitement when a barge, lit up like a Christmas tree, glided past, its engines thrumming in the night air.

Nat's real estate training kicked in. He quickly calculated what the house alone must be worth, not even considering the grounds. Even in the dark they appeared extensive and manicured. The newspaper business had been good to Russell P. Franklin.

"Nice place." The cabdriver switched off the engine.

"Not bad," Nat agreed. But impressive as the house was, he wouldn't want to live in it, and he couldn't picture free-spirited Jess here, forced to spend her childhood behind locked gates. He was beginning to understand how lonely she'd been as the only child at Franklin Hall.

Opening the car door, he was greeted by the friendly scent of a fireplace in use. That heartened him, although he doubted the setting was as cozy as the living room at the Rocking D in Colorado. But he didn't need cozy right now. He needed information. He hoped to God her parents had some.

He turned toward the driver. "Listen, I don't know how long I'll be, so I'm sure you could wait in the house, where it's warmer."

"Nah. Thanks, anyway, but I'd rather stretch my legs and have a smoke, if it's all the same to you. I'll be here whenever you're ready to go."

"Okay." Nat was too impatient to argue the point. "Knock on the door if you change your mind." Leaving his backpack in the cab, he exited the car and mounted the steps to the front door, which looked as proper as a starched shirtfront. He lifted the brass knocker and rapped twice.

Almost immediately a uniformed butler opened the door.

Nat introduced himself. He was ushered quietly inside and relieved of his leather jacket. The butler had a strong British accent, and Nat remembered Jessica mentioning him. Barclay. Her father had hired him away from the Savoy.

The foyer lived up to the promise of the outside. A crystal chandelier sprinkled light over antiques that had been waxed and buffed until they shone. A table against one wall held a small bronze that Nat thought might be famous. He wasn't up on art, but it looked familiar.

On a larger table in the center of the large entry, a bouquet of fall flowers filled a blue-and-white urn taller than a two-year-old child. Nat would bet the flowers were replaced every day. Their scent mingled with the tang of paste wax, and something else—maybe the smell of money, Nat thought. The contrast with the poverty he'd recently left made the elegant setting seem almost obscene.

''Mr. and Mrs. Franklin are in the library,'' the butler said. ''If you'll follow me.''

As Nat walked down the hallway, an Oriental carpet that looked old and priceless cushioned his steps. He glanced at the gleaming railing on the stairway spiraling up to the second floor, and a vivid image of Jess sailing down the banister tugged at his heart. She'd only gotten away with it once, she'd said, but she'd never forgotten the joy of risking the forbidden.

He'd been having trouble finding evidence of her in this formal setting, but the banister looked as if it had been made for sliding down. Still, she'd probably never swung on a tire in the backyard or played hopscotch on the front walk. He was glad he'd seen this place, if only to understand Jess better.

His last picture of her tortured him—her long red curls tousled from lovemaking, her brown eyes filled with angry tears. *Don't you love me enough?* she'd cried.

He'd left without answering the question, which effectively gave her an answer. He'd heard some object hit the door and shatter after he'd closed it behind him.

For Jess, love meant marriage and children. He hadn't been willing to give her either one, because he'd thought he'd be lousy at it. He still thought so, but she'd haunted him the entire time he'd been gone. Another worker in the refugee camps, a sweet and willing woman, had offered herself. He'd gladly accepted, but to his chagrin he discovered that he couldn't make love to anyone but Jess.

Finally he'd faced the truth. Sometime during the year he'd been seeing Jess, while he'd thought he was guarding his heart, she'd crept past the gates and set herself up as a permanent resident. He could either live the rest of his life alone, or he could try to overcome his fears and give Jess what she wanted.

Bad risk though he was, she'd been eager to take a

chance on him once. He wondered if she still would. In the refugee camps he'd dealt with people who'd been ripped away from loved ones by force and had to scratch for every bit of human connection. After witnessing that, tearing himself from Jess seemed like ego run amok. He'd been offered so much, and he'd foolishly rejected it.

The thought of having kids still scared him to death, but maybe, in time, he could get used to that, too. If he expected to create an adoption program for war orphans, he'd be a real hypocrite if he didn't at least consider that option for himself.

But first he had to find Jess. And he had no clue where she was. For seventeen months he'd pictured her in her little Aspen apartment. When he hadn't been able to locate her there, he'd gone slightly crazy.

The butler paused in the doorway of the library to announce him, and Nat was so lost in thought, he nearly ran into the guy.

"Mr. Nat Grady to see you, sir," the butler said.

"Show him in, Barclay," boomed a voice from the interior of the room.

The butler stepped aside and Nat tried to control his eagerness as he walked forward. These people could lead him to Jess.

Russell P. Franklin, a robust, silver-haired man, rose from a leather wingback in front of the fireplace and came toward him, hand outstretched. Mrs. Russell P. remained seated in her wingback. She strongly resembled Jess, but Nat assumed the red hair was a beauty-salon copy of the color she'd been born with. Still, he couldn't help thinking that this might be how Jess would look in twenty-five or thirty years. He wanted to be around to see that.

Adele Franklin smiled a greeting, but at the same time she surveyed him carefully. Under her scrutiny Nat remembered how grungy he was in comparison to his hosts. No doubt their sweaters and slacks were everyday casual wear, and they probably cost three times what Nat would spend on his hotel room tonight. Good thing neither Adele nor Russell knew yet that he had designs on their only daughter, or he'd probably be thrown out on his ear.

"Glad to have you stop by, Grady," Russell said. His handshake was warm and firm. "Come over by the fire. What will you have? A drink, something to eat?"

"Scotch would be great." Nat didn't plan to drink much of it, but he'd been a real estate broker long enough to know the value of accepting someone's hospitality if you wanted to make the sale. This might turn out to be the most important sales call of his life. He would have preferred a beer, but this didn't look like a beer-drinking household.

"Good." Russell looked pleased as he signaled to Barclay. "And have the cook rustle up a few sandwiches," he added. "This man's been existing on airplane food."

Airplane food was gourmet fare compared to what the refugees had to eat, Nat thought. But this wasn't the time to tell them that. "I hope you'll excuse the way I look." He stroked his beard. "I came straight from the airport."

"No excuse necessary," Russell said. "A man involves himself in a cause such as you have, he doesn't have time to worry about appearance."

"It does rearrange your priorities." Nat sat on a love seat positioned between the two wingbacks and directly in front of the marble fireplace. The stout logs crackled smartly, as if aware of the honor of adding heat and ambience to Franklin Hall.

Windows on either side of the fireplace looked out on the inky flow of the river and the dark shore beyond, where only an occasional light showed signs of civilization. Books, mostly leather-bound, lined the other three walls of the room. There was even a rolling ladder to reach the top shelves.

Adele and Russell each had a book resting on a table beside them, a bookmark inserted in the pages. Then he realized there was no television in the room. Apparently the Franklins still believed in reading as a way to pass an evening.

Nat's career in real estate had centered primarily on land, but he'd handled a few homes, and some had been real showplaces. None of them equaled this house. The cost of running Franklin Hall for a day would probably feed a refugee family for months.

Adele leaned forward. "You are quite a humanitarian, Mr. Grady. The rest of us may have sent a little money over to help those poor people, but you invested something far more precious—yourself. I commend you."

Her voice startled him. Jess's voice. He wanted to close his eyes and savor it. "I don't really think of it that way, Mrs. Franklin," he said. "I just had to go." And not only to escape his demons concerning Jess. That was another thing he needed to settle with his ladylove. If she'd found out about his work in the refugee camps, she probably thought he'd only run away from her. But his decision to help the war-torn country was far more complicated than that.

"Call me Adele," Jess's mother said with a warm smile.

Her eyes were gray, not brown like Jess's. But otherwise she reminded him so strongly of her daughter that he couldn't stop looking at her. She wove her fingers together in her lap the way Jess did, and when she spoke she wrinkled her forehead slightly, as if putting real thought into what she was about to say. He remembered loving that about Jess.

"By all means," Russell said. "Let's not stand on formality."

At that moment Barclay arrived with Nat's scotch, a tray

of sandwiches, and what looked like mineral water for Adele and Russell.

"Here's to your dedicated efforts on the part of the refugees," Russell said, raising his glass toward Nat. He took a swallow and sat back. "Now, why don't you tell us what you have in mind?"

"I'll be glad to." He was passionate and absolutely sincere in his dedication to the war orphans foundation, but he'd used it without remorse as his ticket into Franklin Hall. Once he'd discussed the foundation, he planned to casually mention Jess. He forced his attention away from Adele and concentrated on Jess's father.

Russell had brown eyes the color of Jess's. But where her gaze had reminded him of a wild fawn's, Russell's could have belonged to George Washington when he led his troops across the Potomac. The man was a fighter and an empire builder. No one who looked carefully into those eyes would underestimate Russell P. Franklin.

Nat thought briefly of his own father. Nobody underestimated Hank Grady, either, least of all his son. Nat especially didn't underestimate his father's ability to be cruel. Yet Nat had been fed and clothed. Now he appreciated the luxury of that.

Shutting out the image of his father, Nat carefully outlined his plan for a foundation that would oversee the welfare and possible adoption of the orphaned children he had recently left. He had several potential backers in mind for the project. If Jess had still been living in her apartment, as he'd expected when he'd called from London, he wouldn't have put Franklin on the list and risked causing Jess problems. But she hadn't been in her apartment. The phone had been disconnected.

Both Russell and Adele seemed eager to hear the details of his plan, and he realized that getting their support for the foundation was a done deal. He was happy about that, but it wasn't the most critical part of the interview.

"We'd be honored to have the Franklin Publishing Group be part of that effort," Russell said when Nat finished. "I'll talk to my accountants in the morning and see how much of your budget we can cover. Your ideas are well thought out."

"Thank you." Nat smiled. "I've had a lot of thinking time."

"Some people could think for years and not come up with a practical scheme," Russell said. "I appreciate dealing with someone who has a head for business. Philanthropy is a fine thing, but some of these confounded do-gooders quiver at the very idea of fiscal responsibility, and that makes me nervous. It's too easy to pour money down a rat hole if you don't have some checks and balances in place."

"That's why it was important for me to be over there so long," Nat said. "I've lined up some excellent people who are ready to help run the program."

Russell nodded and sat back in his chair. "Are you planning to approach other backers about this while you're in town?"

"Yes, I am. But I wanted to see you first."

The older man regarded him like a benevolent uncle. "I'm sure you'll get the backing you need. But I should probably warn you that not everyone is as liberal as I am. You might want to shave."

"I probably will." Growing a beard had been practical when hot water and shaving gear had been scarce and cold wind had chapped his bare skin. He'd also blended in better with the refugees, and after a few months, the beard had seemed natural to him. Now that he was back in this country, seeing it in the mirror every day would serve to remind him of his mission. Still, Russell had a point. And then there was the matter of Jess. She had very tender skin....

"I rather like your beard," Adele said.

"Yes, but you're not a conservative businessman, Adele," Russell said. "Some of these fellows get suspicious if they see a lot of facial hair. A mustache, now that's no big deal, but a full beard conjures up the idea of radicals and hippies, y'know. It could affect whether Nat can get them to turn loose of their money."

"I understand," Nat said. "Besides, I might give my secretary a heart attack if I walked into the office looking like this."

"You sell mostly unimproved land out there in Colorado, don't you?" Russell said.

"That's right." Nat spied an opening. "Have you ever visited the state?"

"No, I never have. Flown over it many times, but never did stop. Pretty country, I understand."

"It is that." Nat thought he saw a flicker of emotion in those brown eyes. Adele gazed down at the fingers she'd laced tightly in her lap. Nat waited to see if either of them would mention that they had a daughter living in Colorado. Neither of them did. He'd have to plow this furrow on his own.

His pulse rate spiked. This was undoubtedly a touchy subject, but he didn't intend to leave without getting into it. "Unless I'm mistaken, your daughter, Jessica, lived in Aspen for a while."

The atmosphere in the room changed immediately. The camaraderie disappeared as Adele and Russell tensed and looked uneasily at each other. Finally Adele gave an almost imperceptible nod, as if to let her husband handle the comment.

"And how would you happen to have come by that information?'' Russell asked. His question was quietly phrased, but the tone was one of command.

''I met her,''

They regarded him in stony silence.

Nat forged on. ''But I've lost touch with her. I tried calling her from London and found out the number I had for her isn't good anymore. I thought you might be able to tell me where she is,'' he finished, matching his tone to Franklin's as he met his gaze.

Russell had not changed position in his chair, but somehow he seemed bigger, more formidable. The publishing tycoon had replaced the affable philanthropist. ''What is she to you?'' he demanded.

''She saved my life.''

Adele gasped.

''And exactly how did she do that?'' Russell asked. A muscle twitched in his jaw.

Nat had wondered if she'd ever mentioned the incident to her parents. ''She might have told you about helping four clueless cowboys who'd decided to go skiing,'' he ventured.

''No, she did not.'' Russell continued to drill Nat with his gaze.

''We...she's a very independent person.'' Adele laced and unlaced her fingers. ''She doesn't fill us in on all her doings.''

''That's an understatement,'' Russell barked. ''So, what happened out there in Colorado?''

''Well, some friends and I went skiing and stayed at the lodge where she worked at the desk. I guess she figured out we were beginners who might get in trouble, so she offered to go along and watch out for us. Unfortunately we didn't give enough credit to her warnings. We blundered into an avalanche, and I was completely buried. She figured out where I was and told my friends how to dig me out. If she hadn't been there, I might not have made it.''

Adele sagged back against her chair, her face pale. ''An avalanche.'' She glanced over at Russell. ''She could have ended up in it, too, Russ.''

''Of course she could have!'' Russell's jaw worked. ''But she thinks she knows best, so what the hell are we supposed to do?'' His voice trembled with obvious pain and frustration.

Nat had only heard Jess's version of the difficult relationship she had with her parents, and of course he'd sided with her in her bid for independence. But seeing the strain they were under because of her leaving, Nat couldn't help sympathizing with them. She was their only child, and they were frantic with worry because they could no longer watch out for her. Nat could relate.

''Is she still up in Aspen?'' he asked.

Russell lost his tenuous hold on his composure. ''We don't know where the hell she is! We—''

''Russell.'' Adele's quiet authority stopped his tirade immediately. ''Jessica calls,'' she continued, sitting up straighter and sending another warning glance at her husband. ''She updates us every couple of weeks. About six months ago she decided to see a bit of the country, so she's traveling around.''

A cold chill zipped up Nat's spine. Something about this scenario didn't sound like the Jess he knew. She was a nest-builder, not a vagabond. She'd loved her setup in Aspen, and she'd told him it was the perfect place to begin her study of herbs. ''Traveling where?'' he asked, trying to keep the panic out of his voice.

''God knows. She's behaving like a damn gypsy!'' Russell shot a belligerent glance at his wife.

Her voice remained low and well-modulated. ''Russell,

we don't know this young man that well. I think perhaps you should—''

"I think I should reconsider supporting this foundation, is what I think!" Russell turned back to Nat. "Tell me, Grady, how did you know that Jessica is our daughter? As I recall, she wanted to 'fade into the woodwork' as she put it, so she could—and I quote—'live a normal life.' She didn't intend to tell anyone she was related to me. How did you find out?"

"She told me," Nat said. Concern for Jess tightened his chest. "After the avalanche we became friends." It was all he dared admit in this charged atmosphere. "I don't think she ever told anyone else, but she told me. Now that I'm back in the country, I wanted to…say hello." Yeah, right. Say hello. And then kiss her until neither of them could stand. And make love to her for about three days straight.

Adele leaned forward, her gray eyes intent. "Did you have a close relationship with our daughter, Mr. Grady?"

He'd been demoted from that first-name basis pretty quick, Nat thought as he wondered how to answer her.

"What the hell kind of question is that, Adele?" Russell asked. "The man said they were friends. Don't go making something more of it."

Adele ignored her husband and continued to study Nat. "She never mentioned being involved with someone," she said, "but I knew it had to happen, sooner or later. She's a beautiful girl."

Nat's throat went dry. "Yes."

"She didn't trust many people," Adele continued, her gaze steady. "If she trusted you enough to let you know who she is, then I suspect you're more than a friend to her."

He'd hoped to avoid getting this specific, but he wasn't going to lie to her parents. "We're more than friends," he said.

"Oh, that's terrific!" Russell said. "Are you telling me you left my daughter high and dry while you went running all over God's creation helping strangers in that little piss-ant country over there?"

"I…" Nat cleared his throat and faced Russell. He'd come into this room thinking of himself as a world-weary champion of the underprivileged. But he was beginning to feel more like an irresponsible teenager. "Yes, sir, I'm afraid that's exactly what I did. And I'd like to make it up to her."

"You'll have to catch her first."

Nat damn well intended to do that. At least it didn't sound as if she'd found herself another guy. "Do you happen to remember where she was the last time she called?"

Adele's poise cracked a little. "She won't tell us," she said, a quiver in her voice.

The tightness in his chest grew. "What do you mean?"

Adele's knuckles showed white under her delicate skin as she clenched her hands in her lap. "She only says she's on a grand adventure and she'll fill us in later."

"What?" Nat set down his drink and stared at her, incredulous.

"She apparently uses a pay phone," Adele said, "and she gets off the line before we can—"

"This is unbelievable!" In his agitation, Nat got to his feet. "I know she wants to live her own life, but refusing to tell you her whereabouts is ridiculous!"

"I wanted to hire somebody to track her down," Russell said, sounding defeated. "Adele won't let me. She says if we do that, we're liable to lose her forever."

"At least now she calls!" Adele stood, as well. "If you get heavy-handed, she'll stop doing that!"

"Then I guess I'll have to find her," Nat said. And she'd better have a damn good explanation for her behavior when he did. Maybe her mother and father were overprotective, but it was obvious to him that they loved her. They deserved better treatment than this. Either something was terribly wrong, or his darling Jess had turned into a brat.

"Don't tell her you came to see us," Adele said. "Please. She might think we asked you to find her for us."

"Don't worry, I won't involve you."

Russell levered himself from his chair. "But if you want that foundation money, you'll tell us where she is when you locate her," he said.

Nat gazed at him. As fair as that sounded, he couldn't agree to it. First he had to talk to Jess and find out what had caused her to take off like this. "I can't make that promise. I will try to convince her to come out of hiding so you don't have to worry so much about her, but under the circumstances, maybe I should withdraw my request for foundation money."

"No, no, you shouldn't." Russell's mouth twitched in a ghost of a grin. "But you can't blame me for trying to use some leverage."

Nat smiled at him. "No, I can't."

"My accountants will contact your Colorado office in a few days."

"What if Jessica finds out that you're helping with this foundation? Won't she make the connection?"

Nat had had enough. He'd learned that life could be short and brutal, and he didn't have time for games. "Look, the welfare of those orphans is too important to let Jess interfere with the fund-raising. Unless she's a different person from the one I knew, she wouldn't want to interfere, no matter what her personal situation is. And I intend to find out exactly what that is."

"You sound so sure you will," Adele said.

"That's because I am sure I will." He refused to consider any other possibility.

''You called her Jess,'' Adele said. ''Does she go by that now?''

Nat looked at her. ''No. I just…I call her that.'' He realized how familiar that sounded. Her parents didn't shorten her name when they spoke of her.

''I see,'' Adele said. Obviously she saw everything.

Russell cleared his throat. ''I don't know your exact relationship to my daughter, and I don't think I want to know,'' he said. ''Maybe you left her high and dry and maybe you didn't. But if you find her and can let us know, this number will get you straight through to me.'' He handed Nat an embossed card.

''I'll find her.''

Russell extended his hand, and there was an unspoken plea in his gaze. He was obviously too proud to voice it, but it was there, nevertheless. ''Good luck to you, son.''

CHAPTER THREE

JESSICA DIDN'T BOTHER to follow the road around to the house. She moved through the trees, greeting each one as an old friend while she tried to decide what to do once she arrived at the mansion. She couldn't imagine what Nat was doing there. She was afraid to hope he was looking for her.

Her first glimpse of the house brought a rush of home-sickness. Glancing up to the second floor, she picked out the darkened windows of her bedroom. Her parents wouldn't have changed it. She and her mother had flown to Paris to choose the golden toile de Jouy fabric that draped the windows and the antique canopy bed. The bed probably had sheets on it, just in case she returned.

Most of the time she'd felt trapped in this house, but she'd also felt incredibly safe. Safety sounded good right now.

But if she walked into the house and accepted the pro-tection her parents would love to give her, she'd lose all the independent ground she'd gained. And the fight wasn't only about her now. Elizabeth deserved to grow up like a normal child instead of being followed by bodyguards wherever she went.

Oh, but the tug of home was strong, even after all this time. They were burning oak in the fireplace. The familiar smell of the smoke made her throat ache. She could picture her mother and father, each in their favorite wingback chair, reading glasses perched on their noses as they settled down with a favorite book. The love seat had been designated as hers, positioning her right between them.

When she'd been small, before she'd begun feeling stifled, the love seat sandwiched between her parents' chairs had been a good place to be. She hadn't exactly been allowed to sprawl on that seat while she read, but they'd let her tuck her feet under her as long as she took off her shoes first.

In those early days, at precisely nine o'clock, Barclay would arrive with refreshments—lemonade in the summer and steaming cocoa in the winter. And gingersnaps. Jessica could almost feel the crunch between her teeth.

She wondered if Nat was sitting on the love seat at this very minute. What on earth was he saying to her parents? A horrible thought came to her. If she told Nat about Elizabeth and the stalker, he might insist that she come back here and inform her parents. If he wanted to tell them himself, she wouldn't be able to stop him.

With Elizabeth's freedom at stake, maybe she'd better not tell Nat too much until she was sure he wouldn't go running to her parents with the information. She didn't think he'd sell her out, but she couldn't be sure. After all, he'd come here tonight.

But she needed a plan.

The cab Nat had arrived in sat empty in the driveway as the driver strolled around smoking a cigarette. He returned to the cab to stub it out in the ashtray, which was a good thing, she thought. Herb, the gardener, would have a fit if he found a cigarette butt lying on his velvet lawn. He had enough trouble contending with the autumn leaves, which he snatched up the minute they dropped from the trees.

Still, she missed Herb and his persnickety ways. She missed all of the staff, even stuffy Barclay. She hadn't realized how much until she stood in the shadows looking at the house that had sheltered her for so many years. But then, she supposed zoo animals would miss their keepers if they were suddenly turned loose. You had to give up something to get something, as her father was so fond of saying.

The cabdriver walked away from the car again and headed for the slope leading down to the river. About that time, the lights of a barge appeared from upriver, and the rumble of the boat's engines drifted toward her on the night air. The driver stood with his back to her, his hands in his pockets as he gazed at the approaching boat.

Jessica's pulse leaped as she recognized her opportunity. Nat had ridden in the front seat on the way out here. No doubt he'd do the same on the way back. While the cabbie watched the barge sail past, she could hide on the floor of the back seat. The boat's engines would muffle the sound of her opening and closing the car door.

Unless Nat happened to come out at the exact moment when she was sneaking into the cab, she'd be able to hitch a ride without being noticed. When they arrived at Nat's hotel, she'd reveal herself and hope that the cabdriver didn't have a weak heart.

As for Nat, maybe he deserved the jolt she'd give him. For all she knew, he was telling her parents about her involvement with him, which she definitely didn't appreciate having him do without checking with her first. To be fair, he would have had some trouble checking with her first, but still, in coming here he'd overstepped his bounds.

The rumble of the boat's engine grew louder. Good thing *she* didn't have a weak heart. It was skittering around like crazy while she waited for the noise to reach its loudest point. Okay. Now. She hurried toward the cab. The back door was locked.

She lost precious time opening the front door and reaching around to lift the button on the back door. Fortunately the barge's engines drowned out the sounds she made. Or at least she hoped they did. The rhythmic rush of blood against her eardrums made it difficult to gauge how much noise she was making.

Luck seemed to be favoring her. The cabdriver didn't turn around and the front door remained closed. She climbed into the back seat and shut the car door as quietly as possible. The driver stood watching the barge edge down the river. He probably didn't think he needed to watch over his cab when he was inside the gated confines of Franklin Hall.

Putting her backpack on the floor, she lay on her side across the hump and put her head on the backpack. Not so good. And she'd thought she was roughing it when she'd had to give up first-class for coach.

She shifted position several times trying for some level of comfort. Finally she gave up. Comfort wasn't in the cards for this ride. She'd have to hope, when the cab reached the city, that she wouldn't be too crippled to walk.

Now if she could only stop gasping for breath, she might actually be able to pull this off. She forced herself to inhale slowly and deeply. She almost choked on the stale cigarette smell wafting up from the carpeting.

I'm doing this for Elizabeth, she told herself. She turned to face the back seat instead of the front, which gave her a little more breathing room. Gradually she became more accustomed to the obnoxious odor.

Nat's backpack was within reach on the back seat. She stroked the frayed canvas, as if that would somehow start the process of connecting to him. He was not the same man who'd left her in Aspen, that was for sure. But then she wasn't the same woman, either. Maybe they'd find no common ground other than the most obvious—their child. But Elizabeth's welfare was worth any amount of sacrifice she had to make.

Despite her awkward position on the floor of the car, she

began to relax. Then she heard the front door of the house open and close. Suddenly she couldn't breathe. Nat was coming.

"All set?" the cabdriver called.

"Let's go," Nat replied.

His voice splashed over her, drenching her with longing. She wanted him. No matter how she'd tried to stamp out her feelings, the sound of his voice brought back a flood of memories—tender, lusty, explosive memories. And of all the times they'd made love, the most electrifying had been the night they'd conceived Elizabeth. He'd become such a part of her that night that she'd thought for sure he'd agree to break the code of silence.

Instead, he'd smashed their love to smithereens.

Her heart beat wildly as the front doors of the cab opened and the dome light flicked on. If either of them decided to look in the back seat during that brief time, they'd see her.

They didn't.

The engine started, and she discovered one other unpleasant fact. She could smell car exhaust down here. Wonderful. Now she could worry about asphyxiating herself.

As the cab began to move down the driveway, Jessica was sure she could feel every rock and pebble in the road, especially when the tires threw them up under the car. But she didn't dare move, at least not until they were well on their way back to the city.

"Did you get your business settled?" the cabdriver asked.

"Not exactly," Nat said. "But it was a start."

Please let this be a nosy cabdriver, Jessica prayed. She just might find out something that would partially make up for being crammed in here like a doomed mobster.

Unfortunately for her, the cabbie wasn't all that interested in Nat's business at Franklin Hall and started talking about the World Series instead. Jessica clenched her teeth as Nat happily traded opinions on the relative merits of each team in the playoffs. Guys and their sports.

Yet even though the conversation bored her to tears, she loved listening to Nat's voice, and his low chuckle was enough to trip the switch on her libido. She didn't focus on his words, but absorbed only his tone.

Maybe because she was lying in the dark, she began to think of how it had been lying with Nat in the dark. Gradually her mind replaced his talk about baseball with other words, polished gems from her treasure-house of memories. *I could spend forever looking at you, Jess. And kissing you. Your skin tastes like milk and honey. Come here, woman. Come let me make love to you. For the rest of the night. Who cares about sleep when we can do this?*

She hadn't forgotten a minute of the time they'd been together. She wondered if he'd forgotten it all. But if he didn't want anything more to do with her, why had he traveled to Franklin Hall the minute he set foot on U.S. soil?

Cautiously she wiggled over so she could see out the window. It wasn't a great view, and the hump on the floor forced her to arch her back to an uncomfortable degree, but she'd be able to tell when they reached the city. She was more than ready to get there. The exhaust fumes were making her woozy.

"There's the Franklin Tower," the cabbie said. "They say Franklin's office takes up the entire top floor. A huge office, they say, with a three-hundred-sixty-degree view of Manhattan."

She knew that office. Jessica brought her attention back to the conversation in the front seat. Maybe the driver would finally try to get some gossip out of Nat.

"I've heard about his office," Nat said.

He'd heard it from her. Nat had been the only person who knew about her background, and when he'd abandoned her, she'd lost more than a lover. She'd lost the one person she could talk to without constantly guarding her speech.

When she'd left New York, she'd severed all ties with friends because she couldn't be sure they wouldn't somehow give her away and leave her open to the kidnappers her father spoke about endlessly, the ones waiting to snatch a rich man's child. She'd heard his warnings for so long that she believed him. She'd just wanted to find a different way to avoid that fate.

She'd made new friends in Aspen, but none of them knew she had a famous father. Only Nat. Keeping the secret had been more of a burden than she'd planned on, and confiding in Nat had been a welcome relief.

"That Franklin, I guess he's a real wheeler-dealer," said the cabbie, obviously fishing for information. "I've also heard he's tough to get along with."

No joke, Jessica thought. *Try having a different opinion from his and see what happens to you.* The lights of the city were all around her now, with horns blaring and even more fumes coming up through the floor of the cab. Her head started to pound, and she closed her eyes to see if that might help.

"Someone did tell me that Franklin was hard to get along with," Nat said. "But he seemed like a reasonable guy to me."

Jessica's eyes snapped open. Nat thought her father was *reasonable?* What sort of a turncoat was he, anyway? Her headache grew worse.

"So you two got along pretty well, then?" the driver asked.

"I think so," Nat replied. "Anybody with that much power is bound to rub people the wrong way once in a while, and he makes for an easy target, but he struck me as a decent man who tries to do the right thing."

Jessica couldn't decide which was worse, the fumes or Nat's praise of her father. Both of them were making her sick.

"And I also think the person who told me he was hard to get along with probably has some authority issues to work out," Nat added.

Authority issues? What the hell did he know about it? Jessica's automatic yelp of protest was halfway out before she remembered that nobody was supposed to know she was hiding in the back seat. She clapped her hand to her mouth, but it was too late.

"Jesus!" the driver cried. "Somebody's in the—"

"You watch the road! I'll handle it!" Nat climbed into the back seat and grabbed Jessica by the front of her jacket.

She was too stunned to speak.

Gasping for breath, he hauled her up to a sitting position, which knocked her glasses askew. She pushed them back into place and tried to keep from throwing up. The exhaust fumes had really made her nauseated.

"My God, it's a woman," Nat said in amazement.

"What's a woman doing in my cab?" the driver babbled hysterically. "Is she armed?"

"I don't know," Nat said, breathing hard. "Are you armed?"

She shook her head, still trying to keep from tossing her cookies.

"She's not armed," Nat said to the driver. As his breathing slowed, he peered intently at her. Multicolored lights streamed in through the cab windows and slid across his face, making it difficult to read his expression. But he seemed to be studying her, as if trying to solve a riddle.

"I'm heading for the nearest cop shop," the cabbie said.

"Don't do that yet," Nat told the driver quietly. "Let me see if I can find out what's going on here." He looked down at Jessica. "Where did you come from?"

She didn't trust herself to open her mouth without losing her lunch, so instead she took off her glasses and gazed up at him.

He stared at her, stared at her hard. Then, while he kept his gaze locked on hers, he reached up with his free hand and hit the switch on the dome light.

She blinked in the glare of the overhead, but when she could once again meet his gaze, she saw the dawning recognition there.

"Jess?" he whispered.

She nodded. Then she scrambled for the window, rolled it down and threw up.

ENDLESS HUMILIATING moments later, Jessica was finally ensconced in the bathroom of Nat's hotel room with the door locked. Swearing under her breath, she stripped down, pulled off her wig and stepped under the shower. In all the scenarios she'd played in her head about this meeting, none of them had included barfing.

Fortunately she'd only baptized the side of the cab and the sleeve of her coat. In the hullabaloo following her hurling incident, she'd been too embarrassed to be able to gauge whether or not Nat was happy to see her. It would have been difficult to factor out the vomit in that calculation, anyway. Not many men would be happy to see a woman whose first move was to spew all over the place.

Once in the shower, she gave in to the urge to wash her hair with the luxurious hotel shampoo. Much as it pained her to admit it, she missed the five-star treatment. In the years since she'd left Franklin Hall, she'd tried not to dip into her trust fund at all, but once she quit her job and went on the lam, so to speak, she'd had to draw some money out. She begrudged every penny she spent, because it was her father's money.

Consequently, she could hardly describe her accommodations in the past few months as first-class. Maybe fifth- or sixth-class.

Knowing Nat and his lack of pretense, she'd expected him to opt for a low-to-medium-priced hotel while he was in New York, but for reasons she couldn't fathom, he'd directed the cabdriver to the Waldorf. From the reaction of the clerk at check-in, she'd figured out Nat hadn't made an advance reservation, so it was a spur-of-the-moment decision.

Maybe he'd done it for her, although she'd died a million deaths standing there in the glittering lobby in her bag-lady clothes decorated with barf. Now, however, as she rinsed her hair under the most excellent showerhead she'd enjoyed in months, she blessed him for his choice.

Ah, the thick towels. Oh, the rich scent of the body lotion. She wanted to be a good girl and not care about such superficial things, but she'd been raised with them, and the sense of deprivation had been more acute than she'd planned on.

She smoothed at least half the tiny bottle of lotion over herself, both because it felt so good and because, once she was finished, she had to face putting on something wrinkled and musty from her backpack. She was sick to death of wrinkled and musty.

From years of experience with luxurious accommodations, she knew that in the room's closet a thick terry robe would be hanging ready for just this moment. Technically it was there for the use of the person who'd rented the room. That person would be Nat.

She pictured herself coming out to talk to him in the wrinkled and baggy jumper and turtleneck she had stuffed in her backpack. Then she pictured herself having the same conversation wearing that thick white robe. The discussion would be difficult enough without looking bad while she had it.

Wrapping a towel around her, she went to the door and opened it a crack. "Nat?"

"Yes?" Instantly footsteps hurried in her direction. "Are you feeling okay? Should I call a doctor?"

"I'm feeling better than I have in ages," she said. "But I have a big favor to ask. Would you mind if I put on the hotel bathrobe that's hanging in the closet? My clothes are…well, they don't look very…the thing is, I—"

"Here." A wad of white terry poked through the crack in the door. "Enjoy."

"Thanks." She opened the door enough to pull the robe through. Oh, yes. Egyptian cotton. It felt like heaven as she pulled it on and belted it around her waist. In the steamy mirror she fluffed her still-damp hair. For the first time in months, she looked and felt like herself.

And now she had to face Nat.

She fluffed her hair again. Then she ran a quick comb through it. She wasn't happy with the last cut, which she'd got done at a beauty school to save money. It took an exceptional stylist to deal with her thick, naturally curly hair. This one had left it too bulky around her shoulders. She tried to tame it with her fingers, but it was no use.

Maybe a little lipstick.

While she'd been on the run, she'd pared down her cosmetics needs to lipstick, mascara and blush. She had the tube of lipstick halfway to her mouth when she stopped to stare at herself in the mirror. What was she doing? Trying to come on to him?

She rolled the lipstick back down, capped it and tucked it into her backpack. She'd take him the herbal supplements she'd brought, though. Fishing them out, she started toward the door. On the way she happened to look down at her feet.

Now, *there* was a sorry sight. She paused to consider her unpainted toes, clipped with a toenail clipper. Not buffed, not filed, not pampered. Her last pedicure had been before she'd had Elizabeth. Nat had always loved her feet.

Stop it, she lectured herself. He probably didn't love any part of her anymore. What she looked like didn't matter. Elizabeth was the only person who mattered in this whole mess.

"Jess?" Nat rapped on the door. "Are you sure you're okay in there?"

"I'm okay."

"Then what's taking so long?"

"I was, um, thinking."

"Well, could you do that out here? We need to talk."

"Yes, we do. We most certainly do." Drawing in a bracing lungful of air, she opened the bathroom door. She found herself staring at his shirtfront. He stood right outside the door, crowding her, invading her space. She would have to walk around him to move any farther into the room.

His masculine scent surrounded her, making her quicken in all sorts of strategic places. She gathered her courage and looked up into his eyes. Her heart stuttered at the fire burning there. "Nat?"

"What's that?" He glanced down at the two bottles of supplements.

"Herbal stuff for you."

His gaze lifted. "Why?"

"Because…" *Because I love you and worry about you.* She didn't dare say it.

He made an impatient noise deep in his throat. "Jess, I have to ask you something."

"Okay." Her heart hammered.

His words were as intense as his gaze. "Is there anyone else?"

Joy rushed through her. *Hallelujah. He still wanted her.* "No. No one else."

With a gusty sigh he took the vitamin bottles and tossed

them on the floor. Then he pulled her into his arms. "Excuse the beard," he murmured. Then his lips crushed hers.

Overjoyed as she was to know that he still cared, she was distracted at first by the beard. Kissing him was like smooching a stuffed animal. But then…then he coaxed her mouth open. She forgot all about the beard as she rediscovered why kissing Nat had been one of her all-time thrills. He could pack more sensuality into a kiss than other men could manage in an hour of whole-body sex.

A few moments of kissing Nat beat a day at the spa for making her tingle all over. One kiss from him and she was so awake, from the tips of her curling toes to the tiny hairs at the nape of her neck. His fingers stroked there, and she turned to melted butter in his arms.

Boiling butter might be more like it. She wriggled against him, trying to get closer.

He shifted the angle of his mouth and tugged at the bathrobe's sash while he muttered something that sounded like *have to.*

Oh, so did she. Had to. She started on the buttons of his shirt. But wait. She hadn't planned on this.

"Need you so," he breathed, backing her toward the bed as he continued to kiss her senseless.

"Wait," she said, gasping.

"Can't." He pushed open the terry cloth and closed his hand over her breast with a groan.

"Nat—" She tried to tell him she wasn't on the Pill. He kept coming, thrusting his tongue in her mouth, making her crazy with wanting him. The back of her knees hit the edge of the bed. She fell against the quilted spread and he came right with her.

Panting, she tried again. "I'm not—"

His mouth silenced her once more.

Oh, God. How many times had she fantasized about his weight pressing her into the mattress, his hand between her thighs, his mouth at her breast? Both of them going wild. If this was a dream, she'd kill whoever or whatever woke her up.

Even his beard was wonderful, brushing her skin like the pelt of some exotic animal. She'd never realized kissing a bearded man could be so erotic. She pulled him closer, arched into his caress, moaned his name.

"God, I need you," he groaned.

"I need you, too." But one unplanned baby was enough. She forced herself to choke out the words. "But I'm not on the Pill anymore. We can't—"

"Yes, we can." He nuzzled his way back to her mouth.

At first she thought he meant that he wouldn't care if she got pregnant. "We can?"

"Yes." He covered her face with a million kisses. "We can. I want to be inside you, Jess."

Could he really be telling her that he'd changed his mind about children? Her heart expanded with the possibility. "Why can we?" she asked breathlessly.

"I had room service bring up condoms. Don't worry." He kissed her cheeks, her eyelids, her nose. "I won't get you pregnant."

She went still. "Would that be so terrible?"

He paused and lifted his head to gaze into her eyes. Although it seemed to take some effort, he gained control of his runaway desire. Then he took a deep breath. "I don't want to start out with a fight, Jess."

A pulse hammered in her throat. "Neither do I. But I need to know. Would it be so terrible if you got me pregnant?"

"You mean right now, at this very moment?" Without giving her a chance to answer, he barreled on. "Yeah, it would. We have a lot of talking to do, and that's one of the things we need to talk about, but I wouldn't want to make a move like that without taking all kinds of things into consideration. I am willing to give it some thought, much more so than when I left. Maybe…I'm not saying positively, but maybe…someday. But not right now.''

The hope swelling in her heart died. Damn, but he was a pain in the butt. She'd meant to find a gentle way to tell him, but suddenly she didn't want to be gentle with this incredibly sexy but frustratingly stubborn man. She wanted to hit him between the eyes.

''It's too late to talk about it, Nat,'' she said. ''Eight months ago I gave birth to our daughter.''

CHAPTER FOUR

NAT STARED down at her as a sick feeling worked its way through his gut. "No," he whispered.

"Yes. I'm sorry to spring it on you like this. I hadn't planned on that, but I've carried this secret for so long that I—"

"No!" He scrambled from the bed, as if eliminating all contact with her would change the message she was trying to deliver. He jabbed an accusing finger at her. "You were on the Pill!"

Jess sat up, drew her robe around her with great dignity and retied the sash. Sometimes, at moments like this when she adopted an almost royal air, he realized that some of her upbringing had stuck with her, whether she wanted it to or not.

"Yes, I was, but—"

"You stopped?" The fear boiling in his stomach erupted into accusations. "You stopped without telling me, didn't you? You thought if you couldn't hook me one way, you'd try something else!"

"How dare you!" She leaped from the bed, rigid with anger.

"What else am I supposed to think?" Oh, God, he remembered how she'd pleaded with him to commit. Her pleas could have come from the desperate knowledge that she might be carrying his baby.

Clenching her fists, she faced him, her eyes dark with betrayal. "You could try thinking that it was an accident."

Her voice quivered. "I had a cold that weekend, remember?"

"Yeah, I remember." She'd suggested their not seeing each other because she hadn't wanted to infect him. But he'd talked her into it by saying he had a great immune system. He'd told her they'd spend the weekend in bed. Which they had. Her cold had made their final argument that much more miserable, because she'd been crying and coughing and sneezing through it all. He'd felt like the worst kind of heel, but she'd been the one pressing the point, not him. And he'd run.

Her tone grew bitter. "I was so worried about you catching whatever I had that I decided to get a prescription for antibiotics, hoping then I'd be less contagious."

"I remember that, too. What does that have to do with—"

"See? You don't know, either! Antibiotics can make birth control pills useless!"

So it was true. The realization washed over him in an icy wave. A child. He had a child. His baby wasn't a refugee, yet still the images of those sad-eyed orphans rose up to taunt him. Life had let them down, and sure as the world, he would let down any child that called him father.

When panic threatened to overwhelm him, he looked for someone to blame. "If that's true about antibiotics, it should be common knowledge! The doctor should have told you!"

"How could he think to? I ran over to one of those all-night clinics, and they were busy as hell. The guy who prescribed the antibiotics didn't know me or my situation, and let's not forget that I was supposed to keep it so damn secret that I was involved in a sexual relationship."

He looked away from the accusation in her eyes. Guilty. He was so guilty. Loving a woman like Jess had been a mistake from the beginning. After only a couple of days of knowing her, he'd realized she was a white-lace-and-promises kind of gal. Pursuing her had been pure selfishness on his part.

But he'd wanted her in a way that reason and fairness couldn't touch. He still did. One glance in her direction and the urge to take her came roaring back, especially now, when he was vulnerable and afraid. He'd discovered making love to Jess was magic. Holding her, pushing deep inside her, his fears always went away.

He could still taste her kisses. Her mouth was red from them, her skin rosy from the brush of his beard. The scattering of freckles across the bridge of her nose had been something he'd missed more than he realized. He loved her more now than ever before, as she stood there defiantly challenging him, her wild mane of red curls a riot of color around her tight, angry expression.

Then it finally struck him that she'd announced that they had a child, but she was here alone. "Where is the baby now?"

The defiance whooshed out of her in no time, and her expression became heartbreakingly sad. "In Colorado," she said quietly. "At the Rocking D."

"With *Sebastian?*" Alarm zinged through him. "Sebastian doesn't know a damn thing about babies! How long—"

"Maybe we'd better go over there and sit down." She gestured to a polished cherry table and two side chairs positioned by the window. "We have several things to talk about."

He couldn't come up with a better plan. It was as good a spot as any for him to be while she flung one hand grenade of information after another. Walking over to the window, he opened the drapes. He'd closed them while she was in the shower as part of his preparation for seducing her. Now he needed a feeling of space.

Below them the city still bustled even though it was nearly midnight. Which meant it was early morning in London. If his body ever stopped pumping with adrenaline, he'd probably keel over from lack of sleep. As it was, he felt as if he'd never be able to sleep again.

"Are you going to sit down?" she asked.

He turned. She was seated primly in one of the Queen Anne chairs, her elbows resting on the arms, her fingers laced together and her feet crossed at the ankles. He thought again how well she fit into this environment. She looked like a younger version of her mother.

He also had the ignoble thought of going over to that chair and trapping her within its arms while he ravished her. There was something very provocative about that bulky terry robe covering her naked body, and the untidy mass of her just-washed hair made her look like a woman in need of ravishing. She had freckles across the top of her breasts, too, and he'd been too busy to take proper notice of them the first time he'd opened her robe. Those freckles called to him.

She'd given birth to his child. He couldn't take it in. His mind kept trying to reject the whole concept.

"I guess you're not going to sit down," she said. "I can understand you being agitated. I really had hoped to break this to you more gradually. But before I say anything more, I need to know if we can keep this between us, or if you will feel some obligation to contact my parents."

He thought of the worry etched into Adele's forehead, and the desperate gleam in Russell's eyes. "They're worried sick about you. They said you've been traveling…" He paused to stare at her. "Have you been hauling that kid around all over the place?"

"Her name is Elizabeth, and no, I haven't. Like I told you, she's been at the Rocking D."

Elizabeth. Her name made her more real, which was not a good thing. "Since when?"

"Since March."

"Holy shit! Is she okay? Is Sebastian—"

"She's fine. I keep checking by phone." Her knuckles whitened as she clenched her hands in her lap. "I had to do it like this, Nat. But first I have to know. Are you going to call my parents and tell them everything?"

"Don't you think they deserve to know? My God, it's their grandchild, Jess!"

"I know." She swallowed. "But they'd want to swoop back in and protect me, and this time they'd include Elizabeth in their net. She'd become a little prisoner, just like I did. Once they knew the whole story, they might even get a court order giving them the right to do that."

Gradually he began to piece things together. Her disguise, her separation from the baby, her traveling around. He walked over to stand directly in front of her. "What's the problem, Jess?"

"I need your word that you won't call my parents."

"You're not getting it. That might be the thing to do."

She looked frantic. "No, it's not! I won't have my daughter grow up that way." Her eyes begged for his understanding. "Please, Nat. Promise you won't bring them into this."

He shook his head. "No promises. I understand what you're afraid of. I've seen Franklin Hall and I'm sure you were very lonely there. But there are worse things than being lonely." And he was the guy who could testify to that. "You'll have to trust me. I wouldn't contact them unless I thought it was absolutely necessary, but if they're your best alternative, and you're being too pigheaded to see that, then—"

"You never lived there." She pushed out of the chair and brushed past him, headed for the bathroom. "Tell you what. My main objective was to tell you about Elizabeth, and I've done that. All I ask is that if anything should happen to me, you'll see about our baby.'' She went into the bathroom.

He was across the room with one hand bracing the door before she could close it. ''Stop right there.'' His heart hammered in his ears. ''What the hell do you mean, if something should happen to you?''

She looked at him. ''There are no guarantees in life, are there? Now, if you'll excuse me, I'll get dressed and out of your way.''

''The hell you will.'' Seventeen months ago he wouldn't have thrown his weight around. That was before he'd lived in the middle of a war zone, where life could be snuffed out in an instant. He grabbed her wrist and pulled her back into the room. ''You're obviously in some kind of danger, and you are, by God, going to tell me about it.''

She resisted, trying to struggle out of his grip. Her color was high, and she was breathing hard. ''This macho routine isn't like you.''

''I've changed. Now tell me.''

''Why should I?''

Both fury and passion put the same bloom in her cheeks and the same hitch in her breathing, he noticed. He might not recognize the difference, except for the look in her eyes. ''Well, for one thing—'' he grabbed her other wrist ''—you're the mother of my child.'' Saying it made him shudder, but the fact gave him some rights.

Her eyes spit fire. ''I have always put Elizabeth first, and I always will. I'll make sure she's safe, no matter what happens to me.''

''She needs you.'' He tightened his grip on her wrists. ''And damn it, so do I.''

''No, you don't!'' Tears of frustration filled her eyes. ''You just need me for sex!''

His throat ached with remorse. Of course she'd think that. He forced the words past the lump in his throat. "Oh, I need you for sex, all right. Like you wouldn't believe. But that's only the tip of the iceberg, sweetheart."

Her response was low and choked with tears. "I don't believe you. Now let me go."

"No. Tell me what danger you're in. I have a right to know."

She gazed up at him and he could tell from the turmoil in her eyes how hard she was trying to be tough, how desperately she wanted to handle whatever she was dealing with by herself.

He couldn't let her do it. "Tell me. For Elizabeth's sake." Saying the baby's name, acknowledging her personhood, took another major effort on his part, but he figured it might turn the trick with Jess.

It did. Her shoulders slumped. "Someone's trying to kidnap me," she murmured.

"Oh, God." He didn't remember letting go of her wrists to wrap his arms around her, but all at once there she was in his arms, and he was holding on for dear life as he rocked her back and forth. He buried his face in her hair. "Oh, God, Jess." He knew about kidnapping. In the political upheaval he'd just witnessed, people had been kidnapped all the time. They never came back.

"It's just like my dad predicted!" she wailed, hugging him tightly. "In Aspen I thought someone might be following me. Then a car tried to force me off the road one night. Thank God Elizabeth wasn't with me. I got away, but I saw the same car following me another time, and I knew for sure then. Somebody has found out who I am. They've decided to snatch the Franklin heir."

With growing horror he listened as the story came tumbling out. She'd traded in her car for a different one, packed up the baby and taken her to the Rocking D for safekeeping. For the past six months she'd been on the run. But it had been a creative run.

Using different disguises and modes of transportation, she'd tried to elude the kidnapper. But just when she thought she had, a man would follow her along a crowded street, far enough away that she couldn't positively identify him, but close enough for her to suspect he was the same man. By keeping her wits about her, she'd stayed out of his clutches.

When she was finished, Nat held her tight for a long moment. Then he sighed. ''We're calling the police.''

''No!'' She backed away from him. ''The minute you do that, my parents will be all over this situation, and then my life as we know it will be over.''

''Your life as you know it is totally screwed up!''

''No, it isn't.'' She tucked her wayward hair behind her ears, which made her look like a schoolgirl. A sexy schoolgirl.

He was determined not to be distracted. ''The hell it isn't. You have a kidnapper on your trail and you can't even risk being close to your baby as a result.''

''I can risk it now that you're home.''

''Now, wait a minute. Flattering as that sounds, I can't have you thinking I'm an adequate bodyguard.''

''You just said you'd changed. And I can see it. You're more aggressive than you were seventeen months ago.''

''I'm not a trained bodyguard, and your parents are exactly the people who could—''

''Oh, gee, look at the time.'' She glanced at her bare wrist and started back toward the bathroom. ''Gotta run.''

''Oh, hell.'' He clamped a hand on her shoulder to keep her from disappearing behind the closed door. Holding her firmly by the shoulder, he heaved a gusty sigh. ''Are you telling me that if I call your parents, you'll take off and leave me to deal with them?'' He didn't relish the thought of facing Russell P. Franklin alone and announcing he'd gotten the Franklin heir with child.

She glanced over her shoulder. Jess was the sort of woman who could be provocative without even trying. "I guess that's about the size of it, Nathaniel Andrew."

"That's blackmail, Jessica Louise."

She smiled a vixen's smile. "I know."

He couldn't decide which he'd rather do, strangle her or kiss that saucy mouth until she moaned. He did neither. "You're blackmailing your parents, too, you know. Your dad wants to put a private detective on your trail so bad he can taste it, but your mother won't let him because she thinks you'll go away for good if he does."

"She's right."

Turning her to face him, he grasped her other shoulder and barely stopped himself from giving her a shake. "Jess, what if this kidnapper gets ahold of you? What if he decides, after getting the ransom money, to just kill you? Have you thought of that?"

She nodded. "That's why I needed to talk to you and tell you about Elizabeth," she said in a matter-of-fact tone. "So everything would be okay for the baby."

The thought of something happening to Jess had the power to paralyze his mind, so he didn't think about it for long. "Setting aside the issue of how the rest of us would fare in that event, let me emphasize that if you got yourself killed, it would *not* be okay for the baby." Panic nibbled at him some more. "I'm a lousy candidate for a parent, and you know it."

"I don't know it, but if you call my parents, we'll never get a chance to find out. They'll have Elizabeth behind the gates of Franklin Hall before you can say boo."

"Sounds like a plan to me." Then he wouldn't have to worry about the baby. He had a business in Colorado, after all. He could pay support, although the Franklins would probably scoff at the pittance the courts would ask of him.

"And I'd have to go with her," Jess said softly.

Ah, there was the rub. The woman he loved would be safe but unhappy. And he would be…lost. Lost without hope of redemption.

"You see, it has to be this way if you and I are to have any chance. If Elizabeth is to have any chance."

As he gazed into her eyes and saw the glimmer of hope there, his feelings of inadequacy threatened to swamp him. "I would botch the job of being Elizabeth's father, Jess. We've been through all that, and you know how I feel about having kids of my own. I'll admit that on the flight over I began thinking that maybe someday I could consider adopting an orphan from one of the refugee camps. But see, that would be different. The kid wouldn't have that many options, and even having me as a parent would be better than nothing."

"Oh, Nat." She moved in close and combed her fingers through his beard so she could cup his face in both hands.

He loved her touch, and decided at that very moment that he wanted to shave so nothing interfered with the feel of her soft hands on his face.

"I've never met your father," she said, "but I know you're nothing like him. You would never beat a child the way you were beaten, or belittle them until they felt worthless, the way your father did."

"You don't know that. It's the pattern I saw for eighteen years. Some of that behavior has to be lurking in me, waiting for the time when I have a kid, and that automatic conditioning kicks in."

Her gaze searched his. "Don't you at least want to see her?" she asked gently.

His stomach churned at the thought, but yes, he'd admit to a flicker of curiosity. "Maybe, from a distance."

Jess smiled. "How far a distance?"

"One of those videophones would be about right."

She held his gaze. "I think she has your eyes."

That rocked him. All along he'd pictured her with woeful brown eyes, like the children he'd left in the camps. "Blue?"

"They probably are by now. The color was still a little indistinct when I...when I left her at the ranch." Her breath caught and her eyes began to glow with longing. "Oh, Nat, please. Let's call the ranch and tell them we're on our way. It's been an eternity. Please. It's still only ten there. They won't be in bed. Let's call them now."

One thing had become obvious—he wouldn't in good conscience be able to shift this new and unwanted responsibility to Jess's parents. Neither could he expect Sebastian to keep on taking the burden, although Nat wasn't wild about heading out there to face this massive change in his life. He'd ten times rather hold up in the Waldorf for a few days and calm his fears by making endless love to Jess.

But it looked as if he needed to take Jess to Colorado. "Okay. Yeah. We'll do that."

"Oh, thank you!" She wrapped her arms around his neck and planted a kiss right on his mouth.

She might have meant it as a friendly gesture instead of an invitation, but it didn't matter how she'd meant it. His body flipped to automatic pilot as he grabbed her and pulled her in tight. He couldn't have kept his tongue out of her mouth for all the gold in Fort Knox.

With a little whimper of delight, she molded herself against him the way only Jess could do. Her body dovetailed with his as no other woman's body had ever done. It was as if they'd been carved from the same block of stone so that when they came together, the seam of separation disappeared.

But she wasn't stone—she was warm and pliant. When

he pushed his hand into the invisible gap between them, she magically made way for him. He tugged at the sash of her bathrobe and the thick material loosened instantly, gaping open over the smooth curve of her breast.

He was there in an instant, cupping the weight, almost out of his mind with the joy of caressing her silken breast again. He brushed the erect nipple with the pad of his thumb and she gasped against his mouth. She'd always been so sensitive to his slightest touch, which had made him feel like a god when he made love to her.

Tonight her reaction seemed even more sensitive, and subtly different. Or maybe it was all in his mind. Once upon a time, he'd thought he knew every intimate detail about her. But in his absence she'd given birth to a child—his child. The knowledge made her body mysterious and exotic. He needed to reconnect with her, if only to convince himself that she was still knowable, still within his reach.

He lifted his mouth a fraction from hers as he rubbed her nipple with his thumb. "Did you nurse her?" he murmured.

Her breath blew warm on his lips. "Yes."

He traced her open mouth with his tongue. "Tell me how it was."

"Sweet." Her breath quickened.

He looked down at her upturned face, her auburn lashes lying against her freckled cheeks, her lips parted, her breathing uneven as he stroked her taut nipple. "So you liked it." He was hard, so hard.

Her eyes fluttered open, and her glance scorched his. "I loved it."

"I wish I'd been there."

"So do I."

Holding her gaze, he deliberately pushed aside the lapel of her robe. Lifting her breast in his hand, he leaned down, heart racing, and slowly drew her nipple into his mouth. She tasted like heaven. He closed his eyes in ecstasy.

She sighed his name and tunneled her fingers through his hair to hold him against her breast.

When he thought he might come apart from the pressure of wanting her, he lifted his head and gazed into her passion-dark eyes. "I'm taking you to bed."

"What about…the phone…call," she whispered weakly.

He scooped her into his arms and the robe fell away as he carried her to the bed and laid her on the quilted spread. His throat went dry at her beauty, and his vocal cords felt like the rusty hinge on an old screen door. His hand went to his belt buckle. "In the morning," he said.

CHAPTER FIVE

WITH A SENSE of inevitability, Jessica abandoned control
of the situation and allowed her desire to take her where it
would. Making the phone call tonight wouldn't get her to
her baby any faster, anyway. Nat needed sleep before he
went anywhere.

But sleep didn't seem to be on his mind. She watched
him shuck his clothes and remembered all the lonely nights
she'd dreamed of his virile body moving in rhythm with
hers. She wanted that as much as he did. Needed that, to
give her a taste of what she was fighting for.

Her gaze swept hungrily over him. She'd always loved
looking at him naked. Maybe it was the long absence, but
he seemed even more beautiful now, leaner, stronger-
looking, his chest and shoulder muscles more defined. With
his thick beard, she couldn't help thinking of some Norse
god with thunderbolts in each clenched fist.

When he put his knee on the mattress and braced his
hands on either side of her, she reached up to stroke his
chest. The muscles under her hand were rock-hard.

She glanced into his intense blue eyes. "You must have
worked like a field hand over there."

"I dug a lot of ditches." He leaned closer and nibbled
on her lower lip. "I worked until I was so tired, I couldn't
stand. And still I couldn't sleep for needing you."

His beard tickled her skin. She longed to give herself to
the sensuous delight of his kiss, but first she had to know.

''And did you…find someone to help you with that problem?''

When he stilled, her heart twisted. Cupping his face in both hands, she drew back and looked into his eyes. She saw remorse there, and a crack started to form in her heart. ''You did, didn't you?''

''No,'' he said quietly.

''No? Then why are you looking so guilty?''

''Because it just hit me how she must have felt when I turned her down.''

''A refugee?''

''God, no. I would never take advantage of those vulnerable women. Another camp volunteer, from England. She wanted me, or at least she wanted someone like me. I thought I could go through with it. I tried to go through with it.'' His gaze bored into hers and he sounded irritated. Whether with himself or her, she wasn't sure. ''I wanted to forget you,'' he said. ''I wanted in the worst way to be able to make love to her.''

The thought of him even considering getting naked with another woman drove her crazy. ''So, did you kiss her?''

''Yes.''

She couldn't leave it alone. ''French-kiss?''

''Yes.''

''You had your tongue in another woman's mouth? How could you do that?''

A faint smile touched his lips. ''Forget it, Jess. Nothing happened. Not that I wasn't hoping it would. I just… couldn't.''

Jessica was pretty happy about that. ''Did you take her clothes off?''

''Yes, and now I'm going to take off the rest of yours.'' His mouth came down, cutting off her next question as he worked her arm out of the bathrobe sleeve.

She shoved him away and gasped for breath. ''Not so

fast, buster. I want to get this straight. Were your clothes off, too?''

''Mostly.'' In one smooth movement he pulled the robe off her other arm and tossed it on the floor.

''And even after all that, you didn't make love to her?''

''No.'' He pushed her flat on the mattress and followed her down, pinning her there with his chest.

Oh, yes. She loved the satisfying weight of him, the slight abrasion of his chest hair against her breasts. And he needed her. Only her. She gazed up at him, overjoyed with the news that he'd had a chance to make love to someone and hadn't been able to.

Yet she still could hardly believe it. ''Is that normal?''

''I doubt it. I think you've ruined me.'' He framed her face in both hands, and his eyes searched hers for many long moments.

''What is it?'' she questioned softly.

''I can't believe I'm really here with you. I'm afraid I'm going to wake up.''

''Me, too.'' She reached up and touched his cheek. ''Make love to me, Nat, before we both wake up.''

With a groan he lowered his head and kissed her. His kiss was deep and sensuous, as it always was in her dreams, and she arched against him, praying that he wasn't an illusion. Deepening the kiss, he slid his hand between her legs and caressed her inner thigh, but that had been a part of her dreams, too. Even when he slipped his fingers into her moist channel and stroked her until she whimpered, she couldn't be sure he wasn't a figment of her imagination.

But in all the nights she'd fantasized about loving him again, she'd never dreamed of the soft whisper of his beard against her skin. As if that alone could convince her that he wouldn't disappear in a puff of smoke, she combed her fingers through it.

He lifted his mouth from hers. "I should have shaved," he murmured.

"No." Oh, his fingers could work magic, winding her tighter and tighter. "I...like it."

"It must be like making love to a furry animal." As if to make his point, he nibbled his way down her throat, his beard tickling her all the way.

"Uh-huh."

He stroked his beard deliberately over the tip of her breast. "Or some caveman."

She closed her eyes in ecstasy. "Uh-huh."

"And you like this?" he asked in a husky voice as he swept his beard back and forth across her tingling nipples.

She struggled for breath. "Uh-huh."

His low chuckle was laced with excitement. "You're kinky, woman."

"And you love it."

His voice roughened. "Damned if I don't." He moistened each nipple with his tongue and then brushed them dry with his beard. He repeated the process, all the while coaxing her higher with the persistent rhythm of his fingers.

The effect was incredible. She climaxed with a wild cry, arching away from the mattress as he buried his bearded face between her breasts. And he'd only begun. As she lay helplessly gasping from his first assault, he kissed a path down her quivering body until he'd nestled himself between her thighs.

"Oh, Nat." This was no dream. In a million nights of fantasizing she couldn't have imagined the delicious sensation of his mustache right *there,* while his beard feathered her inner thighs, and his tongue...there were no words for it, only sounds. And she filled the room with her moans of delight.

He gifted her with another shattering climax before making his way back to her mouth, revisiting his sites of conquest along the way. By the time he kissed her again, she would have done anything for him, if only she had a smidgen of strength left with which to do it.

"And I thought this beard was only good for keeping my face warm in a cold wind," he whispered.

She could barely move, let alone talk. But she wanted him to feel this euphoria, too. It was only fair. She liked her dry lips. "What about…you?"

He lifted his head and gazed down at her, his eyes alight. "I'm getting to that." He kissed the tip of her nose and his voice was gruff with emotion. "But you know how guys are when they've been frustrated for this long. It'll be fast and furious the first time. You needed a head start."

"Mmm." She figured she'd already finished the race. Twice.

"Don't go away." He leaned over and opened the bedside-table drawer.

She turned her head and watched him put on the condom. Observing him rolling the latex over his stiff penis turned out to be an arousing activity. After the way he'd thoroughly loved her, she was amazed she was still capable of being aroused.

He hadn't worn a condom any of the other times they'd made love, and she wondered if she'd feel the difference. They'd both trusted in her birth control pills, which had ultimately failed them. But she couldn't be sorry about getting pregnant. Even if Elizabeth ended up tearing them apart, she couldn't be sorry.

He slid back into bed beside her and turned on his side. His gaze locked with hers. She grew restless, wanting him again, but the ache was deeper this time. She no longer had that frantic craving for release. This time she wanted connection.

Still looking into her eyes, he took her chin in his hand. Then slowly he stroked down the curve of her throat, and his gaze followed the path of his hand as it swept past her collarbone and over the slope of her breast. His touch seemed to define the shape of her body as his palm glided past her hip and down her thigh. His penis twitched impatiently, yet he took his time, propping himself up on one arm so he could reach all the way to her ankles.

She'd never seen such intensity in his eyes. Under his scrutiny, she became self-conscious. She hadn't lost every ounce she'd gained with Elizabeth, and most days the few extra pounds felt good, womanly. Now she wasn't so sure. "I…guess I'm not quite the same as I—"

His voice trembled slightly. "You're perfect." He met her gaze and there was a sheen of moisture in his eyes. "And after how I treated you seventeen months ago, and even just now, accusing you of trying to trap me into marriage, you should have forbidden me ever to touch you again."

Her throat closed. He was so hard on himself, more judgmental than she could ever be. "Nat, don't—"

"But you let me touch you, let me love you, because you have a good and generous heart." He moved over her, his gaze holding hers. "And for that, I'm eternally grateful."

"I could never turn you away," she whispered.

"You should." He eased the tip of his penis inside her and closed his eyes. "God knows you should."

"I can't." She cupped his buttocks in her hands. "I want this as much as you."

He opened his eyes. "Then, besides being too generous, you're a fool, a bigger fool than I am. And I'm going to take advantage of that, Jess. One more time." He thrust forward and closed his eyes with a groan. "So sweet. Oh, Jess."

She dug her fingers into his buttocks and held him tight inside her. Yes, the condom made a difference, separating them in a way that seemed unfair. She wanted him flesh to flesh, as close as they'd been before. But she couldn't have that, and what she could have was very good indeed. He filled the emptiness that had tortured her ever since he left.

He opened his eyes, and they were blazing with passion. His voice was thick with restrained desire. "When I'm inside you like this, I own the world."

She stroked her hands up the knotted muscles of his back and slipped them around to cradle his beloved, bearded face. "So do I." Her smile quivered as she gazed up at him. "I thought this was going to be fast and furious."

"It will be, the minute I move. I just want to savor this part, the first time I push deep, and I'm leaning over you like this, looking into your eyes, watching them get all dark and soft, seeing your cheeks flush. And your freckles stand out."

"They do?"

"Yeah, and I've missed that so much. I've missed every crazy thing about you, Jess. Your herbal teas, your bossiness—"

"I'm not bossy."

He chuckled. "Yes, you are."

"I've missed your laugh." She felt his penis stir within her and knew he'd begin to move soon.

"I've missed your happy little moans." He eased down onto his elbows, so that his chest brushed her nipples. "Lace your fingers through mine," he murmured. "Like we used to do."

She knew exactly what he meant. It had been their favorite way of making love. She slipped her hands under his so they were palm to palm, fingers intertwined.

Looking deep into her eyes, he gripped her hands tightly in his. "I've missed the way your mouth opens, just a little, when I start stroking." He eased back and came forward again. "Like you want to be open…everywhere." He picked up the rhythm.

"I missed the look in your eyes when you're close to coming," she whispered breathlessly. "You look like a fierce warrior."

He pumped more vigorously, and his voice was hoarse. "Then I must look pretty fierce right now."

"Yes. Magnificent." The grip of his hands was almost painful, but she didn't care. His frantic desire drove her straight to the edge of the precipice with him.

"Oh, Jess." He gasped for breath as he plunged into her again and again. "Can you?"

"I'm there, Nat. Love me. Love me hard."

He groaned. "Oh, *Jess.*"

They came apart together, clutching each other wildly as their control shattered.

As they lay panting and spent, she caressed his sweat-soaked back. "Welcome home," she murmured.

ALL HIS LIFE people had accused Steven Pruitt of being an egghead. By now he was damn proud of the label. In fact, he figured that his eggheadedness was the key to making him enormously rich. Someday he'd be the one staying at the Waldorf. Right under Russell P. Franklin's nose.

In the meantime, he had to be patient. When he thought of the money he would wring out of Russell P. when this thing came down, he could be patient. Trailing Jessica wasn't so different from some of the investigative-reporting assignments he'd had. He'd never needed much sleep, and catnapping on a bench where he could keep tabs on the entrance to the hotel was uncomfortable but bearable.

Some people might think six months of trailing someone in order to kidnap them was too long. But they didn't understand the thrill of the chase. He hadn't understood it, either, until he'd begun following Jessica. Once he'd found out what a rush this cat-and-mouse game could give him, he'd decided to enjoy it for as long as his money lasted. He'd probably never get to feel this much like James Bond again in his life.

He ought to be good for another month or two. What a feeling of power he felt whenever he made her run. By now he knew her well, probably better than the guy she was shacked up with in the Waldorf.

The guy was an unexpected turn of events, but Steven didn't consider him a major obstacle. He might even be of some help. He and Jessica obviously had something going between them, and there was nothing like a little hanky-panky to make people careless. That was all Steven needed to make his dreams come true when he was finally ready to make the snatch—one careless moment.

A KNOCK AT THE HOTEL DOOR woke Nat from a dreamless sleep caused by pure exhaustion. He staggered out of bed, not quite sure where he was.

"Maid service," called a woman through the closed door.

Everything came back to him, and he glanced over at the bed to see if Jess was still in it. The bed was empty. He panicked. She'd left him after all. She didn't trust him not to call her parents and give her location away.

"Come back later!" he called to the maid. Then he heard water running and dashed into the bathroom to find Jess calmly brushing her teeth. Naked.

"What's wrong?" she asked around a mouthful of tooth-paste foam.

"I thought you'd taken off." He grabbed her and kissed her, foam and all. And just like that, once they were skin against skin once more, he was in the same condition he'd been ever since he and Jess had arrived in this hotel room. Apparently he'd stored up a lot of sexual tension in the past seventeen months, and he'd become very particular about who could relieve it. He'd narrowed the candidates down to one, as a matter of fact.

He filled both hands with her breasts. "Come back to bed," he coaxed between kisses.

"We need to call the ranch," she said.

"We will. But I need fortification first." A true statement. And despite her protest, she was responding, heating up like the blast furnace he knew she could be.

Her words came out breathy and excited. "We'll call right after?"

"We'll call right after. I promise. Please, Jess." He was begging and he didn't much care. Besides, it looked as if he could win this one, and making love to her one more time would give him courage for that phone call. He started backing his way out of the bathroom, bringing her with him. "Come in where the condoms are."

She tugged on him, and she'd found a very effective handle. "I have a better idea."

"There *is* no better idea." God, he loved it when she wrapped her fingers around his erection like that. He wondered if he should try some caveman tactics and throw her over his shoulder, except he hated to interfere with all that terrific fondling she was doing.

"Toothpaste," she whispered against his mouth.

"Yeah, I know." In his gusto to kiss her he'd smeared both of them with the foam. It was all over his beard and her chin. "I probably have it everywhere."

"Not quite." Leaning back, she grabbed her toothbrush from the counter where she'd tossed it, stuck it in her mouth and worked up another head of foam.

"What in hell are you—"

"Tell me if you like this."

Before he understood her intentions, she'd dropped to her knees and taken his penis in her toothpaste-filled mouth.

He gasped as cool tingling foam met hot pulsing flesh. Then he groaned in delight as she added embellishments with her tongue. Gripping the counter, he closed his eyes. Oh, this was good. This was very good. Heaven. He wanted it to last forever. His grip on the counter tightened as he trembled and fought for control.

Then he made the mistake of opening his eyes. The mirror running the full length of the counter reflected Jess, totally involved in her task. He came in a rush. The sensation was so intense that if he hadn't been holding on to the counter, he would have toppled over.

He stood there gasping and quivering as she licked him clean and slowly rose to kiss him gently on the mouth.

"How was it?" she murmured.

He sucked in a shaky breath. "Okay, I guess."

"Liar." She kissed him again. "I wasted you."

"You did." He managed to focus long enough to look into her laughing eyes. Then a really unpleasant thought occurred to him. "Where did you learn that?"

She chuckled. "I'm so glad you can be jealous, too."

The wonderful languor that had settled over him disappeared. He'd asked her last night if there *was* anyone else, but he didn't ask if there had *been* anybody else. He slid his hand behind her head and held it gently but firmly so she couldn't look away. "Where, Jess?"

Her expression wasn't the least bit evasive. Instead, she seemed extremely proud of herself. "I read it in a book."

His tension melted, and he smiled. "Oh."

"Unlike some people in this bathroom, I haven't even been naked with anyone since you left, unless you count my obstetrician, Cliff."

Nat wasn't sure he could tolerate even that thought. He didn't know where this possessiveness was coming from, but it was very strong. "Is he single?"

"No."

"Good."

She wrapped her arms around his waist and laid her cheek against his chest. "And now that we have that settled, can we call the ranch?"

He knew the time had come. Although he didn't look forward to talking with Sebastian about the situation, he couldn't postpone it any longer. "Okay."

"Before you do, I need to tell you something."

His gut tightened. "What?"

"I wanted to make sure I was the one to tell you about Elizabeth, so I didn't tell Sebastian you're her father. When you call, he'll be hearing that news for the first time."

Nat grimaced. If he'd been dreading the phone call before, he purely hated the thought of having to make it now.

CHAPTER SIX

SEBASTIAN DANIELS got down on all fours so his wife, Matty, could prop Elizabeth on his back.

"Giddyap, horsey!" Matty said.

Elizabeth chortled and bounced as Sebastian whinnied and started off around the living room. Matty walked alongside to steady the baby and make sure she didn't fall.

Sebastian hated having only one week in three to spend with Elizabeth, but it was the only fair arrangement, and Sebastian valued fairness. When Jessica had named him the baby's godfather, she'd also included Travis Evans and Boone Connor in that honor. The kicker was that each of them thought they might be Elizabeth's daddy. All three of them had been pretty drunk the night of the avalanche reunion party, and each of them vaguely remembered making a pass at Jessica, who had stayed sober and driven them back to their cabin.

Ever since Jessica had left Elizabeth on Sebastian's doorstep eight months ago, the men had hotly debated the baby's parentage. Finally they'd submitted to paternity testing and discovered none of them was the baby's father. Trouble was, they and their wives had become so darned attached to the little cutie-pie. Until the real father showed up, or Jessica came back to clear up the mystery, they'd agreed to take turns with Elizabeth.

The baby trade always took place on Saturday morning, and whenever he picked up Elizabeth, Sebastian was on top of the world. The following Saturday, which happened to be today, was a different story. But both he and Matty tried to keep their sadness from Elizabeth.

Besides having to deal with Elizabeth leaving, Matty was extremely hormonal in this fifth month of her pregnancy. He loved the way her belly had begun to round out, and she seemed softer all over. She wore her blond hair loose all the time now, and Sebastian could barely keep his hands off her. But he'd noticed she could get weepy at the drop of a hat, and this morning he'd noticed her swiping at tears when she thought he wasn't looking.

Elizabeth seemed oblivious to their distress. Decked out in denim overalls and a bright red shirt, she laughed and bounced happily on Sebastian's back. Every so often she kicked his ribs with her moccasined feet, which was his cue to snort and pick up the pace. His knees were sore and his ribs were getting tender, but he didn't care a bit. He hoped that just this once Travis and Gwen would be late.

They weren't. The doorbell chimed at eleven, right on schedule.

"That'll be them." Matty lifted the baby off Sebastian's back.

"Travis never used to so damn punctual," Sebastian grumbled as he got to his feet and brushed off the knees of his jeans.

"I think it's Gwen's doing. Marriage to her has really domesticated that man." Matty propped Elizabeth against her hip and started toward the door.

"Here, let me take her," Sebastian said, hurrying after her. "You shouldn't be carrying—"

"I'm fine. Let me keep her a little longer," Matty said, a slight quiver in her voice.

Sebastian backed off. When she got that little tremble in her voice, he knew she was close to tears. He'd adjusted to her frequent crying, but she hated turning into a water faucet all the time. She'd cried more in the last couple of months than in the entire ten years they'd been neighbors, before they got married, and he knew it embarrassed her to be so emotional. It made him feel manly and strong, but he didn't dare tell her that, or she might whack him with the frying pan.

He was doing everything he could to stay on Matty's good side, because then he could enjoy one of the other side effects of pregnancy. Much to his surprise, Matty wanted to make love more often than ever, and he was quite happy to oblige.

He thought about that as Travis and Gwen came in, all smiles because they were about to make off with Elizabeth. Once they left, he'd coax Matty back to the bedroom. A hot session in the old four-poster would help ease the pain of having to be without the little girl for two weeks.

Gwen was dressed to emphasize her Cheyenne ancestry, with her long dark braid and a fringed outfit. Sebastian had seen the combination on her before, but for some reason he couldn't put his finger on, she seemed different today. Maybe she was trying out some new brand of makeup or something. Gwen was much more into that sort of thing than Matty.

Travis was his usual debonair self, strolling in with one hand behind his back. "Hey, Lizzie!" he said. "Lookee here!" He brought his hand out from hiding and waggled the raccoon puppet he held. "Hello, Mizz Lizzie," he said in a falsetto. "Wanna come home with me?"

Elizabeth squealed and wiggled impatiently as she held out both arms toward the puppet. Matty relinquished her to Travis.

Sebastian had always been a little jealous of the way Travis could charm the baby in two seconds. "Show-off," he muttered.

Travis whipped the puppet's head around toward Sebastian. "Spoilsport," he said in falsetto.

"Okay, you two," Gwen said, stepping forward. "Play nice."

"We always do," Sebastian said with a wicked grin aimed at Travis. Then he looked at Gwen. "Say, are you trying out a new shade of lipstick?"

"No." Gwen seemed taken aback.

"Lipstick?" Matty chuckled. "You are the last man on earth I expected to comment on a woman's lipstick color."

"I just think Gwen looks different today. I thought it might be the lipstick."

Gwen gave him a startled glance. "You really think I look different?"

"I'm probably imagining things."

Travis gazed fondly at his wife. "Oh, I wouldn't say that."

"Then there *is* something different."

Gwen looked at her husband and smiled. "In a manner of speaking."

Matty figured it out before Sebastian did, and she hollered with delight as she threw her arms around Gwen. "When? When did you find out?"

"About a half hour ago," Gwen said, hugging her back. "We wanted you two to be the first to know."

Sebastian eyed Travis and tried to pretend great seriousness. But inside he was jumping for joy. To his way of thinking, the more babies around, the better. "Seems to me the last time this happened, the guy responsible got tossed in a snowbank," he said. Travis and Boone had lost no time wrestling him out the door the night Matty announced she was pregnant.

"See, I plan these things better than you, Daniels." Travis looked ready to burst his buttons with pride. "I waited until the snow melted and I had a baby in my arms. Plus, you don't have Boone around to help, so I reckon I'm pretty safe."

"Don't count your chickens, buddy. The day's not over yet."

"This is so wonderful," Matty said. "Does your mother know, Travis?"

"Not yet. Like Gwen said, you two are the first."

"Luann will be out of her head with happiness," Matty said. "I'd love to see the look on her face when—" She stopped as the kitchen phone rang. "Excuse me a minute," she said as she started toward the kitchen. "That might be the vet. Stay right there until I get back, okay?"

"They will," Sebastian assured her. "Anybody for coffee? We have leaded and unleaded around here these days, so we can handle your new regime with no problem, Gwen."

"Thanks, but as soon as Matty gets off the phone, Travis and I need to get home. We have a ton of chores waiting, and besides, Luann counts the minutes until she sees Elizabeth again."

"I can relate to that," Sebastian said. "I—"

"Sebastian?" Matty hurried back in, a smile on her face. "You'll never guess. It's Nat! He's in New York!"

"He's back?"

Matty nodded.

"Hallelujah," Travis murmured.

"About time," Sebastian said. "This is turning out to be a real red-letter day." Relief and happiness washed through him as he started toward the kitchen. Nat's decision to help war orphans made some kind of crazy sense, given his background, but Sebastian had worried about his safety. They all had. Nat pretended to be so together, but inside he was one of the walking wounded. As a result, he took chances he shouldn't take, and it would be just like him to get himself killed doing something stupid and heroic. Apparently he'd escaped that fate…again.

"Tell him to get his sorry ass back to Colorado," Travis

called after him. "I want the sheepskin vest I loaned him, and I want it before the snow flies."

"I'll tell him," Sebastian said. He was grinning as he picked up the receiver and put it to his ear. "Hey, you crazy son of a gun. What the hell do you mean staying over there so long? We thought you'd gone native!"

"Hey, Sebastian." Nat's voice was thick with emotion. "It's good to hear your voice again."

"I'm glad, because I plan to run up your long-distance bill while I chew on your ear for being gone so damn long on that extended vacation of yours. When you finally show up at the Rocking D, I suggest you bring some identification. We've all forgotten what you look like."

"Yeah, I know I was gone too long." Nat sighed.

Sebastian's grin faded. He'd expected at least a chuckle out of Nat. A chilly finger of anxiety ran down his backbone. "Are you okay? Don't tell me you got shot up over—"

"No, no. I'm fine. But…look, Jess is here with me."

Sebastian almost dropped the phone. "She *is?*" He felt as if somebody had short-circuited his brain. "You mean *our* Jessica?" he repeated, his mind still not operating on all cylinders.

"Yeah. And that baby of hers you're watching is… mine."

"Yours?" Sebastian roared. "What the hell do you mean, *yours?* You weren't even *there.*"

Matty hurried into the kitchen followed closely by Gwen and Travis, holding the baby. They all stared at Sebastian, and Elizabeth started to fuss.

"Yeah, I was there, the night before you arrived," Nat said. "Is that her?"

The night before. Sebastian couldn't figure how Nat had been there and nobody had known about it. "Is what her?"

"I hear a baby. Is that her?"

Sebastian felt shell-shocked. And absolutely sure that Nat Grady was not Elizabeth's father. He couldn't be. "Yeah, that's her. But I don't know why you think—"

"I don't think. I know. After the avalanche I started seeing Jess. We had a…relationship…for almost a year, and—"

Pain sliced through Sebastian. "You were seeing Jessica for an entire year and you didn't tell me? I thought we were friends!"

"I'm sorry. I should have trusted you more. Should have trusted all of you more. But I was afraid you'd be after me to make a commitment, and I didn't think that was going to happen, so I asked Jess to keep it between the two of us."

Anger followed on the heels of Sebastian's sense of betrayal. Matty came forward, as if to offer her support, and he waved her off. Later he'd cling to Matty like there was no tomorrow, but at the moment he needed to concentrate on this conversation and make sure he understood what Nat was telling him. "Go on," he said to Nat in a tight voice.

"The week before the avalanche reunion party I went up to Aspen to spend some time with Jess before the rest of you arrived. The night before you guys came up, Jess and I had a big fight. She wanted to end the secrecy."

"Imagine that."

Nat sounded desperate. "She wanted marriage and a family, Sebastian! I knew I couldn't do that."

"Then you should have been a wee bit more careful, shouldn't you?" All the muscles in Sebastian's body clenched in denial. Shifting Elizabeth around every week wasn't a great solution, but at least he hadn't lost her completely. Now he might. He couldn't bear to look at Matty, and especially not at Elizabeth, so he stared down at the worn linoleum.

"Yes," Nat said quietly. "I should have been more careful."

"So now what?" Sebastian asked dully. "Are you coming back to pick her up? Is that what you called to tell me?"

"No. I'm still not sure what to do about the baby. I'll provide all the financial support Jess needs, of course, but I'm not a fit person to take on a little kid, as we all know."

"Why not? You've been over there taking care of nobody *but* little kids!"

"They had nothing. No one. And there were plenty of other people around, so I never worried that I'd do the wrong thing. But put me in a house with my own kid, and I don't trust myself."

"That's pure, unadulterated bullsh—" Sebastian caught himself as he remembered that Elizabeth was in the room. He'd vowed not to use those words around her, because in another seven or eight months she might start talking, and he didn't want…. Then he realized that in another seven or eight months Elizabeth could be gone.

"Call it what you want," Nat said. "It's the truth as I see it. I'm bringing Jess back to her baby, and we'll take it from there."

Sebastian fought so many conflicting emotions he couldn't think straight. He couldn't imagine a man turning away from Elizabeth, and he took it as a personal affront. Yet he wouldn't want a man to claim her if he wasn't planning to be an A-number-one dad. "When will you be here?"

"That's just it. I'm not sure. We might have to take a roundabout route. Jess has someone on her trail, somebody who's apparently trying to kidnap her. That's why she left the baby with you."

"Good God. Why would they want to kidnap Jessica?"

"Ever hear of a guy named Russell P. Franklin?"

"Why, sure I—" Then it all clicked into place. "Well, damn." He'd always suspected Jessica had come from money. Maybe it was the way she held a fork, or her posture, or her choice of words. Sebastian hadn't dreamed how *much* money, though.

He glanced over at Elizabeth in sudden fear. The child he loved so fiercely was an heiress, and that was potentially life-threatening. "Is the baby in danger?"

Travis frowned and wrapped his arms tighter around Elizabeth.

"Apparently the kidnapper doesn't know about the baby," Nat said. "Neither do Jess's parents. Now that Jess has been separated from Elizabeth for six months, she thinks it's safe to come back and see her." Nat lowered his voice. "She needs to, Sebastian. This has been really tough on her."

It's been tough on all of us, Sebastian thought. *And it doesn't promise to get any easier.* But complaining wouldn't get them anywhere. "Has she notified the police about this?"

"No. That would bring her parents into it. According to her, they'd swoop in and bring the baby back to New York to live on their estate. They could probably swing it, too, considering the legal firepower they have. Jess doesn't want that."

"I wouldn't want that, either," Sebastian said. "Unless it's our only choice to keep Elizabeth safe."

"I'd rather catch the bastard and not have to worry about him," Nat said.

Sebastian heaved a sigh. "Finally we have an area of agreement." Then he paused to think. "It's mighty strange that he's been following her all this time and hasn't snatched her yet."

"I've thought about that, too. Either he's crazy or inept."

"Let's hope he's inept. I don't suppose you have a weapon on you."

"You know I hate guns," Nat said.

"Yeah, I know. Listen, get here as best you can and as soon as you can. Be careful. Once you arrive, we'll find a way through this."

Nat didn't respond for a moment. Then he cleared his throat. "You're a better friend to me than I deserve."

Still smarting from Nat's betrayal, Sebastian was tempted to agree, but then he remembered the stories Nat had told of his childhood. Thinking of the cruelty Nat had endured made compassion easier to find. "You've always been too hard on yourself, buddy," he said. "Come on home and we'll straighten everything out."

"Home," Nat said, his voice husky. "That's how I think of it, too. Listen, Jess wants to ask you about the baby. Here she is."

Sebastian braced himself.

"Sebastian?" Jessica sounded very unsure of herself. "How...how is she?"

"Good." Sebastian discovered that the lump in his throat made talking difficult. "Big. Growing. She has four teeth."

"Four. Wow."

Sebastian could hear her swallow. Her struggle to stay composed touched him. "This must have been a nightmare for you," he said softly.

"Yeah," she murmured. "I hope you can forgive me for all I've put you through, but I couldn't think what else to do. And I didn't realize Nat would be gone so long."

"No kidding. None of us did."

"Is she...what color are her eyes now?"

"Blue." And now Sebastian could see it. They were Nat's eyes. "She has a sock monkey named Bruce," he added, not sure why he'd said it. "She dotes on that silly monkey."

"She does? That's...so cute. I wish—'' Jessica broke off with a little sob. "Here's—here's Nat,'' she choked out.

Nat's voice was rough with emotion. "We'll be there as soon as we possibly can. Goodbye, buddy.''

"Take care, Nat.'' His heart heavy, Sebastian slowly hung up the phone and turned to the little cluster of people waiting in the kitchen doorway. They all looked anxious except for Elizabeth. She'd stopped fussing and was playing happily with the raccoon puppet Travis had brought her.

Sebastian's chest grew tight as he looked at the baby. He'd known life couldn't go on indefinitely like this. He'd told himself hundreds of times that someday Jessica would turn up. But the longer she'd stayed away, the more he'd built a case in his mind for challenging her right to Elizabeth. Now he could see that she'd stayed away for a good reason, an honorable reason. She'd tortured herself in order to protect her baby, and he wasn't about to challenge her claim now. And that meant his days with Elizabeth were numbered.

"I think we'd better get Boone and Shelby over here,'' he said.

JESSICA HUDDLED on the bed and tried not to cry. No matter how hard she worked at it, she couldn't picture her little baby with four teeth. Four. And blue, blue eyes instead of the smoky gray-blue they'd been at two months.

Elizabeth was so different now, but all Jessica could imagine were tiny hands, impossibly tiny fingernails, a gummy smile. She didn't look like that anymore. And she'd found a favorite toy, a monkey named Bruce. Jessica had missed it all.

Nat hung up the phone and put his arm around her. "It'll be okay,'' he said gently.

"Will it?'' She looked at him through eyes blurred with tears. "She's changed so much. If someone walked by me on the street holding Elizabeth, I probably wouldn't recognize her!''

"Sure you would.'' He gave her a comforting squeeze. "I'll bet she hasn't changed all that much.''

The knot of misery tightened in her stomach. "Maybe that's true,'' she said, pushing each word out as if it were made of lead, "but even if I didn't know her right away, that's not really what I'm afraid of.''

"Then what?''

She gulped back tears. "Oh, Nat, after all this time…*she* won't recognize *me!*''

CHAPTER SEVEN

JESSICA LONGED to hop on a plane and be in Colorado by nightfall, but in order to do that she'd have to use her real identity at the ticket counter. She didn't want to risk it.

"I think you'll have to rent us a car," she said as they ate a room-service breakfast, she wearing the hotel robe and Nat in jeans and a T-shirt. "I'll be glad to pay for—"

"Don't you dare start that." He put down his coffee cup and glared at her.

"Start what?"

"Assuming all the responsibility."

Even when he got gruff and bristly, she couldn't stop the surge of lust she felt every time she looked at him. When he talked, the movement of his mouth reminded her of his kiss, and everything he touched reminded her of his caress. "But I'm the one who should have known about antibiotics and how they affected birth control pills," she said. "If I'd been smarter, this wouldn't have happened."

"If you'd been smarter, you wouldn't have been involved with me in the first place." His tone was bitter. "I should have been proud to tell everyone that you…that you cared for me. Instead, I kept you hidden in the shadows."

"You didn't hold a gun to my head, Nat. I stuck around because I wanted to." She'd noticed that they were both avoiding using the word *love* to describe their feelings for each other.

For her part, she hesitated because she didn't want to saddle him with even more guilt. With Nat, it was probably a way to maintain some distance, despite their obvious sexual need for each other. He might figure that if he claimed to love her, she would expect certain things.

"Nevertheless," he persisted, "if our relationship had been out in the open, you might have gotten some advice from a girlfriend about those antibiotics."

"But then there would have been no Elizabeth."

"My point exactly."

Jessica could no longer contemplate a world without her baby in it, and the fact that Nat could imagine such a thing shocked her. She put down her fork and leaned toward him. "We need to get a few things straight. I don't regret one single minute I spent with you. I had a fabulous time. And I especially don't regret that I became pregnant with your child. But I assume you're not happy about the baby."

"You assume right."

Although she'd been expecting him to agree with her, his statement still hurt. She hurried on, not wanting him to know it. "That's why I want to take all the responsibility, as long as I can do it. I don't want Elizabeth's needs handled by a man who begrudges her existence."

"I didn't say that, damn it!"

She stood and tightened the belt on her robe. "Yes, you did. Do you want the shower first, or should I take it? We need to get on the road."

"Not until we settle this we don't." He pushed back his chair and nearly upset the breakfast tray as he got to his feet. "When you say I begrudge her existence, you make it sound like I'm upset because of the inconvenience. I don't give a damn about the inconvenience! What I regret more than I can say is bringing a child into the world by accident, when I have zero confidence in my abilities to be a father to that child."

So they were back to that. But things had changed since the last time they'd had this argument. She played her trump card. "If that's so, then what were you doing in some hellhole taking care of *orphans?*"

He flinched, and then his voice rose. "Maybe I was testing myself, okay? Maybe I wanted to see if I'd have the urge to get violent with those children."

She thought there was a lot more to his work with the refugees than that, but she wasn't going to question him on that point now. "And did you get violent?"

He looked away from her to gaze out the window. "No."

"Then you must know you'll be fine."

He swung back to face her. "I don't know that! You'd have to be a monster to lay a hand on those kids. They'd been through so much, patience was easy." He ran a hand over his face. "Some of them, especially the boys, tried so hard to be tough, but you could see that inside they were terrified."

Like you were as a child. Gazing at his anxious expression, she could picture the frightened little boy he must have been. She wanted to wrap her arms around him and let him know he'd never have to be that frightened again, but she didn't dare trespass on that minefield strewn land. "It must have been terrible," she murmured.

"It was." He stared into the distance.

She guessed he'd seen his own experience in every child's face. Nat might as well have been orphaned, with no mother and totally at the mercy of a violent father who didn't know how to love. Living with a father like Hank Grady might not have been so different from living in a war zone. "You wouldn't have to worry about being violent around Elizabeth," she said gently. "I'll be there."

He snapped out of his daze and glanced at her. He looked so heartbreakingly vulnerable. "I don't know how to do this, Jess. With the orphans, it was easy. Get them clothes, get them food, find them a bed. Comb through the donations coming in and look for a stuffed animal they could hold.''

The picture of him doing that brought a lump to her throat. ''And did you hug them when they got scared?''

''Well, sure, but—''

''And when they were sad, did you tell them funny stories to make them laugh?''

''Once I learned the language, but—''

''And if they did something wonderful, if they were kind or generous or brave or smart, did you tell them they were great?''

''Of course.''

''Nat, that's all there is to it, whether you're talking about a refugee child in a faraway country or Elizabeth. That's all you have to do.''

''The hell it is! What if they do something stupid? How do you keep them from doing dumb things?''

She thought about her restrictive childhood in which she'd hardly been allowed to make a mistake. She'd broken free of that, and maybe she'd been stupid when she accidentally got pregnant. But as a result she had Elizabeth.

''Got you there, haven't I?'' he said.

She met his gaze. ''I think, within reason, you have to let them be stupid.''

He snorted in derision. ''Yeah, so they can get themselves killed, and maybe somebody else in the process.'' He said the words so automatically he seemed to be reciting a memorized lesson.

''Is that how your father justified beating you to a bloody pulp? That he was keeping you from killing yourself?''

''Sometimes.'' He glanced at her. ''Sometimes I think it was for the pure enjoyment of it.''

Talk about monsters, she thought. ''You have to know you're nothing like him.''

He didn't reply as he continued to hold her gaze.

"Nat, you're not like him! I'm sure of it."

"Better go take your shower."

She recognized the wall he'd just put up between them. She'd seen him construct it often enough in the year they'd been seeing each other. Once that wall went up, she had no hope of breaking through to him. But he hadn't seen Elizabeth yet. Jessica clung to the hope that the baby, *his* baby, might be the one thing that could breach that wall.

"Okay," she said.

"I'll call and arrange for a rental car, and I don't want to hear about you paying for it."

She hesitated. Letting him pay for things seemed almost as if she'd be giving him the easy way out. She didn't want his money. She wanted his participation in raising Elizabeth, or she wanted nothing.

"Please, Jess." His mask slipped a little. "It's what I can do for now. Can you accept that?"

She took a deep breath and nodded. "Okay. For now."

"Good. I'll call and get us a car."

As he walked over to the phone, she went into the bathroom and started the shower.

Nat was liable to break her heart all over again, she thought as she slipped out of the robe, tied her hair into a knot on top of her head and stepped under the hot spray. She wanted to believe that he would see Elizabeth and fall in love with the baby, so deeply in love that he'd be willing to rethink his position about marriage and children.

But that might not happen. He'd walked away once, and if the baby scared him enough, he would walk away again.

With that possibility hanging over her head, she probably shouldn't continue to make love to him. She was only setting herself up for a worse fall if she became accustomed to his sweet loving on a regular basis. If he couldn't cherish Elizabeth as she did, then she'd have to tell him goodbye.

But she'd better let him know they wouldn't be making

love. She needed to tell him before they started on their trip to Colorado. Considering her behavior up to this point, he would be justified in expecting to continue their physical relationship. After all, she hadn't made sleeping with him contingent on anything. She'd simply fallen into his arms at the first opportunity.

She didn't want to set up contingencies for when they would make love again, as if he had to agree to marry her before he could enjoy her body. That was too much like blackmail. But she had to create some distance between them. Surely he'd understand that she was only protecting both of them from worse heartache.

She turned off the shower, fumbled for a towel on the rack nearby and dried herself while standing in the warmth of the leftover steam. That's when she heard the steady snip of a pair of scissors.

Wrapping the towel securely around herself, she stepped out of the shower to find Nat standing there wearing nothing but his low-slung jeans. He'd propped a wastebasket up on the counter to catch the hair from his beard as he clipped it very short.

Apparently he'd just finished that part, because he set the wastebasket on the floor, lathered up the remaining stubble and picked up his razor. The spicy scent of his shaving cream brought back vivid memories of all the times she'd watched him do this little chore. Often he'd capped off a shaving session by making love to her and rubbing his baby-soft chin all over her body.

Yet she missed that beard already. Then she remembered the vow of abstinence she'd just taken in the shower. Whether he had a beard or not meant nothing to her now. "I see you're shaving it off," she said.

"Yep. I want to go out of here looking different from the way I came in, in case your friend saw us together."

"That's a good idea." And it was, but she still struggled

with disappointment as he stroked the razor over his chin. On the other hand, she liked seeing his strong jaw emerge from under the lather. And his skin would be very smooth after this first shave. He'd be heaven to kiss, all spicy scented and silky to the touch.

As he paused to meet her gaze in the mirror, his eyes seemed bluer than ever before. "If you stand there much longer with that look on your face, you won't be wearing that towel anymore," he said.

A familiar tingle of desire settled between her thighs. Keeping her vow wouldn't be easy. "We need to talk about that."

He continued to watch her as he shaved. "I wasn't thinking of having a conversation."

A deep, trembling need seized her. "All things considered, maybe it would be better if we didn't make love anymore."

He paused and narrowed his eyes. "Ever?"

"Well, at least not until…we know where we stand with…with each other, and the baby, and everything." That sounded like a contingency, after all, but she really didn't mean it that way.

"Mmm." He continued shaving, but his hand didn't seem perfectly steady. "Are you trying to bribe me?"

"Absolutely not!"

"Might work." He shifted his weight and stopped leaning against the sink. "I want you pretty damn bad."

"I don't operate that way." Heat sizzled through her veins as she realized he'd moved back from the sink because the edge of the counter was pressing into his erection. She swallowed. "I'm trying to think of both of us. Maybe we should protect ourselves."

"It might have been better if you hadn't made that speech while you're standing there wrapped only in a towel. Funny how when someone says you can't have something, that's the only thing in the world you want.''

So did she. Right this minute. "I think it's for the best, don't you?"

"Jess, guys *never* think going without sex is for the best. But if that's the way you want it, that's the way it'll be."

Her glance took in the fit of his jeans from behind. She'd forgotten what a fabulous view that was. She licked dry lips. "That's the way I want it," she said.

"Then quit checking me out," he said in a low voice, "and go get dressed."

"Right." Heart pounding, she left the bathroom.

STEVEN DAMN NEAR MISSED Jessica leave the hotel. He'd known she'd have on another one of her crazy wigs. It was blond this time. He got a real high out of knowing she was going through all this trouble hoping to fool him, especially when he knew she'd lose in the end. The fact that he was playing with her gave him a buzz that was almost sexual.

Once he had her and got the money from Russell P., the challenge of the thing would be over. Maybe he'd be too rich to care about challenges at that point, but he wasn't altogether sure about that.

Her boyfriend might present some real obstacles, though, and the prospect of a new player in the game got his blood pumping. The boyfriend was obviously sharper than Steven had given him credit for.

Steven had been keeping an eye out for a scruffy guy with a beard. He'd noticed the tall, clean-shaven man who'd come out to claim a rental car, but he hadn't made the connection because everything was smooth about this character. His suit and hat were technically western in style, but the look was far more polished than Steven had ever seen on a cowboy. Even the longish hair looked avant-garde. He hadn't realized it was Jessica's boyfriend until she hurried out and hopped in the car with him.

In the past six months Steven had become an excellent carjacker. He had an instinct that allowed him to spot a car with the passenger door unlocked, and he found one now. No one on the busy street noticed when he got into the green sedan and quietly put a toy gun against the driver's ribs.

Once he'd explained to the gasping, quaking man that all he wanted was for him to follow the white rental car, the guy complied with Steven's request, as everyone so far had had the good sense to do. Once they were on the open road, he launched into his well-rehearsed covert-operations speech and showed the driver that the gun wasn't real. His altered press card looked official enough for most people. In all his carjackings, he'd never had to pull the .32 out of his boot.

He always made the drivers feel as if they were part of something really big, something top secret and connected with national security. When Jessica and her boyfriend stopped for gas, he let both driver and car go back home and he located another chauffeur. The routine worked like a charm, as it had for the last six months. So far no one had ever been hurt. Steven took pride in that.

NAT DROVE ALL DAY and into the night, ready to get this trip over with. Jess offered to take the wheel, but he knew once she did that, he'd fall asleep. Jet lag was playing havoc with his system, but he didn't want to sleep while she was driving and allow her to be at the mercy of whatever dangers were out there.

At a diner where they'd stopped for dinner, she'd said she thought the guy was around. She hadn't seen him, but she'd claimed to have developed a sixth sense about him, and Nat was willing to believe that. He'd kept his eyes open, but the man would be hard to spot. Jess had described him as average build with brown hair. He could look like a million other guys.

The best plan seemed to be to keep driving. They didn't talk much, for which Nat was glad. Even the sound of her voice got him hot. Her every movement was like the flick of a match against the dry tinder of his need. He wasn't sure how he'd travel with her all the way to Colorado without making love to her again. Exhaustion would help, he decided, so he pushed himself until he was afraid he was a hazard on the road. "We need to stop," he said about two in the morning as he took the exit to a motel right near the highway.

"Of course." She stretched her arms over her head and yawned. "I was beginning to think you'd decided to drive nonstop from New York to Colorado."

He pulled up in front of the motel lobby. "I didn't trust myself to stop for the night until I was totally wiped out."

"Oh."

He could see from her expression that he didn't have to explain himself any further. "We're getting one room, for the safety factor, but you don't have to worry about me attacking you. I'm too beat."

"I've never worried about you attacking me."

He glanced at her. "Maybe you should." He wasn't crazy about the blond wig and the elaborate makeup she'd included as part of her disguise, but in another way it was a turn-on. He'd never made love to her as a heavily made-up blonde, and it might be kind of fun. Her stretchy zebra-print dress was too tight to be fashionable, but it sure fueled the imagination. "Come on in with me. I don't want to leave you alone in the car."

"Don't worry. I wouldn't stay behind." As they started toward the lobby's front entrance, she chuckled. "You know what they're going to think, when we come in at this time of the night, with me looking like a—''

''Hooker?'' he finished for her.

''I was going to say high-class call girl,'' she said primly.

''Hooker,'' he said, and opened the door for her. Damned if his libido wasn't kicking in now that he was out of the car and moving around. He wasn't tired enough. Maybe there was no such thing as too tired where Jess was concerned, especially when she was decked out like this.

But he didn't think he could drive another mile, so he was stuck with this frustrating situation. He approached the reception desk, where a sleepy-looking young man gave Jess the once-over as she crossed the lobby to glance through a rack of travel brochures. She'd slipped on her coat over the stretchy dress, but hadn't bothered to button it. She was dynamite.

Nat restrained the impulse to challenge the clerk's obvious assumption. He'd be wasting his breath, anyway. No matter what he said, the clerk would think he knew exactly what was going on.

Sure enough, the guy turned a coconspirator's gaze on Nat, as if congratulating him man to man on his score. ''You folks need a room?'' he asked, barely controlling a smirk.

''Two double beds,'' Nat said. As if that would make a difference.

''Oo-kay.'' The clerk typed a few things into his computer and took Nat's credit card. ''Need help with luggage?'' he asked as he slid the keys across the counter. He looked as if he didn't expect luggage was part of this deal.

''No, thanks,'' Nat said. ''We can handle it.''

''Okay. Have a nice night.'' The clerk stopped short of licking his lips when he gazed at Jess.

Once again Nat bit back a reprimand. Given the look of things, the clerk couldn't be blamed for his behavior.

"We're all set," Nat said to Jess. "It's in the back. We'll drive around."

"Fine."

He held the door for her, and as she went through it looking for all the world like his playmate for the night, his temper began to fray. Then when he held the car door for her she managed to show quite a bit of leg getting in. She'd better not be teasing him. He closed the door with a little more force than was necessary.

"You slammed that door. Is anything wrong?" she asked as he got in and started the engine.

"Nope." He backed out and pulled around to a parking spot near their room on the second floor.

"Your face is all scrunched up, like you're upset about something."

"Just tired." He'd be damned if he'd admit that he felt randier than a teenager paging through a smuggled porn magazine. He was supposed to be more in control of himself than that, but damn it, she hadn't made life easy for him, wearing that getup of hers.

"I can understand you being tired. I wish you'd let me drive some of the time."

"It's better if I do it." He got out of the car and opened the back door so he could haul out their two backpacks.

She was beside him instantly. "Nat, let me carry my—"

"I've got it." He knew he sounded unfriendly. But he was too tired to be friendly and still keep his hands off of her.

"Okay." She lifted both hands and backed off.

He slung a backpack over each shoulder and they trudged up a set of outside stairs to the second floor of the motel. All the while, Nat was picturing that cozy room with two very available beds in it. He handed a key to Jess and she opened the door and flicked on the wall switch.

Moving into the plain but serviceable room, she glanced

around. "It might not be the Waldorf, but it's nicer than some of the places I've stayed in recently." She took off her coat and laid it on a chair. Then she walked over to the window and reached for the cord on the drapes.

He shoved the door closed with his foot and stood there holding the backpacks and watching those zebra stripes wiggle as she moved. Damn, but she was hot stuff. He slung the backpacks on the floor and when he spoke, his voice was razor-sharp. "Quit fiddling around and pick your bed. We need to get some sleep."

Surprise lifted her eyebrows as she turned toward him. "You are upset."

He laid his hat brim side up on the dresser and stripped off his suit coat. "I don't suppose you could have organized a different disguise for today," he said, an edge of sarcasm in his voice. He wanted the words back. He hated sarcasm. His father had used it all the time. Stress brought out those traits in him, which was why he worried about what he'd be like around a kid of his own.

She finished pulling the drapes closed. "What do you mean?"

He threw his suit coat on the nearest bed. "When you climbed into the taxi last night, you looked like a bag lady. Under the circumstances, couldn't you have come up with something more like that for this trip?"

"Circumstances? Oh! *Those* circumstances."

He allowed his anger to build. Maybe blowing off steam this way would keep him from doing something crude and unforgivable. "I mean, first of all you announce that we're not having sex, and then you put on a dress that looks like it came from Frederick's of Hollywood. Don't you think that's a little unfair?"

"For your information, I consider your outfit equally unfair."

"Mine?" He held out both arms and looked down at the

pearl buttons on his black western shirt. "What's wrong with mine?"

"When you said this morning that you had to go out and pick up a few things, I had no idea you were planning to buy that suit."

He'd been proud of the fact he'd found something decent to wear, given the short time he had to look for some clothes. He'd left all his spare shirts and jeans with the refugees, keeping only the sheepskin vest that belonged to Travis and the clothes on his back. On his quick shopping expedition that morning, he'd been glad to find something on short notice that he could actually wear once he started dealing with clients again. "What's wrong with it?"

"The cut of those western pants is so...blatant."

"They fit. What's the crime in buying pants that fit?"

"They fit like a glove, you mean! I've been watching you all day in those pants, and all I want to do is..." She paused, her color high. "Never mind what I want to do."

Oh, yeah. If she cracked first, then she couldn't blame him, could she? He began unsnapping his shirt. "You're the one who made the rules, darlin'," he said softly.

CHAPTER EIGHT

BOONE CONNOR HEARD the clock chime two-thirty in the morning as he lay staring into the darkness thinking about all that Sebastian and Travis had told him today. On the one hand, he was glad Elizabeth's father wasn't some stranger. On the other, it hurt to think that Nat hadn't seen fit to tell them that he was involved with Jessica for an entire year.

And the most troubling part of the news was that Nat wasn't enthusiastic about being a daddy to Elizabeth. Boone knew about Nat's crummy childhood and his fear that he wouldn't make a good father, but he should have tried to overcome that fear, in Boone's estimation. And marry Jessica, while he was at it.

But whether Nat decided to cooperate or not, Jessica was coming back to get her baby, which meant Boone wouldn't have the pleasure of playing daddy to Elizabeth every third week. He didn't like to think about that too much. He'd taken the little girl into his heart, and letting her go was going to be one of the toughest things he'd ever done.

Thank God he had Shelby and Josh to ease the pain. With a sigh he rolled to his side and gazed at his wife sleeping beside him. He couldn't see her clearly in the faint light, but he could see her clearly enough in his heart. He'd never known he could be this happy.

Having Shelby was wonderful enough, but now that they'd officially adopted her nephew Josh, Boone's world was nearly perfect. Josh's sociopathic father was behind bars awaiting trial for murder, and with the evidence against him, he wasn't likely to bother Shelby and Josh again.

Boone cherished the notion of having his own little family and thought Nat was a fool to turn his back on the chance to have one, too. A family steadied a man.

Shelby's hand, so small and delicate, lay on the pillow beside her cheek. Boone stroked it with the tip of his finger. He still couldn't believe that a tiny thing like Shelby wanted anything to do with a big lug like him.

Luckily she wanted a *lot* to do with him. They were trying for a baby and hoping for a girl. Another baby wouldn't replace Elizabeth, of course, but Josh had loved having a little sister. Boone and Shelby had both figured the day would come when they'd have to give up Elizabeth, so another baby seemed like a very good idea.

Trying to get Shelby pregnant had been an extremely satisfying project, although Boone was a tad bit worried about whether carrying his child would be too much for her small frame. She insisted that a woman's body was amazingly adaptable, and he'd have to say that sure was true when he made love to her. Despite the difference in their sizes, they fit together beautifully.

He hadn't realized she was awake until she spoke.

"You're thinking about this business with Nat and Jessica, aren't you?" she murmured.

"Yeah. I guess I woke you up with my tossing around."

"No." She snuggled against him, bringing with her the tempting scent of her body. "You woke me up with that feathery touch on my hand. For a big man you have the most gentle touch in the world."

He reached under her nightgown and cupped her sweet bottom with more force than he usually used. "Don't go making me sound like a sissy," he said, pulling her toward him.

Her low chuckle was rich with arousal as she wiggled closer. "No one could ever accuse you of that, Boone. You're gentle with the ones you love, but you're hell on anybody who tries to hurt them."

Holding her close, he stroked her blond hair and breathed in her special aroma, a blend of shampoo, cologne and woman. "That's what's bothering me. Nat's one of my best friends, but if he won't be a proper daddy to Elizabeth, that's going to hurt her. Maybe not right away, but down the line, she'll wonder how come he doesn't pay attention to her."

"I can't believe he's going to ignore her. She's too darned cute." She massaged the nape of his neck. "Each one of you worried yourselves sick about the responsibility until you laid eyes on her, remember? Once Nat sees her, he won't be able to help himself. He'll be a good father."

"I hope you're right, but he's going to have to prove himself before we just turn her over."

There was a smile in her voice. "Oh, I'm sure of that. Elizabeth definitely has her champions."

"Yeah." Holding her like this was having a predictable effect on him, which was just fine, because she was in her best time of the month for conceiving. And a man had to do his duty by his wife. His hot, sexy wife. His body throbbed with anticipation. "Well, enough of that," he murmured, easing her nightgown higher.

"I was wondering if you were going to talk for the rest of the night," she said.

"Nope." His mouth found hers in the darkness. As she kissed him with abandon, passion rose in him, blocking out every other thought but one. Maybe this time his seed would find fertile ground and Shelby would ripen with his baby.

JESSICA TRIED to remember all the reasons why she shouldn't make love to Nat as she stood in the motel room watching him strip off his shirt. Next, he hooked an arm over his shoulder, grabbed his T-shirt from the back and pulled that off over his head. Beneath a light pelt of dark chest hair, his muscles flexed as he tossed the T-shirt to the chair where he'd thrown his shirt.

No doubt about it, seventeen months of manual labor had sculpted him into a love god. He probably didn't realize it, but he'd gone from having a decent build to being calendar quality. Even his hair, which was longer than she'd ever seen it, added to his muscular appeal. And she had to find the strength to turn away from him.

His gaze challenged hers and his voice was dangerously soft. "Are you planning to get undressed for bed, or are you waiting for me to help you?"

Her pulse rate climbed. "I…" She paused and cleared her throat. "I'll undress in the bathroom."

"Suit yourself." He broke eye contact as he sat on the bed and pulled off one of his boots.

Without looking at him, she hurried across the room. She gave him as wide a berth as possible, which still meant she nearly stepped on his feet as she grabbed her backpack and ducked into the bathroom. She closed the door and leaned against it, breathing as if she'd run a footrace. Then she glanced at herself in the mirror and saw what Nat had seen—a blatant invitation.

She pulled off the blond wig and unpinned her hair. She hadn't been trying to tease him, she told herself while running her fingers through her hair and massaging her scalp. This was simply the next outfit in the rotation she'd developed.

She'd bought and discarded clothes and wigs along the way—this particular disguise was a fairly new addition to her bag of tricks. But as she shimmied out of the zebra-print dress, she had to admit that she'd been glad this was the outfit for today instead of another truly ugly one, especially after seeing how he filled out the shoulders of his western-cut suit.

Rummaging through her backpack, she found her teal sleep shirt. Usually that was all she wore to bed, but tonight maybe she'd better leave her underwear on, too. Oh, God, how she wanted him. The few hours they would be closed into this motel room would be so packed with tension she'd never sleep. He probably wouldn't, either. Maybe, for both their sakes, she should just go back out there and climb into his bed and be done with it.

No. She had to think of Elizabeth's welfare ahead of all else. Love me, love my daughter. Nat didn't seem at all prepared to do that, which meant she had to stay out of his bed.

After scrubbing all the makeup off and brushing her teeth, she started toward the closed door of the bathroom. The night before, she'd come out and he'd been standing right there waiting for her. If he did that again, and pulled her into his arms, she wasn't sure she could resist him. One kiss and she'd be a goner.

She opened the door slowly and peeked out. With a sense of disappointment, she realized he wasn't there. Apparently he wasn't planning to use any caveman tactics that would let her off the hook. That was just as well. Of course it was.

Turning off the bathroom light, she walked out into the room and discovered he was already in the bed closest to the door, lying with his hands tucked behind his head while he looked up at the ceiling. He'd left the lamp on between the two beds, and he'd only pulled the covers up to his waist, so his chest was bare.

She wondered if he had any idea of the picture he made. Probably not. He'd never been aware of his sex appeal. And damn it, she wanted to know if he was naked under the covers. She'd never known him to wear anything to bed.

Averting her gaze from the tantalizing sight of him lying there, she walked over to the far bed and pulled back the sheet.

"You're right, you know," he said.

"About what?" She got into bed and pulled the covers up to her chin.

"Not making love to me."

His tone of voice pierced her heart. "I don't know what's right," she said. "I only know what I have to do, for the baby's sake. I can't let myself be involved with someone who doesn't love her as much as I do."

He continued to stare up at the ceiling. "I knew you'd be a devoted mother, ready to sacrifice anything. That's good. You were meant to have kids, Jess. Too bad your first one had to be with me."

"As I said before, I don't regret that." She started to reach for the lamp switch and paused. Something had been nagging at her ever since the night before, and now she had to know. "Nat, why did you go to see my parents?"

He sighed. "Because I'm weak. Even though I'm the wrong guy for you, I keep thinking there must be a way for this to work, because I want you so much."

There is, if you can let go of your fear, she thought, but she didn't say anything. They were both tired, and this wasn't the time to get into it.

"I tried calling your apartment before I got on the plane in London, to tell you I was coming home," he continued. "When I found out the line was disconnected, I was determined to find you. I started with your parents."

The thought that he'd gone looking for her warmed her considerably. Maybe all wasn't lost. "And they agreed to see you just because you asked about me?" she asked. "That doesn't sound like them."

"They agreed to see me because I told them I wanted to talk about my foundation for helping the orphans in the refugee camps. I didn't mention you until later."

She propped herself up on one elbow to stare at him. "What foundation?"

Finally he turned his head to glance at her. "That was my main purpose in going over to that country, to see if I could set up some sort of program that would take care of the kids and find homes for them, either over there or over here."

"I had no idea."

"It'll be terrific." His tone grew more excited. "I have some great people lined up to administer it from that end, and I've used my own money to set things in motion, but this will be a huge project. Obviously I need more funding, but I think I can get—"

"I can't believe this." The injustice of it shot through her and she sat up in bed. "I vaguely remember you mentioned the idea of adopting an orphan at some time in the future, but I had no idea you were going to head up an entire operation."

"I'm already doing it," he said. "It's desperately needed, and once we clear up this situation with the person who's trying to kidnap you, I'm planning to give it my full attention."

"Are you?" Anger seethed within her. "Not that I don't think it's a wonderful idea, Nat. It is. I'm sure you'll be a hero. But how can you enthusiastically throw yourself into this program to save little children you don't even know, when you won't consider being a father to the one who belongs to you?"

His gaze was bleak. "You still don't get it, do you? I'm helping those kids because it's what I can do. I understand them, and because of that, I don't expect much from them. I can't relate to a little girl who's never known anything but loving kindness, because I'd probably expect her to be perfect. Hell, I might even envy her, and because of that I wouldn't cut her any slack.'' He paused. ''I would ruin her, Jess.''

She glared at him in frustration. ''When you get an idea, you sure do clutch it to your breast forever, don't you?''

His glance flicked over her. ''I've been known to. Now cover up.''

She understood his implication and slid under the covers. ''I'm too mad at you to make love, anyway,'' she said.

''Now, there's the difference between us,'' he said, reaching up to shut off the light.

''What difference?'' she said into the darkness, knowing full well she should keep her mouth shut.

''I can get so mad at you I could chew nails, but at the same time I want to strip you naked and go at it until we're both moaning and soaked with sweat.''

She gulped as the vivid mental image rocked her with desire.

''Sweet dreams,'' he murmured.

''Up yours,'' she said under her breath.

''We can try it any way you'd like to, darlin'. I'm open to suggestion.''

With a groan, she turned her back to him. She would get no sleep tonight. •

NAT DIDN'T EXPECT to sleep, considering that every rustle of the sheets in the other bed made him clench his jaw against a new wave of desire. When he closed his eyes he still saw her, sitting up so indignantly when she'd heard about his plans for the orphans. He'd thought she'd be pleased. He hadn't figured out how it might look from her perspective, and she probably had some justification for being angry.

In fact, she had every reason to be upset with him. He

wasn't giving her what she needed and deserved, and yet he wanted…all of her. In his imagination he could still see the proud thrust of her breasts under the cotton nightshirt and the wild tangle of her red hair as she challenged his behavior.

She might not remember, but some of their best times in bed had come about after a heated argument. That spitfire quality of hers really turned him on, maybe because he liked the idea that she'd never allow herself to be dominated by anyone or anything. A tiny voice told him that where he was concerned, her demands might be his salvation. But he didn't care to listen right now.

She'd come by her grit the hard way. After he'd met her father, he understood that she'd learned to be tough by having to go up against Russell P. Franklin. And maybe she was more like her father than she would like to think.

But she could be soft and vulnerable, too. Back in the days when they'd been together, he'd loved watching the transformation that took place as his lovemaking burned away her anger and left only molten passion surging between them.

Remembering, he lay in the dark and ached. If he'd hoped to get any sleep in this motel room, he'd probably wasted his money.

But finally exhaustion must have claimed him, because before he knew it, light was seeping around the edges of the closed drapes. Somewhere down the hall a vacuum cleaner whined. They needed to get back on the road.

He should just get out on the far side of the bed and go directly to the shower. Instead, he rolled to his side and lifted his head to glance over at Jessica, which was a definite mistake.

She was asleep, but she must have had a hell of time achieving that, because she was completely tangled in the covers. One smooth leg was revealed all the way up to the high-cut leg opening of her briefs. Irresistible.

Propping his cheek on his fist, Nat studied that bare leg way too long. He'd forgotten how much he loved her knees, which were small and finely shaped. He used to tease her about them, saying they were the most aristocratic part of her body.

And the backs of her knees were two of her most sensitive spots. Several times he'd driven her to the brink of orgasm simply by nibbling and licking those delicate creases.

He was punished for his reminiscences with a desperately rigid penis. If he knew what was good for him, he'd head for the shower now, before she woke up.

While he was still trying to gather the willpower to do that, she opened her eyes. The fiery belligerence that had lit those brown eyes the night before was gone. In its place was the soft acceptance of a woman wanting to be loved. He sucked in a breath, hesitating. Her pupils widened and her lips parted.

Heart pounding, he held her gaze as he started to get out of bed. But even before his foot made contact with the floor, he saw the change in her eyes as she became more aware of her surroundings. As memory, no doubt, returned. The welcome faded, to be replaced with grim determination.

"No," she whispered.

He groaned and flopped back onto the bed. "It was yes when you woke up, and don't try to tell me different."

"I can't control my dreams."

He looked over at her. "You were dreaming about me?"

She didn't answer, but he knew by the expression on her face that she'd been dreaming about him, all right. Hot dreams. He knew all about those kinds of fantasies. They'd been his constant companion the entire time he was overseas.

He might still be able to force the issue and love her into submission, considering that she wasn't that far removed from those potent dreams. Her mind might be trying to shut down her desire, but her body would be slower to obey. She'd still be moist and ready, and he could break down her defenses easily enough if he climbed into that bed with her and ignored her protests.

But that wasn't his style. She'd told him to back off, and that's what he intended to do, unless and until she changed her mind. "Guess I'll hit the shower," he said.

"Okay."

Maybe his wounded ego was causing him to imagine things, but he could swear she sounded disappointed. Maybe she wanted him to override her objections. After all, she'd never said no to him before, so how the hell was he supposed to know if she meant it?

Damn, but she had him twisting in the wind. And if it was a game she was playing, he wanted to raise the stakes. He wanted her to twist a little, too. "And I'd appreciate some privacy while I'm in the shower," he said.

"You don't have to worry about that." She sounded huffy.

He realized she didn't get his implication, so he'd have to make his hint broader. "The thing is, a man can only stand so much before he has to find relief any way he can. I wouldn't want you to come in and be embarrassed by what's going on."

Her freckles stood out against the pink flush on her cheeks. She obviously got it now. "I wouldn't dream of barging in on you."

"Good." He had no intention of following through with what he'd hinted he might do in that shower, but he wanted her to think that's exactly what was happening. From the heat in her eyes, he had a good idea of how the concept was affecting her.

Later on he might be ashamed of himself for torturing her like this, but at the moment he couldn't seem to help it. He wanted her so much he could barely walk.

He rolled to the far side of the bed and swung his feet to the floor. Somehow he made it to the bathroom and closed the door. This was hell. If he'd thought living without her for seventeen months had been horrendous, that was only because he hadn't imagined what it would be like if she was right within reach...and forbidden.

CHAPTER NINE

THE MINUTE NAT closed the bathroom door, Jessica propelled herself out of bed and tore through her backpack looking for the most unattractive outfit she could find. When she heard the rush of water from the shower, she tried not to think about what might be going on behind the shower curtain.

He wouldn't really do it. He was only implying he would to mess with her head. But then again, she'd never been around a sexually frustrated Nat Grady. In fact, she and Nat had spent many hours in bed making sure that didn't ever happen. So maybe he *was* in the shower giving himself the pleasure she had denied him. The idea should repel her, but instead it made her hot.

Forcing her attention back to her task, she pulled what she needed from her backpack—faded, baggy overalls and a nondescript gray shirt to wear underneath. She was going to do her part to cut the sexual tension between them. In this getup she wouldn't look sexy and she definitely wouldn't feel sexy.

She could even get dressed right now and skip her shower. Then she totally would not feel sexy. She started to take off her nightshirt and paused. With the way Nat was driving, they'd probably make Colorado on this leg of the trip. Jessica didn't care what she was wearing when she saw Elizabeth again, but she'd like to be reasonably clean.

So she put her clothes in a pile and stalked back and forth in the small area between the beds and the double

dresser while she listened to the drumming noise of the
shower. He was taking too damn long in there. Probably
he was shaving in the shower. That was it. He used to do
that sometimes.

A quick whispering noise by the motel door made her
turn in that direction and she noticed a piece of paper lying
on the carpet in front of the door. Thinking it was the bill,
she walked over and picked it up. The message was typed,
and very short:

Don't think your boyfriend can protect you.

With a sharp cry she dropped the paper and backed away
from the door, almost expecting to see the knob turn.

In an instant the bathroom door flew open and Nat came
out, dripping wet with a towel held around his waist.
"What? What happened?"

Shaking, she pointed toward the paper she'd dropped on
the floor.

He snatched it up, read it and cursed. Dropping the note
back on the floor, he whipped the towel from his body and
grabbed his suit pants from the chair.

"What do you think you're doing?" she cried as he
struggled into them and headed for the door while pulling
up the zipper.

"Lock the dead bolt behind me," he said, "and don't
open the door until you know it's me."

"No! You can't—"

"I won't debate this with you." He wrenched open the
door. "Now lock it behind me!"

She could either do as he asked or run outside after him
in her nightshirt. She didn't relish being kidnapped in her
nightshirt. After bolting the door behind him, she scrambled
into the gray shirt and overalls, her heart pounding in fear
for Nat. Stupid fool. Stupid, impetuous fool. She was shov-

ing her shoes on her feet when a knock came at the door followed by Nat's voice calling her name.

With only one shoe on, she hobbled quickly to the door and opened it. He looked to be in one piece, and she sighed with relief.

He came in, breathing hard, his hair still damp and his pants spotted with the moisture he hadn't bothered to towel off before he put them on. Locking the door, he leaned over and put his hands on his knees while he got his breath back.

"Couldn't find him," he said at last, glancing up at her, his hair falling down in his eyes.

"You shouldn't have tried! What did you think you were going to accomplish, racing out there half dressed like that?"

"The element of surprise. Even if I didn't find him, he might have seen me. And that's good."

"How do you figure?"

He straightened and combed his hair back with his fingers. "I know his kind, Jess. He's a bully, and there's nothing he likes better than to know someone is scared. I've been thinking about this. Sebastian wondered if the guy is inept, considering he's been after you for this long and still hasn't caught you."

That got her dander up. She braced her hands on her hips. "Did it occur to Sebastian that I might be outsmarting this jerk and that's why he hasn't caught me?"

A faint smile touched his lips. "Oh, I'm sure that's part of it. Your disguises make it tougher for him, and you've let him know by your actions that you're smart. He understands that when he makes the snatch, he'd better make it a good one or you'll get away. But I think there's something else going on here."

She was proud of her efforts so far, and didn't much appreciate Nat's comments. "Such as?"

"If he's the bully I think he is, he's getting such a charge out of scaring you that he hates to finish the job too soon. That would put an end to his fun.''

Jessica's indignation faded and she shivered. ''That's sick.''

''Yeah, well, sick people are out there. Sometimes they appear to be perfectly normal, too.''

She gazed at him and knew without a doubt that he was talking about his father. He understood bullies because he'd been raised by one.

''We'd better get on the road,'' he said. ''The sooner we pull into the Rocking D, the better. This guy's had a field day stalking you while you've been running all over the country by yourself. He won't have it so easy when a bunch of us are around to protect you.''

''Do you think there's a chance he'll forget the whole thing?''

''No. Sorry. I'm sure you'd like to believe that, but anybody who's this persistent will want the pot of gold at the end of the rainbow. Maybe, when he realizes you're less accessible at the Rocking D, his frustration will cause him to make a mistake.''

''You think so?''

''I kind of figure it that way.'' The corner of Nat's mouth tilted up. ''I know a bit about frustration, too.''

That reminded her of their previous conversation, and suddenly she wondered what activity she'd interrupted when she cried out.

His expression softened. ''Aw, hell, Jess. Don't look at me like that. Nothing X-rated was going on it that shower. Now let's get moving. We need to hit the road.'' He glanced at her outfit, as if seeing it for the first time, and started to laugh. ''Is that the plan for today?''

''It's not *that* funny.''

''It's not funny at all. It's cute as the dickens. Is it for my benefit?''

She bristled. "You said yesterday's outfit was too sexy, so—"

"Jess, I appreciate the effort. I really do. But I realize now I gave way too much credit to your outfit yesterday. It wasn't the tight dress turning me on, it was the body inside it. And covering it up with those overalls only makes me want to take them off so I can get a better look. You can't win this one."

She threw out both arms. "Then what am I supposed to wear?"

"Anything you want, darlin'. The guy already knows what room we're in, and he'll probably watch us come out. I'd say a disguise isn't going to do you much good today. Got any ordinary clothes in that backpack?"

"Some jeans and a sweater." She'd kept them with her during the entire six months. The jeans were her favorites and she'd needed their familiar comfort for days when she'd felt as if she was losing her identity. And the sweater—well, Nat had given it to her for Christmas.

"Then wear those," he said gently. "And get ready as quick as you can. I'll call Sebastian and tell him to expect us late tonight."

Her stomach began to churn. "For sure?"

"We can make it if we eat on the run."

"Okay." She wanted to see Elizabeth desperately, but now that the moment was so close, she was even more afraid of Elizabeth's reaction to her after all this time. She'd never intended for the separation to be this long, but the weeks had slipped by while she waited for Nat to come home. "It's a long way," she said. "Are you sure you're up to it?"

"I'm up to it. You need to see your baby, and another night in a motel room with you would probably kill me."

She picked up her backpack and started for the bathroom. "Same here," she said over her shoulder.

NAT'S DRESS PANTS were damp and uncomfortable after he'd pulled them on straight from the shower, so he put on the only other clothes he'd bought when he'd made the quick shopping trip before leaving New York, jeans and a collarless knit shirt. The jeans were new and stiff, so he'd do well to keep his mind off Jess during the drive today or he'd do his privates some serious injury.

Once he was dressed, he sat on the bed and reached for the phone. Punching in his credit card information, he dialed Sebastian's number. He got Matty again and wondered why she'd answered Sebastian's phone both times he'd called.

"Is Sebastian in the neighborhood?" he asked after assuring Matty that he and Jess were fine. He decided not to relay the information about the note slipped under the door. No use worrying people who couldn't do a damn thing about it.

"He's down at the barn. Do you want me to go get him?"

"That's okay. I just wanted him to know we'll be rolling in tonight, but it might be late. I hate to make him wait up for us, but with this bozo running around loose he'd better not leave a key under the mat."

"Don't worry about keeping us up," Matty said. "In fact, we might—"

"Uh, Matty?"

"Yes?"

"Has there been a…change in living arrangements while I was gone? You keep saying 'we' like you're, um…how can I say this without being offensive?"

Matty laughed. "You want to know if we're shacking up?"

"I guess I do." Nat found himself grinning. "Are you?"

"That's one way of putting it. I guess Sebastian didn't get around to telling you the news. We're married."

"Seriously?" Nat's grin widened. What a perfect match. It was amazing that nobody had thought of it before.

"The truth is, we're hardly ever serious," she said, her voice teasing. "We save that for when we have to worry about you."

"God, I know this has been a mess." The burden of the problems he'd caused his friends settled heavily on his shoulders. "I hope someday you'll forgive me. In the meantime, I'm sure happy for you, Matty. That's great news. When did you tie the knot?"

"Five months ago. We have Jessica and Elizabeth to thank for bringing us together, as a matter of fact. Sebastian desperately needed help with the baby, and I wasn't much more knowledgeable than he was, but we muddled through together, and in the process figured out we couldn't live without each other."

"Hot damn." The knowledge that Sebastian and Matty were together lightened his load of self-blame. "I'm glad to know something good came of all this."

"Oh, lots of good came from it. Having Elizabeth around has changed quite a few lives. While we went on our honeymoon, Travis took care of her, and when she caught a cold, he went to Gwen Hawthorne for help, and now—"

"Evans having a new girlfriend isn't news, Matty." Nat leaned back against the headboard. "It'll blow over, like every other love affair he's ever had."

"I doubt it. Not considering they've stood in front of a preacher and are expecting a baby."

"*What?*" Nat sat up straight. "You're kidding. Are you sure we're talking about the same Travis Evans?"

"One and the same. He's domesticated, Nat."

"I find that hard to believe. Next you'll be telling me that Boone—"

"Ah, yes. Boone. On his way up here from New Mexico to see about Elizabeth, he met Shelby McFarland, who became, as of two months ago, Mrs. Boone Connor."

''My God.'' Nat rubbed his temples with his free hand and tried to take it all in. He focused on the first bit of information she'd given him about Boone. ''Why would Boone be coming up to see about Elizabeth?''

''Jessica didn't tell you what she did?''

''Well, yeah. She left the baby with Sebastian.'' He glanced up as Jessica came into the room in the green sweater he'd given her two Christmases ago. The sight of her in that sweater did funny things to his heart.

''She didn't tell you about the letters she wrote to each of the guys?''

''Not that I remember.'' He watched Jessica move around the room collecting any stray belongings. The forest-green sweater was cashmere, he remembered. He'd loved stroking her breasts through the soft material. He wanted to do it now. ''What letters?'' he asked to be polite, although he was fast losing interest in the conversation.

''She wrote a letter to each of them, asking them to be a godfather to Elizabeth.''

''That's nice.'' Nat liked the soft drape of the sweater on Jess, but it was even more effective combined with the snug fit of her jeans. He remembered that combination had seduced him quite thoroughly the last time she'd worn it.

''I don't think you understand,'' Matty was saying. ''They were so drunk that night of the avalanche reunion party that Jessica drove them to their cabin and tucked them in. Elizabeth was born nine months later, so they each assumed the godfather label was a smoke screen.''

Finally what Matty was saying penetrated his erotic musings about Jess. His gut clenched when he realized her implication. ''Wait a minute. What do you mean, a smoke screen?''

''I mean that every last one of them thought he was the baby's father.''

Nat stared at Jess as jealousy washed over him in uncompromising waves. "Why the hell would they think that?" he said much too loudly.

Jess closed a dresser drawer and turned to gaze at him in alarm.

"Oh, you know," Matty said. "Because they each vaguely remembered making a pass at her in their drunken stupor. Stealing a kiss. Harmless stuff, I'm sure, but they imagined they'd gone beyond that and fathered this kid."

Nat could barely breathe. The fact that none of his friends had known a thing about his involvement with Jess was a point of logic that didn't matter right now. He still wanted to wring each of their necks for even *thinking* of touching her.

"It's sort of funny, looking back on it," Matty said. "But believe me, it wasn't funny at the time. And now that I realize this is all news to you, I should probably warn you that these guys still feel very fatherly toward that little girl. They're extremely possessive. They've found out they're not her father, of course, but the bond is formed, and I doubt it'll ever go away."

"I see." New and strange emotions coursed through Nat. He should be happy that his friends were so attached to Elizabeth. That took some of the responsibility off his shoulders. Hell, they probably didn't need him around at all, with three of them ready to take over as the baby's father figure.

So why was he feeling as if he needed to charge in and trumpet his claim like some wild stallion warning off rivals?

"I'm glad I had a chance to talk to you," Matty said. "I'm guessing that everybody will be here when you arrive tonight. You should be prepared. They'll probably give you the third degree regarding your intentions toward Elizabeth." Her voice softened. "She's cute as a bug's ear, Nat. Once you see her, you'll understand why the guys are so protective. Why we all are."

Nat's head began to ache. "I appreciate the information, Matty," he said. "We'll get there as soon as we can."

"Don't break any laws doing it," she said. "Bye now."

"See you soon." Nat put the receiver back in the cradle and gazed at Jess, who was standing motionless by the dresser. "You failed to mention the letters you wrote to my friends."

"Did I? Well, that was part of my plan to make sure Elizabeth had plenty of protectors. I asked Sebastian, Travis and Boone to be her godfathers. I thought it was ingenious of me."

"Oh, it was that."

"Then why are you looking like a thundercloud?"

He stood and walked toward her. "Because each of them assumed he was Elizabeth's father, that's why!"

Her jaw dropped.

"What went on the night of the avalanche reunion party, Jess?" He prayed she'd laugh and give him a logical answer. "Why would all three of them think that?"

She didn't laugh. Instead, her eyes grew bright with anger. "What in hell are you implying?"

"I'm not implying anything." He drew closer. He desperately wanted her side of the story. "Matty said they all got smashed and remembered making passes at you. I just want to know—"

"How can you even *think* to question me about this?" She trembled with rage. "Is that the sort of opinion you have of me?"

"No!" He lifted a hand as if to touch her cheek, but after seeing the look in her eyes he thought better of it. "I just—"

"You just want my word that I didn't go to bed with all three of your best friends in the same night!" Her voice quivered. "Well, you're not getting it. Only an insensitive idiot would ask the question in the first place, and I will not stoop to explaining myself."

"Damn it, Jess. Less than a minute ago I found out that three other men thought they were the father of my baby. Any guy would want to know what that was all about!" Deep in his heart he knew she hadn't done anything wrong, but jealousy had him by the throat. *Something* had gone on that night. He wanted her to tell him it had been nothing, like Matty said. Harmless. He wanted her to assure him that she felt nothing but friendship for each of those men.

"*Your* baby? As I recall, you don't want anything to do with her."

"That's beside the point. She's my baby, and those guys have no right—"

"All of them rushed to take care of her, as I hoped they would," she said. "While *you* were out of the country and completely out of touch. In my book that gives them a ton of rights."

"I didn't know about her!"

"You ran away, so how could you know?"

"I didn't run away." But he had and he knew it. So did she. Then he remembered the rest of Matty's news. He delivered it with some relish, knowing it would shock her as it had him. If she'd secretly thought one of his stalwart, responsible friends would be a backup if he bowed out, she could forget that fantasy. "Well, they're all married now."

"They are?"

"Surprised at that, aren't you?"

"I sure am! I had no idea—"

"So if you had some plan that included roping one of them into marriage in case I didn't work out, you can forget it. They're taken."

Her open palm stung as it connected with his cheek. He resisted the urge to put his hand against the spot, which hurt like hell. They stared at each other, both of them breathing hard.

"We need to get going," he said.

"Fine. Let's go. The sooner I'm rid of you and your

insinuations, the better.'' She spun on her heel, snatched up her backpack and headed for the door.

"Don't go out there by yourself, damn it!" He hoisted his backpack and charged after her.

"Maybe you should let me be kidnapped," she replied harshly, flinging open the door. "Shoot, if I play my cards right, I might even be able to bribe the guy into marrying me. After all, any man will do, so long as I have a ring on my finger."

He slammed the door and caught up with her, grabbing her by the arm. God, the cashmere was soft. The first time she'd worn it, she hadn't put on a bra, and when he'd rubbed his palms over her breasts, her nipples had puckered instantly under the material. She'd said it was like being stroked with mink. He really didn't want to fight with her.

He took a breath. "Maybe I shouldn't have said that," he murmured. "But I think you still owe me some explanation for—"

"I owe you *nothing*." She pulled her arm away and marched down the balcony toward the stairs.

Nat didn't know where the creep might be hiding, but letting Jess get so far ahead could be the invitation the guy was waiting for. He caught up with her again and took her arm. When she struggled, he gripped her harder than he'd intended. Seventeen months of digging ditches had given him that kind of strength.

"Let me go."

"No." He lowered his voice as he propelled her down the stairs so fast she nearly stumbled. "You may not owe me anything, but I owe you something, and that's to see that you get safely back to Elizabeth. Now, don't pull away from me again."

She struggled for breath as they hurried across the parking lot toward the car. Her voice was sharp with fury. "I'll bet you're finally mad enough not to want me."

He opened the car door and practically shoved her in. "You'd lose that bet," he said.

CHAPTER TEN

As THEY RODE in silence, speaking only when they stopped to order a fast-food breakfast to go, Jessica tried to control her curiosity. She was dying to know who each of the guys had married, and whether it had happened before she'd dropped off the baby or after. But she'd be damned if she'd strike up a conversation with a man who, however briefly, thought she was capable of engaging in some sort of orgy the night after he'd dumped her.

She hadn't been able to gather any personal news about Sebastian, Travis or Boone during her quick calls to the Rocking D in the past six months. She hadn't dared spend any time on the line when she'd phoned for fear the kidnapper would somehow trace the call and go there to find out what the fuss was about. Even now she worried that she was leading him to Elizabeth, but now that Nat knew he was the baby's father, Jessica was ready to make a stand.

So all three men were married. The idea caused her to smile. Each of them in his own way would make some woman very happy, even a confirmed bachelor like Travis. Jessica had always suspected there was more to Travis than the playboy image he projected, which was why she'd wanted him to be part of the group watching out for Elizabeth.

If three women had joined Elizabeth's chosen circle, so much the better. They'd have to be fantastic ladies if they'd hitched up with three of her best friends. She could hardly wait to meet them.

She peeked over at Nat. His expression was grim and he'd pulled his Stetson down low over his eyes, which was always a sign he didn't feel like having a conversation. Not that she had much to discuss with him, after what he'd said.

But the drive seemed endless with no communication between them and all the questions hanging in the air. She gazed out the window at the stubble of harvested fields and willed the time to go faster.

They picked up more fast food for lunch. Continuing to drive was fine with Jessica, but she began to feel sorry for Nat, who bore the brunt of the task. She shouldn't feel sorry for him. After all, at the first hint that all was not fitting and proper, he'd practically accused her of being a tramp. If he didn't trust her any more than that, she didn't want to have anything to do with him.

That was a lie. The only reason he'd been able to hurt her with his questions was that she was in love with him. From the feel of it, she wouldn't ever be in love with anyone else. She'd hoped to fall out of love with him sometime during the seventeen months he'd been gone, but it hadn't happened.

And he still loved her. He might not *trust* her completely, but he still loved her. She could see it in his eyes every time he looked at her.

Before they reached the western border of Kansas, he apologized. "Look, I'm sorry," he said quietly. "You're right, I shouldn't have even asked the question."

She sighed and relaxed against the seat. She hadn't even realized how stiffly she'd been sitting until the last of the anger flooded out of her in one big gush. "Thank you for that." She glanced at his tense profile. That apology had cost him a lot of pride and she admired him for sacrificing it. She could do no less. "Would you like to hear about that night?"

"Doesn't interest me in the least."

"Liar."

The corner of his mouth tilted up. ''Okay, I want to hear every last detail, but you don't have to tell me a damn thing.''

She couldn't ever remember wanting to kiss him as much as she did now. But they were driving, and even if they weren't, she'd said no lovemaking, which naturally meant no kissing, either. ''I guess I should be flattered that you're jealous.''

''You can be flattered if you want, but I'm furious with myself.''

''Jealousy's a natural emotion.''

''That could be, but in my opinion, the only men who can treat themselves to jealousy are would-be husbands, so that lets me out.''

The words hurt, so she tried to make light of them. ''Oh, I don't know. It seems to be the in thing these days.''

''No kidding.''

''Before I tell you about what happened that night in Aspen, will you tell me who the guys married? I'm dying of curiosity.''

He glanced over at her.

''Nothing but curiosity, I swear,'' she said with a smile.

''I wouldn't blame you for being attracted to any of them. They're good men, and I guess they're okay-looking.'' His grin was genuine this time. ''Not as handsome and manly as me, of course.''

''Of course. But obviously someone found them irresistible. Who was it?''

''Sebastian married his neighbor, Matty Lang. Her husband was killed a while back, flew his Cessna into a mountain, and she's been running her ranch by herself, except for Travis helping out in the summer. Now that I think about it, she's the perfect match for Sebastian. But I guess now I'll never be able to buy his ranch. He's probably there to stay.''

''You wanted to buy a ranch? You never told me that.''

"It's a beautiful piece of property." He straightened his arms against the wheel and flexed his shoulders, stretching the kinks out. "I could sell it for a huge profit someday, but that wasn't my motivation. I'm not sure what my motivation was."

"You grew up on a ranch. Maybe you'd like to get back to that."

He shook his head. "Probably not."

"Maybe you'd like to run a ranch for kids with no place to go," she suggested gently.

He gave her a startled glance. Then he returned his attention to the road. "You sure have a way of getting inside my head, Jess. I hadn't put it all together, but you might be right. The orphans in the refugee camps aren't the only ones without a home. But it was a place to start."

Such noble dreams, she thought. How she'd love to be a part of them. But she came with a kid attached. How ironic that he wanted to save all the children of the world except one. She'd been upset about that at first, but she was slowly beginning to understand his reasoning, and it didn't seem so contradictory now.

"So who did Travis marry?" she asked.

"Gwen Hawthorne, who runs a bed-and-breakfast in Huerfano, the little town down the road from the Rocking D."

"I know where it is." Just hearing the name of the ranch brought back the pain of the night she'd abandoned her child.

"Do you know what the town's name means in Spanish?" Nat asked.

"No. I took French in college."

"It means *orphan.*"

"Really?" She wondered if that had been one of the reasons he'd been attracted to the area in the first place. "Maybe it's fate that you're supposed to start something like that near Huerfano."

"If I do, I'll have to find a piece of property besides the Rocking D to do it on."

"Guess so." She tried to sound as if where he ended up didn't really concern her, when in fact it concerned her tremendously. If he chose not to link his life with hers, then she wanted to locate far, far away from him. "What about Boone, then? Who did he find?"

"A woman named Shelby McFarland. He met her on the way up from his folks' place in New Mexico to the Rocking D."

"You mean both he and Sebastian got married *after* I left Elizabeth at the ranch? That's weird."

He nodded. "Travis did, too. Matty said it was the baby that pulled each couple together, in a way."

"Wow." She'd never anticipated causing such havoc, even though it seemed to be a good kind of havoc. "And each one of the guys thought he was Elizabeth's father. That blows me away. It never occurred to me they'd think such a thing. I only wanted to surround Elizabeth with people who would watch out for her. I knew I could trust them to do that."

"So what did happen that night?" Nat asked the question as if he was only mildly curious.

She smiled at his obvious attempt to sound casual. "Your friends assembled in the bar at the lodge and got totally plowed, that's what." She still chuckled whenever she thought of the raucous drinking songs, the arm-wrestling contests and the corny jokes that made them all laugh until their sides hurt. They'd pledged eternal friendship to each other that night, but she'd never expected to put that pledge to such a test.

"I gathered they got smashed. Then what?"

"They'd booked that same little cabin you guys had the year before, which is about two miles from the lodge, if you remember. It was nasty out, and I didn't dare let any of them behind the wheel, so I drove them back to the cabin.''

He glanced over at her. "You didn't have anything to drink?"

"Somebody had to stay sober and keep them out of trouble." She didn't want to admit she'd been so heartbroken that even one drink might have caused her to lose control and start sobbing in the middle of what was supposed to be a celebration. She shouldn't have continued to feel an obligation to keep her relationship with Nat a secret, but she had—all this time.

"So you drove them home and that's it?"

"Well, of course not. I knew they'd be miserable in the morning, so I made them take some vitamin C and B-complex. I tried to get them to drink some chamomile tea with honey, but they wouldn't hear of it. Said it was a sissy drink and they were studly cowboys who could hold their liquor, by God.''

Nat chuckled. "Good for them."

"I'm not surprised to hear that from you, considering how you've reacted whenever I've tried to guide you to some natural cures."

"You wanted me to drink stuff made with weeds!"

She bristled. "Those *weeds,* as you call them, are loaded with nutrients. People have no idea what a bountiful harvest they have in their own backyards! Why, if only everyone would—"

"I think I've heard that lecture a few times, Jess."

"And it's had zero effect."

"If I promise to drink the next cup of weed tea you offer me, will you finish your story?"

"There's not much more to tell. I helped them out of their clothes and into bed, and then I went home. The next morning—"

"Hold it. Back up the hay wagon. What do you mean, you *helped them out of their clothes?*"

Her anger from their morning argument threatened to return. "I don't like your implication, Nat."

"Okay, okay. I'm not implying anything was wrong, but I'm getting a mental picture here, and it's bugging me. Be fair, Jess. You weren't too happy when you found out I had my tongue in another woman's mouth."

"I *never* had my tongue in any of their mouths."

"But you undressed them."

"Down to their T-shirts and shorts! They were in sad enough shape the next day, without adding the discomfort of sleeping all night in their clothes."

"I guess," he mumbled. "Did any of them try to kiss you?"

"Sure they did. So what?"

The muscles in his jaw bunched. "I'm going to strangle them."

"Nat, they didn't know about us! They were drunk, and goofing around." She paused. "But I sure never imagined any of them thought they'd done more than try to kiss me. Is that even possible? To do the deed and not remember the next day?"

"That's never happened to me, but I guess it's possible." He blew out a breath and glanced at her. "None of this would have happened in the first place if I'd been there that night. I should have been there. But I thought I was doing you a favor by leaving."

"A *favor?* By walking out of my life completely? By putting yourself totally out of reach in a country across the ocean with no reliable phone or mail service? How was that supposed to be a favor?"

"I thought if I was out of the picture, you would find someone else."

Her throat tightened. "Is that what you want?"

"Hell, no, that's not what I want! I'm going crazy thinking of you in the clutches of my friends, even though I know it was all completely innocent. I don't dare imagine you in bed with another man. It would drive me nuts.''

''I can't imagine that, either,'' she said quietly.

He groaned. ''I love hearing that, and I shouldn't love it. I should want you to go out and find yourself a nice, marriage-minded guy who loves the idea of having children of his own.'' He slapped the steering wheel. ''I am beyond selfish to want you, when I'm not capable of giving you everything you need.''

She felt bathed in warmth, and absolutely sure he was wrong about himself. He had no idea what he might be capable of, given a chance. ''But you do want me?''

His jaw clenched again. ''Every minute of every day.''

She restrained herself from reaching over to touch him, although she ached to do that. One touch and they'd be exiting the freeway and parking on some side road so they could climb in the back seat together. Exciting as that sounded, she believed that making love now would only confuse the issue. Nat thought sex was all he could give her, and she wanted to show him they had far more going for them that that.

Because she dared not touch him, she could only reach out with words. ''Don't give up on us yet,'' she murmured.

He responded with silence, and although she would have preferred more encouragement, she was glad that at least he didn't argue with her.

MANY LONG, frustrating hours later, Nat drove down the dirt road leading to the ranch turnoff. The sun had set hours ago, and he thought he deserved a medal for making it all the way to the Rocking D without swerving onto some dark back road and finding a place to make love to Jess. He felt certain she wouldn't have stopped him if he'd tried that.

The closer they came to the ranch the more nervous he was. While he was overseas he had imagined reuniting with his buddies would be a homecoming of sorts, but Jess's bombshell of an announcement had changed all that. He desperately needed the sense of safety that making love to her would bring, but she'd chosen to pull the rug out from under him on that, too.

Her decision to stop having sex was a shaky one, and they both knew it, but his pride wouldn't let him challenge her decree. He wasn't entirely clear on what would have to happen before she'd take him back into her bed, but he figured it hinged primarily on his attitude toward Elizabeth. A marriage proposal would probably do the trick, too.

She'd be amazed if she knew how much he'd thought about marrying her, and how close he'd been to asking— right up to the moment he'd found out about the baby. He'd worked it all out somewhere over the Atlantic. He'd planned to propose, and when she inevitably brought up the idea of kids, he would then suggest adopting one of the orphans from the refugee camp as a first step.

That process would have taken some time, time he desperately needed to adjust to the concept of being a father. If he'd managed okay with an orphan child, then he'd have been ready to consider having a baby of his own. It had been a carefully thought-out compromise that he'd believed he could live with.

Of course, once he was in a hotel room alone with Jess, he hadn't been able to think at all. Making love to her had taken top priority. And then he'd been hit with the news about Elizabeth.

He wasn't ready. He didn't know if he'd ever be ready, but he didn't have the luxury of more time to find out. Everything was on the line right now, and he felt as if he'd been told to take an exam he was doomed to fail. Worse yet, he would fail in front of his three best friends, men whose respect he wanted.

They had a head start on him with his baby thing, too. During his work at the refugee camps, he'd steered away from the really tiny ones, leaving them to the women volunteers. He'd concentrated on the ones who could walk and talk.

The vulnerability of a baby terrified him. He knew damn well that if his mother hadn't been around during the first three years of his life, his father would have killed him for doing something as innocent as crying. Then he'd gained another couple of years' advantage while his father drowned his grief in the bottle.

By the time Hank Grady had looked around and noticed he had a son to bear the force of his rage and frustration, Nat was old enough to run and hide most times. A smart kid could usually avoid the worst of the abuse, but a little baby had no defense at all.

As he turned down the lane leading to the ranch house, he took a deep breath. He wasn't much of a praying man, but he found himself praying now. It wasn't a specific prayer, just a general plea to somehow have things turn out okay for everyone concerned.

Stands of juniper trees dotted the approach to the ranch house, shielding it from view until the final bend in the road. The place was lit up as if it was a holiday. He'd driven up here at night many times, and the first glimpse of the rustic log house with its wide porch, large windows and native-rock chimney was usually a welcome sight on a chilly night. Tonight Nat was intimidated by it. All those lights blazing from the windows seemed to be announcing the coming of Judgment Day.

"Nat, I'm scared," Jess said.

"Me, too."

"What are those other pickup trucks doing here at this hour?" she asked, sounding easily as nervous as Nat felt. "It looks like they're having a party or something."

"Matty warned me about that." He pulled into the circular driveway and parked behind a purple truck he didn't recognize. Travis's fancy black rig was in front of that, and Boone's battered king-cab was in the lead. Nat looked around for Sebastian's Bronco and saw it parked down by the barn.

"What'd she warn you about?" Jess asked, her eyes wide.

He turned off the rental car's engine. The little sedan looked out of place in the lineup of cowboy Cadillacs. For the first time ever in his visits to the Rocking D, Nat felt out of place. "Matty said everybody would probably be here—all the guys and their wives. I gather they've become very protective of Elizabeth, and they're not...well, they're not eager to give her up."

"That's too bad!" A frantic note crept into her voice. "I'm her mother, and I—"

"Hold it." He reached over and put a reassuring hand on her shoulder. Dealing with her panic would help him push aside his own. "I didn't say they weren't going to do it. But when you think about it, they've spent more months with Elizabeth since she's been born than you have. It's understandable that this will be tough for them. I'm sure once everyone gets used to the idea that you're ready to take her back, they'll be fine with it."

Jess gazed at the house and her lower lip trembled slightly. "This show of strength doesn't indicate they're going to be fine. They could take me to court, you know. They could charge me with abandoning her, and they'd have a pretty good case, too."

He gave her shoulder a gentle squeeze. "They're not going to do that," he said quietly. "Come on. Going in to face everybody will be the hardest part. Let's get it over with."

She turned to him. "Nat, I've said this before, but I want to say it again. Whatever happens in there, however this gets screwed up, I want you to know that I don't regret the pregnancy. I don't regret that you and I brought a little girl into this world. I realize we've caused a lot of people a ton of trouble, but I would do everything the same, just to have Elizabeth.''

He loved her so much at that moment that the feeling was painful in its intensity. ''That's all the people in there will have to hear,'' he said, his voice gruff with emotion. ''Now, let's go face the music.''

CHAPTER ELEVEN

As JESSICA REACHED for the handle of the car door, a familiar tickling at the back of her neck told her she and Nat were being watched. She'd learn to dread the sensation, but she was grateful for it, too. It left her less vulnerable. "I think he's followed us here," she said.

Nat tensed. Then he turned to look through the back window of the car.

"You won't be able to see him unless he wants you to," she said. "I've always had a feeling that when he shows himself, he means to do it."

"The guy's a damn psycho," Nat muttered as he continued to peer into the shadows. Then he looked over at Jessica, and his words took on an edge of steel. "And you know what? I'm glad he followed us. Now that we're here, we can figure out a way to catch that son of a bitch."

She was grateful for a champion, and now that they were at the Rocking D she would have four of them. Until the moment that she sensed her stalker was watching, she'd been nervous about going into the house and facing Sebastian, Boone and Travis. Now she wanted to be close to all that protection. "Let's go in," she said, opening the car door.

"Close the door and lock it. Then wait there until I come around and get you out."

"Help is close by, if he tries anything."

"Doesn't matter. Before I could get there, he could use

you as a hostage and we wouldn't be able to do anything about it. Wait there."

"Okay." After closing and locking the door, she kept her attention on Nat as he rounded the car. Then she unlocked the door and took his hand as he helped her out.

"I can't imagine how you've lived this way for six months, having to be afraid all the time," he said.

"Simple. You can't stay afraid all the time. You can get used to anything, if it goes on long enough. I—" A movement on the path coming up from the barn caught her eye. "Nat."

His grip on her hand tightened and he glanced over his shoulder. "What?"

"Over there." She pointed toward the barn. "Someone's—"

"I see him." Then his grip relaxed and he blew out a breath. "It's Sebastian. And Fleafarm."

"Fleafarm?" In her relief, she found that name funnier than it might have been otherwise.

"She was a stray, and Sebastian's ex-wife named her that. Sebastian wanted to change it once he found out what a great dog she is, but it's tough to change a name once it sticks." He tugged on her hand. "Let's walk down to meet him. I wouldn't mind breaking the ice by talking to Sebastian first."

"Good idea." Her feeling of being watched had begun to fade, and trusting the instincts she'd developed over the past few months, she decided that her stalker had retreated for the time being. She became more aware of her surroundings—the clean scent of juniper mixed with wood smoke, and the faint sound of country music and male laughter coming from the house. "I think the guy's gone now, anyway."

"You're that tuned in to him?"

"After six months, it's become a habit." Not a pleasant

one, she had to admit, but a necessary one. "Now let's go meet Sebastian."

As the sense of danger passed, she once again had the luxury of being nervous about facing Sebastian. Watching him walk toward them, she didn't know how she'd ever mistaken his purposeful stride and solid build for her stalker. There wasn't a sneaky bone in Sebastian's virile body.

When she'd made that fateful decision to leave Elizabeth at the Rocking D, she'd been blind to every concern except protecting her tiny child. Yet the arrival of the baby had drastically changed Sebastian's life, as well as the lives of the people waiting inside the house. She had to take responsibility for that. No matter how noble her motives, she'd created chaos.

She felt it whirling inside her, too. In a short time she'd see her child again. Logically, Elizabeth couldn't be expected to know her. Illogically, Jessica prayed that she would recognize her mother, that something about Jessica's voice, her touch, her scent would awaken memories. But even if that happened, Elizabeth would be hesitant at first. She'd prefer the people she'd lived with since March to some vaguely familiar woman. The pain of watching Elizabeth choose someone else over her own mother would be excruciating.

Sebastian spotted them and quickened his pace. "Nat? Jessica? I thought I heard a car drive up."

"What are you doing down here?" Nat asked as he drew closer. "Did Matty banish you to the barn?"

"I'll thank you not to say that in front of her and give her ideas," Sebastian said, his grin flashing in the darkness.

Fleafarm bounded forward with a bark of welcome.

"Hey, Fleafarm," Nat said, leaning down to scratch behind the dog's ears. "I'm surprised you remember me."

"I'm surprised *I* remember you," Sebastian said as he

reached them. He grabbed Nat's outstretched hand and clapped him on the back. "How the hell are you?"

"Surviving," Nat said with a faint smile.

"That's a start." Sebastian gave him a level look before turning to Jessica. "How about you, little one?"

She'd forgotten he used to call her that, and the endearment brought tears to her eyes. "I'm okay, Sebastian. But I'm afraid I caused quite a ruckus around here."

"You could say that." He stepped toward her. "But that doesn't mean I'm not glad to see you. I'm happy you're safe, Jessica." And with that, he enfolded her in his arms for a bear hug, just like old times.

Tears dribbled down her cheeks at his uncomplicated welcome. "I'm sorry for what I've put you all through," she murmured as she hugged him back. "I had no idea you'd all think that you might be Elizabeth's father."

"You didn't?" Releasing her, he tipped back his Stetson with his thumb and gave her a puzzled look. "By the way you dropped her off, asking us to be godfathers and everything, I thought you meant for us to think one of us was."

"Oh, God, no." She put a hand to her chest. "That would have been diabolical, to lead you to believe that and then keep the real father a secret. Did you really think I was capable of something so mean?"

"Well, no." Sebastian looked uncomfortable as he glanced over at Nat. "But then I didn't think Nat would carry on a yearlong relationship with a woman and not tell me, either."

Nat squared his shoulders as if ready to take whatever blame might be heaped on him. "Like I said on the phone, I was wrong to keep that from you."

"Then why did you?" Sebastian asked quietly, hurt shining in his eyes.

"Because I have a yellow streak a mile wide running down my back," Nat said, glancing at Jessica before he returned his attention to Sebastian.

"I wouldn't put it like that," Jessica said. Her heart went out to him. This moment was difficult for her, but it had to be sheer hell for Nat. In her experience, men didn't like to admit their vulnerability and mistakes to other men.

"I don't know. I think it sounds about right," Sebastian said evenly.

Nat met his friend's steady gaze without flinching. "Not going to cut me any slack, are you, Sebastian?"

"Not when I stop to consider that little baby in there."

Jessica heard the warning loud and clear as the men faced each other like two bucks vying for the same territory. Either Nat agreed to take full responsibility for Elizabeth, or Sebastian, Travis and Boone would step in and do the job. But she didn't want Nat to be bullied into doing his duty. Then they'd all lose.

She took a deep breath. "Is Elizabeth awake?"

"Probably not," Sebastian said, his glance softening as he turned toward her. "She generally goes to bed about eight. She must have picked up on the excitement, because we had a little more trouble than usual getting her to sleep tonight. Then again, it could be another tooth coming in." His voice was filled with love as he spoke about Elizabeth.

Jessica battled a surge of jealousy. She was being extremely petty to be jealous. After all, having everyone become so attached to her baby was the best she could have wished for. But she *was* jealous—of all the time and experiences they'd shared with her daughter and the strong bond that had been created as a result. She couldn't stand her own separation from Elizabeth a moment longer "I want to see her," she said. "I promise not to wake her up."

"I expected you'd want that. We need to get on in, anyway, before Matty organizes a search party."

"Why were you down there?" Nat asked again as the three of them started toward the house. "You never did say."

"Just jumpy, I guess. Ever since your call I've been on edge, thinking about the guy you told me about. I was probably imagining things, but about twenty minutes ago I had the biggest urge to go out and take a look around. I didn't see or hear anything, so I'm sure it was just nerves."

"I'm not so sure," Jessica said. "I think the guy's around here somewhere."

Sebastian paused and gave her a sharp look. "What makes you think so?"

"After all these months, I've developed a sixth sense about when he's nearby and when he's not. When we pulled up tonight I had the definite feeling that he was watching us."

"And now?" Sebastian asked, glancing around him.

"Now I think he's gone again, but I'm guessing he knows I'm here."

"And you're sure he doesn't know about the baby?" Sebastian sounded agitated.

"Yes, I'm sure."

"That's good." Sebastian started up the path again. "As far as I'm concerned, his days are numbered, anyway."

"They sure as hell are," Nat said. "He's not getting near Jess or Elizabeth."

Jessica drew comfort from those words, but as she approached the house she had a horrible thought, one that would explain a great deal. "I'm not really sure he doesn't know about the baby," she said as anxiety churned in her stomach. "In the beginning he might not have, but he might have found out, somehow. Maybe that's why he's waited all this time, so he could snatch Elizabeth and me together. With both the Franklin child and grandchild, he could demand anything he wanted from my parents and expect to get it."

"Doesn't matter," Sebastian said, "because he's not getting either one of you."

"I know, but…" She paused at the steps leading up to

the wide front porch and her stomach twisted as she remembered the agony of leaving Elizabeth there. The sacrifice had seemed necessary. It might still be necessary. "Maybe the best thing for me to do is go away again," she said softly. "I've kept him distracted so far. Maybe I should—"

"No!" Nat gripped her arm as if he thought she might run off into the woods at any minute. "You can't do that."

"I second the motion," Sebastian said. "I love that baby as much as I would my own kid, but the fact is she's *not* my kid, and she belongs with her mother." He paused and sent Nat a challenging look. "And her father."

Before Nat could respond, the front door opened and Travis came out looking handsome as ever, a grin on his face and a longneck in his hand. A tan Great Dane bounded out with him and began to cavort around the porch with Fleafarm.

"I thought I heard somebody carrying on out here!" Travis said. "Thanks for letting us know, Sebastian, old buddy. Sadie, cool it."

"They just got here," Sebastian said.

"Yeah, yeah, yeah." Travis crossed the porch in two quick strides. "Admit it, you were monopolizing them." He bounded down the steps and swept Jessica off her feet as he kissed her loudly on the cheek. "So you finally decided to show up, Jessie-girl. If you weren't so damn pretty and I didn't like you so much, I'd tan your hide for what you've pulled."

Same old Travis, she thought, smiling in spite of herself. "I—"

"Don't you be mauling that woman, hotshot," Boone said as he came thundering down the steps looking even bigger than Jessica remembered. "Not all females appreciate that kind of treatment."

"Name one," Travis said as he set Jessica back on her

feet. "Hey, Nat." He stuck out his hand. "Hope you don't mind me giving your girl a friendly hug."

Nat cleared his throat. "She's not my—"

"Hello, Boone," Jessica said, wanting to cut off Nat's denial of their relationship. Sebastian, Travis and Boone might want to argue the point, and this wasn't the time to get into it. "I'm so sorry for all the trouble I've caused you." She stood on tiptoe, put her hands around his neck and placed a kiss on his cheek.

Boone returned her kiss with a brotherly hug. "I don't blame you," he said. "You were trying to protect your baby, is all."

"Thanks for understanding." With all four men gathered together, her fears eased. These guys were a match for anyone. That's why she'd left Elizabeth here in the first place.

"Everything's gonna work out." Boone gave her a reassuring smile before turning to Nat. "It's good to have you back home, buddy," he said as he shook Nat's hand.

"I'm glad to be home."

Jessica wondered if he really was glad, or if he regretted leaving the refugee camp.

"I'll bet he is glad, at that," Travis said. "Looks like they were short of barbers over there."

"They were short of a lot of things," Nat said. "And barbers were—"

"Well, I have two things to say," Boone cut in. "First off, I want you to know I'm real proud of what you did, going over to help those orphans. And the length of your hair is of no concern to me."

"Thanks," Nat said.

"I wanted to say that first off," Boone added, "because the second thing is of great concern to me." His cheeks reddened, but he soldiered on. "If you won't try and be a real daddy to this baby, I'll kick your butt from here to the New Mexico line."

Jessica was amazed that someone as mild-mannered as

Boone would make such a threat, but she'd had enough of this coercion talk. "Listen, I don't think anybody should be forced to—"

"Now, Jessie-girl," Travis said, "Boone and me, we have a point to make with our buddy Nat, so don't be implying that he'll be let off the hook. In fact, we asked the ladies to wait inside so we could get a few things straight with him before he goes in to see Lizzie."

Lizzie? Jessica's groan of protest was out before she could call it back.

"What's wrong?" Travis asked.

"Um, I…uh, didn't expect you'd all be calling her Lizzie," she said.

"Don't worry," Sebastian said. "Travis is the only one who calls her that. She's Elizabeth to the rest of us."

"Oh." Jessica told herself to be reasonable. A nickname wasn't the worst fate that could befall her baby. But she loved her daughter's name, and didn't like someone fooling with it. Still, it was probably a small matter. "I suppose in the grand scheme of things it isn't important, but I'd always thought—"

"There's not a thing wrong with the name Lizzie," Travis said. "Considering she's smart and funny and loves to play, I'd say it fits her personality a lot better than a long handle like *Elizabeth,* which sounds like somebody in one of those movies made in England."

Jessica winced. She'd been a fan of such movies in college. She'd chosen the name Elizabeth *because* it sounded elegant and British.

"I happen to like her name the way it is," Sebastian said. "It sounds pretty to me."

"Me, too," Boone said.

"Nope, way too formal," Travis said. Then he glanced at Jessica. "No offense. I figure you named her that because it's flexible, and you can make a lot of names out of it.

There's Beth, and Betty, and Liza, and just plain Liz. But the way she's turning out, Lizzie fits best. You'll see."

"She's not going to see a damn thing unless we let her go into the house," Sebastian pointed out.

"I guess we can go in now," Travis said, "as long as Nat understands our position on this baby thing."

"Oh, I understand it," Nat said. He gave the impression of great nonchalance. "But I'm afraid you've raised the bar too high for this ol' boy. I tried to tell Sebastian that I—"

"Hey." Boone clapped a big hand on Nat's shoulder. "Listen, I don't talk about it much, but my old man whupped me when I was growing up, too."

"Yeah," Nat said, "but I'll bet it wasn't the same."

"No kidding," Travis said. "Boone probably outweighed his dad by the time he was ten."

"Doesn't matter if it was the same or not," Boone insisted stubbornly. "He still beat us, but I'm not like my dad, and you aren't like yours, either. I'd lay money on it. So don't give up on this program so quick, before you ever see her."

"Yeah," Travis added. "She'll melt your heart, buddy."

"That's a fact," Sebastian said.

Uncertainty shone in Nat's eyes as he glanced around at his three friends.

Jessica put a comforting hand on his arm, and when he looked down at her, she gave him a reassuring smile, in spite of the butterflies fluttering in her stomach. "Let's go see our daughter," she murmured.

NAT DREW what strength he could from Jess's gaze. He wished he could hold her for a minute before they walked through that door, but that wouldn't be happening.

He glanced once more at his three friends, but their expressions had no give to them. They expected too much, but he couldn't bring himself to tell them so, straight out.

He already felt like a failure for getting Jess pregnant and leaving her to face the experience alone.

"I'll do the best I can," he said.

"In that case," Sebastian said, "everything will work out just fine. Now let's get in and enjoy that fire!"

As they all trooped into the house Nat had come to consider his second home, he was bombarded with the many changes there. A mesh-sided playpen filled with soft baby toys was set up behind the old leather sofa. He noticed a floor loom in a corner and remembered that Matty was a weaver. A new picture hung over the fireplace, and a pretty display of pinecones and autumn leaves decorated the mantel. Sebastian would never have thought to do such a thing.

Matty greeted him and Jess with all the confidence befitting the lady of the house. And she was definitely that, pregnant belly and all. But he had no time to comment on that development. As Matty took their coats and began the introductions, he sensed Jess's tension as she waited for the moment she'd be able to go see their baby. *Their baby.* The reality still hadn't hit him.

But before they could take that long walk back to the bedroom, it was only right that they acknowledge the women who had helped nurture that baby for six months. They met Travis's wife, Gwen, a tall brunette he vaguely remembered as one of Matty's good friends, and Shelby McFarland, Boone's petite, blond wife. They learned that Shelby and Boone had recently adopted Shelby's three-year-old nephew Josh and that he was also asleep in the room with Elizabeth.

The big surprise was Travis's mother, Luann, a tiny, gray-haired woman in her fifties who'd come to live at Gwen's bed-and-breakfast. Nat had always assumed Travis's playboy existence had continued when he'd returned to Utah every winter. Apparently he'd gone home to watch over his widowed mother.

At last the introductions were complete.

"I'd like to go see her now," Jess said quietly.

"Of course." Matty started down the hall, and everyone followed, bumping into each other as they tried to squeeze into the hallway. Jess and Nat brought up the rear.

Matty turned and held up her hand, like a traffic cop. "Hold on, here. We can't all go. In fact, Jessica should be allowed to go alone, if she wants."

Amid mumbled agreement, everyone backed out of the hallway.

Nat could live with Jess going in first. He wouldn't mind taking it slow, easing into the situation a little at a time.

"I'd like Nat to go with me," Jess said.

So much for taking it slow. With his buddies giving him the evil eye, he had no choice but to agree. "Okay. Sure. Good idea."

Everyone stepped aside.

"She's in the guest room, Nat," Sebastian said. "The room you used to use when you came down from Denver. Matty redecorated it."

"And I just want to add that Sebastian picked out that girly crib," Matty said. "I wanted something plainer."

"We left a night-light on," Boone said. "Josh likes that, especially when they're together, so if he opens his eyes he can see Elizabeth over there in her crib."

"Oh, and about the pacifier," Travis said. "Some people purely hate them, but Doc Harrison said it wouldn't hurt her, and so we use it sometimes."

"I hope you like her sleeper, Jessica," Gwen said. "Travis and I couldn't decide which one to put on her when we brought her over tonight. We went with Winnie-the-Pooh."

Jess turned to her with a look of surprise. "Brought her over? I thought she stayed here all the time."

"Oh, no," Shelby said from her position beside Boone. "We all take—I mean, we all *took* turns. You see, everybody…'' She trailed off and glanced around nervously, as if afraid she'd spoken out of turn.

"Everybody wanted her," Sebastian finished, his voice rough with emotion.

Oh, God. Nat had never seen his friend so emotional. It made him feel about an inch tall, knowing he'd helped cause this fiasco.

Jess swallowed, and her voice shook. ''I don't know how I'll ever be able to thank you all, or make it up to you for…for…''

Feeling the need to do something of value, Nat reached for her hand, which was ice-cold. ''Let's go,'' he said gently.

She blinked rapidly, swallowed again, and nodded.

Nat started down the hall. Through their linked hands, he could feel Jess trembling. He laced his fingers through hers and gave her hand a squeeze. If he could have forced words past his tight throat, he would have said something reassuring, but all he could give her at this point was the comfort of touch.

Ahead of them, the guest-room door was open a crack, and a faint light showed around the edge. It wasn't often, Nat thought, that stepping through a door could so completely divide ignorance from knowledge. This was one of those times. Once he went through that door, he would never be the same.

CHAPTER TWELVE

As Nat gently pushed open the door, Jessica gripped his hand and vowed not to cry. Crying would only wake Elizabeth and little Josh and frighten them both. Besides, as long as Elizabeth stayed asleep, Jessica could hang on to the fantasy that her child would remember her.

A zoo of stuffed animals covering every available surface, and bright cartoon wallpaper left no doubt this was a beloved baby's room. The crib was against one wall and a double bed against the other. Jessica barely spared a glance for the small boy in the bed as she started toward the crib, heart pounding so loud she thought the sound might wake Elizabeth.

She was so big! Tears swam in her eyes and she wiped them away swiftly. She wanted to see.

Oh, God. Her daughter was so beautiful. Jessica pressed her fist against her mouth to stifle the sob that rose in her throat as tears rushed down her cheeks. Beautiful. The pain of being separated from this child, this flesh of her flesh, rolled through her unchecked. Until now she'd refused to give it room in her heart, but now, at the sight of Elizabeth, it blasted past her defenses, threatening to engulf her.

She fought for control, reminding herself that the separation was over. No more time apart. Now she could mend the rift between her and this precious child. Elizabeth would be confused, so it was up to Jessica to be strong, to be up to the challenge.

Elizabeth slept on her tummy with her bottom up in the

air. Jessica had never seen her do that. But then, she'd
never seen her crawl or pull herself up, and she probably
could do both of those things now. Her dimpled hand lay
over the tail of a sock monkey with black-button eyes. Her
favorite toy, Sebastian had said. Jessica's heart grew heavy
as she thought of all she'd missed.

The baby's hair, which used to be so wispy and light
brown, looked redder now and more abundant as it curled
in ringlets all over her head. She had Jessica's hair. *Her
child.* Possessiveness flowed hot in her veins. *Hers.*

Before she knew it, she'd dropped to her knees in front
of the crib and was reaching through the bars. She stopped
herself just in time. No, she didn't want to wake Elizabeth.
Not yet. To keep herself in check, she gripped the bars
while she peered into Elizabeth's face.

Oh, yes, she was older and bigger all over, but the same.
Same uptilted nose, same rosy cheeks, same Cupid's bow
mouth. Jessica's breasts ached with the memory of how
sweet it had been to nurse her and how agonizing to switch
her to the bottle.

She heard a steady *plop, plop, plop* and finally realized
it was the sound of her tears, dripping on the edge of the
crib mattress. Drawing back, she felt the imprint the crib
bars had made against her cheeks as she'd tried to eliminate
the barrier between her and her daughter.

When an arm came around her shoulders, she jumped.

"It's me," Nat whispered, crouching beside her. "Only
me."

She turned her head in surprise. She'd forgotten he was
even in the room.

He stared at Elizabeth as if totally amazed by her. When
he glanced at Jessica, even the dim lighting couldn't disguise the wonder in his expression.

"We did this?" he murmured.

She nodded, unable to speak.

His attention returned to the baby, as if drawn by a magnet. "Amazing."

Hope swelled within her. Maybe, if he was as awestruck by this miracle as he sounded, he would find a way around his fears. She looked back at Elizabeth and her craving to hold the baby was like a live thing she had to wrestle every moment she stayed near the crib. Her mouth grew moist with the need to touch her child. Not yet. Soon.

"She's so small," Nat said quietly. He kept his arm around Jessica and kneaded her shoulder gently.

Jessica swallowed hard and managed a whispered comment. "I was just thinking how big she is."

"She looks like you."

"A little." She battled the urge to snatch this baby up and never let her go. "Her eyes are the same shape as your eyes." Jessica had fantasized this scene a million times—picturing how it would feel to be gathered inside the protective circle of Nat's arm as the two of them watched Elizabeth sleep. "And look at her fingers," she said. "They're long and graceful, like yours."

He made a brief noise of protest. "My fingers aren't *graceful.*"

"They are." Her emotions pooled like wax around a candle flame, ready to spill over at the slightest tremor. "Especially when you're—" She caught herself.

"When I'm making love to you?" he asked softly as he increased the pressure of his easy massage.

She'd thought Elizabeth had laid claim to all her needs for the moment, but she discovered Elizabeth's father had a grip on his share, after all. She glanced at him. He was gazing at her with that primitive glow in his eyes that told her exactly what was on his mind.

She shook her head. "I didn't mean to say that."

"How can you help it, when right in front of us is the evidence of me being deep inside you," he murmured.

She tried to be rational. "This isn't the time to be thinking of…that."

"Maybe not. But I don't think I've ever wanted you more than I do right this minute."

His gaze was mesmerizing in its intensity. She could no more stop her instinctive response to him than deny her need for this baby. He leaned down, as if to kiss her. Then a rustling from the crib broke the spell.

Elizabeth smacked her lips and heaved a sigh.

Jessica froze in place, sure their whispering had caused the baby to wake up. Now she'd have to bear the heartache of watching those eyes open and show absolutely no recognition. Jessica felt too fragile to deal with that yet.

But the baby's eyes remained closed, her lashes creating a pale, feathery crescent against her soft cheek.

"We'd better go," Jessica whispered. "Before we wake her."

"Yeah." Nat stood and then helped Jessica to her feet. He held both her hands, and for a moment it seemed he might pull her close. Then he squeezed her hands and released them. "Let's go back to the others. It's been a long night, and they'd probably like to get home."

It TOOK SOME DOING, but finally Matty and Sebastian hustled everyone out the door, including a very sleepy Josh. Nat could see that nobody was happy about leaving Elizabeth, knowing that once they returned, Jess would be in charge as the baby's mother.

Finally the last vehicle pulled out of the driveway, and Nat brought in his and Jess's backpacks. He wasn't sure what to do with them because their sleeping arrangements hadn't been decided, so he leaned them against the wall by the front door. Matty had just eased into the rocker and she looked glad to be off her feet for a change. He decided not to ask where to put the backpacks and risk sending her into her hostess mode again.

While Sebastian made the rounds checking the locks on all the doors and windows, Jess stood warming her hands by the fire. Because Nat couldn't be near her without wanting to put his arms around her, he roamed the living room, examining all the feminine touches Matty had added.

From her position by the fire, Jess turned so she could look at Matty. "I want to thank you for bringing everybody together tonight and giving me a chance to let them know how much I appreciate all they've done."

Matty smiled. "You're welcome, but I probably couldn't have kept them away with a loaded shotgun." A small sigh of weariness escaped her as she laid her head back against the rocker.

"But you're exhausted," Jess said. "I feel terrible that this has been so much work for you."

"I'm a little tired," Matty admitted, laying a hand over her rounded tummy. "But don't feel guilty. I wouldn't have missed any of it for all the tea in China. Besides, being tired at this stage probably goes with the territory."

"I'm afraid it does," Jess said. "I never slept so much in my life as when I was pregnant with Elizabeth. I even took naps, and I never do that."

Matty nodded. "Around this place we've turned into Naps 'R' Us. It's embarrassing how much sleep I need these days."

As the two women exchanged an understanding glance, Nat felt cheated that he hadn't been there to experience Jess's pregnancy, naps and all. As a man, he couldn't be expected to know what it was like to be pregnant, but if he'd gone through it with Jess, he'd at least have some reference point.

Instead, he felt shut out. But it was his own damn fault that he hadn't made sure she was all right before he left the country. "I didn't get a chance to congratulate you before, Matty," he said. "But I think it's great. When's the baby due?"

"We're hoping for Valentine's Day," Matty said.

"We're *planning* on Valentine's Day," Sebastian said, coming into the room and moving behind the rocker. He reached over and began massaging Matty's shoulders. "Little Rebecca will be right on time, like the sweetheart she is."

"You already know it's a girl?" Nat said.

"No, we don't," Matty said.

Sebastian continued to massage his wife's shoulders. "Yes, we do. I don't mean we've looked at an ultrasound or anything. I just know in my bones we'll have a girl."

Matty chuckled. "I sure hope your bones aren't misleading you. A boy isn't going to be happy wearing that hand-tooled belt you're making that says *Rebecca* across the back."

"Sounds like you really want a girl, Sebastian." Nat was fascinated by the concept. He would have sworn Sebastian would want a boy, at least the first time around. Not that Sebastian was sexist, exactly, but the female of the species had always puzzled him. He'd be on firmer ground during the raising process with a boy.

"I surely do want a girl," Sebastian said. "Baby girls are something special, Nat. You'll see."

"Guess so." By now Nat had a good idea how attached Sebastian had become to Elizabeth. Insisting that Matty would have a girl probably helped him cope with giving Elizabeth back to Jess.

"I thought you two could take that double bed in Elizabeth's room for now," Matty said.

Nat tensed and decided not to look at Jess. He didn't know which way she'd choose. She'd asked him to be with her when she'd gone into the bedroom to see their daughter, so maybe she'd want all three of them to be together tonight, too. He could go for that. Having the baby in with them would be nerve-racking, but he'd brave it through if it meant being with Jess.

But she had to know that if they shared a double bed, they'd end up making love, even if they did it softly and quietly so as not to wake the baby. After what she'd said that first morning about no lovemaking, this was her call, not his.

"You might be a little cramped," Matty continued, as if she'd decided their silence meant they weren't happy about the size of the bed, "but it should do until we've worked out…" She paused as if searching for the right words, and glanced up at her husband.

"Well, until we figure out…" Sebastian didn't seem any more able to define the situation than his wife.

"Is that the only spare bed?" Jess asked, her question tentative, as if she didn't want to sound rude.

So she didn't want to share the bed with him, didn't want to feel his arms around her. Nat was bitterly disappointed, but he accepted her decision with as much gallantry as he could muster. He glanced over at her. "There's a daybed in Sebastian's office. Why don't I take that and give you the bed in Elizabeth's room?"

She met his gaze, and her expression was carefully neutral. "I'd appreciate that," she said quietly.

No one spoke for a moment, and finally Matty stood. "Well, guess I'll get some sheets for the daybed."

"I'll make it up," Nat said. "You and Sebastian go on to bed. We've put you to enough trouble as it is."

"Better yet," Sebastian said, "*I'll* get the sheets for the daybed, while the mommy-to-be goes nite-nite." He steered his wife toward the hall.

"It's no trouble. I—"

"I want you horizontal, woman. You've been on your feet long enough. Go on now. You can warm up the sheets for me." Sebastian gave her a quick kiss. "See you in a little while."

Matty's gaze flicked from her husband to Nat. "Okay. Don't be too long."

"I won't."

"Guess I'll turn in, too." Jess walked over to pick up her backpack.

"Here." Nat crossed to her. "Let me take that in for—"

"That's okay." She stepped out of reach. "Thanks, anyway. I can handle it. Good night, and thanks again for everything, Sebastian." With that, she headed down the hall toward Elizabeth's room.

Nat's heart twisted. He wanted to be able to pamper her a little, the way Sebastian pampered Matty. But you couldn't pamper a woman if she wouldn't let you, he thought sadly.

He'd also noticed the eagerness in her eyes as she'd turned to go down that hall. She wanted to be with her baby, and he didn't blame her for that. The idea of spending the night in the same room with her daughter probably thrilled her as much as it would have terrified him. But he would have done it, if that had meant he could hold Jess all night long.

He watched her walk quickly to the end of the hall and nudge the door open. Then she slipped inside and closed it behind her. The whole procedure felt very wrong to Nat. He should be in that bedroom with her.

"I'll get you those sheets," Sebastian said.

"Thanks." Feeling totally unnecessary, Nat walked over to the fireplace and set aside the screen so he could rearrange the coals with the poker. It didn't particularly need doing, but he had the urge to busy himself with something.

He had to maneuver around the dogs, who were asleep on the braided rug in front of the hearth. They both raised their heads, gave him a look as if they thought he was making a fuss for nothing, and went back to sleep.

"You wouldn't understand if I explained it," he muttered to the dogs, who didn't stir.

Crouched next to the fireplace, he looked at the elegant tool in his hand. Boone had made the set five years ago, using his blacksmith's skills to create a gift for Sebastian's thirtieth birthday.

How things had changed in five years. Sebastian had been married to Barbara then, and Matty's husband had still been alive. Come to think of it, Gwen had been at that party with the guy she used to be married to, Derek somebody or other. Travis had brought a date, and so had Nat. He could barely remember who he'd been seeing then. Maybe it was Marianne, or then again, he might have brought Tanya to that party.

Funny how not a single woman from his past stood out in his mind except for Jess. Until he'd met her, he'd never believed in the concept of soul mates. He still didn't, not really. She might be the only woman for him, but he wasn't right for her at all.

"Somebody gave Matty and me some very old, very expensive brandy for a wedding present," Sebastian said.

Nat glanced up to see him standing by the sofa, the day-bed sheets folded over one arm. "That's nice," Nat said.

"I thought so, but Matty hates brandy. Besides, she's on the wagon until after the baby's born. I've got a hankering to try the stuff."

"That's okay, Sebastian." Nat flashed him a brief smile. "You don't have to stay up and keep me company. Go on to bed with your wife."

"Or to put it another way, you don't have to stay up with me." Sebastian tossed the sheets on the sofa. "I'm opening that brandy, but if you don't want any, I guess I'll have to drink alone. Which would be a hell of a thing, when you consider it. A man hasn't seen his friend in seventeen months, and that friend would rather go to bed than share a little brandy and polite conversation. Did I mention that it was old and very expensive?"

Nat grinned and pushed himself to his feet. Sebastian obviously wanted to talk and it wouldn't be very gracious of him to refuse, especially considering that he hadn't been much of a friend to Sebastian recently. "Yeah, I believe you did mention it." He returned the fireplace poker to its place on the wrought-iron rack. "A man would be dumb to turn down an offer like that."

"Then come on in the kitchen and I'll get you a glass. Or a snifter, as the trendsetters say."

"You've got snifters?" Nat hadn't realized how much he'd missed Sebastian and his wry sense of humor.

"Hell, no. Years ago Barbara tried to talk me into getting some. She even bought me a box of Cuban cigars and a smoking jacket."

Nat laughed at the mental picture of Sebastian in jeans, boots, a Stetson and a smoking jacket. "She never did get you, did she?"

"Guess not." Sebastian reached into a cupboard and took down two juice glasses and the promised bottle of brandy, which he carried over to the scarred oak kitchen table. "Did you know she had an affair with Matty's husband, Butch?"

Nat stopped dead in the middle of the kitchen. So that nasty little bit of information had come to light at last.

Sebastian poured the brandy into the glasses before he looked up. "You did know, didn't you?"

"Yeah." Nat didn't like admitting that. He was getting a real reputation for being secretive. Maybe the best thing to do was to get it all out in the open. "She told me about it, and you might as well know the circumstances. She propositioned me, too, and when I turned her down, she said it didn't matter because she always had Butch to fall back on."

A flicker of anger came and went in Sebastian's gray eyes. "Now I wonder who else she came on to. What about Travis?"

Nat sighed. "Yeah, she tried to get something going with Travis, too. Barbara was a real alley cat, and neither of us knew how to tell you. I have a hunch she went after Boone, as well, but he's the kind of guy who wouldn't mention that fact to a soul, even if you put a branding iron to his feet.''

''I guess I can see why you wouldn't tell me. A man tends not to want to believe a thing like that about the woman he married. Instead of waking me up, it probably would have come between you, me and Travis.''

''That's what we figured. So we kept quiet.''

Sebastian took one of the glasses and handed it to Nat. Then he picked up his own. ''To friendship.''

Nat saluted him with his glass. ''To the best damn friend I know.''

Sebastian sipped the brandy and grinned. ''Not bad. Not bad at all.''

Nat had to admit the dark liquid felt good going down. He took another sip and felt himself begin to relax. ''Real good, in fact.''

''Now that we've discovered it doesn't taste like rat poison, pull up a chair,'' Sebastian said, taking a seat at the table. ''We don't charge extra for that.''

''Don't mind if I do.'' Nat settled into a wooden chair worn smooth by countless denim-covered butts. After another swallow of the brandy, he felt the tightness loosen in his chest. ''This really is good stuff. So you scored this just for getting married?''

''That's all I had to do. Here, let me top that off for you.''

''Why not?''

Sebastian poured Nat's glass nearly to the brim and set the bottle down. ''That oughta put lead in your pencil.''

''Now there's a problem I don't have. I have just about every other problem you can name, but lack of interest in sex isn't one of them.''

Sebastian eyed him. ''I was only being a smart-ass, but as long as we're on the subject, how do things stand between you and Jessica, anyway?''

"I figured you'd get around to that." Without the relaxing effect of the brandy, Nat might have been more defensive, but the more he relaxed, the more he felt like talking. Of course, Sebastian had planned it that way.

"How you're getting along with Jessica is pretty damn important," Sebastian said. "If you two are fighting, then Elizabeth will know it right off. That's not good for a little kid."

"We're not fighting," Nat said. "At least, not like you think. We've had a few heated words, but mostly…mostly I need time to get used to this whole situation, which I told her. At this stage of the game I can't make promises. So she decided we shouldn't sleep together."

Sebastian nodded. "That sounds logical."

"Oh, it's *logical* as hell. But logic doesn't keep me from wanting her."

That made Sebastian smile. He took another swig of brandy and set it down carefully on the table. Then he swiveled the glass back and forth between his fingers, staring at the contents as he spoke. "You dated her for a year, right?" He glanced up. "That's quite a long time for a free spirit like you."

Nat met his gaze as another wave of remorse washed over him. "Yeah, and I should have told you guys about it."

Sebastian shrugged and leaned back in his chair. "Hey, forget it. That's water under the bridge. We've established that you're a regular chickenshit when it comes to matters of the heart." He grinned to take the sting out of his words. "Besides, you thought we'd try to interfere, and you were right about that. I would have told you to marry that woman if you'd enjoyed each other's company for an entire year. Lucky for you that you get another opportunity."

"You know, when I was on my way home, I'd pretty much decided to ask her to take a chance on me. I figured that if I loused things up in the first few months because

I'd reverted to being like my father, then she could divorce me.'' That concept of divorcing Jess soured his stomach when he said it out loud. He took another sip of brandy. ''But now, with the baby, it's more complicated. And I don't want to put that little kid at risk.''

''From you?'' Sebastian gazed at him.

''Yeah, from me.''

''That's—''

''Don't tell me it's ridiculous. It's not. I've seen what happens to people under pressure. They do things they wouldn't otherwise do.''

Sebastian stared into the depths of his brandy. ''What was it like over there?''

''Rough.'' Nat wondered how Sebastian would have reacted to seeing a child of three sobbing over her mother's body, knowing that the mother's death had been the result of a senseless act of violence. It might have broken Sebastian's big heart beyond repair. Sebastian liked to believe the best of people.

''It was hell, in fact,'' he added. ''But it some crazy way it was heaven, too. The measure of a person working or living in the camps wasn't how they dressed or how much education they had or the size of their bank account. It was all about character.''

''And you thrived there, didn't you?''

''I guess I did.'' Nat had always valued the way Sebastian could help him sort out his thoughts. ''I know I felt worthwhile for the first time in my life.'' He looked over at his friend. ''I have a project under way to get some of those war orphans adopted, but that's a short-term thing. On the way here Jess brought up the idea of me running a ranch for kids in this country who have no place else to go. I kind of like the idea.''

Sebastian looked interested.

Encouraged, Nat continued. ''I could still broker real estate on the side, to keep the cash coming in, and I could use whatever I've learned about sales to get some backers. What do you think?''

''I think that if you don't hook up with a woman who has that much insight into what you need to make you happy, you are the biggest fool who ever sat in this kitchen.'' He chuckled and drained his glass. ''And that's saying a mouthful, because I'm no Einstein when it comes to relationships, either. Now, let's go to bed. I've learned what I came in here to learn.''

Nat chuckled. ''Which was?''

''That you're pie-eyed in love with the mother of your baby. If we have that to work with, we'll be all right.''

CHAPTER THIRTEEN

JESSICA DIDN'T WANT to sleep. She wanted to lie in the double bed and listen to her baby breathe. Whenever sleep started to claim her, she'd wake herself up, get out of bed and pad barefoot over to the crib. She'd stand there watching Elizabeth until the urge to touch her became too strong, and then she'd go back and crawl into bed again to listen to her breathing.

And all the while she carried on a silent conversation with her daughter. *Mommy's here now, sweetheart. When you wake up, I'll be able to lift you out of your crib, the way I used to do. I can change your diaper and play those little tickle games that we used to play. You can show me your new teeth, and how you've learned to sit up, and crawl, and pull yourself up. Mommy's here.*

She lay in bed planning how she would approach Elizabeth when the baby woke up. Obviously she should take it slow and let Elizabeth get used to her again. Knowing that the baby had been swapped between three couples made her feel more confident that Elizabeth wouldn't be as inflexible as she might have been if Sebastian had kept her at the Rocking D the whole time. Still, Jessica didn't kid herself that the transition would be easy.

For now, though, she was content to be in the same room with her child at last. Nat hadn't been happy about sleeping elsewhere, but having him in this bed with her would have overloaded her circuits. For one thing, she wouldn't have been able to concentrate on her child, and right now, that was very important.

Besides, she really believed in the ban on lovemaking she'd imposed. If Nat had shared this bed with her tonight, he would have made love to her. It would be ridiculous to suppose otherwise, with both of them crammed into the double bed together for hours.

The thought was not without appeal, however. She breathed in the scent of wood smoke that pervaded the house and snuggled under the down comforter. No, the idea was not without appeal.

Although she would have sworn that she hadn't slept at all, she opened her eyes and realized the room was filled with the gray light of dawn.

"Ba," cooed a soft voice. "Ba-ba."

Her pulse rate skyrocketed. Elizabeth was awake. Cautiously she moved the comforter aside so that she could peek over at the crib.

On her hands and knees in her footed Pooh sleeper, Elizabeth faced her. Oh, yes, she had her daddy's blue eyes. But they were fringed with light eyelashes, not dark ones like Nat's. Her tousled hair was a riot of coppery curls, and her cheeks were flushed pink from sleep. Jessica could have looked at her forever.

She was staring intently at the bed, and Jessica smiled at the puzzle she must have presented to the baby. When Elizabeth had gone to sleep, a little boy had been in this bed. Now he'd been magically transformed into a grown woman.

"Ba-ba," Elizabeth said again, and drooled. Keeping her attention on the bed, she used the bars to pull herself up until she was standing. Standing.

Jessica stayed perfectly quiet and watched, fascinated by the developmental strides Elizabeth had made in her absence. She swallowed a lump in her throat. So much had happened while she'd been away. Too much.

With a firm grip on the railing, Elizabeth began to rattle the crib. "Ba!" she called, exposing her new teeth as she rattled the crib some more.

"Hi, baby," Jessica murmured. Seeing those teeth made her eyes blur with tears. Her little girl was so grown-up.

Elizabeth stopped rattling the crib and stared some more.

"It's me, your mommy," Jessica said softly.

Elizabeth didn't seem alarmed, only curious.

"You sure are a pretty girl." Moving slowly, Jessica propped herself up on one elbow. "Do you remember me at all?"

A flicker of worry settled in the blue eyes.

"It's okay." Jessica kept her voice low and soothing as she sat up and pushed the covers back. "You'll get used to me again. "You'll—"

Elizabeth's screech of fear froze Jessica's blood.

"I won't hurt you, darling," she pleaded as Elizabeth began to cry. Instinct drove Jessica out of the bed and over to the crib. "Don't be afraid." She reached for the baby. "Please don't be afraid. It's me. Your mommy."

With an even louder wail, Elizabeth flung herself backward to escape Jessica's extended arms and banged her head on the far side of the crib. Then she began to cry in earnest.

"Oh, no." Jessica released the latch on the railing and leaned over. "Oh, sweetheart! Please let me—"

"I'll get her." Matty hurried into the room and over to the crib, lifting a squalling Elizabeth out of the crib and out of Jessica's reach, as if she were a menace.

Jessica knew Matty didn't mean to make it seem that way, but it did, anyway. Tears streamed down her cheeks. "She hit her head," she said. "P-please check her and m-make sure she's okay." The fact that she couldn't comfort her own child was the worst pain she'd ever endured. "I didn't mean to scare her. I didn't mean to."

"Of course you didn't." Matty ran her hand over the

back of Elizabeth's head. "And she's fine. There, there, little one." Matty held the baby against her shoulder and rubbed her back. "Easy does it. You're fine."

"What happened?" Sebastian appeared in the doorway, fastening his jeans.

"I—" Jessica found she didn't have the power to tell him. Her throat was closed with grief and shame. Her baby didn't want her.

Then Nat came up behind Sebastian. He, too, was wearing only a pair of jeans. "Is everybody okay?"

"I think Elizabeth got a little spooked, seeing Jessica for the first time," Sebastian said.

"She'll be okay," Matty murmured as she continued to stroke the baby. "We'll have to ease into it, that's all."

"Oh, Jess." Nat's eyes clouded. "I'm sorry."

She was more than sorry. She was destroyed. And she couldn't stand to be in the room a minute longer. She managed to choke out an excuse that she needed to go to the bathroom. Then she pushed past everyone, went into the bathroom across the hall and shut the door.

Once there, she grabbed a towel and buried her face in it while she sobbed. Elizabeth didn't want her anymore.

Eventually the tears slowed, although she didn't think the pain in her heart would ever go away. She'd lost her baby. Because of that horrible man who was after her, she'd lost Elizabeth. She was ready to search him out and kill him with her bare hands. He'd robbed her of her child.

A light tapping on the door was followed by Nat's voice. "Jess? Can I come in?"

"No."

"That's what I get for asking," he muttered, opening the door.

She turned away and made herself busy hanging the towel on the rack and making sure it was aligned perfectly. "I don't know what ever happened to the concept of privacy," she said in a voice still thick with tears.

He came in and closed the door behind him. "You don't need privacy right now." He took her by the shoulders, eased her around and wrapped her in his arms, tucking her head against his chest.

She was too weak to resist. "How do you know I don't?" Her words were muffled against his shirt. Apparently he'd taken the time to put one on before coming to see about her. She appreciated that. As needy as she felt right now, his bare chest against her cheek might cause her to do something unwise.

"I know because I saw the look on your face when you ran in here to hide. You only think you need privacy. What you really need is somebody to hold you."

He was absolutely right. Her arms had gone around him automatically, and she was clinging to him like a burr. "And you're some sort of expert?"

He laid his cheek against the top of her head. "As a matter of fact, I am."

Come to think of it, he probably was, considering all the times he must have been called upon to comfort grief-stricken people in the refugee camps. His own knowledge of grief was hard-won as a small child.

"I don't know much about this baby stuff," he said, "but Matty told me that Elizabeth will get over this, and I figure Matty knows what she's talking about. She blames herself for setting up the sleeping arrangement that way. She didn't think about how Elizabeth might react when she woke up and found a str—uh, someone she wasn't…well, wasn't used to, in the room."

"I'm her *mother*," Jessica wailed, tightening her grip on him. "And she's afraid of me."

"She'll remember," Nat said softly, rubbing her back in the same way Matty had rubbed Elizabeth's.

"Maybe not." Jessica felt the tears welling up again. "Maybe I'll have to start all over, and it'll be as if I adopted her. Oh, Nat, why couldn't you have come home sooner?"

He groaned. "I wish to God I had. Oh, Jess. It's going to take me a hundred lifetimes to make it up to you for the pain I've caused. And may still cause. Damn it."

Immediately she regretted making a scapegoat of him. She held him close. "Nat, I shouldn't have said that. This whole problem is mine. I'm the one who got pregnant. I'm the one who thought I could keep my wealthy background a secret."

"If we're passing blame around, I should have walked away from you the minute I laid eyes on you. I knew it, too. But I was weak, and I kidded myself that if we kept everything quiet and sort of contained, it wouldn't get messy."

"It's messy."

"I'm aware of that. The Exxon *Valdez* has nothing on us. We could probably qualify for a Superfund."

She surprised herself by chuckling.

"Now, that's music to my ears." He kissed the top of her head. "Any more where that came from?"

She leaned back to gaze up at him and realized her heart no longer felt like a stone in her chest. "You did it."

"No doubt. Name any crime you want and I'm probably guilty."

"Oh, for heaven's sake!" She took his stubbled face in both hands. "Must you always think the worst of yourself? I only meant to say that—"

"Don't try to whitewash the situation, Jess. Everybody knows that birth control fails sometimes. I made love to you…a lot. I should never have left the country without making sure you were okay. If I'd done that, none of this would have happened."

"I would still have this creep on my trail."

He shook his head. "Nope."

"No?"

"I would have eradicated the guy long before now."

She sighed. "You're a good man, Nat." She continued

to cradle his face between her hands. "And thank you for comforting me so well. I do feel better."

He held her gaze, and the anxiety in his blue eyes cleared. "That's good." There was a husky note in his voice as his attention strayed from her face. For the first time he seemed to be taking inventory of the scooped neck of her sleep shirt and the obvious fact that she wore no bra underneath. He swallowed and looked into her eyes again. "Sleep well?"

"No."

His tightened his grip on her. "Jess—"

"No." The look in his eyes set off fireworks in her tummy.

"I'm going crazy."

So was she. She felt her resolve slip a little as heat licked through her. "Nat, we're in the bathroom, for heaven's sake."

"That counter would support you," he murmured. He cupped her bottom and snugged her up against his erection. "I'm a desperate man, Jess. Give me five minutes. I know we can manage in five minutes. We once did it in four, remember?"

She remembered it all, and those memories weren't helping keep her strong.

"I need you. Need to be inside you," he coaxed, seducing her with a rough-edged tone that never failed to arouse her to a frenzy.

And she wanted him there, too. But she shook her head. "Not a good idea," she said, although her breathing was no longer steady. "Besides, you don't have birth control."

He kneaded her bottom through the material of her sleep shirt. "That's what you think. I guess you've forgotten that I was a Boy Scout."

"You actually have a—"

"I do, and I will. At all times. In case you change your

mind.'' He gave her one last nudge and released her. ''See you at the breakfast table.''

FORTUNATELY FOR NAT, when he left the bathroom no one was in the hallway. He ducked into Sebastian's office where he'd spent a miserable night longing for Jess and worrying about Elizabeth. After taking a few deep breaths to get his raging hormones under control, he put on his boots, grabbed his jacket and Stetson and left the room.

The living room was empty but he could hear Matty, Sebastian and the baby in the kitchen. He whistled for Flea-farm and got Sadie, Matty's Great Dane, in the bargain as both dogs trotted out of the kitchen.

''I'm taking the dogs out for a run,'' he called, and didn't wait for an answer before heading out the front door. He needed some time alone before he dealt with that baby again. Or with Jess.

He crossed the front porch and bounded down the steps while the dogs cavorted in front of him like a couple of puppies. Pausing in the circular driveway, he filled his lungs with cool mountain air. Nothing matched the pine-scented air of Colorado.

Damn, but he'd missed this country. And how it loved to show off in October, with cobalt skies and mountains splashed with gold from the stands of aspens turning color. The two white-barked trees Sebastian had planted in his yard beyond the driveway shimmered in the light breeze, the leaves dripping from the branches like coins from a pirate's treasure.

The dogs glanced back at him as if wondering which direction he planned to take. Nat longed to get a good horse between his thighs and ride until he was saddle-sore. But he hadn't stopped long enough to ask Sebastian about taking a horse, and he couldn't presume to do that without asking, even if the answer was sure to be yes.

So he set off toward the trees on foot. He hadn't been

much used to walking before he volunteered to go overseas, but he'd done a lot of it in the refugee camps. Vehicles were in short supply, and if the refugees had owned any horses they probably would have eaten them instead of riding them. Sebastian knew he would never take the basic comforts of his life for granted again.

Fleafarm and Sadie frisked along ahead of him, pausing every now and then to glance back and make sure he was still following. The dogs reminded Sebastian of some other plans he'd made for when he came home. He'd decided to get a dog. But the dog had only been part of the plan.

While living among the refugees, he hadn't missed his luxury apartment in Denver or his well-run real estate office or dealing with clients. He'd missed spending time at the Rocking D. And although he didn't want to go into ranching, he wanted to own a piece of land like this, maybe not quite so large, but big enough that he could have a barn, some horses and a dog.

He'd hoped Jess might like that idea, too, because he'd pictured her there with him. Her suggestion of opening a ranch for orphans intrigued him, but he didn't know if she had any interest in being part of something like that. And there was also the matter of the baby.

This constant, pounding need for Jess made thinking about anything else nearly impossible, though. Nothing was clear to him except that he needed to make love to her. Then maybe he'd be able to consider the other aspects of his life. But obviously she thought he should figure out his life first, and then, depending on what he'd decided, they might be able to make love again.

She wasn't being unreasonable. Even Sebastian thought her decision not to go to bed with him until he knew his own mind made perfect sense. But neither of them understood that trying to sort through his feelings while he needed Jess so desperately was like trying to learn to cook while the kitchen was on fire.

A jay flew across his path in a flash of blue, and from the cloudless sky above, a hawk cried out as it circled, looking for breakfast. A chipmunk bounded out of Nat's path and scurried into a hollow log so it wouldn't *be* breakfast.

Life was so simple for these creatures, Nat thought. Instinct told them when to hide, when to mate and how to take care of their young. He wondered when, in the evolution of humans, the act of breeding had become so surrounded with land mines.

The breeze blew down from the hillside in front of him. The dogs paused to sniff the air at the same moment Nat saw a movement ahead, up higher in the trees. The dogs barked and headed in that direction. At first Nat thought it might be a deer, but then sunlight glinted off something metal.

"Fleafarm! Sadie! Come!" His stomach lurched. "Come here!" he called again, and fortunately the dogs turned around with great reluctance and started slowly back to him. "Good girls!" He patted his thighs enthusiastically while he kept an eye on the spot where he'd seen movement.

All was still now. Although he had a premonition that wouldn't quit, logically he didn't know who was up there. Could be a hunter trespassing on Rocking D land, or a bird-watcher with a pair of binoculars that caught the light of the sun. Or it could be Jess's stalker. He needed to get the dogs to safety and then alert Sebastian. If they saddled up a couple of horses, they could take a look around.

Once the dogs were with him, he started back toward the house, glancing over his shoulder often to see if he noticed anything more on the hillside. Nothing. If it hadn't been for the reaction of the dogs when they'd obviously caught the scent of something, he would have wondered if he'd imagined the whole thing.

Then he heard the rumble of a vehicle on the road, and

before he reached the driveway, Travis pulled up in his shiny black muscle truck.

Travis hopped down from the cab and gave Nat a grin. "Out for a morning stroll, cowboy? What's the matter, did you forget how to ride a horse while you were over there?" His grin faded as Nat drew closer. "What's the problem? Is Lizzy—"

"The baby's fine. At least she was last time I saw her. I need to get these dogs inside and grab Sebastian. I think I might've seen the guy up on that hill. If we saddle the horses and ride up there, we might get lucky."

"Did he know you saw him?"

"I'm not sure. Maybe. But we have to try."

"I'm on it. You get Sebastian and I'll start saddling the horses." Travis hopped back in his truck and spit gravel as he shot off toward the barn.

NAT HEARD the shower running when he walked in the door. He headed for the kitchen, where he found Sebastian feeding Elizabeth cereal, and Matty measuring coffee into the pot. Nat looked into the baby's blue eyes and felt his heart get all tangled up in that gaze. Quickly he looked away. He didn't have time for that now. "Is Jess in the shower?"

Matty glanced up. "Apparently. She hasn't come into the kitchen, and I'll bet she's afraid to. I was wondering if you'd go convince her to—"

"No can do." Nat looked over at Sebastian. "Our guy may have been up on the hillside just a minute ago. Travis is saddling the horses."

"Right." Sebastian put the spoon into the cereal bowl and set it on the table out of Elizabeth's reach. "Matty, take over here, and set the alarm once I'm out the door."

Matty was by his side instantly, grabbing his arm. "I don't think you should go charging up there without a plan."

"I have a plan. I'm getting my rifle." He pulled away from her and brushed past Nat as he headed through the living room.

"Watch the baby, Nat," Matty said as she ran after Sebastian. "Listen, cowboy, you can't just ride up there like the Three Musketeers, you know!"

Sebastian's voice drifted back as he kept going down the hall toward his bedroom. "Don't argue with me, Matty. We don't have time to waste if we want to catch him."

"He could pick you off!" She charged down the hall after her husband.

Nat glanced over at Elizabeth sitting in her high chair with cereal smeared all over her mouth. She was staring at him with wide eyes. He sure did recognize the color in those eyes. He saw it every morning in the mirror. Then her face scrunched up like someone was squeezing it, and she let out a howl of protest.

"Aw, don't do that," Nat said. "Matty will be back soon."

Elizabeth only cried harder and spit out whatever cereal she'd had in her mouth.

Nat panicked. For all he knew, she might choke or something if she kept crying like that. He could still hear Matty and Sebastian arguing back in the bedroom, and here was this kid who might be in serious danger, and he didn't have the foggiest idea what to do. *"Matty!"* he bellowed.

And just like that, Elizabeth stopped crying. But the look on her face was no improvement. She looked petrified. Of him. Nat's insides twisted as he remembered how he'd felt whenever his father had yelled like that. And here he was, scaring his daughter the same way.

"I'm sorry," he murmured. "I'm sorry, baby."

She gazed at him, and tears quivered on her lower eyelids.

"I won't yell at you anymore," he promised, looking into those big blue eyes. Oh, God. She was getting to him.

His chest grew tight and his throat felt clogged up. That little face, that tear-streaked, cereal-smeared little face, was getting to him.

"Let's go." Sebastian came into the kitchen wearing a jacket and carrying his rifle.

With relief, Nat turned toward Sebastian.

"You are idiots, all of you!" Matty said, coming in behind him. "We should call the sheriff."

"By the time we do, Jessica's stalker will be long gone," Sebastian said. "Now set the alarm once I leave, and if we're not back in an hour, then you can call the sheriff."

"Peachy," Matty said. "Should I ask him to bring body bags?"

"Stop it. We'll be fine." Sebastian glanced at Nat. "Ready?"

"Ready," Nat said. As he started out the kitchen door behind Sebastian, he chanced one more look over at the baby. She was still watching him. "See you later, Elizabeth," he said softly.

CHAPTER FOURTEEN

JESSICA HAD NEARLY FINISHED her shower when she heard the commotion in the hall as Matty and Sebastian came by arguing about something. With guilt her constant companion, she couldn't help wondering if it had to do with her. She needed to come out of hiding and find out.

Toweling off quickly, she dressed in jeans and an ivory long-sleeved T-shirt. Then she ran a comb through her hair. As she left the bathroom she heard the kitchen door close.

"Men!" Matty's disgusted voice carried down the hall from the kitchen. "I tell you, Elizabeth, most guys don't have the brains God gave a goat."

Jessica approached the kitchen doorway with caution. "Matty?" she called out before she showed herself "Do you think I should come in the kitchen?"

"Absolutely," Matty said. "Elizabeth and I need reinforcements, don't we, sweetheart? The guys just took the morning train to Stupidville."

"Ga!" came the delighted response.

Jessica's heart hammered as she edged into the kitchen doorway. From her wooden high chair Elizabeth looked her way, and Jessica braced herself for more tears. Instead, the baby almost seemed to give a mental shrug as she returned her attention to the spoonful of applesauce Matty was holding out.

Indifference was better than fear, Jessica told herself. "What did you mean about the guys?" she asked, keeping her voice low and nonthreatening. "Where did they go?"

''Nat thought he saw your stalker up on the hill.''

Jessica put her hand over her mouth to stifle a gasp that would probably scare the baby.

''Travis arrived when Nat was coming back to tell us, so those three dimwits saddled up and rode out to find him. Sebastian took his rifle.'' Matty continued to feed Elizabeth, but the line of her back was rigid.

''Oh, dear.''

''I've set the alarm, so we'll know if the fellow shows up here, but I think we should have called the sheriff. The guys didn't agree.''

Despair washed over Jessica. Calling the sheriff would inevitably lead to the sheriff contacting her parents, but she couldn't continue to avoid that if people were placing themselves in danger. ''Maybe I should just call my parents and be done with it. I can't have all of you risking yourselves like this.''

Matty glanced at Jessica before resuming the feeding as she slipped the spoon neatly in Elizabeth's mouth. ''If you come in slowly and sit at the table, I think that would be a good way for this little gremlin to become used to you again. Then you can tell me about this situation with your parents.''

''All right.'' Jessica eased herself over to the table. She resented every second she had to spend carefully and cautiously renewing the bond with Elizabeth. She wanted to scoop the baby up and smother her with kisses. Of course, it was normal for a baby her age to be fearful of strangers, but Jessica shouldn't be one of them. The world was out of kilter and she wanted to blink her eyes and make it right again.

Elizabeth watched her warily as she came to the table and sat down about four feet from the high chair.

''Elizabeth,'' Matty crooned. ''Have another bite of applesauce, sweetie pie.''

The baby turned back toward Matty and banged her

hands on the high-chair tray while Matty fed her. Matty expertly used the edge of the spoon to scoop up the excess applesauce from around her mouth and tuck that inside, too.

Jessica took note of the procedure with more than a touch of envy. She'd never fed a baby before, but if she and Elizabeth had learned together, Elizabeth wouldn't have noticed that her mother was clumsy at it. Now she'd immediately sense Jessica's lack of experience.

"I take it your parents don't know about the baby or the stalker," Matty said, keeping her tone conversational as she continued to feed Elizabeth.

"That's right. I've been hoping to keep Elizabeth from growing up the way I did, a virtual prisoner because my father was afraid someone would try to snatch me for a huge ransom."

"I guess he had a point," Matty said.

"Unfortunately, he did." Jessica sat gazing at her daughter, her heart breaking. "The way I see it, I can either call my parents and get their protection from this guy, or... assuming the jerk doesn't know about Elizabeth yet, I can take off again before he finds out about her."

Matty turned, her gaze extremely alert. "And then what? Leave her with us indefinitely?"

Jessica didn't miss the barely disguised eagerness in Matty's voice. She didn't blame Matty for ignoring the question of what would happen to Jessica in that scenario. Matty was primarily concerned with Elizabeth's welfare, which was as it should be.

"I would leave her with you forever," Jessica murmured as pain sliced through her at voicing the unthinkable. "If I go away again, I wouldn't come back for her. That wouldn't be fair to anyone, most of all her."

Matty swallowed, but she didn't speak. Then she put down the spoon and picked up a damp cloth that had been lying on the table. Slowly, tenderly, she washed Elizabeth's face while the baby tried to grab the cloth and made little gurgling sounds.

Then, still holding the cloth, Matty looked over at Jessica. Tears shimmered in her eyes. "Of course I would love to have this child forever. Sebastian would be ecstatic. So would everyone—Travis, Gwen, Boone, Shelby, Luann and little Josh." She cleared her throat and continued. "Before I was pregnant, I might not have understood the sacrifice you're suggesting, but now I do, and I can't let you make it."

Jessica gulped back her own tears. "If it's the best thing for Elizabeth—"

"It's not," Matty said firmly. "Did you ever sing to her?"

Jessica blinked back her tears. "Sing? Why?"

"It might be a way back."

"Oh." Jessica had never known a kinderhearted woman than Matty Daniels. Any fool could see how she'd bonded with Elizabeth, and the thought of losing the baby had to be painful. Yet Matty was trying to help Jessica connect again. "Yes, I sang to her," she said.

"I thought so. Most of us do that instinctively, I guess."

Most of us. Jessica wondered if Matty knew she'd unconsciously included herself in the category of mother, even though her own child hadn't been born yet. Well, she should include herself, Jessica thought. She'd been Elizabeth's mother for several months, along with Gwen and Shelby.

"Why don't you try singing now?" Matty suggested.

"Here?" Jessica felt self-conscious singing while her child sat in a high chair four feet away and Matty was still in the room. When she'd sung to Elizabeth before, the baby had been wrapped snugly in her arms. The moment had been cozy and intimate with only the two of them. This would be like a performance.

"She's full and pretty happy right now," Matty said.

"With me right here, she's not threatened by having you around. And she's not being distracted by anyone else at the moment. What do you say?"

"Okay." Jessica gave Matty a tiny smile. "But I'll feel like a Vegas nightclub act."

Matty smiled back. "I promise to be a good audience."

Jessica knew exactly which song she wanted to sing. She could still remember her mother singing it to her when she was a little girl. Jessica had never learned the song's title, only the words, which told of a train bound for dreamland. It ran on a peppermint rail, and only stopped at ice-cream stations to pick up Crackerjack mail.

She'd loved that concept as a child. Although Elizabeth wasn't old enough to understand the words yet, she would be, sooner than Jessica could have imagined.

Blocking out memories of her mother and father had been more difficult for Jessica recently. She'd assumed all along that her parents would be critical and punishing when they eventually discovered Elizabeth's existence. Now she wasn't so sure.

She gazed at her baby as the little girl sat playing with her fingers and experimenting with shoving different combinations into her mouth. Absorbing the beauty of Elizabeth's coppery curls, pink cheeks and innocent blue eyes, she couldn't imagine her parents feeling anything but love for this child. Yet how could she bring them into Elizabeth's life and not expect them to overprotect the baby in the same way they'd overprotected her?

She couldn't. Taking a long, shaky breath and feeling very self-conscious, she began to sing.

Elizabeth looked over at her immediately. With two fingers thrust into her drooling mouth, she focused intently on Jessica's face.

Jessica continued to sing and gradually forgot Matty was there as she searched the baby's expression for the slightest evidence of recognition.

Elizabeth seemed fascinated by being sung to, but maybe she was that way with everyone.

"Keep singing and trade places with me," Matty said.

As Jessica and Matty got up, alarm showed in Elizabeth's eyes. She looked quickly from one to the other while they switched seats, which placed Matty farther away and Jessica right in front of Elizabeth.

Jessica panicked when the baby scrunched up her face as if to cry. Then Matty, who obviously had heard enough of the song to get the melody, began to hum along with Jessica. She couldn't carry a tune in a bucket, but Jessica didn't care. The ploy worked to unscrunch Elizabeth's face.

Elizabeth's attention rotated from one woman to another as the makeshift duet continued, and the look of amazement on the baby's face nearly made Jessica laugh. But she kept singing. She must have started smiling without realizing it, though, because all at once a miracle happened. Elizabeth looked at her and grinned.

Jessica's throat closed and she couldn't sing anymore. But as Elizabeth's grin faded and she began to cloud up again, Jessica made a superhuman effort and began singing again. She even managed a smile, although it quivered at the edges.

Matty began adding words to her humming, but they weren't the words of the song. *"We're doing great,"* she sang. *"How about if you—"*

The sound of hoofbeats came from outside.

Matty bounced out of her chair and looked out the kitchen window. "They're back." She poured a truckload of relief into those two words.

Jessica's heart began to pound. Breaking eye contact with Elizabeth, she went to the window, almost afraid of what she might see. "They're okay," she said with a sigh.

"Looks like." Matty went to shut off the alarm system and then stood on tiptoe to get a better look out the kitchen window. "I don't see any blood."

"Me neither." Jessica couldn't stop looking at the easy way Nat sat his horse. She kept forgetting he'd been raised on a ranch and was a genuine cowboy from the brim of his hat to the tip of his boots. He certainly looked the part now.

She watched the three men dismount and tie their horses to the hitching rail by the back door as if they were part of a western movie. She'd only seen these guys at a ski lodge, where they were out of their natural element. No doubt about it, they were in their element at the Rocking D.

Elizabeth started banging on her tray with both hands.

Matty glanced over at the baby. "I think someone misses the floor show."

Jessica followed her gaze and was gratified that Elizabeth's mood still seemed cheerful. "Do you think we really made progress?"

"I would bet on it. I think singing is the ticket. You should keep that up. Sorry about screwing up your act with my caterwauling, by the way."

Jessica had been brought up to be reserved with people until she knew them well, but it seemed like the most natural thing in the world to put an arm around Matty's shoulders and gave her a quick hug. "Are you kidding?" she said with a chuckle. "Your backup singing saved the day."

Matty laughed. "Be sure and tell Sebastian that," she said as the kitchen door opened and the man in question came through it. "He's threatened to pay me not to sing."

"No, you have that wrong." Still carrying his rifle, Sebastian walked over and gave his wife a swift kiss. "I've said I'd pay you to dance *instead* of sing. I think we should all stick to what we have a talent for, and your talent is definitely dancing." He left the kitchen to put his rifle away.

"Wait a minute!" Matty called after him. "Did you find anything up there?"

"Ask Travis," Sebastian called back.

"So?" Matty asked as Travis came in, followed by Nat. "What happened?"

"We located some tracks," Travis said, shucking his jacket and hanging it on one of several pegs by the back door. "We followed them for a while, but we lost the trail when we hit the rocky section."

Jessica turned toward Nat. "Did you get a look at him before? Do you think it could have been the man who's been following me?"

"Don't know. I only knew somebody was up there, but I didn't get a good look. It could've been anybody, I guess." His grim expression reminded Jessica of the one he'd had when he first got off the plane, a don't-mess-with-me look. There was definitely a harder edge to Nat than there had been before he'd gone overseas. She found it incredibly sexy.

"Might have been one of the neighbors out for a ride," Travis said. "Except if it was, you'd think they'd have come on down to the house for some coffee instead of heading off in the opposite direction."

"I still say the guy deliberately rode across those rocks," Nat said as he took off his jacket and hung it next to Travis's. "He meant for us to lose his trail."

"Could be," Sebastian said as he came back into the kitchen. "But whether he meant to or not, he succeeded." He glanced at Travis. "I thought you were some sort of tracking wizard, hotshot."

"Aw, I just told Gwen that to impress her, considering she has that Cheyenne ancestry and all," Travis said. "I can lose a trail in the rocks the same as the rest of you."

"Wonderful." Sebastian looked at his head wrangler and shook his head. "And for this I pay you the big bucks."

Elizabeth banged on her tray and started gurgling.

"No, you pay me the big bucks to change this little gal's diaper," Travis said with a grin. "Right, Lizzie? Nobody does it like the Diaperman, right?"

The baby laughed and held up her arms to Travis.

"Want me to spring you from that chair, don't you, sweet-cheeks?" Travis unlatched the tray and scooped Elizabeth up in his arms. "Hey, little girl, I do believe you need my services right this minute." He nuzzled her neck until she laughed. "Come with me, darlin'."

As Travis left the kitchen carrying a smiling Elizabeth, Jessica gazed after them in frustration. How long before the baby held up her pudgy little arms to her mother?

NAT WONDERED if he'd ever be able to be as relaxed and charming as Travis was with Elizabeth. Probably not. Ah, but he ached to be. He'd expected to be afraid of the baby, and he was, to some degree. But fascination was quickly overtaking his fear. And he was developing a hunger to hold the little girl and see if he could coax a dimpled smile from her.

"I think Jessica and I made progress with Elizabeth while you three were gone," Matty said. She handed her husband a mug of coffee and poured another, which she gave to Nat.

Sebastian blew across the top of his mug. "Yeah? What did you do?"

"It was Matty's idea." Jess murmured her thanks as she took the coffee Matty poured and held out to her. "She suggested I sing to Elizabeth, thinking she might remember the song and start getting used to me again." She took a sip of coffee. "I think it helped."

"Great idea." Nat figured he was the only one who noticed Jess's slight grimace as she drank the coffee. She would have preferred herbal tea, but under the circumstances, she probably didn't want to ask if there was anything like that in the house. He wished he could have been here to watch her sing to Elizabeth. That would have been a scene to add to his memories.

Damn, but Jess looked good in her T-shirt and jeans. He

would love to be able to go over and sling an arm around her shoulders the way Sebastian felt free to do with Matty.

But he didn't dare. She probably wouldn't appreciate him making such a gesture in front of Matty and Sebastian, and he might lose whatever ground he'd gained earlier that morning in the bathroom. Despite her rejection, he'd been encouraged by the look in her eyes. He still saw a little of that fire now whenever she glanced his way.

"Having you sing to her is a great idea," Sebastian agreed. "But shouldn't you keep that kind of thing up?"

"You want her to go around singing all day?" Matty asked.

"No, although there's nothing wrong with that, either. I meant the contact with Elizabeth." He looked over at Jess. "You could go in and help Travis change her. Then she might start getting the idea that you'll be around all the time, and eventually you could try doing the job and she might not think anything of it."

"You're right." Immediately she set her coffee down on the counter and turned toward Nat. "Do you want to—"

"Let's not have a convention in there," he said, although he wouldn't have minded going. He wanted an excuse to follow Jess around like a puppy, to breathe in her scent and watch the way the light played in her red curls. "Too many of us might overwhelm her."

"He has a point," Matty said. "We'll work him into the rotation later."

"For sure." When Jess glanced at him this time, there was no mistaking the look in her eyes.

His pulse accelerated. Oh, for a few minutes alone with her. But it wouldn't be anytime soon. With a flicker of a smile, she left the kitchen, taking his heart with her.

"And I'll warn you, Travis doesn't sing any better than I do!" Matty called out after her.

Once she was out of earshot, Nat looked at Matty. "Do

you think Elizabeth's really getting over her fear? Or are you trying to make Jess feel better?''

"Elizabeth will get over her fear mainly because Jessica loves that baby more than life itself, and she's willing to do whatever it takes.'' She smiled as the sound of Travis's off-key baritone blending with Jess's more musical voice drifted down the hall from Elizabeth's room. "When she was singing to that baby, I darn near started bawling, it was so touching.''

"It's been tough on her,'' Nat said. And he longed to find a way to ease her pain, one that wouldn't land them both in bigger trouble.

"I'm sure,'' Matty said. "While you three were gone, she began to worry all over again about the danger presented by this character that's been tailing her. She figured her choice was to call her parents and get their protection, or leave now before the guy gets wind there's a baby in the picture.''

Nat's stomach clenched. "She actually said she might leave?''

"Yes, and let me tell you, contemplating that was killing her, but she's willing to consider it if Elizabeth will be better off as a result.''

"She can't leave,'' Nat said, his voice betraying more emotion than he'd intended.

"Whoa, son,'' Sebastian said. "Nobody's gonna let her do that.''

"Couldn't we call the sheriff and get him out here?'' Matty asked. "I'd feel a lot better if we had some law enforcement working on this instead of you guys running around like some posse out of a grade-B western.''

Sebastian gave her hair a playful tug. "Watch how you talk, woman. The boys and I command a heap of respect in these here parts.''

"Joke about it if you want,'' she said. "But I—''

"While we were out trailing the guy, we talked about

the possibility of calling the sheriff's office, Matty," Nat said. "I know this makes you nervous. It makes me nervous. But the problem with going to the authorities is that they'll want to run down leads if they can, and the logical place to start is with Jess's folks."

"Would that be so terrible?" Matty asked. "It seems as if they ought to know about this. Jessica said she was afraid they'd be overprotective, like they were with her, but Jessica is Elizabeth's mother. Surely she could control the extent to which they did that."

Nat thought about the iron gates with the scrolled initials *FH* worked into the elaborate design, and the iron-willed man who lived behind those gates. "I met her father a few days ago, before Jess—well, before she and I hooked up. I can believe that Jess is right about how he'd react if he found out about this situation, and the man's got clout. He'd commandeer the ranch. And Elizabeth would be shipped back to New York so fast it would make your head swim. I'm not sure any of us would ever see her again."

"Oh." Matty glanced up at her husband. "Then I guess we have to come up with a different plan, huh?"

"'Fraid so," Sebastian said. "I'm not about to let some New York bigshot tell me how to run things on the Rocking D. And we're sure as hell not letting him make off with that baby." He leveled a glance at Nat. "Right?"

"Right." Nat had no trouble meeting Sebastian's gaze on that one. Before he'd seen Elizabeth he might have briefly imagined that having her tucked safely inside the gates of Franklin Hall would be the best solution all the way around. Now he knew that was unthinkable. He wasn't sure what part he might end up playing in the little girl's life, but he didn't want either her or her mother hidden away in the Hudson Valley.

"But at the very least we're going to have to beef up security around here," Sebastian said. "I'll have our local expert Jim add a few wrinkles."

"Unless you want me to call the guy who does the security for some of my clients," Nat said, thinking about one particular sale in which a Hollywood star who'd bought property near Colorado Springs had used Seth's expertise to secure his estate.

"Oh, yeah," Sebastian said. "I remember you telling me about him. He's based in L.A."

"He could do a job for us," Nat said. "But he's expensive and slow. Most of the people who hire him are putting in a system they plan to leave in place forever, whereas this would be temporary."

"That's true." Sebastian sipped his coffee. "Let's see what Jim can come up with for now, and keep your guy in reserve in case we need more expertise."

"Sounds reasonable," Nat said. "And in the meantime, we have to convince Jess that she can't leave."

Matty grinned. "I figure that's your job, Nat."

Nat felt the heat climb up from his collar. He rubbed the back of his neck and gave her a sheepish smile while he considered how to explain that he was willing, but Jess wasn't letting him use all the weapons at his disposal. "Well, the thing is, I—"

"Come on, buddy," Sebastian said, obviously taking pity on him. "Let's go unsaddle those nags while Matty cooks us up some of her famous bacon and eggs for breakfast."

CHAPTER FIFTEEN

JESSICA HAD ALWAYS thought of her childhood as lonely, and had supposed she'd love living in a house bustling with people and activity. To her surprise, she didn't love it. After several days of constant visits from all the people who had a stake in Elizabeth, the lack of privacy at the Rocking D began to wear on Jessica's nerves.

Although Matty and Sebastian had moved Elizabeth's crib into their room so there wouldn't be any more scenes when the baby woke up, Jessica had graduated to being able to hold Elizabeth for short periods of time. Still, someone Elizabeth trusted had to remain in the room. If that person started to leave, Elizabeth would begin crying.

Under normal circumstances Jessica would have suggested that they tough it out and see if Elizabeth stopped fussing, but these circumstances were far from normal. Jessica didn't feel she could demand control of the situation and tread on the toes of the people who had been so wonderful to her and her baby.

Because she wanted to spend as much time as possible with Elizabeth, she was forced to have someone else around constantly, too. She'd shared her baby with Matty, Sebastian, Gwen, Travis, Luann, Shelby, Boone and even little Josh.

And most frustrating of all, the third person in the room couldn't ever be Nat. He had to be person number four, or else Jessica was obliged to leave so he could have a chance to hold the baby, too. Jessica had noticed something else.

Whenever she held Elizabeth, changed her diaper or fed her, no one told her how to go about it. But when Nat took his turn, everybody had an opinion.

The women weren't as bad as his three buddies, who were constantly making suggestions and offering to demonstrate a particular skill for Nat. Sebastian, Boone and Travis were definitely guilty of hovering. As a result, Nat had developed no confidence in his abilities with the baby.

He kept trying valiantly anyway, and that was the important thing. He hadn't rejected Elizabeth, but learning to feel comfortable with her while everyone coached from the sidelines might be an impossible task.

Jessica's heart went out to him. And the rest of her body wanted to follow. Sleeping alone in the double bed with Nat right down the hall was becoming increasingly difficult to tolerate. Yet the pattern had been established, and to change it now would cause comment in the household. If and when Jessica invited Nat back to her bed, and she was very inclined to do so, she wanted a more private setting.

Everywhere she turned these days she met with frustration, but she felt ungrateful for having such negative thoughts. Matty and Sebastian had leaned over backward for her. They wouldn't even let her help pay for groceries, and she knew when this was all over she'd have to come up with some way to repay them, to repay all of them. If they were a little possessive of Elizabeth, if they didn't want to rush the moment when Jessica could take care of the baby by herself, that was understandable.

Besides, she was reunited with her child, even if she couldn't be alone with Elizabeth yet. And she felt safe. Now that Sebastian's friend Jim had increased security around the ranch house with a more extensive lighting system, it seemed as if her stalker had grown discouraged and left. After so many days had passed and she no longer had the sensation of being watched, she was daring to hope that the guy had given up.

All in all, her life was going as well as could be expected, she thought as she stood beside Matty at Elizabeth's changing table late in the afternoon of another busy day. They were sharing the job of dressing the baby for Gwen's thirtieth birthday party.

Freshly bathed and diapered, Elizabeth lay on the changing table clutching her sock monkey and chewing vigorously on its arm. Jessica had braced herself for another evening of watching Nat's friends instruct him in the art of baby care.

Earlier she and Matty had decorated the ranch house within an inch of its life. The number thirty had been taped to the walls and hung from the beamed ceilings. They'd even spelled it out on the dining table with Elizabeth's alphabet blocks. Sebastian and Matty had vowed not to let Gwen slide past this milestone without ''raising a ruckus,'' as Sebastian had put it.

''I'm running behind,'' Matty said as she put on one white lacy sock and Jessica put on the other.

''What's left besides getting Elizabeth ready?'' Jessica figured it would take less than ten minutes to put on the baby's ruffled lavender dress and tie bows in her curls. Sebastian was in the shower and Nat was out stringing thirty colored lanterns along the porch railing.

''I still need to stick the candles on the cake and wrap those thirty bottles of Geritol we're giving her.''

Jessica glanced over at Matty. ''I could finish dressing Elizabeth while you do that.''

Matty hesitated.

''We have to keep testing to see if she's adjusted yet.''

''I know, but this might not be the best time. Maybe Sebastian's almost finished. He could—''

''Matty.'' Jessica gave her a level look. ''I think she might be ready.''

Matty's eyes grew moist. ''So do I. I've thought so for

the last couple of days. I just didn't want to admit it, not even to myself.''

Jessica's heart went out to her. With a gentle smile she put her arm around Matty and gave her a hug. ''I'm not going to jerk her out of here right away, and even when we eventually go, I won't take her completely out of your life. I promise. We'll come back a lot.''

Matty swallowed. ''I know that. But it will never be the same.''

''Oh, Matty, I never meant to hurt—''

''Hey.'' Matty gave her a wobbly grin. ''You did nothing but make our lives better around here when you left Elizabeth at the Rocking D. Without this little girl I wouldn't be married to Sebastian. Travis wouldn't be with Gwen and Boone wouldn't have found Shelby and Josh.'' She reached for a tissue in her pocket and wiped her nose. ''I'm very grateful we had her for a little while, but I won't lie to you. When you finally take her, I'll miss her like the devil.''

''Rebecca will help.''

Matty patted her tummy and attempted to look brave. ''You bet she will. And Jeffrey, too.''

''Who?''

''Rebecca's brother. Sebastian's so sure we're going to have another one, and it'll be a boy, that he's started on a second belt. He's using a darker leather, and—'' She stopped talking and glanced at Elizabeth. ''Okay, I'm stalling.'' She took a deep breath and tweaked Elizabeth's foot. ''See ya, toots.'' Then she turned and left the room.

Elizabeth twisted her head to watch Matty leave. Then she glanced up at Jessica.

''Just you and me, kid,'' Jessica said, her stomach churning as she waited to see if Elizabeth would cry. ''Think you can handle that?''

Elizabeth stared at her, as if thinking things over.

The knot in Jessica's stomach began to loosen as she concluded that Elizabeth wasn't going to cry. The baby was definitely evaluating the situation, but apparently she'd decided that Jessica was to be trusted. Finally.

"Just you and me, kid," Jessica said again with a smile. "Sounds pretty good, doesn't it?"

Elizabeth waved her sock monkey in Jessica's face. "Da!" she said loudly.

"I stand corrected." She felt like dancing and singing for joy, but she didn't want to get too wild and alarm the baby. The baby who was finally hers again. "Just you, me and Bruce."

"Any room in that equation for another interested party?"

At the sound of Nat's voice from the doorway, Jessica's heartbeat quickened. Keeping one hand on Elizabeth, she glanced over her shoulder at him.

He leaned casually in the doorway, but there was nothing casual about the way he was looking at her. He'd bought a deep blue western shirt for the party, and it brought out the brilliant color of his eyes. She could have eaten him up with a spoon.

"Is this the first time you've been alone with her?" Nat asked.

"Yes." She glanced down at Elizabeth and saw that she was watching her father with great curiosity, but no apparent fear.

"Then maybe I'd better not come in."

Flushed with triumph, Jessica was ready to be bold. "I'd love you to come in." The three of them hadn't been alone together since the first night, when she and Nat had gone into the bedroom to watch Elizabeth sleep. She still remembered the magic of that moment, and she wanted to experience it again.

"I could stay over here, to play it safe."

Jessica looked back at him. "You know what? I'm sick to death of playing it safe."

A smile flitted across his chiseled lips. "Yeah?"

"Yeah."

He pushed away from the door frame and came slowly across the room as his gaze flicked over her outfit, a pale green sweater dress she'd picked up during a quick trip to town with Matty and Sebastian. If she were honest with herself, she'd have to admit that in buying it, she'd been hoping to incite the lust she saw in Nat's expression.

"Is that why you're wearing that dress?" he asked. "Because you're sick of playing it safe and you want to push me right over the edge?"

"Maybe." Her breathing quickened at the flame that leaped in his eyes. Suddenly not sure if she'd bitten off more than she could chew, she returned her attention to Elizabeth and reached for the ruffled dress hanging from a hook above the changing table.

"Did I hear you say maybe?" he murmured, coming to stand beside her. "That's a country mile from no. Are you aware of that?" He wasn't quite touching her, but electricity seemed to arc between them.

"Yes. No. Oh, Nat, I don't know what I think." Her heart was pounding and she could feel heat spreading through her body and warming her cheeks. "Except that I miss you so much."

"Missing me's a good sign." His voice was gruff with emotion.

Elizabeth waved her monkey in the air. "Da-da!"

Nat went very still. "Did she say what I think she said?"

Jessica glanced over at him. She didn't have the heart to tell him that Elizabeth probably didn't know what she was saying, and that she'd said it before when no men were on the scene at all. It happened to be a syllable she could pronounce, but it didn't necessarily mean she was labeling him. Still, Jessica didn't know that for a fact, now, did she?

He gazed at the baby, his heart in his eyes. "Do you know who I am, Elizabeth? Da-da?"

She waved the monkey again and smiled. "Da-da!"

"My God." Nat looked thunderstruck. And proud, as if he'd been given first prize in some lofty competition.

Jessica took the moment and tucked it away in her memory. No matter how things turned out, she would always remember Nat's expression as he gazed at his daughter. She longed to close the bedroom door and prolong the intimacy of this little group for...for a very long while.

But there would be no closing of bedroom doors. The party would start soon. "We'd better get her clothes on her," she said gently. "Sit her up and hold her steady while I put this dress over her head."

"You're sure she won't get upset?"

"Why should she? After all, you're her da-da."

"My hands are cold." He blew on them and rubbed them briskly together. Then he held them against his cheeks. "Still cold."

"Okay, I'll hold her and you put the dress over her head." She handed him the ruffled outfit and propped Elizabeth up in a sitting position.

"But she likes to play peekaboo when you put something over her head." Nat sounded as if the assignment was way beyond his abilities.

"I'll bet you can play peekaboo."

"I'm not sure if I—"

"Nat." She glanced up at him. "I don't know much about your experience with little children, but I do know what a tender, sensitive and creative lover you are. I'm sure you can manage a game of peekaboo with a little baby."

His gaze grew hot. "You're flirting with me, Jessica Louise."

She smiled and nodded toward the outfit he held in one hand. "Put the dress on the baby."

"Yeah." Without warning, he grasped the back of Jessica's head and kissed her hard, thrusting his tongue firmly into her mouth in a blatantly aggressive gesture. A possessive gesture, a branding gesture. Then, just as quickly, he released her.

She stood there trembling, her mouth tingling and moist, and she was unable to say a word. If she had been able to speak, she could only have uttered one syllable. *More.*

Nat gave her a slow, sensuous smile before turning to the baby. "Hey, Elizabeth, ready for this?"

Jessica hadn't been ready for the kiss, that was for sure. Either her memory of his potent kisses had faded a little or he'd upped the emotional ante. Nat's kisses had been dizzying, arousing, playful, erotic. But she never remembered a kiss that had said forcefully, *Mine.*

Nat carefully lowered the dress so that the material settled softly over Elizabeth. "Where's Elizabeth?" he asked. "Where's that baby?" Then he opened the neck wider and popped it over her head. "There she is!"

Elizabeth laughed happily, showing off her teeth.

"Peekaboo, I see you!" Nat said.

"Da-da!" Elizabeth beamed at him.

"And so I am," Nat said quietly.

"And so you are," Jessica said, looking up at him.

He met her gaze, his eyes glowing with happiness. "Jess, I—"

"How's everything going in here?" Sebastian asked as he strode into the room. "Looks like you nearly have that munchkin dressed. Tying those ribbons in her hair can be tricky, though. I thought I'd see if you needed any help."

Much as Jessica loved her good friend Sebastian, at that moment she could have cheerfully decked him.

Sure enough, Nat's bright expression dimmed and he backed away from the changing table. "Maybe you should take over for the rest of it. I'll see if Matty needs any help in the kitchen."

"Or Sebastian could help Matty in the kitchen," Jessica said, although she had little hope Nat would stay, now that Sebastian was here.

"That's okay." Nat was already halfway out the door. "I'm no good with little ribbons. I'd probably pull her hair or something."

Sebastian glanced from Nat's retreating back to Jessica's face. "Did I just screw up?"

Jessica gave him a halfhearted smile. He was a dear man, but he could be so dense. She started getting Elizabeth's arms through the sleeves of her dress.

"I did screw up, didn't I?" Sebastian said as he came over to the changing table. "I'll bet the three of you were— you know—bonding."

"Sort of. Could you hold her while I button the back of this?"

"Sure. Hey, peaches." He took hold of Elizabeth and kissed her on the cheek.

"Da-da!"

"Did you hear that?" Sebastian said with obvious pleasure. "What a smart little dickens."

"Uh-huh." Jessica finished the buttoning and gathered her courage. "Sebastian, do you really want Nat to take on the job of being Elizabeth's father?"

"You know I do! Why would you even ask?" He leaned down and rubbed his nose against Elizabeth's. "Nosy, nosy."

Elizabeth chuckled and made a grab for his nose.

"You're very good with her," Jessica said.

"It's easy. I love her. Don't I, sweetheart? Love this little bundle to pieces. Yes, I do." He scooped her up from the changing table and nuzzled her again until she laughed.

Nat would never have had the courage to pick Elizabeth up so spontaneously, Jessica thought. "You're all good with her," she said, "and it's been wonderful to watch because I know how well she's been cared for all these months."

Sebastian glanced at Jessica. "Where are you going with this, little one?"

She was so afraid of sounding ungrateful. But something had to be said. "I'm afraid if you three godfathers don't back off a little, Nat's never going to feel comfortable taking on the role of Elizabeth's daddy."

Sebastian stared at her. "But we're only trying to help him get acclimated. He doesn't know about babies, and—"

"And the more you tell him that, the less confidence he has in himself as a father. And he didn't start out with a whole lot to begin with."

"Neither did I!"

Elizabeth laughed and made another grab for his nose.

He gently pried her hand away. "Neither did I," he repeated more quietly. "When you dropped this little girl off, I was scared to death, afraid I'd do something wrong and cause serious damage. At least Nat's got us to help him."

"And that's good, up to a point. The thing is, you didn't have the kind of father Nat had, and his insecurities about being a parent run a lot deeper than yours. None of you had experience with babies, but I don't think any of you seriously doubted you could do it once you put your mind to it. I was sure you could, as long as you had a list of instructions and a book to read."

"You must have spent hours on those instructions."

"Oh, I did. I had to throw away the first set because they were all tear-spotted."

Sebastian's gaze was soft. "You've been through so much. Tell me what I can do to help this get fixed the way you need it to be."

"I'm…I'm not sure. But I think that when Nat sees how competent all of you are, he despairs of ever making the grade."

"I'll talk to Travis and Boone tonight."

She touched his arm. "If you do, please tell them that I love the way they are with Elizabeth. I treasure it. But right now, it doesn't give Nat much room to maneuver."

"We'll come up with a plan," Sebastian promised. "I

want the three of you to be a family. Do you think that could happen?''

''I don't know. But for a moment there, right before you came in, I began to believe it might.''

''And I spoiled that moment. I'm so sorry, little one.''

Jessica wrapped her arms around him and gave him a hug. ''It's okay. There will be other moments.'' Then she crossed her fingers and prayed she was right.

THE PARTY WAS boisterous and fun. Jessica found herself feeling guilty that she'd begrudged any of these wonderful people constant access to Elizabeth. As far as Nat was concerned, they'd only been trying to help, and maybe they'd been planning to ease up on their own. Maybe she shouldn't have said anything to Sebastian, after all.

While she was helping clear the table after the meal, she noticed Sebastian in a quiet huddle with Travis and Boone. It looked as if they'd deliberately chosen a time when Nat, Shelby and Gwen were hunched over a game of Candyland with Josh. From the way the men kept glancing in Nat's direction, Jessica was sure they were discussing her earlier comments to Sebastian.

Dear God, if she'd messed up the relationship among those men she would never forgive herself. Maybe Travis and Boone would be offended that she thought their attempts to help had been interfering. She had a strong urge to set down the pile of plates and go tell them to forget what she'd said to Sebastian.

After all, she was the newcomer in this group. They'd all known each other for many more years than she'd been in the picture. Maybe she'd read the situation wrong.

But in the end, she carried the plates into the kitchen. Then, acting on her own renewed confidence regarding Elizabeth, she lifted the baby from the playpen Matty had put in the corner of the kitchen for the duration of the party.

"I'm going to change her and get her ready for bed,"
she announced to Matty, who was working at the sink.

"Good idea." Matty glanced over at Jessica. "I think
she's getting tired."

Luann put away the glass she'd been drying. "Does she
have to go down already?" Then she looked at the kitchen
clock. "Goodness, I didn't know it was so late."

Jessica had a real soft spot for Travis's mother, who so
obviously adored the concept of grandchildren. Although
Jessica had been relishing the idea of being alone with her
baby, Luann looked so wistful that she relented. It was a
darn good thing Luann's daughter-in-law, Gwen, was also
pregnant.

"Would you like to help me with Elizabeth?" she asked.
"I'm sure Matty could spare you for a few minutes."

"Of course I can," Matty said.

"Then I'd love to help with that precious little girl."
Luann couldn't hang up her dish towel quickly enough.

With two of them working, it didn't take long before
Elizabeth was in her sleeper and ready to collect her good-
night kisses from the houseful of people. Being with Luann
always made Jessica think of her own mother and how she
would have enjoyed spoiling a grandchild. Regret that
things couldn't be different prompted Jessica to give Luann
the privilege of carrying the baby back into the living room.

She followed Luann down the hall and was surprised to
notice that everyone was assembled there as if they were
waiting for something. At first Jessica thought it might simply be time for the cake, but Matty was there, as well, so
no one was available to bring the cake in.

Nat no longer sat on the floor by the coffee table playing
the game with Josh. He stood with his back to the fire and
gazed intently at her as she walked into the room.

Her stomach rolled. They were all waiting for her. She
had overstepped by speaking to Sebastian this afternoon.

Someone was about to deliver a lecture on the subject of ingratitude.

"Sebastian has come up with a plan, Jess," Nat said. "He passed it by me, and now we need to know what you think of it."

Jessica clutched her hands in front of her stomach. "I shouldn't have spoken up. Forgive me, all of you. I couldn't have asked for a warmer, more wonderful—"

"Oh, sweetheart." Matty came forward and put an arm around Jessica's shoulders. "You were right, and everybody knows it. I can't imagine how we expected you, Nat and Elizabeth to form a unit in the midst of all this hubbub."

"You need privacy," Sebastian said.

"Privacy and security," Boone added.

"And atmosphere," Travis said with a wink.

Jessica looked from one to the other, not understanding.

"There's an old but serviceable line shack on the Rocking D," Sebastian said. "We're going to check with Jim and see if he can rig up a good enough security system out there, although this might be the time we have to call in Nat's security guy from L.A."

"A line shack, huh?" Jessica was beginning to get the idea, and she hoped she was hearing it right.

"It's not fancy, but it's clean," Sebastian said. "Once the place is secure, Nat can drive the Bronco out there with you and Elizabeth and enough supplies to last a week or so." He smiled at her. "No interruptions. Should make for some of that bonding stuff."

Her glance flew to Nat as her heart began to pound. "That's okay with you?"

His gaze burned into hers. "It's okay with me. How about you?"

She couldn't hold back her grin. "It sounds great to me," she said.

CHAPTER SIXTEEN

AS NAT HAD SUSPECTED, Jim didn't have the know-how to do an adequate job on the line shack, so Nat had called Seth Burnham. But securing the shack had taken three endless days, and Nat had wondered if he'd make it. Following the decision that they were literally going to "shack up" together, Jessica had turned shy on him, almost going out of her way to avoid him.

He'd spent a fair amount of time wondering why that was. The most promising explanation was that she didn't trust herself to be around him and stay in control of her desire. Now that they were facing a situation in which they could make love again, the anticipation might be driving her crazy, too. Any other explanation for her behavior was too depressing, so he decided to go with the one he liked.

Because he was suffering intense sexual frustration, he'd paid an unholy sum to get Seth on site ASAP. Then he'd spent his days out at the line shack with Seth, helping him install the system.

"This is the best technology has to offer," Seth had said when he was finally finished. "But it's no damn good if you forget to turn it on. So don't forget."

"I won't," Nat had promised. But as he'd driven Seth back to the ranch house in Sebastian's Bronco, his mind hadn't been on security systems. He was thinking about the double bed in the cabin, the one he'd made up fresh with clean sheets. He was thinking of the other preparations he'd made—the folding screen he'd constructed to give them a little privacy in the one-room shack, the flowers he'd put in an old mason jar, the herb tea he'd stocked because he knew she was probably getting sick of coffee.

He was thinking about the following day when he, Jessica and Elizabeth would be driving the Bronco out to the line shack. And he was hoping Elizabeth would take her usual two-hour afternoon nap.

AFTER THE CLOSE CALL he'd had that first morning, Steven Pruitt hadn't ventured so near the ranch house again. He had no intention of facing three pissed-off cowboys, especially when one carried a rifle and looked as if he could use it.

So Steven had marshaled his considerable newsgathering skills to get information out of the citizens of Huerfano. His drama training had come in handy, too, just as it had when he'd worked for the Franklin Publishing Group. Franklin had lost a hell of an undercover investigative reporter when he'd had the stupidity to order Steve Pruitt fired.

It might turn out to be the most costly mistake Russell P. had ever made. The residents of Huerfano liked to talk, and they'd told many tales about the mystery baby who'd been living out at the Rocking D for the past six months. It didn't take a genius to figure out whose baby it was, although Steven knew his test scores put him within genius range.

Waiting to make the snatch had paid off in ways he'd never dreamed. Besides the visceral pleasure he'd enjoyed for six months while he stalked and intimidated Russell's precious daughter, he now had a shot at scooping the Franklin grandchild into his net at the same time he nabbed Jessica.

And he would succeed. Luck was definitely on his side. He'd happened to be in the Buckskin, a local watering hole, when a guy named Jim had come in for a beer. Turns out

Jim's nose was out of joint because Sebastian Daniels had brought in some expert from L.A. to set up a security system for a line shack on the Rocking D. Jim couldn't figure out why they wanted such a high-falutin' system for a line shack in the first place.

Steven had made a hot journalism career out of acting on hunches. He'd seen how tight Jessica had become with that boyfriend of hers. No doubt he was the father of that kid. Steven would bet his bottom dollar the three of them were going off to play house in that line shack. At last, the opportunity he'd been waiting for.

"TAKE MY .38," Sebastian urged the next morning as he and Nat loaded the last of the boxes into the Bronco. "I'll feel a hell of a lot better if you have something out there with you."

Nat wondered if he was being foolishly stubborn. He hated guns with a passion, but he knew how to use one thanks to the endless target practice his father had forced on him. And Jess and the baby were depending on him to keep them safe.

Sebastian closed up the back of the Bronco. "I know you believe in all that newfangled technology you and Seth installed, but I'd still feel better if you had a backup."

"Okay," Nat said with a sigh of resignation. "Do you have a locked box or something secure I can put it in? I don't want to take any chances with that baby."

"I'll give you a locked box, but I'd advise you to put the gun on a high shelf and not lock it up. I'm as concerned about Elizabeth as you are, but she can't climb to the top of those cabinets in the line shack."

Nat gazed out at the hillside where he'd seen the flash of metal on the morning he'd taken the dogs for a run. "He could be gone, you know. Any guy who would follow a woman around for six months has to be weird. Maybe he got his jollies doing that, and now that she's not running, he's picked out another target for acting out his strange fantasies."

"If she were just any woman, I'd say you were possibly right." Sebastian rubbed the back of his neck and glanced at Nat. "But you've hooked up with an heiress, my friend."

Nat gave him a startled look. "Yeah, but she doesn't want—"

"Doesn't matter. She may hope to live a secluded life, but I think she's kidding herself on that score. Look at the Kennedys. Look at your Hollywood clients. Eventually some reporter digs up some information on one of the relatives and the whole family's in the headlines again, even if they work to avoid it."

Nat hadn't really thought about that aspect of his relationship with Jess. He'd thought his main concern was whether he'd be the kind of father Elizabeth deserved and whether he dared take a chance on being the kind of husband Jess deserved. The idea of living in a fishbowl didn't sit well with him.

"I can see you haven't thought much about that," Sebastian said. "You know how dearly I want you to make a life with Jessica and Elizabeth. But I wouldn't be a very good friend if I didn't point out that there's a negative side to that program. She can't change who she is."

"For some reason I never thought of Jess like that. As an heiress." Nat considered the homely little line shack he was about to take her to and winced. She'd probably tolerate it with good grace, the way she'd tolerated drinking coffee for days because she didn't want to make a fuss.

"It's been on my mind ever since you told me," Sebastian said. "When we were deciding whether to call her parents or not, I told you I didn't want to turn things over to some bigshot from New York. That's true, but the other thing I didn't want was the media circus that would result."

"Yeah, it would." Nat glanced around. The log ranch house, the sturdy barn and the horses frisking in the corral created a postcard-pretty view of country living. Then he imagined the area swarming with TV vans, reporters, even helicopters overhead. Sebastian's treasured peace would be shattered.

Filled with remorse, he faced Sebastian. "We shouldn't even be here. I should take Jess and Elizabeth and head out, away from the Rocking D. I've known about her background almost from the beginning, but you haven't. It's not fair to expect you to take this kind of risk with your whole way of life when you had no way of knowing what you were getting into."

"Whoa, son!" Sebastian chuckled. "God, but you do manage to focus on the cloud instead of the silver lining, don't you? I intended to give you a little reminder about the hazards on this road, not send you charging off in another direction entirely."

"But—"

"Never mind your buts. I was only saying that I think it's probable this kidnapper hasn't given up, and yet I'm not in favor of calling Franklin if we can help it. I would gladly entertain the whole crew of *60 Minutes* if that meant I could spend more time with Elizabeth, though. I'm crazy about that kid, in case you haven't noticed."

"Yeah, and that's also my fault. You should never—"

"Listen." Sebastian actually shook a finger in Nat's face. "Whether you and Jessica like it or not, we're in this rodeo with you, and we're gonna be part of that baby's life. All of us—Boone, Shelby, Josh, Gwen, Travis and Luann, besides Matty and me. The fact that her granddaddy's a billionaire is something we'll have to accept and find a way to deal with. But we're not letting that baby get away. At least not very far away. Got that?"

Nat grinned. "Got it."

"And I'm not ready to see the last of your sorry carcass, either, despite the fact you are a heap of trouble."

Nat's grin broadened. "I realize that."

Sebastian handed over the keys to the Bronco. "Here come the ladies with Elizabeth. I'll go get the .38."

"I sure wish I didn't have to take it."

"You're taking it." He started back toward the house.

Nat turned to watch Jess come out toward the Bronco carrying Elizabeth. Heiresses, both of them. When he tried to be objective, he could see the evidence of privilege in Jess. Someone had probably coached her, from a young age, how to walk, how to hold her head, how to remain gracious when everything wasn't exactly as she'd like it to be.

He'd made what most people would think was a lot of money as a broker, but his bank balance was laughable compared to her father's. That hadn't been a factor before, partly because Jess had insisted she wanted no part of her father's wealth because she hated that life, and partly because he'd never intended their relationship to go this far.

Now it was too late to consider whether he was an appropriate person for Jess or not. Heiress or not, he wanted her. And increasingly, he wanted that little bundle in her arms. His heart ached looking at them together.

No one would doubt they were mother and daughter. Sunlight danced on Jess's red curls, setting them on fire, but the baby wore a little cap to protect her face from the sun, and her ringlets curled out from under it. They were a lighter shade than Jess's, but Elizabeth would grow up to have hair as fiery as her mother's. She'd be a pistol, too, like her mother. Nat's chest tightened as he realized he wanted to be there to see how Elizabeth turned out.

Jess would probably have her on skis before he could turn around. Elizabeth would be hotdogging down the slopes by the time she was seven. And eventually she'd discover makeup and earrings. And boys. The boys would be wild for her.

He imagined her gliding down the stairs dressed for her high-school prom, her date waiting with a corsage and a nervous smile. Who would be there to give that awestruck boy an intimidating stare and ask a few pointed questions about his intentions regarding the lovely Elizabeth?

He would. His heart expanded with hope as he allowed himself to dream of a future that included Jess and this baby he had helped create. His first reaction to hearing of her existence had been born of fear. But the longing he carried with him constantly now was born of love.

Matty walked beside Jess, and she was doing her best to look cheerful, but Nat doubted she felt cheerful at all. If this week accomplished what it was supposed to accomplish, Elizabeth would cease to be a regular resident of the Rocking D.

"Oh my God, we forgot Bruce," Matty said. She turned and raced back inside to search for the sock monkey.

"Ba-ba!" Elizabeth called after her.

"She's getting Bruce for you." Jess hoisted the baby a little higher on her shoulder. Then she glanced up at Nat, and squinted a little in the sunlight. "It's bright out here. I didn't want to wear my sunglasses because Elizabeth would just pull them off."

"Here." Impulsively, Nat took off his Stetson and put it on her head to shade her eyes. It was big on her and she looked adorable in it.

"Oh, I can't take your hat," she said.

"You can have anything of mine you want," he said quietly.

She held his gaze and her throat moved in a convulsive swallow.

"Here's Bruce," Matty called, hurrying out with the sock monkey in one hand.

Elizabeth twisted in Jess's arms and reached out both hands. "Ba-ba!"

"Thanks," Jess said as Elizabeth grabbed the monkey and began gnawing happily on its arm. "We would have been back here in no time if we'd forgotten Bruce."

"I'm glad I remembered." Matty started to reach a hand toward the baby, hesitated and shoved both hands in the pockets of the denim overalls she'd taken to wearing now that her jeans didn't fit. "Okay, now, you're sure you have enough diapers?"

"Sebastian and I loaded in enough boxes of those things to diaper quintuplets for a month," Nat said.

"And my cell phone? Did either of you remember to pick it up off the dining-room table?"

"I put it in my duffel," Jess said.

Matty rocked back on her heels and smiled brightly. "Well, then, I guess that's it. Where's Sebastian?"

"He'll be right out." Nat decided not to mention what Sebastian had gone into the house to get. Matty was nervous enough about letting them take Elizabeth out to the line shack without bringing up a danger that might not even exist anymore.

"I hope that wooden floor doesn't give her splinters when she crawls on it," Matty said. "Do you have some first-aid cream? I never thought of that. How about bandages and stuff like that?"

"Sebastian said everything's in that first-aid kit he keeps in the Bronco." Nat decided it was time to get this show on the road. He opened the vehicle's door. "Jess, why don't you put Elizabeth in her car seat?"

"Sure thing. Maybe you'd better take this back for now." She handed him his Stetson and started to put Elizabeth in the car. Then she paused and glanced over at Matty. "Want to hug her goodbye?"

Matty took a deep breath. "You know, I don't believe I will. I don't want to take a chance on upsetting her." She grimaced. "Or me." She turned toward Nat as if she didn't care to watch Elizabeth being strapped into the padded seat. "Now, if you have the slightest problem, I want you to call. Someone will be here all the time, and one of us can take a run out there in my truck."

"I appreciate that, Matty." This scene was starting to make Nat emotional, too. "I expect we'll have an uneventful week." He expected nothing of the kind. The events of this week would determine his entire future. He didn't know if he, Jess and Elizabeth could form a happy little unit, but this was as close to a trial run as he was going to get.

He was counting on having a crutch to get him through, and that crutch was making love to Jess. Nothing had seemed quite right ever since she'd proclaimed a ban on that activity, and Nat was sure once he could take her to bed again he'd feel more sure of himself in other areas of his life.

"She's in," Jess announced. Then she walked toward Matty. "Can you risk giving me a hug?"

"I can risk it." Matty squeezed Jess tight. "Take care of yourself and that precious little bundle."

"I will." Wiping at her eyes, Jess climbed into the Bronco. "You'd think we were leaving for a year, the way we're carrying on."

"We'll get better at this," Matty said. "We'll have to." She turned to Nat. "Watch out for them," she murmured.

"You bet." He gave Matty a quick hug and walked around the Bronco to the driver's side. Matty had moved back several feet, as if to give herself distance from the pain of watching them drive away. If Sebastian didn't show up soon, people were going to start blubbering, Nat decided. He got in and shoved the key in the ignition. He was about to lay on the horn when Sebastian appeared.

"I'm coming!" he called as he loped down the porch steps carrying a small toolbox.

Nat got out again and went around to open up the back. No way did he want that thing up front.

"Okay, I found you a lock for the clasp," Sebastian said as he tucked the toolbox in among the pile of cardboard boxes, collapsible baby furniture and bags of groceries. He handed Nat a small key. "It's locked now, but I wouldn't leave it that way if I were you." He lowered his voice. "Does Jess know how to handle one?"

"I don't know. I doubt it."

"Maybe you should teach her."

"I'm not sure about that. The noise would be bad for the baby."

"True," Sebastian agreed. "Well, at least you've got it."

"Yeah, thanks." Nat didn't want a gun, but if it would make Sebastian sleep better, maybe that was reason enough.

Jess turned in her seat. "What are you two doing back there?"

"Last-minute stuff," Nat said as he closed up the back again and held out his hand to Sebastian. "I'm going to do everything in my power to make this come out right for you."

Sebastian's grip was firm. "Don't worry about me. Make this come out right for that little kid in there and I'll be happy."

"I'll give it all I've got." With one final squeeze, he released Sebastian's hand, touched the brim of his hat in salute and walked back to the driver's side of the Bronco. In seconds he was in, seat belt fastened, engine switched on. As he put the vehicle in gear he looked up to see Sebastian standing with his arm around Matty.

Please don't let me be the reason for screwing up this good man's life, he prayed as he pulled out of the driveway, tooting the horn once as he headed down the rough dirt road that cut across the Rocking D property and ended at the old line shack on the edge of Sebastian's land. In the rearview mirror he saw Matty and Sebastian still standing there, their arms raised in farewell.

"If I knew nothing else about you," Jess said, her voice

choked with emotion, "I would know you were special because of your friends."

As THE BRONCO JOLTED over the bumpy road that was little more than a faint track across the countryside, Jessica didn't try to make conversation. Nat had his hands full avoiding rocks and chuckholes, and she wanted to make sure Elizabeth felt safe, so she kept talking to her throughout the ride.

She couldn't see Elizabeth's expression because the car seat faced toward the back, but at least the baby wasn't crying. During one smooth stretch in the road Jessica unlatched her seat belt and leaned over to find out what was going on with her daughter, who hadn't let out a peep so far. Elizabeth looked up at her, eyes wide, as if flabbergasted by the wild trip.

Jessica couldn't help grinning. "Having fun?" she asked.

"Ba-ba!" Elizabeth jiggled in her car seat with every bump in the road and she kept her monkey clutched tight in one fist, but she didn't look remotely ready to cry.

Settling back in her seat, Jessica glanced at Nat. "I think we have a thrill-seeker on our hands."

"There's a scary thought," Nat said as he steered around one large rut and jostled them all anyway when one wheel dipped into another hole in the road.

"At least she's apparently decided to trust us."

"You, not us. The jury's still out on whether she'll tolerate being alone with me. She never has. Come to think of it, she won't be on this trip, either."

"Why not?" Jessica thought this was the very time for that kind of experimentation. "I could take a little walk, so we could test it and see how she does."

"Not this week. This week I'm not letting you out of my sight."

A thrill of awareness arrowed through her stomach. "You mean because the guy still might be out there?"

He didn't take his eyes off the road. "That's right. Besides, it makes a damn fine excuse to keep you close to me." He gripped the wheel tighter as they hit another rocky spot in the road. "Very close."

As heat spiraled through her, she watched those hands control the steering wheel with strength and sureness. How she'd missed his touch. They'd barely begun to enjoy each other again when she'd insisted on ending the physical relationship.

She'd been right to insist on that until he'd had a chance to see Elizabeth and sort out how he felt about her. Unless Jessica was reading him all wrong, he'd made wonderful progress in that regard. Instead of being an obstacle between them, the baby seemed to be pulling them closer together.

And she was ready to be close to this man again. More than ready. Even the bouncing ride seemed to be stirring her up. A week of loving Nat. It had seemed like a long time when the plan had been suggested, but now she wondered if it would be long enough to satisfy the need that she'd built up over the past few days. She didn't want to waste a minute of their time together. She glanced at her watch. Nearly lunchtime. After lunch Elizabeth always took a nap....

"You're pretty quiet over there," Nat said. "Are you having second thoughts?"

She smiled to herself. "Yes."

"What?" He gave her a sharp glance. "So help me, Jess, if you're not planning on making love to me while we're out here, I don't think I can—"

"I'm having reservations about limiting ourselves to one week. Considering how much time I want to spend loving you, I wish we had at least two."

He let out a gusty sigh and shifted in his seat. "Oh, God. We should never have started this discussion."

Immediately she glanced down at the telltale bulge in his jeans, and her pulse began to race. "I probably don't have to ask, but did you bring—"

"Are you kidding? Those little foil packets were the first thing I packed. We have more of them than we do diapers." His jaw clenched. "I want you, Jess. Right here, right now."

The Bronco jolted them all as it hit a large rock in the road.

She was breathing fast, and it had nothing to do with the rough ride. "Here and now isn't what you'd call optimum," she said.

"I'm aware of that."

"How much longer before we get there?"

He glanced at her, his gaze hot enough to melt steel. "An eternity."

CHAPTER SEVENTEEN

JESSICA HAD PREPARED herself for a primitive setting, not that she much cared where she was as long as she could be alone with Nat and Elizabeth. From the outside, the line shack looked about as she'd expected, the exterior weathered to a dull gray and broken up with square windows without curtains. A corrugated tin roof covered with pine needles, leaves and fallen branches topped the structure. The forest debris on the roof almost made it look thatched.

But the shack, humble though it was, sat within a grove of aspens. With their gleaming white trunks fountaining upward to a burst of golden leaves, they were all the decoration the little place needed to make it spectacular.

"It's beautiful," she said as Nat parked the Bronco near the front door.

"Beautiful?" Nat gave her a puzzled glance. "You don't have to pretend it's the Taj Mahal for my sake, Jess. I know you're used to much better."

She stared at him in shock. "Where did that come from?" In their entire relationship he'd never once apologized for their accommodations, and not all of them had been five-star, by any means.

"Well, after all, you are an heiress, and—"

"Nat Grady, have I ever, in all the time you've known me, put any importance in that? In fact, haven't I done my level best to escape that label?"

Elizabeth began to chortle in the back seat as if she wanted to join in the conversation.

"Well, yes," Nat said. "But you can't change the fact that you are connected to Russell P. Franklin."

"As little as possible." She didn't really want to talk about this.

Elizabeth grew louder.

"Are you planning to keep Elizabeth a secret forever?" Nat asked.

It was a fair question if he was considering making a life with her. She looked over at him. "No, I guess not. No matter how I feel about my parents and their power, that wouldn't be right, for Elizabeth or them. I've been thinking about my mother lately," she admitted. "Under better circumstances, I'm sure she'd love the idea of being a granny."

Elizabeth started rocking in the car seat in time to her increasingly demanding babble.

Unsnapping her seat belt, Jessica started to get out of the car so she could tend to the baby. "We should get her inside."

Nat didn't move. "You mean better circumstances, as in a better guy?" he said softly.

She turned to him, saw the naked uncertainty in his eyes and could have kicked herself for her choice of words. Ignoring Elizabeth's agitation for the moment, she reached out and cradled his face in both hands "I have the best guy," she said. "I wasn't talking about you. I was talking about this whole mess with the stalker. I would be proud to tell my parents you're the father of my daughter." *I would be proud to tell them that you were my husband, too.* But she didn't say that. They needed to take care of Elizabeth before they had that kind of discussion.

He covered her hands with his as he gazed into her eyes. "Jess, I never expect to make the kind of money that your father—"

"Nat, shut up," she said gently. Leaning forward, she kissed him. She'd only meant to silence him and stop this ridiculous discussion, but the minute her lips touched his, the need between them exploded.

With a groan he slid his hands around to cup the back of her head and plunged his tongue inside her mouth. In no time they were straining to get to each other over the console between the seats, their breathing labored as their mouths sought deep and deeper access.

"Da-da!" Elizabeth yelled at the top of her lungs.

Jessica and Nat drew back from each other immediately, and she was sure her expression of guilt mirrored his. "The baby," they said together.

"My God, Jess." Nat looked down at his hands as if they didn't belong to him, as if he had no idea they'd already unfastened the first button of her blouse. He pulled away as if he'd touched something hot.

She struggled for breath and fastened her blouse. "We'll...have to be more careful."

"I forgot everything. I was ready to—"

"I know." Heart pounding, Jessica got out of the Bronco on shaky legs.

"If you'll take her out of the car seat," he said, "I'll unlock the place and turn on the security system."

"Right." Spurred by remorse, she had Elizabeth out of the car seat in record time. Silly though it might be, she was glad Elizabeth's seat faced backward and the baby hadn't seen that sizzling, highly sexual kiss. As if an eight-month-old would know what was going on.

Yet she wondered how the interior of the cabin was arranged and whether she and Nat would have any privacy whatsoever. She discovered that she craved privacy, considering some of the uninhibited activities she had in mind.

"Sorry to ignore you like that, sweetheart," she crooned breathlessly to the baby. "Mommy got a little involved with...with Daddy." She liked the sound of that. But Mommy and Daddy would have to exercise a little more discipline from now on. Maybe once they'd taken the edge off their hunger, they wouldn't be so ravenous for each other.

As she stepped through the door of the cabin, the first thing she saw was a mason jar full of yellow and white daisies on a wooden table flanked by two chairs. The second thing she saw was a double bed with the covers turned back, snowy pillows plumped, as if someone didn't want to waste any time when an opportunity arose to climb into that bed. The third thing she noticed was the wooden hinged screen positioned at the foot of the bed. Nat had been thinking about privacy, too. Sensuous warmth poured through her.

Glancing in his direction, she found him watching her with a tense expression. She was so touched and aroused by his careful preparations that she wasn't sure she'd be able to speak. But obviously she needed to say something. "The flowers—" She paused to clear her throat. "The flowers are very nice."

"Wish I could say I picked them in the woods, but the time of year's wrong. I had to buy them in town. I realize the vase isn't—"

"Nat, if you say one more word of apology about this sweet little cabin, I'll—well, I'm not sure what I'll do, but you won't like it."

He looked immensely relieved. "Then the place is okay?"

"More than okay. I can't think of anyplace in the world I'd rather be, or any two people I'd rather be with."

"Me neither." He met her gaze and gradually a slow smile appeared as the anxiety in his blue eyes was replaced by a steady flame of eagerness.

Her breath caught at the beauty of this man. And for the next week, he was all hers. Well, hers and Elizabeth's.

As if reminding her of that fact, the baby began to struggle, wanting down.

Jessica loved knowing her daughter was becoming more

mobile. She got a kick out of watching her crawl and could hardly wait until she walked. "If you'll close the door," she said, "I'll put her down and let her explore the room a little."

Nat looked anxious again. "Are you sure it's safe? I didn't think about her crawling around on it until Matty said something about splinters."

Jessica surveyed the wooden floor and decided it looked smooth enough to her. The lack of throw rugs might even be a plus. "She'll be fine." She crouched down in preparation for lowering a wiggling Elizabeth to the floor.

"Wait, is it clean enough? I swept it, but there's no vacuum cleaner out here, so I'm sure I didn't get every little bit. Let me get her playpen. We can put her in there."

She smiled indulgently at him. "Not for a solid week, Nat. She'd go crazy, and so would we. No, she needs to get down. Would you please close the door? Eventually I'll let her explore outside, too, but—"

"Outside?"

Amazed by his scandalized tone, she glanced up. "Sure. Why not?"

"She could pick up anything. Bugs, dirty rocks, *snakes.*" He shuddered.

Jessica laughed. "I wouldn't turn her lose and forget about her. I'd follow her every minute and make sure she didn't put anything in her mouth that would make her choke. You can help me follow her every minute if it makes you feel better. She's a good crawler, but I doubt she could outrun us."

"I don't care. The idea of putting that sweet little baby down in the dirt doesn't sit right with me."

She excused his attitude, considering he was so inexperienced. No doubt in a day or so of being around Elizabeth he'd get over it, but he was making her a little nervous. He sounded far too much like her father. She wouldn't tolerate anyone smothering her daughter the way she'd been smothered, even if that person happened to be the sexiest man on the planet.

"Let's start with the cabin, and we'll worry about outside later," she said.

"Okay." Nat walked over and closed the door.

Jess put Elizabeth on the floor, and then sat down beside her in order to take off the baby's cap. "There you go, honey-bunch. Free at last."

Immediately Elizabeth rocked forward onto her hands, and with a cry of glee started off toward the potbelly stove.

"Oh, God," Nat said. "We won't be able to use the stove. She might burn herself."

"Sure we can use the stove. When it's hot, we'll make sure she doesn't get close to it." Jessica kept her eye on Elizabeth as the baby bypassed the stove and went on to the table, where she crawled underneath and sat down, looking pleased with herself.

Jessica chuckled. Elizabeth was obviously mimicking Sebastian and Matty's dogs, who both loved to lie under the dining-room table. "Are you pretending you're a doggy?" she asked.

"Ga!" Elizabeth said, giving Jessica a toothy grin.

"Good girl." Still smiling, Jessica looked up at Nat and was surprised at his frown. "What's wrong?"

"I really didn't expect her to crawl around this place," he said.

"What did you suppose she'd do?"

"I guess I thought we'd carry her, or put her in the playpen, or in that backpack thing that Sebastian uses all the time."

"She's really too old to be confined that way for any long period." Trying to hold on to her patience, Jessica returned her attention to Elizabeth as the baby started crawling toward the bed.

"Then maybe we shouldn't have brought her out here."

Her stomach twisted. "Maybe not, if you're going to be like a mother hen about it."

"I just—Elizabeth, no!" He hurried over and snatched her up. "Give me that!"

Elizabeth started to howl.

Jess was on her feet in an instant. "What? What did she get?"

"Well, it's a long piece of wild grass, but it could have been anything!"

"Give her to me."

He seemed glad to get rid of the baby, and Jessica carried her over to the window. "It's okay, sweetie." She rocked Elizabeth and kissed her wet cheeks. "No problem. Easy does it, little girl. Look! Look out the window! See the birdie? Look at that. A pretty little bird has come to say hello to Elizabeth. Can you say hello?"

"Ba," Elizabeth said, snuffling. Then she took a deep breath and swiveled in Jessica's arms to look at Nat.

Jessica followed the direction of the baby's gaze, and Nat's lost expression ripped at her heart. "She's fine," she said.

He shook his head. "I can't do this, Jess. I'm no good at it."

"Oh, for heaven's sake." Still holding Elizabeth, she walked over to him. She could feel Elizabeth shrink away a little, which was all the more reason to erase the last incident from the baby's memory.

"She hates me," Nat said.

"No, she doesn't. You scared her a little. Talk to her."

"And say what?"

"That she's the prettiest baby in the world. You could give her that piece of grass, too."

"But it's been under the bed!"

"It won't hurt her. Deer eat it all the time."

Nat looked unhappy about it, but he held out the long blade of grass. "Is this what you wanted, Elizabeth?"

"Ga!" She reached for it.

"Tickle her nose with it," Jessica suggested.

"Put it on her face?"

"Yes. Play with her. Remember how much she loved peekaboo. Playing with her is important."

He took a deep breath. "Okay. Hey, Elizabeth, you like this?" He wiggled the tip of the grass against her nose.

The baby laughed with delight.

"You do, huh?" Nat repeated the motion and earned himself another baby giggle. "I like the way she laughs," he said. "It makes her nose sort of wrinkle."

"I know." The tension in Jessica's stomach eased as Nat continued to play the tickling game. Had she thought everything would go smoothly once the three of them were together? If so, she was a foolish woman. She and Nat had never had the basic discussions that future parents needed to have about parenting styles and expectations.

She'd had nine months to read up on the subject of child rearing while she formed her ideas of what kind of mother she wanted to be. Although she didn't want Elizabeth to repeat her own childhood, there had been positives in it, including the certainty that she was loved. Nat had no yardstick for measuring how a loving parent should act.

"It's nearly lunchtime," she said at last. "If you'll get her high chair out of the Bronco and set it up, I'll feed her."

"Okay." He turned away and Elizabeth yelled in protest. He turned back, the beginnings of a smile on his face. "She doesn't want me to leave," he said with some surprise.

"No, she doesn't." Jessica found herself smiling, too. "But she might tolerate it if you give her that grass."

He glanced at the long blade of grass in his hand. "I guess I have to, don't I?"

"Trust me, it won't hurt her. I'll monitor the situation while you're gone."

Reluctantly he handed the grass to Elizabeth, who waved

it and chortled with happiness. When she put it in her mouth, he winced. "I hate that."

"I know. Don't worry, I'll make sure she doesn't choke. She'll be fine."

"She has to be." He looked into her eyes. "Because if anything happened to either of you, my life would be over."

NAT UNLOADED the Bronco and set up the high chair first so Jess could feed the baby. While she was doing that, he brought everything else in and set up the portable crib and the playpen, the one Jess had already informed him they wouldn't be using much.

Now that he thought about it, Elizabeth had crawled around the ranch house quite a bit, but Matty and Sebastian kept the place really clean. And besides, at that point he hadn't assumed the responsibility for what happened to Elizabeth when she was on the floor, because there were always several people around who were ready and willing to do that.

He'd been so hell-bent on getting out here so he could make love to Jess that he hadn't fully realized how the responsibility of the baby would settle on him with the weight of an elephant. When he'd contemplated this week, he'd thought his major worry would be whether Jess's stalker would show up. Now he looked around at the small cabin and saw a million dangers to Elizabeth, none of them having to do with some weirdo on the loose.

Matty had packed sandwiches for their first meal, so once he had the baby furniture up, he took Jess's suggestion to stop for lunch while Elizabeth was still awake. He hadn't missed Jess's meaning when she'd made that suggestion, either. Once that baby went down for her afternoon nap, he and Jess didn't want to waste time with lunch.

How he needed that woman. He couldn't remember feeling this raw and vulnerable in his life, and he ached to take refuge in Jess's arms. But the ache deep inside wasn't only about taking. Now that he understood more of what Jess had been through because of him, he desperately wanted to shower her with all the pleasure he was capable of giving.

He barely tasted his lunch. He was too preoccupied with Jess—the moist invitation of her mouth, the gentle movement of her breasts under her shirt, the snug fit of her jeans when she leaned over to pick up the baby. His groin tightened in response to the flash in her brown eyes and the catch in her voice when she caught him looking.

While she used the portable crib as a changing table and got Elizabeth ready for her nap, he washed up the lunch dishes. He could only see the top of her head above the folding wooden screen he'd set up between the crib and the double bed so they'd have some privacy, and he made a mental note to take the screen away when they didn't actually need it. He hungered for the sight of her.

"I haven't seen anything that looks like an alarm system," she said as she continued to dress the baby for her nap. "Where is it?"

"There's a monitoring screen up in the rafters in each corner of the cabin," he said.

She glanced around. "Wow. I didn't even notice them."

"Seth likes to make his systems unobtrusive," Nat said. "The cameras are on the roof, camouflaged with all those leaves and pine branches. If someone doesn't know a security system exists, they won't try to dismantle it."

"Did Sebastian give you a gun before we left this morning?"

He paused in the act of wiping a dish. "Yes. It's in the green metal box I put on the top shelf. Does it bother you to have it there?"

"It bothers me to have to do any of this. I assume you know how to shoot it?"

"If necessary."

"That's good, I guess."

"I guess."

She murmured something to Elizabeth and began singing to the baby.

He couldn't see her anymore and decided she must be leaning over the crib, trying to soothe Elizabeth to sleep.

She'd accepted the presence of the gun better than he'd thought she would. He remembered the last time he'd held one. It was this same gun, and the guys had been joking around about who was a better shot one summer day at the Rocking D. Sebastian had set up a few beer cans on a fence and everybody had taken some shots except Nat. He hadn't wanted to touch the thing.

Finally, the teasing had become so bad he'd given in. He'd told himself he was over the revulsion he felt at holding a gun, but apparently he hadn't been. He'd nailed the cans—*bing, bing, bing.* It seemed all the hours of practice as a kid had stuck with him. Then he'd put down the gun and walked around to the back of the barn so he could throw up.

His friends had thought he had a case of stomach flu, and he'd let them think that. He had no interest in telling them that when he was thirteen, his father had made him shoot a horse. Sure, the horse had turned mean, but only because his father had regularly beat him the same way he'd beaten Nat. When the animal had kicked Nat and broken his arm, Hank Grady had flown into a rage and forced Nat to shoot that poor horse. Nat hadn't fired a gun since.

Jess was the first person who had made all those bad memories fade. Until he'd left her seventeen months ago, he hadn't appreciated the unique brand of magic she'd brought to his life. Loving her healed him. And God, did he need healing now.

She hadn't reappeared from behind the screen, but he realized that her soft lullaby had ended. Maybe Elizabeth was finally drifting off to sleep. Maybe, at long last, he was going to make love to Jess again.

He stopped working on the dishes and gazed at the screen. The silence was encouraging. Very encouraging. At the thought of what was to come, moisture pooled in his mouth. He swallowed and took a deep breath.

Then her head reappeared above the screen, and she turned toward him with a smile. Oh, such a smile. He'd forgotten how seductive she could be when she put her mind to it.

"She's asleep?" he murmured.

Jess nodded.

Nat tossed down the dish towel. Holding her dark gaze, he started toward the bed, unbuttoning his shirt as he went. Now. Right now.

Then she mouthed the word *wait*.

He stopped and lifted his eyebrows in question. *Wait* wasn't the word he wanted to hear at the moment. *Yes* was more like it.

But she'd turned around again, and he wondered if Elizabeth still had some settling down to do. Okay, he'd wait, even if he was frustrated enough to chew a handful of Boone's horseshoeing nails. Once he started on this program, he wouldn't be able to stop, even if Elizabeth woke up again. So it would be best for all concerned if the baby was fast asleep.

Then Jess turned to look at him again and her cheeks were pink. "Okay," she whispered, and came around the screen.

He nearly lost it.

Her shirt and jeans were gone. In their place was an outfit that belonged in a skin flick. He struggled for breath as she walked toward him. She had fantastic legs. Just looking at her bare legs almost made him climax. This presentation of hers was overkill, but he wasn't complaining. He didn't know where or when she'd come up with the black lace number, but it would live in his fantasies forever.

The sheer, tight material undulated with each step she

took toward him. The top cupped her breasts and pushed them up in a way that made his eyes glaze with lust. A series of ties down the front begged to be undone. He loved it, loved her for going to the trouble of making this an unbelievable moment.

"Gwen and I made a fast trip to Colorado Springs," she said, a trace of shyness in her tone. "Do you like it?"

"Oh, yeah," he said, his voice hoarse. "Very, very much. And after all that effort, I hope you won't be offended when I strip it right off."

CHAPTER EIGHTEEN

NAT REALLY MEANT to undo each of the ties so as not to rip anything on her new outfit, but once he got the first few open and filled his hands with her breasts, his control deserted him. He laid her across the width of the bed without much fanfare or finesse, his mouth hot and seeking against her plump breasts. The first taste of her nipple drove him out of his head.

Dizzy from the wild-strawberry feel of her tight nipple rolling against his tongue, her soft whimpers and the urgent way she clutched his head, he became frantic to have more of her. Ties ripped from their moorings as he yanked the sheer lace down to her knees so he could touch...there, where her waist nipped in and there, where her belly heaved, and God, yes, bury his fingers there, where she was already soaking wet. Gasping, she arched away from the bed.

So that's how it was. With savage joy he stroked her quickly to her first climax. She reached blindly for a pillow, and he had the presence of mind to grab it and hand it to her so she could put it over her mouth and scream into it. Now was not the time to be waking babies. Not when he needed to seek the source of her heat with a tongue that thirsted for the gush of her second climax.

Ah, she was so wild for him that she abandoned her inhibitions and spread her thighs as he slid down, kissing a path from her breasts to her belly, tonguing his way over that sweet terrain to her wellspring of precious, life-giving nectar. He felt energy pour into him as he feasted on her sweetness and she quivered in his arms.

He knew her, knew her secrets, her rhythm, her aching need. He was born for this, to make this woman quake and cry out his name. His name. Nothing he'd ever done in his whole sorry life gave him this sense of rightness. Only loving Jess.

She tensed, her body trembling violently as her hips rose again. As she gulped for breath, she gasped out a plea, wanting more. And he knew that she needed that, too. As much as he had to sink into her to become complete, she couldn't be complete until he had thrust deep and made that ultimate connection.

He didn't bother to undress. There wasn't time. The pressure was too great. He unbuckled his belt, opened his fly and put on the condom. Then he lifted her, moving her higher on the bed so he had room for his knees.

Her head was nearly off the other side, and he cradled it in both hands to steady her. Her silky hair flowed through his fingers. Then, looking into her eyes, he pushed home.

She moaned and wrapped her legs around his. "Tighter," she whispered.

He moved another notch closer to her center and could feel the pulsing begin. "Don't shut me out again," he murmured.

"No." She rose to meet his thrusts.

His breathing grew ragged. "I have to make love to you."

"Yes."

"It's…everything." He plunged into her again and again. And it seemed as if each time he went deeper, and deeper still.

"Yes. Oh, *yes*."

He held her gaze. "Everything," he gasped, and clenched his jaw against the cry of release that rose from his throat as he exploded within her.

WHETHER BECAUSE of the strange surroundings or the activity from the nearby bed, Elizabeth took a very short nap that day. Jessica borrowed Nat's shirt to have something to put on when she went to get the baby, who sounded as if she might start fussing if nobody paid any attention to her.

Jessica didn't want any more tears from Elizabeth today if they could be avoided. Tears seemed to make Nat think he'd done something wrong, and Jessica wanted him to build on a feeling of success.

"Put something warm on her," Nat called from the other side of the screen. "Let's get out the baby carrier and take a walk."

"You think that'll be okay?"

Nat came around the screen zipping up his pants. "We can set the alarm before we leave, and we won't go far. We'll keep our eyes open. I don't know about you, but I don't want to be pinned down here to the point that we feel like rats in a cage."

"Neither do I. As I'm sure you can imagine." She flashed him a smile and returned to diapering Elizabeth.

"You look good in my shirt."

"I like wearing it," she said. "It has your scent."

"So?"

"It gets me hot. Pheromones, you know."

"I've heard of those little devils. I vote that you just wear my shirt today and keep that pheromone thing going. I'll go grab another shirt."

"All right." She couldn't ever remember wearing anything of his before. It was one more example of how the barriers were coming down between them. Isolating themselves in this little cabin had been a brilliant idea.

He started to walk away, then turned around and came back. "You know, this pheromone business works both ways. I like breathing in your scent, too."

"Oh, yeah?" She finished snapping up Elizabeth's overalls and glanced up with a grin. "Does that mean you'd like to wear that black lace number for the rest of the day?"

"Nah. I don't have the build for it." He moved in close beside her. "I'll have to try something else."

"Such as?"

He put a hand around her waist. "Hold still for a minute. I have an idea."

"I can't imagine what you're up to." She chuckled as she looked into his eyes. She didn't anticipate his next move at all. When he slid his free hand under the shirt and down between her legs, she gasped. "Nat!" She tried to pull away. "This isn't the time for—"

"Hold still," he whispered. "This'll only take a second." And he slipped two fingers inside her.

Secretly thrilled at his audacity, she nevertheless acted shocked. Pretending indignation made the caress even more arousing. "Nat, for heaven's sake. The baby—"

"Has no idea what's going on. Mmm. That should do it." He eased his hand out from between her thighs.

She sighed with disappointment. Not that she really expected him to continue while they were standing here by the crib, but he'd left her throbbing and ready. "Do what?" she asked, her voice unsteady.

He held his damp fingers under her nose. "Pheromones," he said. "My share. This should hold me until the munchkin goes to sleep tonight." And he rubbed his fingers across his upper lip.

She groaned as desire pounded through her. "We'd better get dressed and go on that walk." She was mesmerized by the glow of passion in his eyes. "Now."

"Yep." He cupped her face gently in one hand and brushed a kiss over her lips. "Besides," he murmured, "it seems to me Matty once said that being out in the fresh air helps a kid sleep better. And I want that little girl to sleep like a log tonight." He brushed her lips one last time. "Because I don't plan to sleep at all."

Neither did Jessica. As much as she'd loved the urgency of their lovemaking this afternoon, she wanted a long, lazy session in bed with Nat. She'd like it right now.

But once they'd dressed and stepped out into the crisp afternoon, she decided that if she couldn't be in bed loving Nat, this was a good second choice. Elizabeth rode happily in the carrier strapped to Nat's back as they followed a path paved with golden aspen leaves.

"How's your sixth sense working?" Nat asked.

"I don't think he's here," Jessica said. "Do you suppose that you three men really scared him off when you rode out after him that morning?"

"That would be nice. Sebastian doesn't think so, but the guy's so weird that anything's possible."

Looking up through the shimmering leaves of the aspens to the cornflower sky as she walked hand in hand with Nat, Jessica believed anything was possible. Anything at all.

The crunch of leaves underfoot and the musty scent of the dry forest floor reminded her of another October day two years earlier. "Remember the time I talked you into raking up a pile of autumn leaves and playing in them with me?"

"I remember everything about you, Jess. I've had seventeen months to concentrate on those memories. They're sorted and cataloged, and there's not a cobweb on a single one."

She glanced at him. "What a beautiful thing to say."

He met her gaze. "What a beautiful person to say it to." He smiled and squeezed her hand before turning his attention back to the path. "That last picture you gave me for the collection was a doozy, by the way. I'm sorry about tearing those little ties off. Maybe you can fix them."

"I probably could." Currents of electricity seemed to be running between their joined hands. "You'd like a repeat performance?"

He laughed. "You even have to ask? Except the next

time, you'd better tie those things looser. Or maybe not tie them at all. A man tends to run out of patience when he has an erection stiffer than a tire iron.''

With a comment like that, she felt almost invited to look at the crotch of his jeans, and sure enough, a telltale bulge was beginning to show. ''How's your patience right now?'' she teased.

''Being tested,'' he said, not looking at her. ''I strongly suggest we talk about something else.''

The sweet certainty of being wanted made her laugh with delight, and the sound of her laughter brought on giggles from Elizabeth. If life could get any more perfect than this, Jessica thought, she couldn't imagine how.

In consideration for Nat's comfort, she switched the conversation to her interest in wildcrafting herbs. Since he'd been gone, she'd taken a couple of classes and thought she might even turn the interest into a career. Because Nat was so encouraging, she allowed herself to imagine that he was picturing a future in which he ran a ranch for abandoned children and she roamed the nearby countryside in search of wild herbs.

It wasn't a difficult fantasy to build, considering the hum of sensual excitement between them, no matter what they were discussing. Throughout the afternoon's walk, and during the evening as they prepared supper and fed Elizabeth, every accidental touch sizzled and every deliberate one nearly destroyed their control.

And Jessica discovered an amazing thing. Having the baby around definitely limited their freedom to make love at every opportunity. Frustration levels were at an all-time high for both of them. But she hadn't thought to value that frustration.

During the year she and Nat had been seeing each other, on the weekends they'd spent together, they'd been free to indulge themselves sexually whenever they chose. Looking back on that time, she realized that they'd begun to take their physical relationship for granted.

With Elizabeth on the scene, for the first time they enjoyed the thrill of anticipation. Jessica hadn't understood what a powerful aphrodisiac that could be.

She suspected Nat had figured it out, too, because he didn't put any pressure on her to rush either dinner or Elizabeth's bedtime preparations. He patiently waited until Elizabeth had finished all the finger food on her tray. When she was ready to be changed, he asked to be taught the diapering process, which meant the job took twice as long. Then they both played peekaboo with the baby while taking off her clothes and getting her into her sleeper.

Throughout the activities, Jessica was constantly aware of Nat—his hand reaching for a dish at the same time she did, his hip brushing hers as they stood side by side at the crib, his eyes on her while she worked. She noticed every glance and exactly where it was focused. Sometimes he'd meet her gaze, but often he'd direct his attention elsewhere on her body, with heated results. A burning look could make her mouth tingle, her nipples tighten, her belly quiver.

Fortunately she had the same power. She could stare at his mouth until his breathing quickened and his blue eyes darkened. If her gaze wandered below his belt, she could watch the imprint of his erection become more distinct the longer she concentrated on that area. Once she even drew a soft groan from him.

Until the moment they finally put Elizabeth in her crib for the night, they engaged in a silent, tension-laced duel that was the most exciting foreplay Jessica had ever experienced.

But by the time she laid the baby down on her tummy and began singing her to sleep, Jessica was ready for the waiting to be over. They'd dimmed the lights in the cabin so the baby would sleep—but they'd left one on beside the double bed so they could see each other when they made love.

Nat leaned against the wall, arms folded, watching Jessica rub Elizabeth's back and sing to her. In order to do the various evening chores, he'd rolled the sleeves of his western shirt back over his forearms.

There was something incredibly sexy about a man with his sleeves rolled up, Jessica thought. He looked ready for action. And a little action was exactly what she had in mind.

Of course, in her current frame of mind, every part of Nat, from his ears to his toes, had taken on erotic meaning. Still, she especially liked admiring the strength of his arms. She visually traced the pattern of russet hair and imagined running her tongue along the groove that formed between muscle and bone when he flexed his wrist. Then she stared with lust at the supple length of his fingers as they curved around his biceps. When she finally looked into his eyes, she nearly lost her place in the familiar lullaby. The message in that intense blue gaze was unmistakable.

With a faint smile, he looked over at the sleeping baby. Then his glance returned to Jessica. With blatant intent he allowed it to rove over her body, lingering at all the places he knew how to awaken. She wondered if any part of her would sleep tonight.

Elizabeth gave a little sigh and her body relaxed under Jessica's hand. Jessica muted the lullaby and lightened her touch. All the while, she listened to Elizabeth's breathing to gauge when she was truly asleep. At last she was. Slowly Jessica lifted her hand and stepped back. In the silence, she could hear Nat's indrawn breath.

She looked up and found that he'd pushed himself away from the wall and now stood with his arms at his sides, waiting for her. Heart pounding and body already moistening with need, she held his gaze as she walked toward him.

He took her hand and led her around the screen. As they

stood beside the bed, he was trembling. With great restraint he drew her slowly into his arms and looked deep into her eyes. His erection pressed against her. "I've never wanted you like this," he whispered. "I'm coming apart inside."

"We have to be quiet at first," she murmured. "Just in case."

"I'll try." With shaking hands he cupped her face in both hands, tipped her head back and lowered his mouth to hers. His kiss was furnace-hot and more insistent than she ever remembered. His tongue probed boldly as he slipped his thumbs to the corners of her mouth and nudged her mouth wider.

He kissed her as if he couldn't get close enough, deep enough. She wrapped her arms around his waist and fit his denim-covered erection between her thighs, holding him tight against her. They were both breathing so raggedly that she wondered if their gasps alone would wake the baby.

His hands slipped from her face to the top snap of the shirt she'd borrowed from him. She wore no bra underneath, and she knew that once he began to caress her breasts, she'd lose her mind.

But this time she was determined to give as good as she got. This time she would be in charge. The night was long and she could afford to be generous. As he worked his way down the snaps, she reached for his belt buckle.

Before he finished with the snaps, she'd unfastened his belt. By the time he pushed the shirt over her shoulders, she'd opened the button on his jeans and unzipped his fly. He moaned softly against her mouth.

The prospect of what she planned to do, and how it would no doubt affect him, made her pulse race. Pushing both jeans and underwear down, she discovered that he was, in his words, stiff as a tire iron.

Drawing back from his kiss, she guided him down to sit on the edge of the bed before kneeling in front of him.

"Jess—"

"Shh." She kissed him quickly before shrugging out of the borrowed shirt. The movement jiggled her breasts, but when he reached for them she caught his wrists. "Not yet," she murmured. "Take off your shirt. I'll handle the rest."

Then she tortured him by making him watch her, topless, taking off his boots. She knew the movement of her unfettered breasts excited him. He'd once joked that he wished skiing wasn't so cold a sport, because he'd love to watch her do it topless.

If his harsh breathing was any indication, he was pretty darned excited now. So excited that he'd left the job of taking off his shirt half done. Apparently, after unsnapping it, he'd become so absorbed in watching her that he'd forgotten what he'd been instructed to do.

"Your shirt," she reminded him with a smile. Her skin flushed with anticipation.

She waited until he had it off and then she took a moment to admire his work-sculpted physique. With his well-developed muscles and hair a bit too long to be fashionable, he looked far more like a calendar model than a businessman. She wanted him now, sooner than now.

But instead she took her own sweet time removing his jeans, making sure she brushed her nipples against his thighs, his knees and his calves as she worked. Last of all, she pulled off his socks, leaning down so her breasts tickled the tops of his feet.

When next she glanced at him, each fist was clenched around a section of blanket and his eyes were squeezed shut. As she'd hoped, he was in ecstatic agony. Now for her final gift.

She moved between his legs, nudging his sensitive inner thighs with her breasts. In the process she gave thanks for not being small in that department. For what she had in mind, she needed everything she had.

He opened his eyes to gaze down at her. "You're destroying me," he whispered.

She merely smiled and leaned forward to place a wet kiss on the top of his rigid penis.

He gasped. "Jess, you'd better not—"

"Shh," she said again. "Give me your hands."

Quivering, he held them out, as if he'd become her slave. She cupped them against the sides of her breasts and showed him that if he pressed gently, he would capture the shaft of his penis in that soft, silken valley. As he complied, he groaned and closed his eyes. His fingers began an involuntary kneading motion as he held her breasts snug against his erection.

She moved gently up and down, treating him to slow, tantalizing friction. "Open your eyes," she whispered. "And watch."

When he opened his eyes, they were glazed with pleasure. He looked down as he kept up the sensuous rhythm, and his breath rasped in his throat. "Jess. Oh, Jess, I'm going to—"

"I know." She watched his face, saw the muscles work in his jaw, knew he was close. She increased the tempo.

He made a noise low in his throat.

"I want you to," she murmured. "Come for me, Nat."

He began to quake with reaction.

When she knew he was nearly there, she leaned over and slid her lips over the smooth tip. With a cry held behind clenched teeth, he came. Flushed and triumphant, she swallowed all that he had to give.

NAT WISHED he could write poetry. Then he would write a poem dedicated to Jessica's breasts. After treating him to one of the most fantastic experiences of his life, she'd shucked off the rest of her clothes and they'd crawled under the covers to cuddle.

And it was a world-class cuddle as he nestled his cheek against one of her deserving-of-a-poem breasts and cupped his hand around the other. Besides the benefit of the pillowy warmth supporting his head, he could hear the steady beat of her heart and feel the rise and fall of her chest with each breath. As if all that wasn't enough, she began stroking her fingers through his hair.

Elizabeth was still asleep, and he figured they could talk now without worrying so much about waking her up. Sebastian had lectured him about that before he left. *Once she's fast asleep, you can pretty much enjoy yourselves, so long as you don't start yelling or anything.* Nat remembered Sebastian presenting this advice with total seriousness, and the memory made him smile. He'd wanted to yell during that last episode, but he'd managed to control himself, God knows how.

He sighed happily and snuggled closer. "You just keep piling memories on top of memories, Jess," he said.

"I can't think of a better plan."

"That's because there isn't one." He caught her nipple between his thumb and forefinger and stroked gently, making it hard. "I love watching this happen." He lifted his head and looked into her eyes, seeing the passion flare as he plucked her taut nipple in a slow rhythm. "I love watching you get hot."

"Do you now?"

He smiled. Her voice had taken on that breathy quality that told him exactly what she was thinking about. But he liked to hear her say it. He cupped her breast and swirled his tongue around her nipple to shake up the rhythm of her breathing. It worked. Then he looked into her eyes as he kneaded her breast. "Tell me what you'd like."

She ran a tongue over her lower lip in a way that drove him crazy. "World peace."

"I'm working on that, smarty-pants. Anything else?"

"Come closer and I'll whisper it in your ear, big boy."

He edged up and took that sassy mouth in a kiss that left her gasping. "Anyone who did what you just did to me can say it to my face," he murmured.

And she did. Explicitly. Using good old-fashioned An-
glo-Saxon words to describe exactly what she wanted him
to do to her. His blood roared in his ears and he grew
instantly hard again.

Now his breathing wasn't so steady, either. "I think I
can manage that," he said.

And manage it he did. He loved her hard, repeating the
earthy words she'd used and getting her to say them again
as he drove into her. He loved to watch her mouth when
she spoke that way, knowing she'd never use that language
anywhere else but here, in this bed, with him.

Thanks to her wonderful gift at the start of their evening
together, he had staying power this time. He could exper-
iment with different positions, looking for ways to give her
a climax while holding himself in check. Rolling to his
back, he took her with him and urged her to ride him until
she lost control. Then he took her from behind and brought
her to another explosion.

The room was cool, but they were slick with sweat by
the time he stretched her out on her back and savored his
old-fashioned favorite. The other positions were great for
erotic adventure, and he enjoyed them all. But this one, he
thought as he slid deep inside her and gazed into her eyes,
was for making love.

He laced his fingers through hers in the gesture he
thought of as theirs alone. Palm to palm, bodies joined, eyes
locked. All was right with his world.

Slowly he eased back and thrust forward again. "When
I'm here inside you, I have everything I need," he murmured. "Nothing else matters."

Tears shimmered in her eyes. "I'm glad."

He continued the slow, sensuous rhythm. "But I'm human, and sometimes I forget what's important to me.
Who's important to me. But then I sink into you and I know
all I need to know."

She gazed up at him, her face luminous with happiness.

He cursed himself for ever giving her a moment's doubt. "I love you, Jess. I always have. I always will."

"Oh, Nat." Her words trembled. "I love you, too."

He tightened his grip on her fingers, increasing the pace. "We can't let each other go." He felt her first contraction. This time he would be with her.

"We won't."

"Then hold on to me, Jess." He thrust harder and let himself explode at the moment that she gave a soft cry and arched up against him. "Hold on to me," he said, gasping. Then he covered her mouth with his as they whirled together into the heart of the storm.

CHAPTER NINETEEN

STEVEN PRUITT WAS RUNNING out of money. Harassing Jessica for six months had been the most fun he'd had in his life, giving him more of a buzz than any game of Labyrinth.

Putting her constantly on the defensive had also gone a long way toward healing the wounds from their college days together at good old Columbia U. She'd thought she was too good for him back then, but he'd kept up the pursuit anyway, knowing she was making a big mistake in turning him down. And she'd just begun to thaw when dear daddy had stepped in and offered him a deal to go away.

Some deal. Sure, he'd been able to finish school at Northwestern on Franklin's money, and he'd been given the promised job at a Franklin Publishing newspaper after graduation.

But had Russell P. let him break the story that would have made him internationally famous? Of course not. Steven, believing this was a free country, had protested being muzzled. That's when he'd discovered that this damn country wasn't so free, after all. Russell P. not only had him fired, he had him blackballed. Fortunately, Steven had savings. He'd invested the money he would have spent on dates if he had dates, which he didn't.

But the savings were nearly gone, which meant it was time to stop the kid stuff with Jessica and stick it to Russell P. at last. Therefore he definitely had to take Jessica and the brat from the line shack. He wasn't going to have a better opportunity anytime soon. Unfortunately, in order to make the most of the opportunity, he'd be forced to camp out.

The great outdoors was highly overrated as far as he was concerned. Once he'd figured out where the damn line shack was, he'd tried to come up with a plan that didn't involve staying out in the wilderness, either before or after the snatch, but he'd finally concluded it was the only logical way to make this work.

He'd spent one whole day finding a cave without a bear or snakes already in residence. Then he'd spent another day gathering supplies, stowing them in the cave and setting up camp. The cave was a good two-hour ride from the line shack, with a stream in between that he could use for covering his tracks. Once he had Jessica and the kid, he'd take the route that went across several large areas of solid granite, to be on the safe side.

It was an extremely isolated spot, and he knew people got lost in this kind of country all the time. If not for his photographic memory, he'd probably never be able to find the cave again himself once he'd left it. But remote as the cave was, it was still only a half hour's ride from something very critical to his plan—a telephone wire. Russell P. was only getting one ransom note, and he was getting it the modern way. Steven was going to hook into that telephone line and use his laptop to send the pompous hypocrite an e-mail.

Finally, on a cloudless morning, he was ready to ride to the line shack and stake it out. Jessica only had one man to protect her there, and by the law of averages, the guy wasn't as smart as Steven. Not many people were as smart as Steven. Sooner or later he'd get his opportunity. And then he'd be rich.

JESSICA DID SLEEP, but not until nearly dawn, when she and Nat finally gave in to exhaustion. Cradled spoon fashion in the curve of his body, she slept so soundly that even Elizabeth's babbling didn't penetrate at first. When it finally did, she started to climb out of bed.

Nat restrained her. "I'll go," he murmured in her ear.

Surrounded in the warm glow of their night together and the unspoken promise of forever-afters, she decided maybe he should be the one to go to Elizabeth this morning. He'd never had her all to himself, and if he had any trouble, she'd be right there to help.

She turned in his arms so she could give him a good-morning smile. "Okay," she said. "That would be nice."

He combed her hair out of her eyes. "I can think of something that would be nicer, but I guess we have to act like parents until this afternoon's nap."

She liked the way he'd said *parents,* as if he'd truly accepted that role for himself. "But have you noticed how exciting it is to want to make love and then have to wait?"

"No, really?" He grinned and tweaked her nipple. "Yeah, I'd noticed. That doesn't mean I can't complain a little that nap time is several hours away." He kissed her quickly and got out of bed.

God, he was gorgeous, she thought as he stood there for a minute looking around for his jeans. "They're over on my side," she said, reaching down to the floor for his jeans and briefs. She rolled back over and handed them to him. "We just left them there after—"

"Don't remind me." His penis stirred as he gazed at her breasts. "Or I'll never get these on. In fact, I'd better not look at you lying in that bed." He turned his back and leaned down to step into his briefs.

"Fine. Just moon me and make me suffer." Front or back, he was an arousing sight. She grew moist as she stared at his tight butt and the bounty just visible between his legs.

"You're the one who said she appreciated the advantages of waiting."

"Yeah." She sighed when he pulled up his briefs, obscuring her view. "I'm trying to remember exactly what those advantages were."

"I think you said waiting would make us want each other more, so the lovemaking would be even better." He stepped into his jeans, and when he zipped them the material tightened up beautifully over his behind.

She had to clench her hands to keep from reaching out and giving him a pat. "I guess that's what I said."

He turned around, a shirtless god in snug-fitting jeans. "That's what you said."

"The fact is, I can't imagine wanting you more than I do right now."

He smiled. "We'll test your theory in a few hours, then. Right now, I'm going to change Elizabeth's diaper." Then he walked around the end of the screen.

Heaven, Jessica thought. She was definitely in heaven.

Then Elizabeth started to cry.

"What's wrong?" Jessica called as she fumbled around on the floor for a shirt to put on.

"Hell, I don't know!" Nat sounded frustrated and scared. "I'm doing everything the way you taught me." His voice took on a coaxing note. "Come on, Elizabeth. I just want to take your sleeper off."

The baby's wail only got louder.

"I'll be right there." Jessica climbed out of bed and thrust her arms into the sleeves of the shirt she'd appropriated from Nat the day before. She snapped it hurriedly, not even bothering to fold back the sleeves the way she had yesterday.

The chill in the cabin gave her goose bumps on her bare legs as she charged around the screen, nearly knocking it over.

Nat stood beside the crib, his hands hanging limply at his sides, his shoulders slumped. He looked emotionally demolished. Elizabeth had crawled to the far side of the crib. Her sleeper was half undone and she was screaming at the top of her lungs.

"Hey, Elizabeth," Jessica crooned. "What's the matter, little girl?"

Jessica looked at her and crawled frantically in her direction, still crying.

"She hates me," Nat said dully.

"No, she doesn't." Jessica picked her up and held her close. "There, there, sweetie. It's okay."

"No, it's not okay," Nat said. "How can I be a father to her if I touch her and she starts to scream?"

Jessica rocked the baby and gazed at him over the top of Elizabeth's head. "Don't you remember that she did the same thing to me that first morning I saw her?"

"Yes, but that was because she had no idea who you were at first. She knows me." His eyes were filled with anguish. "I've been around her for days, Jess. I carried her on my back all afternoon yesterday."

"Yes, but she couldn't see your face. And you were always with me. This was the first time you tried to do something with her while you were alone. She might have thought I'd gone off and left her."

He gave the baby a tortured look. "She doesn't like me, I tell you."

"Nat, that's not so. She's not used to you, yet, but—"

"I can't handle this. I'm going to make coffee." He brushed past her.

With a sigh Jessica put Elizabeth back in the crib and began changing her while dishes clanged in the kitchen. "That's your daddy making all that noise," she murmured to Elizabeth, "and I'm afraid you've really hurt his feelings."

The baby sniffed and rubbed at her nose.

"I know you didn't mean to." Jessica grabbed a tissue and wiped Elizabeth's nose. "But it would help matters if you'd be nicer to him next time." Jessica was determined there would be a next time, and soon. She finished dressing Elizabeth and carried her into the kitchen area.

Nat had put on his boots and a shirt. He sat at the table with a mug of coffee in front of him.

Jessica walked to the cupboard and took down a box of crackers they'd brought for Elizabeth. Propping the baby on one hip, she got a cracker out of the box.

Elizabeth crowed happily when Jessica handed her the cracker.

Hoping that meant the baby was over her fit of crying, Jessica set her down on the floor beside the table. "Would you please keep an eye on her while I get dressed?" she asked.

He glanced up at her. "I don't know if that's a good idea."

"It's a fine idea. I'll only be a minute."

His expression was bleak as he stared at her. "It wasn't her crying that was the real problem, Jess." His voice tensed. "It was the way I felt when she cried. I got angry at her for doing it, when I thought she should be used to me by now. I wanted to shake her."

"Well, of course you did." Jessica felt there were land mines ahead and she tried to figure out where they were. "I can understand that."

"No, you *don't* understand. I got *angry.* Don't you see what that means?" His voice rose. "I'm just like my father!"

Elizabeth began to whimper.

"You are not just like your father." She scooped Elizabeth up so she wouldn't start crying again. "You wanted to shake her, but you didn't! That's the whole difference, Nat. All of us get angry at our children from time to time. But we don't beat them within an inch of their lives. And neither will you."

"You don't know that." He shoved back his chair and stood. "You have no idea what would have happened if you hadn't been right here. Who knows what I would have done?''

"I know!" She wanted to cry, herself. They'd been so damn close, and now he was pulling away again.

Elizabeth's whimpers grew louder.

"See?" He pointed to the baby. "She takes one look at me and she's ready to cry again. Smart kid."

"She's starting to cry again because we're arguing. I'm sure she doesn't like that. Now, will you please watch her for a few minutes?"

"No." He pushed back his chair and stood. "I don't trust myself."

"You're kidding, right?"

"No, I'm not kidding." He walked over to the door and grabbed his hat and jacket. Then he punched some buttons on a small box mounted near the door. "I'm going out to do something aggressive like chop wood for the stove. I just turned off the alarm. Turn it back on when I'm out the door."

She watched him go in total amazement. She couldn't believe he'd give up on himself that quick. Not until he was outside splitting logs did she realize that in their preoccupation with each other the day before, he'd neglected to show her how to turn the alarm on and off.

The tiny hairs on the back of her neck rose, as they used to do when she thought her stalker was nearby, watching her. Well, if that wasn't the power of suggestion at work. She didn't know how to set the alarm, so she was freaking herself out. She'd become addicted to having a security alarm on.

Well, she couldn't do anything about the alarm, anyway. Even if she managed to reactivate it, she wouldn't know how to turn it off again when Nat came back in. And he'd be in soon. After he'd split a few logs he'd realize how ridiculous he was being and come back to try again. In the meantime, nobody would try to storm the house if Nat was outside with an ax.

While she was waiting for Nat to come to his senses, she decided she might as well get dressed. She put Elizabeth in the high chair and gave her another cracker to occupy her while she quickly got into her clothes. She glanced out the window once while she was zipping her jeans and saw that Nat had already worked up a sweat and discarded his jacket. He'd be in soon, and they'd talk about this.

They had to talk about this. Too much was riding on the outcome of this week.

NAT SPLIT LOGS as if each swing of the ax struck another blow at the demons within him. He'd never known such agony. He wanted to believe he wouldn't hurt that little baby in a fit of anger, but given his background, how could he be sure? Jessica didn't know. She thought she did, but she'd been sheltered so much during her life that she couldn't conceive of a grown man wanting to hurt a child.

He could imagine it all too well. Over the years, he'd read all the pop psychology articles he could find, and they'd all warned that an abused boy is in danger of abusing when he becomes a man. So he'd decided not to take the chance, to never get married or have a child.

Then Jess had come along. He hadn't counted on a woman like Jess, who made him dream of things he thought he'd given up. But a man couldn't change who he was, and this morning, when Elizabeth had looked at him with horror and begun to cry, anger had boiled up in him. Hot anger, probably the same kind his father had felt right before he went for the belt, or on some days, the rawhide whip he'd bought in Mexico.

And yet…Nat had to remember that he hadn't acted on his anger. He loved Jess more than life itself, and yes, he even loved that red-faced, crying little girl. What if Jess was right and he had overcome the legacy his father had left him? But if he was wrong, he'd be gambling with the lives of two people who meant more to him than anything in world. He didn't really have a right to do that. He—

Behind him a twig crunched. Jess. His heart swelled with love. She'd come out with the baby, ready to ask him to reconsider. And he would try again, because he loved them both so much. After all, they still had nearly a week to work this out. He started to turn at the moment a million stars exploded inside his skull. Then everything went black.

JESSICA SAT in a chair and fed Elizabeth another spoonful of cereal. She wished she knew how to operate the alarm. The funny tingling at the back of her neck wouldn't go away. She told herself it wasn't anything to worry about, and that Nat was outside to stand guard.

She glanced up at the top shelf where the locked metal box held the gun Sebastian had sent along. Nat probably had the key. Even if the box hadn't been locked, she doubted that she'd have climbed on a chair to get it down. Handling a gun would only spook her worse. She didn't even know if it was loaded.

The tingling at the back of her neck was probably because she'd slept at a weird angle and a small nerve in her neck was going into spasm.

Of course. After all the unaccustomed lovemaking followed by sleeping all tucked together as she and Nat had, it was a wonder that both of them weren't full of aches and pains. Gradually she became aware that the sound of Nat splitting logs outside had stopped.

She sighed with relief. Now he'd be coming back in, and they could set the alarm properly and sit down to discuss his relationship with Elizabeth. And maybe he should teach her how to work the alarm. The gun was another matter, though. She wasn't sure she wanted to learn how to use that.

He should be coming in by now, she thought as the seconds ticked by. Handing Elizabeth another cracker, she got up and walked over to the window to see what he was up to.

The door banged open at the same moment that she realized Nat was lying facedown on the ground next to the woodpile. With a cry, she spun around. Before she could move, the man from her nightmares was inside holding a gun to Elizabeth's head. For a moment her brain refused to register the sight.

When it did, her blood turned to ice and she began to shake. She started toward him, ready to kill.

"Don't do anything stupid, or I'll blow this kid away," the man said. "It wouldn't be any big loss to me. I'd still have you."

Did you kill Nat? She couldn't ask because the answer might paralyze her. Elizabeth needed her to stay alert.

Looking curious instead of scared, Elizabeth glanced around at the man, so that the gun was pointed at her face. Then she tried to grab the barrel.

Jessica opened her mouth to scream, but no sound came out.

With a growl, the man knocked Elizabeth's hand away, and she started to cry.

Jessica saw the action through a red haze. Her ears rang as she started forward again.

"Don't!" the man shouted. "I'm warning you, I wouldn't hesitate. I really don't want to fool with the kid, but I figure her granddaddy will pay extra for her."

Jessica barely recognized her own voice. "If you do anything to her, I'll kill you with my bare hands. So help me God, I will."

"The plan is to get money out of your daddy to pay for the two of you. If possible, I'll do that without either of you getting hurt. How it all shakes out is up to you. Now walk over here and pick her up. We're taking off."

"Where?"

"Never mind where. We're leaving."

Jessica forced her mind to move forward. It wanted to go back and replay the picture of Nat lying on the ground outside. But she had to concentrate on keeping her baby alive. "We can't just leave. This is a baby. She needs diapers, and baby food, and clothes."

The man glanced at Elizabeth, who had stopped crying but was looking at him with fear. He sighed. "I suppose we'll have to take a few things. Otherwise the brat will cry all the time." He looked over at Jessica. "I'll give you two minutes to pack up."

"All right." She tried to remember where she'd last seen the cell phone. There it was, over by the sink. "I have to get her diaper bag. It's behind that screen."

"You're not ducking behind a screen so you can pull something. Move the screen and then get the diaper bag. And make it snappy."

Jessica blanked everything from her mind except finding a way to put the cell phone in the diaper bag. After moving the screen, she packed the bag quickly with diapers and clothes, lotion and baby wipes. At the last minute she crammed the sock monkey inside.

Then she turned. "I need to get some food for her." When she was taking jars from the cupboard, she would slip the cell phone in at the same time, using her body to block his view.

"Hurry up."

Focusing on the cell phone brought a stark sense of calm. She didn't look at it as she went into the kitchen area. For a moment her glance flicked over the coffee can. Nat hadn't put the lid back on after he'd scooped out the coffee.

Nat. For a fraction of a second she thought she might lose her grip on sanity.

"Ga!" Elizabeth said.

She wouldn't lose her grip. Elizabeth's life depended on it. Opening the cupboard, she took down several jars of

food and some canned milk. She moved fast, all the while
creeping closer to the cell phone. In one quick motion she
scooped it into the diaper bag.

"What'd you just do there?" the man asked.

"I'm getting food." But there was a quiver in her voice.
Damn it.

"Bring that stuff over here."

"Just a couple more things." She reached for something
to cover the phone.

"Now!"

Elizabeth started to cry again.

Jessica started back toward him, rearranging things as
she went. "I don't have everything I need yet," she said.
"We should have—"

"Give me that." He grabbed the bag. Holding the gun
next to Elizabeth's ear, he turned the diaper bag upside
down. Baby-food jars broke as they hit the floor, spraying
their multicolored contents over Elizabeth's clothes. And
there, in the midst of the mess, lay the cell phone.

"Food, huh?" He glanced at Elizabeth. "I should pull
the trigger just to teach you a lesson, Miss High-and-
Mighty Jessica Franklin."

"It will be your last act," she said. "You don't have
enough bullets to stop me from tearing you apart."

"Oh, I think I do. But then I wouldn't have anything to
bargain with. And I want your daddy to give me lots and
lots of money." He raised his foot and brought his heel
down on the cell phone with a sickening crunch. Then he
handed Jessica the diaper bag. "Start over."

Elizabeth's crying became more urgent as she spied her
sock monkey in the middle of the mess. She strained toward
the monkey, which was soaked with mashed carrots.

"What's wrong with her?" the man asked.

"She wants her monkey."

"Then give it to her, and no funny stuff!"

Jessica leaned down and picked up the monkey. Poor

Bruce. His face was covered with orange goo. "I need to clean—"

"Nope. Give it to her like that. We're wasting time."

Jessica handed the gooey monkey to Elizabeth.

The baby grabbed her friend and hugged him to her, which transferred the mess to her. But at least her crying slowed and finally stopped.

"Fill that bag!" the man ordered.

Jessica did, and all the while she worked she tried to think of another plan that wouldn't endanger Elizabeth. She couldn't come up with one.

"You don't recognize me, do you?" the man asked.

"Of course I do." She dumped more jars of baby food in on top of a new supply of diapers and clothes. "You're the same jerk who's been following me for six months."

"That, too. But we knew each other, before. At Columbia. I asked you out a few times."

Her fingers tightened around a jar of apricots and she turned to look at him again. A chill sped down her spine. No wonder he'd looked familiar the few times she'd caught sight of him this summer. She remembered now. He hadn't appealed to her, in spite of his brilliant mind. But she'd felt sorry for him. She'd told her father about him, and had said she might go out with the poor guy, after all.

And then, poof, he'd disappeared.

"Didn't you ever wonder what happened to me?" he asked.

Not for long. But she decided that wouldn't be the best answer. "Of course. What did happen to you?" *What was his name? As crazy as he was, he probably would get crazier if she couldn't remember his name.*

"Your daddy bought me off."

She gasped.

"I didn't think you knew. He paid for me to transfer to Northwestern for my last semester, and he promised me a job with one of his newspapers after graduation, so long as I'd stay far away from you.''

Her brain reeled. She had to wonder how many other potential suitors her father had quietly eliminated in the same way. Men she'd dated had seemed to transfer from Columbia at an alarming rate. But she'd never dreamed...

''So what's my name?''

She knew it was a test. Maybe something starting with an S. Sam? Scott? Damn it, what was his name?

''You don't remember.'' His gray eyes grew hard. ''Well, that will make this little caper all the sweeter. But for the record, the name is Steven Pruitt. I don't think you or your family will ever forget my name after this. Now pick up that kid and let's get out of here.''

CHAPTER TWENTY

THE BACK OF NAT'S HEAD hurt like hell and he tasted dirt in his mouth. Pushing himself to all fours, he fought dizziness as he spit out the dirt. What had happened? Then he knew.

His stomach pitched as he scrambled to his feet. No time to throw up now. No time. Jess. Elizabeth. He half ran, half stumbled toward the open door of the cabin.

"Jess!" he called hoarsely. *"Jess!"* Grasping the door frame for support, he looked in. But he knew what he would find. Nothing.

Spinning away from the door, he looked frantically around. "Jess!" He got no answer but the sighing of the wind through the aspens. He ran around the perimeter of the house, screaming her name. Startled birds flew out of his path, but otherwise there was no sign of life in the small clearing.

Finally he forced himself to think. How had they left? He searched for tire tracks and could find none except those made by the Bronco. But there were hoofprints. Automatically Nat started to follow them, until he glanced up at the sun and realized how much time had gone by. He'd never catch them on foot.

The ranch. He had to contact the ranch. Racing into the house, he searched for the cell phone and finally nearly tripped over it in the muck on the floor by the high chair. Smashed beyond repair. Oh, God.

He had to drive there. Digging in his pocket for the keys, he tore out the door again.

The tires had been slashed.

Nat stared at the ruined tires that he'd missed in his first agitated pass around the cabin. Then he lifted his head and let out a howl of despair.

Slowly the sound of his anguish faded into the forest. But as he stood there with his head exploding in pain, a certainty settled over him that he would find her. He would find her and his baby, and he would kill the man who had dared to take them away. It was as simple as that.

He went back into the cabin, reached to the top shelf for the metal box and unlocked it with the key in his pocket. After checking to make sure the gun was loaded, he pocketed the extra ammunition Sebastian had left in the box. Then he left the cabin. He didn't bother to close the door. There was no longer anything of value inside.

Climbing into the Bronco, he laid the gun on the seat next to him…the seat where Jess had sat when he'd brought her out here. He swallowed another roar of self-loathing. He didn't have time to punish himself now. That would come later. Now he had to drive back to the ranch. He'd ruin the rims on the Bronco, but he didn't care. They could be replaced.

When he arrived, he'd saddle up a horse. Sebastian could call the police if he wanted, but Nat wasn't waiting around for them. However, before he rode out, he had one detail that couldn't be left to someone else. It was his job to call Russell P. Franklin.

JESSICA HAD REMEMBERED the baby carrier before they left, and Pruitt had finally agreed that she could transport Elizabeth in it. She hadn't wanted that monster touching the baby, so she'd propped the carrier against the bed, put Elizabeth inside, and then crouched down and worked her arms through the straps.

Not being used to the weight, she'd been a little unsteady at first, and getting on the horse Pruitt had brought for her was tough, but she knew this would be the best way for Elizabeth to travel in relative safety.

Safety. As if either of them were safe in the company of a wacko like Steven Pruitt. More details about him were coming back to her now. At Columbia she'd thought of him as a typical nerd, the kind of guy whose intelligence had hampered his social skills. She'd been torn between wanting to avoid him and wanting to help him fit in. But apparently there was a little more wrong with Pruitt than a lack of social confidence.

He rode ahead of her, taking her through the forest with a lead rope tied to her horse's bridle. Wearing an L.A. Dodgers baseball cap and pleated pants, he didn't look very natural on the horse. She didn't think he'd ridden much in his life, but then neither had she, and it had all been English, anyway. With Elizabeth on her back she couldn't very well try some fancy maneuver and expect to ride away from him.

He'd tied her hands to the saddle horn, and the diaper bag handles were looped over it, too, so the bag bumped her knees as they moved over uneven, rocky terrain. Elizabeth was quiet in the carrier, probably asleep. Jessica gave thanks for that, but the dead weight made her shoulders ache horribly.

A rest was out of the question. In the first place, Steven probably wouldn't allow her one, and in the second place, Elizabeth might wake up if they stopped. Jessica knew she should be planning their escape, but staying on the horse and enduring the pain in her shoulders took everything she had. She did try to keep track of the route they were taking, but other than the stream they seemed to splash through for miles, the forest took on a sameness that was discouraging.

"So your daddy never mentioned that I was working for one of his papers out in L.A.?" Pruitt asked.

"No."

"Remember that California senator who got kidnapped last year?"

"I guess."

"You *guess?* You must not be keeping up. That was the biggest damn story in the country for weeks. I was on top of it the whole way. Had my share of bylines on *Associated Press* as a result, too."

Jessica didn't respond. Obviously he wanted to brag about himself, but she didn't have to encourage him.

"Then I got a real break," he continued, apparently not needing her participation for his monologue. "When they caught the kidnappers, I got 'em to agree to talk to me, tell me their whole story. I had a series outlined—'Inside the Mind of a Sociopath.' I had all the details of their plan. It was a brilliant piece of journalism. I figured once it ran, somebody would pay me to expand it into a book, or maybe somebody in Hollywood would want the movie rights."

Jessica remembered that Pruitt had always had grandiose ideas. She'd wondered when they'd been acquainted at Columbia if he'd only been attracted to her wealth and connections, but he'd denied that vehemently. She'd naively believed him, but now she could see that's exactly where his interest had been.

"The thing is, my editor checked with your daddy before he ran the series, and Russell P. ordered the piece killed. Not only that, he said since I used the newspaper's time and resources to get that story and write it, he was confiscating everything—my notes, my contacts—everything. He said it would give other sick people a blueprint for doing something like that, and he didn't want to be responsible. What a damn wuss! He coulda raked in a Pulitzer for me and his stinkin' paper."

"My father always has had principles." She realized how proud she felt, saying that. She'd never given her father credit for integrity before. She'd been so busy rebelling against his control that she hadn't stopped to think of his good points. And there were many.

The more she thought about it, the more she became convinced that her father had probably offered more than one man money to stay away from her. If he had, it wasn't a bad test of a guy's character. If the man took the bribe, then he wasn't the one for her. But in Pruitt's case, her father must have been more than a little concerned, to pay for a semester's tuition plus offer the guy a job. Maybe he'd had Pruitt investigated and had uncovered a psychiatric evaluation somewhere.

She had to admit, the conversation was taking her mind off the searing pain in her shoulders. That, more than curiosity, prompted her to ask a question. "So you quit?"

"Hell, no, I didn't quit. I figured right was on my side, so I took my case to anyone with any clout who would listen. I think your daddy was afraid I might get somewhere, because he had me fired. Then he called in all his favors and had me blackballed in the industry. Even though he'd confiscated my notes, I remembered most of the story, and I was prepared to write it for someone else, but I couldn't get a job *delivering* papers, let alone writing for them. Even book publishers didn't want to talk to me. Now, I ask you, does that sound fair?"

"It sounds like my father," Jessica had to admit. When someone within Russell Franklin's organization threatened the empire he'd worked so hard to build, Jessica had no doubt he'd use all the power at his disposal to annihilate that person. She'd also like to think that in this case, her father's contacts in the business agreed with him that Steven Pruitt needed to be stopped.

"Well, he blackballed the wrong guy. I'd just had a crash course in kidnapping, and it didn't take me long to figure out who my target should be."

"How did you find me?"

"You can thank my excellent memory. When we were

at Columbia, you told me that if you could live anywhere in the world, it would be Aspen, Colorado. You'd never been there, but you thought the pictures were beautiful and you were sure you'd like it.''

She vaguely remembered the conversation. Sure enough, she had always been fascinated with Aspen. After meeting Nat there, she'd decided going to Aspen had been her destiny. Oh, God. Nat. An instinct for protecting her child had blocked thoughts of Nat, but now her vision filled with a picture of him lying in the dirt.

Was he…no, he couldn't be…she refused to think the word. She had to believe he'd only been knocked unconscious. Once he woke up, he'd come looking for her.

She should have found some way to leave signs along the way. Damn, why hadn't she thought of that earlier? Maybe it wasn't too late. But what sort of signs? With her hands tied, she couldn't very well drop off bits of clothing.

The diaper bag banged against her knee again. She looked down at it and noticed the tail of Elizabeth's sock monkey sticking out between the overlapping flaps that held the bag closed. She'd crammed Bruce in the diaper bag for safekeeping, despite Elizabeth's protests, because she'd figured if Elizabeth held the monkey while she rode in the carrier, she'd drop him somewhere along the way.

Which would have been a perfect plan.

She needed to keep Pruitt involved in the conversation so he wouldn't suspect she was doing anything covert. ''So after all that time, you remembered what I'd said and figured out to look for me in Aspen. That's pretty amazing.'' Watching to make sure he didn't turn around, she worked the diaper-bag handle up so the monkey's tail was almost within reach.

''Amazing to you, maybe. That's just how I work. I test out pretty high on the charts. I was on scholarship to Columbia, and I probably could have talked Northwestern into giving me one, too, but I liked soaking your daddy.''

"I suppose you graduated with honors, then." The ropes cut into her wrist as she strained forward and finally got her fingers around the monkey's tail.

"Could've. But with your old man footing the bill, I decided not to bust my butt. After all, I didn't even have to worry about a job once I got out of college. Why sweat that last semester?"

Her father must have *really* been worried about his guy, Jessica thought. And for good reason, obviously. "Did you like being a reporter?" she asked. Slowly she let the diaper bag drop into its original position, and an orange-stained Bruce popped out through the flaps.

"It was okay. Following you all summer has been better, though. Like espionage or James Bond stuff. I began to wonder if you were having a good time, too. So 'fess up, Jessica. Did I give you a thrill or two?"

Oh, yeah, she'd loved being stalked by a weirded-out nerd like Pruitt. "Sorry, I guess I don't have your sense of adventure." The guy obviously also needed lots and lots of medication.

"You shoulda gone out with me all those years ago, Jessica."

"Maybe so." She had a split second of regret at sacrificing Bruce, but if she didn't find a way to leave a clue for Nat, losing Bruce would be the least of her worries. Keeping an eye on Pruitt, she loosened her grip on the monkey's tail. He slipped down and balanced on the top of the diaper bag.

Saying a quick apology to Elizabeth, Jessica nudged the diaper bag, and Bruce fell to the ground. She was very much afraid that her horse stepped on him. But most important of all, Pruitt seemed to be so wrapped up in his fantasy that he apparently hadn't noticed a thing.

IT WAS LUNCHTIME when Nat banged on the front door of the ranch house. Sebastian opened the door, took one look at him and yelled for Matty.

"He took them," Nat said, breathing hard.

"Oh, God." Sebastian went white.

Matty came rushing to his side and looked from her husband to Nat. "What...oh no. *No*." She clutched her stomach and began to wobble.

Sebastian and Nat rushed to grab her at once.

"I have her," Sebastian said, supporting her gently. "Come on, Matty. Let's get you on the couch."

"Where are they?" Matty wailed.

"I only know which direction they went. He knocked me out first and took them on horseback."

Sebastian guided Matty down onto the couch and turned back to Nat. "What happened to that goddamn alarm? I thought that was supposed to protect you out there? Where was that fancy alarm system?"

Nat had used the long, grinding stretch of road to the ranch to figure that out. The blame was all his, and he faced Sebastian and delivered the damning explanation. "We had an argument. I went out to chop wood, and I turned it off on the way out. I told her to turn it back on after I was out the door. But she didn't know how. I never showed her how. Oh, God." His throat closed and he turned away. He couldn't break down. He had things to do.

Sebastian's hand closed over Nat's shoulder, and his voice was choked. "We'll get them back. I'll call Travis and Boone. We'll get them back."

Nat dug down and found the strength to meet Sebastian's gaze. "I will. I'll get them back."

Sebastian gave his shoulder a squeeze. "We'll do it together, buddy." Then he turned to Matty. "Are you okay? You're not having pains or anything, are you?"

"No, I'm fine." Matty took a deep breath. "And I want to go with you when you look for them."

"No," Sebastian said. "No, Matty. Don't ask that of me, please."

She stood. "I'm not asking, I'm telling! I want to go. I *will* go."

"God, Matty, don't do this."

"But I—"

"Listen to me, you stubborn, can-do woman." He took her by the shoulders. "I know all your abilities, and yes, you could be valuable to us, but I can't risk you, the mother of my child, the person I can't live without. I will be worthless in this search unless I know that you're safe."

She gazed at him, and her throat moved in a swallow. "Okay, I'll stay," she said in a low voice. "But know this, Sebastian. My every instinct is screaming at me to go and find Elizabeth. I am going to stay only out of love for you. And you'd damn well better find that baby."

Sebastian heaved a sigh of relief. "We'll find her. Nat, you and I can saddle the horses while Matty calls Boone and Travis."

Nat glanced at him. "I'll do that, but after Matty calls them, I need to make a call, too."

"If you're thinking of getting the sheriff into this now, I vote we don't waste time with the law. Let's track this guy down before the trail gets old."

"I wasn't thinking of calling the sheriff. I agree with you on that." Nat thought of the promise he'd made to try to preserve Sebastian's privacy. Along with his other sins, he'd have to break that promise. "I want to call her father."

Sebastian regarded him steadily. "Okay."

Nat knew that no man had ever made a greater personal sacrifice for him than Sebastian was doing at this moment.

Sebastian gestured toward the kitchen. "Go do it now. Matty can use my cell phone to call Travis and Boone. I'll meet you in the barn."

Nat gave him a brief nod and started for the kitchen.

"And Nat," Sebastian called after him.

Nat turned.

"Don't worry. The four of us can damn well handle one dude from New York," Sebastian said with the faintest trace of a smile. "No matter how much money he's got."

Nat wasn't thinking of Franklin's money as he reached for his wallet and pulled out the embossed card he'd kept tucked inside ever since he'd paid a visit to Franklin Hall. What he was about to do to Russell Franklin couldn't be softened by all the money in the world.

Nat knew exactly how the man would feel—the helpless panic, the blinding rage, the self-blame. Oh, yes. Nat knew exactly how Russell Franklin would feel. It would undoubtedly be the worst moment of the man's life. But that didn't mean he wouldn't want to know. Nat understood that, too.

Only two rings sounded before Jessica's father picked up. "Russell P. Franklin."

Nat closed his eyes, hating to deliver the blow.

"Hello? Who's there? Jessica?"

"It's Nat Grady."

"Grady! You've found her!"

"Yes, I did. And—"

"Fantastic, son! Hold on and let me call Adele on the other line. She's going to be—"

"There's more." Nat's chest tightened.

"More?" Fear hummed over the wire.

"For the past six months she's been dodging a stalker. This morning he kidnapped her."

This was a deadly silence on the other end. Then Russell's voice roared over the line. "Then what the hell are you doing on the damn phone? Have you called the police? The FBI? Forget that! Tell me where the hell you are! Don't do a damn thing until I get there!"

A cold calmness settled over Nat. "I'm going after her. My friends and I are heading out on horseback from the Rocking D Ranch in just a few minutes. The ranch is near a little town in Colorado called Huerfano. You can stop anywhere in town and get directions out here."

"I've never heard of the place! Probably a bunch of hicks, and sure as the world, you're going to louse this up! Stay put, and I'll—"

"Huerfano's not far from Canon City," Nat said, his tone even. "If you fly into Colorado Springs and rent a car, you can probably get here by tonight. I plan to have her back by then."

"The hell you say! If you so much as move your little finger before I get there, so help me, Grady, you'll wish you'd never heard the name Russell P. Franklin!"

"Sorry, Russell." Nat wasn't even angry at the man. In his shoes, Nat would have issued the same threats. He could completely understand Russell's need for control. He had the same need. "We're going after her. And there's one other thing. The guy didn't get only Jessica. He also took her eight-month-old daughter, Elizabeth."

Russell gasped.

"And yes, in case you're wondering, she's my daughter, too. So now you'll understand why I'm heading out. See you tonight." He hung up the phone. Nothing else they said to each other mattered. Now it was time to go get Jessica.

Matty came into the kitchen. "I got ahold of both Travis and Boone," she said. "Everyone's coming here. The women and little Josh will stay with me while you're gone."

Nat nodded. "Good. I'd better get out to the barn and help Sebastian."

"I'll pack some food for all of you. No telling how long...well, no telling."

"Right." He turned to go out the kitchen door.

"Nat! The back of your head! It's covered with dried blood. Let me—"

"Forget it, Matty."

She grabbed his arm. ''You might even havé a concussion. Let me look at it.''

Gently he pried her fingers away as he gazed down at her. ''I don't have time,'' he said. ''By the way, Russell Franklin should arrive here sometime tonight. With luck we'll be back with Jessica and Elizabeth before he gets here.''

''Nat, I think you should let me look at your head.''

''Thanks anyway, Matty.'' He leaned down and gave her a quick kiss on the cheek. Then he went out the door.

CHAPTER TWENTY-ONE

"PATTY-CAKE, PATTY-CAKE, baker's man." Jessica sat cross-legged on a blanket with Elizabeth in her lap not far from the mouth of the small cave where Pruitt had set up camp. She'd finally been able to clean the carrot juice off the baby, and so far Elizabeth hadn't seemed to notice that Bruce was missing in action.

For Elizabeth, the forest was obviously a wondrous place filled with birds, squirrels and chipmunks. She was excited, curious, and had no idea that the object held by the man sitting on the far side of the clearing had the power to end her days.

While Jessica played with Elizabeth, she glanced around for potential toys to keep the baby amused. Pruitt had ordered her to keep Elizabeth on the blanket so he didn't have to follow them around and make sure they weren't trying to run off. He lounged on another folded blanket, his back against a tree, and watched them.

The shadows lengthened and the air was turning cooler. Before long it would be dark. Jessica's shoulders still burned from the hours Elizabeth had spent on her back in the carrier. They'd reached the camp about midday, but after a too-brief rest for a little food, Pruitt had ordered Jessica to put Elizabeth back in the carrier and climb on the horse again.

Jessica had thought her arms would come out of their sockets, but she'd done as he'd commanded. Then they'd ridden in a different direction until they'd come to a swath cut through the trees and the first sign of civilization she'd seen so far, a telephone line. Jessica didn't want to think of what had happened next, but the scene was imprinted on her retina as if she'd stared into the sun too long.

At gunpoint, Pruitt had demanded that she transfer the carrier with Elizabeth in it to him. He'd thanked her, in fact, for suggesting they bring the carrier in the first place. Then, with the baby on his back and a laptop computer strapped around his waist, he'd climbed the telephone pole. While Elizabeth crowed in delight at the adventure, Jessica had stood below and prayed as she'd never prayed in her life.

God had answered her prayers, and Pruitt had come back down without falling or dropping Elizabeth out of the carrier. Then he'd returned the baby for the trip back to camp. All the way back, Jessica had been forced to listen to him brag about how he'd tapped into the telephone cable and sent an e-mail ransom note to her father demanding a huge sum of money be wired to his bank account in the Cayman Islands. The following day, Pruitt had said, they'd repeat the maneuver so that he could get her father's reply and confirmation of the money transfer.

Jessica had sent up another prayer, this one asking to be rescued before Pruitt made another journey up that pole with her baby perched precariously on his back. So far, that prayer hadn't been answered. Jessica couldn't remember ever being so tired and sore, except after her hours of labor with Elizabeth.

Pruitt would have to sleep sometime, Jessica thought. Of course he'd tie her up, but surely he wouldn't tie Elizabeth, too? The thought made her stomach clench. She couldn't risk that he'd be inhuman enough to do such a thing. She had to think of a way to disable him before he got sleepy enough to think of tying her and Elizabeth.

"Time for you to earn your keep," Pruitt said. "Get a

can of stew and the camp stove out of that box over there.''
He laughed. ''Your turn to cook dinner.''

She gathered Elizabeth in her arms and stood. That answered her question as to whether or not he planned to
build a fire to keep them warm. Apparently he'd figured
out that a campfire would make it easier for someone to
find them. Jessica decided she'd put a couple of layers of
clothing on Elizabeth tonight.

''Oh, and make some coffee while you're at it,'' he said.

Holding Elizabeth on one hip, she struggled with the
camp stove. If only she could figure out a way to poison
his food. Or his coffee. *Wait a minute.* As she continued
to set up the stove, she wracked her brain trying to remember her notes from her most recent class on herbal remedies.
Part of the class had been devoted to the danger of poison-
ous plants.

But what were those plants? Mistletoe, for sure. But even
if she happened to be lucky enough to see some around
here, it would be hanging from a branch, probably impossible for her to get without being noticed. But there was
another one that grew on the ground. *Foxglove.* And she
knew exactly how she'd look for it.

''I'm having a little trouble working while I'm holding
Elizabeth,'' she said.

''Too bad. I sure as hell don't plan to hold her.''

''I wouldn't want—I mean—*expect* you to. But if I prop
her carrier against a tree and tie it to the trunk, I think it
can work like a high chair.''

''Go ahead. Just remember, this gun is cocked and
pointed at that kid's head.''

''Yes.'' As if she could ever forget. Talking animatedly
to Elizabeth, Jessica picked her up and went over to get the
carrier and a length of rope Pruitt had left lying on the
ground. Looping the rope around her neck, she leaned the
carrier against her knees and put Elizabeth inside. ''I'm

going to find the perfect spot for you," she said, picking it up.

"Ba-ba!" Elizabeth chortled, craning her head around to watch what Jessica was doing.

Jessica walked around the campsite and studied the plants growing there while she pretended to be searching out the perfect tree for securing the carrier. She passed one plant twice, not certain it was the right one. Without the flowers it was harder to tell. Finally she decided it had to be foxglove. And it was growing right behind a tree.

"This is the one," she sang out. "Here we go, Elizabeth." She positioned the rigid back of the carrier against the trunk. Securing the seat to the tree was a tricky maneuver while Elizabeth jiggled around in it. Once, it nearly tipped over. Jessica made a huge production of it as she kept up a monologue about making sure the rope was secure.

Elizabeth twisted and turned, trying to follow Jessica's antics, making the process even more difficult. But Jessica noticed that Pruitt seemed to becoming bored with the extended routine, and finally his attention strayed. That's when she tore a handful of the plant from the ground and stuffed it into her jeans pocket.

"That does it, Elizabeth," she said, dusting off her hands.

The baby seemed perplexed by her new perch, but her feet touched the ground, which she loved. With a grin, she practiced balancing while Jessica moved the camp stove a little closer so she could talk to Elizabeth while she heated the stew.

The foxglove, she'd decided, would go in the basket with the ground coffee. She could disguise it better that way. Cutting off Pruitt's view of the coffeepot with her body, she quickly transferred the mangled foxglove to the bottom of the coffee basket and shoveled ground coffee on top. Then she slapped the lid on and put the coffee on to perk.

She'd evaluated everything Pruitt had allowed her access to, in case any of it would work as a weapon. Apparently he'd thought this through himself, because the cookware was all lightweight and he'd packed only spoons, not knives or forks. Unfortunately, everything she considered, even the flame of the Sterno, might only serve to make him mad, not permanently disable him. The foxglove had to work.

She served him the stew first. Then, heart pounding, she poured him a cup of coffee.

"Hand that to me nice and easy," he said as he reached for it. "I can see the wheels going around, and I'll bet you'd like to toss that hot coffee all over me. But even hot coffee wouldn't stop me from shooting that kid."

"I'm not planning to throw coffee on you," she said. But it worried her that he'd read her expression so well. She tried to make her mind a blank so nothing in her eyes would warn him not to drink the coffee. "As long as you have that gun, I'm not going to take any foolish chances."

"Good. I always figured you for a smart woman."

Here's hoping I'm smart enough. "I'm going to feed Elizabeth now, if that's okay with you."

"By all means, feed the brat. God knows I don't want it squalling." He took a sip of the coffee and grimaced.

Jessica held her breath. If he refused to drink it, that was one thing. If he suspected what she'd done…

"Did anybody ever tell you that you make the worst coffee in the world?" he said. "I can't imagine how you screwed it up this bad."

"I…haven't had much practice." Her heartbeat thrummed in her ears. "I prefer herbal tea."

"Oh, I'll just bet you do, Miss Gotrocks. Probably never had to make coffee for a man in your life, have you, Princess? Cook did all that, didn't she? It's a wonder you figured out how to heat up the stew." He held up the tin cup of coffee. "But I'll drink the damn stuff. I didn't pack much coffee, and I need every bit of caffeine I can get. When this is gone, I'm going to supervise the second pot.''

He didn't suspect! She tried to keep the triumph out of her voice. ''All right.''

He glanced up suspiciously. ''That sounded mighty co-operative. How come you're not telling me to make my own damn coffee?''

She lowered her eyes so he couldn't see her expression. ''Like I said, as long as you have the gun, I'm going to cooperate.''

His eyes narrowed, and his gaze became more calculating. ''Is that right? I'll keep that in mind. It could be a long night.''

Her blood went cold. *Oh, please let that be foxglove I put in his coffee, and please let it be strong.*

''DAMN IT TO HELL.'' Leading his horse, Travis walked around shining his flashlight over the rocky ground. ''I've lost the trail again.''

Nat fought panic. They'd been out here for hours—his three buddies and both the dogs, Fleafarm and Sadie. And now it was getting too dark to see. Somewhere out in this darkness a lunatic had Jess and Elizabeth.

Sebastian sighed and leaned on his saddle horn while he watched Travis continue to search the area for tracks ''I have to say you've done better than I thought you would, hotshot, considering your last performance.''

Travis glanced up at him. ''This is Lizzie we're goin' after, don't forget.''

''Oh, I'm not likely to forget.''

''Maybe if we spread out a little we can pick up the trail,'' Boone suggested.

Nat hated to say what was on his mind, but he figured somebody needed to. He didn't want to be so pigheaded about this search that he put Jess and Elizabeth in even greater danger. "Listen, do you think one of us should go back and call the sheriff's office?"

Sebastian looked around the semicircle of men. "What do you guys think?"

"I'm against it," Travis said. "I think we're gonna pick up that trail again, and if the sheriff's office moves in with a bunch of deputies, and helicopters and god-knows-what, we could have a disaster here."

Boone rubbed the back of his neck. "The way I've always heard it, these kidnappers usually tell you not to bring the cops in on it."

"I've thought of that, too," Nat said. "But I also figure Jess's father is probably at the ranch, or will be pretty soon. If one of us goes back, we can find out if Franklin's received a ransom note yet. And we'll get his opinion on what he thinks we should do. He is Jessica's father. And Elizabeth's grandfather."

"There's some sense to that," Sebastian said slowly. I reckon we all know how we'd feel in his shoes. So, if we decide someone should go back, who goes?"

No one spoke.

"I understand that nobody wants to be the one," Sebastian said. "But—"

"Oh, hell, Sebastian," Boone said. "None of us are going back, and we all damn well know it. Ransom note or no ransom note, that baby is out there, not to mention Jessica, and you know as well as I do we wouldn't trust anybody else to get either one of them back. Not even Jessica's rich daddy."

"Yeah, I do know that," Sebastian said. "But I keep asking myself if we've really been following the right set of hoofprints, or if we've messed up somewhere and we're following the trail of a couple of pleasure riders."

"We're on the right track," Nat said.

Sebastian adjusted the tilt of his hat. "I know you want to believe that, buddy, but—"

"We're on the right track," Nat said again. "I can feel it." And that's what was so frustrating. He could feel Jess and Elizabeth out there ahead of them, somewhere through the dark trees. And yet getting to them was such a slow, painstaking process. He almost felt as if he could find them by letting his instincts take over, but he didn't quite trust himself that much.

"Let's fan out, then." Sebastian glanced around. "Now, where the hell are those dogs? I wonder if we did the right thing, bringing them. They've never been trained to track or hunt, so I don't know what I expected."

A sharp, shrill bark pierced the twilight. Then another.

"Well, great," Travis said. "They've probably scared themselves up a skunk."

"Let's go find out," Sebastian said as he reined his horse in the direction of the sound.

Nat told himself not to get excited by the dogs' reaction. Sebastian was right that they weren't trained for this kind of thing and it might have been pointless to bring them. Fleafarm could drive cattle like nobody's business, but she was no bloodhound. And Sadie, Matty's Great Dane, was a great guard dog, but she didn't know anything about tracking, either.

Nevertheless, Nat kicked his horse into a trot and arrived at the small clearing in the trees where the dogs stood, wagging their tails and looking proud of themselves. Something lay on the ground by their feet.

Nat switched on his flashlight and his stomach churned as the high beam shone on a very grubby-looking sock monkey.

Bruce.

THE PLANT JESSICA HAD PUT into the coffee, whether it was foxglove or not, was having an effect on Pruitt. He'd downed three cups, and Jessica could see that he wasn't feeling good, although he was trying to keep her from finding out. The worse he felt, the sharper his temper. Now every sentence was laced with foul language.

It was nearly dark, and the only light in camp was Pruitt's small flashlight, which he used intermittently. He hadn't asked her to make any more coffee, and she suspected that was because his stomach was cramping and he knew he couldn't hold anything down. She wasn't sure what the effects of the plant were, or if she'd even given him foxglove in the first place. But she'd done something to him, that was for sure.

She'd be thrilled if he'd pass out, but he might only vomit. Even then, however, she might be able to get the gun away from him. She remembered what morning sickness was like. A person would have a hard time holding a gun steady while throwing up.

If that happened, she'd have to move fast. So she'd positioned the blanket on which she sat holding Elizabeth close to the carrier that was still tied to the tree. She had to have a quick place to stash the baby when it was time to grab Pruitt's gun. While pretending to sing a lullaby to Elizabeth, she kept a close eye on Pruitt.

Suddenly he let out a sharp oath and staggered to his feet. "I know what's happened! You bitch! You put something in that coffee, didn't you?"

"Of course not!" Her mouth went dry with fear as she plopped Elizabeth in the carrier and crouched down so she was directly in front of the baby, shielding her. "What could I possibly put in it, anyway? We're out in the middle of nowhere."

"I don't know." He held the gun on her while he clutched his stomach with his other hand. "All I know is I have one hell of a bellyache, and I'd lay money that you did it! Hell, your daddy's probably already transferred my money. I should just shoot you and the kid and be done with it."

She readied herself to spring at him. If he was going to

shoot her anyway, she'd take him with her, somehow. His arm was wavering, so his aim would be off. As long as he didn't kill her instantly, she'd find a way to get the gun away and shoot him before he could aim the weapon at Elizabeth.

"Think I will shoot you." He was nearly doubled over with pain. "I don't know why I thought I had to keep you both around, anyway. Your daddy's going to pay that money. He has to. You're the most important thing in the world to him. That's why I knew that if I kidnapped you, I'd—" He stopped talking. His jaw clenched and his eyes began to water.

"Damn you," he whispered, and dropped to his knees, retching violently. He still held the gun, but it was now hanging loosely from his fingers, the barrel pointed at the ground.

Jessica leaped to her feet, ran to him and grabbed for the gun. Although he was still vomiting, his fingers tightened on it and it went off with a roar, the bullet zinging off through the trees.

Jessica was frantic to get the weapon. A wild bullet could kill Elizabeth as surely as one aimed in her direction. She wrenched his hand up to her mouth and bit down hard. As her teeth sank through flesh, he screamed and let go of the gun.

She grabbed it, but she wasn't steady as she scrambled away and tried to aim it at him. Before she get her finger around the trigger, he lunged at her and wrested the gun away again.

"That's it!" he screamed, pointing the gun at her. "You're dead, bitch!"

"Drop it, mister!" called a man from the shadows. The high beam of a flashlight focused on Pruitt.

Jessica gasped in relief as she recognized Sebastian's voice.

"Don't try anything. You're surrounded," called another man, and a second flashlight snapped on.

Boone. They had come for her. Oh, thank God.

From a different direction came a third man's voice and a third flashlight beam. "Just drop the gun and put your hands up. We're in no mood for shenanigans."

Travis. But what about Nat? Oh, God, was Nat out there?

Pruitt squinted as he tried to avoid looking into the glare. Then, in one quick move, he grabbed Elizabeth out of the carrier and held the gun to the baby's head.

"No!" Jessica screamed.

Elizabeth began to cry as Pruitt stood and looked around, staring into the darkness. "Any questions, gentlemen?"

A gun blasted. Jessica screamed again and ran at Pruitt, not caring what happened to her. She was just in time to catch Elizabeth as Pruitt's grip on the baby slackened and he went down, a bullet in the middle of his forehead.

Jessica fell to her knees, clutching the crying baby to her as she sobbed. Instantly she was surrounded by Sebastian, Travis and Boone, all trying to comfort her at once.

Eyes streaming with tears, Jessica looked up into their beloved faces. "Which one of you fired that shot?"

"Never mind that now," Sebastian said soothingly, rubbing her shoulders. "All that matters is that you're okay. Elizabeth's okay."

She couldn't look at Pruitt. "Is he—"

"Yeah, he is," Boone said. "He won't be bothering you anymore."

Finally, she had to know the worst. "What about... Nat?" she managed to choke out.

"I'm here." He stepped out of the shadows, Sebastian's .38 hanging loosely from his right hand.

CHAPTER TWENTY-TWO

JESSICA DIDN'T REMEMBER much of the trip back to the ranch. She wondered if she might be in shock, because despite the blanket she clutched around her as they rode, she couldn't stop shivering. Her horse was sandwiched in between Sebastian's and Travis's. Boone came next with Elizabeth in her carrier on his back.

Nat, the man she most needed to see, brought up the rear, leading the horse that carried Steven Pruitt facedown across the saddle. She'd had no idea Nat could shoot a gun with that kind of accuracy, but from what brief comments the other guys had made, she gathered that they'd all known he was a marksman.

She, for one, was profoundly grateful that he was, and would have liked to thank him for saving Elizabeth's life. But Nat didn't seem to want to talk about it. He didn't seem to want to talk to her, period.

But he was alive. Each time she thought of that, she sent up another prayer of gratitude. She could understand that Nat had a lot to deal with right now. Knowing him, he was berating himself because she and Elizabeth had been kidnapped right out from under his nose. And now he had to face the fact that he'd killed a man.

Jessica felt no remorse that Steven Pruitt was dead. She would have killed him herself, given a chance. And yet, she couldn't know exactly what it was like for Nat to realize he was the one who had pulled the trigger. Especially for a man like Nat, who was so against violence.

She and Nat needed to have a long talk. When they got back to the Rocking D, they would find the time to straighten things out between them. Once they'd settled everything with the sheriff's office, she and Nat could take some time alone. They had a lot to discuss.

But as they rode up to the hitching post by the back door and saw the helicopter in the middle of the corral, she began to realize that she and Nat might not have a chance to be alone anytime soon. People came pouring out of the house, and she gazed with disbelief as she recognized that her mother and father were among them.

JESSICA WOKE in the double bed in Elizabeth's room the next morning, and the first thing she heard was Elizabeth babbling happily to herself as she stood holding on to the crib railing and batted at the foam-rubber mobile over her head. Jessica adjusted the pillow under her head so she could look at the baby, her baby.

Slowly the events of the past two days washed over her. The scene once they'd arrived back at the ranch was a blur. She remembered hugging both her parents and crying, and endless questions from everyone, and the arrival of the sheriff's deputies, but finally someone had propelled her back to this bedroom, along with Elizabeth, and they'd both been tucked in like children.

Jessica suspected Matty had done that. She took a deep breath. They'd all made it through. And now she had to find out if she had a future with Nat Grady.

She swung her legs out of bed. "Hi, baby," she said.

Elizabeth bounced happily and grinned at her. "Da-da!"

"Yes, that's what we have to go see about, you and me. Your da-da." She listened for noises from the rest of the house, but it was quiet, although she could smell coffee brewing. Glancing at the clock, she was surprised how early it was. She'd only slept a few short hours. Maybe Matty had set the timer so the coffee had turned on automatically.

Getting Elizabeth dressed was no problem, but putting on her own clothes was painful. The carrier straps had rubbed her shoulders raw and she was stiff from all the unaccustomed riding. But she was alive, and so was her baby. She hugged Elizabeth gratefully as she started down the hall toward the kitchen.

Sebastian and Matty's bedroom door was still closed, and so was Sebastian's office door, where Nat usually slept. Jessica considered sneaking in and waking him up, but she decided against it. When she talked to him, she wanted him to be wide awake.

The last person she expected to see sitting in the kitchen drinking coffee was her father. But there he was, glancing through some ranching magazine he must have found in the living room.

He was unshaven, and his designer shirt and slacks were wrinkled. Jessica didn't think she'd ever seen him like that in her life. Her heart squeezed. He looked…old. She thought about what Steven Pruitt had said. *He'll pay the money. He has to. You're the most important thing in the world to him.*

She paused in the doorway. "Hi, Dad."

He glanced up quickly. "Jessica." Then the most amazing thing happened. Her father got tears in his eyes.

Her throat grew tight and she blinked rapidly, not wanting her own tears to fall. "I guess…I guess I put you through quite a bit, didn't I?"

"Yes." Her father's voice was gruff. He cleared his throat and glanced at Elizabeth. "She looks like you."

"Dad, I—"

He held up a hand. "Before you say anything, I have something to say. I spent a little time talking to…the baby's father this morning, and—"

"Nat? Isn't he asleep in Sebastian's office?"

"No. Your mother's in there. I took the couch. I think Grady slept down at the barn. When I woke up I went out

for a walk, wandered down to the barn and found him feeding the horses.''

"Oh." Jessica glanced out the kitchen window toward
the barn, as if to catch a glimpse of Nat, but he wasn't in
view.

"So, as I was saying, Grady and I had a conversation.
He helped me understand how much you've needed...
personal freedom over the years. And how little I gave you.
How little I was willing to admit that you're a grown
woman who can take care of yourself.''

She hurried to blame herself before he could. "Some job
I did!''

Her father gazed at her. "Some job you did," he said.
"You have a beautiful daughter and a fine man who loves
you. That's one hell of a job, Jessica.''

Her jaw dropped in astonishment. She'd waited all her
life to hear those words, and she was speechless. "Thank
you," she said at last, fighting tears.

"You're welcome."

She swallowed past the lump in her throat. "Did he—
did Nat—tell you he loved me?''

"Yes, he did. But he doesn't think he's good enough for
you." He gazed at her fondly. "From my standpoint, that's
probably true, because there's not a man out there who *is*
good enough for you. But I figure he might be the best of
the lot. And I have every confidence you may be able to
convince him of that.''

Jessica decided she'd never have a better chance than
now, before the place started bustling again. She walked
over and took Sebastian's sheepskin jacket down from its
peg on the wall by the back door.

Then she returned to the table. "Would you hold her for
a minute?" she asked.

"Me? I don't know if I should."

She gave him a wobbly smile. "I'm sure you've held a
little girl before.''

"That was a long time ago."

Jessica settled Elizabeth in his lap. "Well, some things never change," she said brightly. And then, when she saw her father sitting there holding Elizabeth, tears spilled out of her eyes. "Oh, Daddy." She leaned down and wrapped her arms around both of them. "I love you."

His voice was thick. "I love you, too, Jessica."

When she drew back, he blinked and cleared his throat several times.

She wiped at her eyes and put on Sebastian's big coat. "I'm going down to the barn," she said.

"And leave her here?" He sounded both frightened and excited by the prospect.

"Not this time." She scooped Elizabeth up and tucked her inside the coat. "But soon. This time I need her. She's my bargaining chip."

NAT PUT the rubber stopper in the drain of the big metal sink Sebastian had installed on the front wall of the barn. As the water level rose, he rolled back his sleeves. Then he shut off the water, picked up the sock monkey and dunked him in the water. Some of the loose dirt came off and floated to the surface, but the orange stain that decorated the monkey's face and upper part of its body looked permanent.

Matty should be the one doing this job, Nat thought to himself as he scrubbed the orange stain. She probably knew what to use on something like this. For all he knew, he was making things worse. As usual.

He'd really screwed up this time. At least he'd shot the man who had held Elizabeth at gunpoint. He'd never thought he'd be grateful to his father for anything, but he was glad of all those agonizing hours spent in target practice under his father's stern direction. No, he did not for one minute regret firing that gun.

But he regretted the need for it. If he hadn't left Jess and

Elizabeth unprotected, they never would have fallen into the guy's hands in the first place. He would never forgive himself for that.

The barn door opened and Jess, nearly swallowed in Sebastian's coat, came inside. He wasn't ready to see her yet. He didn't have his speech, the one in which he'd convince her she'd be better off without him.

The coat stuck out in front, and when Elizabeth's curly head poked out, he realized she'd brought the baby along with her. Another person he wasn't ready to see. He dropped the monkey down in the water and hoped to hell Elizabeth hadn't noticed it in his hand.

But she had. She let out a squeal and reached toward the sink. "Ba-ba!"

Damn. He glanced pleadingly at Jess. "He's soaking wet," he said. "I was trying to clean him up, and—"

"You were out here washing Bruce?"

"Yeah. I probably should have let Matty do it, but she's still asleep and I was hoping I might get him in some kind of shape before Elizabeth woke up."

The baby started bouncing in Jess's arms and her cries for her monkey became louder.

"I think that's so sweet." Jess came closer.

"Listen, maybe you should take her back up to the house." That would get Jess out of here, too, so he could plan what he wanted to say. It was hard to think of the right words when she was standing there looking so beautiful in the soft light filtering through the high windows of the barn.

"I think it's too late," Jess said as Elizabeth began to fuss and strain in Nat's direction.

He tried to ignore the warmth in Jessica's eyes. She didn't know what was good for her. "Maybe it's not too late. She might forget that she saw him if you distract her. I'll wring him out and hang him on the clothesline for a while, and maybe by noon he'll be ready to go."

Jess gazed up at him, a little smile on her face. "Wring him out now. I don't think she can wait until noon."

"But he'll still be all wet. And God knows what he'll look like after I squeeze most of the water out. Probably like some alien."

"She won't care what he looks like. She needs that monkey, Nat."

He sighed with resignation. "Okay."

Elizabeth made an unholy fuss while he squeezed as much water out of Bruce as he could. Jess tried to jolly her out of being upset, but she was getting crankier by the minute. Man, she was really raising a ruckus. If his father were here, he'd have backhanded that kid so hard...

Nat stopped wringing out the monkey and stared down at his hands. Yes, his father would have slapped the baby by now. But he hadn't even considered such a thing. And he wouldn't, not in a million years. He could imagine what his father would do, and separate that from what he, Nat Grady, would do.

Turning from the sink, the damp monkey in his hands, he stared at Jess, who was so busy trying to keep Elizabeth happy that she didn't even notice he was looking at her. He wasn't like his father! And he'd figured it out twenty-four hours too late.

He groaned in frustration.

Her gaze met his. "What?"

"I'm an idiot, that's what."

She smiled. "Sometimes."

Elizabeth went wild as she spied the bedraggled monkey. "Ba-ba! Ba-ba!"

"Better give it to her." Jess glanced at the monkey. "Maybe he'll look better when he dries."

"Maybe. Here you go, Elizabeth. Here's Bruce." He extended the monkey by the tail.

Elizabeth grabbed him with another squeal and promptly

stuck the tail in her mouth. As she sucked happily, the rest of Bruce hung down and dripped on Jess's shoes.

"She's going to get you wet," Nat said.

Jess looked into his eyes. "As if I care. Now tell me why you think you're an idiot, and I'll see if I agree."

"I'm not like my father, and if I'd only understood that sooner, then none of this—"

"Back up. Did I hear you say you're not like your father?"

"Yeah, but I didn't figure that out in time, and so you got kidnapped by that creep." He took a shaky breath. "You nearly died, you and Elizabeth, because I was such an idiot."

"But we didn't die. You saved us." She made it sound as if he was a hero. "Where did you learn to shoot like that?"

"My father. You know how some kids are forced to practice the piano? I was forced into target practice. Pretty grim, huh?"

"Why did he do that?"

Nat had hated the whole exercise so much that he'd never paid much attention to the reason his father had given. And he had given one. "He said that he wanted me to be able to protect myself. He wanted me to be tough, and he wanted me to know how to handle a gun, in case I ever got in a tight spot." He glanced at her. "I suppose, in his twisted way, he was trying to prepare me for life."

"I think he was." She moved closer, so that now the monkey was dripping on his feet, too. "How long since you've talked to him?"

"Years."

She hesitated, then forged on. "Do you think that maybe…maybe it's time to let go of some of that bitterness? Especially if you now realize you won't turn out like him?"

He edged around the idea of communicating again with

his father. It didn't look like such a terrible concept, the more he considered it. There was a kind of relief built into it. "Maybe. Not for sure, but…maybe."

"After all, that target practice did come in handy."

And there was the rub. "But the only reason I had to use a gun is because I'd screwed up so royally. Don't you see? I make mistakes, costly mistakes, that mean the people I love can get hurt or killed. I can't expect to shoot my way out of every fix I get myself or others into."

"Nat, I—"

"Let me finish." He took another breath. For some reason he was having trouble breathing, but he had to get this next part out. "That's why I want you to forget about me. I want you to put me out of your mind and out of your life." He hadn't expected the pain in his heart to be so sharp. He nearly gasped from the impact.

"No, you don't." She stepped closer, so that the soggy monkey rested against his chest, soaking his shirt. "You don't want me to forget about you."

"I do! How can I expect you to forgive me for risking your life, for risking our baby's life, if I can't even forgive myself?"

"Nat, there's nothing to forgive. I don't blame you."

"You should!"

"Well, I don't." She gazed up at him. "Because I love you. I will always love you. Of course you make mistakes. So do I. We'll continue to do that until we're sharing rocking chairs on the front porch. Even then we'll probably screw something up once in a while. Mistakes are a part of life. And love."

Oh, God, he wanted to believe her. His throat was tight, and he still couldn't seem to breathe easily. "I want only the best for you and Elizabeth."

"Well, that makes things easy. That means we need you." She lifted her face to his.

"I'm not—"

"Oh, yes, you are. Do you remember telling me to hold on to you?"

"I shouldn't have told you that."

"Too late. You told me, and I'm doing it. Nat, I don't come without baggage, either. Don't forget I have a father who's richer than God."

"That's not your fault."

"Exactly. Just as it's not your fault that you ended up with your father. We have a right to try and make a life for ourselves, don't we?"

The ice around his heart began to melt.

She smiled. "I can tell you're thinking about it. That's a start. Do you love me?"

That he didn't have to think about. "More than my life."

"And Elizabeth?"

He glanced down at the little girl wedged between them.

As she continued to suck noisily on Bruce's tail, she gazed up at him with eyes the same shade as his. Then she reached up and patted her hand against his chin.

His throat threatened to close completely as he thought of what had almost happened to her. When that maniac had held a gun to her head, he'd never known such rage, or such fear. "Yes," he said, his voice gruff with emotion. "Yes, I love Elizabeth."

"Then marry us," Jess whispered. "We need you. And you need us."

He met Jess's gaze, and warmth surged through him, pushing away the last of the cold chill that had surrounded him from the moment he'd regained consciousness and found her gone.

"Put your arms around us," Jess urged, her gaze never leaving his.

Slowly, he did. He didn't deserve this, but maybe he could work to deserve it.

"Will you take us to be your lawfully wedded wife, baby and soggy monkey?" Jess asked softly.

With a groan, Nat pulled them in tight, squeezing more water out of the monkey and sending it cascading down on his boots. It was a stretch, but with some adjustments he was able to touch his mouth to Jess's. He brushed his lips over hers, leaned back and smiled down at her, his love, his life. "Yes," he murmured. "I do."

EPILOGUE

A year later at the grand opening of the Happy Trails Children's Ranch.

JESSICA HUNG UP the phone and hurried through the house to the bedroom, casting loving glances along the way at the hardwood floors, the large windows, the rock fireplace. After only a few months, she already felt completely at home in this place she and Nat had found only a few miles from the Rocking D. And today it was dressed for company.

She ignored the slight twinge in her belly. She would *not* go into labor today.

"Nat." She walked into the bedroom where her husband was fastening the snaps on a white western shirt. God, he was gorgeous. They were approaching their first anniversary and he excited her more than he ever had. "That was the governor's office calling to say he's running a little late," she said, "but he and his wife should be here in time for the ribbon-cutting ceremony."

"No problem." Nat fastened the snaps at his wrists. "Travis has already offered to do some magic tricks to entertain the press if we need to buy some time."

She laughed. "It figures Travis would suggest something like that. But we don't have to worry about entertainment. My dad and Sebastian are putting on a show out in the front yard giving contradictory orders to the television crews. It's like a battle between George Lucas and Steven

Spielberg.'' Another twinge hit her. Probably nothing. ''Of
course, Boone's trying to mediate.''

''I wish him luck on that one.'' Nat grinned as he tucked
his shirttails into a pair of western dress slacks. ''That was
nice of my dad, to send that big plant and the card, huh?''

''It was. Very nice.'' She was thrilled that Nat and his
father were starting to communicate, and she could tell how
much it meant to both of them.

''I'm almost ready.'' He buckled his hand-tooled belt.

''Good. You can go help Boone keep the peace.'' She
allowed herself a moment to ogle the fit of her husband's
slacks, but unfortunately she couldn't linger. As the hostess
of this grand-opening event, she had duties. ''Well, I'd better see how things are progressing in the kitchen.'' She
started toward the door. ''I swear, if Gwen ever wanted to
give up the bed-and-breakfast business, she could make a
fine living as a caterer. Shelby, Matty and I are in total
awe, which is a good thing, because she has us working
like galley slaves.''

''Jess.''

She turned, pleasure zinging through her. Whenever he
spoke her name that way, as if pronouncing the most important syllable in the English language, she melted. She
met his gaze.

''Come here a sec,'' he murmured.

''We have no time,'' she said, even as she walked back
to him, pulled by an invisible velvet rope. Darn it, there
was another twinge. Actually, she couldn't call them
twinges now. It was definitely a contraction.

He reached out and gathered her close. ''The day I don't
have time to hold my wife in my arms is a sorry day indeed.'' He glanced down at her round belly. ''Are you
okay?''

She couldn't go into labor now. She absolutely couldn't.
''I'm fabulous.''

He looked into her eyes and smiled. ''I know that. But

are you sure this whole thing isn't too much for you? I mean, Doc Harrison said it could be any day, and I keep wondering if we should have held off until after the baby came.''

She cupped his face in both hands and willed the contractions to stop. Tomorrow would be fine to have this baby, but not today. ''Are you kidding? We couldn't have postponed a project like this. It's our dream come true, Nat, and we'll be helping so many kids. I can hardly wait until next week when we have our first arrivals, our first little buckaroos, sleeping in those cozy bunkhouses.'' She grinned. ''Just because it feels like I'm twelve months pregnant doesn't mean I can't enjoy this moment.''

He slid both hands down to cup her backside. ''What I want to know is how you can be so pregnant and so sexy at the same time?''

''It's my special talent.'' Another contraction. Shoot! Maybe she'd have to mention it to Nat, just in case.

He caressed her bottom. ''Special talent, huh? In that case, maybe we should have about twenty kids. Because I—''

''Hold on.'' She put a hand over his mouth. ''Do I hear—''

''Babies cryin'!'' Elizabeth raced into the room dragging a sorry-looking sock monkey by the tail. She grabbed Jessica's skirt. ''Come help GammaLu and GammaDell!'' Elizabeth tugged at Jessica's skirt. ''Come *on,* Mommy!''

Jessica gazed in despair at her daughter, who had looked like such a little angel about twenty minutes ago. ''Elizabeth, what's that on your dress?''

The toddler glanced down at her front, where something green was smeared all over the pink material. When she looked up, her matching pink ribbon hung over her eye. ''I dunno. But babies cryin', Mommy! Come see!''

''Lizbeth!'' Josh yelled, pounding into the room after

her. "Come back in there! GrammaLu and GrammaDell *need* us. It's a regular *rodeo.*"

"We'd better go check on things," Nat said.

As Jessica followed Nat down the hall to the bedroom they'd designated as a temporary nursery for the day, Josh and Elizabeth raced ahead of them. Sure enough, babies were crying behind the closed door. And Jessica had another contraction.

Josh flung open the door. "See that? A regular rodeo." He crossed his arms. "That's *girls* for you."

Jessica's mother, Adele, glanced up from her struggle to diaper a screaming Patricia, the three-month-old daughter of Boone and Shelby. Whatever Elizabeth had down her front, Adele had in her hair. It looked like finger paint. And baby spit-up was all over her designer suit. "Oh, thank heaven, Jessica!" she cried above the din. "Can you get Rebecca out of that drawer?"

Jessica started toward Rebecca. Matty and Sebastian's eight-month-old sat in a bottom dresser drawer yelling her head off.

"She climbed in and didn't know how to get out!" Luann shouted by way of explanation as she continued pacing with the squalling four-month-old who belonged to Gwen and Travis. They'd named the baby Luann after her grandmother, but Travis had quickly dubbed her Lulu.

Jessica picked up Rebecca and grabbed a tissue to wipe her nose. Then she turned to Luann. "What's wrong with Lulu?"

Luann grimaced. "She gulped her bottle, like usual, and now she's got enough gas to heat the city of Denver for a month!"

Matty, Shelby and Gwen appeared in the doorway. Matty, with her seven-month-along belly, took up most of the space. She pressed a hand to the small of her back "What's all this noise about?"

Nat stood surveying the room. "The usual," he said with a grin.

Elizabeth waved her hands. "Lizbeth not cryin'," she announced again.

Jessica caught a flash of green on Elizabeth's hands. Uh-oh. Then she glanced down at her linen skirt, the one Elizabeth had been clutching minutes ago. Sure enough, now she had green splotches on her skirt to match the color on the toddler's pink dress. And she had another contraction, this time a hard one.

"Hey, we can hear this racket clear out in the front yard!" Sebastian crowded in behind the women, followed by Boone, Travis and Jessica's father. "What's going on?"

"It's all the girls making noise," Josh said, looking superior.

Jessica glanced over at Nat. "I hate to tell you this, sweetheart, but I think—"

Nat's casual grin disappeared. "It's time?" His voice squeaked.

Jessica nodded.

The group exploded into action. As Nat rushed over to lead her out of the room, Sebastian took Rebecca, Travis scooped up Elizabeth, and Boone picked up Josh. The women followed, with each grandmother carrying a baby.

As they all poured into the living room, someone knocked on the front door.

Jessica's father wrenched it open. "What?" he bellowed.

The television reporter shrank back. "The—the governor and his wife are here, sir. Their limo just pulled up. And I was wondering if—"

"He came in a limo? Great!" Jessica's father turned back to the group surrounding Jessica. "We'll commandeer his limo for the run to the hospital! Come on. Everybody out!"

"But what about the ribbon-cutting ceremony?" Jessica asked as Nat hustled her toward the door.

"It can wait," her father said, beaming at Nat. "Right, son?"

"You bet."

Before Jessica quite realized how it had happened, the governor and his wife were standing on the front porch waving goodbye and all of them were crammed into the stretch limo, crying babies included.

"So," Sebastian shouted above the din as he glanced around at the limo full of people. "What's it gonna be this time, boy or girl?"

Travis, Boone and Nat looked at him, then at each of the screaming babies. The four cowboys grinned. *"Boy!"* they all said together.

For the Baby's Sake
by
Sherry Lewis

To Valerie and Vanessa
who continually amaze me
and fill me with wonder.

CHAPTER ONE

IT WAS ALREADY early evening as Mark Taylor rode the elevator from his office on the twentieth floor to the mall far below. His briefcase was full, and his mind reeled with discovery, exhibits and testimony for his upcoming trial—the trial that would be a turning point in his career.

He paid scant attention to the people around him. He didn't have time for distractions. But when the woman standing in front of the jewelry store caught his eye, his feet stopped moving and his mind lost its train of thought.

Marianne?

He stared, wondering if he could possibly be imagining her. Marianne Holt had disappeared from Boston without a word three years earlier and taken Mark's dream of a home and family with her. He hadn't heard a word from her in all this time, and he'd long ago learned to ignore thoughts of her when they surfaced.

As he watched, the woman turned and gave him a better view of her face. She looked slightly different—her hair had grown from the short cut he remembered—but he'd have recognized her anywhere.

His heart picked up its pace while he hesitated, trying to decide whether to approach her. Mark had never been one to run from a confrontation, and the one he deserved with Marianne was no exception.

He made his way through the crowd and came to a stop behind her. "Picking out an engagement ring?"

She whirled to face him. "Mark," she said, eyes wide.

"Surprised?"

"A little."

Mark didn't know why she should be. He'd worked in this building the entire six months they'd been together, and she knew firsthand about the long hours required to move up in a large law firm.

She glanced away, then met his gaze again. "Actually, I'm here for a conference with an attorney from McAllister and Carter. I thought you'd have gone home by now."

He checked his watch automatically; it was later than he'd thought. "I see. And you figured you'd be safe."

"Something like that. This is late even for you." She laughed uncomfortably, looked behind her as if searching for an escape route, then pulled herself together. "Are you still working your way up the ladder at Jamison and Spritzer?"

"One rung at a time," Mark admitted. "I have a chance to make partner if I can just keep my feet to the fire. And without a home and family, that should be easy enough." He ignored the bitter twist of her mouth and asked, "And what about you? Still practicing law? Or did you give that up along with everything else?"

If his barb found its mark, she didn't show it. "I'm still practicing. I can't imagine not being a litigator."

Her devotion to her career had always been a sore spot between them. Not that Mark had wanted her to give it up. But while he'd indulged in fantasies about a future with a home and children, she'd been planning a life that didn't include those things.

Even after she'd made her feelings clear, Mark had clung to the hope that she'd change her mind…until she'd suddenly ended their relationship by disappearing without a word.

"Well," he said, "as long as you're happy."

"I am, and obviously so are you." She sidled a step away. "It was nice to see you again, Mark, but—"

Resentment Mark had kept buried rushed to the surface. "Don't you think I deserve a few answers before you disappear again?"

Her gaze flew to his. "Answers?"

"Sure." He lifted his shoulders in a deceptively casual shrug. "How about telling me where you went when you left here?"

Marianne took her time responding. Annoyingly cheerful music and chatter of passersby filled the silence, and when her answer finally came, he could barely hear her.

"I went to Idaho."

"Idaho?" He rocked back on his heels, trying and failing to picture Marianne in the rural setting. "Why there?"

"I have family there."

Mark turned his attention to the window display and tried to digest that bit of news. Something didn't feel right. Marianne had never been overly attached to her family. In fact, she'd hardly mentioned them. "I thought your parents lived in Florida?"

A flicker of a smile teased her lips. "I have a second cousin in Boise."

"A second cousin." He said the words slowly, turning them over in his mouth as if that might suddenly help him understand. But it made no sense at all. She'd turned up her nose more than once at the thought of spending birthdays and holidays with his lively bunch of relatives. He couldn't imagine her suddenly developing a yen for family ties. "What made you decide to run off to see this cousin of yours?"

She shrugged as if it didn't matter. "Everything."

He held her gaze, almost daring her to look away. "Don't you think I deserve a better answer than that?"

"It's the only one I can give you." She sounded defiant, but her gaze faltered ever so slightly.

Another man might not have noticed, but Mark had spent years learning to recognize when a witness was trying to hide something. He also knew how to drag out the truth when it was necessary—and it was necessary now, if only for his own peace of mind. "So, you just woke up one morning and realized it was time to go to Idaho."

"Something like that."

"And have you been in Boise all this time?"

"No." She lifted her chin slightly. "I left there two years ago and went to San Francisco."

That sounded more like the Marianne he'd known. "Is that where you live now?"

"Does it matter?"

"Chalk it up to morbid curiosity," he said with a bitter smile. "You know how I hate loose ends. Are you married?"

"No. Are you?"

"No."

Her expression faltered for a moment. "I'm sorry."

"Yeah? Well, so am I." He took a chance and touched her arm lightly. "I loved you, Marianne. And I believed that you loved me. I thought we were building a future together. It took a while to come to terms with losing you, but I managed. Now I just want to know why."

She drew away from his touch. "I had some things I needed to deal with."

"What things?"

"Things." She laced her fingers together and waited while a young couple looked longingly at a ring in the window. "Personal things," she said when they moved away again.

"We were talking about getting married," he reminded her. "What was so personal you couldn't share it with me?"

"You wanted a different life than I did, Mark," she said softly. "Talking to you wouldn't have helped. It would have made everything more difficult."

"Thanks for the vote of confidence." He ran his fingers through his hair, putting three years of frustration into the action. "It's interesting that you'd turn *away* from the man you claimed to love and *to* the family you never saw. What could they do for you that I couldn't?"

Her eyes darkened with anger. "This all happened a long time ago. I don't see any point in talking about it." She took another step away.

Mark knew she intended to walk out on him again.

He made an effort to pull himself together, to hide the anger, hurt and overwhelming sense of waste. "I don't want to get back together with you, if that's what you're worried about. I'm just curious about what made you leave, and why you chose Idaho of all places. It's been three years. What can it hurt to tell me now?"

She sent him a wary glance. "I had things to think about."

"Like what?"

"Like us."

He shook his head quickly. "Don't give me that, Marianne. I might believe taking a month to think things through. I might even understand two or three. But thirty-six? And what about letting me know what you decided...or are you still thinking?"

"I don't need your sarcasm," she warned.

Mark made an effort to drop it. "Look," he said carefully, "I just want a few answers. You ran out and left me completely in the dark. We were fine one day, and you were gone the next. So, what happened?"

She sighed heavily and glanced away again. "You haven't changed at all, have you?"

That stung, but he didn't want her to know that it did. "I guess not. Put yourself in my shoes for a minute. What if I'd been the one to disappear without a word. Wouldn't you want an explanation?"

She remained silent for so long, he began to give up hope. Just when he was ready to forget about trying to tie up loose ends, she turned a troubled gaze in his direction. "If I tell you, will you leave me alone?"

"Yes, of course."

"You won't like it."

"What difference can it make now, other than to fill in the blanks I've been carrying around with me?" He tried to soften everything about his expression—his eyes, his mouth, the set of his jaw.

"Okay." She took a steadying breath and studied his face for another moment, then seemed to come to a decision. "I was pregnant."

The music faded and the people around them disappeared. Disbelief, joy, anger, excitement and bitterness all corkscrewed together in his stomach. But outrage rose to obliterate everything else. "You were pregnant?"

She nodded without looking at him and lifted one hand to pluck nervously at the shoulder of her blouse. "Yes."

"Was it my baby?" He could barely get the words out.

"Of course."

"Then why did you disappear?"

"I had to think," she said in a near whisper. "I had to decide what to do."

What to *do?* What choices were there? Only two—one of which Mark found utterly unthinkable. And he knew without being told which one she'd made. Consumed by outrage, he looked into the eyes of the woman who'd killed his child.

Somehow, he managed to find his voice. "Shouldn't that have been a choice we made together?"

"*You* weren't pregnant."

"It was my child."

"And my body." She met his gaze steadily. "My choice to make."

"We're talking about a life, Marianne. A human being, not a possession you can get rid of because it doesn't fit the color scheme of your apartment."

Anger flashed in her eyes. "I know you don't think much of me, Mark. But I can't believe you're so willing to assume I decided on an abortion."

The roaring in his ears quieted and hope took the place of blind fury. "You didn't?"

"I decided not to. I carried the baby to term." She rested her hand on the narrow ledge outside the store and half smiled at him. "It was a boy."

He had a son. Hope pushed aside every other emotion and made his hands tremble. Tears of joy burned his eyes. "When can I see him?"

"You can't. I don't have him."

The spark of hope died. "You gave my son away?"

"I thought it would be best for everyone."

"Did it ever occur to you that it might not be best for me, or for him? That *I* might want to raise him?"

"With *your* career?" Marianne laughed and brushed a lock of hair away from her face. "Get real, Mark. You wouldn't have had time for him, either. No matter what you say, you're as married to your career as I am to mine, and I thought he deserved a life with parents who would put him first. Besides, I didn't want to see you."

"You wouldn't have had to see me," he said, clenching his fists until the stubs of his nails bit into his palms. "Where is he? What agency did you use?"

Marianne's eyes narrowed. "Why?"

"Because I'm going to find him, and I'm going to get him back."

"Oh, no." She shook her head and backed away. "You can't."

"If you think that, you don't know me at all."

"You can't raise a child alone. Not with the hours you work."

"He's my son, Marianne. Maybe you don't want him, but I do."

"He's been with my cousin for more than two years," she argued. "As far as he knows, she and her husband are his parents. *I* haven't even seen him."

"Is that supposed to make me change my mind?" He laughed harshly. "I don't care where he's been. I don't care who he's been with. You've stolen two years from me, and that's time I can't ever get back no matter what happens now."

Marianne drew herself up and faced him, no longer an ex-girlfriend but the attorney he'd always respected. "You can't take him from them. It wouldn't be right."

"Was it right for you to give him away without even discussing it with me?"

"Maybe not, but I can't turn back the clock and change that. What's done is done—"

He cut her off. "Is the adoption final?"

She hesitated just long enough to give him hope. *"Is it?"*

"I shouldn't have told you," she muttered. "I should have known you'd act like this."

Mark had gone beyond caring what she thought of him. "Tell me now," he said coldly, "or I'll take you to court to find out. It's up to you. I want every detail—his date of birth, the name of the hospital where he was born. Everything."

She looked as if she could cheerfully kill him, but he knew that he'd worried her. He hoped she'd want to avoid a messy personal lawsuit—especially one that was sure to get media attention. That the same love for her career that had made her decide to give his baby away would convince her to cooperate.

Instead, she checked her watch and shook her head. "I'm late. They'll be waiting for me upstairs." She turned to walk away, then added, "I've told you all you need to know, Mark. For all our sakes, leave it alone."

This time Mark let her go, but he wasn't about to take her advice. He had right on his side. He also had connections and training. The law no longer turned a blind eye on the rights of a child's birth father, and he intended to take full advantage of that. If Marianne wouldn't tell him what he needed to know, he'd track down her cousin and see what she could tell him. One way or another, he'd find his son and get him back.

EXHAUSTED AFTER a full workweek, Dionne Black stopped the stroller and unfastened the harness that barely contained Jared's squirming little body. August heat shimmered on the distant foothills, now golden-brown with drying wild grasses. A slight breeze stirred the tops of the cottonwood trees along the riverbank and made it more pleasant here than inside Dionne's tiny apartment with its woefully inadequate air conditioner.

The faint sounds of nearby traffic mingled with the cries of children clambering over playground equipment. Joggers passed her on the trail, huffing slightly, and she caught snatches of conversation as walkers in groups passed. She loved bringing Jared to the park in the evenings. It gave her a good excuse to slow down for an hour or two.

Lifting her excited son from the stroller, she started to wrap her arms around him for a hug, but he wriggled away. She smiled, telling herself she should know better than to expect cuddles from the energy-packed two-year-old before bedtime. Jared had more vigor and curiosity than she and Brent could ever have imagined.

She pushed away the sadness that always came when she let herself think about Brent. "All right, Jared," she said, setting the toddler down, "get moving. Let's work those wiggles out."

Jared started across the grass like a windup toy with wheels spinning. Dionne had always loved living in the heart of Boise, but lately she'd begun to wonder if she should move to the suburbs. There she'd be able to let Jared run and play without worrying that he'd dart out into the busy streets.

Some days, like today, she wondered whether she'd be able to keep up with him. Brent was supposed to be here with her, helping, chasing, laughing, teaching Jared about being a boy. But the accident last year had taken Brent from them.

No amount of wishing could change that, and she'd made a vow to be happy, if only for Jared's sake. Besides, Brent wouldn't want her to mourn forever. She could almost see him scowling at her and the clouds in his clear blue eyes.

I'm fine, she told him silently. *I'm just tired.* Her work at the insurance agency often left her exhausted, physically as well as emotionally. Maybe one day she'd go back to school and get her degree so she could work with disadvantaged children as she'd always dreamed. But right now she had to bring in a steady income, and that meant doing the monotonous work she hated so much.

Tucking her keys into her pocket, she started after Jared. "Don't go too fast, cutie. Mommy can't keep up."

He giggled over his shoulder and ran a little faster on his unsteady legs. "Over there," he said, pointing toward the jungle gym.

Of course he wanted to climb. Jungle gyms, stairs, cabinets—Jared didn't care, as long as he could go up and then jump down again.

"How about the swings instead," she suggested, catching up to him and holding out a hand to help him over the low concrete barrier that separated the playground from the rest of the park.

Jared shook his determined little head and scowled up at her. "Me do it."

"All right, you do it."

The breeze stirred the air again, tousling his dark hair as he worked his chubby legs over the step. Finally successful, he beamed up at her. "Swing."

"Okay. Let's see if we can find one with a belt so you won't fall out."

He toddled across the sand, and she had to hurry to catch him before he moved too close to the flying feet of other swinging children.

Luckily, they found an empty chair complete with safety strap, and within just a few minutes she had him swinging gently.

"More," he cried. "Go high, Mommy."

"You are going high," she assured him. High enough, anyway. In protest, he arched his body, pushing against the harness that held him in place. "You have to sit still," she warned, "or Mommy won't push anymore."

When he bucked against the restraint again, she caught the swing and held it. "Sit still, Jared."

His face puckered into an unhappy scowl and for a moment she thought he'd cry. He tried to twist in the seat to see her. "I wanna... I wanna go high."

"You were going high," she said gently. "Now, sit still or you'll have to get out." She wondered if all two-year-olds were so determined to go higher and faster, or if he'd inherited the trait from one of his biological parents.

Jared folded his tiny arms and scowled at her. "High."

"Shall we get you out?"

"No."

"Will you sit still, then?"

"No."

He looked so serious, she had to bite back a smile. "Either you sit still, or Mommy will get you down. Those are your choices."

They indulged in a silent battle of wills for a few seconds until Jared eventually, reluctantly, gave in. He shifted back in his seat and held on to the front of the chair. "Push, Mommy."

"Good boy." She gave him a gentle shove and let her gaze travel to the benches facing the playground.

If anyone had asked, she couldn't have said what it was about the man sitting there that bothered her. He'd been here every evening for the past week or more. He looked innocent enough—just a kindly middle-aged gentleman taking a rest on a park bench—but every once in a while, when he didn't think she was watching, she could swear he was following Jared with his eyes. Tonight, he had someone with him. A younger man of about thirty wearing a dark suit.

Dionne tried to relax. Maybe the younger man was his son. Maybe they were here enjoying the park and the breeze, just as she was. But she couldn't shake the inexplicable apprehension that pumped through her veins with every heartbeat.

To the best of her knowledge, the man hadn't ever followed her home. She was probably overreacting, but she took every precaution to make sure she and Jared were safe. She never stayed late, always took a circuitous route to her apartment, and avoided deserted streets. She'd even started carrying a can of pepper spray.

And now there was a second man—

If anything, the younger one seemed even more menacing. She studied them circumspectly so she could describe the younger man in as much detail as the older one if the need arose. Dark hair. Thirty to thirty-five years old. And he looked tall. Even sitting, he towered over his companion, and his legs, stretched out in front of him, reached halfway across the sidewalk. She paid only slight attention to his clothing—that didn't matter as much as his features—but she was too far away to get a good look at his face.

Tonight instinct told her to get Jared out of the swing and take him home. Home, to the safety of their tiny apartment with its dead-bolt locks on the doors. She hated the idea of keeping Jared cooped up all day at the baby-sitter's and all evening, too.

But she couldn't bear the thought of anything happening to him.

Scarcely daring to breathe, she waited until a woman she recognized from her building started herding her children away from the playground. Ignoring Jared's protests, Dionne stopped the swing, unbuckled the restraints and managed to hold him close until they got back to the stroller.

She forced a friendly smile and started a conversation with the other woman, falling into step beside her as if it was the most natural thing in the world. Only then did she dare to send a surreptitious glance over her shoulder, hoping she'd find the men chatting casually or watching someone else.

But what she saw sent a finger of ice down her spine. The younger man had risen to his feet and had even taken a few steps after them. The older gentleman was speaking quickly, urgently, motioning him back to the bench, but both men had their eyes locked on Dionne as she took Jared home.

MARK WATCHED the petite blond woman disappear into the trees with his son. *His son.* It had been two weeks since Marianne dropped her bombshell, but he still hadn't gotten used to the idea that he had a child. Now it was even more difficult to believe that the active little boy he'd just watched was his flesh and blood.

"Don't frighten her," Saul Mason growled, tugging him back to the park bench.

Mark sat reluctantly, though every cell in his body urged him to go after them. Saul was right. He didn't want to tip his hand too soon.

He sent the private detective a sidelong glance. "You're absolutely certain that was him?"

"Positive." Saul rested both arms on the back of the wooden park bench. "He was easy to find, the adoption being a private placement and all. And it was pure, dumb luck that I found him and your girl-friend's cousin together. Two birds with one stone, so to speak."

"Tell me about her again."

"Her name's Dionne Black. Widowed. Husband was killed in a car accident about six months after the boy went to live with them. They were trying to get their ducks in a row, so to speak, so they could adopt him." Saul's lips curved in a tight smile. "The husband being gone might make your case easier to win."

Mark had a brief flurry of sympathy for the woman, but who was he kidding? He knew he'd do anything to get his son back—even use the woman's misfortune to his advantage. But he wasn't naive, either. Mr. Black's death might make the judge sympathetic to the widow. A vicious divorce would have served Mark better.

"What do we know about Mrs. Black?"

"She works at Intermountain Health Providers," Saul replied. "It's an insurance agency with an office in the Mead Building downtown. She's been there for a couple of years, working in the claims department. Looks like she went to work for them right after her husband died."

"At least she didn't sit back with her hand out waiting for someone else to take care of her and the boy." Mark stared at the trees again, remembering the way she'd looked back at them as she spirited his son away, wondering what kind of caregiver she was.

Saul crossed his legs and let his gaze travel toward the river. "She has no family to speak of. An uncle somewhere in California, but both parents are gone. Father deserted the family when she was little. Mother passed away when she was sixteen." He flicked a glance at Mark and added, "Her in-laws are still alive, but they live in Florida."

Mark thought that might work to his advantage, as well. He turned his gaze away from the trees. "Did you get financial records?"

Saul pulled a folded document from his shirt pocket and passed it over. "I have the rest here, too. Where the kid goes while she's working, her home address, the whole nine yards."

Mark scanned the paper quickly, noting that Dionne Black didn't have many resources to draw upon. While she earned a reasonable salary, and didn't have a lot of debt, she obviously wouldn't be able to afford a lengthy court case.

"So what's next?" Saul asked.

"Next," Mark said, tucking the woman's financial records into his own pocket, "I take a trip to the courthouse and get the ball rolling. The sooner I get the custody suit filed, the sooner I can take Jared home with me."

"You want me to keep watching them?"

"Absolutely. She looks stable enough on paper, but I don't want to take any chances on her bolting after the constable serves the complaint."

"You got it." Saul stood and spent a few seconds readjusting his shirttail inside the waistband of his polyester slacks. He glanced at Mark, then at the nearly empty playground. "Of course, she'll be more cautious now that you've drawn attention to us. I might need a little more for expenses…" Another quick glance. "In case I need to rent a car or take other precautions to keep a low profile."

Mark pulled out his checkbook and flipped it open. "How much?"

"A thousand?"

A small price to pay, considering what was at stake. Mark wrote the check and handed it to Saul with a warning. "Don't let her know you're watching."

"I got you this far, didn't I?" Saul said, stuffing the check into his pants pocket. "You've seen your kid. And if it hadn't been for the mistake *you* made, she wouldn't have even noticed me."

Mark stood to face him, but he had to look down to meet the man's eyes. "She must have noticed you before this or she wouldn't have taken off like that."

Saul drew himself up to his full height, which put him even with Mark's shoulders. "Maybe. But she's never gotten spooked before."

With effort, Mark bit back a defensive response. Much as he'd like to, he couldn't deny Saul's accusation. He *had* made a mistake by starting after her. He just hadn't been able to stop himself.

He muttered something about checking with the detective the following day and started toward the far entrance of the park—the opposite direction from the one Dionne Black had taken with his son. He turned his face into the slight breeze and hoped it would wipe away some of the tension that seemed to knot every muscle in his body. But it didn't help. He had to struggle against the urge to double back and find the address Saul had given him, just to see where his son lived.

Until he had the court documents on file, he'd be smart to ignore his heart and stay as far away from her and Jared as possible.

CHAPTER TWO

"IS HE STILL out there?"

Dionne shook her head without turning from the apartment window. This was the fourth day in a row she'd seen the man watching them, but just like those other times, he'd vanished into thin air. Evening shadows had already begun to pool beneath the trees and shrubs. Rush-hour traffic had thinned to nothing more than a few stragglers hurrying home. She couldn't see the man anywhere.

Her friend, Cicely Logan, tried to peer through the chink in the living-room curtains over Dionne's shoulder. "Are you sure it was the guy from the park?"

"Positive." Dionne turned away from the window and lowered herself into a chair. Her hands still trembled and her heart thudded as if she'd been running up stairs.

Cicely took her friend's place at the window, and the fading sunlight formed a halo of her curly, dark hair. "It was the older man? The one you've noticed in the park before?"

"Yes." Dionne had trouble getting the word out. "He's been lurking outside all weekend and was on the sidewalk in front of my office again yesterday."

Cicely's dark eyes narrowed with worry. "What about the younger guy?"

"I haven't seen him since that day at the park." Dionne rubbed the bridge of her nose gently, wondering if it really had been only four days ago. It felt like a lifetime.

"Have you called the police?"

"Of course." Dionne's head pounded in rhythm with her heart, the product of nearly sleepless nights and stress-filled days. "They can't do anything unless *he* does something. There's no law against sitting in the park, or being on the sidewalk outside my office, or even across the street from my apartment. I can't say for sure that he's watching me."

Cicely let the curtain drop and turned back to the room. Her expression tightened when she looked at Jared, who was content for the moment with a stack of brightly colored building blocks. "If anyone tries to hurt him, I'll kill them."

Bile rose in Dionne's throat at hearing her own fears voiced aloud. "You don't think—" The rest of the sentence caught on her almost tangible fear.

Cicely seemed to realize she'd made things worse and dropped a comforting hand to Dionne's shoulder. "Maybe it's nothing. Maybe he lives nearby. Or maybe he thinks you're attractive and wants to ask you out."

Dionne sent her a doubtful smile. "He's old enough to be my father."

"Maybe he is."

Dionne gave her head an emphatic shake. "No, he's not."

"How can you be certain? You were only Jared's age when your dad disappeared."

"He didn't disappear," Dionne said, her voice

sharp. "He walked out on us to live with another woman. There's a difference."

"Maybe he's come back again."

"He wouldn't. And if he has, it's too late. My mother killed herself working two and three jobs to support me while he never once looked back. I'll never forgive him for that."

Cicely dropped onto an ottoman near Dionne's feet and grabbed her ice-cold hands. "Forget I said anything. It's probably not him. It's probably nothing at all. But I'll stay here with you if you want me to."

Grateful tears filled Dionne's eyes. "What would I do without you?"

Cicely shrugged away the question. "That's what friends are for. Give me half an hour to get my things, and I'll be back."

Dionne blinked up at her and tried to smile. "You don't have to do that. The doors are deadbolted, the windows secure, and we're three floors up. We'll be fine. I just don't know what I'd do without you to talk to, that's all."

Cicely dropped Dionne's hands and craned to see out the window again. "I don't mind staying."

"Thanks, but it's not necessary. I'm sure I'm over-reacting. I've been alone every night since Brent's accident." As Dionne trailed one finger along the silver frame that held his picture, an unexpected twinge of anger darted through her. If he'd been here, she wouldn't have to worry.

Swallowing guilt, she stood and turned away from the picture. "Just do me a favor," she said to Cicely. "Watch for this guy when you leave. He was wearing brown pants, a green-striped short-sleeved shirt, and—"

When the doorbell cut her off, she shot a panicked look at Cicely and sent up a silent prayer of gratitude that her friend hadn't left yet.

Moving on tiptoe, she crossed to the door and checked the outside entrance through the peephole. To her surprise, a uniformed officer stood on the threshold.

"It's the police," she mouthed to Cicely, who'd moved to Jared's side.

"Good." Cicely scooped Jared from the floor. "Maybe they're going to do something, after all."

Dionne opened the door and took a long look at the man's badge and uniform. "Yes? Can I help you?"

"Dionne Black?" He didn't even bother removing his sunglasses.

"Yes."

Without another word, he held a thick manila envelope toward her. When she took it, he made a notation on a document attached to a clipboard, curved his lips in a facsimile of a smile and pivoted away.

Dionne watched until he reached the elevator, then she closed the door and leaned against it.

"What is it?" Cicely gave in to Jared's wriggling and set him back on the floor.

"I don't know." Trembling, Dionne tore open the envelope, pulled the document partway out and scanned the court heading. "I'm being sued by someone named Mark Taylor."

Cicely's expression grew even more sober. "Who is he?"

"I have no idea." Dionne could almost taste the apprehension now. "This couldn't have anything to do with Brent's accident, could it? It's been such a long time—''

"Read the rest," Cicely urged, closing the distance between them.

As Dionne took in the caption, she grew numb with disbelief.

"What is it?" Cicely prodded again.

"It's a Complaint for Custody of Minor Child." She managed to choke out the words, but every one ripped a piece from her heart. Her worst nightmare had come true. Someone wanted to take Jared away from her.

She let the document drop to the floor and covered her mouth with her hands. She saw her friend scramble for it and pick it up.

Cicely flipped pages, reading quickly. Her soft brown face hardened. Her eyes glinted. "This can't be real."

But it was. Horribly, frighteningly real.

Cicely touched Dionne's arm gently. "We'll call my cousin. He's a lawyer. I'm sure he'll help. But, Dionne, this can't be real. Your cousin, Jared's birth mother, wanted *you* to raise him."

With all her heart, Dionne wished she could believe Cicely, but the vague sense of foreboding that had been plaguing her finally had a shape—someone was coming for Jared. And he had a name.

Mark Taylor—Jared's father.

WITH TREMBLING FINGERS, Dionne dug the old address book from the bottom drawer of her dresser. She turned pages quickly, sustaining a paper cut and accidentally tearing a page in the process. She could hear Cicely in the other room, soothing Jared, urging him to sleep.

She had an old telephone number for Marianne somewhere, but she had no idea if it was still current. Marianne had made it abundantly clear that she had no room in her life for Jared. Her career came first. At the time, Marianne's promise to disappear from their lives had seemed like such a good idea. Dionne and Brent had thought they had plenty of time to gently tell Jared the truth about his birth and to give him a chance to choose whether or not he wanted to meet the woman who'd given him life.

Marianne had assured Dionne over and over again that Jared's birth father would never be an issue. He was, Marianne had told her, completely devoted to his career. She'd given Dionne the impression that the relationship had been short-lived and casual, but the affidavit attached to his complaint certainly didn't bear that out.

Taking one ragged breath after another, Dionne flipped a few more pages and scanned the cramped writing for Marianne's name. They didn't come from a close-knit family, and though they had a relationship of sorts, they really were more like casual acquaintances than cousins. That's why she'd been so surprised when Marianne first approached them about taking Jared.

Marianne hadn't told her parents about the pregnancy. They wouldn't have approved, and she hadn't wanted to deal with their disappointment along with everything else an unexpected pregnancy brought into her life. She'd wanted to make sure Jared was placed with a loving family, but her work in the legal field had left her leery of people in general, so she'd taken a chance with Dionne and Brent.

Though Dionne had never seriously considered adoption before, it had taken less than a minute for her to come to a decision. Brent had been equally thrilled with the idea. Jared had literally been the answer to their prayers and, it seemed, they were the answer to Marianne's.

But she hadn't been in contact with Marianne since the day Marianne had left Jared with them and driven away from Boise.

Now Dionne had to find her. She had to know more about Mark Taylor, and how he'd found her after all this time. She wanted Marianne to explain why the story she'd told two years ago didn't jibe with the affidavit sitting on Dionne's coffee table tonight.

Finally, after what felt like forever, she found the notation she'd made with Marianne's number, written in pencil that was now half rubbed away. She sat on the edge of the bed and pulled the phone onto her lap. Her hands were trembling and she was having difficulty drawing breath.

She turned on the bedside lamp and squinted to make out her writing, then dialed quickly and held her breath while the phone rang four times. When the answering machine clicked on—a generic computer-generated voice that announced the number she'd dialed and instructed her to leave a message—she let out her breath and closed her eyes.

"I have no idea if I've reached the right number," she said quietly, "but if Marianne Holt is at this number, or if you know where to reach her, please ask her to call her cousin Dionne." She left her own number, replaced the receiver slowly, and clutched the telephone.

"Any luck?" Cicely's voice caught her off guard and pulled her head up with a snap.

"I found a number," Dionne said, "but I don't know if she's still there."

"What about your uncle? Won't he know how to reach her?"

"Maybe." Dionne met Cicely's dark gaze slowly. "If I don't hear back from her tomorrow, I'll try to call him."

"You should call him tonight," Cicely urged. "It would make you feel better."

Dionne shook her head quickly. "Uncle Charlie doesn't know about Jared. Marianne wanted it that way." She didn't go into any further detail. Cicely wouldn't understand the stone walls that seemed to separate each individual in her family, the long periods of silence that all of them just accepted.

Sometimes, she envied families like Cicely's where the people seemed to care about one another deeply, where they shared confidences and visited often. But she couldn't change what was, and it did no good to dwell on it.

Cicely came to sit beside her. "Maybe you should call your uncle anyway, if only for your own peace of mind."

Dionne shook her head again and tried to change the subject. "Is Jared asleep?"

"Yes. Finally." Cicely pushed a lock of hair away from her face. "He knows something's wrong."

"I'd be surprised if he didn't pick up on it," Dionne admitted. A yawn overtook her, but she fought it. She'd already been without sleep for three nights in a row, and she doubted she'd get any tonight, either.

As if she could read Dionne's mind, Cicely stood and started toward the bathroom. "Do you have anything in here to help you sleep?"

"Probably. I never did use those pills they gave me after Brent died. But I don't want to take anything."

"You need something, girl. You'll be no good to Jared if you wear yourself out."

Dionne opened her mouth to protest, then clamped it shut again. "I'll try to rest," she promised, "but I don't want to drug myself to sleep. I don't dare."

"Even if I stay here and keep one eye open at all times?"

Dionne hesitated, then shook her head again. "I'll sleep," she promised. But she could tell by the way her friend's eyes narrowed and her mouth thinned that Cicely didn't believe her. "I just need to be alone for a while. I need to think."

"I'll be back in the morning to check on you," Cicely warned, "and you'd better look more rested than you do right now."

That would take a miracle, Dionne thought. And she wasn't going to hold her breath waiting.

DIONNE COULDN'T SIT STILL. She paced in front of the leather sofa, ignoring the receptionist's pitying smile. Dionne had waited three endless days for this appointment with the attorney Cicely's cousin had recommended, and now she had to wait again. She hadn't eaten much in days, hadn't been able to concentrate at work, and couldn't remember the last time she had more than an hour or two of sleep at one stretch. All the waiting and uncertainty left Dionne feeling as if she was teetering on the edge of a cliff.

She'd finally succumbed and called Uncle Charlie, giving a vague excuse for needing to reach Marianne. He'd given her a phone number for Marianne at work—not that it had done her any good. Marianne's secretary had informed her that Marianne was out of town on business until the following week. The woman had taken Dionne's name and number but had seemed completely unmoved by Dionne's repeated pleas about the urgency of her call. Dionne didn't hold out much hope that Marianne would get the message before she returned.

The woman watched as Dionne strode to the end of the waiting area and started back again. "I'm sure Mr. Butler will be here soon," she said, her voice low and soothing.

It wouldn't be soon enough for Dionne. She didn't think she could wait another minute. Her nerves were stretched taut, her ability to cope with even the smallest provocation almost nonexistent.

"Would you like me to find some other magazines for you?" the receptionist asked. "The ones we have out here are pretty old."

Dionne shook her head quickly. "No, thanks. I wouldn't be able to concentrate." Her pacing was probably driving the poor woman batty, but she couldn't seem to stop.

When she'd talked with the attorney on the phone, he'd assured her they had plenty of time to file an official answer with the court. Her response to Mark Taylor's custody suit wasn't due for another seventeen days. Logically, she knew nothing could happen until then, but every minute she wasn't doing something to stop the man felt like time wasted.

Behind her, the outer door of the office opened and a short, heavyset man with thin, blond hair stepped inside. He smiled at the receptionist and checked an upright tray for messages, then turned to Dionne. "Are you Mrs. Black?"

Dionne nodded. "Rudy Butler?"

He held out his hand and engulfed hers for a quick shake. "Sorry to keep you waiting. My court hearing took a little longer than expected."

He motioned her toward a long corridor lined with wooden shelves of law books. "I took a look at the complaint you faxed me," he said as they walked. "Unfortunately, precedent has been set for the kind of case Taylor has filed, so even without complications, it's not going to be as easy to win as it might have been a few years ago."

Dionne's heart squeezed painfully. "Complications? What kind of complications?" When the lawyer didn't answer, she pressed. "We will win, won't we? The court won't let him take Jared away?"

Rudy closed the door to his office, and gestured toward one of his client chairs as he settled himself behind a cluttered desk. Between stacks of files on the credenza behind him were pictures of a woman and three smiling children. His family? Somehow the sight of them comforted her. At least he understood a parent's love.

He leaned back in his seat and linked his hands behind his head. "I have to be honest with you, Mr. Taylor has a strong case."

Her insides turned to ice. The world in front of her shifted and blurred as tears filled her eyes. She tried to make sense of what he'd said, but the words ran together in her ears.

The lawyer leaned his arms on the desk and waited until she got the tears under control. "The first thing we need to do is have you answer some questions for me."

"Yes. Of course." Her response came out as nothing more than a whisper.

"The child has been with you for how long?" Rudy asked, flipping through a document as if he didn't really expect her to answer.

"Jared," she choked out.

"Excuse me?"

"His name is Jared." She tried desperately to sound strong, to act as if she wasn't falling apart. Jared needed her now more than ever. "He's been living with me for the past two years since he was only a few days old. My husband and I had planned to adopt him."

"Yes, of course." He looked at her over the rims of his glasses. "But you never did?"

"No. His birth mother is my second cousin. I know she wanted me to have him, but I didn't feel right about pushing her too hard."

The truth was, she had been afraid that if she pressed, Marianne would change her mind. To this day, she couldn't understand how Marianne had been able to leave Jared and go on with her life.

Rudy's eyebrows furrowed and his dark eyes clouded. "So, she never signed a consent for adoption?"

"No, she—" Dionne broke off and took a ragged breath. "Marianne thought about having an abortion, but I guess all the religious training her parents gave her stopped her. She decided to put Jared up for adoption, but she was afraid he'd go to someone who wouldn't love him as much as he deserves. She told us that she felt better giving him to someone in the family, even if she and I weren't exactly close. I thought she'd eventually sign the consent, but Brent had his doubts. He wanted to go to court and prove that she'd abandoned Jared, but I didn't want to stir up trouble.''

''I see.'' Rudy linked his hands again. ''Well, there's no doubt you'd have a stronger case if you'd started the adoption process.'' He sent her an unreadable glance. ''Or even if your husband were still alive.''

Dionne rubbed her forehead gingerly and tamped down a flash of anger at the callous comment. ''That's not something I can change, Mr. Butler. I want to know how this Mark Taylor person can do this. He isn't even listed on the birth certificate as the father. How can a court of law take him seriously?''

Rudy lurched forward, pulled a large envelope from beneath a file, and held it out to her. ''You'd better take a look at this. I received it by courier this morning.''

Scarcely breathing, Dionne removed a thick document from inside but her mind refused to work and her eyes still didn't want to focus. ''What is it?''

''A transcript of a deposition given by your cousin. Apparently, she's admitted under oath that Mr. Taylor is the child's birth father.''

Dionne's sudden, unreasonable anger at Marianne was almost as strong as her fear. ''What does this mean?''

"This means," Rudy said gently, "that any judge will probably give him the right to take custody immediately."

No! The word echoed through her heart, her mind, her soul. "He's *not* Jared's father," she cried, standing so fast she nearly knocked over the heavy chair. "He hasn't even been around for the past two years. He's never even *seen* Jared. How can he claim to be a father?"

Rudy lifted an eyebrow. "Have you read the complaint thoroughly?"

"Yes, but…"

"Then you know that Mr. Taylor claims he only recently learned about the boy."

Jared, her mind insisted. The attorney's refusal to call Jared by name made her feel as if he saw him as a commodity instead of a person. Maybe she should find another attorney—one who would see Jared as a human being. One who could comprehend the seriousness of this threat to their lives. But she'd never find one who'd agree to work with her on a payment arrangement as a favor to Cicely's cousin.

As if he could read her mind, Rudy's face softened. "I know this is upsetting, Mrs. Black. Believe me, I wish I could offer you more hope."

He sounded so resigned, Dionne wanted to scream. "There has to be something we can do."

"We can try appealing to the court—"

"Then let's do it."

"—but all too often cases end up being about semantics rather than what's fair. Unfortunately, the judge we've drawn for this case is a real stickler for going by the book." Rudy sent her a thin smile. "A lot of us call her a pit bull in panty hose. Not exactly politically correct, but…'' He lifted his shoulders in a gesture of helpless surrender.

Dionne refused to give up so easily. "We can find another judge, can't we?"

"I'm afraid not. Cases are assigned randomly. Litigants aren't allowed to go judge-shopping."

One after another, he was crushing her slim hopes. "Then what *can* we do?"

Rudy shrugged again. "You're aware that Mr. Taylor has petitioned the court for visitation until the matter of custody is settled?"

"Yes, but—"

"I think you should agree to let him see Jared."

Dionne shook her head emphatically. "No."

Rudy held up a hand to quiet her. "Hear me out, Mrs. Black. Right now, your best bet is to at least *appear* cooperative. We can agree to visitation, but request that the judge grant supervised visits, which means you could be there."

"But I don't *want* to be there," Dionne replied. "I don't want to see him. And I don't want him to see Jared."

Rudy linked his fingers together on his desk. "I'll bet my reputation that the judge will grant visitation, whether you agree or not."

"But what if he runs off with Jared? What if he disappears?"

"That's very unlikely. He's an attorney with a large firm in Boston and he has a reputation to protect. I think we can trust him."

"Trust?" The word came out too loud, too harsh. It echoed off the walls of his office for a second or two.

"I understand how difficult this is for you," Rudy

said again, "but I really don't see that you have much choice."

Never in her life had Dionne felt so helpless, not even after Brent's accident.

"In the course of the visits," Rudy went on, "you can try appealing to Mr. Taylor on a compassionate level. Maybe if he sees how deeply you love the boy, he'll change his mind."

At last, a flicker of hope. Small. Almost nonexistent. But it gave her something to cling to. "I'll try," she agreed in a whisper. "But can't we convince the judge to refuse his petition? Won't she understand that this will traumatize Jared?"

"I wouldn't count on it. Many people think two-year-olds are too young to understand what's happening around them. And that if they do have upsetting circumstances, they'll eventually forget."

"That's not true," she argued. "I have memories from when I was that age." Vague ones, to be sure, but she still had images of her mother's hysteria after her father walked out.

Rudy acknowledged her point with a nod. "I agree with you. I happen to believe that children that young can remember. But I don't get to make the decision here."

"We have to try something," she said again, more to herself than to the attorney. "This man has no right to take Jared."

"Unfortunately," Rudy said softly, holding her gaze with eyes that held a warning, "if what your cousin says under oath is true—and I have no reason to believe it's not—Mark Taylor has every right."

CHAPTER THREE

IT WAS ONLY a matter of time now, Mark thought with a smile as he sipped from a glass of wine and watched the waiter clear away the last of his dinner. Candlelight flickered across white-clothed tables, and strategically placed houseplants made most of the tables feel secluded. Soft music playing from well-hidden speakers relaxed him even further.

Everything was going like clockwork so far. Soon, he'd be on his way back to Boston with his son. *His son.* The words still sounded unbelievable to him.

Marianne hadn't liked answering his questions during the deposition in his office back in Boston. Her anger had been evident in every word and gesture. But she couldn't refuse the summons, and once there, she'd been put under oath. Her respect for the law hadn't allowed her to lie—in spite of her unexpected loyalty to her family. He had all the pieces now, the lawsuit was under way, and the woman who'd been raising Jared had been served with the legal documents.

He'd even arranged things so he'd never have to meet Dionne Black face-to-face. The local attorney he'd hired would act as go-between for the custody transfer. Not that Mark was afraid of facing her, but he'd rather avoid that unpleasantness and spare Jared as much emotional upheaval as possible.

All he had to do was wait.

The only thing he had left to worry about was how Jared would make the transition to his new home and family. When Mark called his parents at their home in New Hampshire to give them the good news, they'd been stunned at first that they had another grandchild, but their shock had given way to excitement. In fact, his mother had already started planning a family get-together so that everyone could meet Jared and welcome him home. After living alone with his foster mother for two years, being surrounded by grandparents, aunts, uncles and cousins might overwhelm Jared at first. But he was a Taylor. He'd adjust. And he and Mark could begin to develop a father-son relationship.

Mark sipped again, vaguely aware of a woman in a black dress moving through the restaurant toward him. Even from a distance he could see her murderous expression and he felt a twinge of pity for the poor sucker she was after.

The maître d' intercepted her, and Mark looked away. He let his mind play with the fantasy of holding his son for the first time. He imagined Jared older—the spitting image of Mark, himself—playing catch on his grandparents' shady lawn in Sunrise Notch, rowing with his dad on Sunrise Pond, learning to ride a bicycle…

"Mr. Taylor?"

He jerked out of his reverie and blinked up at the woman who'd stopped at his table. "Yes?" He straightened in his seat and found himself looking into the face of the last person in the world he wanted to see.

Out of long practice in court, Mark managed not

to show his surprise or dismay as Dionne Black stared at him with eyes so cold they sent a finger of ice up his spine.

"Can I help you?" he asked.

She stood facing him. Stiff. Unyielding. Still holding his gaze with a challenging one of her own. "I'm Dionne Black...Jared's mother."

"Yes, I know." He took in her thin angry lips and the slight color in her cheeks. Under other circumstances, he might have said she was an attractive woman, but the stony expression she wore overpowered everything else. He searched for some resemblance to Marianne, but found none except the determined way she faced him. "Please sit down."

She slid into the seat opposite him. "I'm not staying long," she said. Then, in spite of his efforts to keep his face impassive, she seemed to read his mind. "I'm sure you didn't expect to see me."

He shrugged and sent her a confident smile. Leaning back in his chair, he straightened his tie slowly— a gesture meant to show how little her presence bothered him. When he realized his hand shook slightly, he lowered it and said, "I'm curious how you found me."

"My attorney told me where to find you."

"I see." He'd make sure *his* attorney knew about this first thing in the morning. But since she was here, he might as well satisfy his curiosity. "What can I do for you?"

"You can stop trying to take Jared away from me."

He had to admit a grudging respect for her courage. But he wasn't about to reveal his feelings. "Out of the question."

''He's just a little boy. Do you have any idea what this will do to him?'' The glow of the candlelight against the pale waves of hair made her look almost delicate, but there was nothing delicate about the set of her jaw or the dangerous glint in her eyes. ''Do you even care?''

''Of course I care,'' he said, leaning slightly forward. Another intimidation technique from his days in court. ''I'm his father.''

''On paper only.''

''On paper. In the eyes of the law. In my heart.''

''How long have you known about him, Mr. Taylor?''

''A little over three weeks.''

''And in that time, without ever once seeing him, you've grown to love him.'' The scorn didn't show on her face but it sure as hell came out in her voice.

''I've seen him,'' Mark said. ''And even if I hadn't, he is my son.''

''On paper,'' she said again. The words dropped like stones between them. ''I've been his mother for two years. I'm the one who's bathed him, fed him, changed his diapers. I've comforted him when he was sick, stayed up nights with him, bandaged his little knees, held him, kissed his tears away, tucked him into bed at night. I'm the one he calls Mommy. What have you done?''

''I'd have done every one of those things,'' he said tersely, ''if I'd been given a chance.''

''Why *weren't* you given a chance, Mr. Taylor?'' There was nothing soft in the question. The fierce anger in her eyes was that of a mother protecting her young.

He pushed aside another flash of respect and told

himself he didn't owe her an explanation. He could simply walk away and let the court deal with her. But something held him back. "It's a long story," he said.

"I have time."

He smiled without humor. "Maybe you do, Ms. Black, but I don't plan to share the intimate details of my life with you."

"But you're more than willing to dig through the intimate details of mine. I read your complaint again this afternoon, Mr. Taylor. Apparently, you've done your homework. Or did Marianne tell you all about me?"

He shook his head quickly. "Marianne didn't tell me anything willingly. She doesn't want to hurt you. And neither do I."

Skepticism filled her eyes and colored her cheeks. "You've used everything you can against me—my husband's death, my financial situation…"

"It's what I do," he said with a modest shrug.

She didn't look impressed. "And is that what you plan to teach Jared? To exploit other people's tragedies and problems to get what he wants?"

Anger curled like a fist in his stomach and spread its fingers into his heart, even though he knew logically she had every reason to feel the way she did. "I'll teach Jared what he needs to know to get by."

"I'm *so* relieved."

"Sarcasm doesn't become you."

"No more than fatherhood becomes you." She leaned closer now. "Do you have other children? Are you married?"

"No," he admitted, "to both questions."

"Then what can you give Jared that I can't?"

"Family. *His* family. And financial security."

"Not love?" Her lip curled. "What about emotional security, Mr. Taylor? I had hoped, for Jared's sake, that you might have a heart."

"Oh, I do have a heart, Ms. Black. But if you're trying to appeal to it, you're wasting your time."

"So I see." She stood, swayed slightly, and gripped the table for support. Her skin had turned waxy, even in the candlelight.

For some reason, the slight evidence of weakness touched a part of him that her hostility and sarcasm hadn't. He'd intimidated antagonistic witnesses and battled some of the best attorneys in the country, but nobody had ever faced him with such grim determination.

"Sit down, Ms. Black." He softened his voice and added, "Please."

She glanced behind her uncertainly, and the action made him think of a bird trapped in a net.

"We've gotten off to a bad start," he said gently. "Instead of charging into battle, let's try again."

"Will you change your mind?"

Never in a million years, he thought, but he said only, "As I said before, I have no desire to hurt you."

"*Hurt* me?" She laughed bitterly. "Taking Jared away won't hurt me, Mr. Taylor. It will *destroy* me. And I don't even want to think about what it will do to him."

He motioned toward the chair again and waited for her to sit. She hesitated, obviously fighting with herself, then finally gave in and perched on the chair's edge. When he felt reassured that she wouldn't topple over, he said, "Suppose I let Jared stay with you…'' He ignored the flicker of hope in her eyes and the unexpected jolt of remorse for causing it. ''…would you eventually tell him he was adopted?''

''Yes, when he's older.'' Her voice sounded slightly less brittle.

''Even if you get married again?''

''I won't be getting married again,'' she said sharply. ''I loved my husband. I can't imagine ever loving anyone else.''

''So, you'll tell Jared he's adopted.'' Mark leaned his arms on the table and held her gaze. ''How do you think that will affect him? Don't you think he'll have questions about the parents who gave him away? Do you really believe he won't hurt if he thinks I didn't want him?''

''I'd tell him about you,'' she assured him, but her eyes glimmered with unshed tears and he knew she'd made the promise out of desperation. ''I'd even let him get to know you when he's older.''

Mark cursed silently. A woman's tears always stirred a myriad of emotions in him, and Dionne Black's brought out the one he hated most—guilt. He tried to ignore it, but her honest grief touched something deep inside. He stiffened his voice and his shoulders before he went on. ''Unfortunately, that's not enough.''

''But—''

He didn't let her finish. ''If you were in my shoes, would it be enough for you?''

She shook her head slowly, reluctantly, and lifted her eyes to meet his. ''No. But I've raised him for the past two years. Please, Mr. Taylor. If you *do* have a heart, don't do this to him.''

"To him? Or to you?"

"To both of us." She brushed a tear from her cheek with one trembling hand. "I'm the only family he knows. He's the only family I have. If you insist on taking him away—" She broke off with a choked sob, took a moment to pull herself together, and tried again. "I understand that he's your biological son, but you've never even met him. You don't love *him,* you love the idea of him."

"I intend to rectify that."

"Yes, I know. You've asked for visitation." She took a deep, shaky breath. "I'm willing to agree to your request—as long as you'll let me be there when you see him."

It heartened Mark to know that the woman who'd been raising Jared had such a fierce, protective love for him. He inclined his head slightly. "In spite of the fact that you'd probably rather kill me than sit at this table with me, you seem like a caring woman." He let himself smile, hoped he looked reassuring. "And it's obvious that you're concerned about doing what's best for Jared."

"I am. But I don't believe that letting you take him is what's best for him. You're trying to tear his world apart."

"I'm trying," Mark said patiently, "to give him the world."

"*Your* world."

"It's his world, too," he reminded her. "Whether you like it or not, I *am* his father. And if you push me too hard, I can turn into a real hard-hearted son of a bitch."

"*Turn into…?* You mean, this is you being *nice?*"

In spite of himself and the cloud of tension that filled the space between, he laughed. "*Touche,* Ms. Black." He let his smile fade. "So, when do I meet my son? Tonight? I'm through here. I could come with you now."

He watched her struggle with the decision and prayed silently that she'd agree.

After what felt like forever, she nodded, but the effort seemed to cost her dearly. "I have to ask you one other thing, Mr. Taylor. I need your promise that you won't confuse or frighten him by telling him who you are."

Mark could see some wisdom in the request, even though it disappointed him. "It's a deal. For the time being, at least."

Settling back in his seat, he savored the tiny victory. He'd come to Boise ready to pull out all the stops and the rest of the world be damned. But now, face-to-face with the woman who obviously cherished his son, he wondered for the first time about the wisdom of taking Jared away from her.

He shoved the doubts back and reassured himself quickly. She might love Jared, but she couldn't possibly give him what Mark could offer. Family. Roots. *A father.*

From here on out, he warned himself, he'd be smart to remember this woman was an adversary—and a formidable one at that.

THE SUN HAD long since set by the time Mark, driving his rental car, followed Dionne through the city streets from the restaurant toward her apartment. A summer thunderstorm had washed away the dirt and grime from the city and left everything clean. He could still smell the rain, the harsh scent of ozone, through his partially open window.

Of course, he'd seen Dionne's apartment from the outside already, but he'd deemed it prudent not to tell her at the restaurant. He'd had plenty of time during the week to drive the few blocks from the hotel and check out the home she'd been providing for his son.

In spite of his not wanting to be impressed, he'd been touched by the geraniums blooming in clay flowerpots on her two small balconies. She'd obviously made an effort to make a real home for his son. Her apartment was probably much more suitable for a two-year-old than his with all the antiques and objets d'art he'd accumulated over the years.

Dionne braked suddenly, catching him off guard and forcing him to swerve to avoid hitting her. When he came to a stop beside her car, she rolled down her window and almost smiled an apology. "This is the entrance to my parking lot. You'll have to leave your car wherever you can find a space. I'll meet you back here."

He nodded and pulled away again. He found an empty parking space two blocks away and jogged back along the rain-slick sidewalk.

She was still outside the parking structure when he drew up, breathless and light-headed. Gulping air, he motioned her to lead on.

She folded her arms and held her ground. "It's okay. You can take a minute to catch your breath."

"Must be the altitude," he gasped.

"I'm sure that's it." Her lips curved into a stiff smile.

He turned his gaze to the mountains standing sentinel over the city, let it travel to the sky. "This is a far cry from Boston."

"I've been to Boston," she told him, following the direction of his gaze. "But only once, and that was years ago." When she spoke again, her voice had softened, but not by much. "It's probably changed a lot since then."

Finally able to breathe again, he straightened and studied her in the fading light. She looked frightened. Vulnerable. Defenseless. And the guilt he'd felt in the restaurant returned. For the briefest of moments, he didn't want to take the chance of hurting her.

But in the next breath, everything about her hardened again. "If you want to see Jared, we'd better hurry. I don't want to keep him up too long past his bedtime or he'll be cranky all day tomorrow."

Mark laughed softly and muttered, "Sounds like me."

She stopped walking. "Excuse me?"

"I said, that sounds like me. If I don't get enough sleep, I'm a bear the next day. Always have been, to hear my mother talk."

Her face paled in the moonlight. She clutched the straps of her bag tighter and started walking again. "*All* two-year-olds are cranky if they don't get enough sleep."

Victory always left him feeling charitable, and tonight was no exception. He tried to lighten the moment. "Are you calling me a two-year-old?"

She flashed him a look that could have crumbled a mountain. "I'm simply stating a fact, Mr. Taylor."

"Look," he said, "you and I aren't ever going to be friends, but we don't have to be mortal enemies, do we? Considering that we have a child in common, why don't we at least move on to first names?''

''As long as you're planning to take away my son, you *are* my enemy, Mr. Taylor. And I don't intend to soothe your conscience by pretending to like you.''

''Not even for Jared's sake?''

Her step faltered and a deep frown creased her forehead, but she didn't soften. ''Are you going to pretend that you're suddenly concerned about Jared?''

''I've always been concerned about Jared.''

''Always?'' She laughed harshly and stopped in front of the old building that housed her apartment. ''For a whole three weeks?''

''Look—'' he began.

But she cut him off. ''I've agreed to let you see him, but that doesn't mean I'm going to back down from the fight. I *won't* let you take him from me.''

Without thinking about the wisdom of his actions, he grasped her by the shoulders and pulled her around until their eyes met. ''The chances of your winning in court are so remote, they're not even worth mentioning. The courts presume a child has the right to its parents, and no judge is going to let some distant relative keep a child whose parent is ready, willing and able to raise him. I'm a decent member of society, I make a good living, and I've never been in jail. If we went to court tomorrow, I could be on the way to Boston with him by nightfall. But for some reason, I'm willing to make this easier on you.''

''How kind.''

"Like it or not, you have to work with me if you don't want me to separate you from Jared forever."

She jerked away from his touch and put some distance between them, but some new emotion flickered in her eyes. "What do you mean? Your plan *is* to separate me from Jared, isn't it?"

"I mean, *Dionne,* that I'm not a heartless creature, no matter what you may want to believe about me. I can see how much you love Jared, and if you'll pull in your claws maybe we can come to some sort of agreement about letting you see him once in a while."

"Once in a while?" she repeated. "How generous of you. What do you expect me to do now, fall at your feet in gratitude?"

Something like that, he admitted silently. Aloud, he said, "No. But you could try ditching some of the hostility. To be perfectly honest, I don't see that you have much choice."

"That's where you're wrong," she snapped. "I have choices, including not letting you into my apartment tonight to see him."

"You'd only be shooting yourself in the foot," he warned, hoping his eyes didn't betray his sudden panic. He'd come this close, he didn't want to leave now without seeing Jared.

"Maybe," she admitted. "But it's my foot."

"And Jared's." He tossed her own argument into her lap and, with almost morbid satisfaction, watched her lips tighten and her eyes register the direct hit.

"Five minutes," she said, jamming her key into the lock and wrenching open the lobby door. "No more."

He sketched a bow and followed her into the

building. As they crossed the dimly lit foyer to the elevator, he stole another glance at her. For some reason, the stiff set of her shoulders disturbed him. And a small pang of regret inched up his spine.

DIONNE RODE the elevator with her back to the wall, keeping one eye on Mark as if she expected him to murder her inside the tiny box. Foolish, she knew, but the threat he posed was every bit as real as if he'd brandished a knife in front of her.

She didn't want to let him into her apartment. Didn't want to let him see Jared—especially since their features were so remarkably similar. She didn't want the resemblance to spark his paternal instincts. Only the hope that he'd change his mind after seeing how much Jared loved her kept her breathing.

And there was one small traitorous part of her that reacted to this man with something other than hostility. It was the part of her that recognized the curve of his lips when he smiled and the tiny ridge of flesh between his eyes when he scowled. In her heart, she knew she was looking at an older version of the person she loved most in the world. And that heart refused to let her completely hate him.

If not for him, she wouldn't have Jared. But neither would she be in danger of losing him now.

Mark kept his distance, hands locked behind his back, watching the lights on the elevator panel as they climbed slowly to the third floor. "Who's with Jared now?"

"A friend of mine." She almost smiled. If he thought Dionne was hostile, wait until he met Cicely. On the other hand, wait until Cicely saw what

Dionne had done. Dionne knew she'd have some tall explaining to do.

"Male or female?"

"Does it matter?"

"I suppose not...as long as Jared's safe."

The elevator door creaked open, and Mark put a hand against it while she stepped through. Such a gentleman, she thought bitterly, holding the door for her with one hand and snatching away her child with the other.

She watched him take in the narrow corridor, the faded roses in the carpet, the yellowed walls badly in need of new paint. She waited for him to curl his lip, but he turned a smile on her instead.

"Nice."

"Not really," she said, letting her own gaze travel over their surroundings. "I've been thinking of finding a house in the suburbs and moving out of city center."

"I suppose the middle of the city isn't the best place to raise a child."

"Not one as active as Jared." She drew to a stop outside her door and tried to calm the thundering of her heart. "Remember," she warned, "you are not to tell him who you are."

Surprisingly, Mark looked almost offended. "I gave my word."

She supposed that should make her feel better, but it didn't. He'd also given his word to win. With trembling hands, she tried to unlock the door. When she had trouble getting the key to fit, Mark gently took it from her and inserted it himself.

As he turned the knob, his eyes met hers. "Ready?" His voice had lost most of its hard edge.

She couldn't afford to lose hers. This kindness she saw now was probably nothing more than a tactic to put her off her guard. "I meant what I said downstairs. You can have five minutes, then you leave or I call the police."

FILLED WITH ANXIETY and anticipation, Mark didn't say a word. He pushed the door and waited for Dionne to lead the way.

Inside, a woman sat on the couch watching Jared drive his toy trucks across a mound of building blocks. Her face tightened, hardened, when she saw Mark, but Jared popped up and toddled across the room toward his mother.

Seeing the boy up close made Mark's breath catch. Tears of amazement stung his eyes. He still couldn't believe this boy was his son.

"Mommy. Mommy. Come see."

Dionne scooped Jared up and held him close. Mark ached to do the same but he stayed put, waiting for his chance.

Jared squirmed, protesting the too-tight hug, let his body go slack and tried to slide out of Dionne's arms. Slowly, reluctantly, she put him on the floor again. "I love you, Jared."

"Love you." He reached for her hand. "Come see, Mommy."

Mark was aware of the other woman's stony stare, but he avoided looking at her. This moment belonged to him and to Jared. He wasn't going to let anyone ruin it. He tracked Jared's progress across the room, taking in every unsteady step, every feature. Through the tears, he saw his mother in the boy's face. His father's nose. His own chin. It was a miracle, and Jared was the most beautiful person he'd ever seen.

He drew a ragged breath and caught Dionne watching him with an odd expression on her face.

"Who's this?" the other woman demanded, dragging Dionne's attention away.

"Cicely Logan...Mark Taylor."

Mark flicked a glance and a smile at her, but he didn't let his attention leave Jared for more than a second.

Cicely shot to her feet, grabbed Dionne's arm, and tugged her a few steps away. "What are you thinking, girl?" She kept her voice low, but Mark could hear every word. "Are you a fool, bringing him back here like this? Do you have any idea what this will do to your case in court?"

Dionne knew what she was doing, Mark thought. Letting him come here was the smartest thing she could have done. He wondered if she knew just how smart it was.

"We can talk about this later," Dionne whispered back, shrugging away from Cicely's grasp and lowering her purse to the coffee table. "He's only staying five minutes."

"Five minutes too long," Cicely warned.

Mark tore his gaze away from Jared and settled it on Cicely. "I'm not going to hurt either one of them, if that's what you're worried about."

"You've already done that," Cicely retorted.

He'd meant a different kind of harm, but he knew she was right. "Yes," he said softly, turning back to Jared again. "I suppose I have."

Dionne put an arm around Cicely's stiff shoulders and gave her a gentle squeeze. "I'll explain everything later. I promise. But I don't want to talk about it in front of Jared."

The appeal got through to Cicely. She started toward the couch again, but Dionne stopped her. "Why don't you go home. It's late, and you have to work tomorrow." And in answer to Cicely's worried scowl, "We'll be all right."

The assurance gave Mark hope, and Dionne's understanding of his need to see Jared without Cicely's hostile presence filled him with gratitude. While Cicely reluctantly gathered her things, he got down on the floor but still kept his distance from his son.

"Come see, Mommy," Jared demanded again. "Truck's gonna crash."

"In a minute, sweetheart. We need to say goodbye to Cicely."

Jared sent Cicely an unconcerned glance and waved his chubby fingers. "Bye-bye."

Cicely crossed the room and gave Jared a quick hug. She turned tear-filled eyes on Mark, but she held her tongue.

Dionne gave her friend another reassuring squeeze, whispered a promise to call tomorrow, and let Cicely out the door. Then she turned back to watch.

Jared was blissfully unaware of the upheaval surrounding him. Mark picked up a stray block and held it for a moment, then offered it hesitantly to Jared.

Jared scuttled backward and looked to Dionne for reassurance. "Mommy?"

Battling disappointment, Mark got to his feet and backed away to put some distance between them. When Jared relaxed enough to go back to his game,

Mark met Dionne's gaze again. "He's beautiful." A weak word to describe the absolute wonder he felt.

"Yes," she said softly, "he is."

"He looks like my mother. She's going to adore him." Mark let his gaze settle on Dionne's face, sharply aware of the roiling emotions that kept her silent. Guilt twisted through him again. "For what it's worth, Dionne, I'm sorry."

That tore a response from her. "Sorry?" She turned away, folding her arms and clutching them tightly. "If that were true, you wouldn't do this."

He looked away from her and drank in the sight of his son again. Maybe she was right. Maybe he was making a mistake.

He shook off the doubts and pulled himself together. There were many things about this situation he hadn't anticipated, many emotions he hadn't expected to feel. But that didn't make it wrong to fight for his son. Remembering his promise, he crossed to the door, cast one last longing glance at Jared, and let himself out.

DAMN. Mark paced the inside of the elevator as he rode down to the first floor and swore again, this time aloud. *"Damn!"*

He hadn't expected to feel sorry for her, but the pain in her eyes had been too deep to ignore. He hadn't expected to have doubts about his decision, but the bond between Jared and Dionne was too real to deny.

"Damn!" He jabbed at the first-floor button again.

He couldn't explain his reaction to the picture of Jared in Dionne's arms if he'd tried. Maybe he was just relieved to see that Jared had a mother who actually cared about him. She might be related to Marianne, but the similarities ended with their bloodlines. Even a fool could see that Dionne loved Jared as completely, as fully, as Mark's mother loved him. Only a heartless creature would rob a child of that kind of love.

"Damn," he said again as the elevator doors swished open. Jamming his hands into his pockets, he strode through the dimly lit lobby, glaring at the furniture. He pushed through the doors into the night, listening to the rhythm of his steps as they echoed on the wet, empty sidewalk.

Meeting Dionne Black had changed everything. Now what was he going to do?

CHAPTER FOUR

MORNING DAWNED gray and cloudy, the perfect background for the ache in Dionne's heart. She lay in bed, curled next to Jared, too hurt to move. She rarely let Jared climb into her bed unless bad dreams woke him. Even then, she usually comforted him and carried him back to his own room. But she'd needed to keep him close, to feel his small body beside her and know that she still had him with her.

Mark had been as good as his word last night. Five minutes, then he'd disappeared. But anything might happen today. He might show up at the door ready to take Jared. He might—though she held out only scant hope—even change his mind.

She supposed she should take some comfort in knowing that he seemed kind. That he seemed to genuinely care about Jared in his own way. That he seemed capable of loving Jared. But nothing lessened the fear that had lodged in her throat all night and kept her awake, tossing and turning and listening to the soft drumming of rain against her windows.

Blinking back tears, she touched Jared's cheek with her fingertips, softly so she wouldn't wake him, then rolled to her side and stared at the picture of Brent on the nightstand. For the past week, she'd fought against the anger. Today, she let it come.

If Brent hadn't been so reckless, he'd still be here

to fight with her and for her, she wouldn't be fighting the worst battle of her life alone. He'd have found some way to protect their tiny family. She *knew* he would.

She stared at the eyes that had once made her feel secure and the smile that had once given her faith, then slowly, resolutely, turned the picture facedown on the table.

Jared made a noise and shifted position. To keep from waking him, Dionne forced herself to get out of bed and walk on legs as unsteady as his tiny ones to the door of her bedroom. Clutching the frame for support, she looked back at him. Her arms ached to hold him, but she refused to let herself do it until he woke on his own.

She pulled on her robe and made her way into the cramped kitchen. Working automatically, she scooped coffee into a filter and filled the carafe with water, then sat at the table and waited while it brewed, staring with sightless eyes at the gray sky and the wash of moisture on the windows.

A few minutes later, a soft knock pulled her from her reverie. At first she thought it had come from the apartment next door, but the second time, she realized someone was at her door.

It had to be Cicely. Usually, Dionne welcomed her visits, but not today. She couldn't face her friend's questions this morning. She had no answers to give. But neither could she ignore her. Cicely would only knock louder and wake Jared.

Running her fingers through her hair, Dionne hurried to the door and pulled it open. But it wasn't Cicely standing on the threshold. Instead, she found herself looking into Mark's deep brown eyes.

Shock numbed her. Was this it, then? Had he come for Jared? How could she stop him? What could she say to convince him?

Her heart slowed and her mind raced. "What are you doing here?"

With his hair and shirt wet from the rain and shadows forming deep circles beneath his eyes, he looked almost as haggard as she felt. "We need to talk."

"Talk? About what?"

"About Jared. About what's best for him."

Hope that he'd come to say he'd changed his mind sprang to life. Fear that he hadn't shadowed it. She stepped aside and let him in, vaguely aware that she hadn't bothered to pick up Jared's toys last night.

Mark didn't seem to notice. He walked toward the couch and motioned for her to join him.

She perched on the edge nearest her bedroom, ready to fly toward the door if she had to. The splatter of rain against the windows mixed with the gurgle of the coffeemaker. The earthy scent of coffee filled the air, but it didn't soothe her as it usually did.

Mark studied her with agonizing slowness, letting his eyes roam across her hair, her face, and finally settle on her eyes. "Did you sleep at all?"

She shook her head, wondering why he asked. Why would he even care?

"Neither did I."

The confession surprised her, but she tried to keep her face from showing any expression at all.

"I've been doing a lot of thinking," he said, pushing to his feet again. "I've thought about what you said at the restaurant, and about the way you and Jared interacted last night. It's obvious you love him."

"Yes. With all my heart."

"And it's equally obvious that he loves you. But he's still my son…" Mark broke off and rubbed his face with both hands. "The fact that I've only known about him for a short time doesn't change that."

He reached a hand toward her, then seemed to think better of it. "Are you all right? Say something, so I know you're still alive in there."

"You're going to take him." Her voice rasped and her throat burned with the effort.

He studied her for a long moment. "I called my office this morning and asked for another two weeks here. That should give both you and Jared time to get to know me. Maybe then you won't worry about him so much when I take him back to Boston."

She stared at him, incredulous. "Two weeks won't change how I feel."

Mark rubbed his neck slowly, tilting his head to work out the kinks. "I believe you." He sent her a thin smile and lowered his hand. "I realized last night that I don't want to put Jared through a long, ugly custody battle. He's too innocent and trusting, and I don't want to change that. I'm hoping we can work out a compromise—a way for all of us to win."

Dionne eyed him warily, trying desperately not to get her hopes up. "How?"

"First, I think he should get to know me here in the setting he's used to. I don't want to frighten him by changing everything too fast."

"I think that's the best idea you've had so far."

"I'd like to be here while he eats breakfast, play with him in the park, read him bedtime stories. I'd like to do all those things you talked about last night."

Dionne hated the idea of him insinuating himself into their lives and robbing her of her precious time alone with Jared. But it was preferable to having him spirit Jared away. And maybe, once he saw how difficult life with a two-year-old could be, he'd change his mind about taking on the task.

"All right," she said reluctantly. "You can spend some time with us."

His quick, pleased smile seemed genuine. He closed some of the distance between them. "Good. When can we start? Today?"

Today? No! She held back her automatic response and remembered her attorney's advice. Refusing wouldn't accomplish anything except, perhaps, postpone the inevitable. She forced herself to nod and said again, "All right."

"Great." Another pleased smile curved his lips and excitement sparkled in his eyes. "I also think it would be a good idea for us to try to get along. Jared will pick up on the hostility and it won't be good for him."

Much as she hated to admit it, he was right. She forced herself to say, "I agree."

Mark visibly relaxed as if he'd been worried about her answer. "What time does Jared get up in the mornings?"

"On the weekends, I let him sleep until he wakes up. On weekdays, I get him up at seven and leave for work at seven-thirty. But I can't have you around on workdays. I'm always racing against the clock as it is."

"Then let me help. Let me feed him breakfast while you get ready. Let me take him to the sitter. Or, even better, let me watch him while you work."

She shook her head quickly. "I don't think that's a good idea."

"Why not?" His smile faded and his dark eyes clouded. "Are you afraid I'll abscond with him while you're at the office?"

That's exactly what she feared, and his perception caught her by surprise—just as the almost kind look in his eyes did.

He leaned closer, propping his elbows on his knees. "You don't have to worry about that, Dionne. I won't do that to Jared."

While that offered some small relief, it didn't completely allay her fears.

"I know you're afraid," he said, "and I can't say I blame you. I barged in here like a storm trooper ready to do battle. But you weren't exactly trying to make peace either, you know." His expression softened even more. "If you'll be honest with me, I'll be honest with you. I won't steal Jared while you're at work if you won't try to disappear with him while my back's turned. I really want to work out a compromise," he said. "For Jared's sake."

Dionne bit her lip and glanced at her son's door. For Jared's sake, he said. If he meant that, if he really wanted to do what was best for Jared, maybe he wasn't quite as bad as she'd first thought. She had to believe that. Like it or not, she had to trust him a little.

She just hoped she wasn't making the biggest mistake of her life.

MARK SAT on the faded carpet of Dionne's living room, trying not to be hurt by his son's continuing wariness. The overworked air conditioner in the window did little to relieve the afternoon's intense, dry heat. Sounds from neighboring apartments drifted through the thin walls and added to his frustration.

He didn't expect miracles. He'd known Jared would be apprehensive at first. But after nearly two days together, Jared was still wary. He behaved as if Mark was a stranger in spite of Dionne's introduction of Mark as a friend. But Dionne didn't treat him as a friend, and even a child could sense she was lying.

At least Dionne had finally left them alone for a few minutes. She'd been standing guard, watching every move Mark made, no doubt judging his performance. He knew they both needed time to get used to him, but time was the one thing he didn't have much of. He couldn't stay away from Boston and his career indefinitely.

Determined to break through Jared's wariness, Mark stacked a couple of blocks near Jared and watched his reaction. The boy studied them for a moment, then reached out one tentative finger to touch them.

Progress!

"Do you want these?" Mark asked gently.

Jared pulled his hand back quickly. "No."

Mark held back a frustrated sigh. He hated Marianne for putting them all through this and resented her bitterly for walking away unscathed and leaving three innocent people to deal with the fallout of her decision. Her body, her choice—those had been her words. Yet *her* life was the one least affected by the choice she'd made.

The clatter of dishes in the kitchen pulled him back to the moment and he caught Jared watching him, eyes round with distrust, a deep scowl on his face.

Mark sent him a reassuring smile and hoped he hadn't ruined everything by thinking about Marianne and letting his anger show. "Do you think Mommy dropped something?"

Jared backed a step away.

"Should we go see?"

Jared gave that some thought, then nodded. But when Mark reached out to pick him up, he threw himself onto the couch, face first, as if by hiding his eyes he could also make the rest of his body disappear.

Mark backed away and held up both hands. "All right, sport, you're safe. I won't pick you up. Why don't you show me where the kitchen is."

Jared peeked out from behind his hands, then scooted off the couch and pointed. "Over there."

"Do you want to lead the way? I'll follow."

Jared nodded and toddled off toward the door, checking behind him every few steps, either to make sure Mark was behind him or that he hadn't gotten too close.

Dionne looked up when they entered, smoothed her hands along the legs of her jeans, and frowned slightly. "Is something wrong?"

"No." Mark leaned against the door frame and hooked his thumbs in his pockets. "We heard a crash and got worried."

She glanced at the dishes on the counter. "I'm a little clumsy today for some reason."

Mark laughed. "Couldn't be that you're nervous, could it?"

She half smiled in response. "No, of course not."

Then, as if talking about herself made her uneasy, "How's Jared doing?"

"Still a little shy."

She riveted her attention on the casserole in front of her. "That's to be expected."

"Yes, I know. I have some experience with two-year-olds."

"Really?" She glanced quickly at him. "Who?"

"Nieces and nephews and cousins—lots of them."

"Oh." Moving stiffly, she pulled a carton of milk from the refrigerator. "How many?"

"Three nieces, three nephews, and two dozen cousins—most of whom have several children apiece. We're a close family, so I'm around the kids several times a month."

She looked back at him over her shoulder. "How nice for you."

Mark laughed. "I can tell you really mean that." He took another step into the kitchen. "So what's the matter? You sound disappointed."

"No." The answer came quickly—too quickly. "Not at all. Why should I be?"

He shrugged lazily. "I don't know. Maybe you were hoping to discourage me by letting me see what life with a two-year-old is really like."

"Don't be ridiculous," she said with a laugh, but color flamed into her cheeks and convinced him he'd hit the nail squarely on the head.

He shrugged again and let his gaze travel across the tiny kitchen. It couldn't even begin to compare with the spacious kitchen in his condo, but everything was clean and neat. "Okay. I won't read anything into the situation that's not there."

"Good." Her cheeks went from pink to red.

She looked small and fragile, but Mark had seen the steel in her backbone and knew what an illusion that was. "Do you mind if I make a suggestion?"

Her gaze flew to his. "About what?"

"It's not about Jared," he assured her, making himself even more comfortable against the door frame.

"Well, that's a relief."

He gave in to the urge to smile, surprised to find that he was enjoying himself. "It's just that I don't think you should ever try to play poker. Your face gives you away."

She opened her mouth to protest, then clamped it shut again and turned her back on him. "I'll keep that in mind."

Mark picked up a toy truck and pushed it close to Jared, then crossed to the counter and leaned on it to watch her. "Have you talked to Marianne?"

Her quick glance gave him the answer even before she spoke. "I've tried to reach her, but she's away from her office. Apparently *you* know where to find her, though." She wiped her hands on a towel and reached for a bowl in the cupboard. The material of her blouse stretched tight across her breasts and sparked an unexpected response inside him.

He looked away quickly. "She's staying at the Marriott in Boston," he said, his voice gruff, "I can give you the number if you'd like."

Her eyes narrowed. "Why?"

"Because I'm sure you have questions about me, and she's probably the only person you'd trust to answer them."

Dionne closed the cupboard and eyed him speculatively. Shadows tinted her eyes a deep blue, and he wondered if they always revealed her moods so clearly. "I'm not sure I'd trust her, either," she admitted softly. "I'm so furious I could hit something. I hate her for doing this to Jared."

"And to you."

"And to me," she admitted softly.

"She hurt me, too, you know. She knew how much I wanted children of my own, yet she hid Jared from me."

"Maybe she had reasons for keeping him from you."

"Oh, she did," he assured her. "She knew I'd never agree to give him up."

"Then I can't say I'm sorry she didn't tell you," she said quietly. "Having Jared in my life is the best thing that's ever happened to me."

"Even now?"

"Even now. I wouldn't trade the past two years for anything—not even to avoid this."

"Then maybe you can understand how I feel."

Dionne nodded reluctantly. "I guess I can in a way. But I also know that Marianne gave him to Brent and me because she wanted him to have a stable family life. Obviously, she didn't think you could give that to him."

For a second—and only that—Mark felt a twinge of guilt. After all, Marianne *had* known him well. With the hours he worked, could he really give Jared the security and stability he needed? Was he being fair to his son? To Dionne?

Of course he was. Jared deserved to know Mark and his family. He deserved the love of his father. And Dionne deserved...

Hell. Dionne *wasn't* Mark's responsibility. He had to remember that.

"You don't have to worry about Jared," he said. "He'll have everything he needs."

"Except his mother."

Mark was saved from having to respond when Jared tripped over a block, tumbled to the floor, and hit his head against the leg of a chair. Instantly, Mark started toward him, Dionne beat him. And she was the one Jared reached for.

She swooped Jared into her arms, checked him thoroughly, and cradled him against her. Jared's howls subsided and his tears slowed. He clutched the fabric of her blouse, and Mark's guilt increased.

He'd come to Boise determined to win, but with every passing hour he grew less certain about what winning would mean.

SOFTLY, so as not to wake her son, Dionne closed Jared's bedroom door and walked slowly back toward the couch. She curled into one corner and stared at the telephone, trying to work up the courage to pick up the receiver and make her phone call.

Earlier, she'd pleaded a headache to convince Mark to leave. And he'd gone, just as he had the first time, without argument.

Outside, the sounds of an occasional passing car stirred the stillness. Inside, the hum of the air conditioner working to cool the small rooms teased her already jangled nerves.

She needed answers. She needed to know what kind of person Mark was, what happened between him and Marianne, why Marianne had kept Jared hidden from him, and what had made her tell him after all this time. And Dionne desperately needed to release some of the anger that had been propelling her through each day and affecting her sleep at night.

Yes, she was angry with Mark for showing up and wanting to take Jared, but she was far more upset with Marianne. How could Marianne promise Dionne that she could have Jared and then tell Mark where they were. Marianne must have known Mark would come after his son. Marianne should have *some* loyalty toward her—shouldn't she? They were family, after all. Distant, to be sure, but family none-theless.

Expelling a deep breath, Dionne picked up the receiver, dug the scrap of paper with the number Mark had given her from the pocket of her robe, and dialed before she could talk herself out of it. It seemed to take forever for the connection to go through and the phone to ring on the other end. Another eternity for Marianne to answer. When she did, her soft, rich voice caught Dionne off guard.

Dionne identified herself and found some small satisfaction in the silence before Marianne said, "I knew you'd probably be calling me. My dad told me you'd been looking for me. This must mean Mark's been in contact."

"In contact?" Dionne caught her voice rising and forced it to remain level. "He's filed a lawsuit for custody, Marianne."

"I'm not surprised."

"No? Well, I was. But, then, *I* didn't know about him." Dionne glanced at Jared's door and pulled her voice under control again. "Why didn't you warn me?"

"I guess I hoped he wouldn't actually follow

through,'' Marianne said. ''I honestly thought there was a chance he'd think about it and decide to leave things the way they were.''

Dionne brushed a lock of hair from her forehead. ''*Did* you? I hardly know him, and I can't imagine him backing down from anything. You certainly knew him better than I do. How could you ever have thought he'd change his mind?''

She could almost hear Marianne's shrug, casual and unhurried. ''Because he's so locked up in his career. He might think he wants a family, but I'm not sure he does. Not really.''

That gave Dionne a moment's hope, but it evaporated almost immediately. What if Mark didn't really want a family, but didn't realize it until *after* he'd taken Jared away? She took a steadying breath and tried to keep her agitation under control. ''I need the answers to some questions, Marianne.''

''Such as?''

''For one thing, why did you change your mind about telling him?''

''When I heard about Brent's death, I thought you might have second thoughts.''

''How can you say that?''

''It's just that things were different when your husband was alive. There were two of you to take care of Jared, someone else to help support him—''

''*I* can support him,'' Dionne snapped. ''I can give him everything he needs.''

''Yes, but there's more to life than just the basics,'' Marianne argued, her voice irritatingly smooth and unruffled. ''What about the extras? Can you send him to camp? Enroll him in sports programs? I hear people talking all the time about how expensive those things are. And what about a college education when he's older? Will you be able to provide one for him?''

Trembling with rage, Dionne fought back. ''There's more to life than material things. What about love? Security? I grew up without things, but I knew my mother loved me.''

''So did mine. And so will Mark. He's a decent man, Dionne.''

''Then why didn't you tell him about Jared in the first place?''

''I wasn't ready to do the family thing, and he was. I thought if he knew there was a baby, he'd try to convince me and that wasn't a battle I wanted to fight right then.'' Her voice softened. ''Maybe you need to think about whether you want the burden of caring for Jared all by yourself.''

''If you think raising Jared is a burden,'' Dionne said through clenched teeth, ignoring all the warning bells and whistles jarring inside her head, ''then it's a good thing you gave him up.''

It was only afterward—after she'd slammed down the receiver and stormed into the kitchen—that she began to wonder if antagonizing Marianne had been such a good idea.

CHAPTER FIVE

THREE DAYS LATER, Dionne sat on the park bench under the blazing afternoon sky and watched while Mark played with Jared. In just one short week, the child had adjusted to having him around. Jared seemed to like him—just as Mark had hoped. Just as Dionne had feared.

They looked so much alike, it hurt. Two dark heads bent together, two identical laughs, two terrifyingly similar faces. And they acted so much alike, Dionne felt a pang of jealousy. No matter how close she and Jared were, they didn't share physical attributes or mannerisms.

Mark helped Jared climb up the short plastic slide, then jumped down the steps and raced to catch him at the bottom. When Jared slid into Mark's arms, Mark whooped triumphantly and swung Jared high onto his shoulders.

Jared crowed with delight and pointed at the slide. "Again!"

"Are you sure?"

"Again!"

Mark tromped through the sand, obviously unaware of how out of place he looked in his starched white shirt and suit pants, and started the process all over again. The delight on his face was a far cry from the expression he'd worn when they'd first met. The warmth of his smile when he saw Jared each morning, the glow of love in his eyes, the softness on his face when he kissed Jared good-night at the end of the day all touched her deeply. And in spite of herself, she was beginning to believe Jared deserved a father—*his* father.

Under other circumstances, she might even have liked Mark. But she didn't, she reminded herself firmly. She couldn't afford to get softhearted just because he'd teased an occasional giggle from Jared, shown concern over a scraped knee, or continued to treat her with quiet respect. She couldn't let down her guard even though he seemed genuine about easing into Jared's life instead of bulldozing his way in.

The bottom line hadn't changed. He still intended to take Jared to Boston. Eventually, he'd marry and some other woman would take her place as Jared's mother. At most, Dionne would be left with occasional visits, playing the part of a doting aunt or close family friend.

Laughing at something Jared did, Mark settled the boy on his shoulders again and carried him toward her. "Look, you're bigger than Mommy."

Jared giggled with delight and leaned down to kiss her. "I'm big, Mommy."

Her heart constricted painfully. "Yes, sweetheart, you are. Very big." She reached for him, but he shook his head and pulled away again.

"No, Mommy. Me stay up here." He clapped his hands to Mark's head and held on to his hair, as if he thought she might force him down.

She swallowed the bitter taste of betrayal and reminded herself Jared was only a baby. He *couldn't* betray her.

As if he could read her thoughts, Mark held on to Jared with one hand and disentangled his hands with the other. "You'd better get down, sport."

Annoyance, sudden and unreasonable, flashed through her. "Let him stay if he wants to."

Mark ignored her and pulled Jared from his shoulders. Of course, the child set up a squall, and Dionne watched while Mark teased him into a better mood. He seemed to know how to handle a distressed two-year-old, and for Jared's sake, she was glad.

When he'd calmed Jared down again and had him happily digging in the sandbox, Mark dropped onto the park bench beside her, moving his suit jacket out of the way as he did. "He's a great kid, Dionne. You've done a remarkable job with him."

But now that job was over? She studied him intently, trying to read the expression in his eyes. "It hasn't been a job," she assured him.

"I know." Mark shielded his eyes against the sun and watched Jared for a minute. "I know how you feel about him, Dionne. Any fool can see that. And I know how he feels about you." He let out a heavy sigh and turned to face her. "Any chance you're willing to relocate to Boston?"

The question caught her completely off guard, but she recovered quickly. "What do you mean?"

He shrugged and leaned back against the seat. "You have to admit, it'd make this easier if we lived in the same town."

"Yes, it would." She spoke slowly, trying not to let the observation get her hopes up. "Any chance *you're* willing to move to Boise?"

To her surprise, Mark laughed. It started out as a

low rumble deep in his chest and worked its way out. "Has anyone ever told you that you're stubborn?"

"Not recently." She bit back an unexpected smile and told herself she wasn't enjoying the banter. "Has anyone ever told you that you're pushy?"

"Every day." He leaned back and rested one arm on the bench behind her. His gaze settled on Jared protectively. "I'm serious, Dionne. If we lived in the same city, we could work out an easy arrangement."

"But we don't," she said unnecessarily.

"No, we don't. So what do we do?"

Dionne shook her head, surprised to find herself in this position, yet strangely comfortable with it as well. "Could you move here?"

"I can't leave my career in Boston. I've worked too long and too hard to get where I am."

"And your career is important to you."

"Of course it is." He glanced at her quickly. "Isn't yours?"

Dionne smiled halfheartedly. "Not especially."

Mark shifted toward her eagerly, his eyes glittering so that they looked almost black. "Then *would* you consider moving?"

"I don't know. It's not something I've ever thought about before."

"Maybe you should."

Suddenly her future looked a little brighter. But the idea of leaving everything familiar—home, job, Cicely—frightened her. She rubbed her forehead gently. "I—I don't know. I need some time to think—"

"We don't have much time," Mark warned. "I have to get back to Boston soon."

"But you'll be back for the court hearing."

He didn't speak for a long time. When he did, his voice came out hushed. "We could avoid a hearing if we could work out a compromise. Personally, I'd like to spare Jared all that. It's no kind of memory to give a kid."

Dionne shifted to look at him better. "You're really serious, aren't you?"

"Completely." He sent her a hopeful smile. "Just promise me you'll think about it."

She nodded slowly. "All right."

"I'll stay out of your way tonight so you can think without me around."

He really *was* serious, Dionne thought. But could she seriously consider such a proposition? Of course, if she won in court, she wouldn't have to take such a drastic step. But Rudy Butler wasn't offering much hope on that score.

She could almost hear Brent telling her to refuse. But Brent had never been good at compromising. Besides, he wasn't here. She'd have to make this decision on her own.

SEVERAL HOURS LATER, vaguely unsettled, Mark tugged off his shirt and tossed it onto the bed of his hotel room. He thought about his comfortable bed back in Boston, about his view of Boston Harbor, about the life he'd made for himself. No matter what happened now, it would never be the same.

He briefly considered calling his parents to give them an update, but he didn't know how to tell them that everything was less settled, less certain than it had been last week or the week before. The last time he'd talked to them, they'd been full of plans. Not that they wouldn't understand his confusion, but

Mark had always been the kind of guy who set his mind on something and then got it. He rarely wavered...until now.

He dropped onto the bed and turned on the television, scanning channels in an attempt to find something in the late-afternoon programming that would take his mind off Dionne and Jared. The ball was in her court tonight. All he could do was wait.

Finally settling on an episode of *Biography,* he dimmed the bedside lamp. Though he usually found the show fascinating, tonight it didn't hold his interest.

He turned up the volume and tried to pay attention to the story of Thomas Jefferson's life, but Dionne's image kept interfering. Her infrequent smile, her shaky laugh, the utter love on her face when she held Jared.

Mark blinked, and Jared's image joined hers. His laughter, his little-boy voice calling out to her, his chubby legs churning as he ran toward her.

Mark thought of his own childhood as he had a million times in the last few days and wondered what life would have been like if he'd been taken away from his own mother. What kind of heartless jerk would do something so devastating to a child? Or to the woman who'd been his mother for all of his short life.

After spending only one week with the boy, Mark was so attached to Jared he couldn't imagine life without him. But if *he* felt this way, how must Dionne feel? He might argue bloodlines in court, but he knew that families were made in the heart.

In the middle of a commercial, the telephone rang and startled him back to the moment. He dropped the remote on the floor, scrambled for it and muted the set, then grabbed the receiver. The voice that greeted him was the last one he'd expected.

"Mark? Royal Spritzer here."

Mark dropped onto the bed again. Why was his boss calling? He had no cases pending in court, no imminent trials, no depositions scheduled. He'd given his secretary the hotel's number in case of an emergency, but he certainly hadn't expected one— especially not on a Saturday afternoon.

Royal's voice boomed through the wire again. "Mark? Are you there?"

"Yes. Sorry. What can I do for you?"

"It's very simple, my boy. You can come back to Boston."

Mark turned off the television. "Now? But I have another week of leave."

"Change of plans." Ice clinked against a glass on the other end of the connection and Mark pictured Royal leaning back in his leather chair. "Oscar Nee-bling and I met with a new client yesterday, and after talking about it today, we've decided we want you in on the case."

"No problem," Mark assured him. "I'll review the file and get up to speed when I get back. Or Anna can fax me the pertinent documents here on Monday."

"Not good enough." Royal let out a sigh and set his glass on a hard surface near the telephone. "I don't want to fax anything. I don't want anyone to get wind of it. It's a precedent-setter, my boy. A real landmark case."

Mark reached for a notepad and pen from his briefcase. He could feel the adrenaline begin to rush through his body. He'd been waiting for a case like this. "Can you tell me anything about it over the phone?"

"A little, I suppose." Royal took another drink and let out another sigh. "Very little. We're filing suit against a major national company. Alleged malfeasance with their employee pension plan."

Mark let out a low whistle. "Who's our client?"

"It's a class action suit," Royal told him. He sounded pleased with himself. "A group of former employees who allege that the CEO knew of and condoned siphoning funds from the pension plan to get himself out of financial hot water elsewhere."

Interesting, but hardly a landmark case. Mark ran his fingers through his hair and paced as far as the short telephone cord would let him. "You said it would set precedent…?"

"That it will, my boy. And I'll fill you in on all the details when you get back here where you belong."

"Yes, but— Things still aren't settled here."

"That's unfortunate." Royal's voice sounded anything but sympathetic. "But you've already been there for two weeks. Can't you handle the rest from here? How tough can a simple custody matter be?"

"I'm afraid not. It's a little tougher than I expected."

"What's the holdup? I thought you had everything you needed to get the boy and come home again."

Everything but a clear conscience, Mark thought, but he couldn't admit that aloud. Royal wouldn't understand. "I thought I did."

"You need a little pressure from the firm?"

Hell, no. "Thanks, but I think I've got a handle on it."

"Give me the judge's name and let me make a phone call," Royal said with a laugh. "Put me in touch with opposing counsel. If you can't bring him around, I'll do it."

"I'm sure I can wrap it up if I can just have a few more days."

"How many?"

Mark pulled a number from thin air. "Until Wednesday? I can be back in the office on Thursday morning."

Royal's chair creaked again. "Do whatever it takes, but get yourself back to the office by Wednesday afternoon. We need you on this case."

"Yes, sir."

"Pull out all the stops and get what you went there for. You're an associate with Jamison and Spritzer, my boy, not some country-bumpkin attorney. You don't want me to start wondering if you have what it takes to be a partner here."

Mark had always taken pride in his association with the firm, but he resented the thinly veiled threat behind Royal's warning. When Royal disconnected, Mark replaced the receiver slowly and paced to the window. Shoving aside the curtain, he stared at the mountains and sighed heavily.

He'd postponed as long as he could. There was one solution to the problem. It was pretty radical, but maybe she'd go for it.

WHILE JARED PLAYED contentedly at her feet, Dionne put away groceries in her tiny kitchen. Even with the window cooler on high, the apartment was sweltering. She pulled a cold soda from the refrigerator and held it against her cheek. Emotional and physical exhaustion swamped her, scratched at her eyes, and made her almost light-headed. Worry kept her moving.

She should call Cicely. Mark had taken up so much of her time, she hadn't spoken to Cicely in days. Her friend was probably half out of her mind with worry. But Mark had given her an evening alone with Jared and she didn't want to lose a minute of it.

She glanced at the top of Jared's head and smiled. His resemblance to Mark still disturbed her, but it no longer filled her with terror. Nor did the similarities in their personalities.

There was something high-voltage about Mark. Something almost larger than life that drew her in even while it frightened her. Much as she hated to admit it, there were many things about him she liked—his sense of humor, his unselfish concern for Jared, his generosity—but she never completely lost that sensation of danger when he was around. And it wasn't only the danger of losing Jared. There were other things going on inside her as well, and those had nothing to do with Jared. But she didn't want to think about that. Even the briefest acknowledgment of it felt disloyal—to Brent, to Jared, and to herself.

Jared banged two blocks together and beamed up at her. His broad smile changed suddenly as a yawn puckered his mouth and put a deep scowl on his sweet face.

"You're sleepy, aren't you, big boy?"

Jared shook his head firmly. "No." Even though his eyes watered from the huge yawn and another soon distorted his face. He dropped the blocks and rubbed his ear.

"Silly me," Dionne said, closing the cupboard and picking him up. "Of course you're not tired. But what do you say we get you into your jammies, anyway?"

"No."

"I think we'd better." She pushed the blocks aside with one foot and started toward the living room. "We can read a story."

Jared's eyes lit. "Baby Blue Cat?"

"Sure." Stifling a yawn of her own, Dionne kissed his cheek. Not surprisingly, Jared's favorite story was *The Baby Blue Cat Who Said No.* He could listen to it over and over again. "And then we could read *Mama, Do You Love Me?* if you're still not sleepy."

Jared snuggled against her shoulder and worked his fingers into her hair. "Okay."

For once, Jared didn't struggle while she changed him into light summer pajamas. Instead, he cuddled up to her, put his tiny hand on her cheek, and yawned again.

Such love filled her, it seemed as if her heart would explode into a million tiny pieces. But the uneasiness that had been with her ever since Mark appeared on the scene and the nagging reminder that she needed to think seriously about his suggestion, still hovered nearby, just waiting to destroy the moment.

Doing her best to push that problem aside, she gathered Jared and his books and settled into her favorite armchair to read. But before they'd even reached the part where Baby Blue Cat refused to eat his supper, a knock on the door interrupted them.

Since Jared was nearly asleep, Dionne settled him in the chair and hurried to answer before another knock could wake him. But when she checked through the peephole and saw Mark standing there, she hesitated.

Then slowly she opened the door. "I thought we agreed that I'd have tonight alone with Jared."

"We did. But something's come up."

Dionne checked on Jared, pleased to see that he'd fallen into a deep sleep. His cheek rested against the arm of the chair and a lock of hair fell across his forehead. "Fine," she said with a resigned sigh. "Come in. Just give me a minute to get Jared into bed."

When Mark didn't ask to help, she knew something was bothering him. As she carried Jared into his bedroom, she heard Mark shut and lock the door behind him. While she arranged the covers over Jared, she heard Mark pacing the living room like a caged animal.

She kissed Jared and let her gaze linger on his face for a moment, then took a deep breath to steel herself and rejoined Mark in the living room. He'd stopped pacing and had made himself comfortable on the couch, but his expression was troubled.

"What is it?" she said. "What did you want to talk about?"

"We have a problem," he said, running his hand through his hair and leaving soft tufts in its wake. "I got a call from the senior partner in my firm this afternoon. I have to be back in Boston by Wednesday of next week. We have to make some decisions."

She froze. This was it, then. To her dismay, she realized that she'd started getting used to having

Mark around. Now he'd be leaving, and when he did, he'd expect to take Jared with him. He was suddenly, irrevocably, her enemy again.

He stood and crossed to Jared's door, pulling it shut with a soft click. "Have you given any more thought to moving to Boston?"

She watched him warily, her senses almost numb. "You want a decision now?"

"I need to be back in Boston," he said again. He came back to the couch and sat beside her. The light caught his hair and made it look almost black. "And I don't want to leave Jared behind when I go."

A knot curled in Dionne's stomach. "What will happen if I do move to Boston? Will Jared live with me or with you?"

"We could work out a visitation schedule."

"But he'd live with you."

Mark tilted his head to one side. "Yes, most of the time, but—"

She couldn't bear it. She couldn't. But what options did she have? "How do I know you won't lure me there just to get Jared closer and then take him away?"

"If the court grants me custody, I promise that you'll always have a place in his life. You're his mother, Dionne."

"Marianne is still his legal mother," she reminded him, hating the way the words sounded.

"Yes, but she doesn't want to raise him. She chose you to do that."

"But she's never signed the consent for adoption. Either of you could take Jared away from me any time you wanted. I can't live like that."

"If the court grants me custody—"

"So you say," she snapped, jerking to her feet. "But I'm not sure I can trust you."

He ran a hand across his chin. "What do you want from me, Dionne? I'm giving you all I can."

She shook her head, unable to voice her own needs.

"Do you want me to go away and pretend Jared doesn't exist? That none of this happened? I can't do that, Dionne. I won't."

"But you expect me to give him up and be happy seeing him only a few days a year?"

He remained silent for so long she began to worry. At long last, he spoke. "There is another solution. A way we can both have Jared in our lives."

"How?"

"It's kind of extreme," he warned.

"What is it?"

He held her gaze steadily for what felt like forever before he spoke again. "We could get married."

"Married?" She reeled as if he'd shot her and jerked her hand away. *"Married?"*

"I warned you it was extreme. But let me explain before you toss me out on my ear."

He was crazy. Unspeakably crazy. But a small voice told her not to reject the idea outright. "All right. Explain."

"As Jared's legal father, I can establish custody with the court and that would ensure that he would stay with me. As my wife, you'd be his legal stepmother."

Legal. The word seduced her, gave her hope, and made her want to hear the rest.

"You've already said you're not planning to get

married again,'' Mark went on. ''You're still in love with your late husband, right?''

''Yes, but—''

''And I'm… Well, let's just say that I've been burned one too many times to have any romantic notions about finding true love.'' His mouth twisted bitterly, making her wonder what had happened between him and Marianne. He composed himself quickly. ''But we both love Jared, and we both need him in our lives. More importantly, he needs both of us.''

''Yes, he does,'' she admitted reluctantly. It was a hard admission to make, but like it or not, Jared did need his father.

Mark's eyes darkened with gratitude. ''So, why should either of us have to give him up?''

She must be demented to even consider it. But his argument made a strange kind of sense.

He touched her softly, just a flicker of his fingers across her hand, but his touch affected her deeply. Its gentleness was strangely healing. ''We'd keep the relationship purely platonic, of course. I don't want you to worry about that. We could find a house in the country, where Jared would have plenty of room to play. One with at least three bedrooms.''

''But—''

''We'd need to live within commuting distance of Boston, though. As I said before, I'm not willing to abandon my career. But I'm more than willing to provide for my family and let you stay home with Jared—unless you *want* to work, of course. Full-time. Part-time. Nothing at all. That will be your decision. You'd be my wife in every sense of the word except one.'' He held her gaze again, almost pleading with her to agree. "And most importantly, you'd be Jared's mother."

How could she even consider saying yes? How could she refuse? He held all the cards, yet he was offering her an unbelievable chance. And if she married him, she could ensure that no other woman would ever take her place in Jared's life.

She let her gaze travel over his face, taking in every detail—the thin scar above his lip, the tiny smile lines around his eyes, the way his eyebrows arched when he laughed, just like Jared's. She closed her eyes for a moment, feeling instead of thinking, remembering everything Marianne had told her about him.

Brent had always chided her for making decisions with her heart instead of her head. But in some instances, there was no other way to choose.

She opened her eyes again slowly. "Why are you doing this?"

"I told you before I'm not an ogre." Mark smiled gently. "I'm a fairly decent guy. And I've realized that I don't want to take Jared away from his mother. I'd like to be able to look at myself in the mirror without hating who I see there."

Again, a tiny piece of her brain warned her to think. A sliver of logic made its way to her heart. She knew so little about this man. To even consider his proposition was insane, at best. She should refuse. But Jared chose that moment to toddle out of the bedroom door, his feet scuffing softly along the carpet as he walked, his tiny fists rubbing his eyes, the cupid's bow of a mouth open in a wide yawn. And she knew she was lost.

No matter how illogical, how foolish, how... frightening, there was only one decision she could possibly make.

CHAPTER SIX

"THIS IS INSANE," Cicely snapped as their waiter positioned salads in front of them the following day. "You can't do it."

In spite of the air-conditioning, Dionne could feel patches of perspiration beneath her arms. She'd chosen a neutral spot for this conversation, but even the crowded restaurant didn't inhibit Cicely. Dionne kept her attention on her plate and didn't speak until the waiter walked away.

"I *can* do this," she said softly, "and I'm going to. I won't give Jared up."

Cicely pushed her plate aside. "I can understand how you feel, but there has to be some other way."

"If there is, I'd like to know what it is."

"What about your job?"

"I told them this morning I'm quitting. Today's my last day."

"Without notice? That's great. What about all your things?"

"Our clothes and a few of Jared's toys will fit into suitcases. We'll ship what we can't carry, and Mark's paying a moving company to pack up the furniture and dishes and take them to storage."

"But this guy's a stranger. How do you know he's not psychotic or abusive or...or—" Cicely broke off and waved one hand to encompass all the other possibilities.

"I've talked to Marianne about him," Dionne reminded her, "and she had nothing bad to say about him. Considering what he's prepared to do, I'd say it's obvious that he has a kind heart." Dionne kept her voice low, hoping none of the other customers seated nearby could overhear. "He's offering me a way to keep Jared. How can I walk away from that?"

Cicely reached across the table and covered one of Dionne's hands with hers. "I'm just worried about you. I don't want to see you hurt."

Dionne gripped her friend's hand gratefully. "No matter what happens, I won't be hurt as much as I'd be if he took Jared away. Please, Cicely, don't make this harder than it already is. I need you on my side."

Cicely sighed and shook her head, but some of her reservations seemed to fade. "Maybe I wouldn't feel so bad if you were going to be close. But New England..."

"You can always come to visit."

"Oh, I will. I intend to see for myself that this guy doesn't hurt you." Cicely tried to smile and her fingers tightened on Dionne's. "So, when is the wedding?"

"Tomorrow."

"So soon?"

"Mark has to be back at work by Wednesday afternoon, and we'll need time to travel and get settled. And I don't want to leave here without a wedding. I'm not taking any chances."

"How are you going to explain this to Jared?"

"We'll tell him that we're getting married, of course."

"And that Mark's his father?"

Dionne nodded slowly. "He still knows Brent as 'Daddy' from pictures around the house, so we've agreed to tell him that Mark is his new daddy—at least for now. I have a few reservations, but telling Jared the truth is one of Mark's conditions. I suppose he's right. I can't expect him to be happy with Jared calling him 'Uncle Mark.'"

"I guess not," Cicely agreed grudgingly.

"I'm scared," Dionne admitted, "but I have to do this. Will you be there for me?"

"You know I will." Cicely made a visible effort to put her concerns behind her. "It's your wedding day."

"I've had my wedding day," Dionne reminded Cicely firmly, "with Brent. This is a business arrangement, that's all. Tomorrow is just the day we make the contract binding."

"There are a lot of things this is," Cicely argued, "but a business arrangement isn't one of them. You're committing to live with a stranger for the rest of your life."

The words sent a bolt of panic through Dionne, but she tried to ignore it and made a weak joke. "He won't be a stranger for long."

"You're right about that. The man is going to be your *husband*. What are you going to do when he wants to act like one?"

"That won't happen," Dionne insisted. "We've agreed to have separate bedrooms and keep the relationship platonic. But for Jared's sake we're not telling anyone else that, not even Mark's family. Everyone will believe we fell in love and got married."

"That ought to keep you safe," Cicely said sarcastically.

"Mark's no more interested in me than I am in him," Dionne insisted.

"Right." Cicely frowned, then waved a hand in front of her. "Assuming that's true—and for the record, I don't believe it for a minute—how will you explain your sleeping arrangement to Jared when he gets older?"

Dionne ran her fingers along the side of her water glass. "I don't know. We'll cross that bridge when we come to it."

"That bridge and a hundred more," Cicely predicted.

"Maybe. Probably." Dionne met Cicely's gaze steadily. "But no matter what problems we have, it will be worth it."

"What if *you* start liking *him?* Or what if you meet someone else in a year or two you fall in love with? What then?"

Dionne scowled at her. "That won't happen. I had my turn. Brent was my soul mate. No one could ever take his place."

"I know you feel that way now, but—"

"I won't change my mind."

"Okay, what if he finds someone else and falls in love?"

Dionne had had that thought herself. And she also had the answer. "If Mark has custody, I'll be Jared's legal stepmother. Nothing will change that."

Cicely studied her for a moment, then let out a heavy sigh. "You're so damned stubborn."

Dionne could feel the tide of the conversation turning, and let out a soft sigh of her own. "Yes, I know."

"It's not a compliment."

"Okay."

Cicely waved her hand again, this time in resignation. "All right. Fine. If you're determined to do this, I guess I won't argue with you anymore. But if you ever—*ever*—need me, promise you'll call."

Dionne sketched an X over her heart and smiled sadly. "I promise." She reached over to grasp her friend's hand. "Thank you, Cece. I feel a whole lot better having your support."

Cicely's eyes glittered with unshed tears. "I wish something would make *me* feel better."

"How about knowing that Jared and I will be together and happy?"

"Together, yes. But happy?" Cicely tossed her napkin onto the table. "We'll have to wait and see about that."

As if in a dream, Dionne followed Mark into the justice of the peace's office. Behind her, Cicely carried Jared, who wanted to get down and explore.

"Hush now," Cicely said softly. "Stay with me for just a few minutes. Look how pretty Mommy is."

"Down," Jared insisted. When Cicely didn't release him, he took a deep breath and prepared to let out a howl.

Mark stepped forward quickly, as if he'd been dealing with Jared his entire life. He pulled a colorful key chain from his pocket and handed it to the boy. "Hang on to these for me, will you, sport? See if you can make the light shine." He showed Jared where to push the mini-flashlight and ruffled his hair affectionately.

Dionne sent him a grateful smile, then looked around the bleak office that was so unlike the church where she'd married Brent. Instead of flowers, they were surrounded by file cabinets. Instead of organ music, the sounds of morning traffic filled the air.

But it was perfect for this occasion.

At her wedding to Brent, she'd been full of hope and dreams. Now she clung desperately to the hope that she wasn't making the biggest mistake of her life.

Her finger, without the ring Brent had placed on it, felt bare. Within minutes, she'd be wearing one of the matching gold bands Mark had shown her as they'd carried her bags to the car. He'd seemed almost eager for her approval of his choice, but she didn't care. That ring would symbolize none of the things Brent's had.

The justice of the peace, a middle-aged woman with a bad Doris Day haircut, smiled and stood to greet them. "Right on time. We should be able to get you to the airport with no problem." She shook Mark's hand and nodded toward a short, gray-haired man standing in the corner. "I've asked my husband to stand in as your other witness. I hope that's all right."

Mark left Dionne's side to shake the man's hand. "It's fine. I appreciate you taking time out of your schedule to accommodate us."

"Glad to do it," the man said, stepping forward to stand beside Cicely.

Dionne kept her smile in place and nodded in response to Mark's soft, "Ready?" She *was* ready.

Ready to seal the bargain they'd made. Ready to take the step that would allow her to remain in Jared's life. Ready to put the past behind her and move on.

Still, the brief ceremony passed in a blur. She scarcely heard the woman's short speech about the sanctity of marriage and the sacred nature of the vows they would soon exchange.

She responded with a whispered "I do" when the justice of the peace looked at her expectantly. A moment later, she heard Mark's identical response through the roaring in her ears. But her anxiety escalated when she heard the woman pronounce them man and wife and gave Mark permission to kiss the bride.

There really was no going back now.

When Mark hesitated, Dionne lifted her face to him, knowing she had to keep her end of the bargain. Except for Cicely, no one would ever know what a sham this marriage was.

He gingerly kissed her cheek, then stepped away again. She glanced at the simple gold band on her finger and tried to hold back the sudden tears that burned her eyes.

The justice of the peace looked concerned. "Are you all right, Mrs. Taylor?"

Mrs. Taylor.

The name sounded all wrong. Dionne blinked and sent the woman a tremulous smile. "Yes," she whispered. "I'm fine."

"Just overwhelmed, I'm sure." The woman touched her shoulder gently. "Weddings are such emotional times."

The poor woman would be shocked if she knew *which* emotions were racking Dionne at this moment.

Fear, guilt and disbelief mixed with faith and hope. Dionne reached for Cicely's hand, needing a lifeline to cling to if only for a moment. To her dismay, the hand she caught wasn't Cicely's. It was big and rough-skinned, and completely male.

If the contact surprised Mark, he didn't show it. Instead, he closed his hand around hers and gave it a gentle squeeze. Unexpected warmth began at her fingertips and radiated up her arm.

Stunned, she pulled her hand away and glanced at him quickly. She didn't *want* to be aware of Mark. She was, and always had been, in love with Brent and she owed it to his memory not to betray him.

"Well," Mark said, shoving his hands into his pockets. "I guess that's it. We'd better hurry if we're going to make our flight."

Dionne struggled to still her trembling fingers and turned toward Cicely.

Mark followed the direction of her gaze, then looked back at her again. "We have time for you to say goodbye."

Grateful for his understanding, she took Jared from Cicely and surrendered gratefully to her friend's warm embrace.

"Remember," Cicely spoke softly, "if things don't work out, all you have to do is call me."

"But they *will* work out," Dionne insisted. "They have to."

"I hope so," Cicely whispered. Releasing Dionne suddenly, she straightened her shoulders, propped her hands on her hips, and turned to Mark. "If you ever hurt either of them," she said, "you'll have to answer to me."

Mark nodded soberly. "I'll keep that in mind."

"Would you stop worrying?" Dionne said. "Everything's going to be just fine, you'll see."

But as she carried Jared out the door, firmly resisting the impulse to turn around and flee back to Cicely's side, she couldn't help wishing she was as confident as she'd managed to sound.

ONE OF THE THINGS Mark liked best about traveling was coming home to Boston. He always looked forward to getting back to his routine. But now his routine would never be the same. He had a child. And a wife.

A wife who didn't look happy at all.

She held Jared close, cradling him almost as if he was some kind of protective shield. She looked nervous. Pale. Her cheek still bore the imprint from the seat of the cab where she'd fallen asleep on their way from the airport.

Mark watched the cab pull away from the curb in front of his condo, then glanced at their bags on the sidewalk. Dionne shivered in spite of the warm night air and pulled Jared closer.

"Well," he said, shoving his hands into his pockets, trying to hide his own nervousness. He forced a weak smile. "Here we are."

"Yes."

Mark pulled his hands out of his pockets again and picked up their bags. "I think we should both get a good night's sleep," he said, nodding for her to walk in front of him. "We'll have to start looking for a place to live in the morning."

"Yes." She spoke so softly, he could barely hear her over the passing late-night traffic.

He juggled luggage and held the door for her. "I

know this is tough for you, Dionne. Hell, it's not going to be a piece of cake for me, either. But we're going to be together for a long time. We might as well try to be friends.''

She stopped inside the lobby and looked back at him. ''I'd like that. I know so little about you, about your family—'' She broke off and stared at the ornate ceiling, the rich marble floor and pillars. Mark knew she was comparing this building and the one she and Jared had called home in Boise, and for the first time he saw it as gaudy and ostentatious.

Suddenly embarrassed, he nodded toward the elevators. ''We're going to the twelfth floor.''

She made her way across the deserted lobby, but didn't speak again until the elevator doors closed. ''Can you believe this is happening?''

''You mean that we're married?''

''It keeps hitting me in waves,'' she confessed, leaning against the wall and adjusting her hold on Jared. ''Just when I think I've accepted it, something new happens, like realizing Jared and I are going to be living here.'' She ran a hand over Jared's head and sent Mark a weak smile. ''Or realizing that we'll be meeting your family soon.''

''My family?'' Talking about them put Mark back on firm ground. ''You don't have to worry about them. They're great.''

''I'm sure they are, but I've been alone for a long time. My mother died when I was sixteen, and I have no idea where my father is. Brent's been gone for a year. It may take me a while to get used to... everything.''

He appreciated her honesty. It was the first step in

closing the gap between them. "If it helps, I've lived alone most of my adult life."

"But not completely alone. Your family has obviously played a big part in your life." She watched the lights above the door for a moment. "Maybe you should tell me something about them."

He didn't know where to begin, but he welcomed the chance to fill the nervous space between them.

"I have three brothers," he said as the elevator doors swished open again. "David's the oldest, and I come between Jerry and Steve, who's the youngest." He motioned her toward the far end of the corridor and kept talking as they walked. "David's married. He and his wife, Kaye, have four kids. Jerry's divorced. He sees his two daughters twice a month on weekends. And Steve..." He smiled ruefully. "Well, Steve's a lot like me, I guess. He's twenty-seven and shows no signs of ever getting married."

Dionne glanced at him uneasily. "I wonder if I'll ever be able to keep them all straight."

"Sure you will. But that's not all." He stopped in front of his door and ran his finger between his neck and collar. The realization that she belonged inside brought on a fresh wave of apprehension. "There's Aunt Nonie and her husband, Bruce, Uncle Pete and Aunt Shirley, Aunt Pam and Uncle Carl, a couple dozen cousins, their spouses and kids."

Dionne's eyebrows knit. "They won't all be there at once, will they?"

He unlocked the door, pushed it open, and then stopped. Surely she wouldn't want him to carry her across the threshold. He glanced at her quickly, saw wariness etched on her face, and decided to let her walk in on her own. "My parents' house is like Grand Central Station," he went on. "It's where everybody gathers for any occasion—or no occasion at all. Every family has one."

A shadow passed across her eyes. "Mine didn't." She hitched Jared higher on her shoulder. "We won't be expected to spend every weekend with them, will we?"

"No, of course not. David and Kaye practically live at my parents' house, but they own a house in Sunrise Notch, so that's only natural. Jerry and Steve only show up every few weeks. And between my obligations at work and the things I'm sure you'll get involved with, we'll be too busy to go, even if we wanted to." He turned on the light for her and shut the door. "Well, here it is," he said. "Home sweet home." He found himself watching her, waiting for her reaction.

She gazed around slowly at the furniture, paintings, and sculptures, then took a ragged breath. "It's very nice."

He laughed, but it sounded jittery and tense. "Maybe. But it's no place for a two-year-old. I'll have to get rid of most of this stuff or put it in storage until Jared's older."

"Are you going to be okay with that? You must have spent a lot of money getting everything just right."

She looked so uncertain, he almost gave in to the urge to put his arm around her. But the memory of how quickly she'd dropped his hand after the wedding ceremony made him hold back.

"I'm fine with that," he assured her. "It's just stuff."

"Very expensive stuff."

"Maybe, but it's still stuff." He picked up her suitcase and started toward his bedroom. "I'll put your things and Jared's in here. I'll sleep on the couch."

Her eyes widened. "This huge place only has one bedroom?"

"Sad but true."

"You don't need to give up your bedroom for us. I don't mind sleeping on the couch, and I can make Jared a bed on the floor with some of the cushions—"

Mark shook his head quickly. "Sorry. I was raised to be a gentleman."

"A gentleman doesn't dictate to a lady." Her voice sounded almost teasing.

"A lady doesn't turn down a gentleman when he offers her his bed." The instant the words left his mouth, he regretted them. A sudden, sharp image of his sheets clinging to her body formed in his mind, and the air seemed charged with something that hadn't been there a moment before.

To his relief, Dionne didn't seem to notice. She laughed softly, but the warmth of her laugh and the light dancing in her eyes only made the image sharper. "Is that right?"

"That's right." He tried to block out the mental picture, but it wouldn't go away.

Great. He'd promised to keep their relationship platonic, but they hadn't even been married twelve hours and already his sex drive was threatening everything. Dionne would hate him again if she guessed the kinds of thoughts he was having. She'd probably think that he'd lured her here just to take advantage of her.

Maybe this marriage had been a mistake on both their parts. But it was too late now.

Cursing himself under his breath, he tried to keep his mind on the tasks at hand. The task of settling his new wife into his bedroom. The task of embarking on a life with a woman he hardly knew and a child he couldn't live without.

HEART POUNDING, Dionne woke with a start and sat bolt upright in bed. Sunlight streamed through the windows and burned her tired eyes. She'd overslept. She'd be late for work.

When she tossed back the covers, her hand brushed Jared on the bed beside her. In a rush, everything came flooding back—the emotional turmoil of the past three weeks, the wedding, the long flight. Blinking quickly to clear her eyes, she pulled her hand back and lowered it to her lap. And she watched Jared to make sure she hadn't woken him.

She'd slept hard almost from the moment her head touched the pillow, but she didn't feel rested. Judging from the way Jared slept, he'd been worn out by the long flight. Spending the night in a strange bedroom two thousand miles from home had certainly left her physically and emotionally exhausted.

This was home now, she corrected herself. This bedroom with the wheat-colored comforter and matching sheets, the polished hardwood floor and woven rugs, the Native American art and paintings of southwestern landscapes. And the man who owned it all was her husband.

Just when she'd started to relax around him last

night, he'd changed. He'd suddenly become remote and chilly, and had left her and Jared alone in the bedroom as if he couldn't get rid of them fast enough.

Maybe he'd been nervous. Heaven only knew *she'd* been on edge. But his inexplicable mood swing worried her. Her mother had been moody, and the shifts from one to the other without warning had always left Dionne anxious and uncertain.

Old emotions she'd thought long gone rushed to the surface and made her wary. After climbing off the bed gently, she crossed to the bedroom door and pressed her ear against it to listen. She couldn't hear Mark moving around, which was fine with her. She didn't mind a few minutes of solitude and a cup of fresh, strong coffee before she had to see him again. If she was careful, she could find the kitchen and make a pot without waking him.

After closing the bedroom door behind her, she waited for a few seconds to make absolutely certain Mark was still asleep on the couch. She couldn't see him, but she could make out a mound of blankets and the edge of his pillow.

Quietly, scarcely breathing, she tiptoed through the living room, taking in the furniture and obviously expensive paintings on the walls. Bookshelves flanked the fireplace but, unlike her own particle-board bookshelves in Boise that she'd filled with well-thumbed paperbacks, his books were hardbound and looked new.

She moved into the dining room still on tiptoe. There, a large oak table and matching chairs gleamed in bright morning sunlight. Green plants tumbled from baskets in the corners and curled along a sideboard against the far wall.

Nice. Much nicer than anything she'd ever owned. And she was suddenly glad she wouldn't have to protect Mark's valuables from Jared's quick little hands for long.

Sighing, she crossed to a door that she assumed led into the kitchen and pushed it open. But when she saw Mark standing there with his back to her, she froze in place.

Wearing only a pair of sweatpants, he scooped coffee into a filter. His hair was sleep-tousled, and his back and feet were bare. He looked young and vulnerable and strangely appealing. While she watched, he lowered the can to the counter and stretched. Muscles appeared out of nowhere on his shoulders and arms. The sweatpants slipped a little lower on his hips.

Something Dionne hadn't felt in a long time flickered deep within her. Desire? No, she told herself firmly. Not desire. It was just…just…

Trembling, she closed the door between them and leaned against the wall. This would never do. She didn't need this purely female reaction to the sight of a half-dressed man. She wasn't *supposed* to have that kind of reaction to him. Her heart still belonged to Brent.

She squeezed her eyes shut and tried to catch her breath. At least Mark hadn't seen her. She'd have been mortified if he'd noticed her reaction and misinterpreted it as something personal. Because whatever it had been, it *wasn't* personal. She couldn't allow it to be.

Shivering slightly, she pushed away from the wall,

raced back to the bedroom, and closed the door firmly. She started toward the bed, but she didn't want to wake Jared, and the idea of sitting on Mark's bed suddenly made her uncomfortable.

She hoisted her heavy suitcase onto a chair instead and pulled out jeans and a baggy T-shirt—sensible clothing that was decidedly *un*sexy.

Resolutely, she carried her overnight bag into the bathroom, locked the door behind her, and undressed quickly. Even with the door locked, the idea of Mark, bare-chested and undeniably sexy, only a room or two away made her uncomfortable.

She turned the shower to a heavy pulsing rhythm that should have pummeled some sense back into her. Instead, it seemed to make her body more fully aware. She turned it to a gentle spray and leaned her head against the shower wall.

Now that she knew she could feel desire again, she also realized she couldn't act on it. Mark had suggested this marriage because he felt sorry for her, not because he found her attractive. She'd agreed only because she was desperate.

If she'd been in Boise, she'd have picked up the phone and called Cicely. But even Cicely couldn't help her this time.

She'd have to solve this one on her own.

CHAPTER SEVEN

DIONNE STRUGGLED to keep her eyes open as Mark scooped the last bit of creamy chowder from his bowl and slid it into his mouth. Jared played contentedly with a small container of crayons and a coloring book provided by the restaurant. Both of the men in her life looked ready to hit the house-hunting trail again. Dionne would have given anything for a nice long nap.

Her eyes felt gritty from exhaustion and her muscles had long ago turned to gelatin, and all for nothing. After two days of house-hunting, they were no closer to finding a place than they'd been when they stepped off the plane at the airport.

They'd found charming houses with only two bedrooms, large houses located on busy streets, houses that were practically falling apart, and houses even Mark couldn't afford, but they hadn't found anything that would fit their needs. And she'd been so exhausted each evening when they got back to Mark's condo, she'd gone to bed almost the minute they walked in the door.

After that moment in the kitchen that first morning, avoiding time alone with him seemed like the wisest thing she could do. But some traitorous part of her was disappointed that he didn't seem to mind.

Sighing with contentment, Mark leaned back in his

chair. "If all the restaurants around here are this good, maybe we *should* buy that house."

"The two-bedroom one?"

"Don't worry," he assured her with a quick smile. "I'm only thinking about my stomach."

She let herself relax slightly, though she was determined not to let her guard down completely. Smoothing a lock of hair from Jared's forehead, she smiled at the serious look on his face as he colored a cartoon lobster bright blue. "The food is wonderful here," she agreed, glancing at the low-beamed ceiling and the huge fireplace across the crowded room. "But it's also expensive. I think they're charging for atmosphere."

Mark shrugged easily. "Probably. But it's worth it, don't you think?"

"You obviously live differently than Jared and I do."

"I'm not rolling in money," he said, "but I do okay. You don't need to worry."

She felt him watching her, waiting for her to look at him again. Slowly, hesitantly, she forced herself to do just that. "I'm not worried. I'm used to living on a pretty tight budget. I'm *not* used to relying on someone else to fund the budget."

"Did you work while you were married to Brent?"

She nodded. "I've worked since I was old enough to get a job."

"Doing what?"

"You name it," she said with a thin laugh, "I've done it. I've baby-sat, decorated Christmas trees, worked in a garden shop, and cashiered at a grocery store. I've slung burgers and waited tables… I could go on, but you get the general idea.''

He looked confused. ''Didn't you go to college?''

''No.''

''Not interested?''

''No. I would have loved to have gone. I just couldn't afford it.''

He looked almost embarrassed by her admission. ''If you had gone, what would you have studied?''

She smiled to set him at ease. It wasn't his fault she'd spent her entire life without money. ''I used to dream about being a counselor for troubled children. I wanted to help kids who grow up feeling unloved and disconnected because their parents are absent for one reason or another.''

His eyes glinted with approval. ''What made you decide on that?''

''I guess because that's how I felt when I was growing up. My father walked out on us when I was only two, and my mother worked herself into an early grave trying to support me. She wasn't ever home, even when she was alive.'' She still felt strange telling him something so personal, but they'd agreed to work on their friendship and he couldn't understand her unless he also understood her past.

Before she knew what he intended, he put a hand over hers. ''I'm sorry.''

She tried to ignore the sudden flush of heat that swept through her and struggled not to react to the concern in his voice.

''There's nothing to be sorry for,'' she said firmly and drew her hand away, resisting the urge to let it linger in the comfort of his. ''It's just how things were at my house.''

"But you dreamed about helping other kids in the same boat."

"For a while. But real life brought me back to earth in a hurry."

Something she couldn't read flashed in his eyes. "Do you still think about doing it?"

She shook her head and laughed away the idea. "I don't really have time to indulge in dreams."

"Maybe you should."

"No." She folded her napkin and set it on the table. "Life is much better when I keep my feet on the ground."

Mark let his gaze travel slowly across her face and settle on her eyes again. "I don't agree with you. Life goes nowhere when you're afraid to take risks. You could still get your degree if you want to."

She shook her head firmly. "No, I can't."

"Why not?"

"I've got Jared to think about. I wouldn't be able to put in the hours studying that I'd need to. Not to mention the cost of tuition."

Mark's mouth twisted slightly. "You're not the only one around to take care of Jared, you know. We could find a sitter for him while you're in class, you could study in the evenings while I spend time with him, and finding the money for tuition wouldn't be a problem."

Uneasy, Dionne scooted her chair away from the table and started to pick up the crayons from Jared's high chair. "I can't take that kind of money from you."

"Why not?"

"Because…because it wouldn't be right."

"I don't know why not. You *are* my wife."

"Technically, yes. But—"

Mark cut off her next argument. "Besides, I think you should give some thought to what you're going to do when Jared gets older and starts school himself."

"That won't be for a long time," she said almost desperately. She touched Jared's hand gently, suddenly afraid to see him grow older. "He's only two." And three years seemed like an eternity away.

She wondered briefly what their marriage would be like then. Would they still feel like strangers or would they have settled into a comfortable routine? Would she still feel this quickening of her pulse when Mark looked at her with those deep brown eyes, still tremble when he touched her.

"Three years will pass before you know it," he predicted, picking up the dessert menu. "At least think about going to school. Don't cross it off your list yet. I want you to be happy here."

She ignored the fluttering in her abdomen and managed a weak smile. "All right. I'll think about it." At least, she'd pretend to. "In the meantime, there are more important things to think about, like deciding how we're going to split the household chores."

Mark seemed reluctant to change the subject, but at least he didn't argue. "All right. What do you suggest?"

"We could each make a list, starting with the thing we enjoy most and working down to our least favorite. Maybe we'll discover that I don't mind cooking and you like scrubbing toilets."

"I can guarantee we won't discover that," he assured her with a warm laugh. "Do you like to cook?"

"I'm not a gourmet chef, but I enjoy making simple recipes."

"Then the cooking is all yours." He lowered the menu and rested his hands on the table. "I haven't mowed a lawn in years, but I don't mind doing the yard work."

"I like growing flowers," she said, "but I'll be thrilled to let you do the rest. Does your offer include weeding and trimming and edging?"

"Sure. And shoveling snow. What about dusting and vacuuming?"

"I can do those," she offered. "I'll have plenty of time on my hands." She glanced down at the strange gold band on her finger and added, "I think we should each do our own laundry. I'll do Jared's with mine."

"Good idea." Mark cleared his throat, then picked up the dessert menu again, and made a pretense of studying it. Color flooded his cheeks and she could see his pulse beating against his temple. "And it would probably be best if neither of us left our underthings drying in the bathroom."

He looked so ill at ease, Dionne nearly laughed aloud. "Of course."

"Okay." He shifted on the chair, but his eyes never left the menu. "The cheesecake looks good. Would you like some?"

Dionne shook her head and rested one hand on her stomach. "No, thanks. The chowder was too filling."

"Then let's get out of here." His voice came out gruff and hard-edged. He tossed his napkin onto the table, slipped more than enough money to cover the bill onto the table, and started to lift Jared. "Are you ready, sport?"

Jared leaned back toward the high chair, wriggling his fingers at the picture he'd been forced once again to abandon. "My picture."

"Mommy's got it," Dionne assured him, brushing a kiss to his forehead.

"I need to get to the office," Mark said as he started away again. "Do you want me to drop you two off somewhere, or do you want to go home?"

Dionne gathered her things, surprised but pleased by his reaction. "Jared needs a nap. I think we should just go back to your apartment."

"It's yours now, too," Mark said quickly. "At least until we find someplace else to live."

Dionne didn't argue, but she wondered if she could ever get used to calling his condo home. If she'd get used to calling *any* place home she shared with him.

Someday, perhaps. But not yet.

FOR THE FIRST TIME in weeks, Mark felt like himself again. His office with windows overlooking Boston Harbor, his files, the credenza loaded with work—all of it helped to ground him. He stood inside the doorway for a minute or two, then lowered his briefcase to the floor beside his desk, stripped off his jacket, and draped it over a chair.

Royal wanted a draft of the Young Technologies brief by the end of next week, and Mark wouldn't disappoint him. The case would require hours of research, but he'd never had trouble setting aside his personal life for his professional one. Of course, he hadn't had a wife and son before.

Settling himself in his comfortable leather chair, he pulled the file toward him. Just as Royal predicted, it was an interesting dispute, one that could be a landmark decision if the court ruled the way the firm wanted it to. And maybe, if Mark could immerse himself in the case, he could put Dionne out of his mind for a while.

He hadn't planned to be so damned attracted to her, but every moment he spent in her company only made the attraction stronger. The way she rubbed her forehead when something worried her. The way her eyes changed from ice to slate to sky blue when her moods shifted. The soft swell of her breasts and the curve of her hip...

Scrubbing his face with his hand, Mark told himself to think about work. Exhibits. Testimony. Legal research. There was nothing particularly sexy about any of those things.

He opened the file and spent a few minutes skimming the documents inside, but when a soft knock sounded on the door and his secretary of three years, Anna, peeked inside, he abandoned the case eagerly.

"Hey there." Anna stepped into his office and closed the door behind her. "Welcome back. How did it go?"

Seeing Anna's familiar face, her wild red hair and trademark huge round glasses grounded him a bit further. Grinning, he leaned back in his chair and motioned her inside. "It went fine. Great, as a matter of fact."

"Then you were able to bring back your little boy?"

"I sure did."

"Oh, Mark, that's wonderful." Anna's curls

burned in the sunlight—a nice contrast to the blond ones that kept intruding into his thoughts. "When do we get to see him?"

"Soon. After he's had some time to settle in."

Anna dropped into the empty chair in front of his desk and made herself comfortable. "How's he doing? Does he miss his mother?"

Mark tried to keep his gaze steady, but he couldn't do it. He glanced down at his hands and hesitated over his response.

"Mark?" Anna prodded gently. "What is it? What have you done?"

"What makes you think I've done anything?"

"I know you."

She had him there. They'd been friends as well as co-workers for a long time. Anna had provided a listening ear after Marianne disappeared, and he owed her a lot. But he couldn't tell her the truth about his relationship with Dionne. "It's a long story," he said at last.

"I have time."

"Unfortunately, I don't." He made a face and gestured toward the mess on his desk. "Royal wants this complaint by the end of next week, and I haven't even started on it."

Anna's eyes fastened on the new ring on his left hand and her eyebrows knit. She crossed her legs as if she intended to stay for a while and nodded toward his finger. "What's this?"

He glanced at his hand as if he'd never seen the ring before and tried to joke. "This? I don't know. How'd that get there?"

"What did you do?" she asked again.

He lifted both shoulders in a casual shrug. "I got married."

"To—?"

"To Jared's mother."

Anna scowled at him. "You married Marianne?"

"No." He smiled and leaned back in his chair. "His other mother."

Suspicion turned Anna's eyes almost green. "Really. Do you mind telling me why?"

"Not at all. We wanted to get married."

"Why-y-y?" She dragged out the word and tilted her head to one side, as if she could see through him from that angle. And she knew him so well, she probably could.

"Because we fell in love the instant we met." This was only the second time he'd tried saying it aloud, but the words fell easily off his tongue.

"You fell in love at first sight? *You?*"

He smoothed his tie and tried to look like a man head over heels in love. "Me."

"And it just *happened* to be with the woman who's been raising your son."

Her gaze disconcerted him. He shifted his attention to the file in front of him. "As luck would have it, yes."

He chanced a glance at her. The expression on her face told him she didn't believe a word he was saying. "Well, you know what they say." He laughed, but it came out sounding forced and unnatural. "Truth *is* stranger than fiction."

"I know what they say." Anna leaned forward. "But this is me you're talking to. I know you, and I *know* you didn't fall in love with her in three short weeks. What's the real story?"

"That *is* the real story, Anna. We met, we talked about Jared, and in the process we fell in love. Neither of us wanted to be separated by two thousand miles, so we decided to get married."

"And, by the merest coincidence, you both ended up with your little boy."

Mark had always prized Anna's ability to cut through the fog surrounding legal issues and get right to the heart of the question, but having her turn it on him was another matter entirely. "Don't you have work to do?"

She sent him a triumphant smile. "Yeah, I do. And you've got messages." She pulled a handful of pink slips from the pocket of her suit jacket and started creating a stack on his desk. "Alan Cracroft wants you to call him to discuss a settlement on the Patterson matter. Mrs. Billings called about the deposition next week. And your mother has called three times. She wants you to phone her back."

Mark scowled up at her as the light went on inside his head. No wonder Anna had noticed the ring so quickly. "You talked to my mother?"

"Three times."

"What did she say?"

"That she has something to discuss with you."

"Uh-huh." Mark sent her a resigned smile. "And let me guess… She told you about the wedding."

Anna leaned back in her chair again, looking smug. "She might have mentioned it."

"*Might?* My mother?" Mark laughed and set the messages aside. "Okay, spill it. What did she say?"

"The same thing you did, but I didn't believe her, either."

"You should have."

"Don't lie to me, Mark. I know how you felt after Marianne left, and I've spent three years listening to you say you won't ever fall in love or trust a woman again. Either you're lying, or this wife of yours is one hell of a woman."

"She is," he said, surprised to realize he meant it. She had courage and devotion and loyalty like nothing he'd ever seen before—at least to her son and Brent. He wondered if her husband had realized how lucky he was to be loved like that, then gave himself a mental shake and focused on Anna again. "I certainly hope you didn't mention your suspicions to my mother."

Anna waved one hand in the air. "Don't be silly. I'm completely loyal to you. And I figure you must have some reason for trying to pass off this marriage as the world's greatest romance."

He opened his mouth to set her straight again, then gave in to the temptation to tell her the truth. Anna *was* a trusted friend, and it would be nice to have one person he could be honest with. He rubbed the back of his neck and stretched to work out the knots of tension he could feel forming. "Okay, you're right. We got married for Jared's sake. But we don't ever want him to know that we got married for any reason other than love."

"No one will ever hear it from me," Anna promised. "But if you don't love each other, what makes you think you can make a marriage work?"

"We have to," he said, rubbing his neck a little harder. "Neither of us can stand the idea of being without Jared. When I left here, I didn't care about her. I was ready to fight to the death to take him away...until I saw them together."

"And now you do care?"

"I care about Jared. And, I care about her in a way. None of this is *her* fault. She shouldn't have to pay for what Marianne did."

Anna's smile softened. "In spite of your reputation in court, I always knew you were a decent guy. So tell me what she's like, this wife of yours."

"She's intelligent, warm, caring. She loves Jared with all her heart, and she's willing to cook. I can't ask for more than that."

"You could ask for someone who loved *you*."

He shook his head. "I did what I had to do to have my son with me and still be able to look at myself in the mirror. But love? That's not in the cards." He didn't like the sadness that worked its way through him when he said those words, and he didn't like the direction their conversation was going. "Maybe you don't approve, but what's done is done. And I really do have work to do."

Anna stood reluctantly. "I'll let you get to it then." She crossed to the door and paused. "Do you want me to spread the word about your marriage?"

"If you'd like to." He'd have to face the questions sooner or later. Might as well get it over with.

When Anna left him alone, he tried again to concentrate on the brief, but his telephone rang not five minutes later. And his mother's cheerful voice greeted him when he answered. "How's my newly married son?"

"I'm fine, Mom. What's up?"

"Your dad and I have had the most wonderful idea, but we need to check with you before we finalize our plans."

"What is it?"

"We want to give you and Dionne a reception."

Mark leaned back in his chair and rubbed his eyes. "Why?"

"Why?" His mother laughed. "Because you got *married,* Mark. And since we couldn't be there for the wedding, we'd like to do something."

Guilt at denying his mother the wedding she'd been waiting for pricked him. "I'm not sure Dionne will want you to do all that," he said warily.

"Nonsense. Honestly, sometimes you men can be so dense. Every woman wants her wedding to be something special. I don't want to be rude, dear, but getting married in a justice of the peace's office isn't very romantic."

She had a point. Their wedding hadn't been special or beautiful by any stretch of the imagination. And when it came to knowing what women wanted, his mother certainly knew better than Mark did.

"When do you want to do it?"

"How about this weekend? I'm assuming you and Dionne will be here for Labor Day, and the rest of the family is coming. It won't take much effort to add a few things to the menu, order a few flowers, and let friends and neighbors know."

The family always got together for holidays, but with everything that had been happening, Mark hadn't given Labor Day a moment's thought. "I don't know," he hedged, "Dionne's already overwhelmed by the idea of meeting the family."

"We won't go overboard," his mother promised. "Just a quiet barbecue with family and a few close friends. We're all dying to see Jared and meet Dionne. You aren't going to make us wait, are you?"

Mark couldn't ignore the pleading note in his

mother's voice, and he rationalized his decision by telling himself Dionne would have to meet everyone eventually. This way she could get it over with all at once. "Sure, Mom. That sounds fine. What do you want us to do?"

"Nothing at all. Just show up on Saturday. We'll plan to start about six, but you can come early so we have some time alone before the guests show up."

He smiled tiredly. "Okay, Mom."

"You won't be sorry, Mark. Really. This is something I'm sure your new bride will want."

Mark replaced the receiver slowly, hoping his mother was right. Dionne had given up a lot to come to Boston. Maybe this would make it up to her in some small way.

Mark checked his watch and grimaced as he shut the car door. He hadn't intended to work so late, but one minute it had been early afternoon, the next, evening shadows had been drifting across his office and making it difficult to read.

Shifting his briefcase to the other hand, he tried to find the key as he walked through the parking lot toward the condo. He should have paid more attention to the time. Halfway home, he'd realized he should have called Dionne to let her know where he was.

The idea of having someone else around and a part of his life left him slightly off balance. He'd lived away from his family for years. Before Marianne, he'd had only casual relationships that didn't require a commitment from him. And Marianne certainly hadn't been demanding of his time. Their relationship had consisted entirely of late nights in bed and those few weekends when they both took time away from the office.

But Dionne was different. She wasn't married to her career. At the moment, she didn't even have one. She'd spent the entire afternoon alone with Jared, and they were probably both starving, waiting for him to come home. She deserved an apology.

And he was ready to give one as he put his key in the lock. But the aromas that hit him when he opened the door wiped everything else out of his mind.

He left his briefcase on the coffee table and walked toward the kitchen. Soft music played on the stereo. Gershwin. She must have found his CDs.

Pushing open the door, he peered inside. Fresh vegetables lay on the counter waiting for attention. Steaks marinated near the sink. His kitchen had never looked so domestic.

Dionne was there, too, in an oversize blouse and leggings that emphasized the length and shape of her legs, her hair piled loosely on her head, exposing the soft nape of her neck, the tantalizing curve of her hips visible beneath the blouse as she moved in time to the music. She looked anything but domestic, and Mark had the almost overwhelming urge to skip the apology and kiss her instead.

He stepped into the kitchen and looked around for Jared as the door swung shut behind him. "You're cooking."

She glanced back at him, and the deep scowl on her face marred the picture. "You're very observant."

Forget the kiss, better stick with the apology. "I'm sorry I'm late. I—"

She sent him an icy glare, then looked back at a bunch of scallions on the cutting board. "I'm not here to interfere in your life."

He tried again, skipping to the middle of his prepared speech. "I won't always work this late."

"Do what you need to do."

He crossed to the wine rack and reached for a bottle. "It's just that there's a lot to do to catch up."

Dionne snapped the rubber band off the scallions. "Fine."

"Fine?" He let out a harsh laugh. "If it's fine, then why are you so upset?"

She pulled a knife from the block beside her. "Do you really want to know?"

"Yes."

"Your mother called this afternoon to introduce herself. She told me about the wedding reception she's planning for this weekend. The reception you agreed to." Dionne attacked the scallions with the knife. "How could you agree to something like that without talking to me first?"

Mark sank onto a chair. "I thought you'd like something special. Our wedding wasn't anything to brag about."

She shoved the scallions into a bowl and ripped apart a head of lettuce. "Did it ever occur to you that maybe I don't *want* a huge party to celebrate our marriage?"

He tried not to show how much that hurt, especially since he didn't completely understand why it did. "I thought it would look odd if we said no."

"*We* didn't say anything," Dionne snapped. "*You* said yes without even discussing it with me." Fire flashed in her eyes, making her more beautiful than ever. "I know this isn't a real marriage. But I can't tolerate you making decisions for me."

She was right, of course. "I'm sorry. I made a mistake. Do you want me to tell her to cancel the reception?"

She stopped ripping lettuce and rested her hands on the cutting board. Her eyes traveled across his face, studying him intently. "You'd do that?"

"Yes. At least, I'll try if you want me to."

Her expression softened a little. She let out a ragged sigh, then shook her head slowly. "No. The idea of lying to all those people makes me nervous, but I don't know how we'd explain canceling to your mother."

He tried a smile. "Neither do I."

She went back to work on the lettuce, but her movements were far less agitated. "The idea of pretending to be in love has been fine when it's just you and me, but how are we going to pull it off in front of all your friends and family? I don't know very much about you."

"They all know we had a whirlwind courtship," he reminded her. "They won't expect us to know a lot about each other."

"But we should know *something*. All I really know is that you're an attorney, you live in this apartment, and you're willing to do your own laundry. I don't even know your birthday or how old you are. A wife should know those things."

"I turned thirty-one on April twenty-eighth. What about you?"

A ghost of a smile curved her lips. "I'll be thirty on October nineteenth."

He made a mental note of the date and uncorked the wine to let it breathe. "Favorite color?"

"Green. And yours?"

"Black. What else do you want to know?"

Her smile grew a little. "Where did you go to law school?"

"Harvard." He leaned back in his seat and rested an ankle on his knee. "I really am sorry, Dionne. You have to remember, I haven't ever been married before. I'm not used to this."

"But you've been in relationships."

"Not like this."

That earned a soft laugh. "Very few people have ever been in a relationship like this."

"That's certainly true," he admitted. "But most of my relationships have been pretty casual."

Her smile faded. "Even with Marianne?"

The last thing he wanted was to talk about an ex-lover—especially that one. But Dionne deserved answers. "Especially with Marianne. She was so involved with her career, she didn't care what I did. We each did our own thing and got together whenever we could. What about you and Marianne? Were you close?"

She pulled a bunch of carrots toward the chopping block. "We hardly knew each other. Our mothers were cousins."

Her gaze met his and lingered there. The fire had disappeared from her eyes, and something new lurked there. Keeping his gaze locked on hers, he gave in to temptation and crossed the room toward her. "I don't want to talk about Marianne anymore."

She swallowed convulsively but she didn't look away. "Neither do I."

Taking her gently by the shoulders, he pulled her around to face him. For one breathless moment as he looked into her eyes, Mark thought time had stopped.

He wondered what she'd do if he kissed her. Would she respond or push him away? Would their relationship turn a new corner, or would he land them back at square one?

As if she read his mind, Dionne pulled away gently and grabbed a head of fresh broccoli from the counter. "Your mother wants us to be there by noon on Saturday. I told her we have an appointment to see a house on our way up."

Well, he supposed that was his answer. He tried not to let her see his disappointment. "Are you really okay with what she has planned?"

She nodded without looking at him. "I think so."

"I can still tell her to forget it if you want me to."

This time she did look at him, and the gratitude he saw in her eyes lifted his spirits considerably. "I'm nervous," she admitted, "but I'll be fine. Your mother sounded nice on the phone. Just don't leave me alone too long."

"I won't leave you alone at all."

She laughed. "You don't have to hold my hand every minute, but if you see that someone has me cornered, I hope you'll rescue me."

"Absolutely." Desperate for something to do besides look at her, he glanced around quickly and settled on the steaks. "Since you're making the salad, why don't you let me put those on to broil?"

She blinked as if the offer surprised her. "That's fine, if you don't mind."

Mind? She had no idea how much he needed to distract himself. She'd made it clear that she didn't want their relationship to change. And Mark would do his best to honor that. But he had the distinct feeling that, for him at least, things wouldn't ever go back to the way they'd been.

CHAPTER EIGHT

SATURDAY MORNING, Dionne watched Mark turn around in front of the rock fireplace of the old farmhouse. Sunlight streamed in through the huge windows that looked out on the narrow, tree-lined street. From the corner of her eye, she could see the Realtor leaning against her car in the driveway, enjoying a cigarette while she waited for them.

Dionne had been nervous and agitated since that moment in the kitchen two nights before when she'd wanted him to kiss her. His touch had sent flames through her and the look in his eyes had nearly made her forget everything.

If reason hadn't returned, if she hadn't suddenly remembered Brent, she *would* have kissed him. And after that? She couldn't even bear to think about how close she'd come to betraying Brent's memory.

Mark had been quiet, almost withdrawn, as they made the drive from Boston north into New Hampshire to meet their Realtor. But now, standing in the middle of the broad living room, he looked happy.

His expression brought a smile to her lips. "You like the house, don't you?"

"Do *you*? You'll be spending more time here than I will."

"Yes. I like the way the kitchen catches the morning sunlight. I like the view of the pond, and the way the forest closes in around the house. And I like the flower beds in the backyard.'' Not to mention the three large bedrooms.

"I wonder about the woods," Mark said hesitantly. "Will we be able to keep Jared under control?"

"Under control?" She glanced at Jared who was racing toy trucks along the living-room floor. "Not likely. We'll probably need to fence off part of the yard for him to play in."

"We could do that." Mark ran one hand along the mantel. "So, should we make an offer?"

"I'd like that."

His pleased grin warmed her clear through. He hurried to the front door and called in the Realtor, then led Dionne into the kitchen where they spent a few minutes fine-tuning the details of the offer and earnest money agreement. Finally satisfied, Mark scrawled his signature on the documents and pushed them and the pen toward Dionne.

She signed, started to hand the agreement back to the Realtor, then caught herself and added her new last name. To lessen·the confusion for Jared, she'd decided to take Mark's last name, but how long would it be before she'd remember she wasn't Dionne Black anymore? And how long before she could get rid of the twisting guilt every time she thought of Brent?

If the owner accepted their offer, this would be her home from now on. The sunny room upstairs would be her bedroom. And the man standing at the counter, writing out a check, was her husband.

She paced to the window and stared out at the deep forest and the trees, then glanced back at Mark. It was his face she'd see every morning for the rest of her life. His laugh she'd hear. They'd share meals, sit together at Jared's games and school plays. This was undeniably real.

Almost dizzy, she pushed open the door and stepped onto the deck. Gripping the railing, she gulped air and hoped it would calm her a little. She stood that way for several minutes, until the sound of footsteps behind her warned her she wasn't alone.

Before she could turn around, Mark's hand touched her shoulder. "Are you all right?"

She looked back at him, trying to ignore the sudden warmth she felt at his touch. "Yes, of course. Where's Jared?"

"In the kitchen. Don't worry, I can see him from here." The understanding in his eyes made the lump in her throat grow and tighten. To her surprise, he wrapped his arms around her and rested his chin on the top of her head. Her body tightened.

"It's going to be okay," he said quietly. "You'll see. In time, we'll both get used to this."

"I know we will. I'm not having second thoughts," she lied. She took a deep breath and added honestly, "It's just that the thought of waking up to you every morning for the rest of my life suddenly got to me."

He sent her a teasing smile. "Am I really that disgusting?"

In spite of her frayed nerves, her doubts and her reservations, she laughed. And she thanked him silently for his wonderful sense of humor. "No. You're actually quite nice."

He pulled her close again and let out an exaggerated sigh. "Well, that's a relief. I was beginning to wonder."

His lips grazed the side of her face as he spoke and the now-familiar coil of desire shot through her.

"About the other night—" She broke off when he very deliberately brushed his lips softly against her cheek. She turned to face him and rested her hands on his chest. "Please don't."

He drew back slightly and pulled his hands from her waist. "Sorry. You're just so beautiful, I'm having a hard time remembering what the rules are." He glanced at the open patio door and muttered, "Jared's climbing the stairs. I'd better get back inside. Let me know when you're ready to leave."

She nodded, keeping her eyes trained on the twisted trunk of a tree, but she didn't relax until he'd gone back inside and closed the door between them.

Only then did she allow herself to acknowledge that the bone-deep sensation that settled inside her was disappointment, not guilt, and that her feelings at the moment had nothing to do with Brent.

NEARLY TWO HOURS LATER, Dionne leaned her head against the back of the seat and watched the countryside pass by. Here in the White Mountains, the trees were already beginning to change color in some places, and she could only imagine how glorious the scenery would be in a few more weeks. But the closer they got to Sunrise Notch, the greater her apprehension about spending the weekend with Mark's family and friends.

Would they like her? Would she be able to convince them she was in love with Mark? Or would she do or say something wrong and ruin everything?

And what would she and Mark do tonight when they had to share a bedroom for the first time? Thank heaven for Jared. If nothing else, he could sleep between them.

She glanced into the back seat at Jared, who'd fallen asleep in his car seat, then at Mark who seemed relaxed and happy. Of course, he had less to worry about. He was used to being around his huge, close-knit family. He knew and loved the entire bunch.

He must have felt her watching him because he took his eyes off the road for a second. "Getting nervous?"

"A little."

"It'll be a piece of cake," he promised, steering the car off the main road onto a narrow dirt lane. "They'll adore you."

"I hope so."

He glanced at her again. "What else is wrong?"

"Nothing." She turned toward the window and hoped he'd drop the subject.

Instead, he stopped the car in the middle of the lane and shifted in the seat to look at her. "If you'd rather not do this—"

"I want to do it," she assured him, but her voice came out sharper than she'd intended. She glanced away quickly and softened her tone. "I really want to do it. I'm just a little jittery."

"I know you are." Mark touched her arm gently. "I want you to know I appreciate the effort you're making."

She smiled bravely. "Just promise me that when this weekend is over we can have some quiet time."

His thumb stroked her arm lazily and started the

familiar fire roaring through her. "Before or after we move into the house?"

She let out a groan of dismay. "After, I guess."

"Good. Because I was thinking about asking my brothers to help us move. Is that okay with you?"

She appreciated his obvious efforts to discuss things with her before making a decision. As long as they were both willing to try, they stood a chance. She let out a weak laugh. "You don't really think I'm going to say no, do you? *I* certainly don't want to do all that heavy lifting."

"Just checking." He grinned and pulled his hand away. "I might be new at this marriage stuff, but I'm learning."

His smile helped her relax a bit further. "You're doing very well," she admitted.

His grin flashed again. "Thank you, ma'am. Are you ready to go on? We're almost there."

"Yes." She laced her fingers together on her lap to keep from touching him. "Should I wake Jared?"

"Probably. It would be better to wake him now than to have him startled awake by a bunch of strangers, don't you think?"

While she reached over the seat and shook Jared gently, Mark pulled back onto the road. Jared resisted her for a minute or two, then finally awoke. But he wasn't happy. His sobs of protest filled the car and he pulled away from her hand.

"Jared, sweetheart—"

Jared pushed her hand away and dropped his head as if he intended to go back to sleep. She thought about letting him do that to avoid the scene of introducing her new in-laws to their shrieking grandson, but Jared's head popped up again and he let out another yowl.

Mark took his eyes off the road for a heartbeat and glanced into the back seat. "What's wrong with him? Is he hurt?"

"He just wants more sleep." Dionne had to raise her voice to make herself heard over Jared's sobbing. She dug around in his bag of toys and pulled out his favorite plush giraffe.

But Jared wanted nothing to do with it. He tossed it, bouncing it off the back of Mark's seat.

"Maybe you should stop," she suggested when the giraffe landed on the floor near Mark's feet. "Let me try to calm him down before we get to your parents' house."

Mark rounded one last bend and drove across a narrow wooden bridge. "Too late," he said, braking in front of a large white house with black shutters. "We're here."

While Jared screwed up his face and let out another howl of protest, Dionne glanced at the house. The front door flew open and a woman with short-cropped hair the color of Mark's and Jared's came out onto the porch. A tall man who looked almost exactly like Mark followed. His hair was shot with gray, but he still had the trim figure of a young man.

Jared drew a shuddering breath and pushed Dionne's hands away again. "No!"

"Please, Jared. It's okay." She kept her voice low and soothing in spite of the heavy sinking sensation that filled her. This was *not* the first impression she wanted to make on Mark's parents, but Jared left her no choice. On the other hand, it could only get better from here.

Now all she had to do was convince them she was in love with their son.

MARK HURRIED around the car to help Dionne with Jared and watched as she took a steadying breath before she opened the car door. Before he could reach her, she'd pulled Jared from the car seat and tried to soothe him.

"You're here!" His mother ran toward them and pulled Mark into a warm embrace, then turned toward Dionne and Jared. "Oh, look at the baby, Nigel. Isn't he beautiful?"

Mark could tell her reaction soothed something in Dionne, and he was grateful beyond words.

His father clapped a hand to Mark's shoulder, smiled warmly at Dionne, then chucked Jared, whose cries were slowly subsiding, under the chin. "So this is my new grandson, eh? He's a Taylor, all right. Just listen to that voice. And I do believe he's got my nose. But he's hardly a baby, Barbara. He's already a strapping young man."

Nervous sweat pooled beneath Mark's arms. He hadn't wanted to admit it to Dionne, but he'd been dreading this moment. His parents had been skeptical about the hasty wedding. Even his continued assurances that he'd met the woman of his dreams hadn't totally convinced them.

He trusted them not to show their doubts to Dionne, and she was obviously going to keep up her end of the bargain. But he'd still feel a whole lot better once this initial meeting was behind them.

Before he could make introductions, his mother wrapped Dionne in a warm hug. "I'm Barbara, and this is my husband, Nigel. We'd love to have you call us Mom and Dad if you're comfortable with that.''

His mother's enthusiastic welcome, in spite of the misgivings she'd voiced, touched Mark. He studied Dionne's face over his mother's shoulder. She looked tiny and vulnerable.

She caught his worried frown and smiled to reassure him. He knew how much effort that took and he could've kissed her.

His father gave Dionne another friendly smile. ''So you're the woman who finally convinced my son to settle down. Welcome to the family. Glad to have you.''

Dionne hid her nervousness well. ''It's wonderful to meet you at last. Mark's told me so much about you.''

''Well, you're one step ahead of us,'' his mother said. ''We know next to nothing about you.'' She kissed Jared soundly on the cheek and smiled when the boy hid his face on Dionne's shoulder. ''But we'll soon put that right, won't we?''

''Yes,'' Dionne said softly. ''Of course.''

''We'll have lots of time to talk after the open house. We're so thrilled to have two new members of the family.''

Mark smiled at his mother and put his arm around Dionne. ''So, where's everybody else?''

''Inside,'' Barbara said, turning back toward the house. ''They didn't want to overwhelm Jared and Dionne. But they're champing at the bit to meet them both.''

He felt Dionne hesitate for a second, then straighten her shoulders. ''We're eager to meet them,'' she said as they walked behind his parents.

Mark admired Dionne's grit and her graciousness. The worst was over, he told himself. It could only get better from here.

DIONNE HAD SPENT two hours standing beneath an arbor at Mark's side, clutching a bouquet of roses, orchids and baby's breath, meeting relatives, shaking hands, and smiling until her cheeks hurt. Her head whirled from trying to remember so many new names and match them to the unfamiliar faces. If only she could slip away for a while and find a quiet spot where she and Jared could be alone.

She took one steadying breath, then another. She watched Jared climb onto Nigel's lap and tug on Barbara's earring. She listened to her son chortle with delight when Barbara bubbled his cheek, and watched him toddle away when Mark's mother put him back on the lawn.

In spite of the warm sunshine, a chill shook her. She closed her eyes for a moment and tried to hold herself together. Jared was unquestionably part of this family—in looks and in temperament—but his resemblance to them felt like a subtle threat. If she couldn't make her marriage to Mark work, there was no question that any judge would place Jared with these people.

They were all warm and friendly, and every time one of his brothers or his sister-in-law or an aunt or uncle drew her into a conversation, she couldn't help feeling out of place. Her own family was so different. She'd certainly never experienced the genuine affection she saw between members of Mark's family. She had nothing in common with these people. Nothing.

Clutching the arms of her lawn chair, she opened

her eyes again and tried to find peace in the surroundings. Maple, oak and other trees she couldn't identify rimmed the lawn. A few leaves drifted lazily to the ground in the slight breeze. A long table full of refreshments stretched along the far end of the lawn. Paper lanterns hung in strategic spots near the patio, which meant the party would probably go on long after dark.

Barbara and Nigel must have spent a fortune putting all this together. No matter what they said, she knew they'd gone to far greater lengths than they would have for a simple gathering, and that made her feel even worse. She hated lying to them.

As she took another look around, she realized that everyone seemed to have forgotten her for a moment. Seizing the opportunity, she stood quickly. But before she could take even two steps, someone put a hand on her shoulder. Holding back a sigh, she turned to find Barbara and Nigel standing behind her.

''What's wrong, dear?'' Barbara took in every detail of her expression. ''You seem awfully quiet.''

''Leave the girl alone,'' Nigel groused, waving a celery stick in front of him. ''She's just not used to us yet, are you?''

Dionne smiled at him. He really was a kind man. ''I guess I'm a little tired from the trip and all the time we've spent looking for a house.''

''Yes, but Mark tells us you found one in Longs Mill.'' Barbara glanced at Nigel. ''Isn't that what he told us?''

''Nice town.'' Nigel bit into the celery. ''You'll like it there.''

''It's a lovely house.'' Just thinking about it made Dionne feel a little better.

Barbara pulled up a lawn chair and sat down. Nigel took up his position behind it. They looked as if they intended to settle in for a nice, long chat. "I've been wanting to tell you all day what a wonderful job you've done with Jared," Barbara said. "He's a delightful little boy, and I don't say that only because he's my grandson."

"Thank you." Dionne sank back into her own chair and clasped her hands together in her lap.

Barbara let her gaze settle on Jared, who'd found a small pile of rocks to play with. "Does he see much of your folks?"

"No. My mother passed away several years ago."

In a gesture so like one Mark would make, Barbara covered Dionne's hand with one of hers. "I'm sorry. I didn't know. What about your father?"

Dionne decided not to give Barbara and Nigel the sordid details. She was quite sure none of the Taylor men had ever deserted their wives and children. "My father's no longer with us, but Jared does see Brent's parents about once a year."

"Brent's parents?" Barbara's eyebrows knit in confusion. "Who's Brent?"

"He was my hus—" Dionne cut herself off and glanced quickly at Mark across the lawn talking to one of his brothers. Apparently, he hadn't told his family much about her.

Well, too late now. She didn't want any more secrets to worry about, and she certainly wouldn't deny Brent. "He was my first husband."

Nigel lowered the celery to his side and glanced from Dionne to Barbara and back again. "Your *first* husband? I didn't know you'd been married before, did I? Did Mark tell us that, Barbara?"

Barbara's smile faltered. "I don't remember. I don't think he did."

"Brent passed away shortly after Jared came to live with us," Dionne explained.

"A first husband," Nigel muttered. "I wonder why Mark didn't tell us."

"Well, that's all in the past, so I'm sure he didn't think it was important," Dionne assured Nigel, adding another possible lie to her list.

Barbara ticked her tongue against the roof of her mouth and scowled at her husband as if he'd had something to do with Mark's decision. "Honestly, sometimes you men can be so thoughtless." She sent Dionne a smile full of warmth and reassurance. "Mark's my son and I love him, but I don't understand how he could possibly think your first husband was unimportant. Not that it makes any difference to us," she added quickly, "but what if we'd inadvertently said something that hurt your feelings?"

Dionne couldn't imagine either of these kind people hurting anyone. "I'm sure Mark would have said something sooner or later. Things have been pretty hectic for both of us."

"Of course they have." Barbara tousled Jared's head as he came near, chasing a loose ball. "Still, I wish we'd known. I feel utterly foolish."

Dionne scooped Jared onto her lap and wrapped her arms around him. He struggled for a second, then leaned his head against her shoulder and gazed up at her with his big brown eyes. "Mama."

Relief swept through her and uncorked her other emotions, and tears filled her eyes. She blinked quickly, hoping Barbara wouldn't notice. But she was too late.

"Have I upset you, dear?"

"No." She stood quickly, still holding on to Jared for dear life. "No. I'm just a little tired."

"Then maybe you should take Jared inside for a nap. Just slip away and come back when you're ready."

Grateful for her understanding, Dionne started away but Jared squirmed in her arms. "No nap."

"Please," she whispered so softly she didn't know if he could even hear her. "Please, for Mommy?"

He pulled back and looked at her. "No nap."

"Sweetheart, I promise we'll come back and play with everybody."

Jared scowled, made one last attempt to get down, then stuck a finger in his mouth and settled himself more comfortably against her. "Jared wants a story."

She would read a hundred stories if it meant she could find a few minutes alone. Just a few minutes to pull herself together so she could make it through the rest of the day.

MARK TRIED to keep up with his uncle Bruce's story as he watched Dionne carrying Jared across the lawn and away from his parents. The sun beat down on him, as hot as mid-July instead of early September, and he longed for a glass of his mother's lemonade, or maybe something a little stronger from the liquor cabinet in his father's study.

Dionne had been wonderfully gracious to everyone, but he knew the day hadn't been easy on her. He wondered how she was holding up. Maybe she'd had enough of his friends and family.

"So," Uncle Bruce said, hooking his thumbs in

the waistband of his pants, "there we were. And what a mess it was, I tell you…"

Mark smiled but kept his gaze on Dionne. She glanced over her shoulder, as if she wanted to make sure nobody was following her.

"…Nonie threw up her hands and let out a shriek," Bruce went on with a laugh. "The woman nearly put a hole in my eardrums…"

Dionne checked behind her once more, then slipped through the kitchen door and disappeared from view. Mark started to turn back to Bruce, then glanced at the house again. *Had* she reached the end of her rope? Had the reception been one thing too many? Maybe he should have told his mother to forget it, after all.

His wife had looked secretive as she crossed the lawn—almost as if she was trying to hide something—and a knot of suspicion began to form in his stomach. Did she regret her decision to marry him? Was she thinking of leaving with Jared?

Surely she wouldn't do that. Where would she go? How would she get there?

All the logic in the world couldn't take away his sudden anxiety. He hadn't expected Marianne to disappear either. Dionne had Jared back, and Mark was involved with friends and family who wanted to wish him well. Maybe she thought she could call a cab and get away before he noticed she'd gone.

"…So I told Nonie to pull herself together. It's just a little snake, I said—"

"Excuse me, Uncle Bruce," Mark interrupted. "I need to check something."

Leaving the older man staring after him, he hurried across the lawn after her. He told himself again to give her the benefit of the doubt, but his heart raced and his mind whirled with dreadful possibilities.

He managed to sidestep three of his cousins who tried to waylay him, hurried through the kitchen, down the hall, and out the front door. There wasn't a cab in sight, but maybe she'd called earlier and it had been waiting for her.

He ran partway down the driveway, even though he knew he'd never catch a moving cab on foot. He'd have to take the car.

Wheeling around, he dug his keys from his pocket, then realized with dismay that three other cars had his blocked in. Frustrated, he ran back toward the house.

"Hey, Uncle Mark. Come with us." One of his teenage nephews made a grab for his arm. "We're going over to the hill."

Under normal circumstances, Mark might have joined them. But he couldn't relax until he found Dionne and Jared. "Not this time," he said, opening the front door. "Have any of you seen Dionne and Jared?"

Corey nodded, walking backward with the others. "I saw them going upstairs a few minutes ago."

Upstairs? Mark's step faltered. *Upstairs?* Not away in a cab? Feeling relieved—and foolish—he waved a thank-you, hurried inside, and took the stairs two at a time.

He walked quietly down the hall, hoping she'd never know he was checking up on her. As he neared the bedroom door, he heard the soft sound of her voice as she talked to Jared.

Mark ran a hand over the back of his neck, smiled to himself, and started to turn away. But an overwhelming desire to be part of Jared's naptime and the sudden need to make their family real brought him back around.

He pushed the door open an inch or two and looked inside. Dionne lay with her back to him, curled beside Jared whose little legs wriggled and whose arms flew about as he struggled to escape.

She kept up her soothing monologue. Mark felt like a voyeur, but he couldn't tear himself away.

She was like no other woman he'd ever met, not only because of the way she cared for Jared, but because of the way she treated Mark, as well. He'd never met anyone who'd been willing to go to such lengths for him. If Marianne had been in Dionne's position, she would have forced him into court to decide custody. Dionne had respected him enough to make an unbelievable compromise. And the most amazing thing was, she'd never resented him for suggesting it.

Finally, Jared yawned, put one tiny hand on the side of Dionne's face, and closed his eyes. Mark told himself he really should stop watching. But the gentle curve of her hips kept his gaze riveted, and unexpected desire kept him rooted to the spot.

He wanted to hold her, to lie down on the bed beside her, to breathe in her scent and let it surround him. He wanted more than that. He wanted to kiss her, to make love to her, and his sudden need was stronger than anything he'd ever felt for any woman.

But he couldn't do any of those things. Not only did she and Jared need time alone, but Mark knew how she'd react if he tried to seduce her. She'd made it clear from the beginning that this was nothing more than a marriage of convenience, and he'd agreed to that. Hell, he'd suggested it.

If she'd given him some sign that her feelings were changing, he might have held out some hope. But the way she'd pulled away from him that morning left no doubt that she wanted things to continue the way they were.

What bothered him most was the realization that all the time he'd been searching, while he'd been chasing the imaginary cab down the driveway, he'd had two concerns. Of course, he'd been afraid of losing Jared. But, equally important, he'd been terrified of losing his wife.

CHAPTER NINE

FOR THE THIRD TIME in less than an hour—since Dionne brought Jared back outside—Mark caught himself losing the thread of conversation with his brother, Jerry. Jerry had been talking about football, but all Mark could think about was the way Dionne had looked lying on the bed. Now visions of her in a nightgown, the way she'd be when they shared that same bed tonight, kept creeping into his mind.

Think flannel, he told himself firmly. *Long-sleeved, high-necked, hem to the floor.*

He brushed aside a mosquito and tried once again to follow what Jerry was saying. But his gaze drifted back across the lawn to where she sat, legs crossed, in a patio chair.

Her face, tilted to watch a rollicking game of badminton, caught the waning afternoon sunlight. Her fingers, long and delicate, rested on the arms of the chair. The soft blouse she wore drifted over her breasts, outlining them whenever she moved. He couldn't have looked away if he'd tried. Until she looked up and caught him watching her.

Damn. He turned away quickly. But that didn't make him any less aware of her. He still caught the sudden frown, the slight narrowing of her eyes, the stiffening that warned him she'd seen and understood exactly what was running through his mind.

"What's up with you two?" Jerry's voice near his ear caught him off guard.

Mark wheeled to face him. "What do you mean?"

"You seem jittery, and so does she." Jerry propped himself against the picnic table and stretched his legs out in front of him.

Mark forced a laugh. "Nothing's up. We were just a bit worried about the family's reaction to our marriage. After all, it was a very sudden thing."

"Yeah?" Jerry took another drink. "Well, maybe I'm just extrasensitive."

"Maybe you are." Mark knew he sounded touchy, but he didn't want Jerry to guess the truth. He couldn't let anyone shatter the illusion he and Dionne were trying to create.

"So, are you happy?" Jerry crossed one foot over the other and waited, as if he expected the answer to be no.

Mark looked him square in the eye. "Very."

Jerry nodded slowly, but Mark could tell his brother wasn't convinced. He let his gaze shift toward Dionne. "Mom and Dad seem to like her."

"Of course they do. What's not to like?"

"Nothing," Jerry said with a shrug. "She's great. But I will admit Mom sounded worried when she called to tell me you'd got married."

"*She* doesn't have to worry, either."

"Yeah?" Jerry studied Mark's face for a long moment. Too long. "Well, you know how she feels about marriage. If I had a dime for every time she told me not to get married until I'd known Alice for at least a year, I'd be a millionaire."

Mark had heard his mother's advice since David had grown old enough to notice girls. And he'd always seen the value in his mother's warning. A couple shouldn't rush into marriage. Just look at what had happened to his brother and his sister-in-law.

Jerry and Alice had been completely wrong for each other. But they'd married before they'd figured out that they'd had nothing in common except their sex life. That had quickly lost its luster, and Jerry had wound up in the arms of another woman.

When he'd confessed his indiscretion to Alice, the marriage had finally crumbled. Unfortunately for Jerry, his relationship with the other woman hadn't survived, either, and the experience had left him bitter. Mark sympathized in many ways, but he wasn't in the mood for his brother's cynicism today.

He changed the subject. "What are you doing next weekend, big brother?"

Jerry's eyes narrowed in suspicion. "Watching the football game, why?"

"Tape it. Dionne and I need you to help us move."

Jerry groaned aloud. "Move? I *hate* moving."

"Doesn't everybody? But it won't be bad. We'll only have to worry about the things I don't want to trust to the movers."

"I don't know. You want me to give up the game to move all your junk?"

"I don't own junk," Mark reminded him with mock severity. "But I'm not above offering a bribe, I'll throw pizza into the deal."

"That sounds a *little* more tempting. But I still don't think it's quite enough."

"What do you want?

"I *want* to watch the game," Jerry grumbled, then grinned and tried to sound irritated. "But if you're

going to beg, I suppose I'll help.'' He nodded toward
the far end of the lawn where David and Steve were
playing badminton with two of the kids. ''You want
them to help, too?''

''Definitely.''

''Let me tell them.'' Jerry's eyes gleamed, and
Mark could only imagine what he had up his sleeve.
''I'll make sure they're there.'' He started away, then
turned back and added, ''About you and Dionne…
Forget I said anything. I'm sure you're not anything
like Alice and I were.''

Mark watched him cross the lawn, scoop up Da-
vid's youngest son and settle him on his shoulders.
Obviously, he'd put their conversation behind him.
But Mark couldn't forget it quite so easily.

The truth was, he and Dionne *didn't* have anything
in common. They had no shared interests. They
didn't even come from the same kind of background.
The only thing holding them together was Jared. And
for the first time, Mark wondered if that would be
enough.

DIONNE SAT on the window seat by the open window, listening to the breeze whispering through the
trees while Mark said good-night to his father in the
hallway. The temperature had dropped a little, but
the night was still uncomfortably warm. Her body
screamed for sleep, but she wondered if she'd get
any with Mark in the same room.

She'd expected to have Jared sleep with her, but
the entire family had joined the protest that newly-
weds needed one night on their own. Barbara and
Nigel had made a bed for Jared in their room, and
Jared had decided the whole thing was an adventure.

He seemed to enjoy being the center of attention. In spite of her own nervousness, Dionne hadn't had the heart to spoil his fun.

Of course, the family could never know the truth about this marriage, so Dionne had smiled pleasantly and pretended to be happy with the arrangements.

Nigel smiled at her over Mark's shoulder. "You're probably getting fed up with me for keeping Mark out here, aren't you?"

"Not at all," she assured him. *Keep him as long as you want. In fact, take him with you.*

"You're sweet to an old man," Nigel said with a laugh, "but I'll get out of your hair. Good night, Dionne. Pleasant dreams."

"Thank you, Nigel. Same to you."

He turned away, and Mark stepped inside the room and closed the door behind him. The click of the latch sounded as ominous to her as prison doors shutting.

"Well." Mark propped his hands on his hips and leaned against the wall. "Here we are."

"Yes."

"You can have the bed. I'll sleep on the floor." He pulled a pillow and extra blankets from the closet and tossed them to the floor beside the bed. "If you want to change first, I'll...well, I'll look at the moon for a while. I promise I'll keep my back turned."

His apparent nervousness gave her a slight boost of confidence. She had the strangest urge to join him and lean her head against his shoulder, but she couldn't do that. "I can just slip out to the bathroom and change in there."

He glanced back at her and smiled. His almost shy expression touched her on a level she didn't want to be touched. "Good idea. But let me change in there. You can use this room."

He pulled sweatpants from his suitcase, tossed them over his shoulder, and started toward the door again. "Just leave the door open a crack when you're through so I know when it's safe to come back."

"It won't take me long," she promised. She waited until he'd closed the door behind him, then jumped off the bed and dug through her own bag. She'd brought a light pair of summer pajamas, but suddenly the thought of wearing them left her feeling defenseless. Instead, she'd follow Mark's lead and put on her baggy sweatpants and a long T-shirt.

She changed hurriedly and tucked her clothes into a drawer. After draping her robe across the foot of the bed, she opened the door an inch or two, then quickly, before he could come back, climbed under the covers and pulled them up to her neck.

He didn't return immediately, but when he did, he knocked softly before pushing open the door the rest of the way. "All clear?"

"Yes."

He tossed his jeans and T-shirt over the chair and set to work spreading the blankets.

She watched him for a moment, then asked, "Are you going to be okay on the floor?"

He looked at her. "I have to be, don't I?"

She flushed, embarrassed by the thoughtless question, shaken to the core by the look in his eyes. "We can trade places tomorrow night. I don't mind."

"We've already had this discussion once, haven't we?" He turned out the overhead light and crossed the room, illuminated now only by the dim lamp beside the bed and the glow of the moon through the paned windows. "You keep the bed, Dionne." He kept his gaze on her as he moved toward her, robbing her of breath and conscious thought. Just when she thought he might climb onto the bed, he hunkered down to the floor.

She waited until he'd covered himself with the sheet, then turned off the lamp. But sleep didn't come. Too many conflicting emotions raced through her. Too many unanswered questions and unresolved issues kept her mind jumping.

In the silence, she heard the village clock chime midnight. Eyes wide, she stared at the patterns made by the moon and trees on the ceiling. She heard Mark's breathing change as he shifted onto his side, the rustling of the sheet as he tried to make himself more comfortable, the soft groan that escaped his throat.

Did he feel it, too? This pricking of the nerves, this all-over tingly feeling? Slowly, she turned to look at him. Too late, she realized he was watching her. Her breath stopped. Her heart plummeted, then lurched into her throat.

"Can't sleep?" He kept his voice low, which didn't help. The intimate tone made her hands sweat.

She gripped the sheet and shook her head. "No."

"Thinking about Jared?"

She seized on the excuse gratefully. "Yes."

"Do you want me to get him?"

No doubt having Jared curled next to her would help, but she didn't want to disturb him. "No, I'm sure he's asleep already."

Mark sat up suddenly. The sheet fell away, exposing his shoulders and chest. The moonlight revealed dark tufts of hair and the outline of his muscles, and the suffocating feeling in the room seemed to grow. "Are you hungry?"

Dionne let out a nervous laugh. "After all that food your mother had this afternoon? I'm not sure I'll ever be hungry again."

He reached toward her, and for a second she thought he would touch her. Everything inside her stilled, waiting, anticipating, *wanting* to feel his touch. Instead, he reached for the alarm clock, checked the time, and put it back on the nightstand. "We could go down to the family room and watch TV—if you want to."

"Will we wake your parents?"

"No way." His voice caressed her. His breath brushed her cheek. "They can't hear anything from their room. When we were kids, we used to stay up half the night, and they never did figure it out."

"Oh. Good. Then, yes." Anything to get out of this room. She slid out of bed and grabbed her robe as if it were a security blanket. She walked quickly down the hall, far too aware of Mark behind her. When they reached the family room, she stopped abruptly. Someone had closed the shutters, which blocked the moonlight. The room was still unfamiliar to her, and she didn't know which way to turn.

Mark leaned in close, and again she thought he might touch her. But he only reached for the light switch on the wall.

Blinking against the sudden glare, she looked away, not wanting him to see how much she hungered for his touch. How very much she wanted him to kiss her. How bitterly disappointed she was that he didn't try.

Heat suffused her face as she hurried toward a

wingback chair and curled into it as if it might protect her. If he noticed her eagerness to get away from him, he didn't show it. He sat on the couch, found the remote on the coffee table, and turned on the television. The set came to life with a scene from *Casablanca,* and all of her earlier thoughts evaporated.

She and Brent had loved this movie and watched it often together. She'd always snuggled against his side, secure in his love, content with her life. Tonight, the music, the voices, the faces of the actors made her almost sick. Because she suddenly realized that not once all evening—while she'd been fighting her attraction for Mark, while she'd lain there and listened to his breathing, while she'd watched him move around the bedroom and wanted to feel his hands on her—

Not once had she thought of Brent.

THE NEXT AFTERNOON, Dionne sat beneath the shade of a huge oak tree that cut the temperature by several degrees. Jared played nearby with one of Mark's nieces. The heat here was different from the warmth in Boise, filled with moisture that seemed to make the air not only hot but heavy as well.

Perspiration trickled between her breasts, the humidity kept her rooted to her seat, and the sheer numbers of people milling around the backyard again today made her head spin. She'd never get used to this. Just as she'd never rid herself of the nagging guilt each time she lied to one of Mark's friends or relatives.

She closed her eyes and tilted back her head, opening them again when she felt someone touch her hand. Mark's aunt Nonie, a gray-haired woman with a pleasant round face, smiled down at her.

"Are you all right, dear?"

"Yes." Dionne struggled to sit straighter in the chair and checked on Jared, then worked up a smile. "I'm fine."

"You look tired."

"Maybe I am a little. We've had a busy week."

"Busy?" Aunt Nonie laughed and settled into a chair beside her. "I'd say it's a bit more than that, wouldn't you? You've been swept up in a whirlwind, my girl. That's what happens around these Taylor men. I know. I married one."

Dionne couldn't have described it better if she'd tried. Being around Mark *was* like being swept into a storm. Emotions buffeted her from every direction. "The whole family is full of life," she said.

"Aren't they? There's never a dull moment around this bunch, that's for sure." Nonie patted her hand almost tenderly. "Don't let it overwhelm you. You'll get used to us in time."

"For now, I'm just working on learning who everyone is," Dionne admitted with a thin laugh. "There are so many of you."

"Well, yes." Nonie let her gaze travel across the lawn, and studied her family for a moment. "But you've got years and years to get us all straight."

As always, the reality of her situation made Dionne pensive. Years and years as part of this huge, sprawling, noisy brood. She forced aside the uneasiness. "Yes, I do, don't I?"

Nonie made herself more comfortable on her chair and smoothed her hands across her lap. "We're really not so bad."

"Oh, I didn't mean—"

Nonie cut her off with a laugh. "Mark says you're from a small family."

An almost nonexistent family. "Yes. This is very different from what I'm used to."

"Then I can only imagine how overwhelming it must be to you. So let's forget about everyone else for a few minutes. Tell me how you and Mark met. That ought to put the smile back in your eyes. And don't leave anything out. I'm a sucker for a good love story."

Dionne fought the urge to pull away. She didn't want to compound the lie by embellishing it for this nice woman. "There's not much to tell, really."

Nonie laughed as if she'd said the funniest thing in the world. "Not much to tell? Mark leaves town a bachelor and comes back a devoted husband three weeks later, and you say there's nothing to tell?"

Dionne flushed and wondered what Nonie would think if she told her the truth.

Still shaking her head in disbelief, Nonie fanned a hand in front of her face. "None of that, now. I've been dying to hear the whole story. Where did you first see him?"

"In the park."

"Really?" Nonie sighed and put a hand to her breast. "Was it love at first sight?"

Dionne smiled slowly. "I wouldn't say that, but I did have some pretty strong feelings right from the first."

"Well, of course you did. Who could look at Mark and *not* feel something? If I do say so myself, he's a good-looking boy."

Dionne glanced at the "boy" who was deep in

conversation with his father on the other side of the lawn. What kind of little boy had he been? What had he looked like? There was still so much she didn't know.

"And when did you realize you were in love?" Nonie prodded.

"In love?" The afternoon heat intensified and a dull ache started in Dionne's head. "Later. I don't remember the exact moment."

"Of course you remember. Every woman remembers."

Obviously, Nonie wasn't going to give up. "I think it was when I realized how much he loves Jared."

Nonie's face wrinkled with disapproval. "That's all very well and good, my dear. But Jared won't be around forever. You can't base a marriage on a child."

Dionne floundered for a second. "No. I mean, I think that's what made me realize what sort of man he is."

"And *that's* why you fell in love with him." Nonie looked pleased at that. "Well, he does have a kind heart. Wouldn't hurt a fly, our Mark. Not if his life depended on it."

Dionne remembered the look on his face when she first saw him and knew that a good many flies could be in danger if Mark felt strongly enough about something.

"And so you married him." Nonie's voice sounded wistful. "And now here you are, part of the family."

"Yes."

"Well, we're all happy to have you, dear." Nonie

patted her hand again. "To be honest, I was beginning to think Mark would never get married."

"Really? Why?"

"When Marianne left without a word—" She broke off and her eyes grew huge. "You do know about Marianne, don't you?"

"Yes, of course."

Nonie sighed with obvious relief. "It did seem like she would be the one. And he was heartbroken when she left. Moped around for months."

Something uncomfortable darted through Dionne, but she told herself it wasn't jealousy.

"But, of course," Nonie went on, "he's over her now. He must be because here you are."

Dionne forced a smile, but her heart wasn't in it. She stole another glance at Mark and wondered if he was really over Marianne. Not that it mattered. For heaven's sake, she still loved Brent and always would. Her relationship with Mark didn't matter, as long as they gave Jared what he needed. As long as she could stay with Jared and be his mother forever.

But when she remembered the look in Mark's eyes the night before, when she caught the lilt of his laughter and deep rumble of his voice, she knew she wasn't being entirely truthful with herself. Like it or not, her relationship with Mark had begun to matter a great deal.

DIONNE STROLLED aimlessly along the gravel driveway and away from the house. A stiff wind had blown in storm clouds and dropped the temperature by several degrees. She took a deep breath of the clear mountain air and walked through a small pile of orange and yellow leaves. Autumn had always been her favorite season, and spending it in New England was a dream come true.

She'd put Jared down for a nap and then slipped out the front door instead of rejoining everyone in the living room. Sooner or later, someone would discover she'd disappeared. But until then, she had a blissful few minutes alone.

Children—nieces and nephews and cousins whose names she'd never remember—played together on the broad expanse of lawn that rolled downhill toward a grove of trees. Shouts of laughter and an occasional playful roar filled the air.

She stopped at the crest of the hill and watched them, envying them their easiness together, their shared childhood, the memories they were making. A wistfulness tinged with envy filled her heart. She'd long ago stopped wishing for something that would never be, but the noisy bunch of kids laughing and shouting together brought back all the familiar pain of childhood.

She didn't want to feel that today, so she turned her thoughts to Jared. Her son would have a different life than the one she'd had. He'd grow up loved and secure. He'd never suffer the loneliness and isolation, the sensation of being disconnected.

She smiled at the children in front of her, then turned away and started toward the house to check on Jared. But when she saw Mark standing only a few feet behind her, her step faltered.

The breeze tousled his hair, and the faint shadow of whiskers darkened his cheeks and chin. In his faded jeans and gray T-shirt, he was ruggedly handsome.

Wrapping her arms around herself for warmth, she

walked slowly toward him. "They look as if they're having fun," she said when she drew nearer, purposely keeping her tone light.

His gaze roamed her face and settled on her eyes as if he could see right through the mask she wore. "It is fun. We used to do the same thing when we were kids."

"You and your brothers?"

"And the cousins."

Another pang of envy shot through her. She forced it away, just as she had the others. "I'd better get inside and check on Jared."

"I just looked in on him. He's fine." Mark took a step closer. "And if he wakes up, someone will hear him. Mom and Kaye are in the kitchen. Dad's watching the game with the guys, and Nonie's reading in her room. Just relax and take a moment for yourself."

Dionne shook her head. "I don't want them to take on my responsibilities."

Mark laughed. "You can't honestly think any of them will mind. They all adore Jared. They wouldn't care if you and I disappeared for hours."

Dionne knew he was right. "I'm glad they love him so much. It means a lot to me."

"And to me," he admitted, his voice low. "They're all completely smitten with you, too."

Dionne smiled slowly. "They're wonderful people, Mark. They really are."

"They're a big, noisy, meddling bunch," he argued mildly. "But they mean well."

"I know they do." She shivered as the wind danced across her shoulders. And when a shout went up from the hill below them, she turned to look at the kids once more.

Boys chased girls who squealed when they got caught. One boy rolled into another, buckling the second one's knees and sending him sprawling into a small pile of leaves on one side of the lawn.

Mark grinned over at her. His dark eyes glittered with mischief. "You want to show them how it's done?"

"You mean play in the leaves?" Dionne backed a step away from him. "I'm afraid I wouldn't be a very good teacher."

"Why not?"

"I've never done it."

Mark's eyes rounded with shock. "Never?"

"Never."

"You're joking, right?"

"I'm not. I was an only child, remember? And I didn't get to play with friends often. My mother liked knowing I was safe inside while she worked."

"Well, then, I say it's time you learned."

She took another backward step. "I'm too old."

"Old?" He shook his head. "Hell, Dionne, you're not even thirty yet. Even grown-ups need to play."

His enthusiasm was infectious, but Dionne didn't give in to it right away. "I *do* play," she argued halfheartedly.

"When? *I've* never seen you play."

She propped her fists on her hips. "You haven't known me very long. And for your information, I play with Jared all the time."

He shoved aside that argument with one huge hand. "I'm not talking about that kind of play. *This* is what I'm talking about." Without giving her a chance to react, he scooped her up and barreled down the hill, letting out a shout that sounded almost like a battle cry.

Surprised, she wrapped her arms around his neck to hold on. "Stop," she squawked. "You're going to drop me."

"Me? Drop you? Never."

"I'm serious, Mark—"

He stopped suddenly and held her gaze. "That's your trouble." His cheeks burned red from the chill but his eyes were pure fire. "You need to stop being so damned serious." Before she could respond, he lowered her with a soft plop into the pile of leaves. They cushioned her fall and billowed out around her.

"That wasn't fair," she protested weakly.

"No?" Mark laughed again, a teasing rumble that sounded more like a fourteen-year-old boy than a thirty-one-year-old man. "Well, then, come and get your revenge." He backed a step away, daring her to try.

Strangely exhilarated, Dionne scrambled to her feet. "You think I can't?"

"You said you didn't know how," he reminded her, but there was nothing harsh or mean in his tone.

"Yeah? Well, it doesn't take a brain surgeon to figure it out." She scooped up an armful of leaves and tossed them straight into his face. But when the shower of red and gold stopped and she could see his face clearly again, the almost-predatory gleam in his eyes made her turn and run.

He came after her, just as she'd known he would. His laughter warmed her and the shouts of the children, some urging her to run faster and some calling for him to overtake her, filled the air.

He caught her easily and they fell back into the leaves together. He stretched along the length of her, his body hard and unyielding, his male scent slightly heady.

Mark lay there, panting, his face just inches from hers, his breath warm on her cheek and faintly scented with mint. "You didn't really think you could outrun me, did you?"

"Apparently not." She was breathless from the unaccustomed exertion but she felt wonderful, and joy bubbled up inside her. She made an attempt to get away, but he held her fast.

"Right. And don't you forget it." Their eyes locked, and the teasing light in his slowly died away. Something else, something white-hot and intense, took its place.

His eyes searched hers for answers to questions he'd never asked, and she knew what answers he found. They came from the bottom of her soul, laid bare by the moment they shared. She wanted him to kiss her, to cover her mouth with his, to hold her in his arms and never let her go. She waited, breathless, hoping, wanting, needing.

His eyes darkened and sent chills of anticipation through her. He dipped his head and brushed her lips with his, only a feather-light touch but it rocked the world beneath her and left her aching for more. She responded eagerly, savoring the feel of his lips on hers.

The kids swarmed around them, shouting, jeering, calling out encouragement. "Kiss her, kiss her," one unmistakably male voice taunted. Another hissed for the boy to be quiet.

The mood was shattered. The passion in Mark's eyes dimmed. The need inside her faded.

"Kiss her again," the boy demanded. "Whatcha waitin' for?"

Mark looked away slowly and his entire countenance changed. "I'm not going to kiss anybody with you watching," he said with a laugh. Then, growling playfully, he took off after the boy Dionne recognized as David's oldest son.

With her heart still rocketing and her head swimming, Dionne watched him. She marveled at all the different sides she'd seen in him in the short time they'd known each other. Jared was lucky to have him for a father. And she…

Well, she had to admit the truth. She was lucky to have him for a husband. Brent had been many good and fine things, and she'd always love him for his steadiness and dependability. But he hadn't kept her off balance. He hadn't embraced everything with abandon the way Mark did. If anything, Brent had been almost resistant to change.

Once, Dionne had needed that. But somehow— maybe as a result of Brent's death, *certainly* because of the upheaval over Jared—she'd grown past that need. Now she was a different person from the frightened, lonely young girl who'd fallen in love with Brent.

Rubbing her arms for warmth, she watched for another moment while the kids tackled Mark and sent him to the ground. They heaped leaves over him, nearly burying him.

Smiling, Dionne caught the eye of three young girls. Their eyes danced in anticipation of her next move, and Dionne suddenly realized they'd accepted her as one of them.

Her smile widened. Her heart began to race again. Motioning for them not to give her away, she took a deep breath and threw herself into the fray.

CHAPTER TEN

LONG AFTER DINNER was over and almost everyone else had gone home, Mark sat on the long, leather couch in his parents' living room, and gave up the pretense of reading his novel. Near the front windows, bathed in moonlight, Dionne rocked Jared in the old wooden chair that had been Mark's grandmother's. Dionne's eyes were closed, but she spoke softly to their son.

The boy snuggled close to her, his fingers alternately clutching his own hair, reaching for something on a nearby table, then settling on her arm before starting all over again. His small mouth puckered for a moment, then stretched wide as he yawned.

Barbara's laughter erupted in the kitchen followed by Aunt Nonie's a moment later. His dad and Uncle Bruce sat across the room, heads together, solving the problems of the world. Mark couldn't remember when he'd last felt so content.

It didn't get much better than this. His wife and child across the room, other family members he loved nearby. Of course, things could get a *little* better. Although he had no idea what would happen when he and Dionne closed the door to their bedroom tonight, he did know that brief kiss on the hill had left him wanting much more.

The change in her that afternoon as she'd tackled

him and stuffed leaves down his shirt had been nothing short of miraculous. And she'd been more at ease
around the rest of the family all evening. He'd
thought her attractive before, but she was damned
near irresistible now.

Even Jared sensed the difference. He'd picked up
on her mood and had seemed more settled all evening.

If Mark could have had his way, he'd spirit Dionne
to the bedroom and make love to her. But doing the
wrong thing now could ruin the tenuous relationship
they had. He didn't want her to go back to the quiet,
almost somber woman she'd been the past few
weeks.

He made another unsuccessful attempt to read a
few pages until his father left Uncle Bruce and came
to sit beside him on the couch. Nigel propped his
hands on his knees and groaned as he lowered himself into position. "What a weekend this has been."

"It's been a great weekend," Mark said, lowering
his book to his lap. "And the reception you and
Mom pulled together yesterday was really nice.
Thanks again."

"Nothing to it, son. Nothing at all." Nigel sank
back in the seat and let out a sigh of pure contentment. "Certainly made your mother happy."

Mark nodded and set the book on the couch beside
him. "I think it did. She's really incredible, isn't
she?"

"Your mother?" Nigel looked surprised by the
question. "She's a good woman, son. But I believe
you've got one, too. She's a good mother to that son
of yours." His father retrieved a sailing magazine

from the coffee table and propped it open on his knee. "You've done well for yourself, my boy."

"Thanks." His father's praise meant the world to him.

"Now just make sure you don't blow it."

Mark's smile faded. "I don't intend to."

"Intentions aren't everything, son." His father marked his place in the magazine and sent him a sober look. "Jerry didn't intend to cheat on Alice, but it happened anyway."

"I'm not Jerry," Mark reminded him.

Nigel chuckled softly and loosened the top button of his shirt. "No, you're not. But you can be stubborn when you want to be. And you're single-minded. Once you decide what you want, you go after it and everybody else be damned."

That hit a little too close for comfort. "I've always been that way, Dad. But you've always seemed proud of that."

"I have been proud." His father turned to face him more fully. "Damned proud. That stubborn streak of yours is what kept you in law school when the going got tough and wouldn't let you quit the football team your senior year of high school. All I'm saying is, don't turn it on your wife or you could be in trouble. Listen to the voice of experience."

"I don't intend to—" Mark broke off with a laugh and held up both hands. "I know, I know. Intentions aren't everything."

"Just be flexible." His father opened the magazine again and glanced at the page. "That's my best advice. It'll be especially tough for you. You've been on your own a long time. You're used to having things your own way. But if you want to keep that woman happy—and I'm *sure* you do—'' He accented this with lifted eyebrows.

''Of course I do.''

''Well, then, you've got to put her first and yourself second. Find out what she needs to be happy and then make sure you give it to her.'' His father propped his feet on the coffee table. ''I'm not talking about the big things, now. I'm talking about the things that are hard to do, like respecting her when you're in the mood for romance but all she wants to do is go to sleep, or pulling yourself away from the television long enough to recognize when she's too tired to cook dinner, or just listening to her when she's complaining about something even if you've had a lousy day.''

Mark nodded slowly. It sounded simple enough.

His father glanced toward the kitchen and lowered his voice before he went on. ''Nothing I do makes your mother madder than when I try to step in and fix something without her asking.'' He shook his head and sent Mark a wry smile. ''I don't understand it, but it's the way things are. So I've learned to just stand by until she asks for my help or my advice.''

Mark laughed. He'd heard a few ''discussions'' between his parents when he was younger that bore that out. ''I'll keep that in mind.''

''See that you do, son, if you love her.'' He lifted an eyebrow and looked at Mark meaningfully.

Mark felt his smile freeze, but he managed to keep it in place. He'd certainly begun to care for her, and he couldn't deny the physical attraction, but did he love her?

For some reason, he had trouble getting the words

out of his mouth. "Of course I do. I married her, didn't I?"

"People have gotten married for all sorts of reasons that didn't include love," his father said. But he turned his attention back to his magazine as if Mark's answer had pacified him.

Mark breathed a sigh of relief and picked up his book again, but the conversation left him faintly uneasy. He didn't love Dionne, he told himself firmly. He'd sworn off love after Marianne's betrayal and had vowed never to leave himself that vulnerable again.

But that had been before she'd responded briefly to his kiss. Had her reaction meant anything more than the fact that she was vulnerable right now? She'd put everything she had on the line to marry him and move here. Anyone could see her emotions were painfully raw. Only a complete jackass would take advantage of that.

A few short days ago, the idea of their living together as polite strangers had seemed not only possible but easy. Now... Now, it felt like hell.

THE FOLLOWING SUNDAY, while Dionne tried to organize her bathroom in the new house, she listened to the banter between Mark and his brothers downstairs. They were all so relaxed, they'd put her at ease almost immediately. And the boom of deep voices as they tangled over which one had to carry the heaviest boxes, over who got to drive the truck back into Boston for the last load, and over which of them had to sit in the middle made her smile.

She sat back on her heels, enjoying the sound of their good-natured bickering. Even if, God forbid, things between her and Mark didn't work out, she could never take this away from Jared.

The thought brought her up short. Of course, if things didn't work out, taking Jared away from his family wouldn't be the issue. *She* was the one who'd have to leave.

"Hey there." A deep voice cut into her thoughts and brought her around quickly. Mark's youngest brother, Steve, snagged Jared from a stack of boxes he'd climbed in the hall while she wasn't watching. "No climbing, sport. We don't want you to get hurt."

"Jared wanna climb." Jared started back toward the stack, his determined little face set in a scowl that matched his uncle's. "Jared show you."

"No you don't." Steve caught him by the waist and pulled him away from the boxes, jiggling him as he did and earning a delighted laugh. "I'm serious, Jare-Bear. No climbing." He set Jared on the floor again and looked him straight in the eye. "All right?"

"Uncle Steve is right," Dionne put in. "You might get hurt."

"No," Jared said stubbornly.

"Yes," Steve argued. "Why don't you build me a house with your blocks instead? Show me that, okay?"

Jared thought about that for a second, then scurried off. Steve turned back toward Dionne. "Sorry. I didn't think you saw him. You looked like you were a million miles away."

"I was," she admitted. "Thank you."

Steve waved a hand as if to say her thanks were unnecessary. "So what had you so far away?"

"Besides serious sleep deprivation?" she asked with a laugh. "I was just listening to the four of you downstairs together and thinking how lucky you are to have such a great family."

"It's your family now, too, you know. And your humble brother-in-law is at your service. Mark, David and Jerry took off for Boston to get the last load. They left me here to help you."

"What happened?" she teased. "Did you lose the coin toss?"

"No." He leaned against the wall. "I won."

"What a charmer," she said, grinning easily.

"It's a family trait."

It certainly was. One she noticed a little more each day. She nodded toward a stack of boxes against the far wall. "If you're supposed to help me, I suppose we ought to get started. Most of those belong in Jared's bedroom."

Steve pushed away from the wall and bowed elaborately. "Your wish is my command."

Dionne stepped over a stack of towels and checked to make sure Jared wasn't climbing something else. "With an attitude like that, how on earth have the women let you stay single?"

Steve sniffed comically and hitched the waistband of his jeans. "It's been a tough fight, but I've managed to escape the noose... Begging your pardon, ma'am. Nothing personal."

She bent to retrieve a pile of Jared's pajamas from the floor. "I'm sure it has been tough. Your resolve is commendable."

"We Taylors are famous for it," he said, starting toward the boxes. He tested a couple for weight, then hefted one with a groan. "We always get what we go after."

"Oh?"

"You're here, aren't you?" Steve waggled his eyebrows at her, disappeared with the box, and returned a minute later.

Dionne had to admit he was right. Her presence in New Hampshire on a sunny autumn afternoon *was* the result of Mark getting what he wanted—his son. But she was determined to keep the lightness between them. "Does it ever backfire?"

"Rarely." Steve's face clouded for a second, then he grinned. "Well, it did once for Jerry, but the rest of us are a lot smarter than he is."

"Poor Jerry." She stopped working and sat on the side of the bathtub. "How did the famous Taylor determination fail him?"

"He lost his wife and kids when he cheated on Alice."

"I shouldn't have asked," she said quickly.

"Why not? Jerry won't mind if you know. We're a pretty open family. Nobody has secrets."

Little did he know, Dionne thought. "Really?"

"Yeah. My parents have always been big on honesty. Drilled it into us from the time we were kids."

"It's a good trait to have."

"Yeah, it is." Steve sat on the corner of the box and wiped his forehead again. "And safe. There's nothing worse than getting caught in a lie by my parents."

That was an experience Dionne hoped to avoid. She cast about for some way to change the subject. "Is that the last of the boxes?"

Steve laughed, a warm, rich laugh that sounded

exactly like Mark's. "Are you kidding? It'll take us all day to bring in Mark's junk. But where's all your stuff?"

Dionne's gaze faltered. "I didn't bring anything with me."

"Really? Why not?"

"None of my things were as nice as Mark's," she said honestly. "Besides, it would have cost more in shipping charges than any of my furniture was worth."

Steve's eyebrows knit. "Yeah, but still— Don't you want a few familiar things around?"

More than he could possibly imagine. "The only thing I really miss is my rocking chair," she said, brushing a lock of hair off her shoulder. "And Mark already bought one of those for Jared's room, along with the new bed for mine—" She broke off and her eyes rounded when she realized her mistake.

"Yours?"

"My...study. The guest room. It's going to do double duty."

"As a study?" Steve propped one foot on a low-lying box and his chin in his hand. "I thought Mark said you weren't going to work away from home for a while."

"I'm not," she assured him, and added another lie to the list. "But I am thinking about going back to school."

"Oh yeah?" Steve looked impressed. "What will you study?"

"I've always wanted to work with disadvantaged children." At least *that* wasn't a lie.

"Good field. What school will you go to?"

Dionne picked up an armful of towels and started

into the hallway. "I don't have all the details worked out yet, and I probably won't until we're settled in here."

Steve followed her slowly. "And you won't get settled unless your lazy brother-in-law gets back to work, right? Fine. I can take a hint."

Much as she liked talking to him, it would probably be a whole lot safer to work in silence. The worst part about lying, she thought sadly, was that you couldn't ever relax.

A FEW HOURS LATER, Mark lugged another heavy box up the stairs. In spite of the chilly weekend weather, sweat ran down his forehead and dampened his shirt. His brothers had gone home, leaving him alone with Dionne at last. But the day's work had left him worn out. His knees had taken a beating running up and down the stairs, his arms ached from lifting, his back felt as if it could snap in two.

He stopped just inside the bedroom door and propped the box he carried on his knee. Dionne glanced up at him from a spot on the floor where she'd surrounded herself with towels, blankets, sheets and tablecloths. Jared had abandoned his trucks and blocks and was contentedly playing in an empty box beside her.

She lifted her hair from the back of her neck and fanned her face with her hand. She smiled, thoroughly unaware that she'd set his blood boiling just as she had so often during the week since their visit to Sunrise Notch.

Again he was reminded of that brief kiss in the leaves and again he wanted another. He remembered the way she'd looked with her lips parted slightly, her eyes dark with emotion, her face flushed, her breath labored. He remembered the feel of her lips beneath his and the thrill of her response. And, as he had every time the memory surfaced, he shoved it away firmly.

"Where do you want this?" he asked, lifting the box slightly.

His voice caught Jared's attention. The boy scrambled out of the box and raced across the room toward him. "Come see my house."

"You have a house?" Mark couldn't resist. He set his box aside and followed Jared toward his makeshift playhouse. "Can I come in?"

Jared frowned up at him. "No. You're too big."

"Well, shoot. I guess I am at that." Mark dropped to the floor in front of Jared and peered inside. When Jared seemed satisfied, he turned back toward the box he'd abandoned and realized Dionne was still watching him. Oddly self-conscious, his step faltered. "So where do you want it?"

She motioned toward the closet. Then asked, "Have you put up Jared's bed yet?"

Before answering her question, he let his gaze drift across her bedroom. It landed on the bed they'd picked out for her and stayed there. *Wrong thing to look at, old boy. You'll give yourself ideas.*

He shook his head quickly and stuffed his hands into his pockets. "Not yet. I'll do that now."

"That would be nice. Thank you." She sounded tired, and he realized she must be as exhausted as he was.

On impulse, he turned back to face her. "Come with me."

"Where?"

"We've been at this all day. I think we need a break."

"Of course. You must be tired."

"Me?" He sent her a teasing smile. "I'm too tough to get tired. I'm just thinking of you."

She laughed and stood in one fluid movement, so graceful he thought his heart would fly out of his chest. "How thoughtful. Yes, I am exhausted after folding all this linen. I'm really grateful that you and your brothers wouldn't let me carry in any of the boxes."

"Just doing our job, ma'am." He coaxed Jared from his new toy, then followed Dionne down the hall toward the stairs. "Seriously, Dionne, now that my pesky brothers are gone, let's take advantage of the peace and quiet for a minute."

She looked up at him so quickly, he wondered if she'd misinterpreted him.

He tried to set her mind at ease. "To talk."

Her expression remained wary. "About what?"

"About the weather. About movies we've seen recently, or books we've read." *About whether or not our relationship will ever change.* "You were right that night back in Boston. We *do* need to know more about each other."

He cleared a path through the boxes, found a safe spot for Jared to play and led her to the couch. When she'd made herself comfortable, he sat beside her and cocked one ankle across his knee. "Why don't you tell me more about your childhood."

Her smile faded and he knew he'd touched on a delicate subject. "What do you want to know?"

"What kind of little girl were you?"

"Pretty typical, I guess."

He doubted that. She was anything but typical now. "Did you play with dolls, or cars and trucks?"

"Whatever my mother could afford or whatever some nice neighbor's kids had outgrown." She made a visible effort to push aside her wariness. "What about you? Dolls or trucks?"

"Trucks. Cars. Bulldozers. I didn't care as long as they had wheels and made noise."

"I'm not surprised."

"Why not?"

"Because Jared's so much like you."

It was, he thought, the first time she'd acknowledged a similarity between Jared and him, and it touched him. "Do you mind?"

"That he's like you?" She shook her head slowly. "Not anymore."

Her smile, her eyes, and her scent were driving him to distraction. How was a guy supposed to be a buddy to a woman who looked and smelled like that? He tried desperately to keep up his end of the conversation and changed the subject to one he knew would cool him off. "Tell me more about your marriage."

She studied her fingers for a minute. "What do you want to know?"

"Were you happy?"

"Yes." The word fell softly between them, and he tried not to acknowledge the direct hit to his heart. She lifted her gaze again. "Were you happy with Marianne?"

He gave that some thought, then nodded. "At the time, yes." But, as always, talking about Marianne made him uneasy and brought up the worst of his emotions. "What was your husband like?"

"I guess the best word to describe Brent would be dependable. He was quiet. Reserved."

Although Mark considered himself dependable, nobody had ever accused him of being quiet and reserved. If that was the kind of man she'd fallen in love with, Mark didn't stand a chance to win her heart.

That thought pulled him up short. Did he *want* a chance? He tried to convince himself he didn't. That it was only physical attraction that held him spellbound. But the truth was, he wanted to win her heart very much, indeed.

ON THEIR THIRD NIGHT in the new house, Dionne sat up suddenly, her sleep broken by a scream of pain from Jared. Outside, the wind howled and branches scratched against the side of the house. Clouds blocked the moon, leaving the room inky black. Without thinking, she tossed back the covers and started from the room, stubbing her toe against the dresser in the process.

Biting back a cry of her own, she plowed toward the door and hit her hand against a sharp corner. When Jared screamed again, she forced the pain out of her mind, yanked open the bedroom door and hurried into the hallway...

And ran straight into someone else.

"Sorry." Mark's voice, sleep-rough and deep. Mark's chest, bare, solid, strangely comforting.

Too late, she realized she'd forgotten to grab her robe, but another cry from Jared convinced her not to go back for it. As if they were connected, she and Mark turned at the same time and started toward the third bedroom.

Mark turned on the hall light, momentarily blinding her. But she didn't stop. She ran toward her son's bed and came to a stop just half a step in front of Mark. Jared sat up, holding his blanket against his face.

"What is it, sweetheart? What's wrong?"

"Mommy?"

"Yes, sweetie. Mommy's here. What's the matter?"

"Hurt."

"Hurt?" Mark's voice came out sharp. "What happened? How did he get hurt?"

Dionne motioned for him to be quiet, then sat on the edge of the bed. "What hurts, sweetheart?"

Drawing in a shuddering breath, Jared covered his ears with his hands. "Hurt."

Mark moved closer, his face pinched with worry. "What's wrong with him?"

Dionne pulled Jared onto her lap and attempted to cradle him, but he tried to get away and covered his ears again. "I think he has an earache," she said to Mark. "He has them occasionally."

"What do we do? Should I call the doctor? There's a hospital about twenty miles away—"

A mixture of gratitude and relief filled her. It had been a long time since she'd had anyone with her when she faced a crisis in the middle of the night. "He'll need to see a doctor," she said. "The infection won't clear up without an antibiotic."

"Then, let's get him one." Mark turned and started across the room. When Jared's howls increased, Mark turned back again. "Is there anything we can do for him now?"

Still holding Jared, she stood. "We could give him some children's pain reliever."

"Are you sure? Is it safe?"

"That's what the doctor in Boise had me do."

Mark didn't look at all relieved. In fact, he looked downright skeptical. "Do we have any?"

"I always keep some on hand."

Like a windup toy, he changed direction once more, raking his fingers through his hair as he walked. "Where is it?"

She held back a laugh. "Calm down, Mark. It's in my purse."

His step faltered and hesitation flickered across his face. "Maybe you should get it."

"All right." She settled Jared into his arms and smoothed his hair again. "Stay with Daddy, okay?"

Jared nodded solemnly and another sob shook him, but he snuggled up to Mark.

"Daddy?" Mark's eyes softened in the dim light. "I think that's the first time you've called me that since we got married." He touched her gently with his free hand and his fingers trailed up the side of her arm. As if someone had yanked a veil away, she became acutely aware that he wore nothing but a pair of boxers, while she wore only a thin nightgown.

"I'll be back in a second," she said and rushed from the room. She dug the baby Tylenol from her purse and threw on a robe before she rejoined her husband and their son.

Jared's cries drove everything else from her mind until they'd seen the doctor. But when Jared was finally able to sleep again on the return drive from the hospital, she thought about Mark's earlier comment and realized just how much she'd changed over the past few weeks.

Mark *was* Jared's father, but even more—he was a daddy in all ways. He was a kind and gentle man who'd given up his own chance at love and happiness for his son. He'd been as concerned about Jared that night as any father would be for his child.

Sudden, unexpected love for him surged into her heart and tears blurred her eyes. She looked out the window to keep Mark from seeing them, but she couldn't turn away from the emotion.

She didn't delude herself into thinking he loved her. He'd made that very clear. But he did care for her in some way. She'd have to be senseless not to know that. And he was certainly capable of loving. She only had to watch him with Jared and his family to know that.

Maybe one day he'd begin to love her. In the meantime, she'd be wise to keep her feelings to herself. The days would be easier that way.

And the nights far safer.

CHAPTER ELEVEN

COMFORTED BY THE FACT that Jared seemed a little better this morning, Mark had gone to work. But he'd made Dionne promise to call if Jared took a turn for the worse.

Now, checking the signs on each building as she walked, Dionne pushed Jared's stroller slowly along the Front Street sidewalk and looked for the pharmacy. Quaint buildings lined the narrow road. Shade from an occasional tree covered the sidewalk and half a block away a dog lazed in the autumn sunshine.

To her, the village of Longs Mill looked like something out of a movie or a Norman Rockwell painting. It was utterly charming. Exactly the kind of town she'd dreamed of living in as a young girl.

When the sign she'd been looking for caught her eye, she stopped walking. "Looks like we've found it, sweetheart. After we get your medicine, you'll feel better in no time." She maneuvered the stroller into the recessed doorway, skimming a bright orange piece of paper taped to the glass announcing the Longs Mill Autumn Festival the following weekend.

She smiled softly and let her imagination run for a second or two, picturing the scene. But when Jared shifted fitfully, she forced her attention back to the present, propped open the door with one foot, and worked the stroller up the single step and inside the building.

It took only a moment to get her bearings. Three narrow aisles flanked by packed shelves ran the length of the building to the pharmacy in back where a woman of about Dionne's age, with softly curling shoulder-length brown hair finished a telephone call.

Dionne pushed the stroller toward her and waited until the woman replaced the receiver. "Dr. Miller said he'd call in a prescription for my son this morning. It's for Jared Taylor."

The woman smiled, her warm brown eyes friendly and welcoming. "So *you're* Mrs. Taylor. I was wondering when I'd finally get to meet you."

"Really?"

"We've all heard that you bought the old Preece place, of course. Someone new moving in is always big news." She turned away to speak over her shoulder to the pharmacist, then smiled again at Dionne. "I'm Patsy Wagner. We live out on the Old Post Road not far from you. I've been meaning to stop by and say hello, but I've had a houseful of sick kids. Looks like you're in the same boat."

When Jared reached for something on the shelf in front of him, Dionne took it from him and moved the stroller back a few inches. "My son has an ear infection."

"Same with two of mine. The others have regular colds. It's that time of year. My kids always get sick when the seasons change." Patsy straightened some papers in front of her and leaned both arms on the counter. "I just hope they're all well by next weekend."

Dionne glanced over her shoulder at the door. "For the autumn festival?"

"Yes. I love the festival and I don't want to miss it. You'll be there, won't you?"

"Oh, I—" Irritated by the response that rose automatically to her lips, Dionne cut herself off. Why did she immediately think "no"? She longed for friends and family, yet she instinctively held back from both. "I didn't know about it," she finished lamely.

Patsy waved one hand toward the street. "You really should come. It's not a big deal. Just a party we hold every year in the square. But it would give you a chance to meet everyone."

"It sounds wonderful," she said tentatively. "But we wouldn't want to intrude."

"But you wouldn't be intruding," Patsy assured her. "You're a part of Longs Mill now. You're *supposed* to be there."

The sense of belonging warmed her clear through. "In that case," she said with a smile, "I'll mention it to Mark. If Jared's feeling better, we may come."

"Hopefully, he'll be better, and so will all of mine." Patsy checked behind her to see if Jared's prescription was ready, then leaned over the counter to smile down at Jared.

To Dionne's surprise, Jared sent her a toothy grin and tried to climb out of his stroller. Though he'd never been shy, he'd always been slightly wary of strangers. But he'd lost even that since becoming part of the Taylor clan.

"If you do come," Patsy said, "bring something with you for the potluck dinner. And there's dancing afterward."

"It really does sound like fun," Dionne said.

"It is," Patsy said, laughing. "And you'll be doing yourself a disservice if you don't have some of Hazel White's crab cakes or Nancy Wiggs's blueberry cobbler. And there are always lots of people around," Patsy went on, "so there'll be someone to watch this cute little bundle while you and your husband dance."

Dionne glanced down at Jared, who'd lost interest in his surroundings and had started fussing quietly. She found his toy giraffe on the seat where he'd dropped it and offered it to him. He clutched the toy tightly, then rested his head on its plush body.

The idea of skimming across a dance floor in Mark's arms certainly had appeal, she thought, suppressing a delicious shiver of anticipation. "The party sounds perfect," she said to Patsy.

"Then you'll be there?"

"I hope so," Dionne said, a little surprised by how deeply she meant it.

After paying for the antibiotic, Dionne pushed the stroller back into the warm September morning. She found herself hoping she and Patsy would become friends. Losing Cicely was the one deep void still left in her life.

She drank in the sight of the quaint little town, the shops, the narrow road, the weathered buildings. She and Mark had been right to buy the house here. This was a perfect place to raise a family.

That thought caught her by surprise. She pondered it for a moment, testing the idea of giving Jared brothers and sisters. Did she really want that?

Yes, she realized with a start. She did. But she

couldn't give him brothers and sisters unless her relationship with Mark changed drastically.

What she wanted, what she *longed* for, was to be loved again. And she couldn't help wondering if she'd locked herself into a life without any hope of that happening.

EXHAUSTED AFTER a lengthy deposition that had left him frustrated, Mark put the last file he needed in his briefcase and took another long look at his desk to make sure he hadn't forgotten anything. Through the open door, he could hear Anna moving around in her office, closing file cabinets, locking her desk, getting ready to call it a day.

Usually, Mark stayed long after Anna went home. His most productive hours were those spent after the phones stopped ringing and the support staff disappeared. But tonight, he was leaving on time.

He'd been worried about Jared all day, in spite of Dionne's promise to call and the doctor's diagnosis. Even talking to his son for a minute on the phone that afternoon hadn't made him feel much better and he'd been watching the clock, just waiting for five o'clock to roll around.

To be honest, concern for Jared wasn't the only thing drawing him home. More and more, he found himself wanting to be with Dionne.

He was still thinking about his family as he reached for his jacket. But before he could put it on, the door to his office opened wider and Royal Spritzer poked his head inside. "Got a minute?"

Mark bit back a groan of dismay and nodded. Royal's "minutes" were notoriously long. But he couldn't very well refuse the boss. "Sure. What is it?"

"I need to talk to you about the Young Technologies case." Royal closed the door behind him and settled his long, lanky frame into one of Mark's client chairs. He cocked an ankle across one knee and made himself comfortable.

Obviously, Mark wasn't going anywhere soon. He dropped his suit jacket to the second chair again and sat on his own. "Is something wrong?"

"Not at all." Royal smoothed his silk tie across his stomach and sent Mark a smug smile. "As a matter of fact, everything's right as rain."

"Great. What's up?"

"We lined up a witness this afternoon who's willing to talk to us."

"No kidding?" They'd been floundering so far, trying to find someone who could give them evidence that Young had filtered money from the employee pension plan. "Who is it? How did we find him?"

Royal's smile grew larger by the minute. Mark couldn't remember ever seeing him so pleased. "He's a former employee who worked directly with the pension plan at Young's national office in New York."

Mark grinned. "Chalk one up for our side. Why is he willing to talk?"

"I don't have all the details, but apparently Young fired him under some pretty questionable circumstances. He's what you'd call disgruntled."

"And he's willing to talk to us?" No wonder Royal looked so pleased. "That's the best news I've heard all day. Do you need me to pull something together for Oscar before the meeting?" Mark glanced at the clock on his desk, calculating the time it would take to get what Oscar needed and make the drive home. It was still doable.

"Oscar's not handling this witness." Royal leaned back in his chair and linked his fingers together on his stomach. "You are."

"Me?" Mark stared at him, dumbfounded. "Why?"

"Because you've been doing a good job for the firm. Oscar tells me you've given your all on the cases he's worked on with you. And I think it's about time to give you a leg up. You've earned it."

"Thank you, sir." Mark made a mental note to also thank Oscar next time he talked to him.

Royal waved away his gratitude. "You have a sharp legal mind, Mark. We value that. You're loyal. Dependable. Devoted to your career."

Mark tried to look appropriately humble, but it wasn't easy. He wanted to punch his fist into the air and shout, "Yes!"

"And now you're also a family man. A wife *and* a son in one fell swoop." Royal smiled again, rested his elbows on the arms of the chair, and linked his hands together in front of him. "That's what we like to hear, Mark. Stability has always been at the core of Jamison and Spritzer's success. It's an image we like to promote."

Mark wasn't sure how to take that. He'd always considered himself stable, even when he wasn't married. But he wasn't about to argue. He'd been waiting a long time for Royal to give some sign that Mark's efforts hadn't gone unnoticed.

"Things are going well at home?" Royal sounded

casually interested, but Mark suspected there was a reason behind the question.

"Very well."

"Glad to hear that, too. A family can be a real asset. Makes a man look successful."

They could make a man *feel* successful, Mark thought with a smile. "I appreciate you letting me get more involved in the case, sir."

"Nonsense. It's well deserved. Just have your secretary book you a room. The firm will pick up the tab, of course. The meeting's scheduled for eight o'clock."

"Tonight?" Mark couldn't keep the dismay from his voice.

Royal's close-set eyes narrowed slightly. "What's the matter? Do you have a conflict?"

"Sort of."

"Well, whatever it is, cancel. This witness can give us everything we need to prove our case at trial. We could blow the other side right out of the water." He leaned forward slightly and held Mark's gaze. "We can't afford to lose him."

"I know that. It's just—"

"Your wife will just have to understand that this sort of thing comes with the territory." Royal's thin lips curved into a smile as he spoke, but Mark heard the warning in his words.

"Dionne will understand," Mark assured him, knowing she would. He was the one who was disappointed at not being able to be with his family.

"Well, then, what's the problem?"

"No problem," Mark said. "Which hotel?"

"We'll put you up at the Seaport." Royal's eyes gleamed with satisfaction, and Mark knew he'd passed the test. "We want to make sure the firm looks good."

Mark had never stayed in the five-star hotel, but he tried to find some pleasure in knowing that if he had to be lonely, at least he'd be doing it in style.

"You'll have to handle the witness with kid gloves," Royal warned. "He's agreed to talk to us, but he's still pretty skittish."

"Don't worry. I'll get what we need."

Royal's smile widened. "I know you will."

The vote of confidence pleased him. "I won't let you down."

He watched Royal stand and stride across the office, waited until the door clicked shut behind him, then picked up the phone and dialed. Though he liked knowing that Royal's confidence in him was increasing, he hated having to make the choice between his career and his family. And he wondered how many times he'd be asked to make a similar choice in the future.

DIONNE GAVE the kitchen counter a final sweep with the cloth and stepped back to survey her handiwork. Dinner was over. Dishes were done. The kitchen was spotless. Jared had already drifted off to sleep, Mark was probably already settled in at the hotel in Boston, and she had absolutely nothing to do.

She sighed softly and wandered into the living room. She'd already put away Jared's toys, the furniture gleamed from polishing, and the carpet still bore tracks from vacuuming. She'd never been this efficient with housework. But then, she'd never had so many hours to get it done before.

Curling onto one end of the couch, she turned on

the television and watched for a few minutes, flicking between channels and trying to find something that would hold her interest. Unfortunately, her only choices seemed to be mindless sitcoms, a shoot-'em-up police drama and a melodramatic movie of the week.

She turned off the television and looked out the window at the sunset. The sun hovered on the horizon. Streaks of orange and deep red tinted the clouds. The sunset was beautiful, but she couldn't find any satisfaction in watching it.

With a sigh, she picked up a magazine and leafed through it. When none of the articles looked even slightly interesting, she tossed it onto the coffee table again.

What was wrong with her? She'd been in the strangest mood since Mark called to let her know he wasn't coming home. But why did that bother her? She'd only been living with him for a month. It wasn't as if her entire life revolved around him.

Or did it?

What else did she have? In Boise, she'd had work and her friendship with Cicely to fill the hours and keep her connected to the adult world. Here, she had Mark. No friends. No job. Nothing.

Not good, she told herself. Not good at all.

Without thinking twice, she picked up the cordless phone and dialed Cicely's number as she walked back into the kitchen. When Cicely answered, she lost herself for a moment in the excitement of hearing her friend's voice again and catching up on all that had happened during the past few weeks.

But it didn't take long for Cicely to drop the social

niceties and zero in. "Tell me the truth," Cicely demanded. "How are you doing?"

"I'm doing fine," Dionne assured her. "You really should see this place. It's like something from a Christmas card. There's a covered bridge just outside of town and everything."

"That sounds great," Cicely said patiently. "But what I'm interested in is how things are going between you and Mark."

"Things are going well. We've stopped arguing all the time and we're even becoming friends."

"Seriously?"

Dionne laughed. "Seriously."

"No trouble yet?"

"No trouble." Dionne put the kettle on to boil and pulled a tea bag from the cupboard. "Honestly, Cicely. You sound as if you *want* us to have trouble."

"Don't be silly. Of course I don't. I just want you to be happy. So...*are* you?"

"I'm not delirious," Dionne admitted as she lowered a mug to the counter. "But I'm certainly not miserable. You really can stop worrying about me."

"Right." She could almost see Cicely rolling her eyes in frustration. "You could be living a million miles away for all I ever hear from you. And you want me to stop worrying. It's not going to happen, girl."

Dionne sat at the table where she could look out into the backyard. "Well, then, try not to worry so much. Mark is terrific with Jared. And his family— Well, they've welcomed us both with open arms."

Cicely was quiet for a moment, then asked, "What are you doing? Falling for Mr. I'm-Taking-My-Son-Away-and-You-Can't-Stop-Me?"

"I'm getting to know him," Dionne hedged. "He really is a great guy."

Cicely humphed in disbelief.

"Wouldn't you rather hear that I like him than to find out he's beating me or something?"

"Of course." Cicely's voice softened considerably. "You know I would. But I still don't trust him."

"Well, I do," Dionne assured her. "And I'd rather talk about something else."

"Okay," Cicely said. "Are you working yet?"

"No."

"Are you looking for work?"

"No."

"You're staying home and playing housemaid, then?"

"I'm not playing housemaid," Dionne said firmly as the kettle began to whistle. She turned off the burner and poured hot water over the tea bag. "I'm raising my son. *Our* son."

"And doing dishes. And cleaning house. And keeping the home fires burning while he goes to work every day. Is that enough for you?"

That was a tough question. "For now."

"I don't believe you." Cicely's voice took on a sharp edge. "What about all those dreams you once had?"

"I still have them. In fact, Mark offered to loan me the money so I can get my degree."

"Really?" Cicely didn't sound impressed, but that came as no surprise. "Are you going to take him up on it?"

"I don't know." Dionne sipped and wrapped both

hands around the mug. "I feel funny accepting money from him."

Cicely let out a harsh laugh. "You can't be serious. You're already accepting money from him—rent money, food money, utility money. Why not tuition, too?"

"That's different," Dionne argued, though she couldn't explain how. She sighed. "I didn't call you so we could bicker, Cicely. I called because I miss you."

Cicely's voice softened. "I miss you, too. You know that. But I'm worried…and maybe just the tiniest bit jealous."

"Jealous? Why should you be jealous?"

"Because I feel as if I've lost you as my friend. I feel as if Mark has taken you away from me."

Dionne smiled. She'd always valued Cicely's honesty, even though it sometimes felt brutal. "I'm still your friend. I'll always be your friend. And I miss getting together as much as you do. I miss shopping and having lunch and hanging out on Saturdays." Just talking about the things they used to do brought tears to her eyes. "I wish you could come for a visit."

"So do I. But I don't have vacation scheduled until Christmas, and I've already promised to spend that with my parents."

Dionne's heart sank. She hadn't realized until that moment how much she'd been hoping to see Cicely again.

The conversation drifted on to other topics until Cicely finally pleaded fatigue and an early-morning meeting the next day. Hanging up reluctantly, Dionne battled an odd sense of disquiet as she walked through the kitchen and climbed the stairs to her bedroom. But as she undressed for the night, she put a name to it at last.

She was bored.

Yes, she loved being home with Jared, but Cicely was right. She did want more out of life than cooking meals and straightening the house while Mark pursued his career. If she wanted to be truly happy, she'd either have to go back to work or accept Mark's offer.

Cicely was right about another thing, too. Accepting a loan—and Dionne still couldn't justify taking Mark's money any other way—was no different than accepting everything else he'd been providing. That he did so without complaint only endeared him to her more. And his encouragement seemed genuine. He wanted her to follow her dream.

She pulled on her thin cotton nightgown and sank onto the foot of the bed. If she moved quickly, maybe she could still enroll in classes for the fall semester.

Excitement began as little more than a tingle close to her heart, then worked its way up to an almost electric charge. If only she could talk to Mark immediately, but she'd have to wait until tomorrow.

Too worked up to sleep, she descended the stairs again, poured a glass of wine, and carried it to the living room. She didn't bother with a robe. It was a warm night, and except for Jared she had the house to herself. Nor did she bother turning on the light.

Instead, she curled in a corner of the couch and looked out at the night. She thought about Cicely's question and whispered, ''Happy? Yes, Cicely, I really think I am.''

CHAPTER TWELVE

AT A LITTLE PAST MIDNIGHT, Mark pulled into the driveway and turned off the engine. Clouds hid the moon, and a breeze brushed the tops of the trees. In the distance, a dog barked. He smiled and reached for his briefcase. Home, sweet home.

Maybe he'd been foolish to drive for more than an hour after his meeting instead of staying at the hotel overnight. But after getting what he needed from the witness, the idea of celebrating alone in a lonely room—even in the posh hotel—hadn't appealed to him. He'd rather stumble over toys than sit alone in an elegant hotel room any day.

He was, of course, too late to see either his wife or his son tonight. Jared had been in bed for hours, and Dionne rarely stayed up this late. But if he got up early, he could spend a few minutes with them in the morning.

Giving in to a huge yawn, he grabbed his suit jacket from the seat beside him and hurried up the front walk. He let himself in and flipped the light switch, then froze at the sight that greeted him.

Dionne, wearing only a thin white nightgown that left little to the imagination, lay curled on the couch. A glass of wine, nearly untouched, sat on the floor beside her. The gown had twisted slightly, and its hem skimmed the tops of her thighs.

His breath caught at the same time his pulse began to race. He turned away quickly, closed and locked the door, then looked back at her. He could just leave her there, but she looked uncomfortable.

And that's how he justified his next move.

Slowly, cautiously, he crossed the room and touched her shoulder. Her skin felt warm—too warm, and far too soft. He should have pulled his hand away, but he didn't want to. He let it rest there for a moment, then shook her gently. "Dionne?" He shook her again. "Dionne? Wake up."

She mumbled something and curled closer to the cushions, and he had to fight the sudden craving to have her snuggle against him that way.

"Dionne?" He leaned a little closer, catching the scent of her hair.

This time, she opened her eyes. But she seemed disoriented, unaware of him for a second. In the next breath, she lurched upright and tugged at her gown. "What's wrong?"

"Nothing. I just thought you'd be more comfortable in bed." He held out a hand toward her, only half-convinced he could touch her again and still maintain control. "Come on. I'll help you up."

She took it warily. "What are you doing here? I thought you were staying in Boston."

"I was. I decided to come home instead. I was worried about Jared. Is he okay?"

"He's fine."

Mark helped her stand, which brought her to her feet mere inches from him. Light traces of her scent floated toward him, but more enticing was the scent of her skin he caught beneath it. He released her hand quickly. After all, he could only resist so much temptation. "Maybe I should have let you sleep, but you, uh…" He ran his hand over his face and backed a step away. "You looked uncomfortable."

Her eyes clouded for a moment. She rubbed the back of her neck, testing for kinks. "I guess I must have drifted off. I didn't plan to fall asleep there."

With the dim light behind her, the nightgown seemed to vaporize. Mark told himself to look away, but he couldn't. It had been a long time since he'd been with a woman and this one had gotten completely under his skin.

He cleared his throat and tried to pull himself together. "Why don't you go up to bed. I'll double-check the doors and windows." Anything to get away from her before he did something they'd both regret.

Obviously unaware of her effect on him, she started past him, then stopped and smiled. "I made a decision tonight."

"Oh? What kind of decision?" *Please, let it be that she wants a real marriage—starting now.*

"If your offer to loan me tuition still stands, I've decided to take you up on it."

He did his best not to look disappointed. "Yes, of course. But what brought about this change?"

"A lot of things." She ran a hand through her hair, tousling it even more, making him want to work his hands into the curls and do it for her. "Mostly I realized that I can't teach Jared to reach his fullest capacity if I don't even try to meet my own. Actions say more than words ever can. I need to teach by example."

Mark dropped onto the couch to put some distance

between them. "I'm so glad," he said honestly. "I'd like to see you doing something you enjoy."

"I enjoy being home with Jared." She sat beside him, and Mark couldn't decide if the distance between them was too little or too great. "But I also need to do something more personally challenging than housework."

"I think that's great," he said. "Just find out how much you'll need for tuition and books, and let me know. I'll have the money for you by the next day."

Dionne smiled, and the room brightened. "Thank you. You know I'll pay back every penny."

He shook his head emphatically. "I don't want you to pay back anything."

"But I do." Her smile faded for an instant. "You're already doing so much—"

"I'm doing nothing." The words came from the deepest, most honest part of himself. "You're the one who's making all the sacrifices in this marriage."

Something flitted through her eyes too quickly for him to read it. "We're both making sacrifices, Mark. And I need you to know how much I appreciate what you've done."

Were those tears glinting in her eyes? Mark's heart sank. He didn't want her to cry. He didn't handle tears well. They made him feel inadequate, rough, coarse.

He did the only thing he could think of. He put a comforting arm around her. But the instant he touched her again, desire overtook him. Pulling her closer, he lowered his mouth to hers and brushed it softly. When she didn't move away, he let the last remnants of control disappear and deepened the kiss.

Her mouth felt warm and soft, and he lost himself in it.

This was right. So very right. He didn't want to stop. When he realized she wasn't going to pull away, he tugged her onto his lap and wrapped his arms around her waist, exploring her mouth with his tongue, running his hands along her back, her thighs, her hips.

He told himself to hold back, to stay in control, but some logical piece of his brain reminded him that they were husband and wife, that there was nothing wrong with what they were doing, that everything he'd done for the past two months had been leading up to this moment.

When she whimpered softly, waves of fresh yearning rolled through him and his thoughts jumbled again. "You feel so good," he whispered when he could finally drag his mouth from hers. "So very good."

"So do you." Her breath caressed his neck and sent another surge of need through him. He ran his hands along her sides and slipped them beneath the top of her nightgown. She was beautiful. Sexy. Desirable. And he was more alive than he'd been in a long time.

He half expected her to pull away from his touch. When she didn't, he grew braver. Groaning softly, he cupped her breasts with both hands and closed his eyes. She moaned, responding to his touch. Every nerve in his body flamed. "I want you," he muttered as he claimed her mouth again.

It seemed to take forever before she could catch her breath enough to whisper, "Yes."

He pulled away slightly. "Are you sure?"

"Yes."

Groaning again, he caressed her one more time. Then, holding himself in check, wanting to make the moment special for both of them, he carried her up the stairs to his bedroom.

He kicked the door shut behind them and lowered her onto the bed. And he slowly, patiently, lovingly took them both over the crest into paradise.

DIONNE WOKE before the sun came up, before Mark's alarm went off, before Jared stirred. She lay tangled in the sheets, cradled in Mark's arms.

Rolling onto her side, she watched him for a moment. His mouth was parted slightly. His dark lashes fanned on his cheek. He looked young and defenseless.

She touched his hand with her fingertips, but when she remembered everything they'd done, when she realized the extent of their intimacy, she blushed furiously and pulled her hand away.

She'd never been so uninhibited during lovemaking before, not even with Brent. She realized, in the soft gray of sunrise, that though she'd loved Brent and enjoyed his lovemaking, it had never been like this.

Slowly, without disturbing Mark, she inched out of bed, pulled on her nightgown, and stepped out into the hall. She needed to think, to decide exactly how she felt about this change between them, and she didn't want to wake him.

Padding softly across the hall to her own bedroom, she checked on the sleeping Jared, changed quickly into jeans and a T-shirt, then hurried downstairs and slipped out onto the deck where she could enjoy the solitude of the morning.

The air felt clean and cool against her still-fevered skin. The scent of earth and trees and water soothed her. Maybe, she thought with a wry smile, she should have felt guilty. But she didn't. She felt alive and achingly feminine and surprisingly hungry for more. But there was one thing missing.

Mark hadn't said he loved her.

He'd said a thousand wonderful things last night, but he hadn't used the word *love*. And she'd held back her own confession, afraid to let go of that one last piece of herself, afraid he'd answer with silence. She could have borne many things, but she didn't think she could bear that.

So what was she going to do now?

She could continue the physical relationship with Mark and hope he'd fall in love with her. But what if he didn't? What then? Would her love alone be enough? Or would the pain of knowing Mark didn't love her eventually drive a wedge between them?

They couldn't afford that. Neither of them could. They'd be right back where they'd started—battling each other for Jared. She didn't want to go through that again, and she wouldn't put Jared through it. And she knew Mark would feel exactly the same way. That's why they'd gotten married in the first place.

Sighing, she walked to the edge of the lawn, tilted back her head, and let the silence wrap itself around her. She'd like to think she could still protect her heart, but the truth was, she'd already moved far beyond that point. The only choice left to her was to protect Jared from the pain that adults could impose on their children.

WHEN THE ALARM WENT OFF, Mark stretched and reached across the bed for Dionne, but his arm encountered only the pillow and rumpled sheets. He sat up, blinked, and looked around the room. The sky had just begun to lighten but he could see she wasn't there.

Wondering if Jared had woken her, Mark pulled on his briefs and a pair of jeans and hurried into the hall. But Jared's bedroom door stood open, and Mark could see the small mound of his son under the sheet on his bed.

Next he checked Dionne's room. To his relief, her bed was empty and unrumpled. At least she hadn't had second thoughts about this new phase in their relationship and gone back to her own bed.

Yearning to hold her again, to taste her sweet lips and feel her against him, if only for a moment, he looked for her in the kitchen, the living room and the bathroom. Each time he left an empty room, his uneasiness grew.

Finally, he caught sight of her through the patio door. She stood on the far edge of the lawn, her face tilted to catch the rising sun, her hair the color of ripe wheat where the sun touched it. She was heartbreakingly beautiful.

Smiling, he slipped outside and watched her for a moment. The need he'd thought they'd satisfied last night twisted through him again, stronger than ever now that he knew the absolute joy of making love to her.

More than anything, he wanted to take her back

to bed so they could spend the rest of the morning discovering each other all over again. But Jared would be up soon. And Royal and Oscar would be waiting for him. Clients needed him. He couldn't stay.

More irritated than he'd ever been with the demands of his job, he crossed the lawn and came to a stop behind her. If she heard him approaching she gave no sign, but kept her face turned toward the sky.

He wrapped his arms loosely around her waist and pressed a kiss to the back of her neck. "Good morning."

She must have heard him because she didn't seem surprised by his touch. Neither did she turn toward him. "Good morning."

"How long have you been up?"

"Only a few minutes."

He wanted her to snuggle against him, to turn and kiss him, to wrap her arms around his neck and hold him close. But she did none of those things. He moved his hands to her shoulders and turned her around. Her eyes were shuttered, as if she had something to hide from him, and his mood took a nose-dive.

"What's wrong?" he asked gently.

Her gaze lifted to his almost reluctantly. "I've been thinking about last night."

"Not having second thoughts about what we did, are you?" he said lightly. A joke. And he longed for a denial.

Instead, she met his gaze slowly. "Are you?"

"No. Not at all." He brushed a tentative kiss to her lips, but she didn't respond as she had last night.

He struggled to keep his tone light in spite of the heaviness that settled around his heart. "So, what's wrong? Did I hog the blankets? Keep you awake with my snoring?"

She laughed softly. "No. And no. You're an absolute gentleman in bed." Her cheeks reddened and she lowered her gaze again. "In all ways."

That helped, but he could still sense her withdrawal. "Then what is it? You seem distant this morning." When she didn't respond immediately, he said, "We didn't do anything wrong, you know. We *are* married."

"Married, yes." She glanced at him, and her eyes clouded with some emotion Mark couldn't name. "But what is our relationship, really?"

"I think it's better than ever," he said. "I'd much rather take you to bed than argue with you."

She stepped away from him and folded her arms across her chest. "Is it really better? Or have we made it more complicated?"

The question stunned him. "Complicated? How?"

"Everything's changed now. There's more at stake. There's a greater risk." She studied his face for a moment, searching for something, sighing when she didn't find it. "And yet nothing's changed, has it?"

A strange sort of dread began to churn in his stomach. What was she asking? What did she want him to say? If he knew, he'd say it in a heartbeat. "Like what?"

"We don't love each other, Mark."

Until that moment, he hadn't realized how much he wanted to believe she felt differently about him— about them. And realizing that she didn't, hit him like a fist in the gut. "What we have is a good start," he argued. "It might turn into love in time."

She shook her head and looked away, speaking so quietly he could hardly hear her. "That's not how you start a relationship. Not if you want it to last. You don't make love first and then try to fall in love afterward."

He shivered, more from the chill between them than the morning breeze. "Is that what you think we did?"

"Isn't it?" When he didn't answer, she prodded. "Do you love me, Mark?"

One part of him believed he did love her, but what was love, really? He'd loved Marianne, but what he felt for her now was anything *but* love. She'd claimed to love him, yet she'd betrayed him. Jerry had loved Alice, but he'd hurt her and destroyed their marriage. Mark said none of this to Dionne. Instead, he spoke softly. "I thought we'd agreed to this marriage because neither of us had any delusions about love. But I care about you, Dionne. A great deal."

"I see." She turned away and rubbed her arms. "I guess that tells me everything I need to know."

The knot in Mark's stomach grew. "You could have stopped me at any time last night. You could have pulled away and locked yourself in your own room. But if memory serves, you were pretty damned willing."

"I was. I won't deny it."

"Are you saying *you* love *me?*"

She hesitated long enough to make him wonder. Long enough to make his pulse slow and his fingers grow numb.

"I don't know," she said after a long pause. "But

I do know that just because we have a piece of paper that says it's legal for us to make love, that doesn't make it morally right if our hearts aren't involved. And it wouldn't be fair to Jared to put our relationship at such risk.''

Mark clenched his jaw and worked hard not to let her see his disappointment. ''So, you're saying you don't want what happened last night to happen again?'' He could hear the defensive coolness in his voice, but he made no effort to change it.

Something flashed across her face too quickly for him to identify. ''It *can't* happen again. Wonderful as it was—and it was great—I don't want a relationship with you that's only physical.''

He laughed bitterly to hide the pain. ''Well, you don't have to worry about it. I'll control myself in the future.''

Without giving her a chance to make things worse, he pivoted and strode across the lawn toward the house. She was right about one thing—it would have been much easier to take the rejection if they hadn't shared last night.

FOR TWO DAYS, Mark tried to keep his anger and disappointment under control. He left in the mornings before Dionne came downstairs and he didn't come home again until he knew she'd be in bed. That meant he also missed seeing Jared, but he didn't trust himself to be near Dionne and not tell her everything that was boiling inside him. He couldn't go on this way for long. He'd fought to have Jared with him, and he wasn't going to let this come between them. He and Dionne had to work through this.

Mark was torn between the rational argument that

people had sex all the time without love, and the painful knowledge that that's exactly what ruined so many relationships. The bottom line was, he had only himself to blame. In one thoughtless, hormone-driven moment, he'd ruined everything.

He ran his hand across his chin and glanced at Anna, who stood in front of his desk holding a stack of legal books he'd asked her to find an hour earlier. Normally, he'd have gone to the firm's library himself, but he'd snapped unnecessarily at one of the interns the previous afternoon and he'd decided not to risk a repeat performance today.

He tried to shake off his frustration and focus instead on his job. Logic. Law. Rules. Regulations. At least they made sense to him. "So, did you find them all?" he asked.

"No, unfortunately." Anna lowered the heavy books to his desk along with the list he'd given her. "But I found most of the cases you wanted."

He could feel the scowl forming and tried to wipe it away. Anna shouldn't have to pay for his mistake. "Just tell me you've got Fed Second 367."

Anna shook her head and flashed an apologetic smile. "Don't get mad, but it wasn't in the library."

That figured. His bad luck was holding. "Can you find out who has it?"

"I can E-mail everyone, but we still may not find it in time. Lots of people are out of the office."

"Great." The word came out unnecessarily harsh. Even he knew that.

Anna matched his scowl. "You want to tell me what's wrong with you?"

That was the last thing he wanted to do. "Nothing's wrong."

"Right. You're always this pleasant."

"I'm fine. I just have a lot of work to do."

"We all do," Anna reminded him and swept an arm toward her desk. "I'm not exactly partying out there. This new case has put us all in a bind."

The reminder brought him back down to earth with a jolt. He sent her an apologetic smile. "I know you're busy. I didn't mean to imply that you weren't."

"Good." Anna looked slightly mollified. "Then tell me what's really bugging you."

He looked away from her and opened one of the books. "Nothing important."

As usual, Anna wouldn't take no for an answer. "Money trouble?"

Mark shook his head.

"Has Royal done something?"

"No."

"Shoes too tight?"

He flicked a smile at her. "No."

"Then it must be something to do with your new bride."

Mark's smile faded. "I said I don't want to talk about it."

Anna sat in the chair facing his. "I heard you, but *I* don't want to put up with this foul mood you've been in for the past two days."

"If you go back to your desk," he pointed out, "you won't have to."

"That's not true." Anna made herself even more comfortable and crossed her legs. "You're so cranky, it's seeping out from under the door. I can't escape."

He glanced at her, caught her smile, and relented

a little. "I appreciate your concern, but it's personal."

That didn't faze her. "It's not as if we've never talked about anything personal before. I thought we were friends."

"We are." He closed the book slowly. "Of course we are."

"Then tell me what's wrong."

He sighed heavily, ran a hand along the back of his neck, and leaned back in his chair. "I did something stupid, okay? And I'm not exactly proud of it. So, if you don't mind…"

"*You* did something *stupid?*" Anna's eyebrows rose. "I find that hard to believe."

He let out a thin laugh. "Okay, so it's not such a rare occurrence."

"You'll feel better if you talk about it."

"I don't think so."

He reached for the book again, but she leaned across the desk and put a hand over his to stop him. "All kidding aside, Mark, I hate to see you like this. You know that whatever you tell me won't go out of this room."

"I know."

Her lips twitched, a sure sign that she was about to wallop him with one of her one-liners. "I'll just bring everyone in here when I tell them."

The joke broke through the last thin wall of his reserve. He pulled his hand away, stood, and paced to the window. "I think I've ruined everything."

"With Dionne?"

"Yes."

"How?"

He turned to face her, feeling as sheepish as a

twelve-year-old who'd been caught necking on the school playground. "I made love to her."

Disbelief and amusement darted across Anna's face. "Excuse me?"

"I said, I made love to her."

"How did that ruin everything? She's your wife, isn't she?"

"You don't understand." He shoved his hands into his pockets and turned back toward the window. "We got married so that we could share Jared. I promised I wouldn't take advantage of her. But when I got home the other night..." He shuddered just thinking about it. But the shudder wasn't entirely self-loathing.

"Did she mind?"

"Yes. Of course she minded."

"*Of course?*" Anna stood and came behind him. "You didn't force her, did you?"

"No." He shook his head quickly. "I wouldn't do that."

"You had me worried for a minute. So, explain, please. You made love to her, and she minded."

"Not at the time," he said with a bitter smile. "But she sure as hell minded the next morning."

"What happened? Did you shout out another woman's name or something?"

"Of course not. She just doesn't want it to happen again."

Anna scowled. "Why not? Has it escaped her notice that you're a fairly good-looking guy?"

"It's not about that," he said sharply, then tempered his voice again. "It's about trust. It's about breaking a promise—an *important* promise."

"Okay." Anna lifted a hand as if she intended to

put it on his shoulder, then dropped it to her side. "I understand that. But if she didn't resist, if she didn't tell you no, if she didn't belt you in the nose and tell you to stop—"

"She didn't."

"Did she…" Anna blushed slightly. "Did she respond?"

"At the time." He looked down at the windowsill.

Anna folded her arms and stood beside him. "Maybe the important question is why you made love to her in the first place."

"Because." He glanced up at her quickly. "Because she was just so damned beautiful lying there, and because she was wearing a thin cotton nightgown, and because—" He broke off, uncertain what else to say.

"So, did you make love to *her?* Or did you just have sex with a beautiful woman?"

"Both."

Anna sighed with impatience. "If you'd walked in and found some other beautiful woman there, would you have come on to her?" She moved a step closer and held his gaze. "Were you just horny, or was it Dionne?"

"It wasn't just physical."

"Do you love her?"

He frowned at her. "That's what she asked, but I don't know."

Anna smiled knowingly. "Then I suggest you figure that out. And when you do, make sure she's the first person you tell."

She pivoted and crossed to the door. And with one last, silent glance, she stepped through and pulled the door shut behind her, leaving him alone and utterly confused.

CHAPTER THIRTEEN

EXCITED AND APPREHENSIVE at the same time, Dionne clutched her purse and followed a group of students into the crowded room being used for registration. The sheer volume of students—all at least ten years younger than she was—left her feeling slightly dazed.

Taking a deep breath, she squared her shoulders and tried to orient herself. She'd made the decision to come back to school, and she'd do her best to succeed. Looking around for the first instructor she wanted to see, she finally settled on a tall, good-looking man about her own age near a long table. He didn't look like an instructor. No suit. No tie. Just Dockers and a pale blue shirt. But several students flanked him, and he had the confident air of someone in charge.

She took her place in line and checked the cell phone in her purse once more to make sure the baby-sitter Patsy had recommended could reach her in an emergency. Within minutes, a young girl of about twenty joined her in line and let out a sigh. "Have they started the waiting list yet or is there still room to get into this course?"

"Waiting list?" Dionne hadn't anticipated that. "Does that happen often?"

"It happens a lot, especially with Eskelson's

classes.'' The girl shifted her purse to her other shoulder. ''You look nervous. Are you new here?''

''Very,'' Dionne admitted with a smile. ''I haven't had to study anything for years. I'm afraid I'm out of the habit.''

''Well, you picked the wrong class to start with,'' the girl told her. ''Eskelson's famous for being tough even in a first-level course like Introductory Psych.''

Dionne could have gone all day without hearing that. ''Is that Eskelson up there in the blue shirt?''

''That's him.'' The girl folded a piece of gum and wedged it into her mouth. ''One of my roommates, Trish, took this course from him spring semester. She said it was really hard.'' The girl dug something else from the depths of her backpack. ''I think it's because of the amount of homework he assigns.''

''Great.''

The girl laughed, but she sobered again immediately. ''If I could have gotten this credit any other way, I would have done it. But this is the only time it's offered, and if I don't get it this semester, I can't take Applied Psych next semester.'' She waved a pair of glasses in the space between them as she talked. ''It'll throw my whole schedule off and I'll end up having to wait a couple of semesters to graduate.'' She started to put on the glasses, then smiled at Dionne again. ''I'm Heidi, by the way.''

''It's nice to meet you. I'm Dionne.'' She stole another glance at Mr. Eskelson. ''What kind of homework are you talking about?''

''Trish said she had to read fifty pages a night just to keep up. *And* he doesn't go over the reading material in class.''

Fifty pages? Dionne's heart thudded to the floor

and landed between her feet. How would she find time to read fifty pages a night? The last time she'd tried to read a novel, she'd fallen asleep long before the end of the first chapter.

"And Trish says there's a lot of writing," Heidi added with a frown. "Like, a paper due every other week or so."

Dionne took a steadying breath and tried to force away the sudden feelings of inadequacy. She'd find a way. If she ever had to support Jared on her own again, she wanted to do it right.

Thinking about Jared reminded her of Mark, and the familiar ache in her heart worsened. She hadn't expected Mark to be happy about her decision not to continue the physical part of their relationship, but she hadn't expected him to pull away so completely.

Very often, when she let herself dwell on it, she found herself remembering her father. He'd turned to another woman when a second difficult pregnancy for her mother interfered with his sex life. Mark's mistress might be his career but the effect was the same.

He'd kept his word and left a blank check for tuition and another for books on the dining-room table one morning. But what did his money matter? What she wanted was his heart.

Today wasn't the time to think about that, she reminded herself.

She lifted her chin and asked Heidi, "Is there anything else I should know?"

The young woman thought for a moment, then shook her head. "I don't think so. Don't worry. You'll be fine as long as you keep up—that's what Trish says, anyway."

Sighing softly, Dionne looked around at the others in the room. They were all so young and full of energy, they looked as if they could conquer the world. Dionne doubted she had the stamina to conquer the piles of laundry waiting for her at home.

When she realized that the line had inched forward, she moved with it. She could do this. She'd just have to make a few adjustments, that's all.

Mark or no Mark, she could do this. No more self-pity. No more self-doubt. She had the chance to fulfill her dream, and that's exactly what she was going to do…come hell or high water.

OUT OF HABIT, Dionne checked for oncoming traffic before pushing Jared's stroller into the deserted intersection of Front and Sycamore Streets. She had plenty to do at home, but she'd deserted it all to take a walk. She needed the exercise and she wanted to play with Jared. But she'd also needed to get out of the house, away from her never-ending homework, and away from the nagging discontent she felt whenever she thought of Mark.

She wasn't sure which of them was avoiding the other, but one by one the days ticked past and nothing seemed to be getting better. For three days he'd left early in the morning and come home late at night—when he came home at all.

When they did see each other—always briefly in passing—his eyes were unreadable. His muttered excuses about a big trial that was demanding all his time didn't make her feel any better.

She could forgive him for not loving her. That had never been part of their bargain. But she couldn't forgive the confusion she saw in her son's eyes when

Jared asked for his daddy at breakfast and dinner, or when Mark wasn't there to tuck the little boy in at the end of the day.

Jared twisted in the stroller to look at her. "Jared wants juice, Mommy."

She smiled down at him and bent to smooth a lock of hair from his forehead. "I'm thirsty, too, sweetheart. Let's see if we can find something to drink, shall we?"

Jared nodded solemnly, twisted back in his seat, and reached toward one of the concrete planters on the edge of the sidewalk. The summer flowers had been removed and the planters stood stark and empty, but bunting draped the fronts of the buildings and reminded her that the autumn festival was that night.

The town still made her think of the movies she'd watched as a young girl. The ones where parents loved each other and children didn't have to question their parents' devotion to one another.

Such a fantasy. Such a foolish dream.

And such a foolish dreamer.

Biting back a self-mocking laugh, she stopped in front of a narrow building with a carved wooden sign and peered in through a picture window at a cluster of old-fashioned tables and a long, gleaming counter.

"Well look at this," she said to Jared. "It's called Mabel's. Shall we go inside?"

Jared started to climb from the stroller, but the safety strap held him in place.

"Hold on a minute. Mommy'll get you out." She hunkered down to undo the belt and glanced up when a shadow fell over the sidewalk and a friendly voice said, "Hi, there. Out for a walk?"

It took her only a second to recognize Patsy. "We're exploring the town."

"You picked a good day for it." Patsy glanced up at the sun overhead, then at the shaded doorway. "Are you going inside?"

"Yes, for a few minutes."

"Then I'll join you…if you don't mind."

"I'd enjoy the company," Dionne said, realizing she sounded almost desperate for a friendly face. Determined to put Mark out of her mind, she chose a table near the front window and situated Jared away from the aisle so he'd have to get past her if he wanted to take off exploring on his own.

While they placed their orders, she dug the tiny trucks and cars she always carried from her purse and gave them to Jared, then turned back to Patsy. "You're not working today?"

"I have the day off to get ready for the festival. You're still planning to come, aren't you? Jared's obviously healthy again."

Much as Dionne wanted to go, she didn't want to face all her new neighbors without Mark. She didn't want to face them *with* him, either, she realized. She swallowed hard and said, "I don't think we can make it."

"Oh, but you have to come," Patsy insisted. "I've already told everyone you'll be there, and they're all looking forward to meeting you."

"I'd like to meet them, too," Dionne assured her. "But Mark's been putting in so many extra hours at work, he doesn't get home until late."

"Then come by yourself."

Dionne waited while their waitress settled their

drinks on the table, then helped Jared onto his booster seat. "Another time, maybe. Next year."

Patsy's dark eyes filled with concern. "But I hate to think of you staying home alone tonight."

"I don't mind. I have plenty to do."

"Is everything all right? You sound kind of sad."

The temptation to confide in her was almost overwhelming, but Dionne didn't give in to it. She didn't know Patsy well enough to share confidences. "Everything's fine. I'm still adjusting to the move, to living in a new house and strange town, *and* to going back to school."

"Not to mention having a new husband," Patsy interjected.

"And that." Dionne looked away and let her gaze travel down the street, hoping to keep Patsy from seeing the truth in her eyes. "Actually, I've still got a few boxes from the move left to unpack."

"Do you want some help?"

Dionne looked back at her quickly. While the offer sounded tempting, she couldn't risk Patsy finding out that she and Mark didn't sleep in the same room. Nor did she want Mark to come home while Patsy was there. Patsy would immediately sense the strain between them. "No, thanks. I can manage. It's just a matter of making myself do it."

"I'd be glad to help. I love organizing things," Patsy said with an easy, infectious laugh that helped to lift Dionne's spirits. "Especially when they're other people's things."

"What I'd really like," Dionne said, trying to change the subject, "is to find out more about the town. Tell me what I should see."

Patsy shrugged. "There isn't much *to* see, really. It's a perfectly ordinary town."

"You only say that because you're used to it. There's nothing ordinary about it. It's fascinating."

Patsy looked out the window, as if seeing the town for the first time. "Do you really think so?"

"I really do. It's very different from what I'm used to. Even the countryside is different." She picked up a stray car for Jared. "I'm used to a place where trees are an import and water might as well be on the endangered species list."

Patsy laughed again. "I guess what we find fascinating is relative, isn't it? I've never been out west, and I'd love to go. The pictures I see are so raw and wild, and this all seems rather boring by comparison." She sighed and reached across the table to touch Jared's cheek. "So is my life when I get right down to it. I envy you."

"Me?" Dionne's hand froze just as she reached for a truck that teetered near the edge of the table. "Why?"

"Why not?" Patsy waved a hand toward her as if to take in everything. "You're having a grand adventure and you're living that thrill of new love. George and I have spent our entire lives within fifty miles of Longs Mill, and we've been married so long, we've lost the magic."

Dionne handed the truck back to Jared. "There's something to be said for being together a long time. You become comfortable with the other person, you know how they think, and what they like and dislike."

"True." Patsy frowned thoughtfully. "But it was so exciting to *discover* all that about George when we first got together. And to watch our love grow as we did.'' She toyed with her napkin for a moment. ''I miss it, but I didn't realize how much until you came to town.''

Just as Dionne missed being at ease, the way she'd been with Brent. ''How long have you been married?''

''Ten years.''

''That's a long time.''

''It's forever.''

As long as Dionne would have been married to Brent if he'd lived. She wondered if they'd have eventually reached the same point in their marriage, if she'd have been bored and yearning for adventure. But that was one question that would never be answered.

Unexpectedly, Mark's image took the place of Brent's, and she had the uncomfortable notion that life with him would never be boring. He had too much electricity and the emotions she felt around him were too sharp-edged to ever become dulled.

Slowly, she became aware of Patsy watching her. She fidgeted with her napkin, and laughed softly. ''Sorry. I was thinking about something else for a moment.''

''You don't have to apologize to me. I just can't wait to meet the man who puts that look in your eyes.'' Patsy smiled mischievously. ''In fact, I'm looking forward to introducing him to George. Maybe some of it will rub off.''

Dionne laughed. ''Maybe.'' But the yearning she saw in Patsy's eyes made her wonder if she'd been overlooking the positive things about her relationship with Mark.

She'd loved Brent the first time they made love, but not fully and completely. And she hadn't been absolutely certain that he loved her. That kind of love took time to grow. So why hadn't she been willing to give Mark a chance? Was she afraid he'd leave one day like her father had? Or was she afraid of living through another horrible loss like Brent's death? Had she been holding Mark at arm's length to protect herself?

With brutal honesty, she admitted the answer was yes. She also had to admit she'd failed miserably. Pushing Mark away, and convincing herself it was all *his* fault, hadn't protected her at all. With him around or without him, she still felt everything. And if she lost this time, the loss would be of her own making.

"HERE COME the peas. See?" While Dionne's dinner cooled on her plate, she swooped the spoonful of vegetables in front of Jared, hoping to tease him into eating.

He clamped his mouth shut and pulled away. "No," he said through tightened lips.

"Peas are yummy," Dionne argued gently. "Mommy loves peas, Jared. Try some."

"No." Jared folded his arms and scowled at her.

A miniature Mark, she thought, and her heart gave one of its familiar skips. She didn't know when she'd see him next. Nor did she know what she'd say when she did. She only knew she had to try to explain what she'd been afraid of and then pray that he'd understand.

She urged the spoon at Jared again. "Come on, sweetheart. For Mommy?"

"No. Jared want ice cream."

"You can have ice cream when you've finished your peas."

Jared's scowl deepened and wariness flashed in his dark eyes. But before he could argue again, the sound of a car in the driveway had him squirming frantically to get out of his high chair and knocking the spoon from her hand. "Daddy."

Dionne glanced at the clock. It seemed early for Mark, but she hoped Jared was right.

She didn't have to wonder long. Her body gave her the answer almost before she heard his key turning the lock. Her heart began to pound, she couldn't draw a breath, and her knees felt wobbly. But she tried to look normal when she lifted Jared from his chair. "You're right, sweetie. Let's go say hello."

Jared didn't have to be told twice. The instant she set him on the floor, he took off at a dead run. Dionne followed more slowly, reaching the middle of the living room just as Mark opened the door.

When he saw them, he froze for a moment, and all Dionne's insecurities come rushing back. In the next breath, he dropped his briefcase and suit jacket and scooped Jared from the floor.

"Hey there, big boy." Mark pulled back, noticed the bib, and added, "I'm late for dinner again, aren't I?" He turned his gaze toward Dionne slowly, hesitantly. "Am I too late?"

Dionne shook her head. "Not at all. We just started."

"Do you mind if I join you?"

"Of course not." She stopped, then forced herself to add, "We've missed having you around."

He met her gaze over the top of Jared's head. "I've missed *being* around."

Time slowed, then stopped altogether while he held her gaze. She could almost hear her pulse as her heart tapped out a staccato rhythm.

Mark kissed Jared's cheek, then lowered him to the floor and took his hand, all without taking his eyes from hers. "We need to talk about the other night."

"All right." She forced away the dread that had replaced the anticipation.

"I acted like a jerk. I promised I wouldn't take advantage of you, but that's exactly what I did. I know you're angry with me and you have every right to be, but I've been miserable this week. I'd like to put it behind us so I can come home again."

"You can come home whenever you want," she said quietly. "I never asked you not to."

"I know, but I was afraid to look in your eyes and see how much you hated me."

"I wasn't angry with you."

"You sure avoided me as if you were."

"Well, yes. But only because you made it pretty clear nothing had changed for you."

"Are you kidding?" He looked shocked. "*Everything* changed for me that night." He reached a tentative hand toward her and touched her cheek, sending flames to every extremity. "I've done a lot of thinking since then."

"So have I."

"Maybe what we have isn't exactly what you had with Brent—"

She touched her fingertips to his lips to stop him.

"This isn't about Brent," she said softly. "This is about us."

"But it is about him," Mark insisted. "I know I can't give you the kind of love you had with him, but I do love you, in my own clumsy way."

Tears filled her eyes and her heart threatened to jump out of her chest. "I don't want the kind of love I had with him," she said honestly. "I want something new. I want what *you* can give me."

His eyes turned a soft golden brown. "Do you think you can learn to love me?"

She laughed, nearly choking on her tears. "I already do."

He kissed her briefly, gently, but she knew his entire heart was in it. Before he could deepen the kiss or she could respond, Jared tugged on his hand. Mark pulled away, smiling. "I guess we can stop avoiding each other then, can't we?"

"I guess we can. But I wasn't the only one who missed you this week, Mark. It's been hard on Jared, too."

His gaze faltered. "I'm sorry."

"Just promise me that whatever happens between us, you won't let it affect your relationship with him."

"I won't. He'll always be my son. Just as I hope you'll always be my wife."

"That's what I want, too," she told him gently.

He responded to another impatient tug from Jared by taking a couple of unsteady steps toward the kitchen. "What's going on in town tonight? Everyone seems to be going somewhere."

"It's the autumn festival." Dionne reached for

Jared, to put him back in his high chair. "It's a big deal around here, I guess."

"Why aren't you there?"

"Because I don't really know anyone, and I didn't want to show up alone and have to answer a bunch of questions."

He sent her a rueful smile. "Because your husband's a jerk and a coward who won't come home before you're in bed?"

"Not exactly. I'm the one who created this rift between us."

He shook his head quickly. "Wrong. But we can work all that out later when Jared's not listening. The question of the moment is, would you like to go?"

She turned to face him. "I would. But what about you? Aren't you tired? You haven't had much sleep all week."

He waved away the question. "Sleep? Who needs sleep? I'm in such a good mood right now, I could go another three or four hours without it." He met her gaze again. "Seriously, if you'd like to go, let's do it…unless you're too tired after being in class all day."

His willingness to please her and his concern touched her deeply. "I'm not tired, and I think it would be fun. I'd like to get to know the people in town. I've only met a few of them."

"Then you're a few up on me." He loosened his tie, then stopped and made a face. "Is it casual, or do I have to stay dressed?"

"Patsy told me it's casual."

"Great. I'll change after dinner."

"Maybe I should change, too," she said with a glance at her own faded jeans and T-shirt.

His eyes traveled slowly, appreciatively, over her. "You look great just the way you are."

Everything felt different and wonderful between them. "Thank you," she said with an embarrassed smile, "but I could look better."

His gaze settled on her again, took her in almost hungrily and left her tingling with anticipation. "Maybe," he drawled, "but you'll have to prove it to me before I'll believe it."

Amazed at how right this new mood between them felt, she grinned. "Okay, I will."

She fixed Mark a plate and gave it to him. "I should warn you," she said as put the plate in front of him, "everyone in town knows we're newly-weds."

"Then I say we give them what they're waiting for." He trailed a finger down her cheek and used it to tilt her chin. He kissed her thoroughly and left her nearly breathless. "What do you say we show them a pair of newlyweds so in love they can't see straight?"

She grinned, feeling mischievous and excited, desirable and wanted all at once.

He kissed her again, quickly. "Are you ready?"

"Yes." For that and a whole lot more.

CHAPTER FOURTEEN

THE EVENING WAS PERFECT. Outdoor lanterns cast a magical glow over everything, white-clothed tables holding refreshments lined one end of the square, music from an unseen stereo wafted through the crowd and blended with the laughter and conversation.

Patsy had found them immediately, guiding them from one knot of people to another, introducing them to everyone in town. A few faces looked familiar—Mrs. Wiggs from the post office, Arlen Harris from the small village grocery store, a tall blond man with a rugged face Dionne had seen outside the hardware store, who turned out to be Patsy's husband, George.

To Dionne's delight, Mark and George hit it off immediately, and the Wagner children took to Jared as if he'd always been one of them. Visions of family outings and shared barbecues filled her head and left her floating. And the food— It was everything Patsy had promised and more. Dionne gathered promises of shared recipes with every dish she tasted.

"I forgot to tell you," Patsy said as the music started and people began to gather around the temporary dance floor in the center of the square. "You two are supposed to lead off the dancing."

"We're what?" Dionne glanced up at Mark, but he didn't look at all surprised. She'd been anticipating a dance with him, but not with the whole town watching.

"The dancing," Patsy said, taking Jared from her. "The newest and oldest couples always lead off. That'll be Hattie and Arlen Harris—they've been married sixty-two years last May—and the two of you since you're the newlyweds."

The background music stopped for a moment, then began again, louder now. Dionne recognized the tune. A waltz, of course. The most romantic dance in the world.

"Well, I'm sure not going to flout tradition," Mark said, holding out his hand. "Shall we?"

Dionne put her hand in his, relishing the thrill of his touch. He led her onto the dance floor, and though she was vaguely aware of everyone's eyes following them, she no longer cared. She would have danced on hot coals at that moment, as long as she could do it in Mark's arms.

A few feet away, an elderly couple moved into the spotlight and began to dance. Arlen held his wife as if she were a new bride, smiling into her eyes with such love and devotion, Dionne's heart stilled for a moment.

Mark pulled her close, wrapping an arm around her waist and holding her hand as if they'd done this a thousand times before. Dionne closed her eyes and submerged herself in the nearness of him. He tightened his arm to hold her more securely and whirled her in time to the music, for all the world to see. The soft gleam of the lanterns and the dim hum of conversation faded and there was nothing else in her world but Mark. Mark and the music.

He nestled his cheek against the top of her head. "You dance divinely, Mrs. Taylor."

She smiled up into his eyes. "So do you, Mr. Taylor."

"Every man in this place is seething with jealousy. They're wishing they could hold you like this."

She laughed, as he'd intended her to. "It's the women who are jealous."

His delighted smile warmed her clear through. "Poor things. We could really make them suffer."

"How?"

"Like this." Without warning, he dipped her so low she couldn't hold back the tiny scream that escaped her lips. While she lay back, vulnerable and completely dependent upon him to hold her, he waggled his eyebrows comically. "I think we got 'em."

Dionne glanced at the people watching, at the staid, respectable couples standing on the sidelines, the eager young ones, and at Patsy and George a few feet away. Someone laughed aloud, and other couples moved onto the floor with them.

Mark pulled her upright and cradled her against him. "They're *all* jealous."

Dionne laughed again and pushed playfully at his chest. "I thought you were going to drop me."

"Never." He tightened his arm on her waist again, but the teasing light left his eyes. "You can trust me, Dionne."

It was impossible to keep grinning at him when he looked so earnest. "I believe you."

"Do you? I'm glad." The light in his eyes returned, and he whirled her until she lost her breath.

Somehow, she managed to match his footwork and keep up with him. No one but Cicely knew how many hours she'd spent watching old musicals and fantasizing about dancing this way. The only thing missing was a swirling ball gown and heels. But even jeans and tennis shoes couldn't spoil the mood.

Mark slowed, then stopped completely. His chest heaved as he panted slightly, his eyes narrowed with concern. "What's wrong?"

"I was just trying to remember if I've ever had a moment that felt so absolutely perfect before."

The worry left his eyes and a twinkle replaced it. "You haven't."

She scowled at him playfully. "Well, now, how would you know?"

"*I've* never had one," he said, running a fingertip along her cheek and sending delicious shivers of anticipation through her. "So it wouldn't be fair if you had."

He let his gaze travel from her eyes to her lips and linger there. She waited, breathless, knowing he was going to kiss her again, and wanting it with every fiber of her being.

"Mommy? Daddy?" Jared worked his way between them and held up his arms.

Mark laughed, released her for a moment, and settled Jared between them.

"Jared, sweetheart—" Patsy tried to intervene. "Come with me, okay?"

"He's fine," Dionne assured her. "He belongs right here."

"You two were incredible," Patsy said. "Where did you learn to dance like that?"

Mark put an arm around Dionne's waist and they turned together to face Patsy and George. Grinning, she said the first words that came to mind. "From the movies."

"Believe it or not," Mark added, "this is the first time we've ever danced together."

"You're kidding," Patsy argued. "You must have taken lessons."

George let out a deep groan. "Please don't say yes, or she'll have me signed up for the damned things before the end of the week."

"Don't worry," Mark said with a laugh and shared a grin with Dionne. "It's just chemistry."

"And magic," Dionne added.

"Yes." Mark met her gaze again and held it. "And magic."

THE MOOD STAYED with them as they walked home. A million stars shone in the clear night sky, but a soft breeze had dropped the temperature enough to make Dionne wish she had a jacket in addition to her sweater. One by one, other couples and families turned up sidewalks toward their homes and left Dionne feeling as if she, Mark and Jared were the only people on earth.

Mark carried a sleeping Jared high against one shoulder, leaving her free to touch trees, fences, anything and everything that invited contact. And, it seemed, everything did.

She stopped to inhale the fragrance of the night air and turned back to find Mark watching her with an expression that made her heart skip a beat.

He put his free hand on the small of her back. "Did you have a good time tonight?"

"I had a wonderful time," she admitted. "What about you?"

"Perfect." His hand brushed her back lazily, stirring the embers of the passion that had ignited when he'd held her in his arms to dance.

"I've only seen parties like that in the movies," she said.

"They're pretty common fare in small towns. But it wasn't just the party that I enjoyed." He looked deep into her eyes again, the rest of his message as clear as if he'd spoken aloud.

"It wasn't just the party for me, either," she admitted.

They walked on in silence for a moment before Mark spoke again. "We're going to be okay, aren't we? This is going to work."

"Yes." She smiled at him. "I think it is."

He stopped walking and stepped in front of her. "Thank you."

"For what?"

"For agreeing to marry me."

"Thank you for asking."

He laughed softly, a delighted laugh that started deep inside his chest and rolled outward to wrap itself around her. A second later, his laughter stopped and he dipped his head to kiss her.

She relaxed, leaned into the kiss, breathing him in. When his tongue brushed her lips, she opened her mouth and invited him in. The kiss grew more demanding, as if neither of them could get enough, until Jared stirred fitfully.

They broke apart guiltily, and Mark took her hand again. "I guess we should get this guy home to bed."

Dionne laced her fingers with his and leaned her head on his shoulder, wondering if they'd pick up where they'd left off when they got home.

Correction, she thought with a silent laugh. She *hoped* they'd pick up where they left off. She knew exactly where they were headed, and she wanted to race toward their inevitable destination.

MARK CAUGHT HIMSELF whistling as he strolled down the corridor toward his office. And why not? Life was damned good at the moment. Perfect, in fact. He was in love with the most remarkable woman in the world. And even better, she was in love with him.

Making love to her all weekend had made him feel powerful. As if there was nothing that could stop him and no one who would dare get in his way. As if he alone was responsible for the brilliant autumn sunshine outside and the changing leaves that lined the highway of his morning commute.

Still whistling, he stopped in front of Anna's empty desk and checked his box for messages, then turned toward his office. But when he saw her standing in the doorway wearing a knowing grin, he checked his step and let his song die away.

"You're certainly in a good mood today," she teased. "I wonder why."

"Nice weather," he said with an innocent shrug.

"Yes. Very." She stepped aside to let him enter and followed him inside. "It must have been warm at your house this weekend."

"Like a tropical island." He took off his suit jacket and set his briefcase on the desk. "And I have you to thank."

"Not having to put up with your bad moods is thanks enough." She rested her hands on the back of a chair. "I hate to burst your bubble, but Royal said to send you to his office as soon as you got in."

"Fine."

"He said he's got another new case for you."

"Great."

"On top of all the others? Aren't you even going to get upset?"

Mark laughed and put on his suit jacket again. "Nope. Nothing could spoil my mood today, not even Royal."

He left her sitting in his office and whistled all the way to Royal's huge corner office. He listened without batting an eye to the details of the case Royal wanted to dump in his lap. He even smiled all the way through his first court case of the morning and stopped at the florist shop on the corner to order roses for Dionne and buy a small bouquet to thank Anna.

But when he settled the flowers amidst the files, documents and other clutter on Anna's desk and caught the look in her eyes, his smile faded. "What's wrong?"

She stood and motioned toward his door. "I'll tell you in your office."

Praying that nothing had happened to Dionne or Jared, he followed her inside and closed the door. "What is it?"

"Marianne called while you were in court."

Mark tried not to acknowledge the apprehension that curled in his stomach. "Marianne who?"

"Your ex-girlfriend. Jared's mother."

"What the hell did she want?"

"She wouldn't tell me," Anna said with a bitter smile. "And believe me, I tried to find out. She just said to have you call her."

He took the message slip she offered with Marianne's name and number scrawled across it, barely resisting the urge to crumple it into a ball and toss it away. Whatever she wanted, it couldn't be good.

Anna obviously shared his opinion. "Be careful. She's up to something."

Nodding grimly, he crossed to his desk and yanked the receiver from the hook. Anna watched him in silence, then let herself out and shut the door behind her with a soft click.

He punched in the long-distance number, taking out his nervousness on the dial pad, clenching his jaw so tightly it hurt. When she answered, he barely kept his fear under control. "What do you want?"

"Mark?"

"Who else?"

"Thank you for calling me back."

"What do you want, Marianne?"

"I've been doing a lot of thinking in the past couple of months."

"If you're calling to say you want Jared back, you can go straight to hell."

"Is that what you think?"

"What else should I think?"

She must have realized that he was in no mood to chat because her voice changed subtly. "All right. I'll get to the point." She took a deep breath, as if she needed courage for what came next. "I have to come back to Boston later this week, and I'd like to see you."

"We have no reason to see each other."

"I think we do. Seeing you again during the summer made me realize that I need to see the baby again, too."

It was his worst nightmare and Dionne's biggest fear come true. "Over my dead body."

Marianne sighed again. "You really do hate me, don't you?"

"Hate is a weak word for what I'm feeling right now."

"For what it's worth, I'm sorry for what happened between us."

"I don't give a damn about what happened between us," he assured her. "It's what you're trying to do now that matters."

"I'm not trying to do anything. I'd just like to see you and the baby."

"Forget it."

She took her time before she responded to that. "Obviously, you're upset. Why don't you think about it? I'll be at the Oyster House at noon on Wednesday. If you change your mind, you can find me there." And without giving him another chance to refuse, she disconnected.

THE WEATHER THAT EVENING matched Mark's mood perfectly. Wind howled and tossed tree branches against the house. Windows rattled, and leaves skittered across the patio. He sat back in his seat and watched Jared playing with building blocks in one corner of the kitchen. And the anger he'd been nursing all afternoon surged again.

Marianne had wreaked havoc on his life once. Now she threatened it again. Worse, she threatened his family. The urge to protect Dionne and Jared swelled within him, and he made a solemn vow not to let her hurt either of them.

Unfortunately, the more he thought about Marianne, the more convinced he became that the only way to stop her was to meet her. If he didn't, there was no telling what she'd do next.

Dionne poured another cup of coffee and raised the pot in silent question. He knew she could sense that something was bothering him, and he tried to hide his churning emotions. Nodding, he pushed his cup closer for a refill.

She filled his cup and poured one for herself. "You really don't mind watching Jared while I study again tonight?"

"Of course not," he told her. "I'm his father, not his sitter. You don't have to make arrangements with me to take care of him. I love the time he and I spend together."

She sat on the seat beside his and her thigh brushed against his. "I know you do. Maybe I'm just looking for an excuse not to study."

He tried to smile, but he knew it probably came out looking more like a grimace. "Why don't you want to study? Don't you like your classes?"

"I love them," she said quickly. "They're fascinating. But between your job and my school, it feels as if we never get time together. And now Patsy wants me to go shopping with her in Boston on Saturday—"

"You're going, aren't you?"

"I don't know." She watched Jared pull some plastic bowls from a cupboard, then added, "I'd rather spend time with you."

She wouldn't want to be around him if she could see the darkness inside. He wasn't fit company tonight. He took a sip of coffee before he responded.

"You should go. It will do you good to go out with a friend."

"You'd have to stay with him," she warned.

"That's fine. I told you already I don't mind."

Her gaze traveled over his face and her eyebrows knit as if she could see right through him. "What's wrong?"

He had to be more careful if he didn't want to frighten her. He took another long sip and lowered his cup to the table carefully. "What makes you think there's something wrong?"

"You seem distracted."

He stood and started clearing the dinner dishes away. "I had a hard day at work. Big case."

"Do you want to talk about it?"

"There's nothing to talk about."

"I wish you would." Dionne stepped in front of him. "I know almost nothing about what you do all day."

"It would only bore you."

"Not if it interests you." She smiled softly. "I'll admit, the law isn't exactly the most fascinating subject to me, but it would help me understand you better if I knew how you felt about the cases you're working on. Or are they all top secret?"

"No, not really. I can't divulge names, but issues of law are fair game for conversation."

"Then tell me about an issue of law."

He tried to think of one, but Marianne's call wiped all the details from his mind. "Maybe later," he said, sidestepping her and stacking the dishes by the sink.

He could see Dionne's reflection in the window, the slight narrowing of her eyes. "I don't like it when you pull away like this."

"I'm not pulling away." He forced himself to face her again, though it was hard to do with the lie between them. "I just have a lot on my mind and I'd rather talk about something else."

She searched his face for a moment, and her eyes looked so sad he wanted to kick himself. "Is this how it's going to be every time something bothers you? Are you going to pull away and shut me out?"

"No." And it wouldn't be, he assured himself. He argued with himself for a moment more, then reluctantly realized he owed Dionne the truth—no matter how frightening it might be, no matter how hard it was for him to tell her. "It's not a case that has me worried," he admitted at last.

"I didn't think so."

He motioned for her to sit and took the seat across from hers. "It's Marianne."

Dionne's eyes widened and the blood drained from her face. "What about her?"

"She called me today at the office. She wants to see Jared."

"No!" The word exploded between them and that same panic that had been so much a part of her when they first met filled her eyes. "Why?"

"I don't know."

Dionne shook her head quickly. "Tell me the truth. She wants him back, doesn't she?"

Mark covered one of her hands with his, trying to comfort her.

She jerked it away and stood. "Don't say anything more. Let me get Jared into the other room. I don't want him to hear any of this."

"You stay. I'll do it."

"No. No, I need to. I want to." Her voice trembled. Her eyes darted frantically around the room as if she expected Marianne to materialize before her eyes.

He waited for her to come back, too agitated to sit still, too angry with Marianne to think clearly. When Dionne returned, he tried again to comfort her. "Don't worry, sweetheart. I'm not going to let her barge in here and start telling us what to do."

"You can't let her see him, Mark." Dionne kept her voice low and put one trembling hand on his chest. "You can't. If she does, she'll want him back."

He covered her hand and tried to calm her. "I'll take care of it, I promise."

Her eyes strayed to the doorway where she could see Jared playing. "Promise me you won't let her see him."

The legalities of Marianne's position rose up in front of him and kept him from making a vow he might not be able to keep. "I'll handle her."

Dionne paced away from him and stared out the patio door into the night. Mark watched her, wishing he could guarantee that Marianne wouldn't be a problem.

He had no idea what he was going to do or say. He only knew his happiness and his family's depended on him.

MARK STOOD just inside the dimly lit lounge and looked for Marianne. The building had been a tavern in colonial times, and the low-beamed ceilings and huge fireplace in the center of the room, the pewter trays and pitchers lining the dark brick and wood walls, all gave the place atmosphere.

Dionne would love it here, though she'd raise her eyebrows at the prices. And he'd love to bring her.

Later.

Today, more important things demanded his attention. The past two days of watching Dionne worry had been pure hell. This morning at the office had dragged by so slowly, he'd started wondering if he'd go stark, raving mad waiting for noon to roll around.

Now that it had, his nerves were shot. The conversation and laughter of the other diners irritated him and his palms were sweat-slick from dread. Just as he began to suspect that Marianne had changed her mind, he spied her at a corner table nursing a drink.

He tried to affect the cool, unruffled look he used in court and made his way through the crowded restaurant to her table. "I want you to stay the hell away from me and my family."

Her smile faltered and died. "That's a nice greeting. Didn't your mother even teach you to say hello before you attack?"

"Hello."

"That's better. Now, I'm here because I want to see the baby."

"No."

"He's my son."

"You gave up that right," Mark said, his voice low. "You gave it up when you gave *him* up."

Marianne's jaw set in the stubborn lines he knew so well. "I haven't given anything up—not legally. Why are you always so quick to assume the worst of me?"

"Maybe because that's the side I've seen most."

She laughed harshly. ''And you've always been a paragon of virtue, I suppose.''

''I have my faults,'' he admitted, ''but I didn't run away when the going got tough. I didn't hide Jared from you. And I sure as hell didn't abandon him.''

She flushed slightly and tilted her head to one side. ''We're butting heads again, you know. This is exactly what went wrong between us in the first place.'' She trailed her finger along the rim of her glass. ''I didn't ask to meet you so we could argue, Mark. And I don't want to take the baby away from you and Dionne, if that's what you're worried about. I just want closure on that episode in my life.''

''Episode?''

''You know what I mean.''

He eyed her suspiciously and tried not to get his hopes up. ''You'd better be telling me the truth, because there's no way in hell I'll ever let you take him.''

She smiled. ''He's really gotten to you, hasn't he?''

''He's my son.''

''And mine.''

''And *Dionne's*.''

''I gave birth to him.''

''She's been raising him.''

''I know she has.'' Marianne turned her glass slowly. ''What is he like?''

''Do you care?''

''I'm curious.''

Touching. Again, he tried to rein in his irritation and hoped she'd get what she needed and go away for good. ''He's a good boy. Stubborn.''

''Like you?''

"Worse." In spite of his apprehension, he smiled.

"And he's totally bonded with Dionne?"

The question chilled him. "She's his mother. The only mother he'll ever know."

Her eyes traveled over his face and to his surprise, he saw nothing but mild curiosity there. "You've really fallen for her, haven't you?"

"Yes, I have."

"Are you in love with her?"

"Yes."

"It's written all over your face." Marianne looked almost wistful. "I'm happy for you, Mark. And for her." She brushed a lock of hair from her cheek and crossed her legs. "And all this hostility I'm getting is because you're worried that I'm going to hurt her?"

"Something like that."

She took a drink and carefully lowered her glass to the table. "I don't want to take Jared away from her, Mark. Truly, I don't. I just need to see him, that's all. I want to see how he's turned out so far Then I'll go away and leave you alone."

"What about later? Will you want to see him again in two years, or ten, or fifteen?"

"Maybe." She pulled her hand away and shrugged. "I don't know. But even if I do, what can it hurt?"

"It can hurt a lot, Marianne. I won't ask Dionne to live with that kind of uncertainty."

"But you're willing to let me live with it?"

"You can't reject a child one day and then decide you want him back the next. You can't place a baby in a mother's arms and then rip him away again." His voice tightened. "It was your choice, Marianne.

And the rest of us have been paying the price for it. If you have to pay one now, that seems only fair.''

Her gaze faltered and some of her certainty vanished. ''I wouldn't have been a good mother, you know. I never was as big on family as you were.''

He didn't respond to that. He forced himself to wait as he would have if he'd been facing opposing counsel across a conference table.

''Will you ever tell him about me?''

He hid his elation and said, ''Probably.''

''He'll have questions.''

''Dionne and I will answer them.''

''Maybe he'll want to meet me. Have you thought about that?''

''If he does, we'll find you. But I'm not leaving this open-ended so you can come and go whenever you please. It wouldn't be fair to Jared or to Dionne.''

She linked her hands together on the table. ''You're quite the papa bear, aren't you?''

''Call it what you want. I take care of the people I love. I'm not going to ask Dionne to live with you lurking in the background, and I'm not going to confuse Jared.''

''You're still as hard-nosed as ever, aren't you? No compromises. No prisoners.''

''I'll compromise,'' he said, feeling the familiar rush of imminent success begin to move through him. ''If you'll sign the consent-for-adoption forms, I'll let you see him once. But you'll have to promise in return that you'll go away and not come back unless we contact you when he's older. You can't come and go whenever it's convenient for you, Marianne. That's pure selfishness.''

"I've already agreed to give you custody," she reminded him, "and the court has approved it. Why do you still need a consent form?"

"It's not for me," he told her. "It's for Dionne and Jared. She needs to know he's really hers. He needs the stability of having a mother around forever."

Marianne thought about it for so long, he began to worry. But she finally conceded. "All right. You have a deal."

"Good." He struggled to keep his face impassive, but the thought of Dionne's reaction to the news made him light-headed.

"I guess the only things we still need to work out are where and when."

"Saturday," he said without hesitation. "Dionne's going shopping with a friend, so I can get away easily."

Marianne's eyes widened. "You're not going to tell her?"

"Not until everything's signed, sealed and delivered."

She laughed and tossed her head to see him better. "So, it's okay for *you* to keep secrets."

The last thing he needed was a lecture on ethics from Marianne. He stood and glared down at her. "I'm not bringing Jared all the way to Boston, but I'll meet you halfway. Riverside Park in Welby's Landing at two o'clock. I'll bring the documents for you to sign."

She laughed again. "You're not taking any chances, are you?"

"No."

"Okay. I'll bring a pen." And when he turned away, she added, "Until Saturday, then."

He left the restaurant quickly, anxious to leave Marianne behind, equally anxious to escape the guilt made worse by her observation. He *was* keeping a secret from Dionne, he told himself as he strode back to his office. But after the way she'd reacted to the idea of Marianne seeing Jared, how could he tell her he'd compromised? Once she saw why he'd agreed, she'd understand. And he fully intended to tell her the truth as soon as he could offer her some peace of mind to go with it.

That made all the difference.

CHAPTER FIFTEEN

NEARLY DEAD on her feet, Dionne trailed Patsy along the sidewalk. The bags she carried—full of pants and shirts for Jared and a fisherman sweater she hadn't been able to resist for Mark—dug into her fingers and dragged at her arms. Thinking about Marianne dragged at her heart.

Mark had promised to think of a solution that would protect them all, but Dionne still hadn't slept well all week. She'd suggested that she talk to Marianne, hoping she could appeal to her cousin, but Mark had discouraged her. He and Marianne had issues to resolve, and Dionne had agreed to let him handle it—for now. But if he wasn't successful, she'd confront Marianne herself. She'd had trouble concentrating at school and she'd started the day exhausted and nearly a week behind in her homework. If she hadn't agreed to come shopping with Patsy, if Mark hadn't encouraged her to do something to take her mind off things, she would have stayed home.

She'd left home hoping he was right—that spending the day with Patsy would help push Marianne to the back of her mind, that some quality time with a friend would help her relax. But it hadn't helped. Instead, the exhaustion had grown so overwhelming, she wondered if she might be coming down with something.

On the plus side, Patsy had changed her mind about driving all the way to the city and had suggested instead that they stop at the outlet stores midway between Longs Mill and Boston. Dionne hadn't argued. The drive through the woods, now deep in the change of seasons, had been breathtaking, but she'd been more than ready to stop when Patsy pulled into the parking lot.

Now, on the sidewalk in front of her, Patsy slowed her step and sniffed the air. "Can you smell that?"

Dionne barely managed to stop before she plowed into Patsy's back. She could smell something, but the aroma made her stomach pitch. "What is it?"

"Food, silly." Patsy grinned back at her. "I don't know about you, but I'm starving. Let's grab something to eat and take it to the park."

Dionne checked her watch and noted with surprise that it was already past two o'clock. She should be hungry after the meager breakfast she'd forced herself to eat, but she wasn't. Worry and her constant state of exhaustion were even starting to affect her appetite.

"And afterward," Patsy said, picking up the pace and heading toward a hamburger stand, "we're going to buy something for you."

"I told you," Dionne said, huffing a little as she hurried after her friend. "I don't want anything."

"Don't be silly." Patsy drew up in front of the building and pushed open the door. "You've completely spoiled the men in your house. Now it's your turn. What do you need?"

For Marianne to disappear and leave us alone, she thought. But she said only, "About ten more hours every day and a long nap every afternoon."

"Can't help you there. What else?"

"A clone. I love the courses I'm taking, but school's wearing me out. I'm exhausted all the time. I feel as if I could fall asleep right here."

Patsy laughed and moved to the end of a line leading to the counter. "Maybe you're doing too much."

"Maybe," Dionne said skeptically. "But this shouldn't be harder than working full-time and being a single mother. Mark's been getting Jared to bed every night while I'm supposed to be studying. Instead, I fall asleep."

"All the more reason to relax in the park while we eat." Patsy moved up in line. "What do you want for lunch?"

Dionne studied the menu, but nothing sounded even remotely appetizing. "Maybe just a salad."

"You should try one of their Philly sandwiches. They're positively wicked. Cheese and onion and peppers, and beef this thick." Patsy held up her fingers to illustrate.

Just the sound of it made Dionne nauseated. She shook her head quickly. "I'll stick with the salad. I don't think my stomach could handle the sandwich."

Patsy eyed her suspiciously. "Are you sick?"

"I'm not sure. I don't feel bad all the time. The queasiness comes and goes. I'm probably just overtired."

Patsy turned to face her. "Is it worse when you're hungry?"

Dionne thought back over the past few days. "Yes, but then I have no appetite."

A slow smile stretched Patsy's mouth. "And in the mornings?"

"I think so."

"As in *morning sickness?*"

The suggestion stunned Dionne and made her take a step back. She'd never been able to get pregnant with Brent. She *couldn't* be pregnant now. "No, it's not that. It can't be."

"Why not?"

"Because…" Dionne shook her head frantically. "It's impossible."

Patsy tucked her hand under Dionne's arm and gave her a gentle squeeze. "Correct me if I'm wrong, but you are a married woman. And I'm assuming that you and Mark have a healthy relationship…if you know what I mean."

"Well, yes. But—" Dionne's thoughts flew in a thousand directions at once. She and Mark had taken precautions after the first couple of nights together, but there *had* been those two nights.

Patsy leaned a little closer and whispered, "Are you late?"

Dionne had stopped keeping track of her monthly cycle after Brent's death, and it took her a few seconds to calculate it now. When she realized she was overdue by several days, her knees grew weak. "I think I might be," she whispered.

Part of her wanted to be pregnant and experience the miracle of creating another life. She longed to carry Mark's child and to give Jared a brother or sister. But she also knew that a pregnancy would complicate everything just when their relationship was beginning to work. And she didn't even want to think about how it would affect school.

Patsy laughed softly. "Now we know what to buy for you. We'll stop somewhere and pick up a home pregnancy test."

Dionne managed to nod. "Thanks. I think that would be a good idea." If she *was* pregnant, how would Mark take the news? Knowing how he felt about Jared, she couldn't imagine him being anything less than ecstatic. Of course, he'd be thrilled. And having a baby would forge another link between them and maybe make Marianne think twice about trying to take Jared back…unless it encouraged her because she figured they'd have someone to take Jared's place.

While she stood by and struggled with her conflicting emotions, Patsy placed their orders and collected their food. Dionne followed her across the street to the park, still too stunned to do much more than listen to Patsy's running monologue about her own pregnancies.

With every passing minute, the idea of being pregnant grew on her. But she told herself not to get her hopes up. She didn't want to be disappointed if the test came back negative.

MARK HELD ON TO Jared with one hand and his briefcase with the other as they walked slowly through the park. Marianne was nearly half an hour late, but Mark wasn't ready to give up and go home. If she didn't show, he'd track her down. One way or another, he'd have her signature on the consent for adoption before the sun set tonight.

Jared stopped to pick up a pebble and held it out to him. "See, Daddy?"

"For me? Thank you, son." Mark slipped the pebble into his pocket and smiled when Jared picked up another for himself. Today, with the threat Marianne posed looming in front of him, Mark understood

Dionne better than he ever had. She had countless memories of time spent alone with Jared, but they would never be enough. The more time Mark spent with his son, the more time he wanted.

It was hard for him to believe that such a short time ago he hadn't even known Dionne and Jared existed. Now, his world revolved around them.

When a man walking a dog caught Jared's attention, Mark let him watch for a moment, then urged him forward again. "Come on, sport. Let's go around the loop again."

When Jared held back, Mark set his briefcase on the ground and lifted the boy onto his hip. "How about a piggyback ride? Would you like that?"

Jared nodded and Mark settled the boy on his shoulders. "Hang on tight and don't let go, okay?"

"Okay." Jared laced his fingers through Mark's hair. "Run, Daddy."

Mark didn't want to go too fast, so he set off at a gentle trot, holding Jared's legs tightly. He circled the briefcase twice, delighting in his son's laughter. On the third circle, he caught sight of Marianne on the edge of the lawn watching them.

He slowed from a trot to a walk, then stopped completely and steeled himself while she hurried across the grass toward them.

"Sorry I'm late," she said when she drew closer. "I got caught in a last-minute meeting about this case I'm working on and couldn't get away."

"No harm done." Mark tilted his head to look at Jared. "Ready to get down?"

"No. Again."

Even with Marianne watching, Mark wasn't going to deny his son. He trotted twice more around the briefcase, then helped Jared down. "Let's get your trucks out, okay? You can play with those for a few minutes."

Jared looked disappointed, but not for long. Laughing mischievously, he set off at a run toward the other side of the lawn.

Mark raced after him, scooped him up again, and carried him back toward Marianne. "I need to talk to this lady for a minute, son. Will you play with your trucks while I do?"

Jared thought about that for a second, then nodded. "Okay."

Mark led them both toward a park bench, spent a few minutes settling Jared on the grass nearby with his trucks, and left the briefcase open on the bench beside him.

"So," Marianne said when he turned his attention to her again, "this is Jared. He looks like you."

"Thank you."

"He seems happy."

"He is."

"I'm glad." Marianne ran a finger along the chain of her necklace and sighed softly. "That's what I wanted for him."

Mark watched Jared for a few minutes in silence. "I haven't thanked you for him, and I need to. He's the most incredible person I've ever met."

Jared chose that moment to drive a truck across Mark's foot and chortle with glee.

"It's hard to believe I had anything to do with bringing him into the world," Marianne said with a sad smile. "I didn't want to see him when he was born, so he's always seemed a little unreal to me. I think that's why I needed to see him now. Just once,'' she added quickly, ''before he's really not mine anymore.''

Mark's heart skipped a beat. ''Then you're still willing to sign the consent?''

She looked back at Jared, then nodded. ''I gave my word.''

Her word had never meant much between them, but Mark had to trust her now.

''I suppose you brought it with you,'' she said.

''I did.''

Marianne leaned against the bench to see him better. ''You know, in one way you haven't changed a bit. But in another, you've become a completely different person. When I saw you running around on the grass with Jared on your shoulders, I thought I was seeing things.''

He laughed softly and ran his hand along the back of his neck. ''I am a different person,'' he admitted. ''But I'll still do anything to protect my family.''

She held up both hands to ward off the warning. ''You don't need to protect them from me. I'm fully prepared to sign. I just needed to see him.'' She trailed her gaze back to Jared and a fond smile curved her lips. ''I was right to give him to Dionne and so wrong to keep him from you. Can you ever forgive me?''

The question wiped away the rest of his wariness. ''Yes, I can,'' he said, touching her arm gently. ''Because everything worked out for the best, just the way you did it.''

MARK'S CAR wasn't in the driveway when Patsy dropped her off, but Dionne thought that might be just as well. This way, she wouldn't have to disappoint him if Patsy was wrong.

After promising at least a dozen times to call with the test results, Dionne watched her new friend drive away. Inside the house, she dropped her bags to the floor and let out a sigh. She kicked off her shoes, resisted the impulse to stretch out on the couch for a few minutes, and started toward the stairs.

First, the pregnancy test, she told herself. Then she could relax and plan how to tell Mark if the results were positive. She hugged the idea to herself as she walked past the telephone table, but the blinking light on the answering machine stopped her.

Wondering if Mark had left a message about where he'd gone, she pressed the button and listened.

"Mark? Mark, are you there?"

Dionne recognized Marianne's voice immediately and she had to clutch the table for support.

"Mark, if you're there, pick up."

Fear slammed her like a fist in the stomach. She covered her mouth and listened, every nerve taut.

"Well, I hope you get this before you leave. I'm going to be about an hour late to meet you and Jared—"

There was more, but Dionne's body reacted so violently she barely heard the rest. She retched, covered her stomach with one hand, and ran up the stairs toward the bathroom. It was a false alarm, but she wondered if she might have felt better if the urge had been real.

Why was Mark meeting Marianne? Obviously, he'd agreed to let her see Jared, in spite of Dionne's objections. But why? If there'd been a good reason, a valid reason, surely he would have told her. So why was he sneaking around behind her back?

The only possible reason snaked through her, making her nausea return even more strongly. Why did any man sneak around to meet a woman? There was only one reason. Only one.

Now she understood why he'd discouraged *her* from talking with Marianne. With a dreadful certainty, she knew that the past six weeks had been a lie. Mark had used her to get Jared. He'd deceived her. He'd made her think he loved her. And like a fool, she'd believed him.

He was planning to leave, just as her father had. The only difference was, Mark planned to take *his* child with him.

She pushed back to her feet, knees wobbling, head throbbing, stomach still rolling. Fear filled her, so strong she could almost taste it. She moved as quickly as she could, and crossed the hall to Jared's room. Praying silently, she threw open the door to his closet. When she saw his tiny clothes still hanging there, tears of relief filled her eyes.

She checked his drawers next and made sure all his favorite toys were still scattered around the room. Yes. Everything was still here. Leaning against the wall to steady herself, she took several deep breaths to restore calm and get her mind working again.

Instinct told her to pack her things and run. But she wouldn't go anywhere without Jared. And she couldn't grab him and walk out the door while Mark was here or he'd stop her. She'd just have to bide her time and wait for the opportunity to get away safely.

Still trembling, she made her way to her bedroom,

sank onto the foot of the bed, and tried to formulate a plan. She had no cash except the leftover grocery money, and that wasn't enough to get them very far. She had Mark's credit cards, but he could track her too easily if she used them.

Maybe running wasn't the answer. Mark had found her once. He could easily find her again. As Jared's legal father, the law would be on his side. No matter how frightened she was, she couldn't do anything illegal or she could lose Jared forever.

And what if she was pregnant?

Her stomach lurched again. The knowledge that Mark would be able to do this again if he wanted to brought on a wave of helplessness.

She stood abruptly and paced to the window. Maybe she should find an attorney. One who believed in her case. But who? And where?

Boston was full of attorneys, but any of them might be friends of Mark's. How would she ever know which of them she could trust?

Dashing away tears with the back of her hand, she pivoted from the window and told herself to be strong. Mark might have connections, he might know his way around the court system, he might have more money than she did and the law on his side, but surely she had rights as well.

First things first, she decided. She'd do the pregnancy test and plan her next move after she saw the results. As she started toward the living room where she'd left her bags, the shrill ringing of the telephone stopped her in her tracks. She stared at it, suddenly unable to move.

Who could it be?

Patsy? She might have some suggestions about where Dionne could find legal help.

What if it was Mark? What would she say to him? How would she hide her fear? Clutching her hands in front of her, she listened while it rang twice more, then forced herself to answer just before the answering machine clicked on.

"Hello, Dionne. Am I interrupting something important?"

Mark's mother. Of all people. Dionne sank onto the couch, fought another wave of tears, and tried desperately to keep her voice sounding normal. "No. I'm just waiting for Mark and Jared to get home."

"Oh? Well, I'm glad to hear Mark is giving you a day off. I'm sure you could use some time to yourself." Barbara's voice sounded oddly strained, but Dionne told herself she was just imagining it. "What have you done with yourself while they've been gone?"

Had my heart broken, she thought. *Had my world destroyed.* But she said only, "I went shopping with a friend."

"Wonderful. You've been so busy, I'm glad to hear you're doing something for yourself."

Dionne closed her eyes and tried to control the tears she felt threatening. This woman had accepted her into the family without question. Barbara had given Dionne a place to belong, and Dionne would miss her horribly.

"Listen, dear, I'm calling because I need to ask you a favor. But if this is an imposition, I want you to say so…"

Dionne refused to let Mark's behavior affect the

way she treated his parents. "Of course, Barbara. What is it?"

"Nigel has to have some tests done at a hospital in Boston starting early Monday morning. We need to check him in tomorrow, and he may need to stay for a few days."

Dionne held her breath. "It's nothing serious, I hope."

"His doctor says it's not." Barbara sounded so sad, Dionne's heart broke for her. "Anyway, I'm calling to ask if we could impose on you for a day or two."

"You want to stay here with us?" How could she face them now? But how could she say no?

"If you don't mind. I wouldn't even ask, but the drive between here and Boston is so long. And I remember Mark saying that your house has a third bedroom." She must have hesitated too long because Barbara's voice changed subtly. "If it's a problem, we can just stay in a hotel."

"It's no problem at all, Barbara." The words came out slowly, hesitantly. She forced herself to sound more certain. "Of course you can stay here."

"If you're sure. We don't want to intrude."

"I'm positive. Mark will be thrilled when I tell him."

Barbara sighed. "We were thinking of driving down this evening. We thought it would be nice to spend some more time getting to know you. And, of course, we'd love a chance to see Jared again."

"That's fine." Maybe having them around would actually help. It might create a buffer between her and Mark and give her time to firm up her plans.

"What time will you get here? Will you join us for dinner?"

"That would be lovely. But don't go to any trouble. Something simple will be fine." Barbara's voice went soft as she spoke to Nigel, then said, "We're leaving now, so we should be there around six."

"Wonderful." Dionne rubbed her forehead and tried to still the sudden pounding there. "I'll have the room ready for you."

When she replaced the receiver a moment later, she rested her forehead on her knees and let out a soul-wrenching sigh. The last thing she wanted was to spend another night in Mark's bed, but she couldn't think of any way to avoid it without tipping her hand.

Slowly, she lifted her head again and stood. She crossed to the door and gathered the bags she'd dropped there. Taking a steadying breath, she pulled out the pregnancy test and carried it up the stairs.

DIONNE STARED at the test-result window in horror while two deep pink stripes formed in front of her eyes. Positive. She was pregnant. It should have been the happiest moment of her life. But it was one of the worst she could remember.

She touched the plastic case with one trembling finger, then drew her hand away quickly as if it might contaminate her. As if she needed more proof, her stomach gave a sickening lurch. She dropped to the floor and leaned her head against the cool porcelain.

What was she going to do?

She couldn't tell Mark. She couldn't tell Barbara and Nigel. She couldn't even call Cicely. Cicely would confront Mark, which would be the *worst* thing she could do. And Patsy would no doubt react exactly the same way.

She couldn't confide in anyone.

It wasn't the first time she'd had to face something difficult on her own. But she'd started getting used to having people in her corner, to feeling as if she belonged somewhere. And having that security yanked out from underneath her made everything worse.

Tears threatened again, but she forced them away. Crying wouldn't help. She had to remain strong.

But when she heard Mark's car pull into the driveway a few minutes later, her resolve weakened. Heart racing, she gathered all the evidence of the pregnancy test and stuffed it into a garbage bag.

Working quickly, before he could come inside and find her, she searched for a hiding place. In desperation, she shoved the bag into her drawer in the bathroom behind her makeup and toiletries. Then she squared her shoulders and slowly walked down the stairs to face the man who'd betrayed her.

WHISTLING UNDER his breath, Mark put his key in the lock and turned it. After his meeting with Marianne, he'd spent a pleasant afternoon celebrating with Jared in the park. Unfortunately, he'd stayed longer than he'd planned at the petting zoo, but Jared had been so entranced by the animals, Mark hadn't had the heart to pull him away.

While he drove and Jared slept in his car seat, he'd planned the best way to give Dionne the signed consent for adoption. Simply handing it to her seemed almost anticlimactic. He wanted to do something special.

Maybe he'd take her out for a romantic candlelight dinner—without Jared—and give it to her there. Or maybe he'd talk to Patsy and make arrangements for Jared to spend the night with her and George. Or he could wrap it in a box and give it to her for her birthday...except he didn't want to wait that long.

He couldn't wait to see the look on her face. And he took great pleasure in the knowledge that he could finally give her the one thing she wanted most—security. He'd finally make her as happy as she'd made him in the past few weeks.

In all the years he'd dreamed about having a home and family, he'd never imagined it this good. The house had become a haven to him, a place where he could escape the pressures of the office, the demands of clients, and the worries of real life.

And Dionne was the main reason their home felt like such a sanctuary.

She managed to soothe him and drive him to distraction at the same time. Her eyes, her lips, the soft curve of her neck. Her inner strength, her courage and that incredible determination, all housed in one deliciously sexy body.

Still whistling, he unlocked the door and stepped inside. But when he saw Dionne standing in the middle of the room, his step faltered. She wore a form-fitting sweater and jeans that hugged every curve. But her eyes looked wild, and he could almost feel the tension radiating from her.

He shifted Jared to his other arm, pocketed the keys, and pushed the door shut with his foot. "What's wrong?"

Her eyes widened with surprise. "What makes you think something's wrong?"

"Because it's written all over your face."

She turned away and folded her arms as if she needed to protect herself from him. He'd seen clients use the same defense mechanism when they faced something unpleasant, and it made all his senses leap to the alert.

"Your parents called earlier," she said. "Your dad has to have some tests run at the hospital over the next couple of days."

Concern immediately replaced his wariness. "What kind of tests?"

Her expression softened slightly. "Your mother didn't give me any details, but she assured me they're nothing serious."

"But you don't believe her?"

"I don't know. She sounded worried."

"I'm sure she did. My dad's never sick." Mark put Jared on the floor beside his blocks and studied her cool expression. "What else?"

Her shoulders stiffened, but she forced a smile. "They want to stay here with us so your mother can be close to the hospital. Nigel has to check in tomorrow."

He let out a relieved laugh and closed some of the distance between them. "I'm glad that's the only problem. I was beginning to think I'd done something wrong."

Her eyes flew to his face, then away just as quickly.

"I know you're not used to having people around all the time," he said, sliding his arms around her waist. "But my parents won't be any bother. And we do have an extra bedroom now, you know."

He expected her to relax. Instead, she grew even

more rigid and stepped away from his embrace. "I know."

Her reaction confused him. He took a step back and studied her face for a long moment. "Do you want to tell me what you're really upset about?"

"I'm tired," she said, picking up Jared and holding him to her. "I've just spent the last hour getting the bedroom ready for your parents."

"You should have waited. I would have helped you."

"If you'd come home earlier, I would have let you."

He still had the unsettled feeling that she wasn't telling him everything. "I didn't plan to be so late. I took Jared to the petting zoo and lost track of time."

She smiled, but there was no warmth in it. "How nice."

For the life of him, he couldn't figure out why she was behaving so coldly toward him. He hadn't done anything wrong. He hadn't even been around. A few hours ago, she'd been looking forward to shopping with Patsy, and she'd kissed him so thoroughly before she left, he'd been tempted to try coaxing her to stay.

Now, the inexplicable chill brought back vivid memories of his last few weeks with Marianne. "I know you had a lot to do, but this isn't my fault."

She leveled him with a glance, but she didn't say a word.

Confusion made his next words come out a little too harsh. "Why are you angry with me? *I* didn't tell my parents they could come."

"*You* weren't here to take their call."

"Is that what you're upset about? That I went somewhere with Jared?"

She took another deep breath and let it out slowly. "No."

"Well, you can't possibly blame me because my dad needs to have some medical tests done."

"Of course not."

"Maybe you should have told my parents not to come."

She rounded on him, eyes blazing. "Are you telling me I should have sent them to a hotel?"

"If having them here is going to upset you—and obviously it is—then maybe you should have."

She laughed bitterly. Obviously affected by the anger and harsh words, Jared squirmed to get back onto the floor. She put him down, but she seemed reluctant to let him go. "Of course, your parents aren't a problem, Mark. I'm just tired."

He wanted desperately to believe her, but the truth glared out at him from her icy blue eyes. He pressed a little harder. "I don't want to be arguing when my parents get here, so why don't you just spit it out—whatever it is."

"We won't be arguing." She turned away from him, making it clear she didn't want to talk about it anymore.

Mark bit back his frustration. For one desperate second he thought about showing her the papers Marianne had signed in the park. But he wanted that to be a happy moment, not a last-ditch attempt to coax her out of a bad mood.

It was pretty damned clear to him, though, as he watched her leave the room without a backward glance, that home wouldn't be much of a sanctuary tonight.

AT LONG LAST, Mark closed the bedroom door to shut out the rest of the world. His parents were settled in Dionne's old room and Jared was sound asleep across the hall. Mark could finally have some time alone with her and, hopefully, get to the bottom of whatever it was that had her so edgy.

He turned slowly and looked at her. She sat on the foot of the bed, hands linked on her lap, gaze averted.

After their initial argument, she'd put up a convincing front all evening. But he could tell by the set of her shoulders and the grim look on her face that she was still upset with him.

And he still had no clue why.

He turned out the overhead light, leaving only the soft glow of a bedside lamp to illuminate the room. And he tried not to notice how beautiful she looked, or how intimate the setting was. It was obvious she wasn't interested in romance tonight.

Mark could live without it, even though he wouldn't have turned down a chance to explore that new facet of their relationship. Right now, it was far more important that they clear the air between them. And to do that, he needed her to talk to him.

He took his loose change from his pocket and put it on the dresser. "Are you still upset?"

She glanced at him, just a flick of the eyes. "I'm not upset."

He took off his watch and tried to act as if he believed her. "So how was your shopping trip today? Did you and Patsy have fun?"

"Fun?" She sent another contemptuous glance in his direction. "Not especially."

The look on her face gave him an idea and a tiny bit of hope that maybe this wasn't about him, after all. "Did something happen between you and Patsy?"

"No. She's a good friend," Dionne said evenly. "And don't worry. I didn't spent much money."

"I don't care about how much money you spent. I've already told you that." Frustration was making him tense and he resented having to beg for an explanation when something was so obviously wrong. He unbuttoned his shirt slowly, letting that latest clue sink in for a moment. "Is that what's bothering you? The money?"

She stood quickly and turned her back on him. "It's not the money. It's not anything. What will it take to make you drop this?"

"How about the truth?"

"I'm telling you the truth."

He closed the distance between them and took her gently by the shoulders. "Are you? I don't think so."

She shrugged away from his touch and glared at him. "When did *you* become so interested in telling the truth?"

The question—the accusation—set him back a pace and he wondered if she could possibly know how he'd spent his afternoon.

No. Impossible. She *couldn't* know.

But that didn't stop the guilt from churning in the pit of his stomach. "Is that what this is about? You think I'm lying to you about something?"

"Are you?"

Again he resisted the urge to tell her the truth. He

really wanted it to be a special moment when he handed her the consent for adoption Marianne had signed. "What do I have to lie about?"

Her eyes narrowed, and for an instant he thought she might actually tell him. Instead, she took a step away. "I'm tired, Mark. I have a ton of homework to do for class tomorrow. And this discussion is getting us nowhere."

That was certainly true. He tossed his shirt over the back of a chair and stripped off his pants. She averted her gaze as if they were still strangers.

Increasingly frustrated, he tried to decide whether to let the conversation drop, or if he should push a little harder. He'd been oblivious with Marianne, and look where that had gotten him. He loved Dionne enough to try again.

He walked slowly toward her and touched her again. "Come on. Let's go to bed. Whatever it is, you can talk to me. I love you, Dionne. Trust me."

She jerked away and climbed into bed, turning her back toward his side. And a flash of memory, of Marianne turning away from him exactly the same way, taunted him.

Was this a sign that Dionne was changing her mind? Was she having second thoughts? But if so, why? He was as clueless as he'd been when Marianne left. But this time, he had far more at stake. His son. His dreams. His heart.

CHAPTER SIXTEEN

MARK LAY on his side of the bed watching shadows drift across the ceiling. Noises—an occasional passing car, a dog barking, the soft sound of Dionne sleeping next to him—were magnified by the stillness of the night air and kept him awake. Or maybe it was the fear that once again he was failing at love, and he didn't know how or why.

Too agitated to relax, he climbed carefully out of bed and walked to the window. Shadows from the moon pooled beneath the trees and undergrowth rimming the backyard. He rested one hand on the wall and rubbed his eyes with the other.

Dionne shifted in the bed behind him and let out a breath soft as a baby's sigh. His heart constricted, and he wondered when she'd become so necessary to him. He'd gone into this marriage for Jared's sake; and though keeping Jared happy was still important, somehow everything had shifted and the relationship with Dionne had become his top priority.

He couldn't lose her. No matter what it took, no matter what price he had to pay, he wouldn't screw up again.

Dionne stirred and rolled over in bed. She'd been so exhausted lately, he didn't want to wake her so he padded across the room, let himself out into the darkened hallway, and closed the door behind him almost soundlessly. Using both hands to feel his way, he stumbled down the stairs toward the kitchen.

Inside, the neon light over the range was on, a sure sign that his mother was prowling as she often did when something worried her. He searched for her in the shadowy room. "Mom?"

"Over here, son." Her voice came from somewhere near the patio doors.

Squinting to make out the furniture between them, he crossed the room and stood beside her. There, in the glow of the moonlight, he could see her at last. The tattered bathrobe she'd been wearing as long as he could remember, the slightly tousled hair, the face scrubbed of makeup.

He put an arm around her shoulders, taking comfort from the familiar scent of her face cream. "What are you doing up?"

"I couldn't sleep."

"And why not?"

"I'm worried about your father."

"I thought you said the tests were nothing to worry about. Is there something you're not telling me?"

She flapped a hand at him as if to wave away the suggestion. "Of course not. Unless the doctor's lying to me."

He drew back and looked down at her. "You don't believe him?"

A sad smile curved her lips. "I'm trying to."

Mark gave her a gentle squeeze. "I'm sure he'd tell you if there was anything to worry about."

"You're probably right. I'm just not used to anything being wrong with your father. You know he's always had the constitution of an ox."

Mark finished the family joke for her. "And the disposition of a mule."

His mother laughed, then sobered again. "We've been married nearly forty years, and suddenly I find myself staring mortality right in the eye. For the first time, I'm facing the possibility that he could go before me, and I don't know what I'd do without him."

And for the first time in his life, Mark understood how she felt. "Do you want me to go with you tomorrow and talk to the doctor myself?"

"I'd like that very much. But you know your father. He'd think we were trying to baby him, or that I was keeping something from him."

"You're right. He would." Mark let his gaze trail away again.

His mother took a deep breath and smiled at him. "We'll be fine. It's you I'm really worried about."

"Me?" He laughed nervously. "Why me?"

"Because something's wrong between you and Dionne. I can sense it."

She didn't need his burdens added to her own, nor did Mark want to make them real by voicing them. "Everything's fine," he said quietly.

He could see her scowl in the moonlight. "Don't lie to me, Mark Taylor. I know when something's wrong with my children."

"We had a little disagreement earlier," he admitted. "But everything's fine now."

"Every couple has disagreements. Heaven knows, your father and I have had our share. But it's not one minor disagreement I'm talking about. It's something more substantial. I felt it the first time I saw you together."

Mark tried to laugh away the suggestion. "What did you feel?"

"If I knew that, I wouldn't have to ask. It's just an uneasy feeling I experience at times. Don't get me wrong, I adore Dionne, and I don't think you could have picked a better wife. And she's a wonderful mother to Jared. But there's something…" Her scowl deepened. "Do you love her?"

"You can't even imagine how much," he said truthfully.

That seemed to relax her a little. "And she loves you. I can see that whenever you two are together. But I've been worried. I had doubts about whether you truly loved her, or if you only married her because of Jared."

Mark kept his face impassive, his body from reacting in any way. "What made you think that?"

"You have to admit, it's a bit of a coincidence that you'd go in search of your son and then fall madly in love with the woman who's been raising him."

Mark kept his gaze riveted on a lawn chair on the patio. "Coincidences do happen."

"Well, I'm glad to know you two *are* in love. Marriage is tough enough between two people who love each other. And trying to keep a marriage together when there's not love involved isn't only foolish, it's dangerous. Look at Jerry."

He laughed sharply. "Jerry had an affair, Mom."

"It's not *what* he did as much as *why* he did it. You know as well as I do that he and Alice never did really love each other. They got married for the wrong reasons." She sighed softly. "I'm not condoning what he did by any means. I'm just saying that the affair didn't cause their problems. It was a symptom of what was wrong between them. If that hadn't ended their marriage, something else would have eventually.''

Mark believed that, but he sure as hell didn't like thinking that his marriage to Dionne was headed toward the same fate.

"The saddest part," his mother went on, "is what it's done to the girls. Children are always the victims when a marriage goes bad."

That made him feel even worse. Were he and Dionne setting Jared up for disappointment and heartache? "You don't have to worry, Mom. That's not going to happen to us."

"I'm glad, sweetheart." She leaned up and kissed his cheek, then patted it gently. "Maybe now I can get some sleep. Are you coming upstairs?"

"Not yet. I don't want to wake Dionne."

"Well, don't stay up too late. You need your sleep."

He forced a laugh. "I'm thirty-one years old, and you're telling me when to go to bed."

"I'm still your mother," she said, and patted his cheek again. "And I still care."

He smiled in spite of the ache in his heart and watched her cross the room. But when she disappeared, his smile faded. And the new doubts she'd raised began to tear holes in his resolve.

He wanted desperately to believe he could hold his marriage together, but he wondered if he could do it on his own.

THE NEXT MORNING, Dionne felt as if she were walking on a tightrope. She'd slept fitfully all night, waking in the middle of the night to find Mark gone. She had no idea where he'd gone or if he'd ever come back to bed. His side of the bed had been empty when she woke again and finally got up.

He'd been thoughtful all morning, stepping in to help with breakfast and Jared. At least he'd stopped pressuring her to confide in him. But she kept waiting for him to do or say something about last night, and her emotions were so close to the surface, anything might push her over the edge.

She filled a plate with scrambled eggs and tried not to let the smell make her sick. As she turned to carry them to the table, Mark stepped in front of her and took the plate from her hand.

Nigel was hidden behind a section of the newspaper. Barbara sang softly to Jared as she fed him cereal. The realization that she'd have to leave them soon brought tears to Dionne's eyes, but she forced them away.

Barbara glanced at her with a bright smile. "Are you sure I can't help you with something?"

"You're already helping," Dionne assured her.

Barbara lowered the spoon to the table slowly. "You look pale this morning. Are you feeling all right?"

Dionne sat at the table. She could feel Mark watching her, but she didn't let herself look at him. "I'm fine," she said, trying not to look queasy when the breakfast aromas hit her full force. "Just a little tired." She stood quickly to get away from the eggs and bacon and mumbled something about making more toast.

Barbara helped Jared with his apple juice. "Why don't you let Mark do that." She sent him a pointed glance that would have made Dionne laugh under other circumstances.

And when he popped up again like a puppet and hurried to do his mother's bidding, she had to force away a rush of affection.

Nigel lowered his newspaper and peered at them over the top. "If you ask me, you ought to get this wife of yours some help around the house. Can't expect her to keep up with school and the house and Jared, too." He ruffled Jared's hair and chucked him under the chin. "We want Mommy to be happy, don't we?"

Jared giggled and reached for his apple juice again.

"I want Mommy to be happy, too." Mark pulled two slices of bread from the bag, but he kept his gaze riveted on Dionne. "Would you like that?"

"You mean, a maid?" The offer surprised her. Mark had always been generous with his money, but why was he talking about the future when he was planning to desert her? Or was he just putting up a front for his parents? She shook her head slowly. "I don't think so. It's terribly extravagant."

"Money's not the issue," Mark said firmly. "If we found someone who could come in a couple of days a week, maybe you wouldn't be so tired all the time."

If Patsy's stories about pregnancy were anything to go by, nothing would help that for a few months. Dionne started to nod, then stopped herself. She couldn't let Mark hire someone to help her when she didn't intend to stay.

Out of nowhere, tears filled her eyes. She blinked them away and shook her head. "No, I..." She pushed aside the coffee that was making the nausea worse and tried to still the rolling of her stomach, the swaying of the room.

Mark dropped the bread into the toaster, still without looking away. Barbara stopped feeding Jared to watch her. Even Nigel had lost interest in his newspaper.

Barbara put a hand on hers. "Dionne, dear, what is it?"

"Nothing." She nudged herself back from the table and tried to take a deep breath, but she could feel sweat beading on her forehead and knew she had to get away—and fast.

Jumping up, she rushed from the room, ran up the stairs, and shut herself in the bathroom. She didn't have time to lock the door before she had to give in to the nausea that had taken over her entire body.

Just as she began to feel a little better, someone knocked softly on the door. Barbara's voice followed a second later. "Dionne? Are you all right?"

She closed her eyes and leaned her head against the wall. "I'm fine," she lied.

The door opened a crack and Barbara looked inside. "You're most definitely *not* fine. Is there something I can do?"

"No." Dionne forced herself to stand, even though her knees barely held her. "Thanks, but I'll be all right if I can just lie down for a while."

"Let me help you get to bed, then."

Dionne backed a step away, her eyes brimmed with tears, her throat thickened with emotion. Why did Barbara have to be so nice to her? It only made everything harder.

The concern on Barbara's face deepened. "Do you want me to get Mark?"

"No." The word fell between them, the desperation behind it obvious. She tried to smile it away. "He has enough on his mind, and so do you. Go ahead and have breakfast without me. I don't want you to be late getting to the hospital."

Barbara didn't turn away, but studied her for a long moment. Slowly, Dionne saw recognition dawn in her eyes and a knowing smile curve her lips. "Does Mark know?"

"Know what?"

"Why you're so tired and nauseated all the time?"

"There's nothing *to* know." Dionne turned to the faucet and splashed her face with water. "Nothing at all."

Barbara's smile died but the light in her eyes didn't dim. "If you say so, dear. Don't worry, I won't say anything. This is your surprise to give him. But if you're worried about how he'll react, don't. He'll be thrilled."

Dionne kept her face impassive as she patted it dry with a towel. "There's nothing to be thrilled about, Barbara. I'm sure it's just a reaction to stress."

Barbara stood there, watching her for a few long, agonizing seconds. "All right," she said at last. "I guess I was mistaken."

After what felt like forever, she closed the door and walked away. And Dionne sank onto the edge of the bathtub and buried her face in her hands.

Of course Mark would be thrilled. No matter how he felt about her, he loved his son. And she knew with unwavering certainty he'd feel the same way about the baby she carried. That's what frightened her most.

Her time had run out. Like it or not, she had to leave. She couldn't stay here and keep the pregnancy a secret from Mark. Barbara had already figured it out. He wouldn't be far behind.

MARK DROVE quickly along the winding road leading home. Late-afternoon sunshine spilled in through the car window. Leaves drifted lazily from the huge old trees lining the highway to the pavement in front of him. It was a perfect autumn day and he was in a good mood.

His mother's call earlier that afternoon telling him that his father's tests were going well and that the doctor had ruled out the more serious conditions he'd suspected had been a good start. Drawing up the petition for adoption so Dionne could sign it had only made things better. And when Royal left the office early, Mark took advantage of the opportunity to sneak out, as well.

Smiling, he glanced at the box of roses beside him on the front seat. He drove through the center of town and was pleased when he passed the green. He wanted the rest of his and Dionne's lives to feel as magical as the night of the autumn festival. And he had the means to a very good start in his suit pocket.

Tonight was the night. He'd talk his mother into staying with Jared for the evening. Over dinner in some wonderfully romantic restaurant, he'd tell Dionne everything. He couldn't wait to watch the stress vanish from her face and the clouds leave her eyes.

When he saw Patsy coming out of the drugstore,

he honked lightly and waved. To his surprise, she didn't return the greeting, but propped her hands on her hips and glared at him. Her reaction bothered him for a moment, but by the time he turned off Front Street toward home, he'd decided she probably hadn't recognized him.

Feeling like a kid on Christmas morning, he pulled into the driveway, gathered the roses and his briefcase, and jogged up the walk. But when he let himself into the house, unexpected silence greeted him.

"Dionne?" He left his briefcase by the door and the roses on the end of the couch. "Jared?"

Still nothing.

Maybe she was putting Jared down for a nap. He took the stairs two at a time and peeked inside Jared's room. It was empty.

Great. The one day he got away from the office at a reasonable hour, and she wasn't here. Trying hard not to be disappointed, he hurried into their bedroom to change. Before he could do more than take off his jacket and tie, he heard someone come in the front door.

He raced down the stairs again, hoping to reach Dionne before she could look inside the florist's box. "You're home," he said as he rounded the corner into the living room.

"Yes." His mother dropped onto the empty end of the couch and leaned her head back. "And exhausted. What are you doing here so early?"

Mark tried not to let her see his disappointment. "I snuck out. I was hoping to surprise Dionne, but she's not here. Have you talked to her today?"

His mother shook her head and closed her eyes.

"I didn't even try to call. I assumed she'd be in classes all day."

He stole a glance at his watch and scowled. "She was, but she should be home by now."

"Maybe she's gone to the grocery store. Or maybe she's studying late at the library."

"That's probably it." He sank into a chair and propped his feet on the ottoman. "I was thinking of asking if you'd watch Jared so I could take her out to dinner tonight. But if you're too tired I'll do it another night."

Barbara opened her eyes again and smiled. "What a lovely idea. I think the two of you could use some time alone, and I'm never too tired to watch Jared."

He grinned and stood again. "Thanks, Mom. You're the greatest." He hurried upstairs, took off his suit pants and opened the closet to grab a hanger. When he realized that Dionne's clothes weren't on the other side of the closet, his hand froze in midair.

As if in slow motion, he pushed the closet door open the rest of the way and stared at the empty hangers and the bare space on the floor where her shoes had been that morning. But it wasn't until he crossed the hall into Jared's room and found his son's favorite toys gone, his drawers empty, and his closet bare, that the realization finally hit him.

Moving on autopilot, he walked back to his bedroom and dressed in jeans and a sweatshirt. His mind still refused to take it in, but his heart screamed the truth with every beat. He sank onto the foot of the bed and buried his face in his hands.

He had no idea how long he sat there before he heard his mother's tread coming up the stairs and moving down the hall toward the guest room.

"Mark?" She paused with her hand on the door-knob. "What's wrong?"

Slowly, painfully, he lifted his gaze to meet hers. "She's gone."

"Gone? What do you mean, gone?"

"I mean gone." The pain was too intense. He couldn't bear to feel it. In the blink of an eye, it turned into anger. He stood and threw open the closet door again. "Gone. Her clothes are gone, and so are Jared's. Apparently, I've failed again."

"Mark—" His mother's dark eyes filled with sympathy.

He looked away. He couldn't bear her sorrow or her pity.

"Mark, sweetheart—" Barbara moved into the room to stand behind him and put her hands on his shoulders.

He jerked away and mopped his face with his hand. He fought tears and tried to hold on to the anger. It was, he thought bitterly, much easier to handle.

"Do you know why she left?"

"If I did, I'd know how to fix it. Maybe I work too much. Maybe I'm just an insensitive jerk. Who the hell knows?" He paced toward the window and glared out at the lawn. "I tried my best this time, Mom. I really did."

"I don't know Dionne well," Barbara said quietly, "but I find it hard to believe that she'd leave without telling you why."

He thought back over the last few conversations they'd had. Once again, he had the uncomfortable suspicion that she'd found out he was hiding something from her. But how?

He turned to face his mother again and slowly, hesitantly, told her the whole story.

MARK PACED in front of the drugstore, watching the sun set, rubbing his hands together for warmth while he waited for Patsy to get off work. Dionne and Jared had been gone for nearly a week. He'd given his anger free rein for the first day or two and tried like hell to convince himself he was better off without her.

But every time he came home to that empty house, his heart broke all over again.

For the last few days, he'd tried everything he could think of—short of hiring a private detective again—to find her. He'd even called Cicely, who'd insisted in a cold, flat, unemotional voice that she hadn't seen Dionne.

He didn't believe her, of course. And tomorrow, he'd fly to Boise and begin his search in person. But he had one last step to take before he did.

Patsy had been with Dionne the day everything turned sour. If anyone knew what had suddenly made Dionne change, Patsy would. And he wouldn't undertake the most important argument of his life without preparing for it.

He glanced through the window and paced to the corner, then turned back toward the door again. The last customer had left at least fifteen minutes ago. Surely, she'd come outside soon.

Maybe he should have gone inside, but he didn't want to have this conversation in front of anyone else. It was bad enough that he had to beg a relative stranger to tell him why his wife had left.

At long last, the front door opened and light spilled

onto the sidewalk. A moment later, the light extinguished and Patsy stepped outside.

As she turned to lock the door behind her, Mark closed the distance between them. "Patsy?"

She whirled to face him. "Hello, Mark." Her voice was cool and brittle. She knew, he thought with a surge of hope. Whatever it was, she knew.

Now, if he could just convince her to share it with him. "Do you have a minute?"

She glanced up the sidewalk, then shrugged casually. "I suppose. What do you need?"

"Have you talked to Dionne lately?"

Her eyes flashed, but she managed to keep the rest of her face emotionless. "Not since the day after we went shopping."

"She hasn't called you?"

"No."

He stepped more fully in front of her. "Did something happen to upset her that day?"

Patsy's shoulders tensed and she looked again toward the end of the street, as if she was searching for an escape route. "Dionne is my friend. I don't think I should talk about her with you."

"And she's my wife." His shoulders sagged and he raked his fingers through his hair. He abandoned the few ragged bits that remained of his pride. "She's gone, Patsy. She left me."

"Yes, I know."

A flash of anger tore through him, but he tried not to show it. He couldn't afford to alienate her. "Do you know why?"

Patsy's mouth settled into a thin line. "I can't believe you need to ask."

He took a steadying breath and tried to keep his

tone level. "I do need to ask. I have no idea why she'd leave."

Patsy laughed bitterly. "Just think about it, Mark."

"That's all I have thought about," he assured her. A gust of wind swirled around them. Cold, savage wind that matched the icy dread in his heart. "I can't eat. I can't sleep. I think back over the last few days she was here again and again, but I don't know what happened. You're my last hope. She seemed fine when she left with you that morning. By the time I got home again, everything had changed."

"You really have no idea?"

"None." He took a ragged breath and let it out again slowly. "I love her, Patsy. If I did something wrong, I'd like to know what it was."

She studied him for a moment and her hostility appeared to fade slightly. She tugged the collar of her sweater closer and shivered in another blast of wind.

"Patsy, please."

She turned her gaze back on him. "Where did you go that day, Mark? Who did you meet?"

Mark's stomach knotted and his mouth dried. "How—" He broke off, then tried again. "How did she find out?"

"Apparently, there was a message from what's-her-name on the answering machine when Dionne got home that day."

That took the wind out of him as surely as if she'd punched him in the stomach. "From Marianne?"

He thought he might be sick. No wonder Dionne had been so cold. No wonder she'd held him at arm's length. He said the only words he could manage. "It was nothing. Why didn't she ask me about it?"

Patsy's smile turned bitter again. "Maybe because she didn't trust you."

"But—"

"And I don't blame her," Patsy said, cutting him off. "You took Jared to meet Marianne without telling her. Why *should* she trust you?"

He looked deep into Patsy's eyes. "It wasn't what you're thinking. Believe me. Marianne agreed to sign the consent for adoption if I let her see Jared one last time. That's *all* it was."

"If it was so innocent, why didn't you tell Dionne?"

"I didn't want to worry her. I thought she'd get frightened if I told her, and I wanted to spare her that. Obviously, I have a lot to learn."

"Yes, you do." Patsy studied him again before she allowed herself a thin smile. "I suppose you look sincere."

"I am," he assured her. "More than you can imagine. And I need to explain everything to Dionne."

"I agree with you," Patsy said, hitching her purse onto her shoulder.

"Then you'll tell me where she is?"

"I would if I could. But I don't have any idea. I haven't heard from her." She patted his shoulder gently and turned away. "For what it's worth, I hope you find her."

"Oh, I will." Now that he knew why she'd run, he knew exactly what to say to get her back. And he knew right where to look.

"YOU'RE GOING to wear a hole in my carpet if you keep pacing like that."

Dionne stopped in her tracks and glanced over her shoulder at Cicely who sat at the kitchen table cradling a cup of cocoa in both hands. She'd only been home from work a few minutes, and she hadn't changed out of her work clothes yet. In her suit, nylons and pumps, she made a stark contrast to Dionne, who hadn't been able to work up much interest in her appearance since she left Longs Mill.

"Sorry," Dionne said, forcing a weak smile. "I'm just restless, I guess."

Cicely's eyes narrowed. "You're still thinking about him, aren't you?"

Every waking minute, Dionne admitted silently. She missed him terribly. She heard his laugh everywhere she went. A dozen times she'd thought she glimpsed him in a crowd, only to discover it wasn't him after all. Every time she closed her eyes, she saw him.

She'd expected the longing to fade. Instead, it seemed to be getting worse. "I'm waiting for the bomb to drop," she said. "It's been almost a week already, and he hasn't done anything."

"Maybe he won't. After all, I told him I hadn't seen you."

She laughed harshly. "Oh, he will. I'm absolutely certain of it."

Cicely sipped cocoa and carefully settled the cup on the table. "Maybe he really is in love with you."

"I'd give anything for that to be true," Dionne admitted. "But if he is, why did he take Jared to Marianne without telling me? He knew how I'd feel about it.'' She shook her head and started to pace again.

"There may be a perfectly good explanation for that," Cicely said quietly. "But you never gave him the chance to explain. I think you should talk to him."

Dionne turned to glare at her. "I can't believe you're even suggesting that. If I call him, he'll know where we are."

Cicely made a face at her and sipped again. "I hate to break it to you, girl, but I don't believe you're really trying to hide from him. This will be the first place he looks, and you know it." She leaned back in her chair and crossed her legs. "You came here because you want him to find you."

Dionne rested her hand on the stomach of her oversize sweatshirt, trying to feel the new life she carried. She glanced at Jared, who drove a fleet of toy trucks across the floor. He'd been unusually quiet since they'd left Longs Mill, and each time she noticed the difference, guilt overwhelmed her.

"I *don't* want him to find us," she argued without conviction. "I just didn't have anywhere else to go."

"Uh-huh." Cicely rolled her eyes and kicked her foot gently. "I don't believe you."

"It's true," Dionne insisted. "Where else was I supposed to go?"

Cicely rolled her eyes again. "All I'm saying is, if you really don't want him to find you, you'd have thought of something else. Admit it, Dionne. You're hoping he comes after you."

Dionne wanted to deny it again, but she couldn't. "Maybe you're right," she said. "I've tried over and over again to make myself hate him, but I just can't stop loving him.''

"Then, talk to him.''

"I can't.''

"Why not?''

"Because." She sat across from Cicely and rested her chin in her hand. "I know he'd come after us if he knew about the baby. Maybe he'd even stay with me. But it would be out of obligation, not love, and I don't think I could bear that.''

"So what are you going to do?''

"Find a job. Get an apartment. Get on with my life.''

"Dionne, listen to me." Cicely rested her hands on the table and faced her squarely. "You're carrying that man's child. Do you really think it's fair not to tell him?''

"And let him take both of my children away?'' Dionne shot to her feet and put some distance between them. "Never. Why are you suddenly on his side?''

"I'm not on his side." Cicely shook her head sadly. "I'm on your side, whether you know it or not. You love him, Dionne. You're miserable without him. And if he was the heartless creature you're trying to make him out to be, you never would have fallen in love with him in the first place.''

"I made a mistake.''

"I agree with you. But your mistake was leaving without giving him a chance to explain.''

Dionne studied her friend's face for a long moment. "Why the sudden change of heart?''

Cicely shrugged innocently. Too innocently.

It sent a rush of apprehension through her. "You know something, don't you?"

"I know you're in love with him," Cicely said firmly. "And I know you're dying inside being away from him."

"So, what do you want me to do? Take Jared back to Longs Mill and hand him over to Mark and Marianne?"

"No. I just want you to talk to him." Cicely took a deep breath and turned away. "He's here in Boise."

Dionne's heart dropped. Her stomach lurched. Her mouth dried and her hands grew moist. And in the midst of it all, her spirits soared. "He's here? How do you know?"

"He came by to see me this afternoon."

"And you didn't tell me? Does he know I'm staying with you?"

"I told you, girl. This is the first place he looked."

She dropped into a chair and held on. "What did he say?"

"Just that he wants a chance to explain."

"Explain what?"

Cicely turned back to her with a smile. "I think you'd better let him tell you that."

"How do you know he's not trying to set me up so he can take Jared away?"

"I recognized the look in his eyes. Pure misery, exactly what I see in yours. Dionne, that man is in love with you and he wants you back."

"What about Marianne?"

"I'll let him tell you."

"What about—"

Cicely cut her off with a wave of her hand. "I'll

let him tell you," she said again. "I'm not getting any more involved than I already am."

Dionne took a deep breath and tried to still the trembling of her hands. "Did you tell him about the baby?"

"Nope. I figure that's for you to tell. I told you, girl, I'm not getting involved."

Dionne managed a weak smile. "Where is he?"

"Outside."

"Outside?" She lurched to her feet and ran into the bathroom. She checked her reflection and noted with dismay that she looked like a corpse. Her cheeks were pale, her hair tousled, her face gaunt and shadowed from lack of sleep. "I look horrible," she moaned softly. "I can't see him looking like this."

"I think you look wonderful."

The deep male voice brought her around sharply. He stood there, blocking the bathroom door, his face creased with worry, his eyes dark with concern. Soft spikes in his hair told her he'd been raking his fingers through it the way he always did when he was worried.

Torn between the urge to rush into his arms and the need to protect herself, she gripped the sink for support. "Where's Jared?"

"In the hall with Cicely. She wanted to give us some time alone." He shifted uncomfortably but he didn't look away. "I talked to Patsy last night. She told me about the message Marianne left on the answering machine."

She nodded, too numb to do anything else.

"It wasn't what you thought, Dionne."

"Wasn't it?" The words came out little more than

a whisper. She willed herself to be strong. "What was it, then?"

"I met Marianne so I could get this." He reached into his coat pocket, pulled out a document, and handed it to her.

Scarcely breathing, she took it. But she couldn't make herself open it.

"It's a consent for adoption," he said softly. He took a tentative step toward her, as if he was as afraid of this moment as she was. As if he had as much at stake. "I wanted to surprise you with it."

She unfolded it quickly, scanned the document, and checked for Marianne's signature. Then slowly, she lowered it to her side and let the relief sweep through her. "Is it real?"

"One hundred percent real." He handed her another document. "And here's the petition for adoption I had drawn up. All it needs is your signature."

"You—" She gulped back tears and met his gaze. "This is what you were doing?"

"This is it."

"I thought you and Marianne were planning to take Jared away from me."

"I know." He moved toward her, but stopped short of taking her into his arms. "I'm sorry, Dionne. I should have told you, but I didn't want to worry you." He laughed at the absurdity of it and touched her gently. "I love you, Dionne. I want you with me always. I need you with me. I didn't even realize how much until you left. If you'll come back to me, I promise I'll always be honest with you."

She dashed tears away with the back of her hand and resisted the urge to throw herself into his arms. There was still one piece of unfinished business.

"Mark, I—" She broke off and studied his face, memorizing the details, loving him more than she could have ever imagined loving anyone. "I haven't been completely honest with you, either."

His dark eyes narrowed. His smile faltered. "What is it?"

"Well, I—" The words wouldn't come. She gripped his hands for strength and forced herself to say it. "I'm pregnant."

For one heart-stopping moment, time stood still. His eyes registered shock and she waited. Then he threw back his head and let out a whoop loud enough for everyone in Cicely's building to hear. "Pregnant?"

"Yes."

He pulled her into a bear hug and held on as if his life depended on it. "You've made me the happiest man in the world."

"But—"

He touched her lips with his fingertips, then pulled them away and replaced them with his lips. He kissed her gently, thoroughly, putting his entire heart into it. When he let her go again, he smiled into her eyes.

The last of the reserve between them vanished as if it had never been. He kissed her until she was gasping for breath, then released her quickly and dropped to one knee on the cold tile floor. "Mrs. Taylor, will you do me the honor of marrying me…again?"

The tears came freely now. She couldn't have stopped them if she'd tried. "Oh, Mark—"

"I'm serious." He took her hand in his and held it. His eyes danced with joy that matched hers.

"You've got to admit, that first wedding was nothing to write home about."

"I don't need a big, fancy wedding," she whispered around the lump in her throat. "I just need you and my children, forever."

He stood slowly and wrapped her in his arms again. "Then that's exactly what you'll have." He kissed the top of her hair, trailed his lips to her temple and down the line of her jaw.

Nothing had ever felt so right, so wonderful, so much like heaven on earth. "I've missed you so much."

"And I've missed you." He gathered her close. "I love you, Dionne. You hold my heart in your hand. Please, say you'll come back to me."

She buried her face in his shoulder and sighed. She belonged with him, in good times and in bad. "Can we tell everyone the truth? I hate lying."

"Absolutely. No more lies. Not to anyone."

She took a ragged breath and smiled up at him. "Take us home, Mark. All of us."

Baby, Baby
by
Roz Denny Fox

PROLOGUE

MICHAEL CAMERON TURNED UP his coat collar before he stepped out of the cab. He took care to shield his medical bag from the cold, relentless rain blowing into New York City. "Keep the change," he told the cabby, thrusting a folded bill through a slit in the window. Hunched into his topcoat, Michael stared up at the window of his luxury midtown Manhattan penthouse. Now he wished he hadn't asked his secretary to phone Lacy and forewarn her of his arrival. She would be furious at his leaving her in the lurch again. "As if I have a choice," he muttered, taking the front steps two at a time.

Bettis, the attendant on duty, opened the building's main door. He extended Michael a large umbrella. "Nasty weather, eh, Doc?"

"Thanks." Michael shook wet hair out of his eyes as he ducked under the canvas. "Nasty all right, but at least it hasn't turned to sleet." He lingered, making small talk. The longer he avoided the scene that surely awaited him upstairs, the better.

"Home early today, huh?" Bettis closed the umbrella and reached around Michael to press the button summoning the private elevator. "Big evening, I guess." The older man winked. "Saks delivered Mrs. Cameron's new dress. Oops. Don't tell her I spilled the beans. I think she planned to surprise you."

Michael frowned as he entered the elevator. "Lacy bought a new dress for tonight? Damn," he muttered. Keeping the door ajar with his bag, he pushed back one cuff to check a flat gold watch. "I need a cab out front by two, Bettis. I'm scheduled on a five-twenty international flight. In this weather, traffic to JFK will be hell."

The doorman nodded briskly, but his eyes were sympathetic as Michael let the door close. Michael hoped he hadn't revealed his own unsettled feelings. It galled him to think the staff had probably discussed his rocky marriage—although it shouldn't surprise him that Bettis was aware of his and Lacy's problems. After all, the doorman occasionally dated the Camerons' housekeeper.

Michael dug for his door key as the elevator glided to a stop outside his apartment. Could he really blame staff for talking when the situation between him and Lacy had gone from bad to worse over the past ten months? That was why he'd arranged a night out, hoping to mend their latest rift. An unexpected trip was the last thing he needed. But there was no other option. Throwing back his shoulders, Michael braced for battle as he moved to insert his key in the lock.

Surprisingly, the door swung inward. Caught off balance, Michael pitched forward, hands flailing, as Lacy flung herself at his chest. The key flew in one direction and his bag in the other, and Michael's arms circled his wife's too thin frame. His shocked sputter ended with a mouthful of Lacy's fine blond hair. She paid no attention to his incoherent gurgle, only fused her mouth with his as she stripped him of his coat, jacket and tie.

"Mmm, Michael," she whispered seductively. "When Maxine phoned to say you were leaving the clinic early, I sent Mrs. Parker to a movie." Lacy's momentum propelled Michael into the bedroom where they both toppled onto a king-size bed.

"Lacy, what the…?" He'd barely lifted himself onto his elbows when she unfastened her peachy satin robe to expose naked skin. Pressing her lips against his, she wound around him again. The kiss smothered his second attempt to speak. With sure fingers, she unbuckled his belt and released the zipper of his slacks.

"I see you're ready, too," she cooed, leaving his mouth long enough to run a wet tongue from his navel to the bulge of white cotton springing from the open zipper.

Michael exhaled swiftly. "La…c…y." Her name was a groan ripped from his tortured lungs as she quickly slid over his erection with grasping hands and initiated a frenzied ride.

Release came for Michael before he caught his breath. The speed embarrassed him, yet he was more concerned about their rough coupling. It'd been weeks since they'd said two civil words to each other, let alone had sex. "God, Lacy, are you all right?" he gasped, raising his torso enough to ease her aside.

She pouted as she slid to the edge of the bed. Tossing her shoulder-length hair, she matter-of-factly retied her robe. "I thought this would be an incentive for you to come home early more often, Michael. Heaven knows your technique needs practice."

He winced, as much at her underlying rebuke as the bright lamp she'd snapped on. "Lacy, what exactly did Maxie Lucas say when she phoned?"

"That you asked her to let me know you were on

your way home. Why?'' Her blue eyes narrowed in sudden suspicion.

Michael rolled off the bed and raked an unsteady hand through tousled brown hair. ''Maxie was to warn you that I was on my way home to pack. The fourteen-year-old Norwegian girl I told you about has moved to the head of our transplant list. I got a call an hour ago. We have a match. I'm flying out tonight.''

A crash followed by breaking glass brought his head spinning around. Lacy, her pretty face contorted by anger, had cleared the nightstand with a sweep of her hand. Pill bottles lay strewn amid jagged pieces of glass from their smashed wedding photo.

''Dammit! I didn't set out to disappoint you, Lacy. But I *am* the chief surgeon on the international heart-lung transplant team. I'd expect you, of all people, not to begrudge a child her chance.''

''I don't need a doctor now, Michael. I need a husband.''

One of his eyebrows shot up to meet a rain-wet lock of hair.

''I hate that superior attitude you get, Michael. Almost as much as I hate that the first question out of your mouth after we made love was, 'Are you all right, Lacy?' ''

''Not this argument again,'' he growled. ''Getting over-tired, flu, colds—anything causing undue stress can still put your transplanted organs in jeopardy. Dammit, I don't like arguing, Lacy. If it wasn't such awful weather in Norway, I'd take you with me.''

''Wouldn't that be fun?'' she drawled sarcastically. ''I could sit around a hotel while you spend twenty-four hours a day at the hospital. No, thank you, Michael.''

''Then call Faith. She didn't have any time off at

Christmas to visit, but maybe she'd like a break from Boston now. You two can take in some shows. I don't think she's seen the apartment since you redecorated this last time.''

''That's because my sister spends as many hours at *her* hospital as you do at yours. I'll go to the beach house—again. The sailing crowd doesn't treat me like an invalid.'' Her last words were muffled as she pulled a suitcase from the closet and flopped it open on the bed. With an aggrieved air, she folded a new silk dress that hung on the closet door.

''I refuse to be made to feel guilty about this, Lacy. I was a surgeon when you married me, and I'm a surgeon still. Name one thing you've ever wanted that I haven't given you.''

''Your time, Michael.''

He gestured helplessly, then turned away to shed his remaining clothes. He strode into the bathroom and wrenched on the shower, returning to the bedroom just long enough to yank a black flight bag from the closet. ''I took an oath to heal, Lacy. It's what I do.''

''Amen. Not a day goes by that you don't ask if I've taken my pills. If I'm doing my breathing treatments. If I'm warm enough. Et cetera, et cetera.''

''A few precautions seem a small price to pay for enjoying a normal life.''

''Normal?'' Lacy paused in the act of pulling on a pair of slacks. ''Normal women's lives don't revolve around endless checkups and buckets of pills, Michael. The don'ts in my life outweigh the dos. Don't walk in the rain, Lacy. Don't play in the snow. Don't climb mountains. Don...don't have children.''

Michael's jaw tightened. ''Your anti-rejection drugs

place you at risk. Add to that the normal stress of carrying a child—but you know all this, Lacy.''

"Yes, Dr. God. Tell me again how normal I am." With jerky movements, Lacy tucked in her blouse and began flinging clothing into the suitcase.

"There's adoption," Michael ventured after a pause. "But we'd need to solve our differences first."

Stone-faced, Lacy continued to fill the case as if he hadn't said a word.

Doubling a fist, Michael smacked the door casing on his way into the shower. When Lacy wore that closed expression, there was no discussing anything with her. Meanwhile, it was getting late. A kid in Norway counted on him. Lacy had been given a second chance. Why in hell couldn't she appreciate the fact?

By the time Michael dried off and dressed to travel, Lacy had packed the third in a trio of matched luggage. Michael folded two suits and several shirts into his bag. "How long are you planning to stay at the beach?" he asked, eyeing her growing pile of luggage. Not waiting for her answer, he took his shaving kit into the bathroom to fill.

"Why would you care?" She elbowed past him and scooped an array of cosmetics into an overnight case.

"You're my wife. Why wouldn't I care?" His bafflement increased when she slammed the lid, tossed the small case with the others, then went to pick up the phone.

After punching in a series of numbers, she spoke into the receiver. "Bettis, this is Mrs. Cameron. Call the garage and have them send the Mercedes around. Then please come to the suite and collect my bags."

"It's pouring rain," Michael said quietly. "If you must go today, call the car service to take you. I'll arrange a few days off when I get back from Norway. We'll drive back to New York together.''

"Go to hell," she said in a voice that dripped honey.

"Lacy, dammit!" He faced her across the bed. "Why do you always have to pick a fight before I go on a trip?"

"And you're forever off on one, aren't you? For all we're together, I may as well be single. I...I've made up my mind, Michael. I'm filing for divorce."

"Divorce," he said in a strangled voice. "God, Lacy." His knees buckled and he dropped heavily to the bed just as a sharp rap sounded at the front door. Michael couldn't force words past the lump in his throat. He knew things hadn't been good, but—

Lacy left the bedroom. Moments later she led Bettis in to get her bags. The doorman eyed the broken glass. He made no comment, only gathered the cases as Lacy directed.

Michael caught her wrist or she would have gone without saying goodbye. "Don't do anything rash until I get back," he begged in a low voice. "Give me a chance to put things right. I'll take a few weeks off. We'll go to the Bahamas or something."

She jerked from his hold. "It's over, Michael. I've never been anything more to you than your first transplant."

"That's not true."

"Yes. Find another star patient. I want a man who sees me as a woman."

Stunned, Michael watched her walk away. It was some time before he stood and resumed filling his shaving kit. He studied the hands reaching for his razor. A surgeon's hands. His skill had brought them together. Well, technically, Lacy's sister, Faith, had brought them together. She was a nurse at the Boston hospital where Michael had done his residency. Lacy was the one who'd demanded he set up practice in New York.

How had they gone from building a future together to…contemplating divorce? With hands not quite steady, Michael knocked a packet of pills from a shelf in the medicine cabinet. Absently he retrieved it. Lacy's birth control pills. In her haste she must have forgotten them.

Michael dashed out of the apartment to catch her. Halfway to the elevator, he stopped. This was a full dispenser. Probably an extra that Lacy's gynecologist had given her in case they had to travel on short notice.

A shiver coursed through Michael's body as he recalled what had happened earlier. Replaying the scene in his mind, he felt his blood begin to flow again. Granted, Lacy could be impulsive, but she wasn't foolhardy. Those were just angry words she'd thrown out, hoping to make him stay home. Her threats had become habit—a way to manipulate him. And he'd refused to bend. They were both at fault.

Sighing, he retraced his steps. He'd phone her the minute he reached his hotel in Trondheim. Once he turned the patient over to her own team for follow-up care, he'd talk to his partner about taking time off. Dominic would understand.

Michael finished packing and wrote a note to the housekeeper, letting her know that he and Lacy would be away for a week or so. He felt better for having a solid plan in place. Shifting his bags, he locked the door and went down to meet his cab.

CHAPTER ONE

August

A PERSISTENT RINGING dragged Faith Hyatt from a deep sleep. As one hand fanned the air above her nightstand in an effort to silence the sound, her sleepy brain insisted the call had to be a wrong number. She'd just come off two weeks of back-to-back shifts at the Boston hospital where she worked. Half the staff was laid low by flu. Maria Phelps, who scheduled shifts, had promised Faith four uninterrupted days off.

"'Lo," she said in a raspy voice, burying the receiver in the pillow under her ear. Faith covered a yawn and tried to focus on the voice at the other end of the line.

In spite of exhaustion, she shot upright. Her head and heart began to pound, and the receiver slipped from her shaking fingers. Scrambling to find it in the dark, she brought it to her dry lips again and croaked, "Gwen, you're positive the woman admitted through E.R. is my sister? Lacy Cameron?"

Long used to being ejected from bed in the middle of the night, Faith turned on a light and found clean clothes as the caller relayed details. "Yes," Faith said, bending to tie her sneakers, "It's possible she'd revert to Hyatt now that she's divorced. I'll be there in ten minutes, Gwen." Smack! The receiver hit the cradle. Faith's mind continued on fast-forward as she splashed cold water on her face, brushed her teeth and ran a comb through her short brown hair.

Her last contact with either Cameron had been in June. It was now the end of August. Lacy's husband, Michael Cameron, had thrown Faith for a loop when he'd phoned late one night in early June to inform her that he and Lacy had divorced. At the time Faith had been crushed to think her sister hadn't confided in her. But family ties had never meant to Lacy what they did to Faith. In fact, it was pretty typical of Lacy to arrive here in the middle of the night after months of silence, expecting her big sister to haul herself out of bed and put in an appearance at a moment's notice. Lacy had always thought the world revolved around her needs. And when hadn't Faith turned herself inside out for family? Sighing, she strapped on her nurse's watch and rushed from the building. Lopsided though the relationship was, she and Lacy were bound together by blood.

Faith set out to jog the four night-shadowed blocks that separated her apartment building from the hospital. Passing the corner deli, she realized she hadn't asked Gwen what was wrong with Lacy. No one detested being sick more than Lacy did. As her worry increased, Faith broke into a run.

At last, lights spilled onto the street at the corner where Good Shepherd had stood for over fifty years. Breaking her stride only long enough to press the button that operated the front doors, Faith rushed into E.R.

"Hi, Cicely." Breathing hard from her sprint, Faith latched on to the plump arm of a passing nurse, another friend. "Gwen phoned. About my sister," she managed after the next deep breath. "Do you know where she is, or which doctor admitted her?"

"Finegold. He sent her up to Three East. Said he'd

do a complete workup after he finishes the emergency surgery that brought him in tonight. Your sister just dropped in, said she hadn't seen a doctor. Finegold ordered tests, which Lacy refused until after you see her.'' The nurse rolled her eyes. "The great Finegold doesn't take kindly to anyone vetoing his edicts. I don't envy you having to unruffle his feathers.''

Faith gave a puzzled frown. Finegold was senior staff gynecologist. "Uh…Cice, did Lacy say why she happened to be in Boston at this hour? She lives in New York City.'' Faith frowned again. "Or she did. Perhaps Newport, Rhode Island, now. Her husband, er, ex, said she'd received their beach house in the divorce settlement.''

"I thought her chart listed a Boston address, but maybe not. Uh-oh. Hear those sirens? Headed our way. You'd better get out of here, girl, while the gettin's good.''

"You don't have to tell me twice.'' Faith ran and boarded the elevator as two ambulances screeched to a halt under the portico. Loudspeakers began to drone the names of staff who were needed in E.R. Doors opened and nurses spilled out.

By comparison to the E.R. chaos, the third-floor ward was silent. Faith stopped at the nursing station and spoke to a nurse she knew. "You admitted my sister, Lacy Camer…er, Hyatt.'' Shedding her coat, Faith tossed it over a rack. "May I see her?''

Two nurses at the desk appeared to be relieved. "In 312,'' one of them said. "We hooked her up to oxygen, Faith. It was all she'd allow.''

"Lacy hates hospitals.'' *Especially this one.* First, their mother had been chronically ill. She was in and out of Good Shepherd for years. Then, in college, Lacy had developed degenerative cardiopulmonary disease. Faith stared into space as memories of those unsettled years crowded in. Her sister had been terrified of their mom's cystic fibrosis. On their mother's bad days—and there were many—care of the household fell to Faith. She was just seven when she first assumed responsibility for her baby sister, since their dad could only afford part-time help. About the time Lacy hit her teens, life became doubly traumatic for Faith, who by then attended nursing school at night. Her sister rebelled and refused to help take care of their mom. In spite of everything, the family had endured—until worse tragedy struck.

Mrs. Hyatt died and shortly after that, Lacy fell ill. Their dad folded inside himself. Only good thing happened that year—Faith met Dr. Michael Cameron, Good Shepherd's rising star of heart-lung transplant surgery.

As she turned away from the nursing desk and approached her sister's room, Faith guiltily recalled the secret crush she'd once harbored for the handsome, brilliant surgeon. The man who'd ultimately married her sister. How fortunate that Michael had never had any inkling of how she felt. Before she'd begged him to take Lacy's case, Faith had rarely drummed up enough courage to even smile at the man. He'd left her tonguetied and feeling giddy. Nurses didn't feel giddy. It wasn't allowed.

Hearing that Dr. Cameron had fallen in love with her more attractive, more outgoing sister really hadn't come as any big surprise to Faith. The *real* shocker came when Michael telephoned to say he and Lacy had split up.

Now Faith wished her shyness hadn't kept her from asking pertinent details. Michael had volunteered noth-

ing—merely mentioned he'd been out of the country
and he didn't know about the birthday gift Faith had
sent Lacy until a full month after her twenty-seventh
birthday. Michael promised to forward her package to
the beach house, which he said Lacy had received in
the divorce settlement. He'd signed off, leaving no
opening for questions of a more personal nature.

Faith, who'd observed numerous doctors' infidelities,
took for granted that Michael had ended the marriage.
She knew from experience that all sorts of attractive
women stood ready to trap doctors who were as successful and handsome as her former brother-in-law. Few
men had the integrity to walk away from such easy bait.
Michael had fallen off the pedestal she'd placed him
on, and that disappointed Faith. She wondered if her
reaction was a result of being more mother than sister
to Lacy; after all, mothers resented people who hurt
their kids. Lacy had probably been humiliated by Michael's defection. That was, Faith had decided, the reason her sister had slunk off in private to lick her
wounds. The reason Lacy had never returned any of her
calls.

Refusing to dwell on those unhappy circumstances,
Faith cracked open the door to Lacy's room. Her legs
refused to step over the threshold. Was that motionless
body in the bed her once-vibrant sister? Perhaps this
wasn't Lacy's room.

Letting go of the door, Faith tiptoed to the bed for a
closer look. She gasped as her eyes lit on the patient's
swollen belly. She stumbled backward a step, not wanting to startle a stranger.

But…no. The hair, the features, were Lacy's. *Her
sister was pregnant.* Faith muffled an involuntary cry
as the room spun wildly. It was impossible to stop sta-

tistics from running through her head. How many heart-
lung transplant patients had successfully delivered
babies? She battled the hysteria clogging her throat. Because of Lacy's condition, Faith regularly sought out
articles concerning organ transplants. She remembered
reading in a discarded medical journal about one young
woman's successful delivery. *One*. And that woman's
journey hadn't been easy.

In spite of her reluctance to disturb Lacy, Faith must
have made a noise. The dark lashes that brushed her
sister's pale cheeks lifted slowly, revealing unfocused
blue eyes. "Faith?" Lacy's voice was thin, breathless.
Even with a steady infusion of oxygen, it was obviously
a struggle to talk and breathe simultaneously.

"Lacy, honey." Faith dragged a chair to the bed and
sat, grasping the cold fingers. She rubbed gently, trying
to share her warmth. "Michael told me you were living
at the beach, Lace. I tried calling—left quite a few messages—but you were never at home. Or were you too
sick to return my calls?"

Pulling free, Lacy groped in a bedside cabinet. "We,
ah, haven't got much time. In my purse…papers for you
to sign." There was no question that she considered her
request urgent.

"Hush. Save your strength. Admission forms can
wait." Faith recaptured her sister's hand. "I understand
Dr. Finegold ordered some tests. If you'd prefer, I'll
notify your own obstetrician and the two doctors can
consult first."

"I haven't seen an obstetrician since I moved to Boston. That was…three months ago. The papers…are
from my attorney. Sign them, Faith. K-keep a copy and
mail the other. Envelope is attached. I'm giving you full

custody of m-my baby, in case…'' The icy fingers tight-ened on Faith's hand.

"Custody? Oh, hon, I know you feel rotten. It's tough enough going through pregnancy alone, to say nothing of getting sick." Tears squeezed from Faith's eyes. "Why didn't you tell me you were pregnant? Did you think I wouldn't help? I'll be the best aunt ever. And you'll be a wonderful mom."

Lacy again tried to reach the cabinet. "Sign… papers," she panted.

Faith knew it could spell disaster to upset a patient in Lacy's condition. "Okay, if you'll lie still, I'll sign the blasted forms." She hurriedly found Lacy's purse and retrieved the documents. Without reading a word, Faith dug out a pen and wrote her name beside every *X*. "There," she exclaimed, tucking one copy into the pocket of her uniform and the other into a stamped en-velope. "All done. Now will you please relax?"

Lacy tossed her head from side to side. "After it's mailed."

Faith heaved a sigh. "You always were stubborn. There's a postal box right outside the entrance. I'll post this after the doctor examines you." Faith was no stranger to bartering with Lacy. Once it had been a game with them, everything from coaxing her younger sister into eating oatmeal to doing her homework.

"Now." Lacy's demand was punctuated by a siege of choking that turned her lips blue.

"Hey, hey. Breathe slow and easy. See, I'm on my way to the mailbox. I'll just have the duty nurse page Dr. Finegold. Oh, and Lacy, Finegold may act gruff, but he's the best OB-GYN in Boston."

Once Lacy's choking eased, Faith scurried out. After stopping at the nursing station to ask them to hunt up

Dr. Finegold, she completed her mission as fast as humanly possible. Lacy's condition frightened Faith more than she wanted to admit. She was afraid her sister needed more than an OB-GYN. She needed a pulmonary cardiologist.

Passing a pay phone in the hall, Faith was tempted to call Michael. He, more than any heart-lung specialist, had the expertise to help Lacy. But she dared not contact him, not without Lacy's consent. Maybe now that those all-important papers were dispatched, her sister could be persuaded to listen to reason.

Inside the room again, Faith met Lacy's anxious eyes with a smile. "Mail gets picked up from that box at six in the morning. Now let's discuss you. I think we should call Michael. Whatever happened between you two, Lacy, he's one of the world's leading transplant authorities. Plus," she said around a quick gulp of air, "he's your baby's father."

"No. Well, probably not." Lacy's voice rose and fell convulsively. "Sit. Listen."

Faith found that her legs wouldn't hold her. She thought she was beyond shock. Obviously not. Recovering marginally, she sank into the chair, gathered Lacy's clammy fingers and kissed the white knuckles. "I'm here for you no matter what, Lace. I won't call Michael. But don't ask me not to hate him for booting you out."

"Michael, ah, didn't boot me out." Lacy's fingers fluttered. "He…we—he was so rarely home. He loved his work. M-more than he loved me."

"That's doctors, Lacy. Surgeons, especially. I thought Michael was different. The times I visited you, he seemed so devoted. I thought you had everything, honey."

"Isolation. Drawers full of pills. Endless poking and prodding by my follow-up team." Lacy ran a restless hand over her swollen stomach. "I quit taking everything when I found out I was pregnant."

"Oh, Lace! You shouldn't have stopped the anti-rejection pills. Your body needs them to function properly."

"Yes, but I..." After struggling to catch a breath, Lacy whispered, "I...want her to be perfect. N...or...mal."

"You know it's a girl?"

Lacy shook her head and cradled her abdomen again. "No. I haven't consulted a doctor. I just call my baby Abby. You remember my best friend in high school? Abi...gail?"

Faith's flicker of a smile was soon replaced by a frown. "So, if you're not having Michael's baby—then whose?" She bit her lip and glanced away. "I'm sorry to be nosy. But it occurred to me that if you cared for a man enough to make love with him, he ought to be here seeing you through this."

Lacy grew fretful again. "I...I—K-Kipp's on the U.S. sailing team. We, ah, met the day I left Michael. After I fi-filed for divorce, I...I stopped at the club. Kipp...well," she explained haltingly, "he was lonely, too. The next day he took me sailing and we, ah, made love on the boat. In the weeks after, we danced, sailed, combed the beach. He brought me flowers. Kipp never treated me like a...a...an invalid." Lacy took a long time to finish her sentence.

"Sounds...wonderful." Faith didn't want to hear more, and Lacy should rest and save her strength. "Dr. Finegold ought to be out of surgery by now. I'll go see what's keeping him." She rose and started away.

Lacy plucked at Faith's arm. "Let me fin…ish. Kipp's team went to Florida for a race. H-he phoned every day." A weak smile lifted her blue-tinted lips. "I expected him to visit when the team returned. He didn't. A few days before he was due back, I got sick. Flu, I thought. I went to the clinic for antibiotics." She labored to catch her breath. "And…learned I was pregnant."

Again the room fell silent except for the muted puff of oxygen combined with Lacy's raspy breath.

"Shh. We can talk after you've recovered." Lacy's breathing had changed. Her respiration had become so shallow and erratic it frightened Faith. "It's obvious the guy didn't stick around. But don't you worry. I make enough to hire a nanny to help with the baby. Lie quiet now, please," Faith begged.

Lacy wouldn't be denied. "I'd never been to Kipp's house. He always came to mine." Color splashed her ashen cheeks. "I…found his address and dr…ove there." Tears flowed from the corners of her eyes.

Wanting to save her sister pain, Faith wiped the tears away with her thumbs. "Please don't do this, Lacy. Some men are just jerks. Forget him."

"I…I…parked and was admiring his house. His…his wife came out to…see if I was lost. I didn't know he was m-m-married." Tears rolled over Faith's thumbs and onto Lacy's pillow.

"The bastard!" Faith couldn't help herself. She wished she could have five minutes alone with the man responsible for causing her sister this agony.

"The…irony, Faith. Kipp and his wife separated because she couldn't conceive. They ar…gued over adopting. His dad, a bigwig on Wall Street, wants a grandson to carry on the family name. Kipp…dropped by later.

To apologize. Seems his wife heard of a new fertility treatment. He felt obligated to l-let her try it." Lacy's thin body was racked with sobs. "I…he…doesn't know about the baby. I don't want him to."

Straightening, Faith adjusted the oxygen hoses. "Oh, sweetie, don't do this to yourself. You're getting all worked up and it's sapping what little capacity you have to breathe. I'm going to get a doctor." Increasingly worried because Lacy's skin felt clammy and her face now had a waxy cast, Faith sprang up and hurried across the room.

She yanked open the door and bumped into someone coming in. "Dr. Finegold!" she said, tugging him inside. "Faith Hyatt, sir. I've assisted you on post-op rounds. This is my sister." Letting go of his sleeve, Faith waved toward the bed. "Lacy is a post heart-lung transplant patient," Faith whispered. "At the onset of pregnancy, she quit taking her anti-rejection meds. Please, she needs help."

The doctor walked to the bedside and swiftly began an exam. Each time he paused to write in the chart, his scowl deepened. "Who did her transplant?"

"Dr. Cameron. Michael Cameron," Faith added, darting a guilty glance at Lacy.

"I only know him by reputation. Get him on the phone. Stat! Meanwhile, see if our staff cardiologist has ever assisted with a post-transplant delivery. And while you're at the desk, Hyatt, order a sonogram."

At each barked order, Faith nodded. Everyone on staff knew Finegold expected blind obedience. Still she dragged him aside. "You wouldn't know, but Lacy is Dr. Cameron's ex-wife," she murmured. "She won't authorize calling him."

"She's been assigned to my care, Nurse. I'm making the decisions."

"Yes, sir." As Faith turned and grasped the door handle, Finegold swore ripely. She felt the flap of his lab coat as he hurtled past her and bellowed into the hall. "Code blue. Get me a crash cart, on the double." Racing back to the bed, he tore away blankets, sheets and the flimsy oxygen lines and started CPR.

Faith's senses shut down totally until a cart slammed through the door accompanied by a trained team whose purpose it was to restore a patient's vital signs. For the first time since she'd become a nurse, Faith didn't see a patient lying there. She saw her baby sister. Pictures swam behind her eyes. Lacy as a newborn. Taking her first steps. Starting school. Going on her first date. A hospital-room wedding that had somehow led to this debacle. If Michael Cameron had been more of a husband, Lacy would be well and happy and living in New York. Lacy might not blame him, but Faith did. He'd promised to care for her sister in sickness and in health—until death parted them. Panic filled her as Finegold ordered the paddles applied to Lacy's thin chest.

Lacy's body jumped and so did Faith's. She didn't breathe again until a technician gave a thumbs-up sign, meaning Lacy's heartbeat had resumed.

"Dammit, dammit, dammit," Finegold cursed, yanking the stethoscope out of his ears to let it flop around his neck. "We have a pulse but it's thready. Clear me for an O.R. This woman doesn't have a snowball's chance in the tropics if we don't take the baby. How the hell far along is she? What kind of prenatal care has she had? Get Epstein, Carlson and Wainwright to scrub.

Round up an anesthesiologist.'' Finegold all but foamed at the mouth.

As he barked orders, Faith grabbed his arm. "My sister hasn't had any prenatal care, but I'm familiar with her heart problems. Let me scrub with you.''

The doctor shook her off, never slowing his steps toward the door. "I know you're qualified to assist, Hyatt, but you aren't in any shape. Take a seat in the OB waiting room. I'll find you when I'm finished.''

"But I *want* to help!''

"Pray,'' he said, spinning on a heel. With that, he flew down the hall.

The hardest thing Faith had ever done, outside of burying her mother or maybe waiting anxiously through Lacy's long and tedious heart-lung transplant, was to step aside while they wheeled her out of the room. Even though Faith heartily disliked clingy relatives who impeded the progress of staff readying a patient for surgery, she doggedly kept pace with the squeaky cart. At the elevator, she elbowed aside a technician and kissed Lacy's cheek.

Weighted eyelids slowly opened. Oxygen tubes from a portable tank pinched Lacy's nose. IVs ran in both arms. "Take c-care of my b-baby. L...li-like you did me.'' The dark pupils of her eyes swallowed all but a narrow ring of blue. It took every ounce of her energy to breathe. Still, she reached feebly for Faith's hand.

Faith closed the icy fingers between her palms. "We'll take care of your baby together.'' Hardly aware that the elevator door had slid open and someone on the team had roughly disengaged their hands, Faith's wavering promise bounced off a rapidly closing door. "You fight, Lacy. Hang in there,'' she cried in a fractured voice.

THE WAIT SEEMED INTERMINABLE. At about five in the
morning, Faith walked to the phone to call her father,
just to hear his voice. He and she were all that was left
of Lacy's family. But Dwight Hyatt had escaped into a
dreamworld when his beloved wife died. Though only
fifty-six, he resided in an assisted-living facility. He
played checkers with other residents, watched TV and
occasionally went on supervised outings. He recognized
Faith at her weekly visits, but he rarely asked about
Lacy unless prompted. More times than not, he didn't
know Faith when she telephoned.

Fighting a sense of disorientation, Faith did as Dr.
Finegold ordered. She prayed—until she ran out of
words and tears. Three hours had passed when she wandered over to the waiting room coffeepot and poured a
third cup of sludge. Through the window, she noticed
that pale golden threads had begun to erase a solemn
gray dawn. The promise of a sunny day lifted Faith's
spirits and gave her hope, the first she'd had throughout
her long, lonely vigil.

Muffled footsteps intruded on her optimistic moment.
Glancing up, she experienced another rush of relief at
seeing Dr. Finegold striding toward her. He untied his
mask and dropped it wearily as he drew closer, still
wearing full blue scrubs. The cup of muddy coffee
slipped from Faith's fingers and splashed across her
feet.

Even at a distance, she recognized the look on Finegold's face. ''No, no, no!'' The scalding coffee seeped
through her socks, but Faith felt nothing until a crushing
pain descended and great, gulping sobs racked her body.
She stumbled and fell heavily into the nearest chair. She
wasn't aware that tears obscured her view of the ap-

proaching man or that they dripped off her cheeks when she stared mutely up at him.

"I'm sorry," he said brokenly. "We did everything we could. Her heart and lungs had been overtaxed for too long. Without anti-rejection drugs…" The doctor shut his eyes and massaged the closed lids. "God, I'm sorry," he repeated, as he continued to loom over Faith's shuddering frame. "This part never gets easier," he said quietly, shifting from one foot to the other.

"And the baby?" she finally asked in a wooden voice.

"Babies," he corrected, pulling out an adjacent chair and sinking into it. "A boy and a girl. Both underweight, but scrappy as hell. My best guess is that your sister was seven to eight months along. The male baby weighed in at four-two. The female, an even four. I put in a call to Hal Sampson. If you want a different pediatrician, I'll cancel him."

"Two?" Hysteria tinged Faith's tearful voice. "Twins?"

"Yeah. None of us were prepared. With no history, we were flying by the seat of our pants." Leaning forward, the doctor clasped his hands between his knees. "You've got a lot to deal with. I suggest visiting your niece and nephew before you tackle the unpleasant chores that face you. I think they'll give you the will to do what needs to be done." He stood then, and gripped her shoulder briefly. "Well, I have to go complete the paperwork."

"I, uh, thanks for all you did." Dazed, Faith rose. Automatically blotting her eyes, she stood and held on to a chair back. Order and organization had always been her greatest strengths. Dependability ran a close second. In an isolated portion of her brain, Faith knew she could get through this ordeal by focusing on one task at a time.

Task one: Mop up the coffee she'd spilled.

Task two: Welcome Lacy's babies into this harsh, cruel world.

Task three: See her sister properly laid to rest.

Only after she'd done those things would Faith allow herself to think about the future. Struggling with a fresh surge of tears, she groped in her pockets for a tissue to wipe up the coffee. In doing so, she encountered her copy of the custody agreement. In sad hindsight, Lacy's urgency became all too clear. Lacy must have sensed how badly off she was if she'd had custody papers prepared. Oh, why couldn't she have had the care to preserve her own health?

She hadn't. And Faith had promised to be the babies' guardian. She would do a good job of it, even if right now her loss seemed too great to bear.

Once she'd mopped up the spill—but before she notified the mortuary who'd handled her mother's funeral—Faith took Dr. Finegold's suggestion. She made her way to the nursery. With her first glance into the isolettes, she lost her heart to these two tiny scraps of humanity. The baby swaddled in blue screwed up his red face and bellowed, letting the world know he was a force to be reckoned with. His sister pursed a rosebud mouth and slept on, the barest hint of a sigh raising her chest.

A pediatric nurse placed a bolstering hand on Faith's shoulder. "I'll get you a mask, gown and gloves if you'd like to hold them."

"May I?" Faith's heart fluttered with both joy and sorrow. Joy for herself. Sorrow for the sister who'd never comfort these little ones with her touch.

She made an effort to curb her sadness and concentrated on counting the babies' fingers and toes. "Oh, aren't you sweethearts? It takes both of you together to weigh what your mama did at birth." Lacy had been a solid eight pounds. Faith rocked them and talked on in a low murmur, determined that they should start life hearing about the good, fun-loving side of their mother. "Your mama loved you," she whispered. "She gave up her own life for you. I'm going to make sure I bring you up the way she would have wanted...."

Soon after, Faith fed both babies with special tubes the nurses prepared, tubes designed to teach the babies to suck properly.

By staying, rocking the dear little bodies and holding them close, Faith was able to delay dealing with her loss. Dr. Finegold was right, she decided, staring at the babies who were now curled up, sleeping peacefully.

Lacy's twins gave her the strength to go on. To take the next step, complete the next task.

CHAPTER TWO

THE TELEPHONE WAS RINGING when Faith walked into her apartment the next afternoon. She'd spent most of the morning attending to the numerous details associated with Lacy's funeral. The cloying scent of funeral-home flowers remained in her nostrils. Although she'd walked home in the late-summer sunshine, she still couldn't warm up.

Physically and mentally drained, Faith considered letting her machine take a message. The red light already blinked, so there were others. News traveled fast in a hospital. It was probably someone from the staff wanting to express condolences. But what if it was the funeral home? The director had said he'd be in touch if any problem arose. Maybe she'd neglected something important.

She snatched up the receiver on the fifth ring. After an initial exchange of hellos, it was a minute or two before Faith realized the caller was the hospital's chief administrator.

At first all she heard was his mention of the twins, and she panicked. Her heart flew over high hurdles, while her ears recoiled in fear. She could only think that something had happened to Lacy's babies, even though they'd been fine when she stopped by at ten. The nurses had assured her the babies were healthy, small as they were.

Little by little, Faith's training kicked in, and she relaxed enough to make sense of what Dr. Peterson was saying.

"I don't understand," she ventured shakily when she thought she finally had his message straight. "Two men are at the nursery asking to see the twins? Both claim to be the father? Who are they? How do they…" Her voice trailed off, but before Dr. Peterson could say another word, Faith drowned him out. "It doesn't matter. Allow no one near Lacy's babies. No one but me. I'll be there in five minutes. Tell the nursery staff to have the men wait in the room at the end of the hall."

The taste of fear grew stronger after she dropped the receiver and bolted for the door. The *how,* the *why,* the *who* all whirled in a muddle through Faith's sleep-deprived brain. She'd hardly closed her eyes since Lacy had reappeared so abruptly in her life…and then vanished for good. Had it really only been last night?

The *how* fell into place before Faith reached the sidewalk. Local newspapers had built a headline story out of the death of Michael Cameron's first multiple-organ transplant patient. Faith had briefly glimpsed today's front page. At the time, she'd only registered pain—to think Lacy wasn't to be allowed dignity in death. Her sister had despised the condition she thought had stolen her independence. Lacy had been terrified of becoming a burden to others. She would have hated having her weaknesses exposed to the world.

As she hailed a cab, it struck Faith that the *who*—the two men making demands at the hospital—wasn't really any great mystery. One of them would be the great Dr. Cameron himself. The other, probably the married playboy. Kipp, the sailor with no last name.

It wouldn't be long before Faith ferreted out the *why,*

she thought grimly as she paid the driver, and quickly entered the hospital by a side door. Not that anything either man had to say would change the facts. Lacy's last request had been for Faith to keep her baby safe from the likes of those two. She had papers saying so.

For good measure, Faith stopped by the admitting office and ran off two copies of the custody document. If, by the time she reached the nursery, she still felt as hostile toward the men as she did now, she'd rub their noses in the truth. Neither one of them had loved Lacy enough to stick by her during her pregnancy. As far as Faith was concerned, the jerks didn't deserve to set eyes on the twins—and that went for the actual birth father, as well as Michael, who must suffer delusions of being the dad. Why else would Dr. Cameron be here throwing his weight around?

Staff members glanced at Faith curiously as she hurried along the corridor and took the back stairs two at a time. Obviously the grapevine had spread the word. An interested crowd would be lurking behind the potted plants in the expectant fathers' waiting room.

Thanks to one of the larger rubber plants, Faith was afforded a good view inside the room before anyone noted her approach. Her breath did a half hitch that she couldn't control. Michael Cameron stood near the window. His brown hair, still dark and thick, was mussed as if he'd run a hand through it several times. The inscrutable Dr. Cameron, who rarely, if ever, had a hair out of place.

No matter how hard Faith tried to control her feelings, her heart always did a slow somersault when she came across Michael unexpectedly. It irritated her that she never seemed to have that reaction to other men—eligible men.

Today Faith commanded her heart to be still. She wanted to study these two analytically—the men who'd been her sister's lovers. Cameron's summer khaki suit looked new. He wore a pale cream shirt and a tie that matched the gold flecks in his hazel eyes. He appeared more gaunt than when she'd last seen him more than a year ago, the previous May, at Lacy's twenty-sixth birthday.

Good. Faith hoped his new leanness had something to do with the breakup of his marriage and wasn't because he'd joined a fancy health club. She couldn't tell if he was suffering. His smoldering regard centered on the room's other occupant. But the man at whom Michael glared appeared oblivious of the daggers coming his way.

Sun-bleached hair fell in a perfect cut above the second man's well-tanned brow. An expensive navy blazer hung loose over pristine white pants. Faith couldn't determine the color of the stranger's eyes. They were trained on a magazine with a sailboat on the cover.

Both men exuded an air of comfortable wealth. Faith could only hope their behavior would be as civilized as their appearance. Taking one last deep breath, she moved around the plant and into the room.

Michael was the first to notice her. He uncrossed his arms and straightened away from the window, feeling a jolt of recognition. Faith Hyatt had always been so different from Lacy. He doubted he was alone in finding it hard to believe they were sisters. Tall, blond Lacy had had an athletic build—or rather she had before she'd decided it was chic to be model-thin. She wore makeup with flair and was always experimenting with hairstyles. His ex-wife had been happiest when surrounded by people. Faith, however, was small-boned and quiet to the point of being difficult to talk to. She seemed content to spend hours on her own, yet she had a rare ability to calm the sick with a touch. If she wore any lipstick at all today, she'd chewed it off. Her fresh-scrubbed look made her seem much younger than her thirty-four years. Something about this woman had always fascinated him.

Michael had first met Faith the year before he'd completed his residency. Even then, she'd worn her walnut-brown curls in a pixie cut that emphasized her huge dark eyes. Serious eyes that studied him now as if he were an unwanted specimen under her microscope. Not surprising. She'd played mother bear too long. Lacy had been her cub. Naturally she'd transfer those nurturing habits to Lacy's babies. *His* babies.

From the minute Michael had seen the article in the *New York Times,* describing Lacy's pregnancy and her reputed refusal to take her anti-rejection meds, many things that hadn't made sense to him before the divorce fell into place. For instance, Lacy's little speech about normal women her age having kids. Her odd behavior that day. The unused packet of birth control pills he'd found after she'd virtually attacked him at the door, frantically initiating sex. A lot added up now—now that it was too late to help her. But it wasn't too late to help their babies. The infants were said to be about four weeks premature, and that made them his. Period. Nothing left to discuss. He scowled in the other man's direction.

Because Faith's steps slowed as she entered the room and her uneasy brown eyes seemed to be searching for an escape route, Michael took pity on her and softened his harsh expression. Crossing the room in long strides, he reached for her trembling hand. "I'm sorry Peterson disturbed you, Faith,'' he murmured. ''You must have a million more important things to do today than rush down here. I can't tell you how shocked I was to read about Lacy's death in the *Times*. The report indicated she'd stopped her anti-rejection meds. I wish you'd called me when her pregnancy became obvious, Faith. Whether or not Lacy was mad at me, someone on her transplant follow-up team should have followed her prenatal care.''

Faith swallowed. ''Lacy never contacted me. She never returned any of my calls. The first I knew she was pregnant was when they admitted her to the hospital. She'd had no prenatal care, Michael.''

The other man in the waiting room rose and glanced at the couple engaged in conversation. Closing his magazine, he walked to the center of the room. ''You're Faith, Lacy's sister? I'm Kipp Fielding III. The news story I read in our paper said you'd spent time with Lacy before she, uh, went into surgery. She and I were…ah…quite close in January and February. Did she by chance mention me?''

Faith's head snapped up. She tugged her hand from Michael's fingers. ''As a matter of fact, Mr. Fielding, she did have a few things to say about you. Except that she never revealed your last name—so you *could* have remained anonymous.'' A rustle near the room's entrance forced their heads around. Two nurses stood in the hall, chatting with a technician who was rearranging items on a lab cart. Faith knew at once that all ears were tuned to what was being said inside. Gossip lightened the tedious work at the hospital, provided a distraction from pain and death. In the past, Faith had been as big a participant as the next person. However, now that it involved someone she loved, she had second thoughts about the passing of possibly harmful rumors.

"Gentlemen, let me call Dr. Peterson and see if there's a conference room available where we can talk with more privacy."

Kipp buried his hands in his pockets. "I don't see what there is to talk about. That baby boy is my son. He's a Fielding. I intend to take steps to insure his birthright."

"Now wait a damn minute." Michael wrapped long fingers around Kipp's jauntily striped tie. "Maybe you can't add, Fielding, but I can. Lacy and I were still married in January. Those are my children she carried."

A shrill whistle split the air. Both men swiveled toward the source. They gaped at Faith, who calmly removed two fingers from unsmiling lips. "Maybe you two don't mind airing your dirty laundry in public. It so happens it's my recently deceased sister you're maligning. Have you no decency?"

Michael dropped his hand. "You're absolutely right, Faith." He cast a scowl at the eavesdroppers. "I agree we need a private place where we can settle this issue."

Confident that she'd soon set both men straight, Faith went to the house phone and punched the hospital administrator's number. "Dr. Peterson, please. This is Nurse Faith Hyatt. He phoned me at home earlier. I'm here in the hospital now." She tapped her toe while she waited for him to come on the line. When she'd explained the problem, he told her the conference rooms were all in use but offered the use of his office. "Thank you," Faith said. "We'll be right down."

Peterson brushed her effusive thanks aside. "It's an honor to have Mike Cameron here. I'm on my way to the cafeteria. I'll have them send over a tray of coffee.

Oh, Nurse, when your business winds down, perhaps Dr. Cameron might take a moment to tour our new heart wing. His stamp of approval would be a boon to Good Shepherd.''

Faith sighed. "I'll tell him." She had no doubt he'd prefer a tour of the heart wing over a trip to the funeral home. Of course, she was probably foolish to even think Michael might ask to pay his last respects to his former wife. Hadn't Lacy said Michael loved his work more than he loved her? If that was how things stood between them when they were married, why would he alter his attitudes after their divorce?

"Does Peterson have a room or not?" Michael spoke near her ear, making Faith jump.

"Um, yes. His office. He also said he hoped you had time to tour our new heart facility when we've completed our business."

"Not today. Maybe later in the week. I'll catch him and explain. Once we iron out this mess, I plan to spend an hour or so with my babies. And after that…" He swallowed. "Uh…if you have no objection, Faith, I'd like to see Lacy."

His chin dropped to his chest and his eyelids closed, and she realized she'd misjudged him.

"Of c-course," she stammered. Seeing Michael so emotional triggered her own bleak feelings again. "The service is tomorrow. It's very small." She named the funeral home. "Lacy didn't have many friends left in Boston. Although…I'm not sure of that." Suddenly flustered, Faith clasped her hands and frowned at her fingers. "Perhaps I should have an official funeral notice placed in the afternoon paper." Peering up at Michael through her eyelashes, she asked him, "Were you aware Lacy had moved back to Boston?" Unexpectedly her eyes filled. She had to blink hard to contain the tears. "That's another thing I don't have any explanation for—why she didn't let me know. It might have made a difference if she had." A tear did creep out and slip down her cheek.

Michael gently clasped her upper arms. "Don't beat yourself up, Faith. It's taken me some time since she asked for the divorce to realize that Lacy always did what Lacy wanted, and to hell with how it affected others. I believe she planned this pregnancy from the get-go. It wasn't accidental."

Kipp broke into the conversation. "Look, I need to catch the three-o'clock shuttle back to New York. Do you suppose you two could take care of family business after we settle my parental rights?"

Faith felt like hitting his supercilious jaw. "I imagine your wife is expecting you home at the usual time. Does she have any idea where you are and what you're doing, Mr. Fielding?"

"Wife?" Michael repeated, bristling.

The well-placed barb brought a wave of crimson to Kipp's tanned cheeks. "Shelby doesn't know yet, Ms. Hyatt. I assure you she'll welcome the boy into our home once the details here are finalized and I have a chance to tell her. Shelby has wanted to adopt a child for some time." Lowering his voice, he said hesitantly, "My father hasn't favored adoption. He's pressed for a blood grandson. And now he has one."

Faith cocked her head to one side. "Lacy had twins, Mr. Fielding. A boy *and* a girl. You've only mentioned her son. But then girls can't carry on the family name, can they?" she said coolly. In an even colder tone, she added, "Lacy's son will never be Kipp Fielding IV if I have any say in the matter. And I have a lot of say."

Michael stepped between the two combatants before Kipp could rebut. "Shouldn't we go to Dr. Peterson's office before we shed blood on this shiny tile?"

Faith clammed up immediately. She hadn't intended to lose her temper. And she'd forgotten their audience. Aiming pointed glances at the bystanders still lurking in the hall, she squared her shoulders and marched past them. Michael and Kipp fell in behind her. Michael, though, paused at the nursery window and leaned his forehead against the glass. He cupped both hands around his eyes in order to see better.

"Lacy's babies are in the premie unit," Faith informed him stiffly.

Backing away from the window, Michael joined her. "The paper said they were approximately four weeks early. Are they well, Faith?"

Kipp halted midstride. "They are, aren't they?" he demanded. "The article I read said the boy was underweight." He stuffed his hands into his pants pockets. "Lacy never told me she'd had organ transplants. Is there a possibility her son will inherit her medical problems?" he asked, sounding both worried and unsure.

Michael shot him an incredulous stare. "I'm a good surgeon, Fielding, but no one is that perfect at cracking open a chest. If you and Lacy got down to bare skin, fella, it'd be hard to miss her scar."

A flush streaked up Kipp's throat. He fingered his tie.

"Stop it, you two." Faith pasted a smile on her face for the gray-haired woman seated behind a desk outside Dr. Peterson's office. "The world doesn't need to know all the sordid details of Lacy's history. Both babies are in good health. Hal Sampson examined them. Michael, you remember him—he was pediatric chief when you were here."

"Yes, I remember. Sampson's top-notch."

The men dropped back and let Faith address Peterson's secretary. "Mrs. Lansing, I phoned Dr. Peterson a few minutes ago. I'm Faith Hyatt."

Nodding, the woman rose and led the trio into an oak-paneled room. She pointed out a tray with a coffee carafe and cups that sat on a low table. While she withdrew, but before she closed the door, Michael poured Faith a cup of coffee, and then one for himself. "Still take cream in yours?" he asked, passing the carafe to Fielding so he could pour his own.

"Yes," she said, surprised he'd recall such a mundane thing. "Too much straight caffeine gives me jitters. Today, especially, I've got enough acid running in my stomach to charge a battery."

Michael gazed at her over the rim of his cup. "I'm sorry so much has fallen on your shoulders, Faith. How is Dwight handling Lacy's death? Has he been any help, or are you having problems there, too?"

She perched on the edge of one of the three chairs someone had arranged in a triangle around the coffee table, and clutched the hot cup to warm her suddenly cold fingers. "I tried telling Dad we'd lost Lacy. He got it all mixed up in his mind and thought I was talking about Mother. The doctor had to sedate him. I decided there wasn't any sense in putting him through the grief of attending her service."

"What about your aunt Lorraine?"

"Still on the mission field in Tanzania. When things calm down, I'll write her a letter. Or perhaps I should try calling her via the field office. But maybe it's pointless to worry her when she can't come." She broke off abruptly. "Why this pretended concern, Michael? Your obligations to the Hyatt family ended when the divorce was final. By the way, exactly when was that?''

"July.'' Michael shifted his gaze to Kipp Fielding. "The divorce wasn't my idea. Lacy filed in January while I was on a medical mission to Norway. I phoned her at the beach house to ask her to reconsider. She refused to talk, and said she had company. It was too late, anyway—she'd already filed the papers. That was January fifth. Two days later, divorce papers arrived by courier at my hotel.'' He massaged the back of his neck. "I might have convinced her to drop the request if I'd been able to make it home the next week as I'd originally planned. But we ran into complications with the transplant and I couldn't leave Norway until much later. By then, her lawyer and mine had pretty much settled the particulars. Mine said I shouldn't contest. He said she was seeing someone else.''

"That would be you,'' Faith said testily, her soft brown gaze hardening as she pinned it on Kipp.

"Yes, it would,'' he returned without a hint of shame.

Faith's gaze never wavered. "I guess you forgot you had a wife.''

"Shelby and I separated before Thanksgiving. I assumed she intended to get a divorce—not that it's your business. Having spent the holidays alone, I felt at loose ends. Lacy was lonely, too.'' His lip curled slightly. "She said she was on her own a lot. Her husband devoted his life to his career.'' Meeting Michael's angry glare, Kipp continued speaking to Faith. "Lacy hadn't been out with her husband in months. She'd never been sailing. Had never dug for clams. You'd have thought I'd given her diamonds when I bought her flowers. If ever a woman had been neglected, it was Lacy Cameron.''

Michael clenched a hand in the front of Kipp's shirt. "Damn you, Fielding! I didn't neglect my wife."

"That's enough." Faith pulled a tissue from her handbag and mopped up the coffee Michael had spilled when he vaulted from his chair. Their macho posturing irritated her so much she forgot to be shy. "Lacy did feel you were obsessed with work, Michael. But Kipp, although you treated her like a queen for a few weeks, that hardly makes up for concealing the fact that you were married."

The men gaped at Faith's furious scrubbing. They both frowned, and Michael recognized the anger in her movements as she wielded the tissue. The table was more than polished to a shine when she finished.

Michael broke the silence first. "Lacy had all of my heart and as much of my time as I was able to give." If he sounded hurt, he thought dully, it was because he still had his moments. "I took an oath to heal." He thought Faith should understand that, even if Lacy had somehow forgotten.

Getting to her feet, Faith tossed the sodden tissue into the trash. While she was up, she dug in her purse again and removed the copies she'd made of the custody agreement. She shoved one into each man's hand. "What drove either of you to do what you did doesn't make any difference to Lacy now. In seeking love, my sister obviously made some bad choices. Maybe even selfish ones. But in the end, her decisions weren't selfish. No matter how difficult it was for her to breathe when she was admitted, her focus was on the life that had been created within her."

"Custody papers?" Kipp skimmed through the stapled packet. "She can't do this. Her babies have a father." The man scowled openly at Faith. "You just admitted that Lacy was in distress during her last hours. Any attorney worth his salt will prove you coerced her into signing these. Not only that, who witnessed your signatures?''

''I didn't instigate this agreement. Lacy brought it with her, Mr. Fielding. If there was duress involved in the signing, it was directed toward me. Lacy refused all treatment except oxygen until I not only signed the forms but mailed them to her lawyer. If you'll check closely, on page three she acknowledges my signature. And someone notarized each line Lacy endorsed.''

Faith wasn't about to tell them Lacy's witness signature had already been in place when she herself signed the document. That didn't change the facts. Lacy had watched her sign. Most importantly, the agreement represented her wishes.

A range of emotions flitted across Michael Cameron's face as he read the document from start to finish. Sadness. Longing. Grief. But Faith didn't see anything like resignation as he folded the papers and tucked them into the inside pocket of his suit jacket. While his eyes darkened sympathetically, his jaw remained tensed, his posture determined—as though they'd entered a fight ring and the bell had rung.

Fielding drained his cup and thumped it back onto the tray. Wadding a paper napkin, he threw it into a nearby wastebasket. ''Lacy told me a little about her childhood. I recall she said her mom was an invalid. And that you sacrificed your youth to run the household, Ms. Hyatt.''

''I was the oldest child. If Lacy had been born first, it would have been the other way around,'' Faith stated flatly.

Michael moved forward. ''If you have a point, Fielding, I'd like to hear it. But don't try to say Lacy slandered Faith. I know she admired her sister."

Faith gave him a surprised glance. She and Lacy had grown closer after Lacy's marriage—and before her divorce. Faith was pretty sure familial love had existed. But admiration? Her heart swelled at the thought. During all those troubled years, she would have settled for a simple hug from her sister. Faith roused as Kipp spoke again.

"My point is that Faith missed the things kids do for fun. Lacy said Faith never participated in school activities. No dances. No sports. No guys. A while ago, you two talked about her ailing father. If she assumes care of two infants on top of that, I think she's kissing any chance for a normal life goodbye. This is when she should concentrate on meeting someone and getting married."

A startled gasp escaped Faith's lips. But she was too embarrassed by Kipp's rundown of her life to make any comment. More like her *lack* of a life. He'd managed to make her sound pretty pathetic. Oh, she'd dreamed of falling in love, she'd even had a brief affair with a hospital accountant. He'd ended the relationship, eventually marrying another nurse and moving to another state. Faith continued to hope for marriage and a family someday. But she never felt as if she needed a husband to be complete. Her life hadn't been all that bad.

Michael, too, seemed astonished by Kipp's blunt statement. Since no one interrupted, Kipp hammered his point home. "I'm offering you an out here, Faith. Shelby and I have a six-bedroom home. It sits on three acres. She's able to devote all her time to motherhood. I made some inquiries this morning. I know how much you earn. And I know you work some oddball shifts. I

ROZ DENNY FOX   47

sincerely doubt anyone would think you derelict of duty
if you signed Lacy's babies over to their natural father.''

"You're claiming that role, huh, Fielding?" Michael
slapped a hand on the glass table. "We have a difference of opinion on that score. The twins are mine."

"Don't be ridiculous." Kipp's chest expanded a few
inches. "I hate bringing this up with a lady present, old
man. Your ex-wife was pretty outspoken about the in-
frequency of your lovemaking."

Michael's face went suddenly florid. "It so happens,
pal, we were intimate the day I left for Norway. January
fourth. You're welcome to calculate that out."

Kipp seemed shaken by Michael's announcement.
"I—I...that's the day before we, ah, that is...when
Lacy and I first slept together. I think you're lying,
Cameron. Lacy said she had to schedule an appointment
with you to make love."

"Think what you want. Lacy's forte was high drama.
I guess I always knew she was impulsive. I'm only just
realizing *how* impulsive."

Faith slumped down hard in her chair. She blinked
up at them, stomach roiling. "So what you're, uh, both
saying is that it's a mystery as to who fathered the
twins?"

Neither man acknowledged Faith's conclusion.

Kipp checked his watch for about the third time in
five minutes. "I have to get back to New York. I don't
have any more time to argue. Here's the bottom line.
There's a boy upstairs in the nursery with Fielding
genes. Because of that, he's entitled to a legacy. I won't
go into everything that entails. Suffice it to say he'll be
well taken care of. You two will be hearing from my
attorney. That's a promise."

Faith and Michael watched in silence as he stalked out.

"Two can play his game," Michael said, his expression thunderous. "I don't care how many damned Roman numerals he has after his name. Fielding will be hearing from my lawyer, too. Meanwhile, I'm going up to visit the babies. I don't advise trying to stop me, Faith." Giving her only seconds to respond, he, too, stormed out.

Faith's shoulders slumped. "Oh, Lacy," she murmured. "What kind of mess have you left me with this time?"

Sighing, she regained enough composure to pick up the phone and call the duty nurse in charge of the premie ward. "My sister's ex-husband has asked to visit the twins, Eileen. I'm willing to extend him that courtesy today, but make sure everyone on the duty roster knows Lacy left custody papers on file. If Michael or anyone else wants to see the babies from here on out, staff will have to call me for authorization. Is that clear?" When she was certain the charge nurse understood, Faith rang off.

Stopping at the reception area, she thanked Dr. Peterson's secretary for the use of his office. After that, she went upstairs to her own ward, post-surgical. Faith wanted to see the babies again after Michael left. Somehow, she couldn't shake the feeling that he presented a threat.

Her mind not on work, she nevertheless emptied her mailbox. It was full. Among the usual junk was a notice to stop at the finance office and discuss Lacy's hospital bill. Faith stared at the statement. She had a tidy savings account. She'd expected to use it to stock a nursery; she'd also figured it would allow her to take six months or so off work. Last night when she couldn't sleep, she made lists of what the babies would need. Planning for two of everything ate up money fast. To say nothing of the fact that the cost of funerals had skyrocketed since she'd arranged her mother's.

Closing her eyes, Faith rubbed her forehead. It hadn't entered her mind that she'd owe for Lacy's care. But then, what company would insure her sister? Even if she had a policy, it probably excluded her preexisting condition. Faith placed this new worry at the bottom of her stack. The next envelope she opened was almost as distressing. The babies needed names before the state could issue birth certificates.

Faith picked up a pen. Abigail was easy. That had been Lacy's wish. *Abigail Dawn.* It was a middle name denoting hope, and the two went well together, Faith thought. *Hyatt.* She wrote the last name in block letters. Writing it felt good. Like thumbing her nose at Kipp Fielding III and his father.

The form for Lacy's son remained mockingly blank. Faith made a list of names she thought sounded strong. Nicholas kept floating to the top. "Nicholas it shall be," she murmured, then chewed on the eraser while she searched her list for an acceptable middle name. *John.* A solid biblical name. Also, it'd been Faith and Lacy's grandfather's. Faith remembered him as a soft-spoken man with twinkling eyes.

Once that chore was complete, she dispatched her remaining mail quickly. A glance at her watch suggested she'd wasted enough time; Michael should be long gone from the nursery. She dropped off the birth certificate forms in the outgoing mail on her way to visit the twins.

By now she knew the routine and proceeded to don

sterile gear before she entered the nursery. Tying the last set of strings on her mask, Faith pushed open the door to the premie ward. And froze. A fully gowned and masked Michael Cameron sat in Faith's usual chair. He had a baby lying along each of his forearms, their little heads cradled in the palms of his big hands. Both pairs of baby eyes were wide-open. Faith was near enough to see their mouths working. Oh, they looked like perfect little dolls.

Fuzzy dark hair spilled from beneath Nicholas's blue stocking cap. Abigail's wispy curls glinted pale gold in the artificial light.

Faith's gaze shifted to Michael's face. Her stomach knotted and her knees felt watery. There was no mistaking the tears that tracked down his cheeks. An involuntary protest rose in Faith's throat, blocking the breath she tried desperately to suck into her lungs. She didn't *want* to empathize with Lacy's ex. Throwing out a hand, she clutched the privacy screen to keep from falling.

Michael heard the sound. His rapt gaze left the twins. "Faith." He said her name softly. "I know I've been here beyond the time you set, but...but they're incredible. I've never been so humbled. Since Lacy risked everything for them I really hope that somehow she knows how perfect they are."

Faith watched him transfer his attention to a tiny hand that had worked free of its gown and felt the blood drain from her face.

With one gloved finger, he captured the baby's waving fist. "Fielding said they're labeled Babies A and B Hyatt. I stopped in finance to pay Lacy's bill and discovered she'd never legally changed her name after the divorce. Officially the babies are Camerons. As they should be,'' he said sternly, his eyes lifting in time to witness Faith's retreat. Michael called her to come back, to no avail.

Hands over her ears, Faith stumbled into the hall. She needed to get home and call Lacy's lawyer. Maybe the custody papers, which plainly stated Lacy wanted the babies to go by the name of Hyatt, were flawed. She took the time, however, to detour by the nursing station to retrieve the birth certificate forms she'd filled out incorrectly.

What was in a name, anyway? Michael had admitted the divorce was final. And she certainly hadn't *asked* him to pay Lacy's hospital bill. Maybe he was being thoughtful. Then again, he might have an ulterior motive. At any rate, Faith felt disloyal to Lacy as she crossed out Hyatt on the forms and wrote Cameron. As she dropped her gown, mask and bootees in the laundry, she mentally rearranged her budget to include attorney's fees. If Fielding and Cameron expected her to fade quietly into the woodwork, they'd better think again. She intended to be a devoted mom to her sister's babies. The kind she'd never had time to be for Lacy. She'd been too young then and stretched too thin in caring for their ailing mother. Still, the thought of so many lawyers getting involved made Faith almost sick to her stomach.

CHAPTER THREE

ATTENDING LACY'S FUNERAL was even harder than Faith had imagined. She was touched by the number of people from the hospital who came out of respect for her. Likewise, by the number of Lacy's old friends from high school and college who'd shown up. Faith made a mental note to catch Abigail Moore after the service so that she could tell her about her namesake.

A few acquaintances had sent flowers and cards. Including Kipp Fielding III. His was an ostentatious arrangement of red and white roses. They dwarfed Michael's small white basket of violets. The violets brought tears to Faith's eyes; they were Lacy's favorite flower and Michael must have gone to a great deal of trouble to find a florist to provide them at this time of year.

More surprising than his thoughtful gesture, however, was seeing the man himself walk into the chapel. He paused at a back row and greeted two couples who'd arrived earlier. People Faith had never met. Now it was obvious they'd known Lacy through Michael.

He didn't tarry long with his friends. Head bent, he walked slowly down the center aisle and knelt in front of the closed casket. Faith had thought her tears were all cried out until she watched his jaw ripple with emotion several times before he leaned forward to kiss the oak-grained lid. There was a decided sheen to his eyes when he rose. Or maybe she was watching him through her own tears.

She couldn't think of a thing to say when he sank onto the bench beside her. Even if she'd thought of something, she didn't trust her voice not to break.

"I swung past the apartment to pick you up," he murmured. "You'd already gone. You must not have listened to the messages on your answering machine. The last one I left said I'd booked a car service for us. I know you don't own a vehicle."

Faith clasped and unclasped her hands. The truth was, she *had* listened to the message. But Lacy's lawyer ordered her to have as little contact as possible with either of the two men. The attorney, David Reed, had been quite adamant, in fact.

Fortunately, Faith was saved from answering Michael when the minister stepped up to the pulpit. She'd asked Reverend Wilson to keep the service short in deference to the people who had taken time off work. However, his opening prayer droned on and on.

Ending at last, the minister segued into a poem by Helen Steiner Rice. The words celebrated life, and Lacy had been particularly fond of them. Anyone who'd ever received a note from her would recognize the piece, as she'd had it reprinted on the front of her monogrammed note cards.

Next, a singer—a woman Faith had selected from a generic pool on file at the funeral home—had half the people in the chapel sniffing and wiping their eyes with her rendition of "The Rose." Faith chose the song because Lacy had worn out two CD copies of it. Too bad if anyone thought the lyrics inappropriate for a funeral. Faith wanted the service to epitomize Lacy's life.

Her own cheeks remained wet as the minister delivered a tribute she'd written yesterday. The words hadn't come easily, but Faith wanted people to know that her sister wasn't shallow and vain, as some might remember her from high school and college. For one thing, Lacy had artistic talents. Before her debilitating illness, she'd dreamed of becoming an interior designer. If the media chose to cover the funeral, Faith also wanted them to report how selfless Lacy had been, giving her life in exchange for healthy babies. But it was all she could do to listen to the eulogy. The tears coursed down her cheeks and plopped on the lapels of her new navy suit.

Before Reverend Wilson brought the service to a close, Michael turned to Faith and whispered, "May I say a few words?"

"Of c-course," she stammered. When he stood, she was shocked to discover her right hand had been tightly entwined in his. Faith immediately pulled away, but she missed the warmth of his hand as Michael stepped to the pulpit and faced the small gathering.

"Lacy Ellen Hyatt Cameron passed through our lives at warp speed," he began in an unsteady voice. "Her sojourn with us was much too brief." He paused to clear his throat, and Faith saw his fingers tremble. She lowered her gaze to the floor and sucked her upper lip between her teeth, biting down hard to hold off a new bout of tears.

However, Michael didn't dwell on Lacy's death. He invited everyone to remember the woman who'd lived life full-tilt. "The Lacy we all knew brightened a room just by being in it. She hated sitting still. She loved to go and do. She loved to argue and debate." His voice cracked a little, but a semblance of a smile curved his lips as he suggested she was probably even now testing

St. Peter's mettle. "It's that Lacy who'll live on in my heart and I hope in yours as well."

People were dabbing at their eyes as he sat down again. Faith felt as if a weight had been lifted. She'd blotted away her tears while the minister offered a final prayer. "Thank you, Michael," she managed to say once everyone began to mill about. "Lacy kept things to herself this last year. I…we…stopped communicating." Faith licked a salty tear off her upper lip while twisting a tissue into bits. "If I hadn't been so wrapped up in work, I keep thinking she might have confided in me more. I'm afraid I gave up too easily, trying to reach her at the beach house. When she didn't return my calls, I…" Faith didn't finish the statement.

"I'm more at fault than you are, Faith," Michael said, his hazel eyes dark and troubled. "I let our lawyers act as go-betweens after she filed for divorce. I should have sat down with her when I returned from Norway. I can't tell you how sorry I am that she ended up hating me."

"I'm sure she didn't feel that strongly, Michael."

"Then how come Fielding believes I'm a first-class SOB?"

"On the phone, Lacy seemed happy enough at Christmas. She didn't give the slightest indication you two would be splitting up in January."

"When you called, she put on a convincing act. She was pretty upset with me for missing most of the major holiday parties we'd received invitations to. Every passing day, she seemed to feel more resentful of the time I devoted to my patients. I didn't know how to bridge the chasm between us."

"I'm sorry, Michael." Faith stood and bent down to pick up her purse. She started to walk away, then turned back. "Don't be too hard on yourself. Lacy's craving for attention goes back to her childhood. To when our entire household centered on our mother's poor health. At the same time, it terrified Lacy to think her illness might somehow force her to become dependent on others—like our mom had been. Looking back, I believe Lacy assumed the transplant would make her one-hundred percent good-as-new."

Michael tugged at his lower lip. "Which explains why she became so terribly hostile toward follow-up care. I wish you'd said something sooner, Faith. You've answered my biggest question. I never understood how Lacy could act so cavalier about the second chance she'd been given. I'm a doctor, for God's sake. You'd think I'd have picked up on her feelings."

Faith touched his arm. "You were too close to the problem. It dawned on me gradually, after you two had left Boston."

"We were married for five years. How could I completely miss what bothered her so much?" he asked with a snag in his voice. "Kipp got the picture, didn't he?"

"It's a little late for recriminations. Kipp treated her so shabbily he's hardly in a position to judge you." Removing her hand from Michael's arm, Faith backed away. "Uh, Michael, I have to go. The funeral director just signaled that it's time for me to get in the family car to make the trip to the cemetery."

"You're doing that alone? I'd planned to ride with friends." He waved toward the back of the chapel. "I'll keep you company if you'd prefer."

"No. Please don't change your arrangements. Someone from the funeral home will accompany me. Right now, I need a minute to decide which flowers go to the cemetery and which I want sent to the hospital to brighten our waiting rooms.''

''All right,'' he said, frowning. He let her go, yet didn't join his friends until the director approached Faith and the two left the room.

THE ASSEMBLY AT THE GRAVESIDE was smaller than the gathering at the chapel. As there wasn't to be a formal reception, friends took the time to speak with Faith before claiming seats beneath a shade tent. She was so caught up in talking to Abigail Moore, relating Lacy's desire to name her daughter Abby, Faith didn't realize Michael had arrived and had slipped into the seat beside her. Or not until he exhaled sharply.

Abigail sobbed. ''I'm so surprised and…and humbled. Lacy phoned me once after she'd moved back to Boston. Just to talk, she said. I suggested meeting for lunch, but she put me off. I never knew she was pregnant, Faith. I feel as if I let her down. Call me when you take the babies home. I'd love to visit.''

Faith nodded and pressed Abby's hand. She winced when Michael leaned over and hissed in her ear. ''I was under the impression Dr. Finegold lost Lacy during the delivery. When did she name the twins?''

''Before she went up for her C-section. Lacy gave me custody, remember. And she wasn't aware that she carried twins. It's common for women to name their babies, Michael. Abby was what Lacy had called her child. I chose Nicholas,'' Faith said, injecting a challenge in her voice.

Michael's brows puckered. He probably would have said more if the minister hadn't asked them to stand for a prayer. Relieved, Faith tore her gaze from Michael's flinty eyes. Bending her head, she willed her bucking heart to slow. David Reed had specifically warned her not to provoke either Michael or Kipp Fielding III. He said to refer them to him for answers to any and all questions concerning the babies.

She shouldn't have let Michael's earlier vulnerability reach her. Well, it wouldn't happen again. He and Kipp were her enemies. She'd do well to remember that.

Faith was first in the circle of mourners to lay a carnation atop Lacy's casket. An attendant had provided each person with a flower. The director sidled up to Faith as she stepped out from under the awning, asking if she preferred to mingle a bit or return to town. "Town, please," she said with a tremor. "I'll come back tomorrow for some private time with my sister."

The short walk to the waiting car proved to be the hardest part of the entire ordeal for Faith. Her knees wobbled like the front wheel of a novice bike rider. She would have stumbled and maybe even fallen if the director hadn't had a firm grip on her elbow. The shaky feeling kept her from turning back for a last look. Not that she would have had a clear picture anyway. Once she was sitting in the car, her nose pressed to the side window, the lovely hillside with its spreading elms and soft carpet of green all ran together. There was such finality attached to the ritual of leaving the cemetery. Up to now it had been easy to pretend that Lacy was only a phone call away. Watching the blur of row after row of headstones stripped away the fantasy, underlined the truth. Her only sister was gone, and there were too many things left unsaid between them.

On the ride back to town, Faith went through half a box of tissues the director had thoughtfully provided.

It was barely noon when the black car pulled up outside her apartment. So little time, Faith thought frantically—it took so little time to cut you forever from the sphere of a loved one.

The long afternoon that lay ahead seemed interminable as she stepped out of the car into the sunlight. And once she'd changed clothes, she found she didn't want to be confined with her thoughts. She could go mad worrying about what Michael and Kipp might be plotting with regard to Lacy's babies. Yet, if she stayed here, Michael could call or show up unexpectedly and further debate her right to name the babies. He hadn't seemed happy with the names she'd chosen.

She considered going to the hospital nursery. There she could hold part of Lacy close, thus assuring herself and the babies that she'd protect them from the men who'd taken such a recent interest in fatherhood. Though in a worst-case scenario, Faith knew one of the two men was the children's biological parent. She might be more willing to face up to that fact if the loss of the twins' mother wasn't so terribly real just now.

On the spur of the moment, Faith grabbed her purse and left the building, deciding to wander aimlessly downtown; she'd visit the twins later. She had no particular destination in mind—until she found herself in front of a major department store. Then she remembered the list of items needed to set up a nursery for the babies. Why not shop now? After all, David Reed, Lacy's lawyer, had told her to outfit a room. He said a judge would certainly take her readiness to provide the babies with a home as a positive sign if it came to a court battle. In her heart, Faith feared it would come to that. What she didn't want to think about was which of the three combatants would win such a fight. Kipp Fielding III, Michael Cameron…or her.

"Be optimistic," she muttered under her breath as she hurried into the store.

Upstairs, the baby department, with its array of pastels and primary colors, infused warmth back into Faith's cold limbs. Buying for Lacy's babies was going to be fun. Faith so rarely shopped for fun. In her mother's stead, she had learned at an early age to weigh price against serviceable value. To be frugal. It was a practice she adhered to when buying for herself. She was determined to give Lacy's babies all the things she'd never been able to give Lacy. That included lavishing them with her undivided attention. She'd been so young, so totally inadequate as a surrogate parent to her sister. Things were different now. Her life was different.

As she wandered through the baby furniture, Faith chose cribs and dressers with clean, classic lines. Beautiful wood that would endure. Crib bedding was another matter. Faith tried to imagine what Lacy would have wanted for her children. Lacy's taste in clothing and furnishings, had tended toward flashy colors while Faith gravitated toward softer shades. She thought about her apartment done in ivory, gray and mauve, and deliberately purchased two wild circus quilts richly patterned in blocks of green, yellow, orange and blue.

The saleslady steered her toward matching crib sheets, bumper pads and a diaper stacker. Next, she added large clown decals for the wall. She'd already decided to paint the nursery walls four different primary colors. She might even pick up paint on the way home and begin the project this evening.

Toys. Faith spotted them across the aisle. She headed straight for a large plush monkey with a funny face. How foolish, she thought, squeezing its soft body. The stuffed animal was bigger than either of the twins. It'd be far more practical to buy a nice mobile or a couple of small rattles. But she couldn't make herself let go of the monkey. It remained hooked on her arm as she reached for an equally impractical giraffe. Faith had to stand on tiptoe to grab the giraffe from the top shelf. In so doing, she dislodged a pile of bears.

"Goodness!" Bears of all sizes tumbled onto the other side of the display.

"Hey!" Faith heard a faint, gruff protest. She dashed around the corner and almost bowled over a man covering his head with both arms to ward off raining bears.

It took Faith a moment to realize she knew that profile. "Michael? What are you doing here?"

"Uh, hello, Faith." Michael shifted two small teddies to his left hand, and began to pick up the larger ones spilled across the carpet—a move that placed him in direct visual alignment with Faith's trim ankles. Hands unexpectedly clumsy, Michael dropped the bears he was collecting. His mouth felt dry as cotton. Lord, what was the matter with him?

Faith's attention focused on the two bears Michael kept separate. One was pink and the other blue, both washable terry cloth. They matched two soft receiving blankets draped over the crook of his elbow.

Several silent minutes passed before Michael realized he was the only one righting the bears. Faith's gaze remained fixed on his intended purchases.

"I stopped off at the nursery after the funeral," he explained, halting his task long enough to meet her eyes. "A nurse, Teri I think was her name, said premies respond to having the type of blanket they'll be wrapped in at home laid over their isolettes. She also suggested tucking small toys inside. Along with frequent holding, she said, that gives premature babies a sense of well-being.''

A sharp pain sliced through Faith's stomach. Her first reaction was to wonder why Michael hadn't gone straight back to New York where he belonged after the funeral. Her second was more an overwhelming sense of fear than a clear thought. A fear that this situation was cartwheeling out of her control.

''You don't have any idea what type of blankets Abigail and Nicholas will have when they go home,'' she said tartly. ''I'm outfitting their nursery. Not in pink or blue. Lacy liked wild colors. Bright colors.'' She said it almost desperately.

Michael's face appeared so crestfallen, she almost regretted her outburst. Or she did until it struck her that he was going behind her back to gain entry into the nursery, despite her request. No doubt he'd used his status as an eminent surgeon to inveigle his way in.

Faith's voice dropped. ''Go home, Michael. Don't make me get a restraining order against you. I spoke with Lacy's lawyer last night. He said she was very much of sound mind when she came to his office to draw up those custody papers. He further said that if you or Kipp Fielding want visiting privileges, you'll have to request approval through Family Court. Any questions you have are to be directed to him. His name is David Reed. You'll find him in the phone book.''

''Why would you drag Lacy's good name through court? Look at her recent behavior. The doorman at our apartment knows she left me that night in January in a fit of anger. From there she had a torrid affair with a married man. Then she ran off without telling anyone and hid out. *Think,* Faith. She deliberately went off her lifesaving medications.''

Faith heard only the warning that overlaid his apparent concern. Pain exploded in her chest. She should have suspected Michael was being nice at the funeral to put himself in a good light. Now she could believe this steely-jawed man with the hard eyes had driven her sister away. "And you're lily-white?" she said angrily. "Lacy left you because you were obsessed with work. Somehow I doubt a judge will find it *her* fault that Kipp pretended to be single. No one knows better than you, Michael, that Lacy's anti-rejection drugs were experimental. Who'd fault her for not wanting to jeopardize her unborn child?"

"I see. You and Lacy's lawyer have it all figured out, don't you, Faith? Well, I wouldn't spend a lot of money furnishing that nursery if I were you." Michael drew himself up to his full six-foot-three height. "Courts have been more favorable to fathers over the last few years, especially if they have the means to provide for their kids. I have the means several times over. And the desire. Tell that to your David Reed."

Faith watched him stride down the aisle. She felt as if she'd been trampled by an elephant. Michael stopped to pay for his purchases, chatting easily with the saleswoman as she rang them up. He appeared impervious to the fact that he'd left Faith shattered and it struck her how little effect her words had had on him. Michael Cameron intended to apply the same tenacity that had made him a world-famous surgeon to overturning her guardianship of Lacy's babies.

He obviously didn't realize she could be tenacious, too. More determined than ever to outfit the nursery as Lacy would want, Faith finished her shopping and requested everything be delivered. Leaving, she visited a paint store. And lugged the heavy cans up to her third-floor apartment. Then she put all other plans on hold while she ran to the hospital to visit the babies. She needed to touch them. To hold them.

Faith cuddled Abigail first, and then Nicholas. "You're going to love the room I'm fixing for you," she told them both as they gazed at her with unfocused eyes.

The pediatrician came in while she was there. He unwrapped the babies and checked them over thoroughly. "They're gaining like champs," he said over their chorusing squalls. "Two more weeks at this rate and you'll be able to take them home."

"So soon? That's wonderful news! The nurses seemed to think they'd have to stay here much longer." Faith couldn't contain a happy smile.

"If they'd lost a lot of weight, that would have been true. Nicholas only lost an ounce and Abigail two. The way they're chowing down, unless something unforeseen crops up, my guess is they'll both top five pounds soon. Dr. Finegold mentioned your predicament, Faith. For what it's worth, I'll be glad to put in a good word for you. The babies may be stable, but caring for premie multiples can be tricky. I like knowing they'll be under the care of a trained nurse."

"I appreciate your vote of confidence, Dr. Sampson. I'm planning to take at least six months off from work. A year if I can swing it financially. Our administrator said he'd hold a position open as long as possible. Otherwise, I'll use our on-site day care. I've already placed my name on the waiting list. Gwen in E.R., said the day care has openings from time to time."

"If you're able to stay home six months, that's great, Faith. A year would be icing on the cake. After I examine the twins next week, I'll give you a call. I should be able to give you their actual release date then.''

"Thank you," Faith murmured. She watched him cuddle Abigail while she diapered Nicholas. She felt all thumbs and hoped he didn't hold that against her. She hadn't diapered a baby since Lacy was little. "I'll get the hang of this soon," she promised.

Sampson laughed. "I have no doubt you will. Call my office and ask my receptionist to put you in touch with a parents-of-multiples support group. They have a newsletter and meetings where other parents of twins, triplets and upward exchange information. My other advice is to lay in a mountain of diapers. You won't believe how many you'll go through in a day.''

"Diapers." Faith snapped her fingers. "I went shopping today and bought out the store. Even paint for the nursery walls. How could I have forgotten diapers?''

The physician handed her Abigail and gave a wry glance at the wet spot on the front of his lab coat. "Breaks of the trade," he said as Faith apologized for leaving him holding a near-naked baby so long.

"Always remember to diaper Nicholas first. Or he'll decorate those newly painted walls.''

"They aren't painted yet. As soon as I leave here, I'm going home to do that. Two weeks," she mused happily, giving each baby a kiss before she tucked them back into their warm cocoons.

By dinnertime that evening, Faith's muscles ached so badly she could hardly stand up straight. The result of her labors pleased her, however. The walls looked cheery, complementing the soft gray carpet and white ceiling. She liked the room.

It suited her to keep busy and to restrict her thoughts to the subject of the babies. So after eating a light dinner, she went to work recovering the cushions on a comfortable rocking chair—the only piece of furniture she'd saved from the old house. The chair had belonged to her mother. Faith remembered how on good days her mom would sit by a sunny window and rock the infant Lacy. As the cushions cut from jungle-print chintz took shape, Faith imagined herself rocking Nicholas and Abigail to sleep.

It was an image that remained with her until she received a phone call from David Reed the next day. "Faith, could you come down to my office, please? I've got faxes from Kipp Fielding's legal team, and also from Michael Cameron's attorney. I want you to see what we're up against. We need to plan our strategy."

"What strategy?" she asked weakly. "Lacy signed custody of the children over to me, as you know. I agreed to raise, clothe and feed them. What other strategy do we need?" She heard his sigh and the creak of his chair.

"I know you're not naive, Faith. I explained during our first phone consultation how messy custody fights can get. On top of that, this case is quite unusual."

"How so?" she asked, although she knew more or less what he'd say.

"Normally it's a matter of determining visitation rights for a noncustodial parent. Occasionally Family Court has to intervene for grandparents. But your case has two men claiming to be the twins' father, and an aunt—you—to whom the biological mom assigned full custody. To say nothing of a very influential grandpa. Fielding Junior made a fortune on Wall Street. It looks as if he's prepared to use it to guarantee himself a grandson."

Faith's legs wouldn't hold her. She fell into a chair. "So are you saying it's hopeless?"

"No. Oh, my, no. Your position in the triangle is equal to the others at this point. Old man Fielding may have New York judges in his pocket, but his clout won't be half as great in Boston. I've cleared an hour on my calendar at one o'clock. It would be in your best interests to meet with me, I think."

"Of course." Faith barely had time to say she'd be there before he hung up. Her nerves were completely jangled. She could practically see Reed rubbing his hands together. He'd struck her as something of a barracuda. Maybe that was good. She hoped it was. And hoped he was clever enough to solve the matter in her favor, preferably within two weeks.

Faith showered and dressed with care, then left for her appointment. After all, if she expected the man to represent her enthusiastically, it would help if she made a good impression. She hoped his fees would be manageable—another thing that worried her. They hadn't discussed what he charged. Faith had a fair savings account, but she'd need it to allow her to stay home with the twins.

Broad-winged bats beat up a storm in Faith's stomach as she walked downtown to the building where Reed's offices were housed. Passing a corner café, it dawned on Faith that she'd skipped lunch. She didn't think she could eat a bite, but she certainly hoped her stomach didn't growl at an inopportune time during their session.

"You're prompt," said a matronly receptionist when Faith checked in. "Mr. Reed likes that in a new client. Just let me ring his office and let him know you've arrived. Can I get you a cup of coffee or tea, Ms. Hyatt?"

"No, nothing, thanks," Faith murmured, hoping she was the only one who knew her hands were shaking so hard she'd spill a beverage. As she'd only seen one other lawyer in her life, when she needed power of attorney to take charge of her father's welfare, she didn't know what to expect of this so-called strategy visit.

"Come in, come in, Ms. Hyatt," boomed a jolly voice.

Faith leaped out of the chair she'd taken in the corner of the waiting room. No wonder he sounded so jolly. David Reed resembled Santa Claus. Though dressed in conservative blue rather than a red suit, he was round and sported white hair and a full beard.

"You don't look a thing like your sister," he said, clasping Faith's cold hand.

"No," she murmured, "I don't."

He merely nodded, indicating she should take a chair near his desk as he closed his office door. "Well, I hope you're more solid than you look. This fight could be long and nasty."

Faith's heart sank. "I...I assumed the court would uphold my sister's wishes."

Reed steepled pudgy fingers. A fair-sized diamond winked in the sunlight streaming through a window that overlooked Boston Common. "Your sister was less than forthright with me, Faith. May I call you Faith?"

"Please do. How, uh, in what way did Lacy lie to you?"

"For one thing, she led me to believe the baby's father was dead. Oh, she didn't come right out and offer to produce a death certificate, but she implied as much. She never said a word about being divorced. In essence, Lacy let me think the money she willed you and her unborn child had come to her through an inheritance."

"I didn't know she'd left any money. She never said anything. We hardly had time to cover the custody papers, which, to be truthful, I signed quickly to ease her mind. I never expected her to d-di-die."

"I believe you, Faith," Reed said, bouncing his fingers together again. "I hope the judge will. Either of the other two legal counsels could imply you want custody only for the money."

Faith gasped. "Surely not! I'd planned to care for the babies out of my own savings. I doubt that whatever Michael settled on Lacy was a huge amount."

"The living trust your sister set up is approximately half a mil. You, if made custodian, have access to the interest until the babies turn twenty-one. Add to that proceeds from the sale of a beach house. Another seven hundred and fifty thousand."

Faith tried to keep her jaw from dropping but didn't succeed.

"I see you had no idea," David said. "I wish I'd gotten your reaction on video. Now you understand my concern. The Fielding team will surely make an issue of the money. And I've got no doubt that Dr. Cameron knows how much his ex-wife was worth."

Clasping her hands tightly, Faith brought them up under her chin. "I don't want Lacy's money, Mr. Reed. Is there a way to put it completely in trust for the twins?"

"There is. But you might not want to be so hasty. If your aim is to win full custody of those infants, it could get costly."

"Of course that's my goal. As I explained, I have three bedrooms. I rented a larger place, assuming my dad would stay with me after he sold his house. In fact, he's living in an assisted-care facility, so I have lots of space. I've already turned one bedroom into a nursery," she said passionately. "I can't believe either Michael or Kipp will offer the twins as much love and attention as I'm prepared to give."

"Maybe not," David said bluntly. "But one of them is the natural father. That's why I wanted to talk to you face-to-face, Faith. Fielding's team has demanded that the court order DNA testing. It takes four to six weeks after they give the go-ahead—and they will," he added. "The test will establish paternity beyond any doubt. If we dig in and fight after that, we'll be contesting a bona fide parent. I'm not saying we couldn't win, considering the mother didn't think highly of either Cameron or Fielding. It does mean that preparing our case will require a lot of expensive hours. I'll need a full-time legal researcher and a legal secretary assigned exclusively to this." He paused. "To be honest, the case intrigues me. Hell, I foresee it being a tremendous boost to my practice."

For the longest time, Faith chewed the inside of her mouth and stared out the window. "I only want what's best for Nicholas and Abigail," she finally said, her voice barely above a whisper.

"I realize it's a monumental decision. Maybe you'd like to go home and sleep on it. Those men both have the best counsel money can buy. I want you one-hundred-percent committed before we jump into a dog-fight."

Faith refocused and looked into his serious blue eyes. "I am committed," she said. "You just hit on the whole point. Kipp Fielding has money coming out his ears and a Roman numeral after his name. Oh, he wants Nicholas all right. To carry on his prestigious family name. He doesn't give a damn about Abigail. Michael has money, too. But my sister divorced him because he was never home. He's a world-famous doctor, who's completely consumed by his work. Lacy thought I'd be the best person outside of herself to raise her child, er…children. Unless the court can show something colossal to make me change my mind, I'm going to fight. I don't need to sleep on it. If holding on to custody takes every penny of my portion of Lacy's estate—so be it.''

Her impassioned speech set the wheels in motion. All the way to Lacy's apartment, where—as she'd promised Reed—she'd handle the disbursement of her sister's belongings, Faith prayed she was doing the right thing for the babies. Unfortunately, she couldn't shake the image of the tears Michael had shed when he held the twins. A court fight would turn Michael against her. He'd most likely end up hating her. But she'd promised her only sister—and she'd lost her heart to those babies. What did it matter that she'd lost her heart to Michael years ago? That was then. This was now.

CHAPTER FOUR

THROUGHOUT THE REMAINDER of the week, Faith dashed about town in search of the items left on her list. As she entered each store, she looked over her shoulder to see if Michael skulked nearby. After the third day had passed without incident, and since he hadn't popped in at the hospital, she began to relax and enjoy her shopping sprees.

She bought a double stroller that did everything but talk. Before setting out to buy one, Faith hadn't had any idea how many types were on the market. The one she selected was blue canvas awash with white daisies. It included sunroofs and a basket large enough to hold a sack or two of groceries plus a big diaper bag. Perfect for walks in the park. There was mosquito netting to drape over both infants during nice weather and clear plastic that zipped on to make the interior cozy if the weather turned blustery. The whole thing folded easily to fit into the trunk of a car.

Pleased by that purchase, Faith then bought what the clerk referred to as "a diaper system." The microfiber bag had waterproof linings and pullout changing pads and removable totes.

The clerk insisted Faith needed two infant carriers. Those were in the event she had to take the babies in a cab—to their appointments with Dr. Sampson, for instance. Faith wondered if the fact that she didn't own a car could be counted against her at the hearing. But if she purchased one, the men's lawyers could say she was spending Lacy's money on personal pleasures. Not to mention she'd have to take driving lessons.

In the end, Faith elected to drop the problem in David Reed's lap. Let him argue that she'd lived in Boston for thirty-four years without owning a car. If the judge thought she needed one to be a good mom, the expense wouldn't be her decision.

As her purchases arrived at her apartment, Faith assembled cribs and a changing table. She added two small chests of drawers and saw the room shrink. Later, when the twins were older, she'd give one of them the third bedroom. Right now, they needed to be together.

"MY APARTMENT IS BEGINNING to resemble a baby store," Faith confided to Gwen one afternoon when she stopped at the hospital to have lunch with her friend.

"It must be costing you a mint to buy all that stuff new. Babies don't know if you buy their equipment at thrift stores and garage sales."

Faith wrinkled her nose. "True, but Michael Cameron and Kipp Fielding III will." She pushed her nose up with one thumb to imply snobbery.

"You poor thing. I'll bet you wish you'd recorded your conversation with Lacy. From what you told me, she didn't want her babies raised by either of those jerks."

"It all happened so fast, Gwen. I was worried about Lacy overtaxing herself. Because of that, it's probably just as well there were no witnesses. At that point I didn't want to sign any custody agreement. It sounded too much like Lacy was giving up. But I can only imagine how our conversation would come across in court."

"Yeah," her friend agreed glumly. "I still think you need to be lining up potential witnesses. Hey, didn't Sue and Vince from the crash cart team hear your sister make you promise to raise her kid? The day after Finegold lost her, the cafeteria was full of wild rumors. Some were valid, I'm sure."

"Were Sue and Vince on the team?" Faith rubbed at the frown creasing her forehead. "That tells you how rattled I was, Gwen. Much of that night is lost to me."

"Let me hunt them up and find out, okay? You have a heavy enough load. Just ask your lawyer if you need character witnesses waiting in the wings."

"All right. I have two appointments with him before our hearing next Thursday. Reed is coaching me on when to speak and when to keep my mouth shut."

"Is David Reed as good as the lawyers coming down from New York?"

Faith picked at her salad. "I don't have the vaguest idea. I'm sure Michael has someone successful representing him. That's the way he is. And Fielding's father is a big shot. David said we could figure his whole team are top legal eagles. Even if David turns out to be lousy, I'm stuck with him. I'll have to trust that Lacy knew he was good when she engaged him. I do know he wants to win."

"Well, that's a plus. Hey, you've hardly touched your lunch. I hate to bug out on you, but my time is up. Shall I see if Trish can get away to keep you company?"

"No." Faith rose and picked up her tray. "I really have a lot I should be doing. And I'm visiting Nick and Abby while I'm here."

"Stop in E.R. before you leave. If it's slow, maybe we can grab a cup of coffee."

"Maybe. I still have high chairs on my list and a few other things."

"Your infant carriers will double as high chairs until the kids are four or five months old. Two high chairs! Gad. Is there room in your kitchen?"

Faith envisioned scrunching two high chairs next to her table. "What are you suggesting? That I find a house? Even if I had time to look, which I don't, it'd undoubtedly be farther from work, and more expensive. My being able to take at least a six-month leave of absence is based on the rent I'm paying now. I'm determined to not touch the money Lacy left, except to pay attorney's fees."

"I know. And if the babies were yours, you'd make do. I panicked, thinking how you described Michael's apartment. You said it was huge."

"And elegant. And Kipp Fielding's home, from the way he described it, is a mansion."

"Don't you worry." Gwen gave Faith a hug as they walked down the hall. "A house isn't what makes a home. Love makes a home."

"You're right, Gwen. There's so much stuff coming at me, I lose sight of the most important thing. Michael will either have to find a wife or hire a nanny. Kipp has a wife, but no one's heard a peep from her. Lacy said they were separated at the time of the affair. Who knows if the woman's anxious to be a stepmother?"

"See? Beside them, you look like a candidate for mother of the year. You took care of your mom and raised Lacy. You can bet your boots Michael Cameron won't take six months off work."

"Everything you say sounds logical, Gwen. I'm afraid to get my hopes up too high, though. Courts have a way of deciding kids need two parents. Believe me, if there was a man I even remotely liked who liked me back, I'd propose to him." She shook her head. "Three contenders. And frankly, none of us can offer the twins an ideal home."

"Quit being so hard on yourself. It's not like every natural parent who brings a kid into the world has a flawless setup. I hate to break it to you, girl, but nobody's perfect."

"I have noticed that." Faith smiled. "Gwen, did you ever lie awake wondering if you had what it took to be a good mom? What if the judge decides I didn't do such a hot job of raising Lacy?"

"For heaven's sake! You were a kid raising a kid. Now you're an adult. But to answer your question— yes. Parenting is a scary proposition. Unfortunately, nobody's designed a test to see if anyone has the know-how to do the job. While you're buying things, pick up a practical book on parenting. Read as much as you can before you bring the twins home. Speaking as a mother of four, I guarantee you won't have time later."

"What a good suggestion! I hadn't thought of buying a book. Oh, I'm so glad you had time to join me for lunch today."

Gwen laughed. "Off to the nursery with you. Before the shine on my halo tarnishes. And don't mention this discussion to my kids. They'll blow my cover. They think I'm the most inept mom in the world. Not to mention the meanest."

Faith still had a smile on her face when she stepped off the elevator outside the premie ward. Her smile faded the minute she donned her gown and stepped through the door and saw Michael holding one of the twins.

"I thought you'd gone back to New York," she said, scrabbling for balance.

"I did for a few days. The judge assigned to our case suggested Fielding and I have our blood for the DNA testing drawn here at Good Shepherd."

"Oh." Faith saw he was holding Abigail. She lifted Nicholas to her shoulder, where he promptly spit up, then started to cry. "Poor baby," she murmured as she rubbed a hand over his back.

"Teri said he's been spitting up after feedings the past couple of days. She said it's nothing to worry about, just that he eats too fast. What do you think?"

Faith blinked at Michael in confusion. "Teri is a trained neonatal nurse. I would assume she knows what she's talking about."

He lowered his voice. "She's a kid. I doubt she's much more than twenty."

"Hmm. At twenty-eight you were performing heart transplants. Age has nothing to do with credentials. But if you'd like, I'll read his chart. See what nurses on the other shifts noted. Does he act sick?" She kissed the baby's cheek, swayed with him tucked against her breast, and was rewarded with a sleepy yawn. "If he had a fever, they'd separate him from the other babies. I'm sure it's nothing, as Teri said."

"If you're confident, then so am I." Michael let Abigail grip his gloved finger. The baby claimed his full attention, and he and Faith drifted into silence.

She roused after Nicholas fell asleep, walked to his crib and laid him carefully down. After rearranging the blankets, she tiptoed back to peer at Abby over Michael's shoulder. "Why would the judge make you guys come to Boston to have blood drawn when you have perfectly competent labs in New York?" The question had bothered her ever since Michael had explained why he'd returned to Boston.

He cleared his throat. "I don't know if I should tell you. My lawyer says we're adversaries, Faith."

Flushing, she stuttered, "S-sorry. I shouldn't have pried."

"Aw, hell, let our lawyers be adversaries. That's what we pay them for. The legal experts said if Kipp and I came here to have our blood drawn at the hospital where you work, your attorney would be less likely to claim contamination or mishandling."

"I suppose David might do that. I would never have thought of such a thing, but lawyers don't think like normal people. I mean, like lay people," she said when Michael threw back his head and gave a rollicking laugh. It was a laugh that grabbed hold of Faith and sent an uncertain longing deep inside. A longing that, even in panic, made her wish she and Michael Cameron were anything but adversaries. Struggling against the unwanted emotions, she turned her back.

"I'm not laughing at you, Faith," Michael said, sobering quickly. "Your statement was a slip of the tongue, but so very true. Everyone makes jokes about lawyers, and yet we willingly toss our hearts at their feet and shell out big bucks, hoping they can fix whatever's gone wrong in our lives."

"What if they can't fix things in our case?" Facing Michael again, Faith was gripped by such apprehension she barely got the words out.

"Oh, they'll rule in favor of someone. One of us three." Michael, too, sounded cheerless. He crooked the back of his index finger and brushed it lightly over Abigail's soft, translucent skin. "The trouble is, there'll be only one winner. Two of us will lose. That's the sad fact. I've seen lawyers and courts in action, and I've seen that it's often the person with the craftiest, most glib-tongued attorney who takes home all the marbles.''

Faith saw how gently Michael stroked Abby's cheek. Despite Gwen's encouragement, Faith suddenly felt on unstable ground again. "Has something else happened, Michael? You sound so…cynical.''

He tore his gaze from the baby and studied her somberly.

His demeanor prompted Faith to blurt, "I'm afraid Fielding will come off looking better to the judge. Aren't you? He has a stay-at-home wife, and a huge house with a huge yard. To say nothing of a rich papa backing him one-hundred percent.''

"My apartment has twenty-four-hour-a-day security,'' Michael returned, as if in self-defense. "The rooms are big and airy. There's a nice neighborhood park nearby, and good schools less than a block away. My parents aren't super-rich, but I guarantee they'll dote on their grandchildren. They're currently running a free medical clinic for street kids in Sao Paulo, Brazil, but if I need them to strengthen my position in this case, they'll fly home at a moment's notice.''

"Is that a polite way of telling me that my position is the shakiest? My apartment is dinky compared to yours. I suppose you've told your lawyer that I'm also the caretaker of my dad.''

Abigail began to fuss and Michael shifted her to his shoulder. "Apparently, you have a low opinion of me, Faith. I don't know, maybe from your perspective I deserve it. Lord knows, I screwed up my marriage to your sister. This is different. Lacy might have made a conscious decision to cut me out of her life, but the babies aren't in a position to do that. Until they're old enough to pass judgment on my ability to be a parent, they ought to live with me. They're as much a part of me as they are of Lacy. Dammit, Faith, surely you understand what I'm saying. You struggled to keep your family together for years. Lacy told me about the many times you and your mom staved off social workers who would have removed you girls from the household.''

"That's right, Michael. Children belong in a loving environment. My mother was ill, but she loved us. And Dad loved her. Yes, it was tough, but we weren't raised by strangers or nannies. Lacy made no bones about how much your work took you away from home.''

Rising, Michael swayed gently to quiet the baby. ''This is an argument better saved for the hearing. It's easy to see that neither one of us is going to change the other's mind. All we're doing is creating tension. I'd hoped we could be sensible.'' He studied Faith as he rocked, missing the woman he remembered. The old Faith looked at all sides of an issue and never jumped to conclusions. Lacy had a short fuse and a hot temper. Not Faith. At least, she never used to.

"That's some statement coming from the man who stomped off in a huff last week in the toy department.''

"I admit you hit a raw nerve that day. At the moment, though, our arguing has upset Abigail, which I'm sure is the last thing either of us wants.''

"You're right. How long are you going to be in town? Perhaps we should set a schedule for visiting the twins so we don't show up here at the same time.''

"I'm sorry it's come to that, Faith.'' Honest regret darkened Michael's eyes. ''No matter how the DNA shakes out, you are always going to be the children's aunt. Let Fielding act like an uncivil ass. I'd like it if you and I kept an open line of communication.''

"Has Kipp been uncivil?" Faith frowned.

"To me. In the lab. And after he had his blood drawn, he stepped into my cubicle and informed me we'd do all our talking through our lawyers. Which reminds me. Has Reed called you regarding the Fielding's lawyers' latest brief?"

Faith shook her head. "I haven't talked to David today. I have an appointment to see him this afternoon. Tell me. I hate surprises."

"Lon Maxwell, my attorney, faxed me a copy of a complaint Kipp's team filed. They want to restrict our visits to the babies. Apparently Fielding has a boat race in Key West. He'll be gone for the next two weeks. The gist of the brief—Kipp claims it's unfair that we get to spend time with the twins when he can't."

"So the babies are supposed to be deprived of cuddling because he's off sailing?" Faith said explosively. "That's dumb. What's wrong with his wife? Or his father? Couldn't *they* visit?"

Michael placed the now-sleeping Abigail in her bed. He pulled the stocking cap over the ruff of light hair curling around her ears. Absently he set the pink terrycloth bear in the corner nearest her head. "Don't get mad at me, Faith," Michael cautioned quietly as he followed her into an anteroom where they both shed their masks, gowns and gloves. "If the auburn-haired ice queen who was with Fielding downstairs is his wife Shelby, I get the distinct impression that nothing about this situation pleases her."

"Really? Didn't he tell us Shelby was dying to adopt a child? Even Lacy said Kipp and his wife reconciled in order to try a new fertility method. That sounds as if she really wants a baby."

"Maybe so. I could be reading her wrong. If she's

undergone a lot of fertility tests, it's possible that being in the lab is what she found distasteful.''

As the two walked to the elevators, Faith stopped suddenly and grabbed Michael's arm. ''Say you didn't read her wrong. If confronting her husband's infidelity is what's bothering her, why is she sticking with the jerk? I mean…they weren't even divorced, and he was screwing around.''

Michael gave a short laugh. ''I'm only guessing, but the Fielding fortune might be old Kipp's trump card. The lady wore more gold than they found in Cleopatra's tomb. You know the type. She breathed money. Suit looked like a million. Italian shoes. Fingernails that have never seen a chip.''

The elevator arrived and they stepped inside. Because they were alone, Faith broached something that still disturbed her. ''David told me this custody settlement could end up costing all of us a lot of money if it drags on.''

''That's the main reason I hate to see you take a leave of absence, Faith.'' Michael ran a compassionate gaze over her face. ''DNA is going to prove that one of us— either Kipp or me—is the twins' biological father. I can't help but think those results will be the deciding factor. Real dad gets the twins. Case over. That leaves you the poorer for having shelled out your savings to Reed.''

Faith glanced at her watch. ''Do you have time for a cup of coffee? I've got an hour before my appointment with David. There's something I'd like to discuss with you—somewhere other than the hospital cafeteria. I don't want to contribute any more to the rumor mill.''

''I had a list of things to do, but sure,'' he said, peeling the cuff back over his watch. He hesitated to mention his appointment with a furniture rental firm. He'd intended to tell her about taking a six-month lease on a unit next door to her, until Lon Maxwell cautioned him to think of Faith, as well as Kipp, as the enemy. Well, she'd find out soon enough. He'd seen the rental sign the day of the funeral, when he'd stopped by her place. The location was convenient, and he'd thought being neighbors would help maintain good relations with Faith. At Lon's strongly worded suggestion, he'd tried to find other accommodations nearby. There was next to nothing available. Nothing suitable.

"Is the bagel place three blocks over still in business?" he asked, avoiding explanations of private matters. "I came in fasting for the blood test. I could use a bite to eat."

"It's still there. And on my way to Reed's office. I'll buy my own. Okay?"

Resting a hand on her back, Michael guided Faith out of the elevator and toward the hospital's front entrance. "In some ways you haven't changed in six years, Faith. Still prickly as a cactus when it comes to letting a man do anything for you."

"What do you mean?" Her steps faltered.

"Come on," he scoffed. "Don't tell me you don't have a clue how many poor residents' hearts you broke with that *I can take care of myself* attitude. I know the common belief is that interns and residents don't have two dimes to rub together, but we had our pride. Any one of us could have bought you pie and coffee in the cafeteria. Or pizza and a beer if you'd ever gone to Tony Bruchetto's when you were asked. It doesn't take too many turndowns for guys to get the picture."

"Oh? And what picture is that?"

"Back then, we all thought you were a snooty Boston

blueblood. Or that you had your sights set on one of the senior M.D.s. Like Dr. Rubin. Did it break your heart when he married that socialite? I forget her name.''

Faith drew back in shock. ''Dr. Rubin? You mean Steffan Rubin?''

''The very same. You followed him around O.R. like a lovesick puppy.''

''I did no such thing! Dr. Rubin was one of the few surgeons who didn't eat first-year nurses for breakfast. I followed him around because I could learn more from him than from anyone else. The other docs had me cowering in my shoes. Besides, your crowd went to Bruchetto's after the late shift. Mom needed me at home. She was really, really sick. By then the hospice team cared for her while I worked. But she always fretted until I got home and took over. Anyway, it wasn't as if you lacked female companionship, Michael. I was probably the only nurse at Good Shepherd who didn't pay you homage on those evenings at Bruchetto's.''

Michael grabbed for the door to the restaurant as another couple came out. He missed and the door shut in Faith's face. Apologizing profusely, he opened it again and ushered her inside. ''Surely, you don't mean you left the hospital after working a full shift and then nursed your mother all night?'' Michael's shocked gaze said he hadn't known.

''It didn't kill me. Anyway, it's all in the past. My schedule wasn't any worse than yours when you were building your practice. I know, because Lacy used to call and talk my ear off on the nights you stayed with a new transplant patient.''

''She did? I don't recall our telephone bills reflecting that.'' He stared at the board listing coffees and choices of bagel toppings without really seeing them. His mind reeled, back to the year he'd all but turned handsprings in O.R. trying to make an impression on Faith Hyatt. All these years he'd thought she'd brushed him off for no good reason.

"Lacy reversed the charges." Faith chuckled at the way Michael's head snapped up. She gave her order for an iced coffee, paid for it and carried it to a table at the back of the room. Idly. She swirled the ice in her drink. Instead of drinking, she plotted how to introduce the topic of Lacy's estate disbursement, which was what she needed to tell Michael. He seemed to think she hurt for money. In the interest of fairness, she thought he ought to know that in a way, she'd be using his own money against him.

"Why am I just now hearing that you subsidized my wife after we moved to New York? I swear I never stinted on household expenses. Lacy had money. I hope she didn't insinuate otherwise."

"Honestly, Michael. It's no big deal. Lacy said you put her on a strict budget. I was impressed, since I'd never been able to tell her no. Besides, if you must know, I welcomed her calls. I was lonely. Losing Mom and then having to place Dad in managed care so soon after you and Lacy moved to New York was hard. You guys assumed I had Daddy for company. In fact, I was more like his nurse. I did everything I knew to combat his depression. Nothing worked. Lacy said I had to place him in managed care. Eventually I had to agree that was best."

They sat in silence for a moment. Both concentrated on their drinks, and Michael his food. Faith spoke first. "I didn't ask you here to rehash the past. In addition to preparing custody papers in my name, Lacy made me her sole beneficiary.''

"That's good." Michael set his bagel aside and touched the napkin to his lips. He glanced over his shoulder to see what Faith found so puzzling. Or was it something he'd said?

"Do you mean that?" she murmured, her eyes shifting to meet his.

"Of course. Why wouldn't I?"

"The bulk of Lacy's estate came from your divorce settlement. Including a tidy sum from the proposed sale of your beach house." Faith shredded her napkin, waiting for him to tell her that, under the circumstances, he would contest Lacy's will.

Instead he smiled gently. "So? Lacy didn't work. Where else would she have gotten money to live on?"

She let her lashes lift slowly until their eyes met. "I'll use my portion to fight you and Kipp for custody of the twins. You said I should step aside and not waste my savings. But I'll spend every dime Lacy left to carry out her wishes. The last thing she said to me was 'take care of my baby.' Don't forget she didn't know there were two."

"I see." Michael pushed his plate aside and downed the rest of his coffee. "I guess we'll each do what we have to do, Faith," he said in an understanding voice.

"Then you really aren't mad about the money? I thought you'd be furious, but I didn't think it was fair not to tell you. Better you contest the will now, before I spend any of it and have to pay you back out of my savings."

"It was Lacy's money to do with as she pleased. We were partners in marriage, Faith. She apparently had qualms about a lot of issues in our marriage, but lack of money wasn't one. I'm truly sorry for everything that went wrong between us. Sorry I didn't try harder.'' He dug in his pocket and tossed a couple of bucks on the table for a tip. Michael didn't know what more he could add to his apology. Frankly, he didn't know why he even felt a need to apologize. The more he thought about what had gone wrong in his marriage, the more he decided it was as much Lacy's fault for not understanding the nature of his job as it was his for failing to see how deep her unhappiness went. He didn't want to think that he might have married the wrong sister.

A part of Faith's brain knew Michael had risen and pushed back his chair. She concentrated on the last of the melting ice in her drink. She was sorry his marriage hadn't worked out. Or rather she was and she wasn't. And that uncharitable wedge of ambivalence left her feeling like a traitor—or worse. Lacy would probably still be alive if she and Michael hadn't divorced. Still, she couldn't help wondering how differently all their lives would have played out if she hadn't been so shy when she first met Michael. Today she'd learned quite by accident that he'd known she was alive back then. Surprisingly, he'd noticed other men's interest in her, too. And in spite of all the time that had passed, he remembered she'd been absent from the crowd that frequented Bruchetto's.

If... Faith never finished the thought. She had been too shy and too bogged down with work to flirt the way other nurses did. It was far too late to wish she'd been more like Lacy so that Michael might have fallen in love with her rather than her sister. Might-have-beens were futile. Faith would die of embarrassment if Michael ever learned of her wayward daydreams.

''Are you going to stay and finish that watered-down

coffee?'' Michael asked, forcing Faith to look up at him.

"Yes. David's office is only a short walk from here. Don't let me keep you. I know you have things to do.''

"Yeah, but I'm not sure this is a part of town where a woman should walk alone anymore. The neighborhood used to be safe, but a lot can change in five or six years.''

"You're right about that,'' she said. "But not in this particular neighborhood. Thanks for worrying though. I can't remember the last time anyone did,'' she added almost to herself.

Michael thrust his hands into his pockets. "I suppose that's, uh, because you're so damned self-sufficient, Faith. Well, you take care, you hear?''

Her heart beat fast at his words. She was tempted to turn and watch him weave his way through the wrought-iron tables. Instead, she wrapped both hands around her glass and tried to hit the straw with her shaky lips.

Faith waited until she was sure Michael would have hailed a cab or disappeared in whatever other manner he chose. Luckily the street was clear except for a couple of teens, weighted down with backpacks, trudging home from school. She fell into step behind the boys and listened to their banal chatter as she followed them for three blocks. They turned left at the corner where she turned right to go to David's office.

On the ground floor of his building, she spotted a rest room. Faith stopped to comb her hair and freshen her pale pink lipstick. Frowning into the mirror, she tried to see herself the way a man like Michael would see her. Her unwieldy brown hair curled in Shirley Temple fashion. Or it would if she didn't keep it short. Her more generous friends said the cut made her look like Audrey Hepburn. Ha!

Critically Faith decided her brown eyes were boring. Lacy's eyes had shone a flawless sky-blue. Faith hoped both Abigail and Nicholas inherited their mother's eye color.

Chiding herself for letting her mind wander, Faith tucked her comb back in her purse and took a minute to straighten her blouse and smooth the lapels of her suit. At least she had good metabolism. She'd been wearing a consistent size seven since high school. That certainly helped in the wardrobe department. Snatching her purse off the mirror shelf, Faith pushed open the door and hurried across the lobby to catch an elevator heading up to David's floor.

"Hello, Ms. Hyatt." She'd been there so often this past week, the receptionist knew Faith on sight. "Mr. Reed just buzzed out to see if you'd arrived yet. Help yourself to coffee or tea while I let him know you're here."

Smiling, Faith shook her head. "I just finished some before I came. I'll read a magazine until he's ready. If he's started something else, tell him I don't mind waiting."

The receptionist hung up the phone and beckoned Faith. "He sounds anxious to see you. Please, go right in. You know the way."

As Faith reached for the doorknob, David flung his door open. "I'm glad you're a little early," he said. "Come in. Sit down. It's crunch time, Faith. It seems Kipp Fielding has to go out of town for a few weeks. His team convinced the judge to advance the preliminary hearing."

"Advance it? To when?" Faith hovered over the

edge of the chair David had pulled out. She neither
stood nor sat.

"Relax." He placed a beefy hand on Faith's shoulder
and eased her into the chair. "We're to meet in Judge
Brown's chambers at ten tomorrow. Fielding and his
wife are in town because he had blood drawn at Good
Shepherd. They're staying the night. Don't look so horrified. Sooner is better. This way, we'll get some rules
established up front."

"Is Dr. Cameron going to be there, too?" Faith
asked. If Michael had known that the meeting had been
moved up, why hadn't he said anything? He hadn't
heard yet, she decided. He would have shared that information with her.

"The court clerk said Dr. Cameron is also in Boston.
She spoke with his counsel. Maxwell said advancing
the date wouldn't pose a problem."

Faith twisted the topaz birthstone ring she wore on
the middle finger of her right hand. She wore her mom's
wedding band on the ring finger of the same hand. She
gripped it now as if it were her talisman. "I saw Dr.
Cameron at the hospital today. He said Fielding's lawyers objected to our visiting the babies while Kipp's
away in Florida."

David thumbed through a stack of papers on his desk.
"I'd intended to talk with you today about drafting a
response. If you want to object, we'll need to file before
four o'clock. That will force the judge to deal with the
issue tomorrow. Otherwise, I'm afraid the judge might
give in to Fielding's request, at least until results of the
DNA come back."

"That's absurd! Of course I want to object. Don't
these people know babies need to be held and rocked?
Infants who are left on their own fail to thrive. Some

stop eating. Even the good eaters can end up with developmental problems.''

"Good, good," Reed said, scribbling as fast as he could on a legal pad. "I'll have the firm's paralegal look up some specific cases to quote. I thought it was a silly point for Fielding's team to insist on. It's not as if you or Cameron asked to remove the twins from the hospital."

Faith glanced guiltily away, then back. "I thought you said I'd have no problem taking Nick and Abby home when the doctor releases them."

David fiddled with his pencil. "I didn't expect the case to heat up so fast."

"I'm ready to bring them home," Faith said. "I mean, I've outfitted a nursery like we discussed. Dr. Sampson, the twins' pediatrician, said he might let them go home as early as next week."

"Next week? That changes things." David snapped his pencil in half. He raked one hand through his hair. "And the first hearing's tomorrow. I counted on having more time to prepare our presentation, Faith. I haven't hired the extra legal assistant or the secretary I mentioned we'd need."

Faith slipped out of her suit jacket and rolled up her sleeves. "I'm a good typist, David. And I'm a good organizer. I've also pulled back-to-back shifts in my time, so I can run on a lot of caffeine and a little sleep."

He studied her helplessly, massaging his jaw.

"I made a promise to my sister. I said I'd be there for her child. And you promised me you'd work hard and win this case. I'm holding you to that promise."

"I did do that," he agreed. "All right." He slapped a broad palm down on his desk. "By damn, what are we waiting for?"

"Nothing. I'm ready when you are." Faith hoped he couldn't hear how her heart nearly hammered out of her chest. In all her life, she'd never made waves. But this newfound assertiveness felt good. Pretty darned good, in fact.

CHAPTER FIVE

AT FOUR IN THE MORNING Faith yawned her goodbye to David Reed and a legal secretary named Lisa and climbed into a cab leaving the law offices. Reed had pulled Lisa from a temporary pool, then decided to keep her on for the duration of what he'd labeled the Baby A & B Hyatt-Cameron case. The young woman, wife of a sailor who was on a submarine somewhere in the Mediterranean, had performed admirably and without any complaint about the hours.

Before their long night ended, Faith developed a grudging respect for her lawyer. David had dates and cases stored in his head from twenty years back. He assigned Faith the job of finding specific cases in his firm's law library, which she did, one at a time, carting the heavy tomes to him when she'd found each reference. He, in turn, plowed through the legalese and scribbled out the portions of the text he wished to use at the hearing.

Lisa Dorn organized and typed his copious—and by Faith's estimation—almost illegible notes. The points David chose to emphasize were typed on legal forms, then copied and sent by night courier to the opposing teams. According to David, in cases of this nature, the winning side was often the one that followed each and every rule to the letter.

Faith was exhausted at the close of the ordeal, but

she felt she knew where David was headed. The test
cases he intended to present had all been won. He'd
decided to use quotes from ten in all. In each instance,
a grandparent or other family member had been
awarded custody over a biological parent.

Of course, Faith thought, as she let herself into her
dark and silent apartment, Michael's and Kipp's attorneys had probably spent the night at precisely the same
chore. Only, Michael's team would cite cases where a
divorced spouse had won. Kipp's lawyers might have
the hardest job. David said that until the DNA came
back, Kipp had the weaker case. They had only his
word and hearsay evidence from a very ill Lacy that
the couple had engaged in an intimate affair. David said
he expected Kipp's team to present signed affidavits
from friends or staff at the country club who'd seen the
couple together. It was still secondhand evidence. Reed
doubted very much that anyone other than Kipp could
swear to the intimacy part.

If Shelby Fielding attended the hearing, it seemed
less likely Kipp III would want his and Lacy's activities
explored at any great length. Or maybe that didn't matter to him. Faith had heard of open marriages, in which
both partners conducted affairs. She'd hate for Lacy's
babies to be raised in such an atmosphere.

As she tossed and turned in bed, Faith wished she
could drop off to sleep. She'd set her alarm for eight-
thirty. It was now six o'clock. Two and a half hours of
rest would be better than none at all. Then it occurred
to her that a single mother of new twins would undoubtedly have sleepless nights, staying up till dawn
with sick or colicky infants. Maybe the judge would be
impressed to learn that Faith could function on little
sleep.

She finally drifted off. And dreamed of the hearing. A clerk escorted her into a dark, damp dungeon. The judge sat in a throne chair, higher than anyone else in the room. His eyes were empty red holes. When he spoke, tongues of fire licked out over the tables.

Michael looked coolly handsome in a blue suit, white shirt and striped tie. Kipp had on white pants, a navy jacket trimmed in gold braid and brass buttons. Though Faith had never seen Kipp's wife, Michael had described her. Shelby sat regally at Kipp's side. The elder Fielding chewed on a huge cigar and looked exactly like Edward G. Robinson.

In her dream Faith wore her nursing shoes and wrinkled white stockings, hideously unattractive with an apple-green suit that had once belonged to her mother.

Kipp sneered. Shelby smirked, and Michael laughed. The judge whammed an alarmingly gigantic gavel and roared for silence. That was when Faith noticed that the table she'd been assigned was empty. At Michael's and Kipp's sides, lawyers busily sorted stacks of well-prepared documents. David had left her to face the mess alone.

Gasping and panting, Faith shot bolt upright in bed. The clock said six-twenty.

Not wanting to risk a return to the same awful dream, Faith turned on the light and climbed out of bed. As she gathered a towel and clothes to put on after showering, she thought she heard water running in the apartment next door. She pressed an ear to the wall and listened. Nothing. Obviously she was hearing things.

"Another figment of your overactive imagination." The next-door apartment had been vacant for six months. Eccentric old Mrs. Coleman who'd lived there had everyone in the building except Faith convinced she was a witch. The woman had looked the part and habitually said some strange things. Rumors circulated about odd lights and secretive activity in the dead of night. Faith had never seen or heard anything out of the ordinary. However, there was no denying the unit had developed a stigma that made it virtually unrentable. Rumors of that nature had a way of spreading to potential tenants.

Every time she saw the building manager, Mr. Kinney complained about a perfectly good apartment going to waste. Faith thought to herself how fortuitous it was that at least she wouldn't have to worry about a next-door neighbor annoyed by crying babies.

And Nick and Abby did have fine sets of lungs each, she acknowledged around a smile as she spun the shower knobs and stepped beneath a fast, hot spray.

She felt much better after the shower. And more alert. The pale pink suit she'd bought lifted her spirits another notch. It was completely unlike the ghastly outfit she'd worn in her dream. A softly gored skirt gave the ensemble a feminine touch, as did the classic tucked-in blouse. Faith rarely took time to apply makeup. Today she wore a thin gloss of pink lipstick and a touch of mauve eye shadow. The clerk at the cosmetic counter said Faith's eyes were her best feature and had convinced her to enhance them a little. Enhancement couldn't hurt on this all-important occasion, when she wanted to influence the people deciding the fate of Lacy's twins.

Still, she was nervous. She tried not to think what would happen if the judge refused to consider her claim on the babies. To fight a queasy stomach, she carried a glass of milk into the nursery and sat there until the bright, cheery surroundings worked their magic and brought her a measure of serenity.

By the time her stomach stopped feeling jittery, she had only twenty minutes to reach the courthouse. So, for the second day in a row, she splurged on a cab.

As in her nightmare, a clerk did lead her to the judge's chambers. There the resemblance ended. Not only didn't Judge Brown sit on a throne and breathe fire, she was a regal-looking African American woman. David Reed had arrived ahead of her, and seeing him there, sorting through a briefcase full of papers, dissolved the last uncomfortable knot in Faith's stomach.

Michael stood when she approached the horseshoe-shaped table. "You look nice," he said, sliding a hand the length of his tie. He wore a summer-weight khaki suit, not blue. His shirt was pale yellow and his tie was covered with comic turtles. The tie elicited a grin from Faith.

"You like it?" he asked with a smile that deepened the laugh lines around his eyes and mouth. "It was a gift from the last kid I transplanted. A girl in Norway. She's an incredible artist. She drew the turtles freehand and silk-screened them on this material. I think she has a promising future." Growing suddenly sober, he let the tie drop. "Six months ago she was knocking at death's door. You'll probably say this is hokey, but when the tie came in the mail last week, I got this insane notion that it's a lucky charm." Michael lifted one shoulder in an elegant shrug.

"There's nothing hokey about talismans, Michael." Faith opened her purse and fished out a framed piece of glass in which was embedded a four-leaf clover.

Seeming to relax, Michael unbuttoned his jacket and perched on the edge of Faith's table. He flagged an eyebrow toward the left side of the room. "Do you suppose old Kipp is carrying a rabbit's foot?"

She peered around him at the huddle of immaculately dressed people surrounding Kipp, and a pretty woman she assumed was his wife. "I'd say he's relying on the Roman numerals after his name." Unlike in her dream, Kipp wasn't wearing yachting clothes. If his silk designer suit didn't have "Made in Italy" stitched on the label, Faith would eat his conservative navy tie. Mrs. Fielding was pretty much the way Faith had pictured her, up to and including the frosty pursing of her lips. But Faith couldn't have been more wrong about Kipp's father. The man, who could have been anywhere from fifty to sixty, was in total command over there. Fit, tan and blond, dressed in what was obviously a hand-tailored suit, he was clearly accustomed to being the center of attention.

Faith disliked Kipp Fielding Jr. on sight. He had cold blue eyes and a shark's smile.

As if Michael read her mind, he murmured, "I'd do anything to keep that bastard from renaming Nicholas and branding him with that damned number four."

A crew of maintenance workers entering the room through a side door kept Faith from responding. Talk stopped as the men set a small table and a comfortable-looking leather chair at the center of the horseshoe for the judge. The clerk who'd led Faith to the room took her place behind a steno-typewriter.

Judge Brown smiled at the men. "Thank you, gentlemen, for your help. This is a somewhat larger group than I'd expected." Her interested gaze touched on everyone at the table before she opened her briefcase and removed a spiral-bound notebook. Two more people entered the room. A man and a woman. Both wore plain, dark suits. They claimed the empty seats next to David.

"Who are they?" Michael asked Faith in an undertone. "Have you hired a full legal team—like Fielding?"

"I've never seen them before. They're obviously acquainted with the judge." Which was true as the trio exchanged pleasantries.

"In the interest of time," the judge said briskly as she settled in the leather chair and steepled graceful fingers, "I propose we get right down to business." She waved a hand in the direction of the newcomers. "Even though this meeting will be conducted as a hearing, I've taken the liberty of including two senior legal advisors from Family Services. Daniel Burgess and Barbara Lang. In the event this should evolve into a trial, Mr. Burgess and Ms. Lang will represent the minor children on behalf of the state of Massachusetts."

Faith felt her stomach go into spin cycle. Had she been naive, thinking they'd walk out of here today with a settlement? Apparently. Michael caught her eye. He, too, appeared surprised and uneasy.

None of the lawyers scattered around the table, however, seemed taken aback by the announcement. One by one they nodded and jotted notes on their legal pads.

Judge Brown relaxed in her chair. "Shall we continue introductions? In the Fielding camp, Kipp Fielding III, the plaintiff. He's flanked on either side by his wife, Shelby, and his father, Kipp Jr. Their legal team, Bob and Keith Schlegel and Nancy Matz of Schlegel, Schlegel and Matz are from New York City."

There was a faint rustling around the table as everyone eased forward to get a look at the competition.

Judge Brown shuffled her notes. "Plaintiff number two, Michael Cameron, M.D. He's represented by Lon Maxwell, who also practices in New York. Plaintiff three, Ms. Faith Hyatt. She's retained David Reed, who is a partner in the local firm of Masterson, Reed and Jacoby. Now that we have preliminaries out of the way, ladies and gentlemen, we'll begin hearing from each of you in the matter of custody for twins of the deceased, Lacy Hyatt Cameron. I'll recognize one counselor at a time. I trust the main concern of everyone in this room is the well-being of the two minors. I assure you that I will not make any hasty decisions regarding their welfare. Whether we need one meeting or ten, we'll reconvene until I'm satisfied we're doing what's right for the children.''

She sent a withering gaze around the table. Someone in a dark suit entered the office with a glass pitcher and poured water into the empty glasses that sat in front of each person, including the judge. When that had been accomplished and he'd shut the door again, the judge resumed. ''Bob Schlegel filed the first formal request with regard to this case. Mr. Maxwell and Mr. Reed have both responded on behalf of their clients. So I'll ask Bob if he has anything further to add.''

The white-haired member of the Fielding team cleared his throat. ''Your Honor. Mr. and Mrs. Fielding have read the rebuttals. Their position hasn't changed. Mr. Kipp Fielding III is committed to a summer and fall sailing schedule. He's an important member of the U.S. sailing team. He is, of course, also an officer in his father's stock brokerage firm. My client is willing to leave his place on the sailing team at the end of this season. However, he can hardly be expected to let the other team members down.''

''I don't believe anyone has asked him to quit the team,'' the judge said. ''Dr. Cameron merely suggests that Mrs. Fielding assume her husband's visiting privileges until he returns. Ms. Hyatt's counter-brief indicates essentially the same.''

There was a scraping together of the chairs at the Fielding end of the horseshoe. Faith wished she had a clearer view of the proceedings, but she sat in a curve that excluded her from seeing either Kipp or Shelby's face.

The younger Schlegel broke out of the huddle. ''Shelby Fielding is undergoing complicated fertility treatments in New York. I'm sure in this enlightened day and age, I don't have to spell out the delicacy of the procedures. I think it's sufficient to say the success or failure of the process depends in part on the patient's optimal physical and mental condition. We contend the two-hour commute from New York City to Boston would place undue stress on Mrs. Fielding.''

Lon Maxwell voiced what sprang to Faith's mind. ''Judge Brown, I'd like to ask the esteemed Counselor Schlegel how that compares to the stress of caring for infant twins. I hate to be indelicate, but if Mrs. Fielding's fertility quest is successful, she could be dealing with three children under one year of age. Or possibly more.''

David Reed drew attention to himself by leaning back and gesturing widely with one arm. ''Mr. Maxwell has brought up an excellent point, Judge. I'm sure my client would be interested in seeing statistics relative to known numbers of multiples born to mothers who'd undergone fertility treatment. I've read it's a high percentage.''

All three of the Fielding lawyers scowled. Judge Brown prodded them to answer. ''What about that, Counselors? Have you and your client discussed what would happen in the event Shelby Fielding conceives twins or triplets?''

Again the group conferred. Michael nudged Faith. *An interesting concept,* he mouthed silently.

She chewed the inside of her cheek. For the first time she was glad Lacy had found David Reed. He'd certainly thrown the Fielding camp, as the judge had called it, a major curve. Kipp's father's eyebrows waved wildly at the team members.

At last Bob Schlegel rallied. "Your Honor, may we suggest that Counselors Maxwell and Reed are trying to cross a bridge before we come to it? Mrs. Fielding hasn't yet conceived. Perhaps our colleagues are trying to steer us away from the question at hand. That of fair play."

"Nothing of the kind," David broke in gruffly. "You may not be aware that I had the privilege of serving Lacy Hyatt Cameron at the time she took ill. I assure you the Fieldings' fertility issue was very much on her mind when she directed me to draft her custody papers. You see, young Kipp told her he was returning to his wife because she'd found a new fertility method to try."

Faith frowned. *She* had told David that. He'd said Lacy had implied Kipp was dead. She didn't want David lying on her behalf.

"So then Lacy Cameron admitted Kipp fathered her babies," argued the last member of the Fielding legal team. Nancy Matz sounded very pleased she'd picked up on that.

Lon Maxwell twirled his pen. "Seems to me none of the topics under discussion make a lick of sense until we get the results of the DNA tests done on my client and young Fielding."

The judge nodded. "I agree."

"About damn time," snapped the eldest Fielding.

"Dad," Kipp muttered.

Clearly not happy with the elder Fielding's outburst, Judge Brown opened a watch that hung on a gold chain around her neck. "I have to preside in court in half an hour. Up to this point, we've made little progress, although that's fairly standard for a first meeting. I must say Mr. Maxwell has a point. It's senseless to proceed until the DNA results are in. I'd be happy to set a tentative date for…say, six weeks down the line. Or we could wait until the lab has the report and schedule a meeting then."

Lon Maxwell closed the folder he'd been working from. "I vote we wait for the results. My client said the technician told him it could be from four to six weeks."

The Schlegels spoke in unison. "Affirmative." Then Keith Schlegel folded his hands across his pudgy stomach. "I take it we agree that no one visits the babies until our client returns from his trip?"

David Reed all but bounded from his chair. "I'll agree to no such thing! Didn't any of you read the testimony from Dr. Hal Sampson that I enclosed in my rebuttal? Sampson is the pediatrician attending the twins. The babies are up to weight, and he plans to let them go home from the hospital next week."

"Home to where?" chorused Lon Maxwell and all of Fielding's counselors.

"Home with Ms. Hyatt," David growled. "I believe she is the legal custodian, at least until the matter of paternity is settled."

Furor erupted around the table. Judge Brown didn't have a gavel, but she did rap her knuckles on her table until order resumed. "Granted, Mr. Reed, you did properly file custody papers for Lacy Cameron. I'd remind you, however, I can still make the twins wards of the court.'' She nodded at the couple seated to David's right.

"That's correct," Daniel Burgess, said, all the while bobbing his head. "Barbara and I can request they be placed in a neutral foster home until such time as the DNA results come in and another hearing is arranged."

Faith cried out. She hardly realized she'd grabbed Michael's arm. He, too, lost his color and swallowed repeatedly before covering her hand with his.

Reed rubbed his chin several times before he spoke. "I'm not disputing your power to place the children elsewhere, Judge. I guess I assumed you'd grant my client temporary custody, since we all agreed at the beginning of today's hearing that the welfare of the twins is our top priority. Ms. Hyatt, the babies' aunt by blood, has set up a nursery in her apartment to accommodate the youngsters. She's arranged for time off from her job as a nurse. No matter what the DNA proves, she will continue to play a role in Nicholas and Abigail's lives." He gave an eloquent shrug.

Keith Schlegel narrowed his eyes. "Judge Brown. I contend Reed is playing us all for fools. My client would have set up a nursery if he'd been aware the babies were so close to being released."

Michael didn't wait for his attorney to speak for him. "Your client might have known that if he'd bothered to visit the twins. I've seen Faith interacting with the babies. She loves them, and they already know her. I have no objection to placing the babies in her care temporarily."

Again there was a moment of disruption in the room. Then, as expected, the senior Fielding convened his team. They all talked separately and at once. Faith tried not to be anxious, but her stomach rolled like a ship on the high seas. She wanted Lacy's babies permanently and refused to dwell on the word *temporary.* Right now, she prayed they wouldn't fight her taking Nick and Abby home from the hospital. She'd dreamed of seeing them sleeping peacefully in their new cribs. Even if they were torn from her during a later battle, they deserved to spend their first months, with family rather than a foster family—strangers who couldn't possibly love them as much as she did.

Michael squeezed her fingers and gave her a lopsided smile. "Relax," he murmured. "Fielding and his cronies might not want to let you take the kids. But it's clear Kipp and Shelby aren't ready to give them a home."

"I don't know," she whispered back. "With their resources, how long would it take for them to buy out a baby store and install an au pair in their mansion?"

"Do you really think the judge would go for that? She doesn't strike me as a woman who misses much. I may be wrong, but I had the feeling she wondered why, if they were truly excited about taking the twins, Shelby Fielding was still going through with fertility treatments."

"Hmm. I can't help feeling sorry for Shelby. Not too many women would welcome a husband's illegitimate offspring with open arms."

"Oh? Wouldn't you if you loved the man?"

Faith frowned. "Do you doubt there's love between them?" She sighed. "Poor Nick and Abby. They'll still probably go to live with Kipp after the results of the DNA come back."

"Thanks a lot." Michael stiffened in his chair. "Those are *my* babies. Trust me—I can feel they're my own flesh and blood when I hold them."

She pursed her lips. "I know what Lacy believed. She thought her baby was Kipp's."

David shushed them as Bob Schlegel's deep voice rang out. "My client will approve Ms. Hyatt acting as foster parent. He does request that she bring the children to see his father and Mrs. Fielding at least once a week during the time he's away. And another thing," the man concluded, cutting through Faith's protesting gasp, "we object to Ms. Hyatt having named the children. Please stipulate that she refrain from using those names while they're in her care."

David Reed snorted. "My client doesn't own a car. She relies on walking to get to her appointments around town. Before Schlegel suggests she use public transit, may I remind him we're talking about two premature babies? Dragging them back and forth to New York City on a packed commuter train is inviting exposure to all kinds of viruses and germs."

The judge glanced from one lawyer to the other. "Mr. Schlegel, that request does seem a bit excessive. As we've already established it unfeasible for Mrs. Fielding to travel, I'm granting Ms. Hyatt the same privilege—she can keep the babies at home. I will allow the grandfather visiting rights, provided he calls and arranges a convenient time with Ms. Hyatt and doesn't just barge in without notice."

Kipp Jr. didn't look too pleased. Clearly he was a man unused to having people thwart him.

"About the matter of the names, Your Honor…" One of the Schlegels reintroduced his earlier objection.

David jumped in before Judge Brown had a chance to answer. "It's a small matter to request a legal change of name if and when the DNA proves Mr. Fielding III is the natural father. My client was simply following her sister's wishes in naming her daughter. Lacy, you understand, did not know she was having twins. Anyway, at this age, what's in a kid's name?''

Faith felt the argument between the men swirl around her. David hadn't said anything she hadn't said herself. Only now, she'd begun to think of these babies as Nick and Abby. She doubted she'd ever be able to call them anything else. There was David maintaining babies couldn't possibly identify the sound of a name at such a young age. She'd be a fool to refute him in this crowd. But not for a minute did she believe that what he'd said was true. The names fit the twins. And from the moment she'd begun calling them by name, they seemed to respond. It hadn't just been her imagination. It truly hadn't.

Nancy Matz made herself heard above the heated discussion among the male attorneys. ''Gentlemen, perhaps we could settle on a written agreement from Ms. Hyatt. One stating she won't contest a name change at the time paternity is determined.''

David bent his head toward Faith. ''If you don't want them reneging on allowing you to take the twins home, let them have their way on this. They're assuming you won't press your custody suit once paternity is established. It suits me to let them labor under false impressions. Why give them more time to prepare a defense?''

''All right,'' she said slowly. ''I suppose I also have to agree to let Kipp's father visit.''

''Yes. Be happy we won a major victory without really having to get in the trenches and fight dirty. I never expected either of the men to agree so readily to your guardianship.''

''Temporary guardianship,'' Faith said with distaste.

David Reed closed his folder. ''Haven't you heard

that possession is nine-tenths of the law? It applies to custody as well as material objects. Unless you strongly object, I'm about to make a truly magnanimous gesture on your part.''

"Wh-what?" Faith stammered.

"We'll invite Dan Burgess and Barbara Lang to make an appointment to visit you. My thinking here is they'll see what a natural mom you are. It couldn't hurt if they recommended leaving the babies in your care, in the event that we have to take off the gloves and fight Fielding.''

Something about his glee at the prospect of a down-and-dirty fight didn't sit well with Faith. He'd prepared her the other night, of course. But she'd hoped against hope that it wouldn't come to a bitter court confrontation. It was probably naive of her to dream anyone with rightful access to these babies would voluntarily step aside. Her sigh could be heard throughout the room.

David bounced the tips of his fingers together as he talked. "Ms. Hyatt will sign a waiver with regard to names. I'll have it notarized. She welcomes scheduled visits from Kipp's father. We'll include her address when we forward the waiver. Also…" He dragged out the word until he had everyone's attention. "Ms. Hyatt extends invitations to Dr. Cameron and to Mr. Burgess and Ms. Lang. That ought to be quite agreeable to all parties, don't you think, Judge?''

As Michael had said, Judge Brown was nobody's fool. She stared intently at Faith until she almost blurted out that it had been Reed's idea, not hers. Seconds before Faith could disgrace herself, the judge picked up her pen and made a few notations on her pad.

"I believe we've answered all immediate questions," she said at length. "I see we're out of time." She checked her watch again. "Unless some unforeseen problem arises, we won't reconvene as a group until the DNA results come in."

The judge stood and gathered her belongings. Everyone in the room rose and waited quietly while she moved around the horseshoe and shook each hand in turn. "My son has twin boys," she murmured as she clasped Faith's fingers in her cool hand. "I wonder if you know how much work you've let yourself in for." Giving a small laugh, she released Faith's clammy fingers. "Twins are a lot more than twice the work of a single child, believe me. My husband and I went to help our son and daughter-in-law when the boys were born. It took four adults running around the clock to take care of those little tadpoles. I've never been so exhausted in my life."

Faith gave a sickly smile. Judge Brown had hit on the elusive uneasiness that had haunted Faith, but which, so far, she'd successfully held at bay. Competent as she was at her job, when it came right down to it, she was afraid she didn't have what it took to be an adequate mother. Because, in the back of her mind, she'd never believed that she'd handled raising Lacy well.

"Faith?"

She came crashing back to earth. Judge Brown and her clerk had both left the chamber; Kipp's entourage were packed up and scuttling out, too. "Sorry, Michael. I must have, um, spaced out for a minute."

"Looked that way," he teased. "What I said was that the hearing wasn't nearly as bloody as I expected."

"Bloody? I, ah, no. It was quite civil, wasn't it?"

"I suppose this was luck," he mused, loosening the knot on his tie. "Once we get the results of the DNA,

I assume the two of us left in the fray will be more inclined to duke it out with no holds barred.''

"Is that your way of warning me to not expect you to be so nice the next time around?" she asked. "By the way, Michael, if you hope to be taken seriously, don't wear that tie again. Those silly turtles would make anyone want to laugh. But perhaps you missed the look on Judge Brown's face when she stopped to shake your hand.''

"I saw. If you ask me, she said to herself, now that Cameron guy is human.''

"Was there doubt?" Faith said dryly.

"Some people think doctors are a stuffy lot.''

"Really? Well, other people consider them playboys. Surgeons especially have a bad reputation in the family market.''

"Well, if *that* isn't a generality, I don't know what is. I didn't end my marriage. Lacy left me.''

"Mmm. So she said. Because you were never around. How will that play in a future courtroom drama, I wonder?''

The smile lingering on Michael's lips winked out. He studied her cool features a moment, then abruptly dismissed himself. Stepping around her, he struck up a conversation with David Reed, and the two walked out chatting amiably.

Faith was left alone to ponder how her exchange with Michael had gone awry. Sadly, she'd never known how to hold his interest. Not that it mattered now. What *did* matter was that she'd fulfilled her promise to Lacy, if only temporarily.

CHAPTER SIX

FAITH STEPPED INTO the sunshine outside the courthouse
and experienced a shift in her attitude. Why had she
snapped at Michael? After all, she'd successfully leaped
one hurdle today. Only time would tell what lay ahead.
Worrying in advance about something over which she
had no control was of no earthly good, to her *or* the
babies. DNA would make one man or the other her foe.
Faith frankly doubted any custody battle was ever
pretty. Michael had said once before that it would go
easier on everyone if the plaintiffs remained civil to
each other. She wanted to stay on good terms with him.
It suddenly dawned on her—what if Lacy had been
wrong, and Michael *had* fathered the children? Faith
saw Michael relying on her, needing her help as the
twins' aunt.

While contemplating Michael in the role of dad, Faith
was beset by an urgent need to visit the twins. On its
heels came a desire to detour past the cemetery. That
was probably the better choice, since she hadn't asked
Michael if he planned to visit the babies. He'd probably
gone straight there from the hearing. It was likely he'd
go back to New York now and resume his surgical practice until the test results became available. After snapping at him, the least she could do was allow him extra
time at the hospital.

Too used to pinching pennies, Faith caught a bus to

the cemetery instead of taking a cab. In spite of the lovely day, a chill enveloped her when she passed between the wrought-iron angels that served as gate sentinels.

Once she'd found the plot of new-turned ground, Faith wished she'd stopped at a florist's to pick up a fresh bouquet. The last of the funeral flowers had turned brown. This was a perpetual-care cemetery. Why hadn't someone thrown them away? And where was the stone she'd ordered?

As thoughts tumbled disjointedly through her mind, staving off memories of Lacy, Faith recalled the man at the quarry where she'd ordered the rosy headstone saying it'd take three to four weeks. She sank to her knees in the warm, fragrant grass, and idly crushed brown flower petals between fidgety fingers.

"Lacy," she murmured past the lump in her throat. "Today we made some progress toward fulfilling your wish. It's not final, you understand. The judge can still take the babies away from me. Oh, God, Lacy. I hope you knew what you were doing, handing them over to me."

Faith scattered the next handful of petals. She brushed at a curling edge of grass. How long would it take for this bare earth, whose shape reminded her far too much of the casket, to fill in completely with grass?

Darn, she'd promised herself she wouldn't cry today. The tears fell anyway. "Lacy," Faith sniffled, "I wish you could see Abigail and Nick. They're beautiful. Perfect. I'm telling you this so you'll know your sacrifice wasn't in vain."

A discreet cough sounded nearby. Faith straightened swiftly and smoothed the heels of her hands over her wet cheeks. "Michael," she gasped, blinking up into a stabbing shaft of sunlight. "Wha-what are you doing here?"

Going down on one knee, he placed a cemetery-approved cone vase near the site of the crumbling brown bouquet. Dewy violets bobbed among a profusion of white daisies in his new floral offering. "Seems we were of like minds Faith. Forgive me, please. I didn't mean to intrude." Rising agilely, Michael extended her a hand.

Even with his help, Faith was slow to climb to her feet. His flowers were so lovely, she paused to remove the last of the dead ones. An awkward silence fell between them. Both gazed down at the pitifully small plot of ground.

"I came out here," Faith said at last, "because I thought you'd be at the hospital visiting the babies."

"When I walked to the parking garage with Reed, he stated plainly enough that I need to make appointments to see the twins—just like the Fieldings. The way you and I parted, I didn't think you'd be too inclined to grant me visitation privileges today."

Faith raised the hand filled with flower stalks to shield her eyes from the sun as she stared into Michael's face. "About the way I bit your head off earlier—I, well, I'd like to apologize. I can't imagine what made me act like a shrew. Nerves, maybe."

"I'm not blaming you, Faith. The hearing was nerve-racking for everyone."

"It's not knowing how it'll all turn out that makes things so tough. Realistically, I know the custody can go any way. It only makes sense for each of us to spend time getting to know the babies. I won't impede visits by you or the Fieldings."

Michael smiled. "I knew you'd do the right thing,

Faith.'' He wanted to hug her. But he let his half-raised arms drop. It wasn't smart to touch her. Especially not here, standing next to Lacy's grave. Lord help him, he wanted to hold her and comfort her....

''Yes, well, the parenting book I've started reading says children benefit emotionally and socially from active, early involvement by fathers,'' Faith was saying.

''I believe I *am* the father and I want to be a good one,'' Michael said forthrightly. ''I understand your reservations, Faith. And you were right about my profession taking its toll on family life. Do you by chance know of a bootee camp for dads?'' he said teasingly, as much to relieve his own tension.

It was on the tip of Faith's tongue to say she didn't want to be having this conversation where Lacy could hear them. Of course, that was stupid. It was just that Michael stood so tall, so broad-shouldered, so alive that he made her feel weak in the knees. She couldn't help reacting to his disarming grin. The more he brought out these ambivalent feelings inside her, the more she clamped down on speaking candidly to him. As a result, she said nothing at all.

Sensing he'd put her off again, Michael groped for something to say. ''If you're finished here, I can give you a lift back to town.''

She mulled over his invitation. ''I planned to stop at the hospital, first,'' she finally told him. ''It's really better if we stagger our visits, Michael.''

''As you wish,'' he said stiffly. ''I'll be more than happy to drop you off at Good Shepherd and time my visit with the six-o'clock feeding. Feeding them is—'' He broke off, restrained his excitement. ''I get a kick out of it,'' he said softly.

Faith recognized the change in his expression and

deeply regretted that her relationship with Lacy had caused this wall to go up between them. But some realities would never change. She was Lacy's big sister, and he was Lacy's ex-husband. The fact that Faith had once had a terrible crush on him and the fact that he was now single only added to the discomfort she felt around him. She probably ought to feel shame for allowing such yearnings while standing beside her sister's grave.

"Good Lord, Faith," Michael exploded. "A ride into town is no big deal. I wish you'd quit looking at me like I'm the Boston Strangler."

"Thank you for the offer," she said meekly. "I accept." It wouldn't do to divulge even the slightest hint of the thoughts running through her head.

"You have the most revealing eyes of any woman I've ever known," he said as they turned and strolled toward the gate. "No wonder you never joined any of the residents' poker games. You would've lost your shirt."

Feeling the tension slide away, Faith laughed. "At last the truth. You guys *did* play strip poker in the basement dead-record room. And you claimed not to understand why no nurse ever agreed to meet you there."

"Ha! Was that the story you heard? You remember Donna Murphy?"

"Vaguely." Faith frowned. "A busty redhead."

"Yeah." Michael grinned mischievously. "She had freckles…well, never mind where she had freckles. Those were the good old days." He felt less on edge talking about the days before he married Lacy. Removing his suit jacket, Michael tossed it into the back seat of his dark green BMW. After unlocking the passenger

door for Faith, he rolled up the sleeves of his dress shirt
and slid behind the steering wheel.

Michael had dark hair on his arms, but only a dusting
above the knuckles of his beautifully shaped surgeon's
fingers. Faith recalled the knots that had formed in the
pit of her stomach every time she'd been assigned to
his surgical team. Something as simple as watching him
scrub had completely entranced her. Even now as he
looped one elegant wrist over the wheel and turned to
back out of his parking spot, her mouth felt dust-dry.

"I wonder whatever happened to Donna," she said
for the sake of keeping the conversation alive. "Now
that I think about it, she was a terrible nurse. A walking
disaster on the wards."

Once he'd eased into traffic, Michael glanced at
Faith. "She married Daryl Sawyer."

"Daryl Saw—? That little bald guy with Coke-bottle
glasses? Proctologist, right?"

"Right. Except Donna married Daryl's father."

Faith's mouth flopped open. "Isn't he some hotshot
plastic surgeon in Hollywood? I saw him on a talk show
touting a newfangled kind of laser liposuction."

"That's him. I met him at a surgical convention in
Athens. Donna had been liposucked everywhere except—" He abruptly dropped his hand back to the
wheel from where he'd cupped it six or so inches out
from his chest. "She looked okay," he said lamely.

"Men! Why are you all obsessed with breasts?"

Michael's gaze ran over Faith's compact frame. She
still wore the pink suit he'd nearly drooled on at the
hearing. In Michael's opinion, small breasts looked
pretty damned good. Faith had always looked damned
good. He coughed—choked really—and berated himself
for allowing his thoughts to wander.

"You can let me out here," she informed him, stabbing a finger at the south entrance of Good Shepherd Hospital. It was the opposite end of the building from the nursery, but Faith wanted to disappear from beneath Michael's scrutiny. He made her feel self-conscious in a way she hadn't felt in…at least six years. Self-conscious and plain. Unfeminine. She'd never resorted to stuffing her bra, although in high school she'd certainly been tempted. Now friends purported to envy the rapid metabolism that kept her trim. At least the women did. Faith knew men like Michael probably found her too boyish looking.

"You want out here?" Michael jerked his attention back from checking out his former sister-in-law. He felt a stirring below his belt—and an immediate sense of guilt. He should definitely not be thinking what he was thinking. Like how his hands could probably span her waist. Or how he'd like to unbutton that blouse and find out if she wore cotton or silk underneath. She obviously didn't know, but men were obsessed by the mystery surrounding any woman they found interesting. Especially the parts she kept hidden—and not just the physical either. Michael recalled a time he'd been very interested in Faith Hyatt. Before he met Lacy. Back then, Lacy made him feel ten feet tall, while Faith had made it very clear that she needed no one but herself.

"Ah, hell," he muttered, swinging the car in next to the curb. "You want to hike a mile to the nursery, be my guest." Yanking on the emergency brake, he vaulted from the car, circled the hood and jerked open her door.

If Faith had any doubts about coming up short in his perusal, they were obliterated by his actions. "Thanks for the lift," she mumbled.

Did he expect a more effusive show of gratitude? she wondered as she hurried through the revolving glass door. Faith saw Michael reflected in the glass, still leaning on the open passenger door. He seemed to be staring blankly after her, although she was too far away to see the expression in his eyes.

Damn Michael Cameron for making her lose the modicum of self-esteem she'd worked so many years to build. "And whose fault is that?" she asked under her breath while pacing in front of the elevator. "You get within fifteen feet of him and you let your mind turn to alphabet soup," she scolded herself, walking into a thankfully empty elevator. Then she laughed and rotated her tense shoulders. "Maybe he knows. Maybe he hopes someone'll see you talking to yourself. Then he and Lon Maxwell can declare you incompetent to take care of the babies."

Faith was careful to lock her thoughts inside once the elevator door slid open and she stepped out onto the busy ward. She exchanged greetings with several staff members and waved to others as she traversed the halls on her way to the nursery.

A familiar figure stood at the viewing window. Faith's steps slowed, but Kipp Fielding III had caught a glimpse of her reflection. He studied her somberly.

Craning her neck, Faith glanced into the waiting room where she supposed Shelby and his father must be sitting. The room was empty.

"Are you alone?" she asked, realizing the question was inane.

His face didn't change as he shoved his hands into his pockets and gave a brief nod.

"I supposed you'd be back in New York by now,

packing for your trip to Florida, or whatever it is sailors do before sailing off into the sunset.''

''Shelby complained of feeling ill after we left the hearing. We checked into a hotel, which allows her to rest awhile. I leave for Florida on Sunday.''

''Ah. Then your dad's staying with Shelby?''

''No. He went back to New York. I, uh, tried phoning you.'' Incredibly blond eyelashes swooped down to shutter very blue eyes. He chewed nervously on his lower lip.

Something about his lost expression troubled Faith. ''Would you like to take a closer look at Nicholas and Abigail?'' she asked gently.

The curtain over his eyes lifted, revealing an eager light. Almost as if afraid to concur, he spread his hands. ''I know you don't have any reason to like me, Faith. But it's important to me that you understand. I, uh, Lacy wasn't just a one-night stand.'' He cleared his throat and looked everywhere but at Faith. The tips of his ears turned red as he went on. ''We connected…like two shipwrecked souls.''

''You don't have to explain. What's done is done.''

''I want you to know. Lacy said she was on the pill. I took her at her word. Cameron thinks I'm an idiot for not making more of her scar. I did notice. She brushed off my concern, saying she'd been in a car accident.''

''I see,'' Faith said. But she didn't—unless Michael was right and Lacy had systematically planned to get pregnant. If Lacy had arbitrarily picked Kipp to father the child she was determined to have, her plan had backfired when she'd fallen in love with him. Faith didn't think Lacy's tears for this man were an act. ''Although your lives crossed for whatever reason, you both harbored secrets. Neither of you was really free to make a new commitment.''

"Hindsight is always clearest,'' he said, sighing heavily.

"Yes, and now there are two more lives that'll forever be disrupted. Do you love your wife?'' Faith asked abruptly.

If a swift, affirmative reply was what Faith was after, she didn't get it. Kipp rocked back on his heels and stared through the window at the rows of bassinets. Faith had almost given up on getting an answer when he finally spoke. "Our fathers were business associates before Shelby or I were born. Our marriage was preordained from the cradle.'' He shivered. "It would be impossible for me not to love Shel. She was raised to be the perfect mate for me. Included in the life plan she was handed was a requirement that she produce the next Fielding heir.''

"I see,'' Faith murmured. This time she *did* see. The perfect mate didn't feel perfect when she failed to conceive. Judging by her brief peck at Shelby Fielding, Faith would say it was probably the first failure the woman had ever experienced. She had no doubt that in Shelby's privileged circle, only success was accepted. "I've had control of my own life for so many years, I can't imagine what jumping to someone else's command would be like,'' Faith said. "Your wife must be a nervous wreck if both sets of parents are demanding she have a baby.''

"Her parents and my mother were killed when their yacht sank in the Mediterranean. If anything, that made my father more insistent. It was on the anniversary of their deaths that Shelby left me.''

"I want Lacy's babies to grow up in a happy, normal

household. I told Michael, and I'll tell you. I'm going to do everything in my power to keep them.''

"I'd already deduced that. But I'm warning you. If the DNA tests prove they're mine, you won't have a prayer of retaining custody.''

"So we're back to square one. Pity. I was beginning to like you.''

"Does this mean you'll refuse to let me visit the babies today?''

"Not at all. Michael pointed out that I'd be wise to remain agreeable. He reminded me that no matter who the father is, I'll always be the twins' aunt.''

This time Kipp's acknowledgment was curt. While Faith directed the nursing supervisor to provide him with sterile clothing for his visit, she elected not to go in with him. She had learned her lesson watching Michael interact with the babies. Faith didn't think she could stand it if Kipp fell under their spell as Michael had.

Faith hung out with a few pals in the nurses' lounge until Kipp left. As it turned out, waiting wasn't all bad. She'd no more than slipped on her sterile gear when Dr. Sampson walked in.

"By Jove," he announced, beaming at Faith. "These tots have done so well, I'm going to let you take them home on Monday.''

Faith could only grin foolishly as the nursery staff gathered around, hugging her happily.

Word spread through the hospital with the speed of light. Faith's friend, Gwen, showed up with several nurses from the floor where Faith had worked. They pried her away from the babies and hustled her back to the lounge. "This is short notice," Gwen exclaimed, waving a can of soda once everyone had quieted down.

"Cicely and I want to give you a baby shower. How about Saturday evening, Faith? At your apartment? Tacky, we know, but that way none of us will have do a whirlwind housecleaning. Besides, it'll make things easier on you. You won't have to cart so much loot home on foot or in a cab. With twins, people naturally buy double of everything. Oh, and in case I didn't mention it, we're providing refreshments. All you have to do, little mama, is relax and enjoy."

"A shower." Faith had never dared hope she'd ever be the recipient of a shower, neither the wedding or the baby variety. "That's too cool, you guys. But—but maybe you'd better not go to all that trouble," she said with a tremor in her voice. "At the hearing today, it was decided my custody is only temporary. The decision won't be made until the men's DNA tests come back."

"Fiddlesticks. We don't care, do we, ladies?" Gwen said, and she squeezed Faith's arm.

Megan, a young nurse from Faith's ward, piped up. "Faith's pretty brave, taking on two babies at once. She deserves a real blowout. You'd better party hearty, pal," she said to Faith. "From what my friends who have singletons tell me, get-togethers are few and far between afterward. And that's with only one baby."

"Singletons. Aren't you clever," Gwen teased. "What do you call twins or triplets?"

Megan rolled her eyes. "Twins are twingles. Moms of triplets have no time to think up cutesy synonyms."

"I'll take singletons, thank you." Cicely pretended to shudder. "Actually, erase that statement. Don't give me any more. Three of them run me ragged. Add to that a full-time job and a spoiled husband." She wrinkled her nose.

"Amen to that." Gwen grimaced. "Faith has it made on two counts. She's taking a leave from work and she doesn't have a husband making demands on her."

"Lucky lady," someone in the back row was heard to say.

"Oh, you guys," Megan chided. "I, for one, want a husband when I have kids. Don't try to tell me any of you want to be single. Cice, how many times have you had to work overtime? I've heard you call Dan and ask him to pick up the kids from school or from the sitter. Plus, he starts dinner. Why can't you give the man credit?"

Gwen looked sheepish. "My Jerry is a sweetie. He's a wonderful dad. You're right, Megan. It's a bad habit a lot of working women fall into—complaining about their spouses. Some women have to do it all—cook, clean, work outside the home *and* have total care of the kids. They're the only ones who should gripe. Sorry."

Faith observed the pensive, or perhaps guilty, expressions on the faces of her friends. Everything they'd said had started her thinking about her situation. Eventually she'd have to return to work. Maybe sooner rather than later, depending on how much she'd have to pay in attorney's fees. It was entirely possible that she might have to hire a mother's helper. The very thing she'd objected to in Michael's situation. Sadly she wondered if Kipp and Shelby, for all their faults, might not be able to offer the babies greater stability. Her own life seemed bleaker for not having a husband with whom to share the joys and trials of parenting.

"Hey, Faith." Gwen snapped her fingers in front of Faith's blank face. "I asked if seven-thirty on Saturday is good for you? That way, the people who work the eleven-to-seven can attend."

"Any time is fine with me. I'm the one living the easy life, remember?"

"Like Megan said, enjoy it while you can." Cicely tapped her watch and made shooing motions toward the door. "Back to the salt mines, ladies. Two minutes, and our break is over."

They said goodbye to Faith. Soon she was left alone with her thoughts. For all the household chores she'd done while growing up, her dad had shopped for groceries and often cooked dinner, even though he'd frequently worked overtime and come home tired. In the mornings, her mother used to brush and curl both girls' hair. There had been times their mom had barely been able to breathe, but she'd pitched in whenever she could.

A lot of women today raised children on their own, Faith argued as she shed her gown, mask and paper bootees. She was, after all, fit and capable. There was no reason she shouldn't manage beautifully.

As she stepped inside an empty elevator and turned to press the first floor button, Faith saw Michael walk out of the adjacent elevator. He was surrounded by people who carried flowers, presents and a balloon bouquet. The balloons were pink and white. They must be on their way to visit a new mother who'd had a baby girl.

Michael split off from the crowd and angled toward the nursery. The door to Faith's elevator slid closed, blocking him from sight. She probably should have gotten out and told him the news about the twins being released on Monday. No, she decided. Let the nursing supervisor inform him and Kipp. Faith didn't feel like discussing visitations with either of them quite yet. By Monday, Michael would be back in New York and Kipp off to his boat race; she'd be able to start establishing a routine without any interference. After the shower on Saturday, she'd have time to wash and dry any clothing and sheets and blankets she might receive as gifts, and she could finish preparing the nursery. With luck, she'd be granted an entire week to spend alone with the babies.

Was privacy what she really wanted? Or would she rather have a happy marriage like Gwen's? For six years, every time Faith pictured herself married, the man in her fantasy could pass for Michael Cameron's twin.

SATURDAY, GWEN AND CICELY arrived at five to begin decorating for the shower. They brought several bottles of champagne, as well as the makings for punch. Abigail Moore, Lacy's friend, arrived next. She said she'd stopped by the hospital nursery to see the twins and they were gorgeous.

Cicely popped the cork on the first bottle and poured each one of them a glass. ''To Nicky, Abby and Faith.'' She held her glass aloft.

''Before you toast us, come see what I've done in the babies' room,'' Faith begged. Taking Gwen's hand, she dragged her down the hall. Abigail followed.

''Gad! It belongs in *House Beautiful*. Isn't that monkey adorable?'' Ab snatched him up and laughed at the funny face.

Gwen leaned over her shoulder. ''He looks a lot like Dr. Peterson, but don't tell anyone I said so.''

''You nuts.'' Faith grabbed the monkey away and propped him up next to the giraffe again. ''You two are the baby experts. Is there anything I need that I've forgotten to buy?''

Gwen made a slow circuit of the room. ''Cribs,

changing table, diaper stacker, chest of drawers, mobiles, toys and a comfy rocking chair.''

Following at her heels, Abigail named a few things
Gwen had missed. ''Night-light, wedge pillows to keep
them on their backs, diaper pail and baby wipes. I don't
see a bathtub.''

Faith choked on her sip of champagne. ''How could
I have forgotten about bathing them? Lord, how do I
go about handling two?''

''One at a time,'' Gwen said, tongue in cheek. ''Remember from nursing school how slippery babies can
be?''

''Don't even mention it,'' Faith gasped. ''Come back
into the kitchen. I'll add a bathtub to my shopping list.
Darn, I thought I had everything covered.''

''Maybe someone'll give you a bathtub as a shower
gift,'' Cicely said, pausing at the kitchen counter to top
up their glasses.

''Well, if they do,'' Faith said, ''I'll take it off my
list. Are you two driving? If so, you'd better back off
on the bubbly.''

Gwen deliberately drained her glass, smacking her
lips afterward. ''Jerry's picking us up. He offered. Told
me to live it up. He knows what a god-awful week it's
been at work.''

''Why don't you leave E.R. and come back to the
ward,'' Cicely suggested between blowing up pink and
blue balloons.

''Yeah,'' Faith agreed. ''Peterson's going to fill my
slot temporarily. It'd give you a break from E.R. for six
months or so. A year if I can swing it financially.''

''The post-surg ward is stress of a different kind,
that's all. There's a lot more lifting than there is in E.R.

After having four kids and tossing patients around for so many years, my vertebrae are giving out."

"Have you seen an orthopedist?" Faith asked.

Gwen screwed up her face and reached for the champagne bottle again. "Fred Morrison. Until he started talking fusion. It's either that or he wants to prescribe a heavy-duty painkiller that knocks me on my butt. I can't take them and work. And I have to work—we need the money. Jerry has a good job, but he doesn't make enough to put four kids through college."

While Faith made sympathetic noises, Cicely stood up, leaned over the kitchen counter and peered around the kitchen. "Is something wrong?" Faith asked.

"Just checking to see if you had something burning in the oven. Don't you smell it?"

The other two sniffed around. Gwen finally shook her head. "I think the champagne must have dulled my senses."

"I do smell something, but I'm sure it's not in here." Faith opened the bakery box one of the women had brought. It was a beautifully decorated cake. A stork carrying two babies, one blanketed in pink and the other in blue, had been outlined on the icing. Bottles and bootees dotted the rest of the cake. "How wonderful!" There was a loud knock at her door, and she hurried to answer it.

A whole troop of women stood clustered in the hallway. Faith stepped aside to let them in, and several others got off the elevator and ran down the hall.

"Pee-ew," said the last woman through the door, holding her nose. "Your neighbor's really stinking up the hallway. A pathetic bachelor or a newlywed, I'll bet."

"Neighbor?" Faith stared at Betty, who worked in

admissions. "The only other apartment on this floor has been vacant for six months."

"Hmm," Betty drawled. "Then I'd say a hungry burglar broke in."

Faith continued to stand in the hall as the others swarmed into her living room and piled their gifts next to the couch. "I'd better call the manager," she said at last. "I don't see any smoke, but there's definitely a burning odor out here."

She excused herself and made the call. She didn't talk long. With the women all yakking at once, she could barely hear the manager's explanation.

"What did he say?" Gwen asked, slicing a hand through the air to silence the noisy group.

"Apparently he did rent the unit. To a single guy. He said not to worry about anything unless the smoke alarm goes off."

"So you have a new neighbor. Why are you frowning, Faith? Maybe he'll be gorgeous, straight and looking for a girlfriend."

Faith shrugged. "I hope he won't complain every time the babies cry. They're bound to," she said. "It takes time to change two kids and heat their bottles."

"I didn't stop to think," Betty said from the seat she'd found for herself on the floor next to the mountain of gifts. "Bachelors tend to throw wild, noisy parties."

"I wish no one had rented the place," Faith grumbled. "I hope this isn't a bad omen."

"Quit worrying." Gwen tore sheets of paper out of a preprinted pad of baby shower word games. "Now come and play."

"Hey, between changing diapers and feeding babies, maybe you can teach the guy how to cook," Cicely said, prodding Faith with the eraser of her pencil.

That garnered a laugh from everyone in the room. The festive mood continued when Gwen hauled out glasses and poured champagne all around. Soon, everyone was having such a good time the next-door neighbor was forgotten.

By the time the party ended and Faith saw her friends out, she'd accumulated not only the missing bathtub, but a thermometer, two musical swings, more stuffed animals and enough darling outfits to last the babies for a year.

Instead of going to bed, Faith stayed up and wrote a lengthy thank-you for each gift. Gwen had convinced Faith she'd never have time later.

She heard the floor creak next door, and considered popping over to introduce herself. But taking the initiative with a man wasn't something she did easily. While she deliberated, she heard his outer door slam.

Faith glanced at her kitchen clock. One o'clock. Either her neighbor was planning to close the bars, or he worked odd shifts like she had.

Stifling a yawn, Faith sealed the last envelope and shut off her lights. She went to bed, leaving the questions about her neighbor unanswered.

CHAPTER SEVEN

SUNDAY, FAITH CRAWLED OUT of bed, snapped on the bathroom light and groaned as she caught sight of the disheveled image in the mirror. "Champagne, ugh." She popped two aspirins. "Never again."

She felt better after showering. In the process of dressing to visit her dad, she contemplated future visits when she'd be taking the twins. Most residents at the home loved babies. With any luck, her dad would show some interest, too.

Faith hummed to herself as she left her apartment. Motherhood—even temporary motherhood—was going to be such a joy. It was hard to imagine ever complaining about it, even in fun as her friends had done at the shower. Young though she'd been when she assumed care of Lacy, every new phase her sister entered had delighted Faith. Well, not the teen years, but looking back, Faith decided her problems had stemmed as much from all the responsibilities she'd had to juggle: her college classes, caring for her mom, who was quite ill by then, managing the household and mothering a young woman who didn't want to be mothered.

Even after those rough years, Faith had envisioned getting married someday and having children of her own. That likelihood now seemed remote. Not too many men would want to take on raising twins—if she succeeded in gaining custody. And if she didn't, she'd still be involved in the babies' lives. Michael might be the exception. And he'd never mentioned wanting a wife.

The attendant at the front desk told Faith her father was having a bad day. She found it to be true. He was entrenched in the past and confused Faith with her aunt Lorraine. Faith gave up after an hour of watching him flip from show to show on his small TV.

Depressed, Faith didn't take him out to lunch as she normally tried to do. Instead, she left word to have his doctor call her at home to review her dad's medication. If they didn't do something, he'd never experience the joy of knowing his grandchildren.

Having jogged back to her apartment, Faith changed into sweats and took several baskets of laundry down to the basement, where the communal washers and dryers were. It wasn't until her third trip that it struck her she'd have to do this several times a week with two babies. Did she bundle them into infant carriers and cart them up and down the stairs? How could she do that *and* carry laundry? And what if one or other baby fell ill?

A washer and dryer in her own apartment was probably the best solution. But how could she fit them into her already overcrowded place? Dashing upstairs with a basket of things that needed folding, Faith ran into movers struggling to get a tan leather couch through her elusive neighbor's door.

She craned her neck to catch a glimpse of the man as she passed, but saw only two more brawny movers.

Back in her apartment, she noticed the message light blinking on her telephone. Figuring it was her dad's doctor, she hooked the laundry basket over one hip and paused to play the message.

"Faith, it's Michael. I would have called Friday after

I visited the twins, but I had business to take care of in New York.''

"Good," she muttered aloud. At least, now he and Kipp were both out of her hair. Except that wasn't the end of Michael's message.

"While I was at the hospital, Trish told me the twins are being released tomorrow. I was on the road before it dawned on me that you don't have my cell number. It's the easiest way to reach me." He rattled the number off fast. Faith had to search for a pen and back up the message so she could write it down. Although why she'd need to call him she couldn't fathom. As if he'd leave in the middle of a consultation and race to Boston to hold her hand.

In the next breath, he said, "If you need anything, anything at all, Faith, call me. I'll move heaven and earth to help. That's the God's truth. Um, I've rambled on long enough and we're both busy. See you soon. G'bye."

For a moment she pictured them as a team. "Yeah, sure," she snorted, placing her index finger on the button to erase his message. As if she'd ever call on him.

Still, she couldn't help dwelling on his words. His offer *sounded* sincere. Had Michael done the same to Lacy? Reassured her, then not been around to follow through when she needed him?

It was how doctors were. Faith could have told Lacy that. Or maybe not back then. At the time Lacy fell in love with Michael, Faith had only worked at the hospital a year. She'd viewed doctors as kings among men, and Michael Cameron had worn a jeweled crown.

Then he'd married her little sister. And work had become just that. A place to go every day. Something to keep her mind occupied so she'd forget the doctor who'd brightened her life.

Boy, she hated all these windows opening into the past. She ought to be telling herself that Dr. Cameron was only one man in a vast ocean of men. She should flush him out of her mind.

Faith dumped the clean baby clothes on her bed and sat beside them, covering her face with both hands. The bald truth was, she'd never stopped pining for Michael. Whenever Lacy invited her to visit, she used to worry that somehow her sister would guess. Had she ever had an inkling? Surely not.

Hopping up, Faith went into the bathroom and rinsed her hot face in cold water. Studying her dripping reflection with coolly assessing eyes, she knew she'd done the right thing in hiding her infatuation from Lacy. Really, she'd had no choice. But that attraction, that *wanting* had never gone away.

When it came to fighting Michael for the babies, didn't her feelings make her a bit of a fraud? She yearned for him, yearned to share the joy of these babies with him. In court, she might be forced to state, or at least imply, the opposite.

Oh, she was a fraud. It hurt to admit it. The truth was, if it turned out Michael and not Kipp had fathered the twins, she might have to rethink her stand in the custody fight. But never in ten million years could Faith tell him why.

For the remainder of the day, as she raced back and forth finishing the laundry, Faith delivered convincing pep talks to herself. Kipp was her nemesis. After all, Lacy had been sure he'd gotten her pregnant. Or pretty sure. Faith didn't find it hard to think about fighting Kipp Fielding III for custody.

All night she struggled with her conscience, but she couldn't have slept, anyway. Her new neighbor spent the night bumping around, hanging pictures or who knew what.

Bleary-eyed, she showered and heard water running next door. At least the man was an early riser. The chorus before six-o'clock feedings shouldn't upset him.

Faith puttered until nine, when she called a cab to take her to the hospital.

Wrestling a double stroller, an oversize diaper bag weighed down with diapers, blankets, bottles and baby clothing, plus her purse, down the elevator and out the door left Faith panting.

"Looks like you brought the whole nursery and forgot the baby," the cabby said as he helped her fold and tuck the stroller into the cab's trunk.

"Everybody's a comedian," she said, rolling her eyes.

"Hey, you look like you could use a laugh."

"Oh, great. I look that bad?"

He grinned and slammed the back door. "Where to?"

"Good Shepherd Hospital. Without a scenic tour."

The man yanked on the bill of his ball cap and glanced furtively at her in the rearview mirror. "Sorry about the jokes. You shoulda said you had sick kids."

Faith opened her mouth to explain. She closed it again and stared out the window at the passing scenery. She was too weary from lack of sleep to go into the convoluted details with a man she'd never see again. "Thanks," she mumbled.

She tipped him well, as he'd gone to the trouble of opening and stabilizing her not-so-portable stroller. All it took was a flick of the wrist, the salesclerk had guaranteed Faith. Ha! The darn thing required a degree in mechanical engineering to set it up and break it down for travel.

"I'll wait if you want, or come back and pick you up," the man offered as he pocketed the money Faith thrust into his hand.

She squinted up. "It's such a gorgeous day, I'll walk home with the twins. But thank you, anyway."

"Twins! You poor woman." He shook his head. "Good luck," he muttered as he climbed back in the cab.

What she needed luck with was manipulating the side-by-side stroller through the hospital's revolving glass door. She wriggled it in, all right, but the diaper bag got caught in the section behind her. A teenager on his way out gave the door a hefty shove, nearly ripping Faith's arm off. An old man came to her assistance. He saw what was happening and yanked the stroller into the lobby so she could go around again and join up with the dangling bag.

"Phew," she exclaimed, once she'd made the circuit. "*Thank* you."

"You okay, missy? I was afraid we'd need a doctor to amputate your arm."

"Nothing so drastic. I'll soon get the hang of maneuvering this contraption." Thanking him again, she hurried down the hall, only to face a similar problem at the elevators. Faith eventually arrived at the nursery, flushed and more than a little disheveled.

The first person she laid eyes on was Michael Cameron. Arms crossed, he lounged negligently in the doorway of the nursing office. His walnut hair appeared newly cut. He wore brown loafers, tan slacks and a pale gold T-shirt that molded itself to his wide chest. If he'd worn boots instead of loafers, Faith would have said he belonged on a motorcycle—in a *GQ* ad.

Compared to Michael, Faith felt frumpy. Her blouse had come untucked from her walking shorts and a lock of hair had fallen over one eye. She blew it aside in exasperation. "What are you doing here? Yesterday, when you phoned, I thought you were in New York."

"I was. Now I'm here. To help settle the babies in their new home."

If Dr. Sampson hadn't stepped off the elevator then and ambled over with a wide smile, Faith would have exploded at Michael. He'd all but accused her of incompetence, for heaven's sake!

"Anxious to get them home, are you, Faith?" Dr. Sampson reached into a closet and helped himself to a clean lab coat. "I hope you realize you can't bring the kids back, and there are no trade-ins on new models."

"He's such a tease," the nursing supervisor said, holding open the door to let Faith, Michael and the doctor into the examining room, where she'd already wheeled the two isolettes. "As if anyone would let these precious babies go," she crooned. Then, when the couple's situation seemed to dawn on her, she made a strangled sound.

Faith had put her foot in her mouth a few times herself in front of patients or their families. She commiserated. "Honestly, Eileen, I don't know how you can bear to let *any* of them go. It's a good thing I work the post-op ward instead of here."

The nurse gave her a grateful smile. "We hang on to a little piece of each one."

When Michael looked puzzled, she pointed behind him to a corkboard wall of photos. "Most parents send us one of the newborn pictures. Oh, say, hasn't anyone provided you with information on the hospital photographs?''

Faith and Michael shook their heads.

"After Dr. Sampson formally releases you, and after the babies are dressed to go home, a photographer comes to the mom's room and takes the pictures. Wait, you don't have a room. Three-ten is empty. Use it.''

"This dynamic duo is all yours," Dr. Sampson announced. He handed the nurse the twins' charts, squeezed Faith's arm and shook Michael's hand. "I'll leave instructions at the nursing station about when to bring them to the office for checkups, along with sample packs of formula.'' Winking, he strode off, calling over his shoulder, "Now you can get back to the important task of having their pictures taken.''

"I wish I'd known about this earlier," Faith said as she began dressing Abigail. "I just gave all my cash to the cabdriver. Shoot, and I used all my film at the shower the other night or I'd take a roll at home.''

Michael dug out his wallet. "I have money, Faith.''

She clamped her teeth over her bottom lip. Only yesterday she'd sworn she wouldn't accept help of any kind from Michael Cameron. Here she was, breaking the pledge already.

"It's a nominal sitting fee," Eileen assured them. "That entitles you to one free eight-by-ten portrait. You're not obligated to order any. Everyone does, though," she said conspiratorially. "Some of them are ghastly, but there's something special about that first photo.''

"Take the money, Faith." Michael tossed forty dollars on the examining table. "I'd say no strings attached, but I'm going to want copies of the pictures.''

"Of course. I'll insist on repaying you half the sitting fee."

He threw up his hands. "A few lousy bucks. It's no big damned deal."

"Don't swear around the babies, please," Faith said primly.

Michael smoothed a hand over his hair. "I don't make a habit of swearing. But sometimes you can be so exasperating."

Fortunately, before Faith could reply, another nurse opened the door and stuck her head inside. "Do you have one of the babies ready to do the oxygen saturation test in your car seats?"

Faith moved Abigail to one side of the table and covered her with a receiving blanket. She laid out Nicholas's new romper. "I'm taking the twins home in a stroller. We're walking," she said.

"It's a hospital rule. Babies aren't released until their car seats are checked and properly adjusted," the young nurse insisted.

"That's going to be difficult. I don't own a car," Faith told her.

"I came to drive you home." Michael picked up Abigail, who'd begun to fuss.

"Well, I'm walking." Faith pursed her lips. She was having difficulty snapping Nick's romper.

"You can't walk everywhere," Michael argued. "Stay here and get the pictures taken. I'll go buy car seats. Tell me where to find them."

"I have two infant carriers at home. The clerk in the baby department said they'd double as car seats for the next few months. I plan to buckle them into the back seat of cabs when we go for doctor's appointments."

"Those will do." The nurse sounded relieved. "We're required to run the tests."

"Good grief." Faith folded a blanket around Nick. "Are you saying I got that double stroller down here for nothing?" She didn't know why, but tears pricked at the back of her eyes. She'd wanted this day to be perfect.

Michael noticed her mounting frustration. He rubbed a hand along her tense back. "Give me your apartment key and tell me where to find the carriers. It won't take me fifteen minutes to make the round trip. Go have the pictures done before the kids start to squall. We'll decide after the test whether to walk home using the stroller or to pack it in the truck and take the car."

Faith nodded. She didn't trust herself to speak. If she got weepy over something as trivial as this, Michael would have good reason to think she couldn't cope with two babies. It must be because she hadn't slept well for the past two nights. After a decent night's rest, she'd bounce back to her old self.

Nicholas didn't like the photographer's bright lights. Abigail had fallen asleep again, and the woman taking the pictures wanted her to open her eyes. Nick flailed his arms and bellowed so loudly Eileen rushed into the room to see what was wrong.

"I don't have all morning," the photographer said irritably. "These babies weren't on my schedule. I have half a dozen others lined up and waiting."

"Maybe a few sips from a bottle will calm this young man," Eileen suggested. She turned to the photographer. "Why don't you shoot the Benton pictures in 312? That'll give Faith time to settle Nicky."

"All right." Wadding her background sheet, the photographer picked up her portable lights and took off.

"Is it time for Nicholas to eat?" Faith asked anxiously when the woman was gone. "According to the schedule Dr. Sampson gave me, Nicholas ate at ten and isn't due for another feeding until twelve."

"I imagine a taste will suffice. This is generally his nap time. All this activity is new for them." Eileen bustled out; she returned a minute later with a two-ounce bottle. Reporters from three newspapers followed her and barged in to interview Faith and take pictures.

Faith refused to allow the use of flashes, but she didn't know how Abigail could sleep through their noisy questions. Ignoring them, she paced the floor and patted Nick's back. He wasn't about to be appeased. At least, not until she took the bottle from Eileen and popped the nipple in the baby's mouth. His little chest rose and fell a few times, but he latched right on. "Excuse us." She closed the door, shoving the reporters out.

Eileen scooped up Abigail. "Dr. Cameron is back with the car carriers. The Oximotor test takes ten to fifteen minutes. I'll get this one started."

Michael came into the room just as Nick sucked the bottle dry and began to fuss again. He issued a few terse answers to the press crowded around the door, then asked what was wrong with Nick.

"I think he's still hungry. That two-ounce bottle only whetted his appetite."

"So feed him more," Michael said, relieving Faith of the bottle so she could burp the baby.

"It's not his scheduled feeding. Eileen thought a taste would do."

"Isn't the new method to feed on demand?"

"Well, he's demanding, all right," Faith acknowledged, feeling the beginning of a headache. "I hate to ask, but could you go to the nursing station and get another of those sample bottles?''

"Don't hate to ask, Faith," Michael said solemnly. "I want to help. As a matter of fact, I'll feed him if you'd like to go see what's happening with Abby. Eileen disappeared with her through those double doors at the end of the hall."

Faith swayed from side to side, still holding the baby. Would she be shirking her responsibilities if she left Michael to quiet Nick?

"Would you rather I checked on Abigail? I thought you might like to see what they're doing to test the infant carriers." Michael didn't want to step on Faith's toes, but he intended to share in the going-home process. She might as well resign herself to that fact.

"I'll have someone bring you a bottle." Faith handed over the squirming Nicholas. She ducked the press and ran right into the photographer. "Could you go on to the next family?" Faith asked. "They're running a test on Abigail, and Nicholas is still hungry."

The woman checked her watch. "Mrs. Cameron, you've already thrown my entire schedule off. I'm due at another hospital at one o'clock. I'll give you ten minutes. If you're not ready then, you'll have to do without pictures."

Something in Faith snapped. "First, I'm not Mrs. Cameron. I'm Ms. Hyatt. Second, I'm sure other studios have left portfolios with our hospital administrator. Are you quite sure your company can afford to lose the repeat business of so many new mothers? I'm on staff here. And we have the largest birthing center in the city."

"Sorry," the woman mumbled, shamefaced. "Take whatever time you need. I'll call ahead and explain my delay. A lot of new moms eat lunch before they go home. I'm sure it won't present a problem."

"Do that." Faith pushed through the double doors and heard Abigail wailing. And why not? They had her cinched in the infant carrier, which was strapped to a machine rocking her forward and back and alternately bouncing her up and down.

Eileen sprinted into the room. She ripped open a plastic packet and stuck a clear pacifier in Abby's mouth.

"Oh, I hadn't planned on using pacifiers," Faith told her.

Eileen laughed. "All new moms say that, honey. My advice with twins is to stop on the way home and buy a couple of sets. See, it quiets them right down."

"I know, but…" Faith didn't go on. Already she felt as though she was treading water. She'd read the parenting book from cover to cover and had come away with such good intentions. It seemed that in the space of an hour, they'd broken all the rules.

Faith felt her energy—or what remained of it—drain out. Maybe she would let Michael drive them home. He could help her cart all the stuff they'd collected up to her apartment. She hadn't realized the hospital gave care packages to new babies. Knit caps, bootees, diapers and formula, to mention only a few things. If Eileen added anything else, there wouldn't be room for the babies.

"This kid slurped down another full two ounces, which I had to go get," Michael informed Faith when she carried Abigail back into the room. "You'd better ask Dr. Sampson if you can increase the amount of his formula at each feeding."

"Sorry." Faith rubbed at the lines that creased her forehead. "It's probably due to all the excitement. I told you this isn't even Nick's regular time to eat. Anyway, Dr. Sampson has gone. I saw him get on the elevator. The good news is the reporters went, too.''

Michael started to say something, but just then the woman taking the pictures knocked at the open door. ''Good, good,'' she said, quickly setting up her equipment again. ''They finally seem content. Do you want their pictures taken together, separately or both?''

''Together,'' Faith decided aloud at the same time Michael said, ''Separately.''

The photographer arched an eyebrow.

''It occurred to me they'll both want an album someday,'' Michael said, pulling Faith aside.

''I should have thought of that.'' It upset her that Michael seemed to have a better grasp on parenting than she did. ''Someone gave me two baby books at the shower. One for each.''

''In any case,'' the photographer put in, even though no one had consulted her, ''Twins should be treated as individuals, Mrs. Cam—Ms. Hyatt. Although it's not so much a problem with a boy and a girl.''

''Why's she so confused about your last name, Faith?'' Michael muttered.

''She thought we were married.''

Michael arranged the sleepy Nicholas on the background sheet as the idea burned into his brain. *Married to Faith.* An idea he'd entertained six years ago. Obviously not one that had ever occurred to Faith, judging by the way she was giving the photographer the evil eye.

''She made a natural mistake,'' he growled. ''No sense trying to explain. It's no one's business.''

''My thoughts, exactly. Okay,'' she said in a louder

voice, turning to the woman. "We've decided on separate shots."

It took quite a lot of coaxing to film both children with their eyes open. After the woman had handed Faith a receipt for the money and left with the completed address forms, the clock had pushed past one. Nicholas still hadn't had his car carrier examination. Then Abby woke up crying.

"She's wet," announced Michael. "Probably hungry, too. I'll take care of both of those problems if you'll round someone up to give Nick that test."

"I'm sorry for tying up your day, Michael. I didn't realize checking them out would be this involved. When we release patients from the surgical floor, we plop them in a wheelchair and someone escorts them out to a waiting car."

Michael grinned. "This reminds me more of buying a car. You have to work up through five levels of sales pitches and get all the gizmos explained before you can drive it out of the dealership."

"I've never bought a car. Now I doubt I ever will," she said, and sighed, heading out to the nursing station.

"What'll it be?" Michael asked her at two o'clock when they were finally released to leave. "So, are we walking or taking the car?"

"In view of all the junk we've collected," Faith said, "it makes more sense to take the car. Unless you're anxious to go home to New York. By three, traffic out of town gets wicked, or so I'm told."

Michael gazed into her wide brown eyes for a moment, debating with himself as to whether he should forget Lon Maxwell's instructions and tell Faith about the apartment he'd rented—next to hers. He apparently debated too long.

"Never mind," Faith said, bending to arrange the cartons of formula in the stroller's basket. "Transportation is my responsibility. I might as well figure out now how to lug stuff home. I'll be grocery shopping by stroller. This will be good practice."

"I know you want to be independent, Faith. But I told you I want to help."

Faith glanced up, expecting to see some version of I-told-you-so reflected in his eyes. She saw only compassion. It affected her empty stomach more than she cared to let him see. "Then quit standing around, and load this stuff in your trunk while I take Nick for his test. According to Eileen, someone on staff still has to bring the babies and me out in a wheelchair. That should give you time to put the infant carriers in your back seat. Eileen also said someone on staff has to check that they're properly installed."

"Right. You bet." Michael made short work of packing the stroller and taking off. Half an hour later, he stood at the curb jingling the car keys in his hand as a nurse wheeled Faith out, a blanketed baby cradled in each arm. Her small-boned face glowed with pleasure. Michael wasn't prepared for the longing that struck suddenly, without warning. She looked so *right* holding the twins. It forced him to take stock of all that was missing in his life.

Faith looked up then and saw him. She smiled hesitantly. Suddenly it felt too much like she was being wheeled out to meet a loving husband. Why had she ever agreed to let him drive them home?

Michael saw the light fade from her large, expressive eyes. This was a tender, momentous occasion. One usually shared by husband and wife. Michael didn't know what was going through Faith's head, but knowing her, she was probably thinking about Lacy. About how if things had been different and he hadn't been such a jerk, he'd be meeting Lacy here right now. He didn't know how to tell her there hadn't been that kind of tenderness between him and Lacy for a long time before she decided to divorce him. No man liked to face the fact that he'd made a wrong choice. Since this wasn't the time or place to discuss it, Michael offered Faith what he hoped was a friendly smile. A smile of reassurance.

She struggled to stand, still seeming uncomfortable. "Here," Michael blurted. "Give me Nicholas. I'll go around to the other side and strap him in. You handle Abby."

It was this working in tandem with Michael that threw Faith off balance. She was awfully afraid she could get used to having him around to rely on. But he wasn't going to be around. He was going to drop her off at her apartment and head back to his busy clinic. As he should. He had obligations and patients needing his attention. Lacy's babies were her responsibility.

"Have you got her fastened tight?" Michael suddenly said directly over Faith's left shoulder. She jumped and struck her head on the car's door casing. Bright lights flashed behind her eyes, stunning her for a moment.

"Hey." Michael guided her gently to the curb. "Are you all right?" he asked as he massaged the top of her head. He even dropped a kiss on the spot.

"I'm fine." Although she didn't sound it. "We need to hurry and get to the apartment. Abby's starting to cry louder. She didn't have a bottle when Nicholas did."

Unhappy at losing this moment of connection, Michael held the passenger door open for Faith, then closed her inside. It took less than five minutes to travel the five blocks to her apartment. He wished the ride had been longer even though Abigail was screaming her head off well before they parked.

Faith whisked the babies up to her apartment and went straight to the nursery. Michael finished carrying everything in from the car.

"What can I do?" he asked, pausing to look around at the decor of the nursery as he pocketed his car keys.

"Do?" Faith had placed Nick in the crib. He sprawled there contentedly. She was in the process of changing Abby's diaper. "Oh. You can let yourself out. As soon as I wash, I'll fix Abigail a bottle. My door locks automatically. I hope you have an uneventful trip back to the Big Apple, Michael."

He opened his mouth and promptly closed it again as Lon's objections replayed inside his head. Kipp and Faith were his opponents. He'd been warned about getting too chummy. Yanking the string on one of the crib mobiles, Michael listened to the first tinkling strains of Brahms "Lullaby" before muttering, "You have my cell number if you need me." He'd planned to fix lunch, but something in Faith's frosty manner changed his mind.

"Um, yes. I wrote the number down. But don't worry. We'll be fine."

Michael ran a finger softly down each baby's cheek, then waved to Faith and left.

She sat in the rocker and fed Abigail. When the musical mobile ran out, she leaned back and enjoyed the silence. This was what she'd envisioned. Their lives were going to be perfect, after all.

Only not for long. Faith had no sooner settled Abby in her crib than Nick woke up bellowing. A dry diaper didn't satisfy him. It was way too soon for him to eat again. He spit out the pacifier Eileen had included in the packet and kicked and wailed nonstop. In a matter of minutes, paradise had turned to chaos.

Finally, hours later, Faith rocked the fussy boy back to sleep. The babies were reacting to new surroundings, she told herself. Bigger cribs. Both of them—all three of them—would eventually adjust.

By midnight, Faith was dead on her feet. The babies' schedules were completely off. Nothing coincided. They were supposed to eat at the same time. She'd bought a special pillow to hook around her middle in order to feed them simultaneously, but neither baby would take a bottle while lying on it.

Dawn broke and Faith had yet to sleep a wink. She stood tensely at the window and promised herself she'd get them on track today. How hard could it be?

As the second evening rolled around, she was near tears. She hadn't found time to shower or eat more than a few bites. One or the other of the twins seemed to cry constantly. Faith didn't know if she could survive another night without sleep. But, of course she could. Other single mothers did.

At one in the morning, she thought she'd succeeded. Both babies had closed their eyes. Suddenly Nick stiffened his legs and let out a bloodcurdling cry. She walked the floor with him. His cries woke Abigail. As the nursery clock edged up on two, Faith joined their chorus of tears. She'd consulted her book but found no firm answers.

She was making her hundredth revolution around the small room when someone pounded on her front door. ''Oh, no,'' she sobbed. ''We've awakened our neighbor.''

Faith's arms ached from holding both babies for so

long. It wasn't easy shifting either so that she could unlock and open the door the length of the chain.

"Please, I'm sorry," she said into the dim hallway. "I have new twins," she explained. "One's very fussy. I'm planning to phone the doctor as soon as I—the office is open."

"When in hell were you going to call me?" growled a familiar voice on the other side of the door.

"Michael?" Swabbing at her tears, Faith loosened the chain and let it fall. She swallowed back more than tears. The man was barefoot and bare-chested. His formfitting, ratty jeans were zipped but not buttoned. His eyes were heavy-lidded, and his face bore a two-day stubble that made him look dangerous. Sexy and dangerous.

"Wh-what are you doing here dressed like that?" Faith squeaked as he herded her back into the room and kicked the door shut.

"For two days I've been sitting next door listening to these infants cry, waiting for you to call. Which you refused to do—but I'm not letting my babies down to accommodate your stubbornness."

"Next door! You're living next door?"

"Yes. How long since you've slept? Hand me those two. You hit the sack."

Faith jerked back, pulling the babies right out of his hands. "I'm not letting you have them! I know why you're doing this, Michael. To make me look bad."

"Give me a break. I don't have to do that. You already look like hell." With that, he wrenched the babies away from her. Stripping them out of their blankets, he draped two sweating little bodies over each of his broad shoulders. Like magic, after a few snuffles and shudders, the infants snuggled their faces into his neck and both fell asleep.

Faith's shaking legs gave out and she collapsed onto the couch. A part of her muzzy brain wanted to kiss Michael for the blessed silence. Another part wished for the energy to boot his sneaky, sexy body straight back to New York. Before managing to do either, she toppled to the side, snoring softly.

Her last puzzled thought before she fell asleep was, *Michael's living next door. What does that mean?*

CHAPTER EIGHT

FAITH OPENED ONE EYE. She didn't know where she was for a moment. Sunbeams danced in lacy patterns across the wall she faced. Her living room wall, she decided as other familiar objects fell slowly into place. Memories of the twins came crashing back, shooting her upright. Faith shed the afghan that had been covering her.

Dry-mouthed and gritty-eyed, she brushed a hand over the blouse and shorts she'd worn for two days. Or was it longer?

The apartment was silent. Frighteningly so. Faith went dizzy from sitting up too abruptly. Suddenly she remembered a scene from the previous night. Michael hammering at her door, then barging in looking like a *Playgirl* centerfold. He'd taken the two crying babies from her arms.

Had he kidnapped them? A sense of panic overwhelmed her. Michael was a cornerstone of the establishment, so the very idea seemed far-fetched. But every day the newspaper was filled with stories of nice guys doing the unthinkable.

Afraid to see what awaited her in the nursery, Faith prepared herself for the worst. Her heart beat erratically and her stomach churned as she stumbled down the hall and, with badly shaking hands, pushed open the door that stood ajar.

What she saw was the last thing she'd expected. Michael seated in her mother's rocker, a baby lying comfortably in each arm. They were sucking contentedly on bottles held in the long, elegant fingers he'd curved around their little faces.

"How do you do that?" Faith inquired softly. "I've tried and tried. My arms simply don't reach."

His gaze seemed to warm her as it flowed from the top of her tousled head all the way down to her bare feet. "Good afternoon, sleepyhead. I've got to admit it took me two night feedings, breakfast and midmorning snack to finally get the hang of doubling up like this."

"Afternoon?" Her bottom jaw went slack. "I slept that long?"

"I passed a cup of coffee under your nose this morning, after I bathed the kids and had a shower. You didn't twitch a muscle. I figured you needed the rest. They slept well once I placed them in the same crib. Hal Sampson said it might make them feel more secure."

"You bathed the babies?" she parroted dumbly, realizing that Michael had shaved and changed clothes. Now he wore a shirt and gray slacks instead of jeans and...nothing. Thank goodness. Faith felt faint at the memory of how he'd looked last night. Or maybe she just needed sustenance. As a nurse she'd seen plenty of naked chests. Other bare parts of a man's anatomy, too. None had ever affected her with the jolt she'd received last night.

"These two are on the verge of sleep," he murmured. "Why don't you hop in the shower? While you're doing that, I'll see what I can round up for lunch."

Crossing her arms over her breasts, Faith propped a hip against the door. "I'll go when you tell me what's behind this sudden spurt of domestic benevolence."

"That was a mouthful."

"You're stalling," she accused him. "You wouldn't move into the apartment next door unless it served your purposes. And why, by the way, didn't you tell me earlier? You'd better have a darn good explanation."

"Won't you feel more like having this discussion when you're clean and fresh?"

"I feel fine. Greatly rejuvenated after—what? Ten hours of sleep?"

"Um, about that." He gently tugged an empty bottle from Nicholas's mouth and tossed it into the crib. Rocking forward, he tipped the baby up and patted his back until the little guy burped. Climbing to his feet, Michael settled the boy in his crib, still holding Abigail. He then returned to his seat and transferred Abigail's bottle to his free hand. "This little squirt would sooner sleep than eat. I think we should keep prodding her and get them back on some kind of schedule, don't you agree?"

Faith gaped. Of course she did. Erratic schedules were the reason she'd gone without sleep. She'd been in the process of either changing or feeding one baby or the other for a full twenty-four hours. "Let's back up. You're right. I will be able to handle this discussion better after a shower." Vigorously massaging her temples, Faith left the room. Not until she stood naked under a hot spray did she allow herself to think about what might be going on with Michael. Last night he'd dropped the bomb about being her neighbor. A neighbor who'd moved in last week. Which meant his precipitous appearance last night had not been spur-of-the-moment. He'd been behind the wall, waiting like a vulture for her to screw up.

And why had he acted so secretive about moving into her building?

Already sputtering, she stuck her head beneath the

spray. The water might be hot, but Faith's blood ran cold. Even when he was a resident, others on staff had insisted Dr. Cameron mapped out and followed a detailed agenda. Back then, his aim had been to become the number-one cardiopulmonary surgeon. A person didn't have to be too bright to figure out what his goal was now, why he'd barged into her home like this. Michael had his sights set on fatherhood. What Faith found hard to reconcile was that he knew the babies might not be his. Why, then, was he willing to waste his time? This was the man Lacy had complained never took a day off. The man who rarely took an evening away from patients.

Guilt was the obvious answer, Faith decided as she grabbed a towel and dried off. Or at least part of the answer. He felt remorse for not trying harder to keep Lacy from following through with the divorce. There was always the possibility that he was spying on her, looking for ways to damage her position in the custody case. Although it hurt to think he'd be so sneaky... Forewarned now, she vowed to be alert.

A shower and clean clothes refreshed her. Facing Michael didn't seem quite so daunting as it had earlier. He was a man dedicated to saving lives. A load of guilt drove him to act out of character. It shouldn't be too hard to offer absolution and send him back to New York.

After peeking in at the sleeping babies, Faith partially closed the nursery door and followed the smell of food to the kitchen. She had only to see the bowls of creamy tomato soup and the thick turkey sandwiches to admit she was starved.

"Yum." She sniffed the air.

Michael pulled out one of the kitchen chairs. "Better

hurry and eat before the soup gets cold. What took you so long?''

''I washed my hair. It took time to blow it dry.''

His gaze wandered to her short, curly locks. ''I guess you were quick, at that. Lacy used to spend an hour to dry her hair.''

''Because hers was so thick,'' Faith said, after taking her seat and letting him slide her closer to the table. ''When Lacy was little, I burned out more dryer motors making sure her hair was completely dry before she went to bed. Mother was of the era that believed going to bed with a wet head insured pneumonia.''

''Was Lacy as bald as Abigail when she was really little?''

Faith bristled. ''Abigail isn't bald. It's just that her hair is so fine and blond, it's hard to see. Nick doesn't have any more. His is a smidgen darker, that's all.''

''More than a smidgen. But in the child development book I bought, it says that's not unusual. Especially in fraternal twins.''

''You bought a book.'' Faith's eyes snapped up from their concentration on her soup.

''Don't act so surprised. You gave me the idea.''

''What if the twins don't turn out to be yours?''

He stared at her the entire time he finished chewing the bite of sandwich he'd taken. Then he swallowed. ''Is it my imagination, Faith, or are you hoping they aren't?''

She fumbled for words. ''I started thinking, feeling sorry really, for the patients you're letting down by being here. Say the DNA takes six weeks. How many lives could you save in that period of time?''

His eyes grew wary. ''What gives, Faith? Lacy was

the one who resorted to flattery to get her way. Not you. You've always been honest, direct.''

Ashamed, Faith stirred a spoon around and around in her soup.

''Come on, just say what you're thinking.''

''All right,'' she blazed. ''Your patients have always been your number-one priority. What's changed?''

''What makes you think something's changed? Doesn't a man deserve a break from work once in a while?''

She smiled crookedly. ''Now who's being slippery? You've hardly taken a weekend off in the six years I've known you. Suddenly a vacation? Admit you were spying on me, Michael. That's why you moved into my building, isn't it?''

''No, I wasn't, and no, I didn't. Priorities can change.'' He frowned as he bit into his sandwich.

''Have yours? Or is this penance because the first time you called Lacy's bluff, something bad happened?''

Michael choked. ''Well, that's direct enough,'' he said when he was finally able to speak. They both sat there, eyes connected and smoldering for what seemed like an eternity. Michael gave in first. He expelled the breath he'd been holding and got up to stare out of the kitchen window. ''There's no one thing at the bottom of my decision to take a break. Yes, I'd felt my marriage hitting the rocks, and I found myself powerless to stop it. Then to learn Lacy had died…'' He lifted both shoulders and let them fall again. ''It's more than that, though. Something…moved inside me the first day I held the twins. I—I can't begin to explain.''

''You don't have to,'' Faith said meekly. ''The same thing happened to me.''

"My book refers to the spell as *twin shock.*" Michael returned to the table and sat again to earnestly make his case.

"Everyone gravitates toward twins."

"Yes, but the author was referring to parents. A… a…special connection."

"Then how do you account for the fact that I felt it? I know you experienced a sense of bonding, Michael, so you're convinced they're yours. But wouldn't you rather keep your distance until the tests come back, and save yourself a broken heart?" Faith suddenly sat straighter. "Unless men don't suffer broken hearts."

"Of course we do. What do you think? That we're made of iron?" He glared at her. "You've certainly developed a rotten attitude toward men."

She had the grace to avert her eyes, because quite the opposite was true. At least, when it came to Michael. Since the first moment she'd set eyes on him, the attraction had been there. Heaven knows she'd done her best to resist it. To tell herself it didn't exist. Apparently to no avail.

"I'm staying here until the tests come back," he said, when it appeared Faith wasn't going to answer him. "My book also says raising multiples is physically and emotionally demanding on both parents, and I've discovered how true *that* is. After your first couple of days going it alone, can you truthfully say you don't need my help?"

Faith didn't have to think long or hard. Neither did she wish to sound too eager. She slowly counted out fifteen seconds. "I can see the value of having a second pair of hands, Michael. If your mind is made up, I suppose we can split some duties. We need to set down rules, though."

"Rules?" Michael didn't think he liked the sound of "setting rules." Fortunately, one of the twins—Nick, he thought—awoke with a wail. Michael bounded to his feet. "I'll go. You've barely touched your lunch. Rule number one should be that we keep up our strength. So eat." Dust bunnies flew in his wake.

Faith planted both elbows on the table and rested her chin in her hands. She hadn't had time recently to get the housework under control. Scrubbing floors was about the best way she knew to combat irritation. Was that what she felt at having Michael underfoot? Or was it more like sexual frustration?

She didn't want to examine the question too closely. Getting up, she stomped to the microwave and reheated her soup. She promptly burned her tongue, causing her to mutter something unladylike under her breath. "It's going to be a long month."

Michael stuck his head into the kitchen alcove. "Nick has wet through everything. He needs changing from the inside out. Which chest of drawers is his?"

Faith pushed her bowl away and started to get up.

"Hey, sit still and finish your lunch. I'm capable of handling this."

After their baths, Michael must have put them back in the same outfits they'd been wearing. "I'm full anyway," she said. "If we're going to share baby duty, you need to know my system. By the way, does this sharing include us both doing laundry?"

He looked startled. "Laundry is a mystery to me. I send out everything I wear." He always had, even as a resident. His colleagues had teased him unmercifully.

"Everything? Didn't Lacy do laundry?"

"Hers, I suppose. Or maybe not." It flustered him to realize he didn't know.

"Well, here the washers and dryers are in the basement. The other day I thought I should buy a set. Then I couldn't decide where I'd put them."

"I think there's a washer and dryer in my apartment. That'll be much closer."

"Yes, but you aren't going to live there forever, Michael. I need to make arrangements for the long term."

"Now who's second-guessing the court decision?"

Faith wore a sheepish look when she walked into the nursery. "I believe in the power of positive thinking."

"For you, but not for me?"

"I thought we weren't going to argue about this, Michael."

"We did say that. I can't help it, though. It bothers me that you refuse to take me seriously. What do I have to do to convince you I want the twins?"

"This is Nick's dresser," she said, stopping to pull clean sleepers from a drawer. "I stacked crib sheets, blankets and receiving blankets on shelves in the closet. Diapers to refill the stackers are in there, too. The pink packages are Abby's, the turquoise ones are Nick's."

"His and her diapers?"

"It has to do with anatomy, Doctor. Nick's have more padding in front, Abigail's are thicker toward the back."

"Oh. Yeah, I can see that makes sense."

Michael watched the deft way Faith handled Abigail, who had opened her eyes and started to mewl. "I'll confess it's my fault Nick is soaked through. This morning I grabbed the first diaper at hand. Now I see it has little pink animals on the front band and not blue."

"You get a gold star for trying," Faith said. "Say, did I ever thank you for letting me sleep? And, um, thanks for covering me up."

He shrugged. "I tried to wake you and send you to bed. That couch didn't look all that comfortable. But you were dead to the world."

"Saturday night was the baby shower. Everyone stayed late. I was excited about bringing the twins home, and didn't sleep Sunday, either. Monday night their schedules were way off. By last night, I'd gone through my reserves."

"So all that laughter and music I heard until the wee hours on Saturday night was a baby shower?"

"What did you think?" Faith whirled to confront him.

"Frankly, I didn't know what to think. I checked the hall several times, but never saw anyone come or go. I'd never pegged you as a party girl, but the later it got and the noisier it became, I decided you'd changed. Next morning, when I saw you hauling all those champagne bottles down to the Dumpster, I was sure you had."

"You were spying on me!"

"Not intentionally. I glanced out my bedroom window and you happened to be standing by the trash bin."

Faith bounced Abigail on her shoulder. The nursery had shrunk after she'd installed furniture. Now with two adults trying to change two babies, it seemed smaller yet. Every time she bumped into Michael or he brushed past her to deposit a wet diaper in the shiny chrome can, she felt self-conscious. "I have things under control now, Michael. Feel free to go back to your apartment."

He sucked the side of his cheek between his teeth and clamped down to keep from reacting to her brush-off. "What's on your agenda today?"

"Nothing. Why? I'm on leave from work, you know."

"After the babies' next feeding, let's sit down and draw up a schedule. Loose, of course, because babies aren't predictable. We ought to be able to set up some sort of daily planner around their general feeding times."

"After what you said at the hospital, Michael, I decided to let them eat when they wanted to. I'll catch up on household chores while they sleep. Or I can do that whenever you feed them. I know you won't want to hang around all day, every day."

"There's where you're wrong, Faith. I do want to. I want us to share fifty-fifty."

"But...but...but..." she sputtered, her eyes clouding.

"What's the matter, Faith? Do I make you uncomfortable? I certainly don't mean to."

"It's not that," she hastened to say. She didn't want him analyzing and eventually figuring out why he made her nervous. After only a few short hours in his company, Faith was awfully afraid she could get very used to having Michael around. And what would happen to her heart when he up and left, as was inevitable? It had taken her years to get over his marrying Lacy. Faith hated to think what it would be like if he took off after she'd come to depend on him—and on his help with the twins.

"What *is* bugging you, then?"

"I've lived in this apartment house for a long time. I...don't want the residents getting the wrong idea." Faith latched on to the first thought that made sense.

"I hate to be obtuse, but what wrong idea?"

"With regards to our re...lation...sh-ship."

"If anyone read yesterday's paper or saw the TV news, they'll know our relationship." Not that Michael himself hadn't sat next door a number of days indulging in some pretty explicit fantasies.

"What do you mean?"

"I'll bring over a copy of yesterday's paper," he said. "The reporters seem hyped about the custody case. I don't recall them taking our pictures when we picked up the kids. But there we were, together on the front page. They even had a shot of Kipp at the helm of his yacht, and his wife walking into a New York fertility clinic."

"Why?" Faith gasped.

"It's sensationalism," he said bitterly. "Prominent surgeon's ex-wife dies in childbirth. Her sister and the son of a prominent Wall Street millionaire fight the doctor for custody of the deceased mother's twins."

"Millionaire? I had no idea," Faith exclaimed, looking a little sick.

"Lon Maxwell phoned last night. From now on, he wants us to say 'no comment' to any questions. I think he's overreacting. By now, we're yesterday's news. To clear the air between us, Faith—Lon's the one who insisted I not tell you or Kipp that I'd be spending time in Boston. Lon would have a fit if he knew I rented a place next door to you."

"He's not alone," she grumbled. "But back to the news article—I want the reporters to leave us alone. I'll phone David and ask his opinion on how to stop their intrusions."

"You might want to do that now, while the babies are quiet. I can't get over how alert they are. They're already turning toward us when we speak."

"Tomorrow they'll be two months old. According to

my baby book, they'll be playing patty-cake by the time the DNA tests are back and their future is settled.''

Michael's expression softened. ''I'm not thinking that far ahead. I'm taking one day at a time.''

The look of love he focused on the twins brought a rush to Faith's heart. Mumbling an excuse to leave, she hurried out to call her attorney.

BY THE END OF THE SECOND WEEK, it appeared Michael's assessment was more accurate than Lon Maxwell's. At first, any time they took the babies out for walks, it caused a stir. Faith even had to escape a reporter when she made her weekly visit to see her father. The first week, news teams hung around outside the apartment. Then, little by little, as both Faith and Michael refused to speak, the reporters lost interest.

By the middle of the third week, Faith had begun to relax. She and Michael had fallen into a comfortable routine. They shared chores during the day. He cooked as many meals as she did. She'd throw laundry into the washer and Michael would put it in the dryer, or vice versa. Though they spent their days together, every night after the eleven-o'clock feeding, he returned to his apartment. He joined a health club and went there every morning, delaying his arrival at Faith's until after she'd dressed for the day.

She found herself wishing for more. No matter how sternly she chastised herself for thinking foolish thoughts, her feelings for Michael didn't go away. Far from it.

She loved to watch him with the babies. She'd initially assumed he'd gravitate toward Nick—masculine bonding or some such thing. After all, Kipp and his father certainly showed a preference. But Michael divided his time equally. He seemed as delighted over Abigail's blowing bubbles as he did when Nick latched onto his finger and cooed. Faith teased him when he came home from the store with frilly dresses for Abby. Not that she didn't splurge on the babies, but she tended to favor practical cotton outfits.

Faith's phone rang early one morning near the end of the third week, while she was home alone. The call threw the first wrench into her idyllic days with Michael and the babies. Kipp Fielding III was on the line.

"I'm home from Florida," he announced without preamble. "Dad and Shelby have been too busy to visit the twins. We're driving down to Boston today. Should be there by eleven. I'd like directions to your apartment."

Taken completely off guard, Faith stammered out her address. Then after they'd said goodbye, she began to fume. The judge had said to phone ahead and request a convenient time. Kipp hadn't even asked if she had other plans. And he hadn't asked how the babies were, which struck her as odd, considering how silent the Fieldings had been.

In the next instant, Faith panicked. She hadn't vacuumed in two days. The apartment wasn't dirty, but it was cluttered. She had a tendency to leave packages of diapers in every room. It was easier than always running to the changing table.

She looked quite harried and disheveled when Michael let himself into the apartment half an hour later than usual.

"Where have you been?" Faith demanded in such a shrewish tone that he swallowed the catchy tune he'd been whistling.

"Working out. Same as I've done every morning. I

stayed later than usual—ran into an old friend.'' He paused. ''Faith, is something wrong?''

She shoved a stack of medical journals he'd brought over to read into his hands. ''Do you have any other stuff here that's obviously yours?'' she asked, opening the door and literally pushing him into the hall.

''A coffee cup in the kitchen, and a couple of shirts in the guest bedroom. I put them in the closet because I never know when Abby's going to spit up or I'm going to be slow with a diaper and Nick's going to pee all over me. What's this about, Faith?''

''The Fieldings are coming,'' she said, sounding a bit hysterical.

Michael tipped back his head and laughed. ''Sorry,'' he said when she glared at him, hands on hips. ''Reminded me of that old movie, *The Russians Are Coming, The Russians Are Coming.* Why are you so worried?''

''I'm not worried about Kipp and Shelby, although Kipp's father is intimidating. It's more that I don't think they'd be overjoyed to find us consorting. In a manner of speaking,'' she said, blushing wildly when Michael arched a brow and stared at her in a slightly mocking fashion.

''You know what I mean,'' she snapped, throwing up her hands.

''I don't. So spell it out, please.''

''Have you forgotten that Kipp's team of attorneys filed a complaint over the two of us having greater access to the babies? You said yourself that Lon cautioned you to hide the fact you'd moved to Boston.''

''I know he did. But the judge decided old man Fielding and Shelby could visit as often as they wished.

Which, by the way, I haven't seen them doing. Not even once.''

"Please don't be difficult, Michael. You've had three weeks of nearly twelve-hour days with the twins. It can't hurt to let Kipp and his family have one day. They'll probably only spend a few hours. I'll call you the minute they leave. I promise.''

Her dark eyes seemed so genuinely distressed, Michael wasn't able to refuse her. He bent to kiss her forehead. "Okay.''

Faith jerked back as if she'd been burned. "Wh-why did you do that?''

"You still act as if my primary goal in life is to cause you trouble. I just want to convince you that my motives are pure.'' He grinned, but then his expression grew more serious. "I can't see any reason I should disappear while the third party in this case decides to exercise his court-mandated rights. But because it matters to you, Faith, I'll stay out of sight. What will you say, though, if Kipp asks how many times I've visited?''

She chewed disconsolately at her bottom lip. "I'll keep my fingers crossed that he doesn't. I'm not very good at fibbing,'' she said.

"That's a relief. I'd hate to think you'd let them believe I'd fallen off the face of the earth. I have a vested interest in those babies. I don't happen to care who knows it.''

"I'm sorry, Michael. Of course you do. After all, you loved their mother.'' Faith stepped back and gripped the doorknob. "I guess you loved her even after the divorce.'' She avoided looking at Michael as she said it.

He placed a curled finger under her chin, forcing her to meet his brooding gaze. "I've deliberately avoided having this conversation with you, Faith. The truth is, I didn't want you to think less of me. I know Lacy meant the world to you. But our marriage had more downs than ups. While it's true that I wasn't the one who opted out, it's taken me some time to realize I felt a sense of relief when all was said and done. Maybe you'd rather not know it, but I'm telling you anyhow. These last weeks with you have been more enjoyable than all the years I spent with Lacy. Oh, at first, with the move, starting the clinic and arranging her follow-up transplant care, our differences weren't so apparent. I may even discount the second year. After that, though…''

Faith wished he hadn't said a word. And yet she was glad he had. His confession eased some of her guilty conscience over dreaming of things she shouldn't. But she felt a great sadness for her sister, and a disloyalty at her own reaction. Because what he'd said meant he wasn't indifferent to her, and that thrilled her. But poor, misguided, childish Lacy…so unhappy in her marriage.

''Don't look so shocked by my confession.'' Pulling out his keys, Michael turned toward his door. ''I'm camped on your doorstep because of the twins. You don't have to worry that I'll take advantage of you, Faith.''

She said nothing. He'd gone inside his apartment and closed the door before she moved. He'd certainly made himself clear. Had burst the bubble on her foolish daydreams. He might enjoy her companionship, but as far as attraction went…forget it. In bed at night, she'd actually dared to imagine that he might ask her to live with him if it turned out he was the twins' dad. Last night, they'd watched a late movie seated side by side on the couch. The way they'd laughed and talked so comfortably together, she'd let her imagination run wild after he'd gone. Oh, she hadn't kidded herself into be-

lieving he felt for her what she did for him. But they
got along, and they both loved the babies. A marriage
could start with that and build.

Slipping inside the apartment, she quietly closed her
door. It was never going to happen, no matter how
much she prayed. It was time she stopped being naive.

She finished picking up the place and pulled on a
clean T-shirt and a pair of faded denim overalls. Her
hair curled over her ears. She needed it cut. Maybe Michael would watch the babies one afternoon next week.
She might even treat herself to a facial. Funny how he'd
become so entwined in her life in such a short time.
How on earth would she manage things like haircuts if
he wasn't around?

She carefully dressed Nick in a sailor suit and Abby
in a pretty yellow dress. "Wait," she said, slapping her
forehead with a palm. Why give the Fieldings greater
reason to choose Nick over his sister? She removed the
nautical outfit and dressed him in a green-and-white
shorts set that had lambs all over it.

No sooner had she finished with the last snap than
there was a knock at her door. Scooping up the twins,
she strolled through the living room to answer it.

The three who stood there might as well have come
for a wake. Kipp nervously pulled at the neck of his
polo shirt. His father wore a scowl. Shelby hovered behind them, studying the ceiling, the walls, the floor. Her
gaze lit anywhere but on the infants Faith held.

"Welcome." Faith pasted on a phony smile. Actually, it wasn't so phony. There was obviously dissension
in the ranks. She shouldn't be happy about that, but it
was only human nature, she thought.

"They've grown," Kipp observed after they'd all
taken seats around the room.

"Yesterday was their checkup." Faith rattled off a height and weight for each child. "They had their first set of shots. So if they're fussy, that's why." She stopped beside Kipp. "Would anyone like to hold them while I fix us some iced tea?"

No one said a word. Faith whipped a baby blanket off the arm of the couch. She spread it on the floor and laid Nick and Abby down. Both immediately kicked and waved their arms. Abigail blew bubbles and Nicholas began to sputter and drool.

"Why is the boy doing that?" demanded the elder Fielding with a certain degree of revulsion.

Faith tried not to sound defensive—or angry.

"Dr. Sampson said Nick may be cutting teeth. It's early, but the doctor said some babies teethe at six or eight weeks. Drooling is quite common. You've probably forgotten how your son reacted to teething."

"My son never drooled," the pompous man declared.

"Ho-kay!" Faith wasn't about to argue. "I'll get that tea," she said. "Sugar or lemon, anyone?" she asked.

Shelby folded her hands. "Nothing. We can't stay. You said we'd just pop in and out." She aimed her comment at Kipp's father.

Faith thought it was odd that Shelby had appealed to her father-in-law and not her husband.

"Cool it, Shel," Kipp said mildly. He slid to his knees and after some hesitation, picked up Nicholas. Kipp's dad moved to where he could get a clearer look at the boy.

After five silent minutes had passed, Faith hoisted Abby onto her lap. It broke her heart to see that sweet baby being ignored.

All in all, the Fieldings stayed half an hour. Only until the babies began to fuss and Faith said it was time for their bottles. "You can feed Nicholas if you like," she offered magnanimously.

Kipp was indecisive; he might have agreed if his wife hadn't risen and hurried to the door.

"Uh, we really don't wish to disrupt your schedule," Kipp told Faith.

"We only came because Bob Schlegel said we should," Shelby burst out. "Although it makes no sense. All this fuss and you don't even know if that child is your son."

Kipp apologized for his wife's petulance. He placed Nick in Faith's arms and followed his family out. "On Friday I'm off to the Carolinas for another race. I'll touch base when I get back."

"The DNA results might be in by then," Faith said, wanting them just to leave.

They did, without a backward glance, and she went to prepare bottles. Uncommonly depressed, she was reluctant to phone Michael although she'd promised. But within minutes, he was standing in the kichen; he'd obviously been keeping tabs. Faith doubted the Fielding troop had made it down the elevator before Michael used his key and let himself in.

"Short visit. Is old Kipper having second thoughts about daddyhood?"

"Oh, Michael." Faith dropped the bottles and burst into tears.

He caught her in his arms and let her sob against his chest. "Kipp only wants Nick. Shelby doesn't want either baby. How can anyone be so...so coldhearted? Abby's gorgeous. She's going to look like Lacy. Please, Michael, don't let them win."

Michael rocked her, rubbing his cheek across her hair. "I see Abby's resemblance to Lacy, now that you

mention it,'' he murmured. ''Maybe that's Shelby's objection. God, I wish I could promise, Faith. I can't.''
His voice dropped, reflecting his frustration. ''Dammit,
if I could put a rush on that DNA, I would.''

CHAPTER NINE

THEY CLUNG TO EACH OTHER until their heartbeats leveled. One of the babies lying on the blanket in the living room began to wail. Faith separated herself from Michael's warmth, pressing a hand to her lips and running the other through her hair. "I don't know what got into me. Their bottles are ruined. Do you mind seeing to the twins while I mix more formula?" Her voice sounded strained.

He caught her hand. "Look at me."

Her eyes lifted slowly, warily.

"I wish I could promise I was going to win. But you know as well as I do, Faith, the whole custody mess is a crapshoot at this point."

"I know. That's why I'm still carrying my lucky clover. It's called covering all bases," she said as she bent to collect the bottles she'd dropped and then carried them to the kitchen sink.

Michael picked up both babies and snuggled them into his arms. "When I spoke with Lon earlier, he said nothing further can be done on our case until the test results come back."

"David gave me the same story," Faith said, as she handed Michael a bottle and held out her arms for one of the babies.

Michael passed her Nicholas. "Here you go, princess,'' he said, parting Abigail's rosebud lips with the bottle's milky nipple.

Faith settled into a corner of the couch with Nick. ''Kipp's dad had the nerve to imply that something might be wrong with Nick because he drooled.''

''I hope you wrote it down. If Kipp does turn out to be the biological dad, you have a better shot than I do at contesting his custody. Lon said I might be able to ask for comparative DNA from a second lab, but the judge could still grant Fielding temporary custody pending any outcome.''

Faith used her fingers to brush Nick's dark, flyaway hair. ''It's too depressing to dwell on, Michael. I may only have a couple of weeks left as their mom. I'm going to put everything else out of my mind and just savor being with them, watching them develop. They're coming into their own personalities, have you noticed?''

''Yes. Abigail's already an accomplished flirt. Nick is going to rip through life with gusto.''

Faith raised her head. ''Both of those traits describe Lacy.''

''I suppose so,'' Michael mused. ''Fraternal twins only share half their parents' genes, which cuts down on genetic similarities. According to my book, it's too early to say whether Abby or Nick inherited any of their father's features or traits.''

''It'd be easier to accept the DNA results if the children resembled the proven biological dad.''

''The waiting is getting to us, Faith. I like your idea of forgetting all about custody for now. After the twins finish their bottles, why don't we put them in their carriers and drive down the coast? Fall's going to give way to winter soon and it won't be as easy to take them on outings.''

Faith didn't want to say that every time they got in Michael's car and the four of them went somewhere, it made her heart ache. She didn't want to tell him that she'd never felt more poignantly alone than on those occasions. The fact that they weren't now and never would be a real family became more painful with every "family" thing they did. Whenever they went out with the babies, people assumed they were married. There was something about twins that made everyone stop and admire, cooing and smiling. Passersby always took for granted that she and Michael were the parents. Faith thought she'd handled it well at first. Now, because they'd grown closer and they'd fallen into sharing tasks, it got harder and harder to put on an act.

What excuse could she give Michael for preferring to mope around the house? "I'll pack a diaper bag," she said without a lot of enthusiasm. "How long will we be gone?"

"We could drive down to Sandwich. I know a great casual seafood place there. We haven't had dinner out since you brought the babies home. Isn't it time we took the plunge?"

"Why?"

His eyes twinkled. "Well, for one thing, it'll be more enjoyable now than when they're older and can reach everything on the table. For another, you deserve a break from cooking."

"You've cooked as many meals as I have."

Michael fixed her with steady eyes. "Do you argue with every man who asks you out to dinner, Faith, or just with me?"

"Men never ask me to dinner," she said, undergoing a sudden need to flee his inspection. The way he'd put that—*asking her out*—made it sound like they'd be going on a date.

"Then I have serious doubts about Boston's male population. That makes me all the more determined to drag you out today. I've never been through the glass museum, have you? I hear it's filled with items made by the now-defunct Boston Sandwich Glass company. They made the pitcher you have sitting on the kitchen table, you know."

"All right. You win. I'd love to go through the museum and have dinner someplace. But don't say I didn't warn you if Abby and Nick both need to be changed and fed the minute the waiter serves your lobster."

"Success has to do with good planning," he said. "You'll see."

She did, indeed, and couldn't help but rub it in four hours later when both babies set up a howl not two seconds after the waiter served her and Michael steaming bowls of thick clam chowder.

Faith had looked forward to the warm stew. Outside, the day had turned quite blustery. She'd been more than ready to leave the beach and go inside for an early dinner. They'd visited the museum first, which she'd thoroughly enjoyed, and couldn't believe Michael had let her wander to her heart's content.

"What's wrong with them?" Michael whispered, when his attempt to rock the carriers and quiet the infants failed.

"It's called Murphy's Law." Faith loosened the straps holding Abigail in her seat and, after straightening the blanket, picked up the baby and rocked her in her arms. "At the parents-of-multiples meeting last week, the topic was timing. A bunch of parents complained that whenever they sat down to a hot meal or got on the phone or even initiated sex, that was precisely when both babies decided to act up. Or three, in the case of triplets.''

Michael couldn't say why his mind had stalled on her reference to initiating sex. His partner at the clinic, who was always analyzing him, would say it was because he'd been celibate for nearly a year. Michael thought it was more likely because the subject had been on his mind too often lately. Rarely a night went by that he didn't lie in his bed thinking of Faith lying next door in hers. He'd had some pretty vivid dreams after falling asleep, too.

He'd folded enough of Faith's laundry to know what she wore underneath her day wear. She didn't go in for frills. Remembering that made him smile.

Her nightgowns were nothing like the blatantly provocative ones Lacy had preferred. But Faith owned a plain white sleeveless cotton number with a thin bead of lace running around a short hem and a deep V neck that left Michael sweating each time he pulled it out of the dryer.

"Why are you staring at me?" Faith hissed. "Are you going to let Nicholas scream until he wakes the dead?"

Jolted out of his reverie, Michael shot a guilty glance around the busy dining room. "Everyone's looking at us," he said.

"No kidding." Faith delivered a smirk insinuating that he was awfully dense. "Eat your soup," she said, and sighed. "Hand me Nick. I'll go see if the ladies room has a changing table. They might be wet again."

"We changed them before we came in so we wouldn't have to go through this." Michael watched her gather both babies and the heavy diaper bag.

"I could say I told you so," Faith muttered, excusing herself as she banged the diaper bag against another diner's chair.

It was only after she left and Michael plunged a spoon into his soup that he realized every woman in the room glowered at him as if he somehow personified all the articles written about chauvinistic men. It didn't help that everyone in the restaurant could still hear both twins wailing. Michael recorked the bottle of wine he'd foolishly ordered. That, at least, they could take home. As a matter of fact, he thought, motioning their waiter over, they hadn't ordered anything for their main course that couldn't be stuffed into a doggie bag.

"Do you want your wife's entrée delayed?" the waiter asked, nervously glancing toward the alcove from which the chorus continued.

Michael didn't correct the man's assumption that Faith was his wife. He just pulled out a money clip and peeled off a few bills. "Could you box the whole works, including the wine? Here. This should cover everything."

The man backed away from the money. "I could hurry your dinner, sir. No sense both of you eating cold food."

"The idea in coming here was to treat the lady," Michael said, his voice sharper than intended. "We'll pick up our doggie bag on the way out. I'll go give her a hand." Collecting the carriers and Faith's purse, he wove his way through the tables, oblivious to the sympathy directed at him by male counterparts.

Unselfconscious, he tapped once on the door to the ladies' room, then barged in. Faith glanced up, her relief palpable. She balanced both infants on a narrow couch, pinning Nicholas to the back of the seat with one hip while doing her best to keep the screaming Abby from sliding off a slick changing pad. "Michael." Faith blew at a curl that fell stubbornly over her right eye. "This place isn't set up for kids and they were both completely wet again. I'm sorry if we're spoiling your dinner."

Michael lifted Nick and kissed his red little face. "Don't apologize, Faith. It's not your fault. I concede that going out to dinner was a stupid idea."

"It was a lovely idea. Not very practical, as it turned out," she lamented, snapping the last snap on Abigail's pink overalls. "They're so upset, I don't know if we can calm them enough to sit through dinner."

"We're leaving," he said, buckling Nick into his carrier. "They'll be happier at home and so will we."

"I hope so," Faith murmured. "They both seem to have runny noses. More so than I'd expect from this crying jag."

"Do you think it was too windy during our walk on the beach?"

"Too soon for that to have caused problems, I should think. Maybe what Dr. Sampson thought might be teething was really a cold."

"Colds? But the weather's been too mild, hasn't it?"

"Spoken like a surgeon. Colds come from viruses, Doctor. They aren't caused by weather."

"Touché, Nurse. I'm sure I learned that in first-year medical school."

"That's the one drawback to taking the twins to Dr. Sampson. He knows we're nurse and doctor. He expects us to have all the answers." Faith grabbed her purse and the diaper bag. She opened the door, leaving Michael to gather up both infant carriers. "I feel he expects us to know more than we do."

"Well, I'm not above telling him I'm in over my head. The youngest patient I've seen in the last eight years was the girl in Norway, and she's fourteen. Oh, can you grab our sack of food?" Michael asked Faith. The cashier held it out as they passed.

Faith stepped to the front window. A mass of dark clouds had rolled in, and rain pelted the glass. "Why don't you take all the extraneous junk to the car and drive around and pick us up? I'll wait here with the twins."

"I'll do that," Michael agreed. "Boy, this squall came out of nowhere."

"It's a freak storm," said the cashier. "We've been hearing reports all day. They're saying hurricane-force winds. You haven't heard?" Her manner suggested they'd flown in from a different planet.

"Hurricane?" Faith and Michael said together. "We, uh, we've been pretty immersed in the twins, and haven't listened to the news," Michael added. "But we walked on the beach earlier and there were people everywhere."

"Probably still are," the woman said with a grin. "We New Englanders are the hardy sort."

Neither Faith nor Michael responded. They were both too busy staring at the rain that had begun to pound the pavement in earnest. Michael got out his car keys and arranged the items he needed to carry so that he'd have one hand free.

"I put the hoods to the carriers in the trunk, along with some heavier blankets. If it's not too much trouble, Michael, could you bring those after you park out front?"

Nodding, he dashed out into the slanting rain. His

180 BABY, BABY

hair and shirt were both wet through when he returned a few minutes later.

"It's downright nasty out there." Turning to the cashier, he said, "You've been listening to the radio. Any word on how far up the coast this extends?"

"The worst of it is supposed to slam into Plymouth within the next hour or so. There are storm warnings posted all along the coast highway. No relief in sight until after midnight." The young woman turned the volume up on her small radio, allowing Michael and Faith to hear the newscaster.

Michael's scowl deepened as reports grew more ominous.

"What are you thinking?" Faith asked. She was unsettled, even though the babies had finally ceased fussing in their carriers, as she swayed them back and forth. Her arms couldn't take much more of the constant strain. Two carriers and babies weren't light.

"I'm not keen on the prospect of getting blown off the interstate," Michael said. "Did you pack extra formula or any change of clothes for the twins?"

"I always pack a variety of outfits. They have one set of bottles left. That should be enough to get us home."

"I'm thinking we should spend the night here."

"But, Michael! We have nothing for the ten, two and six o'clock feedings."

"They're on a fairly common formula. We'll stop at a store."

The cashier couldn't help but overhear their conversation. She interjected a word of advice. "The inns will be filling up. A lot of travelers have been caught off guard. After all, it's barely into October. No one expected this storm. If the wind picks up much, local businesses will start to board up.''

Worried now, Faith pressed her forehead to the window, angling for a better look at the blustery skies. ''If it was just you and I,'' she told Michael, ''I'd be tempted to try and outrun the storm. I'm not so willing to take chances with the babies.''

''Exactly my feeling.'' Michael blew out a relieved breath. ''Listen, a cardiologist I know pretty well owns an old saltbox somewhere on the outskirts of Sandwich. He's invited me numerous times to join him for a fishing excursion. The place might be no more than a glorified shack, but it should be reasonably warm and dry. If I can reach him, I'm sure he'll let us stay there for the night. I know it has kitchen facilities.''

''I suppose it would be better than trying to take two babies to a B and B or an inn. But even if you reach your friend, how would we get into his house?''

''He's offered me use of the place on short notice if I'm ever in the area. People who live here are the trusting sort. Porter said he keeps a key hanging on a peg near the front door.''

Faith pursed her lips. ''I wouldn't feel right staying there unless you talk to him first.''

''I have his number in an address book I keep in the glove box along with my cell phone. While you're strapping in the carriers, I'll give him a call.''

It so happened that Michael's friend was at home and delighted to be of service. He'd just heard about the storm and been about to phone a neighbor to see if he'd shutter the windows. Now Michael could handle that chore. Otherwise, the two men kept the conversation brief. Michael wrote down detailed directions, including how to find the nearest grocery store.

"I guess we're doing the right thing," Faith exclaimed after Michael eased the car away from the curb and they were rocked by a hefty crosswind.

"I've never seen this place. Like I said, it could be primitive. Porter's a crusty old bachelor. Repairing bad tickers and fishing are all he ever talks about."

They stopped at the store first, rather than having Michael go back out into the storm. Which was a good thing. The proprietor said he and his wife were about to batten down the place and close for the night.

Wind and rain followed Michael into the car. The sack of groceries he plopped into Faith's lap dripped, too.

"Brr." She rubbed at her arms, then reached into the back seat and tucked the blankets tighter around the babies. Both had gone to sleep. "We've lived on the East Coast long enough. We ought to know better than to leave home without taking an umbrella and jacket, Michael. Whatever possessed us?"

"This is our first full day-trip with the twins. We were so concerned with packing everything they needed, we forgot about checking the weather or preparing for ourselves."

"I hope the house has heat," Faith said suddenly.

"It's supposed to." Michael peered through the gusting rain, trying to read the numbers on the houses. "There it is. The gray-and-white clapboard."

"They all look alike, but that one has a porch. At least we can keep the babies dry while you unlock the door."

"I'll go open up and see about heat. You and the babies stay in the car for the time being."

"I'm not helpless, Michael."

"I know you're not," he said irritably. "But I got us into this fix. At least let me see to your comfort."

Faith flinched as he slammed the door and disappeared into a swirl of wind and rain. Should she apologize for stepping on his masculine pride? she wondered. She just wasn't used to having a man look out for her. Furthermore, she shouldn't get out of the habit of looking out for herself. How many more weeks would Michael be around? The call regarding DNA results could come at any time. Four to six weeks they'd said. On Monday it would be four weeks.

Truth be known, she already relied too heavily on Michael for his help with the babies. And for his companionship. She hadn't had any male friend to laugh and share observations and debate ideas with in longer than she cared to remember. She'd miss that once Michael left. Faith had enjoyed their lively conversations. She watched as Michael slogged from window to window, dropping and locking the heavy wooden shutters in place. She'd miss *him*, dammit. Why not admit it?

He arrived back at the car to get her before she had a chance to become too maudlin. "It's not a palace by any means," he panted, hunched over the carriers as he raced with Faith to the porch. "But it's not a total loser, either," he added, his mouth twitching with a grin.

Stepping through the door, Faith wrinkled her nose. "It smells musty."

"Oh? I thought it smelled fishy. But I didn't find one rotting in the fridge or anything."

"Well, it is a fishing cottage," Faith ventured, letting Michael close the door while she did a slow, three hundred and sixty degree turn. Plank floors were covered with bright braided rugs. A leather couch and two overstuffed chairs sat grouped around a cheerfully burning fireplace. Two doors opened off the large square room. One was obviously the kitchen, the other a bedroom.

Faith's gaze skittered around the entire perimeter again. *One bedroom.* Was that why Michael suddenly fell silent and appeared to be awaiting an explosion?

"I plugged in the fridge and put the last two bottles of formula and our leftovers from the restaurant inside," he said, again pausing to give her time to speak. "The stove is ancient," he informed her when she made no comment. "The good news is that we've got a fairly new microwave."

"Now tell me the bad," Faith said, assuming he'd mention that there was only one bed.

"The only heat in the whole house comes from this fireplace. The kitchen, bedroom and bathroom are cold as a polar bear's backside."

Faith noticed then how wet his shirt was across the shoulders and down the sleeves. In fact, he shivered uncontrollably. "This room will be cozy soon. Pull off that wet shirt and drape it over a chair near the fire, Michael. You can sit on the hearth until you warm up. I'll take the twins from their carriers and let them stretch out on blankets on the couch."

"You're a good sport, Faith. But you take the chair. I'd hate for the babies to catch a chill."

"They have terry sleepers in the diaper bag. I will let the room warm up, though, before I change them. They have plenty of extra blankets. It's you I'm worried about, Michael. All those trips to the car and wrestling with those shutters completely soaked your clothes."

"I hate to take off my shirt and, uh, offend you."

"Offend me? Michael, I'm a nurse! I'm afraid there are no surprises left when it comes to the naked body."

"I wouldn't have thought so. But the first night I

showed up at your door, I had the distinct impression you were bothered by my state of dress. Or, rather, un-dress...."

Faith recalled that night vividly. She *had* reacted badly. Only because she'd liked what she'd seen of his lean, tanned torso. He'd caught her off guard and she hadn't had time to hide a purely sexual response. She certainly couldn't tell him that. "I thought you'd gone back to New York, so I was shocked to see you." There. Faith thought she'd covered quite admirably.

"In that case, I guess you won't mind if I shed my jeans as well as the shirt. Wet denim is colder than wet cotton."

"Be my guest," she said, once she determined he wasn't just trying to get a rise out of her. Being a doctor and all, he probably didn't realize it was easier for her to deal with a half-naked patient than it was to make small talk while staring at the navy blue briefs of some-one she had wicked dreams about. She knew the color of his briefs, thanks to their shared laundry chores.

Faith felt her cheeks heat when it suddenly dawned on her that Michael had seen her underthings, too. No big deal to him. He wouldn't fantasize about her white cotton panties. Lacy had always said they were boring. Now Faith almost wished she, too, had developed a taste for silk.

Abigail sneezed and immediately began to fuss, which jolted Faith right out of her flight of fancy. Or it did until Michael stood up and loped across the living room in nothing but those navy shorts.

"Earlier it was Nick doing all the hacking. Should we dilute their next set of bottles? If they're coming down with colds, we don't want to clog them up."

"For pity's sake, Michael. You're the one who'll be

clogged up if you keep prancing around in the altogether. I'm sure there's an extra blanket in the bedroom
you could wrap around yourself.'' Even as the prim-
sounding suggestion left her lips, Faith admitted that
Michael's bare skin looked toasty warm and touchable.

"Tell me again how you find no surprises when it
comes to the naked body.''

Swallowing twice to dampen her dry mouth, Faith
slid her hands around Abigail to keep from flattening
her palms against the crisp dark hair fanning Michael's
chest. A chest hovering all too close to the end of her
nose...

It was the first time Faith could recall being happy
to have both babies crying at once. Thank goodness
Michael scooped up Abby and sauntered back to his
chair, leaving her to soothe Nick.

Good grief, that was worse. Michael Cameron's back
view curled Faith's toes right into the soles of her
sneakers. She went hot, then cold and then hot again.
Her reaction was so intense, she tested her forehead to
see if maybe she'd developed a fever. No, her forehead
felt cool. Clammy, but cool.

"Don't tell me you're getting sick, too?'' Michael
said as he studied her, once more from safely across the
room. He'd had to retreat or risk making a fool of himself by hauling her into his arms.

"I'm fine.'' Faith reached for the diaper bag. "Nick's
wet. I'm going to change him, then I'll switch with you
and get Abby into her sleeper.''

"Sounds like a plan. I'll wash my hands and prepare
the bottles.''

"Dressed like that?''

Michael frowned. He wasn't at all sure Faith *wasn't*
getting sick. She was acting odd. But maybe it was the
storm. For the past ten minutes he'd seen the lightning

crack through small gaps in the shutters. Thunder vied with the pounding of rain. "If you want to fix the bottles, I'll hold both of the little rascals. Remember to dilute their milk."

"Won't they be up twice as often?"

"Probably. I doubt we'll get much sleeping done tonight, anyhow."

"Because we'd have to share a bed?" Faith blurted.

Michael stared at her flushed cheeks and bright eyes. His mind began flipping back over the recent give-and-take. He started to wonder whether he wasn't the only one having thoughts of a sexual nature. What would happen if he laid his cards on the table? If he admitted to having had dreams about taking her to bed? Still, if he'd misread the signs, Faith could really cry foul to her lawyer.

Maybe he'd just put out feelers and see how she responded. "I don't have any problem with our sharing a bed. Do you?"

"I, ah, no. The twins will be quite comfortable in their carriers. But we'll be exhausted tomorrow if we don't nab a few z's."

Now Michael was afraid she hadn't fully understood that his intention included their making love. Why was this so hard? It wasn't as if they were juveniles.

Nothing more was said. Faith changed both babies and prepared their bottles. Michael fed Abby and she fed Nick. Even though their breathing was raspy, both babies drifted off to sleep.

"Are you hungry?" Faith asked when Michael rose and stoked the fire.

"Not for food," he said boldly, deciding it was time to jack up the stakes.

If Faith had any doubts after their earlier pussyfooting

around the issue of bed, Michael had just made his intentions completely clear. Her heart began to pound as she checked to see that the twins' carriers were set solidly on the couch. Straightening, her back still toward Michael, she clamped a hand across her jittery stomach. She felt rather than heard him walk up behind her. Yet she stiffened when he slid his arms around her waist and nuzzled the side of her neck with his lips.

"Second thoughts already?" he rumbled softly near her ear.

Faith didn't trust herself to do more than shake her head. Then she worried about the sudden way this had come to pass. She'd harbored a crush on him forever. Did he know? Had he figured it out tonight? What was she to him—a dalliance? *A substitute for her sister?* The thought caused Faith to shrug off the clever fingers that had unbuttoned her blouse and unsnapped her bra.

As though reading her mind, Michael eased her back against his rock-solid erection. "For the better part of a year after we first met, Faith, hardly a day went by that I didn't picture touching you like this." A rough chuckle crept past her ear. "I know you'll say all the surgical residents were young and horny back then, but there wasn't another woman on the face of the earth who haunted my waking and sleeping thoughts like you did."

Unexpectedly she turned in his arms, and they both caught their breath as her nipples grazed the hair on his chest. Anything she might have said Michael ended up swallowing as his mouth met hers in a deep kiss.

If he relaxed his shoulders and bent his head, Faith didn't have to quite stand on tiptoe. Which was a good thing, since her knees were shaking. Especially when she suddenly found her jeans pooled around her ankles.

Michael stumbled backward, gripping her around the waist as he carried her to the chair, leaving her jeans on the rug.

"Aren't we going into the bedroom?" she mumbled when he sat and pulled her astride his hips.

"Don't think I can make it," he muttered, trying again to fuse their mouths. His free hand plunged into the pocket of his drying jeans. "I have a condom in my billfold. Something tells me you aren't on the pill. Are you?" Michael hesitated.

The desperate urge to find fulfillment, and the quiver in her stomach, didn't abate even though her mind retreated. "You just happen to carry condoms?"

"Always. Or have you forgotten your sister wasn't supposed to get pregnant?"

The mention of Lacy had the effect of a faceful of cold water. It wasn't easy scrambling off Michael's lap on legs made of sponge rubber, but she managed.

Michael could have bitten off his tongue. He'd realized immediately that he'd been a damned fool to bring up Lacy's memory. And he should've known better; he'd long since figured out that Faith felt overshadowed in the presence of her younger sister. "Ah, hell, Faith." He dropped the gold foil packet he'd finally extracted, and swiped a shaking hand across his face. "My marriage was over a long time before the divorce. But as I said earlier, you played havoc with my mind a lot longer, from the first day I met you. Dammit, you're not Lacy's stand-in!"

Faith's hands shook equally hard, making it almost impossible for her to climb back into her jeans. "Then maybe you won't mind telling me why, if you spent so much time thinking about *me,* you chose to marry

Lacy." Anger made the fingers hooking her bra and
buttoning her blouse swift and sure in their movements.

Michael decided his jeans had dried enough, and as
this attempt at lovemaking was obviously going nowhere, he might as well put them on. He spoke through
gritted teeth while struggling to fasten his zipper. "Unlike you, Lacy needed me. You were always so damned
self-possessed, Faith. You didn't need anyone." He'd
lashed out in frustration—and he knew that his words
sounded more vitriolic than he'd meant.

Hurt, and feeling her dreams dissolve around her,
Faith snapped back. "Then nothing's changed, Michael.
I can still get along fine on my own."

He might have refuted such a declaration, but just
then both babies woke up screaming and coughing. Michael's earlier prediction had come true. Neither he nor
Faith did more than doze off for the rest of a very long
night.

By morning, the storm had passed and moved up the
coast. A neighbor told Michael the winds were now
battering the coast of Maine.

He and Faith set out for Boston. Conversation was
kept to a minimum. The babies both sounded congested,
so she asked Michael to swing by Dr. Sampson's office.
By the time his staff was able to fit them in, Michael's
nose had begun to drip and his head ached like fury.
He noticed that Faith had bought a decongestant and
cough drops for herself at the pharmacy.

"I've got a slight sore throat," she said in answer to
his raspy question about how she felt. "Go back to your
apartment and get some sleep," she told him in cool
tones. "I've worked many a night feeling worse. The
babies and I will get along fine. Just fine!"

CHAPTER TEN

IF MEN WERE LOUSY PATIENTS, doctors must be the worst, Michael decided. He stumbled into his apartment and fell across the bed. Then he climbed out again and sat in the kitchen with a cup of coffee. He didn't drink it, just hung his head over the cup, hoping the steam would clear his sinuses. He felt like crap in more ways than one. Things had been going well between him and Faith. He'd screwed up royally.

He'd moved too fast. Had let his interest in her overpower his good sense. But Michael had no idea how to straighten this out. If he'd been equipped with the ability to deal with hurt feelings, Lacy might still be alive and none of this would have happened. No Kipp Fielding. No messy triangle. No legal battle.

No babies.

He listened for any sign from next door that Faith needed his assistance with the twins. All was quiet. The medicine must have done its job. Good. Considering how they'd ended the outing, Michael wasn't anxious to knock on her door and get his head bitten off. For two cents, he'd stay away until she begged for his help. As if Faith would break down and ask *any* man for help. Dammit, she couldn't bend, wasn't capable of it, and he had a history of failure at compromise. Any relationship between them was doomed. It was high time he admitted it. He might—if he could get her out of his head.

Groaning, Michael wished he'd followed Faith's lead and bought himself a decongestant. He hadn't had a head cold like this in twenty years. How long did the damned things last? he wondered as he dumped the now-cold coffee down the sink and flung himself across the bed again.

After tossing and turning for more than two hours, he piled up a stack of pillows and fell asleep virtually sitting up.

AS THE NIGHT DRAGGED ON, Faith did her best to minister to both fussy babies. Her own head felt like a helium-filled balloon. When the light of dawn streaked the sky, she'd reached her wits' end. Nick and Abby had slept in fits and starts. They were hungry but had little interest in their bottles. Abby refused to drink at all. Faith worried that she'd become dehydrated. "Come on, sweetheart," she pleaded with the hot, fussy child. "I know you feel rotten, but if you don't take in some fluids, you'll feel worse."

Between rocking and pacing the floor, Faith listened for any sign of life in the apartment next door. As the morning wore on, she began to wonder if Michael had packed up and gone back to New York. She wouldn't blame him. She'd acted like a twit. She'd acted jealous of a sister who was no longer a threat. Guilt slammed through her. Guilt because for so long, she'd denied being jealous of Lacy. Guilt because now that Lacy was dead, Faith had been about to take what had belonged to her sister. Maybe the guilt was irrational, but Faith still felt it, compounded by the tragedy of Lacy's death. And Faith had dumped all *her* guilt on Michael.

Boy, she was something. If he never spoke to her again, it would serve her right. Tears began to run down her cheeks. Hugging Abigail close, Faith rubbed her face over Abby's soft hair. Ultimately she would be the loser if Michael won custody and never let her see the twins again.

By late afternoon, Faith was certain Michael had gone. There wasn't the slightest sound from his apartment. Her cold had worsened, as had those of the twins. Though both babies had taken in some of the electrolyte drink Dr. Sampson's nurse had told Faith to buy at the pharmacy, they were still extremely fussy.

Following a second night without sleep, Faith decided she couldn't do this alone. She hauled out the telephone book and started down the list of advertisements for agencies providing mother's helpers. Her own throat was so sore she could barely croak out her questions. It turned out she'd wasted her breath. Not one of the agencies had a mother's helper available for short-term assignments.

Faith was tempted to promise them she'd pay a month's wages even though she hoped she'd only need someone for a few days.

Just when she thought her arms would fall off from holding the babies and walking the floor with them, she heard the shower running next door. If Michael had been gone, he was now back. The joy she felt in her heart was overwhelming—and pathetic, she told herself.

He'd probably laugh in her face if she phoned to ask for his help. Practically the last thing he'd said to her had been a bitter comment about her self-sufficiency. And she'd more or less told him it would be a cold day in hell before she needed *anything* from a man.

Words. False pride. They could really get you in trouble.

She waited fifteen minutes after hearing the shower shut off to pick up the card on which he'd written his cell phone number. Twice she punched in the first three digits, then went into a fit of coughing and hung up without completing the call.

As she flexed her fingers and tried again, Nicholas woke up screaming and pulling at his ears. He probably needed to go to the doctor again for something stronger than a decongestant. Faith didn't think she could manage bundling both babies up and calling a cab to go downtown. She'd have to call Michael—but she found it easier to beg for his help on behalf of the twins rather than herself.

Jiggling the distressed baby on one shoulder, Faith quickly punched in Michael's cell number. The phone rang and rang and rang. She hadn't hung up yet when a knock sounded at her door. Trailing the long cord to the entry, she balanced the receiver and Nick, while trying to peer out the peephole. To Faith's surprise, Michael stood there, a frown on his face, one hand splayed against the wall.

She dropped the receiver and flipped open all three locks. Faith found herself offering a teary apology to Michael's back. He'd turned and headed back into his apartment.

He glanced over his shoulder, shock on his face. "Wait a minute, Faith. Don't close the door. I left my cell phone in the apartment and I hear it ringing."

"It's me," she said breathlessly, pointing to the receiver at her feet.

"You? You're calling me?"

She nodded and closed her eyes. Michael looked so

wonderfully healthy. He was clean and shaved, while she hadn't had time to shower since they'd arrived home from their outing. She'd changed her blouse because both babies had spit up on it, but she wore the same jeans. "Oh, Michael! You have every right to tell me to get lost, b-ut...but I need you. Nick has to see Dr. Sampson. I think he's developed an ear infection. I'm so light-headed from lack of sleep, I feel faint. Please..." She extended a hand, then quickly drew it back. The man must think she was a stark, raving maniac.

"God, Faith. Why didn't you phone me earlier? I slept for twenty hours straight."

"So that's why I didn't hear any noise coming from your apartment. I thought you'd gone to New York."

"You really were calling me?" he asked, stooping to pick up the buzzing receiver.

Faith clung to Nick and stared at Michael. "I'd hoped even if you were still mad at me, you'd take pity on the twins."

"I'm not mad at you, Faith." Reaching out a finger, Michael ran it tentatively over the trail left by her tears. "I never was angry at you. I'm sorry I pushed too fast. I had no right to do that when our lives are so up in the air over the custody agreement. I'm hoping we can forget it ever happened and go on as we were before."

Bad as she felt, his declaration ripped through her heart. Or maybe it was her stomach. Faith felt very much as if she was about to throw up.

She was.

Thrusting the crying baby into Michael's arms, Faith covered her mouth and ran for the bathroom.

Michael paced outside the bathroom door listening to her retch, and feeling helpless. He'd poked his head

inside once, only to have her plead to be left alone. He
might have drawn her a glass of water or gotten her a
cool washcloth if Abigail hadn't awakened and joined
her brother's chorus. Both babies were stuffy. Michael
checked the medicine schedule Faith had clipped to one
of the cribs. They weren't due more for another hour.

He listened to them cough and cry for five additional
minutes, then made up his mind. He was taking all three
of them to the doctor.

"Get a jacket," he told Faith when she finally
emerged from the bathroom, pale and shaky. "The
babies are already in their carriers. I'll load them up and
meet you at the front entrance. Can you make it that far
alone?" he asked sharply.

"I just need sleep," Faith said. "Can you manage
both babies?"

"I am man," he joked, beating a fist on his chest.
Faith swayed then, and he cursed and scooped her off
her feet. "I'll put you to bed myself. And I'll ask Dr.
Sampson to prescribe something for flu and cold. Are
you allergic to any medications?"

"No," she mumbled. She was sound asleep by the
time he stripped back the spread and put her carefully
down. He brushed the dark curls off her forehead, thinking she looked terribly fragile. Remembering that he'd
slept better on a pile of pillows, Michael lifted her tenderly and arranged several pillows at her back. "I'll
return as soon as possible," he whispered, pulling off
her shoes before covering her with the spread.

AGAIN, DR. SAMPSON'S OFFICE had to work the babies
into an already overfull schedule. "Sorry I didn't call
ahead," Michael said when Hal finally got around to

seeing them. He explained how they'd all been sick and that Faith still was.

"Flu and colds are both going around," the doctor acknowledged. "Faith was right. Nick has developed otitis media," he said referring to an infection of the inner ear. "We caught it early. I'll want him on an antibiotic for ten days. Continue to push fluids with this young miss," he said, after noting that Abby's ears were fine. "Abigail's lost a little weight. She doesn't have much to play around with."

Michael, who'd been holding Nick, now cuddled the choking girl under his chin. She settled in, curling close to her brother.

"You're a natural at this, Michael," Dr. Sampson said. "If your esteemed colleagues could only see you now."

Michael gave a short laugh. "My partner should see me. He's badgering me to come back to the clinic."

"I didn't mean to make light of your situation. I take it there's no word yet on the DNA?"

"No." Michael shook his head. "Next week, or so I'm guessing. You know," he mused, "I want the results, but I'm afraid to get the call saying they're finally in."

"I can understand that. You've gotten really attached to the twins. So has Faith. And the two of you function well together. It'll be tough if you have to fight each other."

Michael said nothing, but Hal's statement echoed in his ears as he stood in line at the pharmacy. The prophesy nagged at him even after he'd returned to Faith's apartment.

He looked in on her shortly after settling the twins in a crib. Faith was dead to the world. She didn't twitch

a muscle. Didn't know he'd come in. Since she was
sleeping so soundly, Michael decided not to wake her
to give her a dose of the medicine Dr. Sampson had
prescribed. Michael had long subscribed to the belief
that sleep was a profound healer.

As the afternoon waned, Michael figured he'd be
spending the night here. Slipping out while everyone
slept, he collected enough clean clothing to last for several days, and a book he'd been reading, along with the
latest cardiopulmonary journal. It was a magazine that
frequently published his articles, although he hadn't
written any since before the divorce. The Norwegian
girl's case had some anomalies worth publishing.
Funny, but the intense desire that used to drive him
seemed to have deserted him. He hadn't thought about
performing surgery in over three weeks. What did it
mean? Was he burned-out?

He was doing too much introspection. Grimacing,
Michael dumped everything in the guest bedroom.

He checked in on the babies and happened to discover that their laundry hamper was full. This was as
good a chance as any to go next door and throw a load
into the washer.

Before he could toss the clean clothes into the dryer,
however, things changed. The twins woke up wet and
hungry. While Michael was in the middle of feeding
them, Faith stumbled out of her room and made it only
as far as the bathroom door, where she upchucked
again. All over the floor.

Michael felt so sorry for her. "Don't worry about
cleaning up," he murmured. "Take care of yourself. I'll
scrub the floor in a minute. Hal prescribed some medicine to help you ward off the nausea. I left it in the
bathroom. Can you manage to get into a nightgown by

yourself? I'm sure the babies have already been exposed to whatever you have, but just in case they haven't, I'd as soon they not get too close to you.''

"I think this is rather more than you bargained for, Michael. You didn't sign on to take care of me.''

"Like I haven't dealt with worse as a doctor?''

"What would I have done without you?'' she asked in all seriousness, gazing at him as she slumped against the door casing.

A wry smile tugged at the corners of his lips. "I promise not to tell a soul that you aren't a superwoman, Faith.''

"Joke all you want. I honestly don't know how I would have gotten through this siege. Handling the twins by myself is tough. Add to that everyone being sick…'' If she had anything to add to the statement, she didn't. "Oh, no, I'm dizzy again.'' Teetering, she wove her way back to her room.

Michael held his breath until he heard the squeak of her mattress. "Thank God she made it,'' he murmured to the wide-eyed babies.

It was nearly dark by the time he had a chance to clean the tile floor in the bathroom. He quietly entered Faith's room to check on her again and discovered that she'd taken a second dose of her medicine. She lay sprawled atop her covers, still in yesterday's sweaty, wrinkled clothes. Michael debated with himself a respectable few minutes. Then, gritting his teeth, he opened her dresser drawers and searched until he found a nightgown. He was a doctor, he reasoned. Faith didn't have anything he hadn't seen before. It was just too bad that the gown he pulled out happened to be the one he'd had fantasies about.

Michael snapped on the bedside lamp. If she woke

up, she could take care of this herself. She tossed a bit. Even mumbled and licked her lips. Her eyes remained closed.

Her skin now felt warm and dry. She probably still had a fever. Once he'd slipped off her blouse and jeans, he bathed her face and arms in cool water.

As fast as possible, he drew her gown over her head, tucked her arms through the armholes, and rearranged her in the bed. Since the room was warm, he covered her with only a sheet.

Leaving a light on low, he wandered into the kitchen, where he heated himself a can of soup. There was something hugely satisfying about knowing he'd met the needs of three people he cared about a great deal. Oddly enough, despite his medical successes, he'd doubted his ability to nurture for quite some time following the divorce. He'd stayed in Europe for a couple of months, throwing himself into the lecture circuit. His lengthy absence then contributed to his partner's concern about the current situation; Dominic felt he'd been left to manage the clinic on his own for too long. But Michael had needed to stay away after Lacy's rejection. The divorce had shaken something elemental in Michael—his confidence in his own ability to comfort and support. If he hadn't discovered the twins, Michael thought he might have lost a vital portion of himself. The part that allowed him to be a true healer, not just a technician, performing medical procedures. The words *physician, heal thyself* were never more prophetic. In a way, Lacy had given him a wake-up call. Michael didn't think he'd ever compartmentalize the areas of his life again.

The feeling that he'd accomplished something—that he'd made a few life-altering decisions in these past hours—remained with him for the rest of the night.

Toward morning, after cajoling Faith into taking another dose of medicine, he thought she seemed cooler and slept more deeply. She had tried to get up once when the babies cried for their two-o'clock bottles. When Michael assured her he didn't need assistance, she'd burrowed beneath the covers again.

Now it was nine in the morning, and Faith snoozed on. Michael got the twins up. He dressed them and fed them diluted formula. They smiled and kicked their legs happily—obviously on the mend. Nick had slept between feedings, which meant his ear wasn't bothering him as much.

Michael noticed that now the babies were a bit older, they stayed awake for longer periods of time. Both held their heads up without assistance, and they laughed aloud with very little prompting.

Michael opened out the playpen Gwen had lent Faith. He put the babies inside and hunted up a few rattles and squeaky toys. He'd just sat down with a second cup of coffee and begun leafing through a medical journal when he remembered the laundry he'd thrown in the washer yesterday. The darned stuff probably needed to be rinsed again.

Rather than haul two babies over to his apartment, Michael propped open both doors so he could more easily run from one place to the other. That way, he could still hear the babies if they cried, and from Faith's living room he'd hear the washer shut off.

An hour later, on the fourth trip, he dashed out of his place carrying a basketful of newly dried baby clothing and ran smack into a man and a woman headed for Faith's apartment. "May I help you?" he asked coolly, not recognizing them. At least, he didn't until the couple took a second look at him and seemed to do a double take.

"Oh," he exclaimed. "Daniel Burgess and Barbara Lang." Shifting the basket to his other hip, Michael stretched out a hand. "Faith didn't tell me to expect a visit from Social Services."

"We were, ah, in the area and decided to stop by," Burgess said. He opened a notebook and glanced pointedly at the numbers on both apartments. "Are you visiting the Cameron twins today, Doctor?" the man asked.

"Yes," Michael said. Lon Maxwell knew he'd rented the apartment next to Faith. Other than Lon and Faith, no one knew. It was no one's business.

He'd never had to contend with visits from Social Services. He decided to be polite but not go out of his way to be too hospitable. What he hoped was that they'd quickly see the babies were doing well and then leave. Because Michael didn't buy their "in the area" story. Burgess had hesitated too long.

"Judge Brown ordered all parties to phone ahead before visiting," he pointed out as he seated the couple. Michael dumped the basket of clean clothing on the couch, sat and began to fold things.

"Oh, but this isn't an official visit," Ms. Lang assured him. Even as she stiffly balanced her briefcase across her knees, her eyes roamed the cluttered room.

Michael knew how it must look. Burgess had been forced to clear two sets of bottles, various burp cloths and a soiled set of Nick's terry sleepers out of one chair before he could sit down. There was a hodgepodge of blankets lying about. The two carriers were stacked by the door; Michael had left them there following his visit to the pediatrician. Glancing around, he saw books and magazines, assorted toys, a coffee cup. Outside of that, the room didn't look too bad...if one discounted the layer of dust on the coffee and end tables.

Daniel Burgess peered into the playpen. "According to my notes, the babies have seen a doctor twice this week. Colds and ear infections." He shook his head. "And yet it's been a warmer than usual fall."

Michael pushed his medical journal aside to make room for a clean stack of receiving blankets. "Bottle-fed babies are more prone to ear infections." Michael had read that in a parents' magazine in Hal Sampson's office.

Burgess cleared his throat and jotted a notation in his notebook.

Barbara Lang put her case down and bent to pick up Nick. She held him aloft at arm's length and talked baby talk.

"Nick's been known to spit up as long as an hour after feeding." Michael warned, sneaking a peek at his watch. He was getting antsy. They hadn't asked about Faith, but he had no doubt they would if they stayed much longer. Or maybe they'd assume that, because he was here, she'd taken the opportunity to get out of the house and do some shopping.

Ms. Lang returned Nick to the playpen. She wagged a rattle in front of Abby and seemed pleased when the baby grasped the toy. "Well, Daniel, Dr. Cameron appears to have things under control. Maybe we should go."

Yes! Michael said to himself. Rising, he took two steps toward the door, hoping they'd follow. They might have if Faith hadn't chosen that moment to stagger into the living room. Her hair looked thoroughly mussed. Her feet were bare, and she couldn't seem to hit the armholes of a pale yellow, summery bathrobe.

"I can't believe the time, Michael." Her husky, sleepy voice sounded garbled around a huge yawn. "You should've dragged me out of bed." As she covered her open mouth with a hand, Michael was sure she had no idea they even had visitors.

Gurgling helplessly in his throat, Michael sprinted to her side before she could start scolding him for taking off her clothes and putting her in a nightgown. A gown that left all too much of her glorious self exposed. Michael thought she looked delightful. He wasn't, however, overjoyed to see Daniel Burgess's eyes popping out of his head.

"Faith, Mr. Burgess and Ms. Lang from the State Department of Social Services have dropped by."

She gasped, choked, started coughing.

"Faith's been sick," Michael added, aiming an apology over his shoulder at the gawking couple. "Combination of cold and flu. Dr. Sampson ordered her some medicine and said she should stay in bed. Sampson said there's been a lot of different viruses going around the area."

Blotches of red crept up Faith's neck. Hopping backward toward the hall, she pulled at Michael's shirtfront, trying to keep him solidly between her and the pair seated in her living room. "Why didn't you warn me?" she sputtered.

"Didn't have time," he whispered back.

Rising on tiptoes, Faith connected with Barbara Lang's still-shocked gaze. "Give me a minute to dress," she said brightly, doing her best not to hyperventilate. She let go of Michael's shirt and escaped down the hall, leaving him to deal with their visitors.

"Brother." Faith gripped her still muzzy head with both hands. "Throwing up in front of Michael was bad enough," she moaned. "Now I've paraded past state workers in my nightie. Can my day get any worse?" What was Michael telling them? she wondered as she pawed through her dresser drawers in search of fresh underwear. She really needed to shower. She'd worn the same clothes for— Her head shot up and the last thought scrambled and stopped as if it had hit a brick wall. In a sense it had. Her last conscious memory was of throwing up outside the bathroom door. She'd been wearing a blouse and jeans at the time.

"Oh." Her fingers plucked at the lace trim on her nightdress. *Michael. He'd undressed her and put her to bed.*

Faith needed a clearer head to face that fact, if not to face their visitors. She elected to take the time to shower and wash her hair. What could those two want? In her experience as a girl, a surprise visit from Social Services meant trouble. It meant well-meaning neighbors had reported that her mother's condition had worsened, and they thought someone other than a child should look after Lacy.

Standing under the hot, stinging spray, Faith could only worry. Maybe the Fieldings had issued a new complaint. It would be just like Kipp's father to want the babies fostered elsewhere. All kinds of frantic and suspicious thoughts ran through Faith's mind as she showered, then toweled dry.

The whole process of showering, dressing and blowing her hair dry had taken no more than twenty minutes. Still, it was on shaking legs that Faith approached the living room.

Michael sat, a baby balanced on each knee. Otherwise, the room appeared empty.

"Where are our guests?"

Glancing up, Michael took in her wide eyes and colorless face. Even then, Faith looked beautiful to him and he couldn't take his eyes off her. "I think we provided more excitement than either of their hearts could handle," he drawled. "I can't tell you how glad I am to see you looking better."

"What did they want? Who filed a complaint? Have the babies been crying too much?"

"Burgess knew we'd made two trips to the doctor."

"Darn and blast." She flopped suddenly into one of the chairs. "They were gathering dirt. And boy, we gave it to them, didn't we?" Closing her eyes, Faith sighed.

"Dirt? I'll grant you the tables are dusty and the place looked a little untidy." He grinned. "But if they were looking for dirt, they didn't find any. I bathed the babies this morning. They could see the laundry was done."

"Not *that* kind of dirt, Michael. Don't joke about it. I mean scandal. They'll think we're living together."

"We are, sort of. I moved some stuff into the guest room after you got so sick."

"You told them you were sleeping in the guest room?"

"No. They didn't ask. They didn't ask much of anything. In fact, I can't figure out why they bothered to come."

Faith threw up her hands. "I told you. They were snooping."

"For whom? And what conclusion could they draw that would be so bad? Look around you, Faith. Baby things, car carriers, playpen. From where Ms. Lang sat, she could see the rack of bottles in the kitchen. Plus, I had enough clothes spread out here to outfit quintuplets. These babies are obviously well looked after. Anyway, who would report us? And why?''

"Lacy probably didn't tell you—I doubt she was old enough to be aware. Social Services wanted to take us kids away from Mother and Daddy more than once. It was awful.''

"What I'm telling you is they'd have to really twist things to make you seem unfit.''

"They don't lie, but they can word the truth so that a judge might wonder if we're doing a good job. For instance, the report could read, Dr. Cameron *appeared* to have fed the twins. He *left* the babies in a playpen and folded clean clothes throughout our visit. At ten to eleven, Miss Hyatt *wandered* out of the bedroom in her nightgown. Look at the inferences that can be drawn.''

"I see. Someone looking for dirt, as you phrased it, might conclude a number of things.'' He ticked them off on his fingers. "We aren't married. Possibly cohabiting. We're neglecting the babies. I'm doing all the work and you're a lazy bum.''

Faith's lips thinned. "Right. Why did they show up this morning of all mornings, Michael? Did you call them?''

"What?'' He yelped so loudly Abigail started to cry. "Shh…shh, honey.'' Rocking her to calm her, Michael glared at Faith over the top of Abby's fuzzy head. "You don't really think such a thing, I hope.''

She linked her hands and stared at them. "While I was in the shower, I started adding up a few things.''

"Like what? Why do I have the feeling I don't want to hear this?''

"Whose idea was it to drive down the coast? Yours. Maybe you knew about the storm in advance. Maybe you set me up. It wasn't *my* friend who so conveniently had a cabin nearby. Ha! I ruined your plan to seduce and discredit me. How lucky for you I got sick when I did, Michael. Because you still managed to damage my reputation with Burgess and Lang—especially when they saw me waltz out wearing a see-through nightgown."

"For crying out loud! With that imagination, why are you a nurse? You ought to write novels."

"Really? If my idea's so far-fetched, how come I never saw any sign that you were interested in me? Not before you met Lacy, or in the past five weeks."

"The signs were there, Faith. I can't help it if you only see what you want to see. And I don't know how to prove what goes on in my head while I sleep. But I can tell you that if you had a window into my mind, you wouldn't like what you'd see."

She blushed at that. Her fingers flexed several times. She did not lift her head to meet his eyes. If she had, Michael figured she'd see the hunger in them. He considered getting up off the couch, putting down the babies and taking her in his arms. But the phone rang, shattering his intentions.

Faith crossed the room and snatched it up. "David," she said in obvious surprise. "How good of you to call and check on us. I'm recovering from the flu. The babies both have colds. One of Nick's ears is infected. Yes, I'm much better, thanks, and so are they."

Michael saw her grip the phone more tightly. She put out a hand to steady herself against the wall. He knew something was wrong and felt his own stomach tighten in response. If Lang and Burgess had caused trouble, they hadn't wasted any time. He stood and paced the floor behind Faith until she hung up. "Well?" he exclaimed the minute she'd replaced the receiver. "What's going on?"

"The DNA results are back, Michael," Faith said in a flat tone.

"So what did it prove? Am I the twins' father?" he asked.

"David didn't know the results. The judge has them. Apparently they'll remain sealed until we all meet in her chambers again."

"When?" He barely mouthed the word.

"Tomorrow at two o'clock. I'm to arrange for a sitter, David said."

A pent-up breath escaped Michael's lips. "At least, the wait will soon be over. This waiting's making everyone nuts."

"Before I went in to take my shower, I remember thinking my day couldn't get any worse. I was wrong." Tears pooled along her lower eyelids as Faith cuddled Abigail close and kissed her fiercely.

CHAPTER ELEVEN

THE PHONE CALL FROM DAVID REED cast a pall over both of them for the rest of that day. She and Michael fell silent for long periods of time. Then one or the other would burst out with a question.

"Why can't someone just open the envelope from the lab and telephone everyone with the results?" Faith sneezed several times into a tissue after asking.

Michael pulled a handful of tissues from a box that sat on the table beside him, and handed them to her. He uttered what passed as a noncommittal grunt.

Faith blocked a final sneeze. "What does that mean? Do you agree or disagree that we shouldn't all be left hanging?"

"I want to know the results. But at this stage, we can't afford to have anyone cry foul. If Judge Brown opened the envelope, our lawyers could claim grounds to suggest tampering."

"But a judge?"

"Judges aren't all squeaky-clean, Faith. I'd rather wait and watch the envelope being opened." Michael sat forward and rested his elbows on his thighs. He laced his fingers and idly twirled his thumbs. "But part of me wants to put off knowing."

"Why? Earlier you said the wait was hard on everyone."

"I know," he said in a shaky voice, reaching over to

rub the back of Faith's neck. "Guess I'm not as confident about the outcome now as I was during our initial hearing."

Faith moved away to escape the hypnotic touch of Michael's fingers. She placed Abby in the playpen next to her sleeping twin. Nick had drifted off while batting at a soft toy. "Whichever lawyer said it would be harder to give up the twins once I brought them home was a hundred percent correct. I thought I was attached before, but now all I want to do is pack them up and run far, far away."

Michael dropped a soft yellow blanket over the infants. "Funny, those same thoughts have been running through my head. I don't even like the idea of leaving them with a sitter tomorrow while we attend the hearing."

"A sitter! Oh, Michael. I still need to do that. I wish there was someone in the building," she said half to herself. "Most of the people I'd trust will be at work during the time we need someone."

Michael pulled Faith against his chest. They stood in contemplative silence for a moment. Until Faith slipped away and rummaged in the cupboard for a new tissue box.

"This is doubly hard on you, I guess," Michael said, his gaze sympathetic.

"Because I'm sick, you mean? The medicine helps. I'll get in three more doses before the hearing. You know how it is with nurses. Unless we're dead, the hospital expects us to work. It becomes habit to keep on going while we're sick."

"Same with doctors. You'd think the medical profession would be more tolerant of staff illness."

"I remember one time Gwen had pneumonia and our

supervisor scheduled her for back-to-back shifts. Hey.'' Faith snapped her fingers. ''Gwen might know of a reliable sitter. She's particular about who looks after her kids.'' She immediately grabbed the phone and dialed her friend.

Michael listened to one half of the conversation. He heard enough to realize their sitter dilemma was solved. ''Gwen came up with someone, I take it,'' he said when Faith got off the phone.

''It's her day off and her kids are in school all day. Gwen offered to come over here and stay with the twins. Said she's been meaning to call and give me an afternoon out, anyway. Wow, I feel so much better having that settled.''

''Do you feel good enough to eat something? I think you've lost weight. More than I'd expect from the bout of flu you had.''

''It's these sweats. They're really baggy.''

''I don't think so.'' He eyed her critically and it flustered her. He'd seen almost every inch of her, and his look now reminded her that he, too, was aware of it.

''How can you think about food?'' she asked as an obvious diversion. ''I'll be a wreck until after tomorrow's meeting. As a matter of fact, shouldn't you go back to your apartment and call Lon Maxwell to work out your strategy?''

''What good will it do? Any appeal we might file hinges on the DNA results. I don't know about you, but my philosophy is that misery needs company. I was about to suggest I run down to the video store at the corner and rent a couple of movies to get us through the long night. How does that sound?''

She glanced at the babies. ''I probably won't sleep,'' she said. ''And after tomorrow we may not be on speaking terms. Depending on those DNA results, this may be the last night you spend with the twins.''

"Why are you trying to cut our ties, Faith? Regardless of the outcome, we'll continue to see each other, I promise you."

Faith's eyelashes swept down, hiding her thoughts. Michael was treading in deep water. He knew Faith's physical response to him in that cabin hadn't been accidental. He also realized their situation gave them a lot to overcome. In fact, he had reservations himself. Not about the passion he felt toward Faith. The more time he spent with her, the more sure he was that he'd married the wrong sister. However, he wanted to be a father to Lacy's babies more than he'd ever expected. Michael certainly didn't want Faith confusing his two pursuits. Wanting her had nothing to do with wanting the babies. It was important she understand that.

Considering how strong his feelings were, Michael wasn't sure he could keep his hands to himself if he and Faith sat side by side watching old movies.

"I won't stay," he said abruptly. He began to collect his belongings. "You still look pretty peaked, Faith. You could crash at my place tonight if you want. I can sleep here and do the night feedings again."

Faith couldn't keep up with Michael's fluctuating offers. First he wanted them to spend the long, lonely evening together. Now he couldn't seem to be rid of her quick enough. Did it have to do with her fantasy of stealing off with the babies? Or had something triggered a memory of their indiscretions at the cabin? Were his regrets finally surfacing? Faith decided to make it easy for him. "We'll rest better in our own beds," she said. "Don't worry, I'll hear the babies. Last night the medicine knocked me out. Today I've adjusted to it."

"You're sure?" He hesitated at the door until she nodded. "Until tomorrow, then, Faith." Michael undid all the locks. "You will let me give you a lift to the courthouse?"

Faith caught the door before it closed. "I'll take a cab. I'm not sure what time Gwen will get here. Not only that, there's no need to give Burgess and Lang any extra fuel for speculation."

"Those two will be history once Judge Brown opens the envelope from the lab."

Faith set her jaw stubbornly. "So you say, Michael. Have you forgotten I plan to contest either way? Lacy named me guardian. Me." She tapped a fist over her heart.

"I'm sorry Lacy felt so bitter. But the judge will see that and take it into account before rendering a verdict." Michael's dark eyes burned with compassion for Faith.

She read the look as pity. "Good night, Michael. You won't win. My position is too strong. But for what it's worth, I think you'll make a great father someday."

"Someday I'll be a good husband, as well," he informed her. Then, because he faced a closed door, Michael wondered if she'd heard. If she had, would she put two and two together? She was wrong if she thought that slamming a door in his face meant she'd seen the last of Michael Cameron.

ANOTHER OCTOBER STORM SWEPT IN from sea the next day, matching Faith's mood. The nearer it came to the hearing, the more Faith's stomach pitched. The sensation was reminscent of the flu she'd just suffered, but she knew it was nerves. Pure and simple nerves.

It was too bad Michael hadn't popped over for coffee. As he'd said, misery did indeed love company. In spite of how they'd parted last night, Faith was surprised not to hear from him.

Fortunately, Gwen arrived an hour early. "I thought, given how important it is to make a good showing today, you might need extra time to get spiffed up." Hugging Faith, she added, "Knock 'em dead, okay? Show them what you're made of."

"Gwen, you're wonderful. I've been so rattled all morning, I think the twins sense there's something wrong. They've been fussier than normal."

Gwen tossed her purse and car keys on the table and gathered a crying Nick into her arms. "It's baby radar," Gwen advised sagely. "Kids act out every time mom has a chance to go out. The little charmers can turn on the waterworks at will. Their aim is to make mom feel so guilty she'll stay home." Laughing, the mother of four buried her lips in the baby's neck and blew him a raspberry. He snorted several times in response. "See?" Gwen said. "What did I tell you?"

Faith didn't look convinced. "Nick and Abby are too little for that sort of manipulative behavior."

"Don't kid yourself, honey. Babies come out of the womb knowing how to manipulate mom and dad. Speaking of dad, where is that gorgeous hunk of man?" Gwen peered into rooms as she followed Faith to her bedroom.

"Which man?" Faith pretended not to understand her friend. "Until Judge Brown opens the all-important envelope today, Nicholas and Abigail are fatherless."

"You know perfectly well I mean Dr. Cameron. Did you know Cicely's sister works in Hal Sampson's office? Carrie overheard Michael telling Hal the two of you and the babies had spent the night in some fishing cabin down the coast."

Faith's sharp exhalation brought a smile to Gwen's face.

Suddenly smug, she dropped a kiss on Nick's nose. "Hey, Faith, remember how we all used to fantasize what that man would be like in bed?" she said. "Is he as good as he looks?"

"I wouldn't know. We never got that far." Faith's muffled reply came from beneath the folds of a jade-green velour dress she'd dived into. "Hey, you were happily married when we both held retractors for Michael. Back off, Gwen, or I'll tell Jerry what you said."

"Ouch, the girl plays hardball." Abigail let out a wail from the nursery then, ending the women's chat.

But Gwen wasn't one to give up easily. "You look great," she told Faith as Faith swiped on pale lipstick and raced for the door to go meet her cab. "I'll bet Dr. Cameron won't be able to concentrate on anything but you today."

Faith balanced half in, half out of the door. "Gwen! Pu…lee…se! Nothing happened in that cabin."

"Of course not. *One* baby can throw a wrench into any lovemaking plans. But two…" Gwen rolled innocent gray eyes. "The thing you need to remember is that Michael *tried* to get something going. Right?" She smiled widely. "You're not denying it, I see. He's interested, and you know it. Think long and hard about that, Faith. Especially if he ends up winning the daddy pool."

Faith raised both hands in exasperation. "My cab is waiting," she said. "I showed you where the bottles and diapers are. If the hearing runs late, I'll call." Tempted to slam the door, Faith sighed and shut it softly instead. Gwen would have her say, no matter what.

THE STORM CAUSED a traffic snarl-up. Faith arrived late, nearly fifteen minutes after the meeting time. An unsmiling clerk hustled her down the dreary hall and into an already full chamber.

She felt Michael's gaze. Staring straight ahead, Faith slipped into the vacant seat left between him and David Reed. If she'd arrived early, she could have engineered the seating better and found a place well away from Michael. Now she'd have to act stoic while waiting for one or both of their lives to be ripped to shreds.

"I guess Gwen got there okay," Michael murmured. "I'd begun to worry. Is she all right with the twins?"

"Fine. Shh." Faith brought a finger to her lips. "Barbara Lang and Daniel Burgess are watching us." Faith wondered if they thought she looked entirely too well to have been as sick as she and Michael had claimed. Or, on the other hand, did they think she resembled something no self-respecting feline would drag in? As if to emphasize the lingering effects of her cold, Faith's nose twitched and she sneezed several times in succession.

Even Judge Brown glanced up. "Are you all right, Ms. Hyatt? Shall I ask the clerk to bring you a box of tissues or perhaps a glass of water?"

Faith shook her head. Michael had already unzipped her purse, and handed her a plastic-wrapped packet of tissues. "Thanks," she whispered.

"In that case," the judge said, pausing to run a last glance around the room. "I believe we are ready to begin. It pleases me that you were all able to make it on short notice. It shows that your interest in the welfare of the twins has remained strong."

"We're all here," one of Kipp Fieldling's lawyers growled. "Please enter in the record that our client flew home from the Bahamas in order to comply with the request that we all assemble on short notice, as you aptly put it.''

The judge seemed to take a long time to acknowledge Keith Schlegel. ''So entered,'' she said at last, directing a nod toward the stenographer. ''I've also received a report from Daniel Burgess and Barbara Lang as to their preliminary custody recommendations. I'll make copies available to all parties, along with today's transcript, if that's agreeable?'' Judge Brown appeared to be focused on getting a response from each team. If she heard Faith and Michael's audible groans, she didn't let on.

David conferred with Faith in low tones. Lon Maxwell did the same with Michael.

''We can always file a rebuttal later,'' he said. ''I know you were sick. Dr. Sampson will probably attest to that in a signed affidavit if Burgess and Lang get nasty. I suggest we agree to the copies in order to move on to the primary issue—what's in the envelope.''

''If that's what you think,'' Faith said, shredding a tissue. ''As I explained yesterday, they showed up without calling first. I—I suppose the damage from their report is done. I mean, the judge has already read it.''

''Brown is known for her fairness. Look, Faith. I'd hate to make a big fuss about something that might not even be an issue.''

''Does your client have a problem with including the Burgess-Lang report in today's transcript, Mr. Reed?'' Judge Brown asked.

''No, Your Honor,'' David said firmly. ''I assume we'll be able to counter the report if I deem it necessary?''

''You mean, if we don't conclude this case today?''

''I sincerely doubt that's possible, Your Honor,'' David said. "You hold the answer to the question of the Cameron twins' biological father—information which in no way changes my client's claim to custody of the babies, based on her sister's last will and testament."

"So you're saying regardless of DNA, your client will press for custody."

"Yes, Your Honor. That is what I'm saying."

The Schlegel brothers hunched around their partner, Nancy Matz. All shielded Kipp, Shelby and Kipp's father. The six jabbered, gestured and shook fingers. In contrast, Lon Maxwell and Michael relaxed in their chairs as if they'd already anticipated Faith's next move.

The judge spent a few minutes flipping pages in a day planner. "It would please the court to have the domestic fate of these children settled before the holidays begin. Mr. Reed, can you prepare an adequate case for your client by mid-November?"

David studied his own calendar. "That depends, Your Honor."

"On what?"

"On which gentleman fathered Lacy Hyatt Cameron's babies. I hope you aren't asking me to disclose my strategy?"

"Of course not," the judge conceded, her frown easing. "I understand it will take you longer to research case histories that have gone against a married couple than the more conventional cases that have ruled against single dads."

"Could we get on with the reason we're all here today?" Kipp's father complained loudly. "Well, what's the sense in dragging this out?" he said, tossing down his pen. "There are peoples' lives on hold here."

Judge Brown picked up the envelope. Turning to a

clerk who hovered at the back of the room, she said, "Ms. Carlson, could you please walk this envelope around? I want every counselor and client to verify that the seal on the envelope remains unbroken."

The elder Fielding threw an arm over the back of his chair. "Ye gods. We trust you, Judge. Open the damned thing, already."

The judge's well-shaped eyebrows drew down sharply. "Mr. Fielding, another outburst like that and I'll have to ask you to leave. The principals in this case have waited nearly six weeks for these DNA results. Ten additional minutes shouldn't cause anyone hardship."

The young clerk started with the state Social Service representatives. Burgess and Lang each checked the seal and also the postmark and return label.

David and Faith did the same.

Michael gave it a cursory glance, while his lawyer jotted the pertinent details on his legal pad. Finally, every member of the Fielding group examined the envelope. As the young clerk returned it to Judge Brown, Faith slid to the edge of her chair and noticed that everyone else did, too. "The anticipation is nerve-racking," she murmured to David.

Michael heard. "Why are you concerned?"

Faith clamped her teeth over her bottom lip. Under the table she had her fingers crossed that Michael's name would be inside that envelope. Not because she relished a fight with him, but if she ultimately lost, she'd far rather Michael raise the babies than Kipp and Shelby. By now, she would have thought he'd know how she felt.

The silence in the room was taut with suspense as Judge Brown slid a letter opener under the envelope flap. Her agonizingly slow rip of the paper had the same effect on the room's occupants as running a fingernail down a blackboard.

All drew in deep breaths when the judge extracted two sheets of paper from the envelope. "For the benefit of the record," the judge stated, "let it show that I've removed individual reports on blood drawn September fourth by a hematologist at Good Shepherd Hospital laboratory. One report is for Kipp J. Fielding III, the other for Michael L. Cameron, M.D."

Judge Brown perused first one sheet of paper, then the other as the keys to the stenowriter clicked softly. "My stars!" she burst out. Both papers slipped from her fingers and fluttered to the floor. The judge's eyes, indeed her whole face, reflected her shock. Composing herself with an effort, she bent and retrieved the pages. She seemed at a loss for words for several seconds, though she had to be aware that her entire audience leaned forward in their chairs.

"In my twenty years of serving in various capacities with Family Court, I've never run across anything like this. Lacy Hyatt Cameron's twins were fathered separately."

The clients all swiveled and looked to their lawyers for clarification. The legal counselors, in turn, peered confoundedly at Judge Brown.

The elder Fielding tumbled first to what Judge Brown meant. He clapped his son on the back. "I knew it. I knew it all along. The boy is yours. I have a grandson at last. Praise be!"

Pandemonium erupted with his declaration. The noise level in the room rose to deafening heights. In the absence of a gavel, Judge Brown pounded her fist on the desk and shouted for silence. "Stop this!" she ordered in her most imperious voice. "This is not a free-for-all, ladies and gentlemen. This is a child-custody hearing. Now then," she said sternly, tugging down her suit jacket. "Mr. Fielding has the right idea, only he's incorrect in his deduction. According to the DNA test results, the cord blood of the female child who, for the record, bears the name Abigail Dawn Cameron, matches the blood drawn from Kipp Fielding III. Whereas, cord blood of the male, known for the record as Nicholas John Cameron, bears the exact imprint of Michael Cameron's DNA."

Following a stunned silence, voices again escalated throughout the room. Again the judge pounded for order, this time with less success.

Bob Schlegel jumped to his feet. He stood, scowling around the room until talk tapered off, then stopped altogether. "Those tests are obviously erroneous," he bellowed, his face florid. "I've handled custody cases for over twenty years, and I've never heard of anything so preposterous as separate fathers of twins."

Nancy Matz placed a hand on her partner's arm. "I believe it's possible, Bob. Not long ago I saw a television documentary that dealt with this very thing."

He gaped at her. "Twins—with *different* fathers?"

Lon Maxwell, Michael's attorney, straightened his tie. "I can't quote names or dates, but my wife read a true account in one of her women's magazines recently. It dealt with twins having two fathers. She found it so fascinating, she read me most of the article at breakfast one morning. Ahem...we'd need to each document this for ourselves, of course, but here's the gist of how such a phenomena is possible, if I remember correctly." He paused, drawing a hand through his hair. "In a typical ovulation cycle, one or more eggs are released into a woman's fallopian tubes. After that, there's a window of two or three days during which conception can occur. So, as you can see, this phenomenon—two babies, two fathers, one birth—is certainly possible, although it's very rare.''

Judge Brown reread both reports and then thumbed back through her notes. "In our initial hearing, both Mr. Fielding and Dr. Cameron claimed to have been intimate with Lacy Hyatt Cameron within a two-day period. Naturally I'd want to see some expert corroboration before we proceed. But a good place to begin, Counselors, might be with the American Society for Reproductive Medicine.''

"Proceed?'' shouted Keith Schlegel, who'd remained mute during the previous uproar. "The place to start is with new DNA blood work. This must be some lab technician's idea of a joke.''

"It's no joke, Mr. Schlegel,'' Judge Brown informed him. "I'll have my clerk run copies of these data sheets right now for everyone involved. The testing lab is reputable. They do the work on some of our most sensitive criminal cases. What we have is unusual, possibly even a test case involving dual paternity.''

Michael groped until he found Faith's hand. They clung together mutely. Kipp and Shelby both slumped back in their chairs, while the separate attorneys rallied and began to argue loudly.

Nancy Matz, after hastily conferring with her partners, paced before the judge. "This case is really open-and-shut. If we all buy into the premise that the DNA testing is valid, then dispensation is simple. Kipp and Shelby should be awarded custody of Abigail, and Dr. Cameron gets Nicholas. Let's end this today.''

David slammed his hand flat to the table. "Such a

decision doesn't *begin* to address my client's claim. I don't give a damn if the babies have separate biological fathers. They had a common biological mother. A mother who clearly stated, while she was of sound mind and body, that she wanted her sister, my client, to receive custody of her offspring.''

Lon Maxwell punched an index finger in the air. "I believe that even your client said Lacy Cameron wasn't aware she carried twins. That fact, if nothing else, should nullify her wishes."

Bob Schlegel's voice rumbled from the far side of the room. "My client's father has offered to pay for new DNA tests. He and his son both feel a strong kinship to baby Nicholas. They aren't prepared to accept this lab's report."

The judge glanced over sharply. "I'm not sure I'll agree. Further testing would necessitate leaving the twins in foster care another four to six weeks. That's assuming any lab you all agree on could draw blood today. And since the cord blood has already been used, you'd have to petition the court to draw blood from the infants."

"Couldn't they have mouth swabs?" This suggestion came from Nancy Matz.

"As complicated as this promises to be," said the judge, "my bottom-line concern is to impact the children as minimally as possible."

"We agree," chorused the two state social workers. Barbara Lang pulled out her notebook. "The twins have settled in nicely with Ms. Hyatt. Daniel and I recommended in our report that she be allowed to continue caring for the twins until custody can be finalized. In fact, she and Dr. Cameron did a fine job of co-parenting, as we noted."

Faith and Michael both gasped. They hugged spontaneously, expressions of amazement etched on their faces.

A flurry of activity erupted in the Fielding camp. Bob Schlegel hitched up his pants and cleared his throat. "On behalf of our client, Your Honor, we object to Dr. Cameron being allowed a larger role in the twins' lives than are Mr. and Mrs. Fielding. They have a substantial estate to run in New York, as well as other pressing obligations. It places a hardship on them to commute to Boston."

"What would you suggest, Counselor?" Judge Brown shot back. "If you recall, Dr. Cameron's home and surgical practice is also in New York. He obviously thought the babies were worth an investment of his time."

"Surely you aren't taking sides, Judge?" Keith Schlegel interjected in a calm, reasonable voice. "Haven't the DNA results moved us into completely new territory? I suggest we all need time to adequately prepare appeals."

Nancy Matz, who'd been in a huddle with Kipp's father, again got slowly to her feet. "In fairness to all concerned, we respectfully request the babies be placed in state-approved foster care for the duration of this custody settlement."

"No!" Faith's cry pierced the air, echoed by David Reed.

"This is obviously not in the children's best interests," he went on. "And it is unacceptable to my client." Faith gripped the sleeve of Michael's suit coat and implored him with tear-filled eyes.

White-faced, Michael covered her hands. His thumbs rubbed warmth into the backs of hers. "Lon," he directed, never taking his eyes from Faith, "I'll agree to return to New York if I must. But why disrupt the babies' lives? They aren't to blame for how this turned out."

Bedlam broke out again, with the Fieldings' lawyers shouting to be heard. Judge Brown again demanded order.

"You all seem to forget that I'm the one who makes the decisions with regard to placement of the Cameron twins. I say we leave things as they are for now and reconvene in these quarters three weeks from today at the same hour for the purpose of presenting expert testimony." She held up a hand when Bob Schlegel started to register an objection.

"My decision is final. Mr. and Mrs. Fielding are welcome, urged, in fact, to spend time with Abigail and Nicholas. Furthermore, I'm ordering Ms. Hyatt to allow them free access to the babies. By that, I mean whenever they can get to Boston." Her tone held a finality that brooked no requests for change or any dissension.

However, Bob Schlegel was like a dog with a bone. "If the same applies to Dr. Cameron, he'll be in Boston every day. It's evident from the report filed by Social Services that he's been shacking up with Ms. Hyatt."

Michael bounded to his feet, fists clenched. Lon Maxwell yanked him back into his chair. "Don't play into his hands," he hissed.

David said virtually the same to Faith, who'd also bristled at the accusation.

The judge sent Schlegel a withering glance. "I'll ask you to refrain from using crudities in these hearings, please. Mr. Burgess and Ms. Lang verified that Dr. Cameron rented an apartment in the building where Ms. Hyatt lives. Your clients are equally free to take up residence in Boston until this matter is settled, if they so choose. As a matter of fact, I realize I've forgotten to set child support payments.'' She named a monthly fee. ''Both Mr. Fielding III and Dr. Cameron will pay that amount to the court, retroactive to the children's birth.'' This time she slammed down a gavel, which a young clerk had hastened to bring her.

Reed gathered his legal pads and stuffed them inside his briefcase. He all but kicked up his heels in glee. ''Man, oh, man. What a case. Whoever wins this will be assured a niche in legal history.''

Lon Maxwell did rub his hands together. ''Don't get too far from the phone,'' he advised Michael. ''Oh, and refuse to speak with reporters. They'll turn this into a sideshow if we let them.''

''Reporters?'' Michael, who'd stood and caught Faith's arm, turned back. ''Why would reporters show any interest in a simple custody case?'' he asked Lon.

''Old son, there's nothing simple about this case now. It's a lallapalooza.''

He'd no sooner spoken than the door flew inward and reporters and cameramen streamed into the room. Ignoring the judge's admonition to leave immediately, the men and women stuck microphones in the faces of lawyers and clients alike.

Shelby Fielding shrank into her husband's side. Pushing at the microphone, she began to sob against Kipp's shoulder.

''Who leaked this information?'' Bob Schlegel roared.

''Good question,'' Michael echoed. Reaching for Faith, he sheltered her under his arm and began shoving his way through the mass of bodies toward the back door.

At a frantic call from the judge, policemen armed with nightsticks muscled their way into the room. "All right," one sergeant shouted. "This is private chambers. Let's clear the room."

A particularly determined fellow and his cameraman stuck close behind Michael and Faith. Out of breath, Michael handed Faith into the front seat of his car. "No comment," he growled after each question. "Get out from in front of my car, buddy, or I'll run you over."

"What's wrong with these people?" Faith gasped as the flashes blinded her. "Michael, we have to go back to the apartment. Gwen won't know anything about this. We can't have her opening the door and letting these jerks get pictures of the babies."

"Those chamber walls must have ears," Michael said. "There are always reporters hanging around a courthouse waiting for a big story."

Faith looked stricken. "Now they'll exploit the whole sordid mess leading up to Lacy's death." She covered her face with her hands to avoid being photographed by a woman who stepped off the curb as Michael wheeled the BMW around the corner of the courthouse.

His expression grim, Michael took the last corner on two wheels. Once they'd left the prying eyes behind, he slid an arm around Faith and pulled her against his shoulder. "The stories can't hurt Lacy now, sweetheart. My main concern is keeping you and the babies from being hurt."

Faith hauled in a deep breath. Michael's jacket smelled of wool and a light, earthy scent she'd come to connect with him…and with a feeling of safety. It was odd, given the volatility of their relationship till now, but she did trust Michael to make the right decisions when it came to protecting the babies. But could *anyone* protect them from the battle that was sure to heat up over the next three weeks?

CHAPTER TWELVE

GWEN LEAPED OFF THE COUCH as Faith and Michael let themselves in the front door and stripped off their coats. She bounced a twin on each hip. "My word, guys, I turned on the TV in time to hear your story break. There was a mob of reporters at the courthouse. The channel I watched tried to interview Kipp Fielding and his wife. His dad took a swing at a cameraman. How did you two escape the party?"

Faith dropped into a chair. "My knees are still shaking, Gwen. Those photographers are nuts. Michael almost ran over one who stepped in front of the car."

"The media types did seem obsessed. So, the lab found that the twins don't have the same father. A real bummer, huh? What'll happen to the kids?" she asked, handing one of the twins to Michael.

He kissed the baby's downy hair. "It's anyone's guess at this point," he said, heaving a sigh. "Everything's up in the air again."

"Sorry," Gwen interjected, "but aren't congratulations in order for you?"

Faith listened closely. She wanted to hear what Michael had to say, as he hadn't mentioned the DNA results on the way home.

He shrugged. "If you want the truth, I haven't had time to absorb it all."

"If you understand the findings, Gwen, maybe you

can explain," Faith said. "I'm skeptical. Only on rare occasions do some women release more than one egg. Why this time? Why Lacy?"

"I worked in endocrinology for a couple of years," Gwen said. "Extra eggs aren't all that uncommon. What's unusual is for the eggs to be fertilized by sperm from different men," she added dryly. "During the broadcast, one lawyer told a reporter the judge ordered your legal teams to consult with a reproductive expert. I say, good luck. In our clinic, the doctors couldn't even agree on how long eggs stay in the fallopian tubes. Some said three days. Others four. I should think a day could make a huge difference if these lawyers decide to get down and dirty."

"In what way?" Michael asked.

"To put it delicately, if they decide to make each man prove when the deed was done."

Faith took the other baby from Gwen and realized it was Nick. She wondered if Michael even realized he held Kipp's daughter and not his son. "That may have been an arguable point without the DNA, Gwen. But those results were conclusive. Besides, both men submitted depositions before the first hearing, listing the dates they and Lacy were intimate."

"Then what's the problem?" Gwen sounded puzzled. Collecting her purse and her sweater, she kissed each baby, hugged Faith and moved toward the door.

"I'm the problem," Faith said forthrightly. "Lacy signed over her custodial rights to me. And I take that responsibility seriously."

"You aren't totally to blame for the brouhaha, Faith," Michael reminded her. "Kipp's dad is demanding additional DNA testing. He thinks Nick, not Abigail, is his grandchild," he added for Gwen's benefit.

She stopped at the door. "Now who would care which child was theirs? They're both perfect little angels."

The phone rang before either Faith or Michael could respond to her statement.

"I know my way out," Gwen said. "Go catch your phone."

Michael deferred to Faith, since it was her phone. He walked Gwen to the door. "There may be reporters hanging around the main entrance. If you take the elevator all the way to the basement, there's a back door that opens into the parking lot. Try not to let anyone slip inside. That's assuming the media bird-dogs have found us."

"They have," Faith said. "That was a reporter on the phone." Even as she broke off speaking, the telephone rang again.

"Unplug it," Michael suggested. "Lon has my cell number. You can give it to Reed and also Fielding."

"Bye, guys. Sounds like you two have all you can handle." Gwen wiggled her fingers and stepped into the hall.

"Hey, thanks for baby-sitting," Faith called. "I owe you one."

"Honey, I'll collect if you ever get your life in order. Right now, I'd say you have more than enough to keep you busy." With that, she slipped out and closed the door.

Frowning at the insistent telephone, Faith disconnected it as Michael had urged. "How long do you suppose this will go on?"

"I don't want to sound negative, but probably until Judge Brown hands down a final decision."

"Three more weeks?" Faith blanched. "How will we

shop or get out to take the babies for walks in the park? Will I be followed again when I go to visit my dad?''

In a spontaneous move, Michael bent and kissed away the frown that creased Faith's forehead. ''Three weeks only gets us to the next hearing, sweetheart, which I'm afraid will turn out to be another round of arguments resulting in further delays.''

Slipping an arm around his waist, Faith leaned into him. The babies' chubby fingers entwined. Both seemed content to be held by adults they trusted. ''Judge Brown won't really separate them, will she, Michael?'' Faith asked worriedly.

''Separate them?'' Michael seemed to have lost his train of thought. In actuality, he felt more relaxed than at any time since he'd walked out on Faith and the twins last night. When they were together like this, their problems seemed to dwindle in scope.

Faith tipped back her head and searched Michael's face. ''You didn't hear Nancy Matz demand an open-and-shut case? You were sitting there when she proposed awarding Abigail to Kipp, and Nicholas to you. What did you *think* she meant?''

''I didn't hear her say that. I'll admit that after the judge read the DNA results, I was in a fog for a while. What was Kipp's reaction?''

''None that I recall. He and Shelby both seemed shell-shocked by the DNA reports. From what I observed, their attorneys couldn't agree among themselves. I'm hoping that'll be a strike against them with the judge.''

''What planet did that Matz woman fall from? What kind of person proposes separating twin infants for any reason?''

Faith's gaze cut back to the babies. ''If that seems to

be a serious possibility, I'd drop my case before I'd see them split up. I'd recommend they both go to Kipp and Shelby.''

"No." Reacting to the pain in her eyes and the tremor in her voice, Michael angled his head and settled his lips softly over hers. He meant it as a kiss to show support. Things changed when Faith's mouth opened under his. Desire, banked for too long, flamed out of control, triggering a restless longing in Michael. One impossible to quench while they each held a baby.

When Michael finally lifted his head, he discovered his free hand buried in Faith's feathery curls. Her eyes were closed, her breathing quickened—and it was all he could do not to kiss her again.

Faith, who hadn't realized she'd risen on her toes, dropped slowly back onto her heels. She opened her eyes and uncurled the fingers crushing Michael's lapel. Unable to stop a blush, she directed her attention to smoothing the fabric. "It's almost time to feed the babies, and here we are still in our dressy clothes.''

Michael exerted a little pressure on the back of Faith's head and forced her to meet his eyes. "It happened, Faith. We kissed and both felt the floor sway. You have to stop denying honest attraction.''

"Don't you mean lust?''

"Are you so sure it's not more than that?'' Michael continued to knead the tense muscles at the back of her neck.

She drew in a shaky breath. "We're trapped together in the middle of a combustible situation. Emotions run high.''

When Michael refused to make light of what had happened, Faith directed his gaze from her to the infants. "Ask yourself why you kissed me now, Michael. Can you honestly say it wasn't a result of our discussion involving the twins?''

"It was, but not in the way you mean. I share your pain and disappointment, Faith. When you hurt, I hurt. I can't speak plainer than that.''

Faith's smile was brittle and she knew it. A foolish part of her had hoped Michael might say he loved her. What was it about that silly little word that made it so important? In the next heartbeat she answered herself. If a man and a woman truly loved each other, all of life's problems could be conquered. Her parents had shared such a love, and they'd built a happy marriage, in spite of overwhelming odds. Darn it all, Faith wanted no less.

"I'm going to change into sweats,'' she said, handing Nick to Michael.

"Running away is another form of denial, Faith.'' Michael's cell phone rang before he launched a second barrage at her retreating back. Placing the twins in the playpen, he flipped open the phone. "Cameron here,'' he snapped, feeling on the verge of combustible, as Faith had kindly termed it. "Lon, hi,'' Michael expelled a breath. "Sorry I left you to fend off the piranhas. We had a sitter here at Faith's. I wanted to get home before reporters started bugging her.''

He listened a moment.

"Just Kipp and Shelby?'' Michael asked in response to Lon's information. Apparently the couple planned to swing by for an informal visit before they returned to New York.

"We can't very well stop them, can we, Lon? I mean, the judge gave everyone unlimited access.''

Faith reentered the room while he was still talking.

"Your lawyer?" she asked when he'd clicked off. Her stomach tightened as she waited for his reply.

"Kipp and Shelby are stopping here on their way out of town. They've been trying to phone, but of course we have the phone unplugged."

"What do they want?"

"To see Abigail, I guess. Shall we put her in a dress?" he asked, shoving his cell phone into a side pocket of the diaper bag.

Faith watched the babies batting at plush black-and-white cows tied to the slats of the playpen. Gwen must have brought them. "Abby's clean. She looks cute in that pink terry sleeper. And comfortable. Let's leave her."

"Okay." Michael walked over to the window. "There's a van from a local TV station parked out front. I'm going down to wait for the Fieldings in the lobby. We don't want reporters following them inside."

Faith had a bad feeling about this impromptu visit. "Why are you suddenly being so accommodating of our enemies?"

"Enemy? Kipp is Abigail's father."

As Faith watched the door close on Michael's heels, she leaned down and kissed both babies. Then she straightened the magazines on the coffee table and plumped the sofa pillows, wondering how she'd get through the visit.

The couple must have been in the area when Lon phoned. Michael was back all too quickly with Kipp and Shelby in tow.

They'd barely voiced stilted greetings when Kipp made a beeline for the playpen and picked Abby up. He sat on the couch. Instead of joining him, his wife perched on the chair farthest from the babies, and inspected her flawless fingernails.

Kipp stared at the baby for a long time, as if memorizing every feature. "I was hoping by now to recognize something of myself in her."

"She's the spitting image of Lacy," Faith blurted. On hearing a sharp hiss of air to her left, where Shelby Fielding sat, Faith guiltily twisted her mother's ring around her finger. She could have bitten her tongue.

A slow dawning of the truth flashed in Kipp's eyes seconds before he doused it and looked at his wife. "I read that children, even adopted ones, come to resemble the people who raise them," he stammered, seeking support from Michael and Faith.

They remained tense and silent, continuing to hover on either side of the playpen.

"Uh." Kipp cleared his throat. "I have a proposition for you, Cameron," he said, eyes locking with Michael's, closing Faith out.

"What kind of proposition?" Michael crossed his arms and widened his stance. He tried but failed to catch Faith's eye. Michael was pretty sure neither of them was going to like what the man had to say.

Kipp lowered his voice. "Take some time to consider what I'm proposing. I'm sure when you examine all the facets, you'll agree it's the best possible solution."

"Spit it out," growled Michael.

"All right. As you, Shelby and I all live in New York, I'm recommending my wife and I take both babies to live with us. You'd need a live-in au pair, anyway. Whenever you can escape work, it'd be a simple matter of coming by to pick up the boy."

Michael practically tripped over his tongue in his

haste to answer. "What gives you the idea I'd ever agree to such an arrangement?"

Kipp smiled. "My dad is your partner's stockbroker. Dominic is floundering without you. If you don't go back soon, your clinic will collapse. Understand, we aren't asking to adopt Nick. If, after the twins are older, you find more time in your schedule, it'll be easy enough to move him in with you. Under my plan, the siblings can eventually attend the same private school. Last, but not least, family courts generally place children with a couple when faced with an either-or choice. Since the babies technically belong to you and me, if we can reach some kind of terms, it'd save everyone time and expense. Judge Brown pitched a fit over the media blitz. I'd bet big bucks she'll rubber-stamp any reasonable system you and I work out."

Faith couldn't believe how neatly he'd cut her out of the triangle. Frozen inside, she finally dared to look at Michael. She expected, no, prayed he'd be gearing up to explode. The icy knot in her stomach froze even tighter. Michael calmly stroked his chin with a thumb and forefinger. He appeared to be considering Kipp's deal. But why shouldn't he? Faith thought numbly. After all, she'd said she'd bow out rather than separate the twins. Until this very minute, she hadn't a clue how impossibly hard that would be. The room swelled and receded as her world slowly crumbled.

"Tell you what. Give me some time to weigh the pros and cons." Michael aimed a polite smile at Shelby Fielding. "Does Kipp's proposal meet with your approval?"

The woman hesitated too long, in Faith's opinion. But when Shelby did at last issue a scratchy "ye-es,"

Michael apparently found it satisfactory. Otherwise he wouldn't have extended his hand to Kipp.

Whatever else passed between the two Fieldings and Michael escaped Faith. She felt sucked into a muddy vortex. She was vaguely aware of Michael walking the couple to the door. She might have managed a cordial goodbye, or maybe not. The first real emotion that registered after her stomach hit bottom was when Michael struck the living-room wall with a fist, exclaiming, "That pompous son of a bitch!"

Faith's head reeled. She flinched, listening to the inventive curses rolling off Michael's tongue as he paced the room.

"But you treated them so civilly," she gasped. "Why…why didn't you tell him no?"

"Because while he was spouting off, I devised a plan of my own."

"What kind of plan?"

"I…well, never mind. It has a few snags I'll need to work out. We'll talk about it later. Maybe over dinner, after I have time to fill in some of the holes."

"Holes or not, it can't be any worse than Kipp's preposterous plan," Faith insisted, pausing to try and read in his eyes whether his unnamed idea was as one-sided as Kipp's. "I'm not going to like this, either, am I?" she asked, tensing at the nervous way Michael scraped his fingers through his hair.

Both babies, who'd been quietly contented up to now, kicked unhappily and began to squall, allowing Michael a reprieve.

"I'll fix their bottles," Faith said over the din.

Michael scooped the two infants into his arms. "When do they get real food?" he asked, the query coming out of left field.

"Dr. Sampson prefers to start cereal at three months. Maybe later for these guys, since they were premature."

In the flurry of activity centered on changing diapers and preparing to feed two hungry babies, Faith forgot about Michael's plan. What stuck in her mind was something Kipp had said. It surfaced again when she and Michael were settled on the couch, each feeding a baby. "Michael, your clinic isn't really in danger of folding, is it? I mean, you are keeping in contact with your partner."

"Yeah. Dominic's called a number of times."

"So, then Kipp was lying? Or else his dad?"

"Dom may well have complained. My partner goes through a lot of money. He's a confirmed bachelor and switches girlfriends every few months. A guy like that can't fathom why I'd leave a booming practice to spend time with crying babies." Michael grinned. "They were crying every time Dominic phoned."

"Kipp got the story right in another sense, too, I guess," she said. "I never stopped to think, but technically you are just on holiday."

"Where's this conversation leading, Faith? Have I ever implied otherwise?" Michael's dark eyes pinned hers.

"No. No, you haven't," she agreed readily.

"So what's troubling you? I can almost hear the wheels turning."

Faith changed gears without blinking. "Did you ever want to do anything other than be a surgeon?"

Michael laughed. "Sure. When I was six I wanted to be a priest."

That was probably the last career Faith would have expected. But at six… He was probably pulling her leg. "Huh. I'll bet that notion didn't last long."

"Until I was fourteen."

"Really? Fourteen? What happened then to change your mind?"

"Well, my dad caught me necking on the porch swing with a sixteen-year-old neighbor girl. He said with the interest I showed in anatomy, I ought to spend my free time in his office learning to be a doctor. Then he proceeded to lecture me on sex and celibacy. I knew, of course, that priests were celibate. I suspect I gleaned enough about the female anatomy during my swing encounter with Tammy Hurley to decide on a new career path then and there."

"Yeah, right," Faith snorted. Lifting a sleepy Abby to her shoulder, she drummed her fingers lightly on the baby's back, trying to get her to burp. "How long before you and Tammy found a more private place to finish that anatomy course?"

"We didn't." Michael let his son slurp down the last of an eight-ounce bottle. Burping had never been a problem for Nicholas. He let out a big one, then closed his eyes. "This kid's ready to crash. I'm going to stick him in the crib. I'll turn on the monitor, so all you have to do when Abby finally burps is put her down."

As though she didn't want to take a back seat to her brother, Abby emitted three in a row. "I'll go with you," Faith said. "That way I won't risk waking Nicholas later."

The babies still slept together in one crib because they preferred it. Michael placed Nick down first and covered him with a blanket. While Faith settled Abigail, Michael flipped on the monitor, which allowed them to hear the babies from the other room.

Faith led the way to the door. She realized Michael hadn't followed and turned back to see why not. Hands thrust into the pockets of his suit pants, he stood gazing at the sleeping babies. A raw look of love softened his masculine features. "Is everything all right?" Faith whispered. Michael's expression had triggered a coiled ache in her abdomen.

Michael pulled one hand from his pocket and motioned Faith toward him. He slipped the same hand around her shoulder once she stood beside him. "Look at the way Abigail burrows against Nicholas," he murmured. "Have you noticed that their heads and arms always touch when they sleep? I defy anyone to look at this picture and say they should be separated."

"I have film in the camera. Maybe I ought to take some snapshots for the court record," Faith said, resting her own head on Michael's broad shoulder.

"Yes, do," he urged. "There's no way anyone with a heart could see how attached they are and then turn around and split them up."

Good sense told Faith that in the case of three people vying for two small babies, someone had to lose. Not wanting to burst Michael's optimistic bubble, she padded off to get her camera.

Michael was obviously stressed by some worry of his own. He barely said two words during their meal of tangy, taco-baked potatoes and small garden salads that Faith prepared after she'd used an entire roll of film on the babies.

Watching Michael toy with the cheesy topping on his baked potato, Faith decided he must be more worried about the situation at the clinic than he'd let on. It had become easy to forget that either of them might ever have to return to demanding jobs. The fact remained that the long, erratic hours Michael spent attending to patients had been the catalyst for Lacy's leaving him.

It hadn't taken Kipp Fielding long to figure that out and capitalize on Michael's hectic life.

It hurt too much to think about strangers raising her sister's babies. Realistically, Faith knew that was what would happen if the court gave Abby and Nick to their fathers. Neither man was ever home. Although, maybe Shelby would eventually come to love the twins—one or both of them. After all, as Gwen had said, who wouldn't lose their hearts once they got to know these precious little ones?

A dish Faith had always loved and looked forward to fixing suddenly seemed tasteless. Excusing herself, Faith rose and scraped her food into the trash.

Michael wasn't any more able to eat than she was. "Something has to give, Faith," he said, joining her in clearing the table. "Do you agree we can't go on the way we are?"

Faith gripped the edge of the sink, and her throat jammed so she couldn't speak, could only nod.

Michael gathered her hands and turned her around. "At the risk of sounding like Fielding did earlier, I'd like you to listen to me, Faith. Don't interrupt until I finish, then you can have your say."

A ripple of hope coursed through her body, followed by a shiver of fear. Faith did her best, nevertheless, to muster a smile. "I'm trying hard not to be scared, Michael. But I've rarely seen you this intense."

He rubbed his thumbs over the white knuckles of her hands. One at a time, he lifted her narrow hands and pressed a reassuring kiss into each palm. He was grateful that she came easily into his arms. That way he could bury his face in her sweet-smelling neck and not have to face a refusal he was awfully afraid would show first in her eyes.

Faith settled comfortably with an ear to Michael's chest. She had no idea what he was about to spring on her. Nestled in his arms like this, she thought even the most horrible news would be palatable. Her lips quirked in a smile as the first strains of his deep voice rumbled beneath her ear.

"There was one thing Kipp said that grabbed me and refused to let go. Do you remember how he sounded so positive about the court placing the twins with a couple rather than a single parent?" Michael laid a row of kisses along her ear.

Faith stilled, taking comfort for a moment in the steady beat of Michael's heart. She fingered the points of his crisp shirt collar. "Kipp was making a case to suit himself. According to David, the judge will study a range of factors before rendering a decision. Lon must have told you we all have strong points."

Michael's arms tightened around her. "I asked you to listen, Faith."

"Then stop asking me questions," she scolded softly, reveling in the comfort of being held. Hugs had been infrequent in Faith's life.

"But suppose a married couple does look like the better option?"

Faith knew to keep quiet this time. Michael had made it clear he wanted to work through to his conclusion without interruption.

"If I was the one deciding, I might think two people were more capable of caring for two children," he said. "I read the report Burgess and Lang submitted. More than once they praised us for working together."

Loosening his hold, Michael ran his palms in lazy eights over Faith's back. She practically purred and hoped he'd continue.

"What I'm getting at, Faith is straightforward. If we were married, we'd actually look better than Kipp and Shelby. You *are* their aunt, and both of us have experience taking care of the twins, while they have none. What do you think?"

In a stupefied corner of her brain, Faith realized that this time Michael expected some response. She lifted her head. Still, he held her so tightly she couldn't see past his chin. "I'm sure you think you've hit on the perfect solution. But, Michael, I haven't even dated anyone in over a year. Maybe it's easy for you to snap your fingers and come up with a wife. In fact, it probably is." Faith's stomach dived again as she wriggled out of his arms and said in a shaky voice, "Whoever she is, she'd better be sincere about wanting children. Judge Brown doesn't strike me as someone easily fooled."

Michael's face went through various stages of shock before sinking into dismay. He doubled back over what he'd said and how it had come out so wrong. He saw now where he'd made his mistake. Slipping an arm around Faith's stubbornly rigid shoulders, he navigated her into the living room. There, he turned her and pressed her onto the couch. Sinking down on one knee, he again gathered both of her hands. "Faith, honey," he said, with only the most minimal tremor, "I meant that we should marry each other."

"Each other?" Faith practically swallowed the question. Disengaging one hand, she pointed first to herself, then to Michael and back to herself again. Words failed her completely this time.

A smile finally kicked up one corner of Michael's mouth. He managed to nod before he placed a hand on either side of her and leaned forward to capture her lips in a reassuring heartfelt kiss.

The kiss went on and on. Michael followed her lips when Faith toppled backward into the soft cushions.

She tried and failed to get a grip on her senses. At some point, without even being aware of it, she kicked off her shoes. It seemed as if his kisses burned everywhere, from the top of her head to the soles of her feet. Cradled in his arms, she felt her entire body tingle in anticipation of *more* than kissing and being kissed.

Married. Such a beautiful word. It tumbled around and around inside Faith's head, gathering hope. It had been several years since she'd allowed herself to think, to plan, to dream about a husband. About walking down the aisle at the church in Marblehead, where her parents had begun their married life. Oh...Michael probably wouldn't want a church wedding. He'd been content to marry Lacy in her dreary hospital room.

Now that the niggling worry had wormed its way into her mind, Faith thought it quite likely that she and Michael had widely differing views concerning this possible marriage. The word *love* had not crossed his lips. Of course, she'd been rather dense about his proposal at first and after that, his lips had kept her mind on his kisses.

Ooh, and now he was doing remarkable things with his mouth against her bare breast. *Did love matter, after all?* she wondered as she tunneled her fingers deep within the satiny strands of his thick hair.

The thoughts spinning in Faith's head soon gave way to feelings. Feelings she'd flirted with a few times, but mostly had only imagined. The few times the accountant had slept over at her apartment, their fleeting encounters had been nothing like this.

Michael's skin felt slick and soft—on his arms and shoulders and where it stretched over his muscled back and narrow hips. His palms were warm and heavenly on the inside of her thighs. One of his thumbs edged higher until it caressed her moist panties. Faith wanted to weep. She did cry out and felt as though she'd been caught in a downward spiral.

At that moment, she didn't think anything in the world could possibly compare. Especially when his searing kisses moved down her body, and his hands slipped behind her, lifting until he gently removed the cotton barrier and covered her with his mouth.

"Is this your first time?" he murmured.

Unable to speak at first, Faith shook her head. Then she found her voice. "No. But it's been a long while." She was a mature woman, and a nurse. Faith knew the facts of life. Yet she couldn't believe what Michael was doing with his tongue.

He blew softly on her stomach and groaned. "Ah, Faith…"

Faith writhed beneath his mouth. Could a man who wasn't in love do this to a woman? Michael's lips wreaked pure torture. Pure rapture. In a tiny still-functioning corner of her brain, Faith envisioned herself and Michael spending a lifetime of nights like this.

Gwen said babies invariably decided to cry and interrupt their parents during lovemaking. Faith listened carefully but heard nothing except the babies' soft breathing on the monitor. Nothing except the pounding of Michael's heart and then her own moan of pleasure as, moments later, she flew apart.

Michael, her lover. *Could life get more perfect?*

CHAPTER THIRTEEN

THE DISTANT SOUND OF a crying baby prodded Faith awake. The room was black. Normally at night she could see the night-light in the nursery, so either she hadn't turned it on or it'd burned out. She started to get up but was stopped by a heavy restraint across her middle. A moment's panic abated as the memory of how she'd spent the preceding hours filtered into Faith's sleepy brain. Fondly she recalled being initiated into numerous new ways of love and then falling asleep in Michael's arms.

That was why she couldn't see a night-light. This was the living-room couch and not her bed. Michael lay on his side facing her, an arm pinning her to the back cushions. She ached from lying in the same position all night. Well, that was only part of the reason she ached, Faith thought with a blush and a smile as she eased out from beneath Michael's arm.

AN INSISTENT NOISE—crying—penetrated Michael's sleep-fogged brain. He lifted his head and squinted at his watch. Four-thirty according to the night dial. He didn't stop to wonder why he was naked except for his watch. His mind only grasped the fact that the twins had slept for a good long stretch. Michael eased oddly tight muscles. That was when it began to dawn—his limbs were tangled with another pair. Smooth, cool legs and a soft warm body. "Lacy?" he murmured, far from being fully awake.

The body beside him had been stirring, too, slipping away from him. Suddenly it stilled, and a light snapped on, blinding Michael. Behind the harsh glare, a voice filled with pain, answered him. "Faith. Not Lacy. How could you, Michael? How could you?"

His bed partner scrambled over top of him. Michael watched her grab clothes from the coffee table and the floor, stirring a cool breeze across his naked backside. Emitting the cry of an injured animal, Faith exited the room in a flash of bare legs.

Recollection of the night flooded back. An incredible, incredible night. It had come on the heels of their latest custody hearing, followed by an infuriating visit from Fielding, the arrogant bastard.

Michael struggled to sit up. It had been weeks— months maybe—since he'd slept so soundly. More awake now, his question from minutes before kicked him in the heart like a Missouri mule. God, yes, he was awake. Michael groaned and scrambled to find his pants. Faith's unhappiness as she fled the room flowed over him and hammered in his blood. *How could he,* was right. How could he call her by another woman's name after the wonderful way, the welcoming and giving way, she'd received him last night?

"Cameron, you ought to be shot," he muttered as he stumbled out to find Faith. He hadn't dreamed of Lacy in months. Not even in the unsettled days after she'd divorced him. Not even after her death. So what in hell possessed him to say her name and ruin the fragile trust he'd finally won from Faith?

"Faith?" She didn't answer, but Michael saw her rocking the babies in the nursery rocking chair. The light of a waning moon silvered noiseless tears that coursed down her cheeks. Both babies sucked on their fingers. Michael knew they needed bottles. He'd get them, but not until he made an effort to explain to Faith something he didn't understand himself.

"You're not a substitute for Lacy, if that's what's running through your mind," he said urgently. "You're the only woman I've been with since my divorce, Faith." His voice pulsed with emotion as he spoke.

The rocking never slowed, nor did Faith look at him or acknowledge his presence in any other way.

"I was half-asleep, Faith! Tell me—what more do you want from me?"

She buried her head in one of the babies' necks. Abby's, Michael thought. "I already explained that my relationship with Lacy was going down the tubes before we split up." Michael knew she had to be taking this in. Stepping closer, he emphasized his appeal with outstretched hands. "My getting Lacy pregnant was a fluke. She initiated sex that day only because she thought I'd come home early to take her to a party. She went ballistic when she found out I'd come to pack for another medical expedition. We hadn't slept in the same bed for three months, I swear. Dammit, Faith, look at me. It's important that you believe me."

He gave up when both twins started to wail. Time. She needed time to work this through. Once she did, she'd be fair. That was just one of the many things he loved about Faith. She didn't harbor grudges.

Faith heard Michael rattling around the kitchen and assumed he was preparing bottles for the twins. She didn't know why she was acting so…so childish. Michael had never said he loved her. His marriage proposal had been more of a business deal, along the lines of the plan presented by Kipp Fielding. Now that she thought about it, she recalled Michael's saying, after Kipp had left, that he had his own plan to win the custody suit.

Kissing the babies, Faith rocked harder. Michael had never promised her love. At the most, he candidly pointed out a shared attraction. A new trickle of tears squeezed from beneath her closed eyelids. It was her own silly dream that made her want more. She loved these babies and she loved Michael. She wanted them to be a real family.

Michael walked back into the nursery carrying two bottles. Faith wished he'd taken time to put on a shirt. If they were going to make a success of his business proposal, she had to keep a level head.

"Do you want to feed Abby or Nick?" she asked. These were her first words after shedding copious tears and her voice was hoarse.

"It doesn't matter which. You do know that, don't you, Faith? I don't love Nick more than Abigail because he shares my blood."

So, the word love *was* in Michael's vocabulary. He wasn't like some men who could never utter the word. She handed him Nick, anyway, and busied herself settling Abby in the crook of her arm. "I saw something in your face the first day you held them at the hospital, Michael," she said quietly. "I knew then that they'd both found a home in your heart."

"They did." He sat on the carpeted floor and leaned against one of the dressers. After testing the bottle on the inside of his wrist, he offered it to Nick.

Dawn began to spill first light into the colorful room. The primary colors were soothing to Michael, as was listening to the rhythmic sucking of the babies. His babies. He thought about the night he'd spent making love to the woman he envisioned spending the next fifty years with. That filled his heart with a sense of peace. It came to him, then, that he'd been walking a precarious tightrope between his marriage to Lacy and his work for a lot longer than he'd realized. His life had lacked balance. Whatever had been the cause—his fast climb to the top of the prominent community of specialists or Lacy's growing dissatisfaction with his involvement in his work—Michael didn't intend to repeat his mistakes. He'd find more hours to spend with Faith. It was time to make changes in his life. He didn't want to miss these all-too-fleeting moments with his family.

His family. A term that held no meaning without Faith. Alarm edged out the feeling of peace. Did Faith seem mellower? Maybe he ought to give her more time, but something inside warned Michael to act now. "My timing probably stinks, Faith. But you didn't answer my question last night."

Her eyes met Michael's and skittered away quickly. "We should have done more talking."

"I'm not complaining." There was a smile in his voice.

Faith sighed. "Nor am I, Michael. Let's start over."

Her statement started the blood pumping through his veins again. "Will you marry me?"

Faith rocked forward and back and forward again. The only other movement she made was to stroke Abigail's ear and cheek and silky hair. "On paper, Michael. I'll marry you on paper."

"On paper?" Michael scowled. "What the hell does that mean?"

"It means I'll fill out the forms at a justice of the

peace. In the eyes of the court, we'll legally be husband and wife. That's all.''

Maybe he hadn't slept as well as he thought. Michael had trouble understanding Faith's terse little speech. Or…maybe not. He was afraid he knew exactly what she was saying. "I want more," he said softly. Gruffly. "I want our marriage to be real.''

Oh, so do I. Faith's lips trembled. So did her hands. And her heart cracked and bled into a chest already filled with pain. "Those are my terms, Michael. If we don't win custody we'll have an annulment. In the interim, there'll be no repeat of last night.''

"Last night was good," he said lamely. He had to fight the pressure of tears at the backs of his eyes.

"Nick's finished his bottle," Faith chided. "You're letting him suck air.''

Michael tipped the bottle up fast. As he hoisted his son to his shoulder, he noticed the sheen reflecting off Faith's eyes. He'd won his point for now. Any fool could see she hadn't recovered from the blow he'd dealt her in accidentally calling her by her sister's name. He'd make it up to her if he had to work at it a lifetime. Which he had every intention of doing.

He would have started his quest then and there had his cell phone not bleated unceasingly until he extracted the instrument from the diaper bag and flipped it open. "Dominic?" Michael fumbled the phone and the baby, whose back arched as Nicholas burped and pooped simultaneously. "Hold on a minute, Dom." Michael climbed to his feet, trying to shuffle the phone to the hollow of one shoulder.

Taking pity on him, Faith rose gracefully and took the baby from his arms. "I'll change him. Talk to your partner.''

Michael did, but he watched how deftly Faith dispatched diapers. "All right, Dominic, calm down. Admit Cynthia to I.C.U. Put her on the usual monitors. If you think she's rejecting the heart, she probably is. I can be there in two hours. You know the routine—bump her to the top of the emergency list. I left my medical bag at the apartment. If you'll go by and pick it up, I'll tell my housekeeper to have it ready. See you at Mercy General. Tell Cyn I'm on my way." He clicked off and turned to Faith.

"I heard. You have an emergency, Michael. Go. I'll be fine."

"Who'll help with the babies?"

"I'm quite recovered, Michael. I really can do this without help. It's what I intended before you moved in next door."

"But…" The ravages of indecision accentuated the deep creases bracketing his mouth.

Faith waved him away. Bending, she blew a kiss on Nick's exposed belly. The baby laughed out loud, galvanizing Faith and Michael with the thrilling sound.

"Oh-oh," Faith exclaimed delightedly. "I'll have to log that in his baby book. He's giggled some, but I think this is his first real laugh."

Michael held out a hand to the babies. They not only followed his movement with their eyes, each latched on to one of his fingers. "I'll call you tonight," he promised Faith. He didn't want to leave them. Not any of them, but most especially Faith. "Cynthia Fitzhugh was my first dual-organ transplant after I set up practice in New York. It was a near-perfect match. She shouldn't be rejecting."

"So go find out why she is," Faith said gently.

"That's your work and you're good at it, Michael Cameron."

He pulled his fingers away from the babies and leaned down to kiss Faith goodbye. She saw his intention and turned, so his lips barely skimmed her jaw. He knew then that he had a long way to go to dig himself out of the hole he'd fallen into this morning. From experience, he knew how difficult that was to do long-distance.

Still, he had no choice. He'd taken a healer's oath. "I *will* telephone," he said again as he strode out of the nursery. Within minutes he was gone, leaving nothing behind but the faint scent of Lagerfeld that Faith always associated with Michael.

By nightfall, even that small trace was gone. He didn't call, even though Faith had plugged in the phone again and suffered through too many calls from obnoxious reporters. What had she expected? That Michael would somehow be different from other doctors who buried themselves in their work to the exclusion of all else? That he would change his life for her when he hadn't done so for Lacy?

As midnight came and went, Faith sat alone and lonely, staring out the window at a dark, rain-soaked landscape. She'd had her first taste of how Lacy must have felt the many nights she called just to talk. To connect with another voice, she'd said.

Unlike her sister, Faith wasn't one to wallow in self-pity.

Next day, the storm had passed. She bundled the babies, put them in their stroller and headed for the library. She'd no sooner set foot out the door than reporters climbed from two different vehicles and boxed her neatly between them.

"We knew you'd surface one of these days," the younger of the two men announced.

"I'm not making any comment with regard to the case," Faith told them both.

"Did you read the story in the morning paper?" The older man flipped open his notebook and read to Faith from notes he'd obviously jotted down. "According to a news flash out of New York, Kipp Fielding's lawyer declared his client and Dr. Cameron have joined forces against you."

"That's not true," Faith exclaimed. As soon as she'd spoken, she wished she could take back her words. Especially when both men turned to clean pages on their pads, overt interest in their eyes. "I'm not saying anything else. If you want to know my position, talk to my attorney, David Reed."

"We've talked to the lawyers. Schlegel, Schlegel and Matz went over Judge Brown's head yesterday and got her visitation edict changed. Superior Court Judge Reuben Kline overturned Brown's decision. Kline has ordered you to travel to New York with the babies once a week. Cameron's attorney said they couldn't be happier, since the doctor has now returned to his practice. I suppose Reed plans to counter?"

Faith's head spun. Was Michael aware of this? Was that why he hadn't called? If all along he'd planned to side with Kipp, she had certainly played the fool. It was plain what Maxwell could do, if Michael revealed how easily she'd fallen into bed with him.

Her breakfast of toast and coffee threatened to come up. David had once said that Bob Schlegel could neutralize her position by discrediting Lacy. What stopped them from applying the same "loose woman" label to her?

Even if she countered and insisted that Michael had proposed marriage, it'd be her word against his. The sick feeling returned.

"Hey!" the young reporter called as Faith whirled around and walked quickly back to her apartment building. "So far all of you are letting the lawyers run this case. John Q. Public cares about what happens to those kids. They're calling our office in droves. If you play your cards right, Ms. Hyatt, you could probably come up with a book or movie deal. This is the hottest news on the Eastern Seaboard."

"No comment," she muttered, grateful the door opened without a hitch today. Some days, especially following a rain, the door tended to stick.

Upstairs again, she peeled the twins out of their jackets and placed them in the playpen. She picked up the receiver, but the phone rang before she could dial out. It was David calling her.

"What's going on over there, Faith? I couldn't get through to you all morning."

"I unplugged the phone. I've been plagued by reporters. But you're the person I was about to call. Why do I need to travel to New York with the twins every week?"

"So you read today's newspaper? Dammit, Faith, I might have seen it coming and thrown up a roadblock if you'd told me Cameron went back to New York."

"He only left yesterday. His partner at the clinic called with an emergency. One of Michael's patients."

"Huh, probably a lie he and Maxwell concocted to get the ball back in their court."

"What do you mean?" Faith had to sit. Her knees buckled.

"I mean they're making you haul the babies into their

territory because it gives them an advantage, a chance to work a deal. Next they'll say that two of the three principals reside in New York, so the hearings should be moved there. If that happens, it cuts our chances of winning.''

Faith's pulse thundered in her ears. "What do you foresee happening?''

"The truth? My guess is Dr. Cameron will get the boy and Fielding the girl.''

"Nicholas and Abigail,'' Faith snapped. "They have names, David,'' she said, sniffling and blinking furiously.

"Yeah, well, that could change, too. Everything could go topsy-turvy. Kipp's father wants the DNA repeated. That man's ruthless. Cameron's a fool to climb into bed with them. Those old Wall Street types have no scruples. Money greases any wheel, if you get my drift. Next thing you know, the first DNA tests will be declared invalid, and Fielding has himself a grandchild.''

The more Faith listened to David, the more certain she was some mistake had occurred. "You aren't giving Michael credit. He'd never allow that. He agrees with me that it'd be horrible to separate the twins. Hasn't Mr. Fielding seen the studies? Even as adults, most of the twins who were separated as babies said they felt a piece of themselves was missing.''

"The man wants his own flesh and blood, regardless. You have to stop being so gullible, Faith. Cameron has his own agenda. I'll admit those twin studies may be our best defense. If we can keep the case in Boston Family Court, odds are we'll get a fair hearing. But I've got to tell you, the way things have gone in the past two days doesn't bode well.''

Faith hardened her heart. "I'm not paying for gloom and doom, David. We have right on our side. Now, when do I have to transport the babies to New York? And where do we go after I get there?"

"The first visitation is tomorrow." He gave her the address of the Fielding estate. "I believe you know where Cameron lives. Their attorneys have requested the babies spend a full hour at each residence. I'm sorry, Faith, but you'll need to fulfill your obligation this one time, anyway. I've filed a counter that, in essence, says with fall weather turning to winter soon, the new order places an undue hardship on the infants."

"What about the hardship it places on me? I have to take the train because I don't have a car."

"I tried to play down that aspect. We don't want Schlegel or Maxwell challenging your position as temporary custodian. Frankly, the longer the babies remain in your care, the more pressure a judge will feel to leave them be. I'm drafting something now that says the kids are getting used to their surroundings, et cetera."

"I hope it works." Faith couldn't help feeling anxious, given present circumstances.

"I'll phone tomorrow night and let you know how my appeal's been received. Kline is a tough judge. But I happen to know he has five grandchildren he dotes on. I'm not above making a few comparisons to tug at his heartstrings."

"All right, David. I'll be waiting to hear. I'm not exactly sure of the train schedules, but I'll go early and try to be home before dark. I'll call you, okay? Remember I have my phone unplugged. Because of the reporters."

"Nothing like a good court bloodbath involving kids to stir a media frenzy. Plus, half the world knows this could be a trend-setting case. That's why all the lawyers have been interviewed on CNN. We're all in negotiations to appear on *Larry King Live*. It's a good thing you aren't answering your phone. They'll be after you, Kipp and Michael, too. But you should refuse.''

"Why would *you* appear? The media only wants to exploit innocent babies.''

"Remember at the beginning I told you we had a hot case? Those DNA results upped the temperature. Whichever lawyer or legal team wins—hey, he'll be writing his own ticket. Ours isn't the first case of its kind, but it has unique features.''

"I had no idea there were any similar situations.''

"Yes, well, this quite possibly is the first twins-with-different-dads battle where the biological mother doesn't factor in.''

"If Lacy had lived, the court wouldn't be so eager to split up the twins, I'll bet," Faith murmured, unable to hide the sad tremor in her voice.

"At least she had the foresight to appoint you her surrogate stand-in. Which has given me an idea for another angle. I'll do my best to see Judge Kline tomorrow." He paused. "We should conduct our next strategy session in person. Leave my name with your building manager. I'll drop by around seven or eight. Good luck in New York, Faith. Don't let the men intimidate you.''

"No, I won't," she murmured. But David had already hung up. Leaving the receiver off the hook, she sat for some time watching the babies kick and coo. Nick tried several times to turn over. Faith didn't expect him to succeed, and when he did, she grinned and clapped spontaneously. She sobered as she realized she'd been wishing Michael was here to see Nick's big accomplishment.

"Oh, Michael," she sobbed, covering her face with her hands. "Oh, Michael." *I know you don't care for me the way I care for you. But I believed you when you said you loved Nick and Abigail equally. I really thought they were hearts and souls to you, not biological oddities or...or some stupid test case.*

IN SPITE OF A SLEEPLESS NIGHT, Faith was determined to look her best and brightest when presenting herself in New York. Unfortunately, the logistics of transporting two babies for two hours by train had her rethinking her plan to wear a dress. In the end, she changed into comfortable drawstring pants and sneakers. She wore a cardigan sweater over a cotton T-shirt. Instead of taking the stroller, she placed Abby in a front pack and Nick in a backpack she'd been given at her shower. That left her hands free to carry the monster diaper bag. Faith also dispensed with a purse. She tucked her ID and money into one of the bag's pockets and had to smile. No mugger would steal a lumpy diaper bag.

The train ride was actually quite pleasant. A baby always managed to coax good humor from the grumpiest of the grumpy. Two babies who'd just discovered their own ability to smile and flirt garnered much more than twice the interest. She was careful to conceal the children's identity, though. It had taken a bit of ingenuity to sneak out of the apartment house and bypass the reporters who hung around the front entrance. There were even more of them today than yesterday. It still shocked her that so many people found their case riveting. But then, when it came to this case, Faith was thrown off balance a lot.

She allowed herself the luxury of taking a cab to the Fielding address. It was awkward traveling by car without the infant carriers. She buckled in securely, sitting well forward on the seat, and left the babies in their respective packs. Both were fussy. They needed changing and it was time to eat. Faith hated the fact that Kipp and Shelby wouldn't be seeing the twins at their best. On the other hand, maybe if they discovered the babies weren't always perfect, they might have second thoughts about their vigorous pursuit.

Faith's cab pulled into the massive circular driveway at the same time Shelby Fielding slipped behind the wheel of a sleek Jaguar parked in front of the three-story brick home. The woman saw Faith, frowned, climbed out of the Jag again and drummed her fingers on the roof of the automobile.

"What are you doing here?" Shelby demanded, when it appeared obvious that Faith had paid her driver and was set to dismiss the cab.

Jiggling the now loudly crying babies, Faith wasn't inclined to be generous. "As if you didn't know your lawyers and Michael's overturned Judge Brown's visitation ruling! I'm complying with the latest court order—making the requisite weekly visit to your home."

Shelby paled underneath her layer of carefully applied makeup. "You must be mistaken. Kipp left yesterday for a race in Antigua. He'll be gone a week and a half." She inspected a diamond-encrusted watch and exclaimed, "If I don't leave this minute, I'll be late for my final evaluation at the fertility clinic."

"Fertility…" Faith hurried around the front of the Jag and backed Shelby against the car. "I've ridden two-plus hours with two restless babies. One of whom was fathered by your husband. If this is some kind of passive-aggressive game you and he are playing, I'd appreciate being dealt out of it.''

Color flared across Shelby's narrow cheekbones. ''Kipp wouldn't have set something up like this and expected me to handle it. He wouldn't.'' In jerky motions, she extracted a cell phone from her Donald Pliner handbag and punched in a series of numbers.

Meanwhile, Faith did her best to quiet the babies, who'd joined in a crying chorus.

Shelby tapped the toe of the strappy heels that matched her purse. ''This is Shelby Fielding,'' she said haughtily in a tone suggesting she was someone special. ''Put me through to Bob Schlegel immediately.''

Faith patted Abigail's back and made soothing sounds over her shoulder at Nick.

''Bob, thank heavens, I caught you,'' Shelby exclaimed, sounding for all the world as if she meant it. ''The Hyatt woman has arrived at my home with the twins. Kipp's out of town.'' She paused in the middle of her hysterical outburst and listened to the masculine drone on the other end of the line.

''You mean to tell me Kipp isn't aware you overturned the original visitation order? No. That's impossible, Bob. I have an appointment. In fact, I'm late. I can't cancel and entertain her for an hour. All right. All right. I'll give her a lift to Dr. Cameron's apartment. Yes,'' she said in meeker tones. ''I understand Kipp is paying you a lot of money to do a job for him. But you can't expect us to comply with a decree we didn't know about.'' The scowl she wore when she clicked off soon blossomed into a placating smile.

''There's been a mix-up on our side, Ms Hyatt. Bob thought Keith had informed Kipp and me of the change. The news fell through the cracks, I'm afraid. Today the twins will only be visiting Dr. Cameron. Hop in. I'll run you by his place.''

Faith knew that if she said what she felt like saying, she'd be the one who ended up looking bad. She held her tongue for the short ride to Michael's building, even though buckling her and the bulky baby-packs into the sports car proved to be harder than in the cab. Plus, not even the car's movement appeased the wet and hungry infants.

Shelby swung close to the curb outside Michael's luxury complex. She didn't cut the engine, but tapped shell-pink fingernails restlessly on the steering wheel.

''Did Mr. Schlegel know for certain that Dr. Cameron's home?'' Faith craned her neck and eyed the upper windows, all of which looked dark. Michael could be in his den. Faith knew from past visits that it faced the opposite street. ''Could you wait while I ask the doorman if he's home?'' she murmured, leaning back inside the car to haul out the diaper bag she'd wedged by her feet.

''I went out of my way to bring you here. I'm going to learn the results of my latest procedure, and I'm already late. Look, I'm sorry. I really must go.''

Faith slammed the door and jumped back from the curb to avoid the backdraft from the car's muffler. ''Thanks for nothing,'' she muttered, hunching to hoist Nicholas higher on her back as the Jag roared out of sight.

The doorman wasn't one Faith had ever met. Of course, it'd been more than a year since she'd been to the Cameron suite.

''Dr. Cameron did not leave word to expect a person with two babies,'' the man said. The nasal way he said *person* made Faith feel as if she was in the same category as the garbage collector. Or perhaps the garbage itself.

"Will you ring his apartment, please? The babies need attention. Even if Michael isn't home, I'm sure Mrs. Parker will authorize a visit. Tell her it's Faith Hyatt, Lacy Cameron's sister."

"The doctor is at the hospital," the man said after a brief conversation he'd taken pains to not let Faith hear. "Mrs. Parker received no instructions to allow you in. She reminded me that Dr. Cameron and his wife divorced earlier this year. You'll have to have Dr. Cameron get in touch with one of us, I'm afraid."

"Would you explain to Mrs. Parker that I have Dr. Cameron's son with me?"

"Are you going to leave peacefully, miss, or shall I phone the cops? The doc doesn't have a kid." The attendant reached for the phone inside his work station.

"Good grief." Faith started to say something smart-alecky in return, but decided there was no use. Media frenzy or not, it figured she'd run into the one person in New York who apparently didn't read the paper, gossip or watch headline news on TV. "Look, I'm sort of stranded. I promise I won't trouble you if you'll get me a cab."

"Sure thing." The man still didn't seem to trust her. He didn't invite her to stand inside the foyer, and he kept her in sight until the cab pulled up.

The cabbie showed greater sympathy. "Twins. You've got your hands full, missus. Me and my wife had our flock one at a time." He shook his head. "Where to?"

Faith named the hospital where Michael practiced. At least, she hoped that was where she'd find him. Prominent as he was, he'd have privileges at many hospitals in the city. For just a minute, her resolve faltered. She reminded herself that even if he didn't want to see *her,* he'd never turn his back on Abby and Nick.

Faith's head ached from the twins' constant crying. They were hungry and she was tired. She was angry, too. Who wouldn't be? She'd complied with a court mandate, only to be turned away at the two homes she'd been ordered to visit.

"Hope the little guys get better," the cabbie told Faith as she paid her bill. "I don't have another fare, so I don't mind lending a hand to help you get them into the emergency room."

Faith almost cried. Kind words right now had that effect on her. What did it say for her situation that a New York cabdriver—one of a clan reputed to be consistently rude—had been nicer to her than the people who might one day have a hand in raising Abigail and Nicholas? "Thank you, but we'll be fine," she sniffled.

Inside, Faith made a beeline for the main desk. Instead of asking for a ladies' lounge where she could change the babies, she asked to have Michael paged. She did so with authority. Let him see what these games he was playing through their attorneys had done to the babies he professed to love.

She rained kisses down on Abby's red face and paced the lobby, bouncing the heavy carrier on her back to try and quiet Nick. Suddenly Michael loomed in front of her, looking wonderful to Faith even though he appeared to be a bit bleary-eyed himself.

"Faith, what's wrong? Are the babies sick again? Are you?" Michael's questions ran together as he pried Nicholas out of the backpack and helped her remove Abigail from the sweaty front carrier. When, surprisingly, Michael leaned over and kissed Faith soundly on the lips, tears threatened to spill from her eyes for the second time in only minutes. Yet she was determined to stay mad at Michael. After all, he'd had a hand in sending her on this wild-goose chase.

"What did you all think," she asked, clenching her fists. "That I'd ignore Judge Kline's orders to bring Nick and Abby to New York so they could spend time with you and Kipp? You ought to know me better than that, Michael."

"Who's Judge Kline?" Michael seemed genuinely baffled. "These babies are soaking wet. No wonder they're crying."

Michael strode to a bank of elevators. There was nothing for Faith to do but follow him. "Judge Kline is the Superior Court Judge who overruled Judge Brown's visitation decree. Oh, why am I explaining this? I'm sure you already know it. David said the Schlegels and Lon Maxwell filed a joint appeal."

Herding Faith into an empty elevator, Michael rode up two floors, then motioned her off and into a quiet room where there were two soft leather couches. The scent of fresh-perked coffee permeated the air.

"Those packs look incredibly uncomfortable," he said, relieving her of the heavy diaper bag. "I'll change the babies while you shed those things, unless you need help getting out of them."

Faith shook her head. The straps had cut off circulation to her arms, and her fingers had trouble undoing the buckles. *Why was Michael being so nice?*

As if he'd read her mind, he glanced up from pulling diapers and changes of clothing from the bag. "I really don't know what you're talking about, Faith. I haven't left the hospital since I got here. We couldn't get a heart for Mrs. Fitzhugh. Last night I decided to try repairing hers. We've never tried a five bypass on a transplanted heart before. It's been touch and go all day. An hour ago we saw the first sign of improvement.''

"I'm glad," Faith said sincerely. "Wait a minute." She turned from the sink where she was running hot water over the two bottles of formula. "Kipp's out of town and Shelby Fielding claimed she had no clue Bob Schlegel had filed the appeal. Now you're denying you asked Maxwell to act on your behalf? Have the lawyers gone berserk?''

"I don't know, but when we're done here I'll find out," Michael muttered. He accepted a bottle from Faith and stuck it in Abby's mouth. "There, there, honey-bunch. God, I've missed you guys," he said with feeling, staring at Faith as she sat down to feed Nicholas.

Still smarting from being rebuffed twice—by Shelby Fielding and also at Michael's home—Faith wasn't ready to forgive him. "Apparently you didn't miss us enough to have one of your staff phone.''

He looked abashed at that. "You know how it is when a doctor has a patient at death's door. I'd figured on doing a lot of things. Truth is, I haven't had a minute to myself. I'd planned to go to Tiffany's and choose your ring, too. Since you're here, and as Cynthia is somewhat improved, maybe we can go together.''

"Ring?" Faith felt the room recede. "I—I assumed you'd decided not to proceed down the marriage avenue. I mean, according to David, Kipp's legal team and yours are working to get the hearings moved to New York.''

"What's that got to do with our getting married?''

More confused than ever, Faith automatically burped Nicholas. "So, we're still working from plan A, Michael?''

He smiled and the tired lines that had dulled his eyes fell away. ''You, I and the twins are going to be a family, Faith. There isn't going to be any plan B. I promise.''

Faith's heart battled her head. Her heart wanted to believe, but her head remembered all the things that had gone wrong already. Michael was back to his hospital routine. How long before he forgot her and the babies again? For the moment, however, his smile set her world right.

Faith wanted so much to believe that things would work out, exactly the way Michael had promised.

CHAPTER FOURTEEN

THE BABIES FELL ASLEEP almost immediately after eating. Faith fussed over them, smoothing the tufts of hair sticking up on each tiny head. Nick sucked so hard at the bottle whenever he ate that he perspired. He also twisted the fingers of his left hand in the longer strands of hair that fell over his ear. Abigail did the same, only she had less hair to grasp. She pinched her ear, leaving it red and sometimes scratched.

"One of us needs to clip their fingernails," Michael noted as he inspected Abby's scratches and the little fingers he splayed out over his larger forefinger.

"I'll let you do the honors." Faith laughed. "You're the surgeon with nerves of steel."

"Oh, ho. Surgeons never work on their own families."

"I bought special baby clippers. Supposedly there's less chance of slipping and cutting fingers and toes. I guess I could do it. I am a nurse, after all."

"I'll do it. I was only teasing. Remind me when we get home. Are you ready to leave? I need a minute to check on Cynthia and give the nursing supervisor my cell number, then we can take off. The car seats are still in the back of my car."

"You're needed here, Michael. I didn't stop by to ask for a lift home. It was more that I needed a place to feed and change them—and that I was mad about no one being aware of the court order except me.''

''Don't remind me. When I calm down, I intend to phone Lon Maxwell and find out what possessed him. He takes his orders from me and no one else. I'll set my housekeeper and the security staff straight, too. I don't want you ever to have to go through that again. There's no excuse for what happened today, Faith.''

''Gr-r-reat! Then I'll be on everyone's bad-guy list. It wasn't my intention to cause trouble.''

''Well, I don't mind at all. Mrs. Parker knows you're family, and she's well aware that I'm involved in a custody suit. I don't understand her actions and I'll be discussing this with her.''

''That's between the two of you. I could have pressed harder, I suppose, but I remember how much she intimidated Lacy.''

''That's news to me. Lacy never said a word. I hired Mrs. Parker so Lacy wouldn't have to worry about cleaning and cooking so soon after her surgery. It worked out well, and I assumed Lacy wanted to keep Mrs. Parker on.''

''That woman would only ever take orders from you, Michael. And you were so rarely home. More often than not, *she* set the house rules, not Lacy.''

He shook his head in amazement. ''As I said, Faith, things are going to change.'' Digging in his pocket, Michael pulled out a set of keys. ''I'm parked on level one in the fifth slot from the west exit. If you load the babies, I'll be there in less than ten minutes and we can get underway.''

Faith had protested all she was going to. If Michael was determined to drive her back to Boston, she was grateful. The afternoon commuter trains were always full and they stopped at every station. The trip home would be much more pleasant in the luxury of Michael's car.

After he returned, they set off, only to be stuck in heavy traffic for some fifteen minutes. She again apologized for intruding on his day. "I feel guilty, Michael. You look exhausted. Are you quite sure you want to make the round trip to Boston?"

"I have to. Tonight will be critical for Cynthia. I wish I didn't have to turn right around and come back. You do know, I hope, that I'd much rather stay with you and the kids."

Faith didn't know that. She wasn't even thoroughly convinced after he'd said it. After all, who knew more about the pressures on a doctor than a nurse? If it'd been any doctor but Michael, she'd never have agreed to marry him. The man bewitched her. He always had and probably always would. Faith found it impossible to think rationally when he was around. She held no illusions about marriage to Michael Cameron; she knew it meant she'd carry the burden of raising the twins practically alone. She'd heard doctors' wives complain about not receiving any emotional support. Now she would join their ranks.

On closer examination of her feelings, Faith admitted she'd settle for small snatches of shared time with Michael. After all, she understood the importance of his work. And she'd expected to be a single parent to Lacy's babies, in any event. But could anyone blame her for wanting more from marriage?

"I almost forgot," she said, a genuine smile chasing away her troubled thoughts. "Nicholas rolled over this morning! He did it more than once, so I know it wasn't a fluke."

"I haven't been gone *that* long. I can't believe I missed such an important milestone. Did you think to record it on video?"

"No. I don't have a video camera. It would be a good idea to get one, though. The twins will be going through a lot of firsts in the months to come."

"They've gone through a lot of stages just since you brought them home. What's after rolling? Crawling?"

"Dr. Sampson's nurse gave me a brochure with an approximate timetable. She said not to worry if they develop faster or slower than it says."

"That means we shouldn't worry because Nick smiled before Abby and now he's rolled over first?"

"Right. She may walk or speak before he does. Then again, because she was smaller at birth, she may always be developmentally slower than Nicholas."

"Another reason I'd really hate for the Fieldings to end up with the twins. Maybe I'm wrong about them, but I can see them pressuring Abigail to do better than her brother. I mean, she does have that superior Fielding blood running through her veins," Michael drawled sarcastically.

His words brought Faith a whole new set of worries. David had said if the Fieldings managed to get the hearings transferred to New York, they'd be able to influence the outcome. Because Michael's clinic and his legal residence were in New York, he fit into their schemes. If Michael loved her, if he hadn't offered to marry her just to try and win custody, she'd suggest he relocate his practice to Boston. But why would he? He had name recognition where he was, and a partner who was probably more important to his life than a wife of convenience would ever be.

"I shouldn't have said anything," Michael muttered,

darting sidelong glances at Faith. "Now you're worried about the Fieldings placing unrealistic demands on Abigail. It won't happen, I swear. They'd have to get her first. And the babies hardly know Kipp or Shelby. Just because old man Fielding tops the list of rich and famous, that doesn't automatically give them an edge."

"Is there any chance he didn't earn his millions legally?"

"Admirable thought, but Kipp-the-first made a killing in real estate. He married into an old banking family. Our Kipp's father increased their wealth on Wall Street. He chose a wealthy socialite wife, too. Kipp has trust funds from both sides of the family. Shelby's folks had a pedigree, too, but I understand they left her cash-poor when they died. She was at Bryn Mawr when their yacht went down in a storm. Kipp was at Yale. He may have married Shelby for her contacts in the boating world, but that's not a crime."

"Schlegel, Schlegel and Matz can make her sound tragic then, can't they? At least if it were me, I'd play up that angle. Young woman lost her parents, wants desperately to have a family of her own. According to David she's had every fertility treatment known to man. That's where she was going today in such a rush. To a fertility clinic. She was quite obsessed with making the appointment. That's why she threw me out on the curb by your apartment and tore off like a madwoman."

"The story fits Lacy's explanation. I recall hearing you say that Kipp broke off their affair because he felt he owed it to his wife to let her try a new fertility method she'd discovered."

"Yes. It was the final blow, so to speak. The reason Lacy left without telling Kipp she was pregnant."

"And yet," Michael said thoughtfully, "it showed

character that the man would be concerned enough for his wife to stick by her through another process. Fertility tests and treatments aren't any fun for either the man *or* the woman. Some are quite painful.''

"I wasn't under the impression that Lacy thought Kipp stayed out of a sense of love or concern for Shelby. More likely it was because his father demanded an heir to carry on that exclusive Fielding bloodline.''

"I know you want to believe Kipp and Shelby will make horrible parents, Faith. He might be weak and she's snooty, but basically they're above average when it comes to looking at where to place kids. I really don't think we have a prayer of discrediting them in the eyes of a judge. If we tried, our efforts might backfire. We'd be better served to concentrate on making ourselves look *more* desirable.''

"You're right. I have nothing against the Fieldings except a gut feeling that Shelby would rather not be stuck with a reminder of Kipp's infidelity. In a way I feel sorry for her. All her friends and acquaintances must be talking behind her back. They must know every sordid detail, considering how the case has been dissected by the media.''

"Friends, strangers, everyone has an opinion. I still think that, in the end, the judge will weigh all facts and do what's right.''

Almost two hours later, Michael pulled into the parking lot behind Faith's apartment. ''I'll carry the kids upstairs. Then I need to leave again.''

Faith had toyed for over an hour with telling Michael there was no way the two of them would look better than Kipp and Shelby. Kipp might be off sailing in Antigua, but Shelby was home attending to duty. She didn't say anything, however. She had no right to chastise Michael for dashing back to New York. His life and work were there.

"Hey, we weren't harassed by reporters. Do you suppose that means you can keep your phone plugged in?" Michael asked as they slipped jackets off the still-sleeping twins.

"I did last night. You'd promised to call me, remember? When you didn't, I disconnected it again."

Michael looked contrite. "I meant to call. If Cynthia's recovery continues, there's no reason I couldn't phone tonight." He tried to pull Faith into his arms, but she ducked out and missed the kiss he aimed at her lips.

"You'll be back when?" she asked, busying herself with hanging the jackets in the closet.

"In time for the hearing. A few days before that, if I can manage. I have a list of things to do and a short period of time in which to do them." Walking up behind Faith, Michael curved his hands over her upper arms and tilted her back flat to his chest. He laid a cheek in need of a shave against her smoother, softer one. "I wish I didn't have to go at all," he murmured. "I'm ready to get on with the wedding."

Faith allowed herself the pleasure of snuggling into his arms. His solid strength and the steady beat of his heart offered a sense of safety. Turning slowly, she slid her arms around his neck and raised her lips to accept the kiss she'd shied away from earlier. Michael's shirt still carried the faint aroma of the hospital. But Faith wasn't put off. Some might find the antiseptic odor oppressive; Faith found it comforting. She briefly touched her tongue to his lips and then when he groaned, she kissed him as if there was no tomorrow.

Michael was the one to call a halt this time. Heart beating fast, he exhaled a stream of air and permitted only their foreheads to touch. "It wouldn't take much of this to tempt me to stay. But I can't."

Michael took a giant backward step. His gaze lingered on her hungrily, before sliding to the cribs where the babies curled together. "I don't ever remember wanting to ignore responsibility so badly," he sighed. "But I can't. We both know that wouldn't play well with the judge, either. Goodbye, sweetheart. I'm counting on you to keep the home fires burning." Hurrying into the outer hall, he walked quickly to the elevators.

Faith stood with one hand pressed to her knotted stomach and the other to her quivering lips long after Michael left. By initiating that kiss, she'd bared her soul. Hadn't he seen that, or didn't he care? He hadn't said he loved her. Foolishly, she had clung to the hope that he'd at least acknowledge the *possibility* of love in their proposed union. She could only conclude that he wouldn't be offering marriage if he thought he could win custody of the twins without it.

So, what did it say about her that she'd marry him on any terms? Faith weighed the matter in her mind for the remainder of the evening. She finally admitted that she'd loved him for so long, she would accept a one-sided match in order to spend even tidbits of time with him.

If that made her pathetic, so be it. If that made her a traitor to Lacy, so be it.

She was prepared to hear nothing from Michael until whatever day he managed to return to Boston. True to his word this time, Michael phoned that night to let her know he'd arrived safely, and Cynthia had continued to improve. "I can't tell you how many times I almost turned back," he confided in a husky, sexy voice that practically unstrung Faith.

"I'll bet the hospital staff is happy you didn't. It probably makes them nervous to have their star surgeon out of reach." Faith had begun to distance herself from him. It was possibly the only way she'd survive a marriage without love.

If Michael noticed a change in her attitude, he didn't remark on it. "You know how hospital administrators are when someone on staff breaks new ground, Faith. After the surgery, the P.R. department sent out a press release. I could do without the added publicity. I prefer not being in the limelight."

"Boy, can I relate." Faith fell back on the couch and wound an overlong curl around one finger. "I've hung up on five reporters who called since you left. Apparently they found out you'd driven me home. Two of them knew about the mix-up in today's visitation. What do they have, a pipeline to our lawyers?"

"That reminds me. I phoned Lon. Our lawyers are out of control. He tried giving *me* orders, until I reminded him I was the guy paying his bill."

"They all want to win this case, Michael. David told me it'll be a huge legal coup for the law firm whose client ends up with a favorable ruling."

"Yeah. Well, the one working for me had better not go behind my back and cut deals with the other team. Lon blew up when I told him to get me out of the new visitation agreement. I have my doubts that he's attuned to the best interest of the babies. If I didn't think firing him would create total confusion at the next hearing, I'd have done it. I hung up without telling him we'd decided to get married, Faith. I hope you haven't mentioned it to David."

"No." Faith's stomach rolled. A woman on the brink of marriage should be shouting it from the rooftops.

And Michael wanted her to keep it quiet.... No doubt as part of his strategy.

His next words proved her right, "Good. It'll have greater impact if you show up at the hearing wearing an engagement ring. Do you have a preference in cut? Emerald? Marquise? Standard?"

"Not emerald," Faith said quickly. That would remind her too much of the ring he'd given Lacy. "Nothing showy. A ring isn't important, Michael."

"It is to me. I'm also in favor of our wedding being as soon as possible. Most people involved in the case probably think we're sleeping together as it is, so the sooner we make it legal, the better."

Better for whom? Faith wondered. Oh, he meant it would look better to a judge, of course. "Will you arrange a marriage service with a justice of the peace in New York, or shall I arrange one here?"

"Do you mind if we have a church wedding? I never felt right marrying Lacy in the hospital."

"Is that really necessary?" Faith's throat was tight.

"Humor me. I want to see my bride walk down the aisle. Besides, someday the kids will expect to see pictures of our wedding."

"Weddings are costly, Michael." Faith bit her lip as a sharp reminder not to let the excitement that had begun to build get out of hand. His wanting a church wedding meant nothing. Another show for his custody quest.

"Faith, I have money. I've been too busy to spend much of what I made. I told you things were going to change. I'll send you my charge card. Use it for whatever you need. I'm sure Thanksgiving is too soon for a wedding. Shall we shoot for Christmas Eve? Morning, with a brunch afterward for guests? That way we can spend Christmas as a family.''

"All right, Michael.'' The old dream called for a honeymoon in some exotic locale. She guessed honeymoons weren't part of Michael's plan. Not with less than two months to get everything ready. This wasn't a love match, she reminded herself, but a marriage to establish a home for the twins. Fine. She loved the babies. She'd make their first Christmas a special event.

"I have to go, Faith. I'm being paged. I'll overnight my card. We'll finalize any other details after the hearing.''

Faith's heart tripped faster as they said their goodbyes. Somehow, knowing that she'd be planning their wedding made marriage to Michael seem more real. She longed to tell someone, even though he'd said they shouldn't until after the hearing. She sat down and wrote a letter to her aunt Lorraine, who worked in a mission hospital in Tanzania. Tomorrow, she'd visit her dad and tell him. He liked Michael. At one time, Dwight Hyatt had been aware that she carried a torch for Lacy's husband. Sporadically aware, anyway. Her dad had offered his sympathy and his shoulder for her to cry on after Lacy's wedding. If he was having a good day tomorrow, he might share the joy that filled her heart. No one else would, as she'd kept her feelings for Michael well hidden. Maybe her father would even be able to walk her down the aisle.

But the next day, when Faith and the twins visited Dwight, he referred to her by her mother's name. And he thought the twins were Faith and Lacy as babies. The fact that one was a girl and the other a boy meant nothing to the old man, who lived more and more in his own world.

Faith didn't linger at the rest home. Seeing her father's condition deteriorating cast a pall over her already fragile joy. From there, she did go to book a small chapel at the church, but she spent more time lighting candles for her father and Michael than arranging her special day.

During what remained of the week, Faith tried to recapture her earlier delight in planning for her future with Michael. She just couldn't seem to shake the sense of anxiety that surrounded her every move. She lived with the cloying fear that Michael wouldn't show up in time for the hearing and that she'd never see him again.

The fear stuck with her in spite of the fact that he called every night.

"If we didn't have these conversations, I'd go crazy in New York with you guys in Boston," he said one evening when she mentioned how long they'd been talking on the phone. "I can't be there to help you start feeding Abby and Nick cereal. Listening to you scrape the spoon on the bowl puts me closer to the experience."

At that very moment, Nicholas spewed rice cereal and formula all over Faith. "Oh, yuck! I hope you felt that shower, Michael." Laughing, she juggled the phone to her other ear as she wiped Nick's face and her own shirt and chin.

"If you need to clean up, I'll call back later."

"That's not necessary, Michael." The few times he'd phoned after she'd gone to bed, he'd said things that made it impossible for her to sleep afterward. He'd asked what kind of nightgown she had on and had commented on how he'd like to remove it. Slowly...

"It is necessary, Faith. I won't risk losing you from inattention."

Faith closed her eyes. Although Michael hadn't spoken Lacy's name, he might as well have. But she guessed her sister would always be between them.

"Faith, dammit, I can feel you pulling away from me. You do it every time I touch on anything personal. Talk to me. If you're having seconds thoughts, we need to figure out why."

Second thoughts. And third. But not for any reason that must be running through his mind. She tossed the empty plastic cereal bowl into the sink. Bustling around the kitchen, she ran water over washcloths and wiped the babies' faces and hands. "I don't know what you expect, Michael. You call when I'm in the middle of caring for the babies so you can feel involved. But I only have two hands, and between the kids, they have four—all of them trying to push the spoon away. And yesterday Dr. Sampson agreed that Nick's cutting three teeth at one time. I spent the night walking the floor."

"Look, I'm doing my best to wind things up here so I can get back to Boston. Barring unforeseen complications, Cynthia ought to go home next week."

Faith rubbed two fingers across the furrows forming between her eyebrows. "Are we fighting, Michael? I don't want to make your life miserable." She burst into tears.

"Stop. I ought to be shot for leaving you to deal with so much. You need a mother's helper, Faith. Why don't you call an agency tomorrow?"

"It's not that, Michael. I can take care of the twins. But...but David phoned today. He's positive you and Kipp are in cahoots. Nancy Matz told him I don't have a prayer of winning. She suggested I'd be smart to let Shelby have the babies before the hearing. According to Nancy, if I show that much good sense, the rest of you will be more inclined to allow me future visits with the kids.''

''Rubbish. Where in tarnation does that woman come up with her half-baked ideas? More likely she's trying to rattle my cage. Kipp's team doesn't like it that I stopped Lon from negotiating with them. You hang in there, honey. Everything's going to work out fine, you'll see.''

''I hope.'' Faith scrubbed at the unwanted tears. ''Sorry, Michael. I think we're all walking a fine line, and it's difficult.'' She sighed. ''I feel I'm being unfair to David in excluding him from our plans. Frankly, I just want a final decision. If Kipp's team does anything to prevent the judge from deciding on a permanent placement at the November hearing, I'm not sure I can continue on as we are. I'm getting too attached to the babies...even though I promised I'd consider myself a temporary foster parent. How do real foster moms let go? Losing the twins will break my heart.''

''You have to keep a positive attitude, Faith.''

''I can't. There was a sidebar in this morning's paper that listed twenty reasons why family court will favor Kipp and Shelby over either you or me.''

''Stop reading that stuff. The reporters have nothing concrete, so they sit around and speculate. They like to sprinkle sand in an oyster. It provides a constant irritation, if you know what I mean.''

''Right. And who gets the pearl in the end? Michael, these babies are more precious than pearls. I keep thinking maybe none of us should be playing god with their lives.''

''You're tired, sweetheart. Hang in a while longer. I believe our getting married will impress the judge. Social Services already reported that we work well as a team."

"I'll try to be more optimistic. Maybe we should talk about something other than the case for a change."

They did just that. They talked for two hours, covering subjects of interest to both of them, everything from books to movies, politics to art. "Wow, it's midnight," Michael exclaimed around a yawn. "I haven't talked on the phone this long since high school."

"I never have. Not even to Lacy, and we sometimes used to spend an hour on the phone. I don't remember her ever saying you liked paintings of seascapes and old lighthouses. But then she did her best to talk me out of buying the ones I have."

"Wait until you see what I have stored. During one of Lacy's interior renovations, she took down three favorite watercolors I'd hung in my den."

"Why didn't you tell her hands off?"

"Because decorating was something she loved to do. I gave her so little else," he said quietly. "I'm glad now that I let her have free rein with the apartment."

Silence fell between them. Then Michael cleared his throat and Faith thought he was going to say goodbye. She hated parting on a sad note. "It's okay if you still love her, Michael."

"Looking back, I'm not sure I ever loved her as I should have. I know that now. Apparently she recognized it much sooner."

"It's a closed chapter in your life."

"It is that. And thanks to you and the twins, I've been given a chance to correct my faults in part two of the saga of Michael Cameron."

Faith didn't know what to say. It was only after

they'd each yawned in the other's ear that they agreed it was time to hang up.

Tuesday, a week before the hearing, an ice storm hit, greatly curtailing Faith's ability to complete the final tasks in arranging the wedding. On her list had been choosing flowers for the chapel and a bridal bouquet. Michael had suggested they serve brunch rather than cake and coffee. She had planned to check out the menus of three restaurants near the chapel. Instead of going out in the wind-driven sleet, she phoned and asked to have copies of the menus mailed to her.

The storm raged for three days. Fortunately, it let up on the fourth, and a south wind blew in and melted the ice on the streets, or Faith's cupboards would have been bare. At least, preoccupation with the weather had taken her mind off the hearing, which was now only a week-end away. As she pushed the babies through the corner grocery store and people stopped to exclaim over them, Faith underwent a sudden, strange longing to have Michael at her side.

And where was he? She'd grown used to their nightly phone visits. The three days she'd needed most to connect with him, he'd seemed to drop off the face of the earth. No calls, and no answer at home or on his cell phone.

It wasn't until Faith stood at the cash register to pay for her groceries, that the morning's headlines caught her eye—and sent her stomach plummeting. Taking Michael's advice, she'd avoided reading articles having to do with the case. What she read now made her physically ill. Bold typeface stretching across six newspaper columns read Attorneys For Kipp Fielding III Expect A Private Settlement Between Their Client And Dr. Mi-

chael Cameron In Custody Case Involving Twins With
Separate Fathers.

Rooted to the floor, Faith barely managed to produce
the cash to pay her bill. Her fingers shook so badly that
the clerk asked if she was ill.

She didn't trust herself to respond. She bought the
paper and hurriedly loaded the sacks into the stroller,
then raced blindly from the store. On the trek home, her
knees felt as limp as one of Abby's rag dolls. Her mind
refused to comprehend what those headlines might
mean.

When Faith reached the safe haven of her apartment,
she methodically stored her groceries and changed and
fed the babies before she felt calm enough to more
closely inspect the article beneath those shocking headlines.

She'd no more than spread the paper out on the
kitchen table when her telephone rang. It was a reporter
for an opposing paper, asking if she intended to press
on with her lawsuit. Faith hung up without giving her
standard "no comment." She quickly dialed David before another call could come in.

He claimed ignorance. "I have calls in to Bob Schlegel and Lon Maxwell. So far, no one's contacted me.
Last I spoke to Maxwell, he was adamant that Cameron
wasn't interested in working with the Fieldings. The
article is devoid of pertinent facts, Faith. This could be
some reporter's stab at turning up the heat before Monday's hearing."

"Doesn't that open his paper up for a possible slan-
der suit?"

"Not really. Since those guys don't have to disclose
the name of their source, they could later print a retrac-
tion and say their source was mistaken."

"All the same," Faith said, having difficulty swallowing, "I'd feel better if you'd heard from the other camps. I'm leaving my phone off the hook. If you find out anything, will you send your clerk by to bring me up-to-date?"

"Sure. But Lacy's custody papers have stood up under scrutiny by the Superior Court commissioner. I received his ruling yesterday. Since then, my assistant and I have been working around the clock to build your case. Relax, Faith. I can't believe that any split agreement Fielding and Cameron could dream up would look good to a judge. Public sentiment is all for keeping the kids together."

Faith hung up and then took the receiver off the hook, wishing she shared David's confidence. Of course, David didn't know she and Michael had been plotting together in order to increase their odds. That was precisely what made her so uneasy. If Michael dickered behind the scenes with her, what stopped him from doing the same with Kipp? Over the last couple of weeks, she'd let her late-night chats with Michael, and all the wedding talk, lull her into complacency.

Her stomach and legs still felt as if they belonged to someone who'd just climbed off an amusement park ride. Faith grabbed a couple of the babies' favorite squeaky toys and went to sit beside the playpen. Playing with Abby and Nick lifted her spirits. She was actually laughing at Abigail's attempts to roll over when she heard voices in the hall. Someone rapped soundly on her door.

"I'm coming," Faith called. She climbed to her feet and straightened her blouse before releasing the locks. David must have heard back from one of the other lawyers. That was fast. Faith yanked open the door, and it took her a second to realize it was Michael, and not David's clerk, standing there. Kipp Fielding and his father hovered in the space behind Michael.

"Look who I found wandering through our parking lot, Faith," Michael said with a grin.

He carried his medical bag and a black suitcase, Faith realized as he stepped past her. Kipp's hands were shoved into his pants pockets. His father gripped a brown leather briefcase. Neither man cracked a smile.

Michael piled his things in a corner and turned to look at Faith, who'd gone white and still gripped the doorknob. He returned to tug it gently from her hands. After closing the door, he slipped an arm around her waist. "Are you ill?"

She dragged a shaking hand through hair that badly needed cutting. "Please," she said tightly, "Sit, gentlemen. And so will I." She pushed Michael's hand roughly aside and stumbled into the chair nearest the playpen. Idly massaging her arms, Faith murmured, "I have a feeling that what you're about to say is going to knock me off my feet, anyhow, so I may as well sit."

Michael sank into the matching chair, leaving the couch to the Fieldings. "Maybe someone would be kind enough to clue me in. None of you seem surprised by this gathering. Am I the only one in the dark here?"

"Come off it, Michael," she snapped. "I know you said I shouldn't read the newspapers but I did. Sorry, but they let your little cat out of the bag."

Folding his hands between his knees, Michael threw a puzzled glance at Faith and then at the men on the couch. Kipp's eyes shifted to the babies and stayed there. The elder Mr. Fielding opened his briefcase and removed five or six pages of paper. He flicked a thumb across his lips a few times. "We're sorry about the leak to the media,'' he said at last. ''Bob Schlegel has tried for two days to contact you, Cameron. My son and I finally drove over to your apartment today. Security said you'd sublet the place and were headed for Boston.''

''My business in New York took longer than I thought to tie up, or I'd have been here earlier. I assumed Lon told you.''

It was Faith's turn to look startled. ''So you three haven't already met, the way the newspaper implied?''

They all shook their heads.

''Why would we meet?'' Michael asked. ''The hearing is Monday.''

The senior Fielding divided the papers and handed Michael a set. ''My son is prepared to sign over full and complete custody of the female twin to you, Doctor. It's all here in black and white.''

A collective gasp exploded from Faith and Michael. Unthinking, she grabbed Abigail and cuddled her protectively, as if such a move would shield her from a father who was announcing he didn't want anything to do with her.

''I don't understand.'' Michael flipped through the pages, then settled down to reading the top one.

''Shelby's pregnant,'' Kipp blurted. ''She found out while I was in Antigua. If she's to carry the baby to term, she has to be off her feet.''

''You always planned to hire a nanny, I believe,'' Michael pointed out.

Kipp turned to his father, as if for help explaining. The older man had no trouble being blunt. ''This agreement comes as a condition of Shelby staying with my son. You'll notice on page two that Bob Schlegel has arranged a sizable trust for the girl. And a generous monthly maintenance fee.''

"Dad!" Kipp glared at his father. "For goodness' sake, she has a name. Call her Abigail."

"All right. Abigail will be monetarily provided for until age eighteen."

Michael interrupted. "This reads very much like you're handing Abby over to me with no strings attached."

Faith began to feel faint. The Fieldings were offering Michael everything he wanted. He'd have clear rights to both babies. He no longer needed her to act as his wife. A trembling gripped her and wouldn't let go as she saw all her dreams drift away, like so much smoke up a chimney. It was all Faith could do to listen to Kipp's explanation.

"At the risk of sounding like a jerk," Kipp mumbled, "I experienced the true excitement of being a real father when Shelby made her announcement. That forced me to take a good look at where I was in this custody fight. It struck me that I have no paternal feelings for the baby I made with Lacy." He sucked in a breath. "Believe it or not, I want my marriage to survive. It's what I've always wanted, even though I did stray the one time. But I'd like a solid assurance that Abigail will be raised by someone who loves her. I think that's you, Cameron."

Kipp's dad butted in again. "From the beginning, Kipp had grave concerns about splitting up the twins. What do you say, Doctor? Do we have a deal?" Extracting a gold pen from his suit jacket, Mr. Fielding thumbed out the last page on both packets. His son had already signed.

Michael spared Faith a glance before he accepted the pen. As her face remained unreadable, he put the pen to the page. Hesitating, he asked, "God forbid it should happen, but what if Shelby loses the child she's carrying? Can I expect to be dragged through court again?''

Kipp III stood and paced to the window. He jingled the change in his pockets. ''Shelby will never love Abby as she deserves to be loved. If you've got no objection, Cameron, I might call you from time to time to ask after her welfare. But you have my word as a gentleman that I'll never make waves in her life. It's up to you whether or not you choose to tell her about me before she comes into her trust.''

''Done,'' said Michael.

As he pulled the papers toward him and scribbled his name, Faith fought back a sob. All the love she felt for the twins squeezed the breath from her lungs. But the love she bore Michael withered as he uttered that one damning word.

CHAPTER FIFTEEN

UNABLE TO BEAR LISTENING to the men seal the fate of the babies she would now lose, Faith swept them both into her arms and carried them to the nursery. They were beginning to fuss for bottles, anyhow. She wanted, needed, to feed them one last time.

After they ate, it would be nap time. There was sanity in routine.

Suddenly panic tore at her soul. Oh, God, she'd still have to face Michael. She'd have to hide this terrible, wrenching pain.

Blocking out the low murmur of male voices from her living room, Faith mixed formula by rote. She warmed it for Abigail and barely took the chill off for Nick. Since he'd started cutting those three teeth, he preferred his formula on the cool side.

Tears sprang to her eyes, obscuring her view of their sweet faces as she sat in her mother's rocker and offered a bottle to each baby. How long would it take whatever nanny Michael hired to discover each baby's idiosyncracies? A few raced through Faith's mind. Abigail wanted to be tightly cocooned in a blanket before being placed in bed. Nick sprawled across his portion of the crib. If covered, he soon kicked his blankets off. Certain kinds of disposable diapers gave Abby a horrid rash. Nick, on the other hand, had tougher skin and wore any brand. But he woke up and fussed if the night-light burned out. His sister, unless she was sick, could probably sleep through a rocket launch.

Faith hummed one of the babies' favorite lullabies. Her voice cracked, so she stopped humming and rained kisses down on the perfect little heads. Kisses mixed with salty tears.

Both bottles were empty, and the babies had fallen fast asleep by the time Michael appeared in the doorway leading into the nursery. "There you are, Faith." He bent his head forward and rubbed a hand over the back of his neck. "With all the excitement of the last hour, we haven't even said a proper hello." He started walking toward her, but she stopped him by placing a finger to her lips.

"Sorry," he whispered. "Do you need help getting them into the crib?"

She shook her head wildly. Already she felt sick. She'd never be able to hang on to any portion of her pride if Michael touched her.

While she sat in the babies' room, which she'd fashioned with such love, Faith was forced to examine what would ultimately be best for the twins. Their future as it appeared now was the exact opposite of the life she'd dreamed about for the past several weeks. Definitely opposite of what she wanted. A kind word now, or the barest brush of Michael's hand, would risk shattering her resolve to let him have Abby and Nick without a fight.

Michael whispered that he was going into the kitchen to prepare a pot of coffee and that once Faith put the babies down, he'd meet her there.

She rocked for another five minutes. Abby and Nick were already sound asleep, but she needed the extra time to compose herself. Even then, she hoped Michael didn't stay in her apartment long. Things should move fairly fast for him once she stepped aside and called off David Reed. Of course, the court would approve his taking both babies. As she'd told Michael, she had no heart for trying to split up the infants.

The babies could be gone by as early as next week. Faith got up and moved around in a daze. She laid the twins down and crept out of the room.

Michael had perked a pot of the new coffee she'd bought that day. Faith followed the fragrance into the kitchen. It seemed longer than three hours since she'd ground the beans and filled the half-pound bag.

Hesitating in the hallway outside the kitchen, she closed her eyes and smoothed her fingers across them, taking care to rid herself of any last tears clinging to her eyelashes. With a false smile on her face, Faith breezed into the kitchen and plucked a cup off the mug tree.

Michael bolted up from the table, where he'd been reading the article that took up most of the front page. "Here, let me pour you a cup. That's some article," he acknowledged with a jerk of his thumb. "Now I can see why you were upset when I showed up at the door with Kipp and his father in tow."

Folding the paper, Faith tossed it in the trash. She drew in a tired-sounding breath, accepted the full cup and then sat as far from Michael as possible, given the small diameter of her kitchen table. "I really don't see any need to cover old ground, Michael. It's a lucky break for you that Kipp followed you to Boston and didn't wait to drop this bomb until we'd wasted time gathering at Monday's hearing."

"Lucky break for me?" He stopped with his cup

halfway to his lips and stared at her through a curl of steam.

"Yes." She waved a hand over her own cup, keeping her eyes averted. Then she fingered the watch on her arm and cleared her throat. "I, ah, still have time to phone David and tell him he's dismissed from the case. You'll want to call Lon. It's important to get the permanent fate of the twins settled. The sooner the better."

"I think so, too." Michael gazed at her oddly. The moment Faith reached for the telephone that still lay off the hook, not meeting his eyes, he clamped a hand over her wrist.

She flinched but was unable to control a shudder. When he remained silent, Faith was forced to turn and look at Michael, against her will.

"We can sit here and you can tell me what's going on inside your mind," he said carefully, "or we can take our coffee into the living room and duke this out in more comfortable surroundings. Either way, we will get to the heart of the problem, Faith."

"There's nothing to duke out, Michael. You've won. There's no reason for me to appear in court."

"Whoa!" He held up a hand. "That's the wrong pronoun. Don't you mean *we've* won?"

Tears welled again and slid down her cheeks. "Why are you dragging this out? Why are you torturing me? I won't hold you to any of the promises you made before you learned that Kipp was going to relinquish custody of Abigail."

"Big of you, I'm sure." Flinging off his suit jacket, Michael loosened his tie before crossing his arms defiantly. "Could you be more specific? Exactly what promises are we referring to?"

Faith had sucked in her upper lip. She released it with

a sigh. "The wedding farce. There's only the chapel to cancel. It's lucky for you the weather turned bad. I never arranged for flowers or the brunch."

"Wedding farce, you say?" His dark eyes, normally so sympathetic, burned like two smoldering fires. Digging into his jacket pocket, Michael hauled out a blue velvet box. He snapped it open with one finger and thrust it under Faith's nose. A two-carat warm-pink diamond glowed softly against a backdrop of white satin. The ring's setting was unique. Threads of gold wrapped the prongs holding the diamond, and intertwined, forming two hearts around smaller stones in a wide gold wedding band.

A less ornate man's ring with three similar diamonds embedded in its curve, completed the trio of wedding bands. "I would have been here a day earlier, Faith, but the jeweler at Tiffany's, who agreed to make this to my specifications, had a few finishing touches. He knew I wanted them to be perfect before I slipped it on the finger of the woman I love."

Faith's chin rose, then her mouth gaped open. "Love," she breathed in the shallowest of whispers. "But you've never said you loved me."

"Asking you to marry me, to be the mother of my children, isn't telling you I love you? I thought we both felt how much I loved you that incredible night we spent together in bed."

"I, ah, you never said you did. Love me, that is. I…I…thought you just needed a wife to parade past the judge."

Michael leaned over the table and bracketed her face with his hands. He settled his lips on hers briefly, but with feeling, then straightened away. "I love you so much. These last two weeks without you have been pure hell.'' He pursed his lips slightly. ''I loved your sister with the impetuousness of youth. What I feel for you is what a man feels for a woman he can't bear to live a day without. What a man feels for a woman he intends to spend the rest of his life with.'' He kissed her again, as if to punctuate his words. ''I wanted to do everything right for you, Faith.''

''It's all right, Michael. I agreed, with my eyes open, to marry you for the sake of the twins. If you haven't changed your mind, and…and especially if you love me, I'll be happy to keep your house, and cook your meals—and I promise never to say a word about the hours you spend with patients.''

''Faith, hush.'' Dropping his thumbs, Michael ran them lightly over her lips. ''I sold my half of the practice. I'm moving to Boston for good. I've negotiated a teaching post at the medical school. I did it because I want more time with you and the twins. I want us to be a regular family. Is that what *you* want, Faith?''

''Oh, Michael.'' Faith's eyes shimmered with unshed tears. She said with an emotional catch to her voice, ''All I've ever wanted is you. You, and the twins. I want to cheer Nick at football games and Abby at soccer. I want to help them grow into fine adults. I don't need backyard barbecues and weekend camping trips, or…or even a silly little word.''

''I do. I want it all.'' Michael slipped the engagement ring on the third finger of her left hand and pulled her out of the chair and into his arms. Then…then he put all the love that filled his heart into a kiss. His hands skimmed the cool skin hiding beneath her white blouse. Buttons gave way, and Michael's palms soon brushed the fullness of her breasts.

Strident cries erupted from the nursery, driving them

apart. Clearly fighting passion, Michael stepped back and took a moment to repair Faith's clothing.

Smiling wryly, she trailed her fingers lovingly along his smooth jaw. "If we can get through the twins' teething, Michael, I predict we'll be together fifty years from now."

"I'm in for the long haul, lady. The twins will eventually sleep through the night. So make a note of where we left off, please."

"After teething comes potty training," she reminded him gently.

"Yeah, yeah. And sixteen years from now, someone's got to teach two kids to drive cars."

Faith glanced over her shoulder at him as she approached the crying twins. "I don't drive, remember?"

Michael stopped her with a loud, wet kiss. "Make that three learning to drive. I know you're trying to shock me into reality, but honey, I'm looking forward to every minute I get to be a father and a husband. By the way, I love you. I love, love, love you. Let me know if you ever get sick of hearing me say it."

"I never will. Oh, Michael, I love you, too."

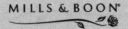

MILLS & BOON®

Modern Romance™

MISTRESS BY CONTRACT by Helen Bianchin

There was only one way for Mikayla to clear her
father's debt to tycoon Rafael Velez-Aguilera: offer
herself in exchange! Rafael was intrigued and
immediately specified her duties as his mistress for a
year! Top of the list was sharing his bed...

MARRIAGE AT HIS CONVENIENCE by Jacqueline Baird

Amber's multimillionaire Greek boyfriend was getting
married—to someone else. Five years later she has put
Lucas behind her—until she inherits half his company.
Lucas, now single again, knows the only way to secure
it: marry Amber!

A SPANISH AFFAIR by Helen Brooks

Georgina was working temporarily at her brother's
company, but when she discovered that arrogant Matt
de Capistrano was taking over, she wanted out! Then
Matt proposed to Georgie that they have a no-strings
affair. Could she refuse?

THE BOSS'S VIRGIN by Charlotte Lamb

Though Pippa refused to get involved when she worked
for him, no man has ever matched up to her ex-boss
Randall Harding. Now Randall is back—and he wants
Pippa. But do all the things that were against them in
the past, still hold true now?

On sale 6th July 2001

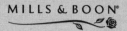

MILLS & BOON®

Modern Romance™

A QUESTION OF MARRIAGE by Lindsay Armstrong

Aurora was horrified when, by mistake, Luke Kirwan obtained her diaries containing her most intimate secrets. He would only return them on condition that she went on a date with him! One date led to another—and Aurora realised she didn't want his teasing blackmail to end...

SURRENDER TO THE SHEIKH by Sharon Kendrick

The last thing Rose expected was to find she was going on assignment to Prince Khalim's kingdom of Maraban. She was whisked away by private jet to Khalim's desert palace—where he treated her more like a princess than an employee...

THE PLAYBOY'S PROPOSAL by Amanda Browning

Joel Kendrick was the sexiest man Kathryn had ever met. Never one to refuse a challenge, when Joel flirted with her, she flirted back! Then suddenly her bachelor playboy proposed...

AT THE BILLIONAIRE'S BIDDING by Myrna Mackenzie

Others might enjoy spending day and night in a luxurious mansion, but to Caroline it was sheer torture! Gideon Tremayne, her wealthy, sophisticated employer, was far too tempting for a poor working girl. However, he'd 'bought' Caroline's hostessing services for the *whole* summer...

On sale 6th July 2001

Available at most branches of WH Smith, Tesco, Martins, Borders, Easons, Sainsbury, Woolworth and most good paperback bookshops

0601/01b